T0357858

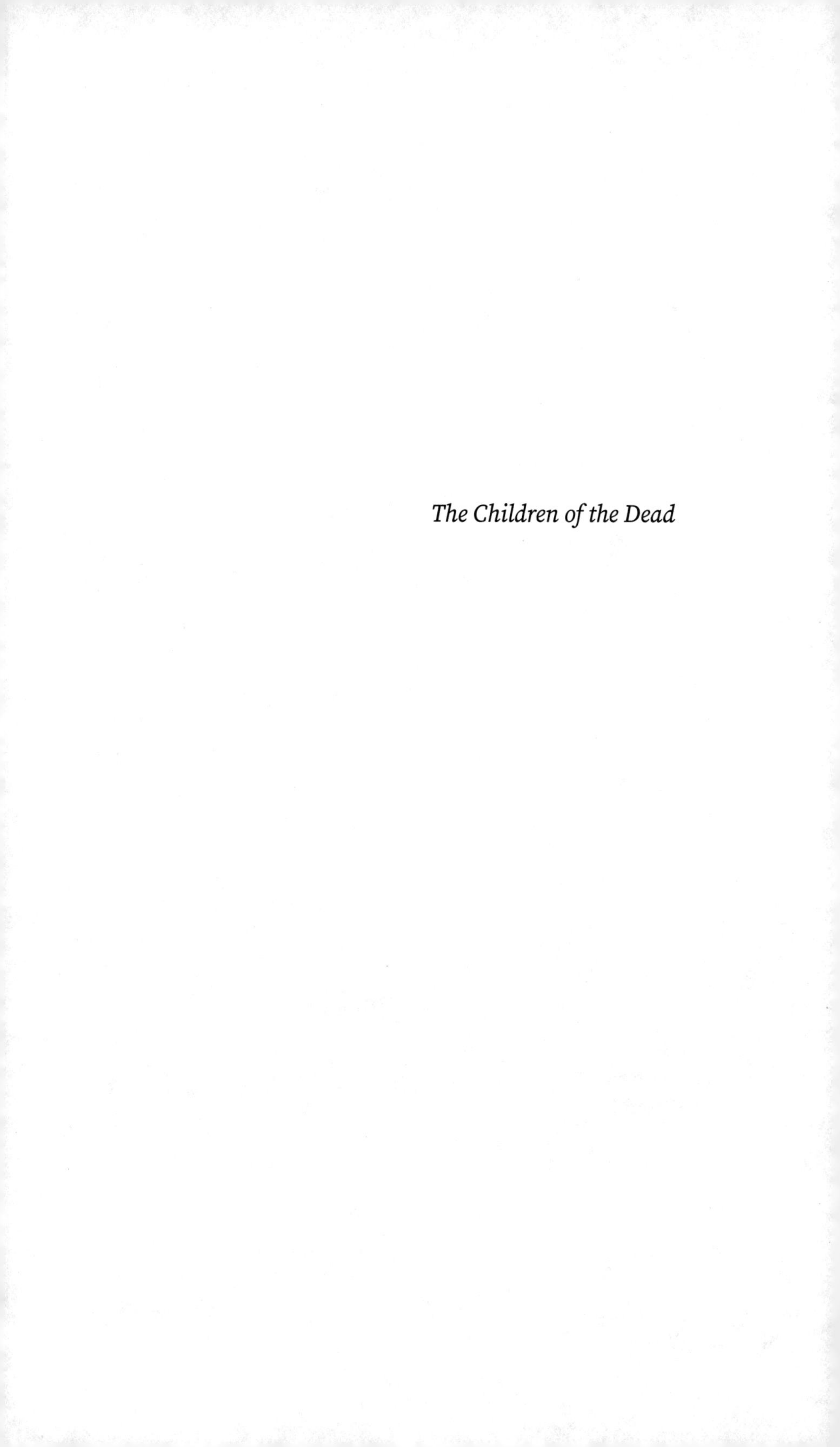

The Children of the Dead

ELFRIEDE JELINEK

The Children of the Dead

Translated from the German by
Gitta Honegger

A MARGELLOS
WORLD REPUBLIC OF LETTERS BOOK

Yale UNIVERSITY PRESS | NEW HAVEN & LONDON

The Margellos World Republic of Letters is dedicated to making literary works from around the globe available in English through translation. It brings to the English-speaking world the work of leading poets, novelists, essayists, philosophers, and playwrights from Europe, Latin America, Africa, Asia, and the Middle East to stimulate international discourse and ceative exchange.

Art: Eran Schaerf, *Mezuzah.*

Among the persons who gave me valuable incentives, I especially thank the satanism expert Josef Dvorak. (E.J.)

Set in type by Motto Publishing Services
Printed in the United States of America.

Library of Congress Control Number: 2023942844
ISBN 978-0-300-14215-0 (hardcover : alk. paper)

A catalogue record for this book is available from the British Library.

This paper meets the requirements of ANSI/NISO Z39.48-1992 (Permanence of Paper).

10 9 8 7 6 5 4 3 2

בואו
רוחות
המתים
שלא
נראו
נושנים
וברכו
את
ילדיהם

Prologue

This land needs a lot of air space for its blessed spirits to move freely above the waters. In some areas it rises over three thousand meters. That's how much nature has gone into this land. In turn, the land—perhaps as a way of paying back its debt to nature—has treated its people quite generously, throwing them right back into it as soon as they take the bait. The great dead, to name just a few, include: Karl Schubert, Franz Mozart, Otto Hayden, Fritz Eugen the Last Breath, Zita Zits, Maria Theresiana, plus everything her namesake imperial military academy, the Theresianum, produced in Wiener Neustadt until 1918 and in Stalingrad 1943, plus several million more destroyed creatures. A place for wheeling and stealing: those sorts of deals and double deals are part and parcel of the tourist trade, in the course of which people, rather than getting worn out and thrown away, return in newer and better condition than they came; they get less for themselves, though, because they have nothing left in their budget. Still, it was worth it. Unfortunately, some also crash in the process. We find ourselves where we can truly find ourselves at the core of our being, in an Austrian village—or, rather, at its outermost reaches, which the mountain has already slipped into its pants pockets. Located rather on the fringe of tourism, the place is largely undeveloped. Only older people and families with lots of children go there, since there are hardly any opportunities for serious sports and entertainment. But all the more fresh air and deep forests. And beautiful mountains, about two thousand meters high, some even higher, though this area does not yet quite belong to the high alpine region. Hiking trails, a small local railroad, brooks, a clear river; however, if the dam is opened too quickly, the trout choke in the mud and they float by the bridge, belly up, countless squadrons, traveling along their choppy route just a moment ago, now driving away the tourists, who want to get to the inn on the other side, which is built into the rock and can be reached only over a sort of chicken ladder, a nearly impassable pathway.

Today some of the guests registered for a trip. They want to visit the Wild Alps region with its lakes and the small castle of the Habsburg archduke Johann, who married the postmaster's daughter from Aussee and then dug up the land like a mole—because besides those daughters above the earth, there had to be some iron left for the sons below the earth that could be processed for plows or cannons, both sharing, as always, a place next to each other in harmony. The earth gave the ore, and in return, the hammer barons from the Mürz River canyon and the iron barons from Vienna returned to the earth her tender children, the cannon fodder. So there is a lot to see in this area, if you are interested in the history of the iron dynasty. Fresh cold air. The minibus they had reserved well in advance stops in front of the inn, which is connected to a farm and a small hotel. Six people registered for the tour. Two of them, a couple from the Ruhr area, are dawdling around the entrance, asking each other for items they forgot and for the place they were to stop for lunch (included in the price); they are joined after a while by a single woman from Halle, (formerly East) Germany, they chat a bit—will the weather hold out, were they dressed properly, might it even be possible to arrange for a tour by one of the archduke's heirs? Would they be able to see the famous speedwell flower that the Habsburg gentleman had planted himself in honor of the postmaster's daughter? The Chrysler Voyager, ready to receive the passengers, pushes her snub nose across the parking lot, she's already gotten wind of her living prey. It's up to her whom she wants to deliver at the destination and in what condition, she has wild horses under the hood. The chauffeur is already slightly drunk, but he doesn't care, around here everyone's always somewhat inebriated, it's the custom of the region, and the regional champions eliminate each other in nightly piss-offs. Mornings at eight not even the players in the qualifying games are playing; they are asleep, leaden from the evening before. After the three passengers have already mounted the best seats, ready to let themselves be pushed out onto the water-gray country road that nearly gets squashed between all that luscious green rolling in from the left and the right, from above and below, four more people arrive—wait a minute, that's one too many, no problem, we'll just squeeze together a bit. On vacation you are more willing to accept things you wouldn't tolerate at home. One of them, a young man, hadn't made a reservation but wants to come along, nonetheless. Others, a mother and a daughter, not exactly a spring chicken either, the daughter, would not want to give up their seats or sit apart. Besides, the old lady wants to sit all the way in the front. That's not possible either. But it's possible to squeeze everyone into the car. We are not that fat, joke the passengers, who like company.

There is a murmur in the air that it will be a sunny day after all, and people are eager, all too eager, to learn about anything assuring them that they are part of this world. Time has passed, the sun has climbed a bit, taking a breath around midday, but the car is merrily rolling along, now she climbs up a mountain road, snaking higher and higher around the steep curves. It seems to be quite warm outside. People on bikes are showing off their bodies. The pavement ribbon, a grayish, living continuum. The alpine panorama reveals itself here, at the Niederalpl, the little lower alp, in all its splendor—mountains are pointed out by name, they nearly drown in all the sunlight, the motor hums soothingly. Now we are approaching the highest point, the summit of this ancient mountain path, and on the other side we'll have to get down again. The summer storms, which hit this area especially hard, took parts of the road down into the river with them. Pretty red-white-red plastic ribbons stretched between poles have been placed along the road in many spots where the concrete had broken off; caution, motorists and fellow travelers! Where there used to be a firm shoulder and just enough room to get out of the way of an approaching SUV, there is a sudden chasm, a jagged wound in the road's side. One doesn't have to thrust anything—a lance—into it to see that the wound is real. Again and again signs commanding extremely low speed limits. A voice from Halle requests in a strange German accent to follow orders—ancient obedience drills keep twitching in this woman's paws—but in this country official orders, which cling to us hungrily and want to ruin all our fun, are on principle not taken quite so seriously. So let's keep driving those sixty kilometers per hour, what can happen. I am telling you: Unfortunately, coincidentally, a tour bus will pass exactly the same part of the road. Tough luck. Here, that giant vehicle harnessed in metal advertisements is irrefutably the stronger. Unexpectedly, that monster which a month ago bit off a side of the road and spit it into the creek gets an unexpected dessert that's not much easier to digest. Only some garnish is missing, but wait—we can still get you some: this bloody multicolored woolen jacket looks quite good, that torn-off shoe over there, yeah, it's a little asymmetrical, the second one's missing, it's still stuck to a dirty, twisted foot. And what's that minibus doing down there all of a sudden, like a careless beetle tossed on its back by a giant step, limbs spread apart, idling in helpless rotations? Lying here are four persons who spurted out of it, not wearing seatbelts, of course, now they lie here, colorful splashes of Miracle Whip and cream dotting the steep grassy incline that merges, together with the debris of the road, into the creek that still carries the floodwaters. One, two uprooted trees in between. But those are left over from the flood. A twisted young man, two twisted women, an old woman, screaming, screaming like a sinner at the tabernacle, hurry, hurry!, before this roadside sale of humans closes. Torsos bent out of shape, arms tossed up high, as if a deep joy had overwhelmed those poor souls. Cool mountain air wafts across it all. The wheels are still spinning. The driver is pinned to the steering wheel that crushed his chest, a bit of liquid trickling from his mouth. But he won't be able to drink it, he was dragged away from his discount beverages; clutching the half-filled bottle of his life, he still seems braced to resist the steering of a higher power. Up on the hill, people are getting off the bus, screaming and crying they are also trying to find their way down the hill to the colorful meadow dotted with humans. Pine trees stand tall. Birds screech because of the disturbance, though deep inside they are unimpressed. The bus driver mumbles something sitting on the steps of the dangerous colossus entrusted to him. In any event, here you really can feel the tangy mountain climate. Like his passengers, the driver is Dutch and no longer understands the mountains or the world or those defeated people around here, this special breed that prides itself as nature's master and can't even master its own cars. Something has been felled here, a clearing opens up, it generously makes room for the sun to shine on like a spotlight. Like rolling stones, helpful inhabitants of the valley clamber across the muddy meadow. From the giant balcony above, the terrace of the tourist center, more human wrecks are tumbling down, unharmed but unhinged by their grief for the victims, they will get in the way of the rescue workers. All are wearing colorful summer clothes until evening. Then they will throw on their sweaters. Like a woolly dog, playful and fresh, nature jumps around her guests, circling them, tossing them in the air but not catching them, because another little stick flying through the air seems suddenly more attractive; capriciously, nature puts her paws on this and that, lets go again, ignoring that her playmate has been completely squashed and torn apart by her. She sniffs at the pieces, howls her song into the light until nightfall, then hauls another song from deep down in her throat. Nature! Jumping about clumsily, she bullies her way across the terrain like her bulldozers, which are already on the way. Endless the thrill of those life-size dolls scattered about, their limbs spread-eagled, their mouths no longer speaking words. Branches are broken off, their leaves already wilting. Rising high in the midday heat are the human slopes, decorations for the landscape, from which this land lives, they stretch all the way up the hill, to the tourist center and even inside, where those still living are scurrying about, rescuing their belongings on the trash pile; they've been saved, now they can spend themselves on the fitness trail. Dark forests below; those recent storms merely ripped the hem, soon construction brigades will have it fixed and rip us off if we dare to speed across it over thirty kph. Let us proceed on foot, into the woods. The sun holds up a lamp to our faces, we think the glare in front of us is a mirror, and bang our heads against the rock that is us. Thus, we throw ourselves down the alpine valley, the dogs bark, something grabs us by the neck, but not the dogs, they want to assure us for now.

1

In the mountains, where tranquillity can quickly be ruptured by lightning, those passing bolts of terror that actually produce little but destroy a lot, up in those mountains several people disappeared. Others returned, who weren't even missed. We, the recovered ones, experienced it all, and now we talk about it as if a word had just brushed against us and, in passing, suddenly stepped on us.

For a while the missing could squeeze into the crevices of the mountain, a mannerly herd seeking shelter according to a brochure that dared to contain it, and then a hand, with the flick of the wrist, ripped them out of there. Those were folks, tourists, who did not withhold their presence anywhere, which makes their sudden absence all the more surprising. They demanded leashes for animals, rules for humans: Figures who one day didn't sign themselves back in at reception; too bad, we had gotten used to serving them. Now they won't touch their food anymore. Who will be touched by the surrounding beauty, now that they are gone? Who took them from nature, their second home? The person of culture swings back and forth inside himself like some vehicle, but if he wishes to rest for a moment, he has nothing to hold on to. He reached for immediacy, which was exactly the way to turn everything sacred to him into its opposite: his simply being here; beautiful mountains! That is what we expect. Nature, that ole barrack leader, who always lets the others do the cleaning! Did these people die in the mountains after an attack that dispatched them to death? Did the Unreal commit a procreative act, which simultaneously bade farewell to the lives of the disappeared? A ceremony that is still in process at this hour?

Not even one bat of an eyelash was left of them hanging in the air. The bats had already returned to the pits. Now rocks burst apart and the batter of the unthinkable that nonetheless had just been experienced is dripping from their skin. Look how brightly the mountains bore through the sky's frosting! (Being nature means being perceivable!) Vigilant and humorous the natives, whose blood contains a high level of confusion. Thoughtlessly we keep them on their toes, those unpolished fellows; not even with the stamp of money can you impress on them the brands of beer or schnapps they should serve us. We must repeat our order every day, and every conversation deals with the dilemma of everything tasting so good on the one hand and not being good for you on the other. The rock gets battered with pitons but does not flinch; that happened earlier, as reported in a special newsbreak, when the pit went up in the air. The mountain is back to being a cuddly pet, pacified, Watch out! Duck!—You are about to enter the text at hand. It slides through your fingers, but it doesn't matter, someone else will have to carry me through to completion, a mountain guide, not you!

All of a sudden, completely useless, the past is here again, it's impossible to love her. Why now? We just sent her out on an errand, to a supermarket where they are selling human spare parts, and now she's back already. We don't yet have any change for bills. Besides, the old supplies must first be removed from the fridge of our memory, where they were kept, frozen and past their expiration date. What's the charge? Whom do we charge? Even fruit trees must accept their fruit being taken from them! But since guests from abroad also dine here sometimes, we must work a little harder. She seems to have stumbled, the past, staggered, just before she reached the finish line—once again the weather was quite rude to her and now—oh no, now she made a wrong turn to boot, and now she shoots right out of the finish line. With determination I now close my path for today and give it a path name before it gets scorched by this red-hot experience. Will we dare to expel this sight emerging from the dark? Or will we be terrified when the past tries to pick our lock and, unsightly and coarse, without any gains but all wrapped up in new bargains, spreads out in our best room, which we, of course, had reserved. Our last topic was rocks. Like the old days that rocked the world, it's impossible to contemplate them romantically when they are five centimeters away from your face and you have no free hand to get yourself out: it wasn't us! People disappeared! Yes, here, from nature, that gingerly beginning of being. Tourists—well, folks who don't know about beginnings, because they are always so quickly finished. And then they regret the end to no end. I offer them the opportunity to do so. This land has always kept still, that is, it has style: as a matter of principle, it explores humans only when they are already hurling into the trash can. The terrain is so difficult, it is impossible to simply keep going. You must learn to economize yourself and your energies, because the road keeps going up and down again so that it appears to be much longer than calculated. For the fun of it, some residents are posing for the photographer now, they don't understand a word they say, but no one gives them a hearing anyway. We don't need any outside judges is how they put it here. Sometimes the youngest among our forever young sing in Austro-Pop schmaltz local dialect, which they zing into the wrinkles we've got because of them. I don't have enough paper to wipe it all off. The rock is opening up, watch out! The creek also opens up in front of us. Terrific! Oh, my dear radio, dearest Austrian broadcasting, I forgot that even if people disappear in crippling catastrophes, you will always be here as long as our rushing mountain creeks keep gushing over the stones. Then the water that used to flow crystal clear into the pipes spouts out a lot of dirt. It is totally confused and doesn't know what's in the pipes. Those are only the loudspeakers, the only ones allowed to come out of the station sometimes, but they are not the up-and-comers, because soon a change of executives is due. Done deal! They all want to stay forever, but they are not allowed.

Guests are snatched from unhappy interactions with each other and the next table; unfortunately, we cannot keep an eye on more than that. There could easily be more sneaking out quietly to other vacation spots. The natives are at our service. In my view they have learned nothing and lost nothing. Who can be helped? Who would pass water onto the insufficient ground into a chasm, where his yellow jet never arrives, where he is nothing but the stone something shines on for a moment and then no more, because the sun has set.

The country inn is like a soul that's shown to a group of tourists: Cursed but not closed, it rests in the body of the mountain and ruins its character. It is old. Years ago, nobler guests left their indentations in the old benches and massive staircases, now it's rather ordinary folks in the beer line. Vigilance and humor are the qualities of the old watchdog waiting with ever reawakening excitement for the lunch hour to end. What a bright vacation day! And how sharp its tool, time—it hollows us out by creating connections between us that will take great effort to undo again. Soon we won't be able to stand any longer the person whom we chose to sit next to not so long ago. With black paws the thunderstorm reaches for the fire wall and then—because it can't tear down anything there—for the lightning rod on the roof, which finally paves the way for the bolt to strike the earth. Will the go-betweens emerge from there, those creatures between life and death? All those time travelers, who timed out long ago, which disqualified them for Olympia? Are the holes in the ground even deep enough? The dead, after all, have been comminuted for their own sake. Will they gather their bodies again from the ashes? Quiet please, existences fall silent here. They are moved through a gate while we are still tossing our spirit in the sizzling grease that's splashing at us from the scenic view with its rest-stop facilities. Sometimes we throw it high up in the air and let it splash back, our great spirit, that is. We open up whining under the impact of the *Sturm,* a homemade storm, the winey juice we brewed and downed and are about to drown in; and that's about the closest we get to being touched.

Fruits crumble and tumble—it is fall—from their stems with a clash and a splash into the grass, where they pop, having puffed themselves up in the trees for so long. Sometimes they land right in the deck chairs, it's a bit late in the season, after all, so risks are part of the deal for anyone still wanting to stay. This is the time of year when retirees can afford a vacation; poor folks, they often have to wake up to the blare of the boom box. It makes them beat their own drum to the tune of the Beach Boys, but they miss and eject themselves from the pleasant harmony. They found nature and they found her beautiful. Nature is empty but holding up. We, at any rate, cannot grasp her; someone else must have done that. We cannot even grasp ourselves once our deeds are over and done with. By then, we simply won't have been at home back then. What, that magazine does not cover us and our worries? That's supposed to be all the celestial fire gifted to us? Who out there is actually prominent and one of those few percent? You would have to set yourself on fire, together with the magazine pages that don't mention you, in the warm oven of a stranger whom you hope to interest in your story on the occasion of a leisurely stroll. That is where the roaring fire of enthusiasm for our local sports club gets stoked. Not even the dog shit on our shoes stays with us as long as that club! Vacations make other people suffer, once the lassos of conversations are thrown around their neck. The gentleman or the lady brushing by them stops walking with a tremble. Their flanks heave, holy, if no longer entirely sober, water runs over them, and in one gush, we throw ourselves with this bathwater all over them. Sitting on the hot floor of a sauna and wanting to jump up any moment, that is vacation: Others are tortured with us. Trees spread out across the slope. We don't even notice that we don't hold our horses, then fire!, the voice box is aflame, and again a new acquaintance has gone up in sound and smoke and video and Photoshop. Folks paint their children's and grandchildren's lifelines in rough strokes until the layers get so thick that the faraway little darlings can't move under all the oil and paint their relatives dipped them into. Vacation. A small response from life, after many months of working up the dough, which means beating, kicking, and punching, with a pinch of salt to taste.

Overweight singers point to their very selves when asked about their artistic goals. Expensive cars linger calmly until they are entered again. The zest of thousands of fans taking LPs home energizes people with no interest at all, to go on singing. So much fire in our artists—it could propel a rocket to shoot those swaying and preying geezers and gals into space, after which they must turn back again when the fire has gone out. A table turns under their record-breaking paws, and the glasses in their hands behave like trained seals. Once on top, always on top. The success of his song makes him very happy, says the singer we call Austrobard because his songs had outgrown beards long before he was even born. It's the kind of music to listen to in the garden while the domestic genies who are still alive, all squeezed into one garret during the season, keep running around busily with trays and bottles and constantly clean up wherever humans and animals, animated by so much intake, both solid and fluid, have had to relieve themselves on the spot.

Logging trucks with their cargo are piling up high on the forest road, the best and fastest model, a Golf GTI offered up to them as a sacrifice before they had a chance to admire it, got underneath their front wheels. But for the time being we prefer listening to Austrian songs on the radio that hangs pathetically tilted under the umbrella of a wooden Jesus's wide-open arms in the farthest right corner you will find in this place (where, by the way, breakfast will also be served) from a board without ever leaving—no, no, God will never forsake us—that board. Everything newly renovated. New showers have also just been installed. And all that time those fresh songs, which also take some time to imprint themselves on us without too much effort, the embossing die is strong, so that the singer can earn some real money. Those songs create a little bit of home in the middle of nowhere, because you've got to sit down right away for such songs, no matter where you are, even if you are not tired at all. But better not let yourself get carried away, because the land's masses are massively represented here. Once the schmaltz is hitting the fan, it would be hard to get it out of its system, and our new guests, whom we now want to welcome with hearty applause, would be trampled down in the resulting stampede.

Anyway, a certain Gudrun Bichler in her deck chair finds herself bothered by a group of female retirettes switching stations, trying to squeeze out a few pounds of *Volk* music so that their muse is also represented. Either tune in, but quietly please, and stay with the station you picked so that your plaster legs and your intercontinental containment pans can easily churn up the ground and only you will fall in. Or turn it off completely! Everyone has a different idea about their vacation, which always must be downsized as soon as the curtain goes up. The retired ladies, among them Frau Karin Frenzel, who reportedly was married to a now-extinct volcano of a man, are still rumbling from the depths of their most innermost selves, where the food dwells, because they want to tease out of life as many sated and stylish tremors as they still can, they don't want to turn them down, who knows if by tomorrow they will have stopped completely? Quiet! Death, this shy game, which the hunter, usually game for anything, prefers not to hit, though more often than not, it hits him: A glob of mustard is all that's left of us when death starts to put the squeeze on for real. These elderly ladies, oh well, they've just been told they are the only recipients of this kind of music, which is evident from the album sales. Now that it's almost too late, those old gals want to fill up big houses, which might turn out to be advantageous if an illness wanted to carry them off. It wouldn't be quite as easy for the illness to find them there. Now that vacationers have been served essential, native-soil agrarian products, they are moving in a completely different direction, more strongly toward local customs to crown the defeat of their lives with a big victory, the victory in the Second World War that this country won in singing and yodeling, won, that is, by simple peasants, workers, and clerks, their music being the sound of weapons: Hard cash from hard hits, which keep the change small in what's a small world after all. And the sacred awakens in us, it hits the news after the hit parade through thousands of miles of light wave cables. Paradise is telecast to ever last, while elsewhere they can only dream about it, in countries that have been silenced.

Around here no one believes anymore that there is anything to get out of another person but a self-knitted touchy-feely pullover, and we certainly don't have to wear that sort of clothing. But since all of us always looked like wild—I mean mild—animals, we could not recognize ourselves in the other, a lady from Erfurth, Germany (formerly East), says to a lady from Steyr, Austria, in the unmistakable tone of innocence. The woman from East Germany had managed to give away nothing of herself and still get away with it, just in time, before they could prove anything. But by then all the others had already left. Time barreled ahead, from thinking to telling and on to yelling and some shelling. Old eyes get turned on one last time by lightning bolts discharged from TV sets and hitting where the passions are kicking and scrambling in baby clothes to get to the goal, all those prettily embroidered covers on top of the couple, yes, there, too fast for the eyes of the elderly, who are close to the heavenly hitter and short of disposable means. The most foreign cultures appear in a box and are carried around, weightless as light, they must reveal themselves like new manifestations of the Holy Eucharist, and still they are not recognized when they appear to us. Those bodies keep silent when stepped on, and nothing returns them to the unspeakable in life as they roll, beat up and broken, down S-Bahn railway embankments. Let our on-screen favorites who don't want us to depart carry on as much as they like, they can squirt their holy miracle whipped filling over the top, those drops are no holy water, they do not bless us.

Those decomposing, dead or alive, haven't yet realized that their future has already begun. The trees all around them have taught them plenty about patience, they can wait for their colors to change. The vacationers, three persons all told, have already collapsed backward as they took off from their folding lounge chairs. Those fruits ripe for fate's firm hand exposed their soft cores in falling, but no one was up to ingesting them. All the other guests are busy taking in Tommy Gottschalk, the famous talk show host, yes, the one who talks up such a storm that they can't keep up getting all those words out of the way again. So they have to burn a few pieces of their furniture to make sure there is enough room for their beloved TV personality. Every vacationer kicks out the past and takes their place—on the floor, if need be. Here folks get a small response out of life, since they remain silent at work. All around live limbs expand crevices and crevasses and encounter their toughest critic: God. On this natural stage all performers are amateurs. Oh dear, look, up there you can see a person transformed into a kite! Or down in the water, that's what they also like, vacationers. The wet can be kept within bounds, since it does not create any boundaries on its own. Edgar G., that young salesman in a sports store, himself an undefined item on his own counter, why, of all people, did they have to pick him? Well, because he pulled himself out and lifted himself up in the air, that's why! There, way up there, the unfortunate in the gliding contraption, that's him! Let's hope he can restrain himself before he crashes into a power line! The way he throws himself up in the air, laughing, every day, as if he had to throw himself on top of anything! So hot for seeing himself as divine, which already proved fatal for our World Cup skier Ulli Maier. The rest of us suffer more decently, maybe from a late lunch that had to be kept warm for us because we chatted away on the bench at the scenic mountain torrent. Yesterday the young hang glider landed in a different place than he had calculated; he woke up to the dull pounding of a tennis broadcast, nothing but a scrap of paper in the air with a man hanging on it, stalling, while the really important things are free to pelt unimpeded through the ether, Boris! Steffi! On the sports channel! Paddling against our domestic wastewater. They, too, are running against their time, but even more so our stars of slopes and concert halls, Anita Wachter, Roman Ortner, and/or Patrick Ortlieb or whatever's his name, in their constant fight against the clock that makes them forget about danger, but those heroes are not to blame for how decisively they decide the race for themselves and the next one, too. Then their last view of life can be milked over and over again, but it will still be dripping, life, because it's not easy to get over it. So we can it. Ulli's time was stopped short by the slalom pole (a scepter of eternity), which dared to spite finity; it broke her neck and ripped the arteries leading to her brain; oh, I feel so sorry for Ulli, the news lady tells us who are stuck, too, kicking in the underbrush, unable to get rid of our leashes. Life is one of many natural climbing schools where our Creator can get rid of as many people as possible as fast as possible. After all, he doesn't have us born as fruit you can squeeze endlessly or stuff into dumplings as their soul. Maybe HE just doesn't want to look at our athletic gear anymore, which is the main thing to us, when we wipe ourselves, all finished, onto paper.

The food of the Wirtin, the innkeeper, is plenty for the eagerly waiting crowd. They sit at the tables pinned to their chairs. And the colas, Sprites, and beers foam like mountain torrents during a tempest into the glasses turned to crystal clearness by the eighty-six-year-old dishwasherwoman temp. Yes, the weather flows into the tourists, it stops right in the middle, just when it's most beautiful. The outfit. In the mountains, it is an intimate part of any athletic burgher, so to speak, the most immediate one, before one can recognize the person underneath, who isn't always waterproof either, still, everyone is special. That's what they all think. The dogs, also those of the guests, are alert yet restless, fat and lazy from all the leftovers fed to them yet ready anytime to sound the alarm, their calling is noise. Here animals also take on duties. Yesterday, down in the valley, a cow dropped an ossified twin calf into the ropes the vet had laid out for it, young as it was. A common mishap. Beyond that no further omens, or we would have paid attention to it, I would certainly hope so. So far, only the weather, our old antagonist, has made an entrance into the Now.

Besides one exception, an unpleasant sight: the forester's two sons two years ago. They filled their gun barrels with water (ammo, however, was also still in them) and blew themselves away, right out of themselves, I mean, each himself out of himself. The self-disappeared. They say one was teasing the other he'd never pass hunter's school. They were so shook up by each other, they finally had to prepare themselves for death: That's what a hunter does, after all, it's his job. They smashed their brains and the pan that comes with each. The village is still talking about it. But what is one to think about sightings of the two—as if the village were an eternal construction site, where all sorts of trash can show up anytime—appearing at the edge of the village, always together, in their forester's traditional costumes (now a horrific sight!), though they both were buried in their one and only Sunday suit, each with a bouquet of flowers, as if for a wedding, maybe so that their smashed heads wouldn't draw too much attention.

The mountains are still distant today: Those alpine athletes are really somewhat childish. Tongue between teeth they scribble themselves into the slope and set themselves as the period behind it. They've said what they had to say with their entire selves, because they've always carried nature, the object of perception, in their soul. This is why they don't really want to read nature; they'd rather erase it, because the previous time they didn't inscribe themselves beautifully enough. So that they could be the end of all, too, but others should follow. Man has always had a moral interest in nature's appearance, which is the essence of her beauty; he forgot it was he who gave it to nature by making the effort to enter her. By nightfall, when fog's furious fumes will roll over the inn's patrons as playing cards smack into hands, the game will change for three of them; they will switch gear and won't need a clutch, nor a crotch that can rot, and become omnipresent. The disappeared return unexpectedly, as opposed to sports, where one also shows up time and again, but this time, let's hope, as the first. In order to scream "Here!" loud and clear. The true athlete remains at the very beginning, which makes him faster than the rest, because he has always already been there. But where would it lead to if all those who left were to come home again? This song wears well! And you are wearing something new today in a stunning new color, good for you! Mother Nature, who always has to get so upset about nuclear power, can for once be happy with us. How could one ever refuse her?

Three people have been fished out of the piles of flesh (and anywhere else where German is spoken) in Austrian cities, which have always made mincemeat of their peoples; all they wanted, these three, was some fun, and suddenly they must funnel a force they hadn't known before. This force wants food, a leather jacket, jeans, nothing but the best; an athletic device humming under us who want to be faster than rivers. Athletes: Austria is like a construction site for those half-finished bodies on their skis chasing each other unrestrained into the chasm, probably because the spaces above were too crowded for them. Then, Bingo!, natural-born actors!, all of them!, this country is in the spotlight, and that can only be good for us! Isn't it often the smallest things—hundredths of a second—that play the most important part? There, the pull of bright light coming from the winners' podium, and later that night you are entitled to drive completely drunk into a house, you don't even have to open the door. Just drive the car right up the wall. Nothingness—and nature is also a part of it, right there, to your right, next to the panoramic view with the ski trails crawling across it like worms measuring the mountain for a new suit she can finally afford, thanks to the profits from tourism, no, still farther to the right, this Nothing has to be fed again and again, or it could happen that it devours people. To put it bluntly: Nature is a pedestrian zone. The gesture of a dead person who is content with an artificial Christmas tree, no, even perfectly happy with just the lights winding around a store entrance, such a small gesture is quite out of place there. Real roots growing into a grave can be quite prickly and annoying. By contrast, look at that drowned face at the bottom of the mountain lake, how beautifully it drifts along—turned into hardwood and wax; minerals, however, are swimming right next to it, making life also pretty hard for the dead:

an entire wedding party at the bottom of the lake! Their horses had taken off with them about a hundred years ago because their cargo was screaming so much, thrilled as to where a mount can lead to: downward. None of the wedding guests could cut themselves a piece from that singing cheesy cake anymore. The vanished and those wasted by sports (Ulrike M.!) won't be missing when we gaze cheery-eyed into the TV screen's bright glow. We simply imagine them up there! But we never thought they would come for real. We would have liked to try, just once, to join the famous races in their place, the Lauberhorn, the Hahnenkamm, why should we be the ones left out, history, after all, had already devoured so many of us who didn't want to get lost either back then. The reserves of our national teams are not infinite to the degree that they don't have to fall back on the resources of those passed in order to shape the up and coming, at weight machines, in fitness spas, under sauna steam, and in the whirls of hot tubs, where the top talents, if they so wish, can be cooked and served in the pretty garnish of their bodies. Why lose sweat over the dead, there will always be plenty new blood and they can suck it or leave it. Either way, they always look so hot on-screen.

Well then, who goes first? This young man here from the National League's former B-Team—what's his name, Edgar Gstranz, a man from the west but not without merit, not just a simple servant of his master trainer. Today Edgar is walking for a change—variety is fun, isn't it?—to the east, can you see his great, almost footloose figure? In the distance. Onto level—take a look at the dipstick—it's not too bad, earthling! Come on now! Something pleasurable swells up inside him and wants out, victories such as: the Super-G, anno Snow, according to the Austrian calendar (meaning way back when), Class Youth II, some have to settle for less. This young man successfully saved himself in a sports shop, where he can purchase at cost the latest outfits in which to constantly present himself as prompter to his customers doing their homework. But they get confused—should they believe him or the Newsies magazine, where they read and saw completely different things. It's even creative in a way to fail at what is hardly wear- and bearable. We deserve it. This is the place, where Edgar will get end-consumed sometime after he placed himself as the full stop behind the National League's B-Team, before he made it all the way downhill. Sometimes the end is closer than you think. Edgar lounges in a deck chair, and some man-eating ladies around him are whispering, hadn't they read in the papers, about two years ago, or was it already three, that he was killed in a CAR ACCIDENT. Can't trust the papers, not even when they disclose all sources and sorts of tips they could tab for the tip-offs. Fast cars are for the master racer, that holiest of all our guiding lights, a danger, because he knows how fast he is and how much faster he must get. Since the athlete can't just jump out of himself, his trainer has to light a fuse in him, and Edgar's is apparently still burning. I live in the capital now, he says, when asked about his uncanny accident more than two years ago. One can't just blurt out, aren't you dead, Herr Gstranz, it would be too embarrassing to publicly admit such an obvious error. Today others are drawing their lines across the telly. That tally is endless, everyone is drawing their life to an end that way—Edgar's life seems to have been a semicolon. A new breath follows, a fire thrown into the soul, how embarrassing to catch such an edge, cutting deeply into the nice virgin snow, which must take so much abuse already.

2

It's been a while since this young man was our guest at our regular Monday night sports rounds, a flaky Napoleon, who kept us entertained. And in return we hound him so viciously! How often did he stand empty-handed before the dreams of his fans, just so he could stay a bit longer in their homes, he was in top shape for it, at least judging by the trial races. No ontological disaster threatened him then. Was he the one who drove up the wall of the house instead of straight ahead? Or wasn't he? Scent tells. Strange, that the dogs don't bark at him, as they do around all the other guests. Disco hunters first admit future winners into our bar, where they go down the un-finitude of our chasms, which we prepared for us so that we could keep off or on track, as the case may be. We spectators sit in front of the tube, the singing of the national anthem went well, and while we pull the thorns of the beginning workweek out of our skin with our wetted beaks, a young man's image crashes on the screen, he throws his arms out of the frame, his song stops, a twenty-five-meter trail of blood in the snow. But nothing stops the calm of conversations about our sons, whom we sent off into the war of sports, and our daughters, who heated our emotions (those are ready anytime to hide again, if a few hundredths of seconds are missing) with a slalom victory. Now we can once again cook the goose for you, dear Austria, you have worn your intrinsic luck long enough, now sleeves must be mended and edges sharpened; woeful babble must slip from the speakers' tongues, as the US boys are winning a bit now, and that sucks! The brightly illuminated home entertainment altar swings open, 85 percent of us let ourselves get sucked dry without having left any effect, and the skier takes a sharp turn at the finish line to drive himself into the haloed hideout of the mike. Words also spring from us, even before we can find the mouth, our estuary for all the knödels and kraut we burned in us. That's what happens sometimes to talents that were spent too soon, they forgot that they were finite, limited: and thus the market was responsible for them to a limited degree only. We, however, we just can't stop anymore. The proof: Formula 1. Every one of us wins it under the collective name Gerhard Berger, no need for you to be fast and furious, a new Walker will do. Just hang on to the big guys in this industry, not even they can smash us small potatoes on our couches. They won't cool our little bit of brio, those windbags! They are not recyclable, that's why we finally need new faces!

What is the purpose of Edgar Gstranz's pompous posturing? Which side of death might he be on? The hereafter or the here here? Some swear that two years ago or so he played a prominent role in the evening news, so it couldn't possibly be him. Why then does he go by the same name as the one who crashed before the cameraman could get to him? Does he look like him? A Lazarus who picks up his bed, no, board on wheels; he seems to have woken up as the role model for our future late existence, or rather, the latest rollerboard model, but the likes of us would have their feet slipping off and under. Still, let's give it a try! In short, his sponsor wants him to test the newest lawn skateboard right here, on the more moderate slopes of the alpine foothills. To get to the point: Edgar's awakening is meant to shield him from the endless cloud of darkness approaching him: timelessness! What's that supposed to mean?, it can't possibly get any worse, since Edgar might be dead already. Time can't be caught in a pointed cap covering our shiny skull; light shies away from the suddenly darkened void and hesitates one moment too long. Today Edgar does not take his mountain bike, he takes his board and, having already been a dish for nature once, prepares himself as a warmed-up meal on wheels for that insatiable omnivore—she might like a second helping, where, in the meantime, friendly creatures have been lolling about: *Yersinia enterocolitica, Salmonella enteritidis, Salmonella* Panama, hemorrhagic colitis, *Salmonella* Braenderup, Agona, Montevideo, Senftenberg, Bredeney, Infantis, Heidelberg, and *E. coli* O157:H7. Oh yes, nature with her rabbit punches.

If you haven't practiced enough to get away from her scent, cars with red and blue lights will come after you. Well, now we'll let nature have it for a change! Today Edgar doesn't take his mountain bike, he takes his skateboard. Summer, unfortunately, limits the kind of equipment that can carry us. But once our clothes are off, folks will be carried away by us, that is, those who also took off most of their clothes. Some manage to get under our skin, but they don't get very far. Edgar came. He laughed, he danced and sashayed about, not bad for a dead man. Will he wear his torn jeans today or the other pants that simulate skin, where human skin would normally begin? Aha, he gets into his cycling pants, actually those are club jerseys, with big numbers, colorful stripes, bright symbols, and sharpened gazes ambling up and down and gliding off now and again from this hilly polyester slope, they glide and swirl like snowflakes, those glances, but they have to watch out for what's down below and for the fire they keep feeding so it won't go out, and without us at that.

One more Coke gulped down to swallow a middle-aged woman's hateful comment, though that comment was laid on somewhat too thick to swallow unpunished by a scale. Something gets outlined on a body, but the sketch got lost midway, and the hidden remains unfinished. The eternal draftsman covers his paper, lest anyone can take a look at it. He'll win again! Another quick look thrown like a sharp pebble over there, where the student Gudrun Bichler—a piece of mediocre architecture, but one of the few around here who are still able to stand up straight without instantly falling, if their crutches were taken away—well then, where this Gudrun sits and studies for the exam. She lifts up her eyes and scoops up a spoonful of Edgar into her own measuring cup, she even treats herself to a second helping on top of all the other mistreats, yes, unfortunately, she is always dependent on other people for such generous gifts. A nice young woman, bent over some written stuff. That's what she does, abandoned as she is inside herself (and that's not a matter of deterioration! It is like passing through one's own nature), which she has done for the past five years. Back then she lay down in her bathtub and cut her wrists thinking that she'd never pass the exams. And that is exactly what happened after they pulled Gudrun—a dripping bundle of a dumpling saved up for absolutely nothing, almost cooked to rags, from the red brew, the red beds. It didn't make the news, so you don't have to be annoyed if you didn't know about it. The old scars, from unlived life, unloved love, are still there. It was groundless, but it did not just seem so. Life is not a bowl of cherries, it's the pits, thus one must either get crushed to death or help things along a bit. One cut on the right, in a rising line above the wrist, one on the left, the significance of it is hard to tell, the young woman always wears long sleeves, even in sweltering heat. This human instrument Gudrun had been tuned by death once and then left behind by death out of tune, because she is so low-strung, and in the orchestra of winners and wannabes (those with their divining rods they hit us with across our calves, as they let everyone have it when they themselves don't make it!), they will not tolerate such lowly fellow players. Thus, for Gudrun everything is always the present, and learning does not advance her either, since there is no future and there is no starting point. Every day is the same, and in the evening thoughts end quietly only to return the next morning, unscathed, unsolved, but once again tortured and tormented by Gudrun. It was Edgar who scooped Gudrun out of the melting pot, as he instinctively recognized a coessentiality: a fellow dead who does not decompose. Just like him. Her parents stopped mourning three quarters of a year ago and turned all their worries toward their second child, a son, who already had problems passing high school. Can't split yourself in two, especially for the dead, we'd have to join them, wouldn't we, and that wouldn't do them any good, they are more than enough for their own elimination rounds, truth to tell, they are already too many to get a good helping of the holy into the souls, the kind of holy that comes with a poster of your favorite star, who, sadly, also had to die. Then we'll all burn, while we are still alive, in the purgatory of our never-ending worship! I can hardly wait. Gudrun, of course, is the kind of person who never uses makeup. Under normal circumstances she wouldn't be worth a pit stop, say those who launched an opinion poll, and now they are gathering all the votes around them that they had collected themselves. However: This is what makes a vacation so special, when you only attend the show in which you have a part, you can pick all the other actors. Edgar's awakening goes back the longest time to when he was still alive, and quite by accident here is a girl who is going through the same thing, she turns here, she turns there, but nothing changes. The wind is blowing, the mind is blown, but that won't help the two to escape the construct they got themselves into wantonly. Something inside them must have been locked too tightly when they died because their passing, owing to circumstances, could not get through to them. The locksmith is still trying his picks on those zombies, which can make one's life a living hell, but those two, as much as they struggle to get through the door, remain at the reception, even though others have been handed their keys quite a while ago and now are tossing about in a steamy bath (maybe it was Gudrun's death bath that dealt her the immortal blow, but strangely enough, not through the big door but through a combination of hairpin curves zigzagging within themselves, through which she could not get because she was not thin as a fish stickie. All those who won't eat those tasty fried fish-waste chippings will be chopped themselves and not get to heaven, thus they won't be welcomed by gilded little children. Upper ski, catching an edge, endless backtracking, this won't get you anywhere today, but in Toni's time it still was possible and common, you could sidestep back and still win. Well, our equipment got faster), so then, lying in the bathtub, having already brought their passions, plain alphabet pasta, to a boil.

Occasionally they live together, content with each other, then again on their own, that's the magic of a vacation fling; bodies do the talking, pretty prints on T-shirts tell entire novels while faces play cool. There we have two young deceased people facing each other, not knowing they are already crossed out on their own ID cards. They look one way, then the other, they briefly show themselves off to each other, though not yet in words. Gudrun did not get any lighter from her final bloodletting. She had just finished some morning leafing through her books and now, encircled by shadows of shivering trees, she quickly drops her glances, blind against anything happening in the twinkling of an eye. The athletic Edgar is on his way to the slope to schuss and shoot down the landscape in a squatting position in which they no longer bury people. The women of the world, though currently in Bosnia (they are staging a play there) and unable to be here, have sent word that the dead may pick the smart sportswear out of the postmortal pile of Goodwill so that they can again be the target of starry eyes. A god has performed at his peak.

Soon the weather will have to yield to dusk and a chill. What happens if someone won't step down, even though he is already dead for the team manager and the downhill coach? Who will sound him the death knell? No matter how friendly the eliminated member's demeanor, it will always just mean an angry stomping: that his presence should be given the chance to remain a bit longer in the luminous squad, for the Plunge into Anonymity is worse than death. This young athlete fitted his character to a T, his team T-shirt, that is, and did not notice that his whole body had vanished underneath: The wall came closer and closer, and it is still coming closer, in an eternal approach, first a soft knock on the wall, but nature slept so soundly, she did not come to in time. The Sacred is unapproachable, thus Edgar has to stay although he is long gone. This is how far ambition can take you, if paired with patience and able to wait to get fielded: eternity does get opened. Edgar has been working for such a long time—almost indistinguishable from the pros squeezing into their ski boots—in a sporting goods shop, starting the clock with his heel (push start), but the clock simply won't move! So Edgar, let go by Time, has to push harder and harder to catch up with the living. His clothing is streamlined, which shaves off a few hundredths, even tenths, of seconds before one has to climb up again like a stag to his stupid does. Why do those fellows in their fashionable gear always look like they have already beaten their own time? Still, they depend on us consumers whether anyone will follow them or not. If not, they have to get right back to the start, no matter how fast they were. Mediocrity wins, we win, we have to suggest to nature what she should look like, yes, we, the simple folk, we have an alarm, we have a sense, we chase us and others, blind to the moment, scared to death of boredom. You would not believe it looking at us. And the way we want to prepare for death! There are outfits simulating wholeness you wouldn't want to wear in the coffin, let alone having anyone take a picture of us. Because our maimed, knowing faces, not to speak of our bodies that finally experienced what a little rascal God can be, how young and cute like an animal, how else could he have the idea to let our whole family get burned alive in a car—we, that is, what is left of us, simply don't belong into those camouflage suits (we can't be seen!). Luckily, those suits are open in the back, so we, the dead, maggots in the bacon of the rich, can easily slip out. As advertised, such outfits come with a top to go with the skirt, and a jacket with the pants, but what's left of us is just a charred trunk and the sawed-off twigs of our children's arms and legs. Now then, we pass! We are on the road again, a great song is devoted to us, God has dedicated it to us. Let's go. Edgar cracks the whip of his clothes as if nothing had happened. And the forest waves with its hem, which is a bit torn and trampled down. In the distance a moving train, people screaming inside, they see an emergency stop coming but they can't find anyone to hold on to before their scaffolding collapses on top of the neighbor who had just offered them a candy. A slight motion somewhere. A thought, a dangerous, radiant mass particle, temporarily stored in the head, will soon jump up and start its travel. It will have to do this outside, because the skull, before it could have a talk with its living partner, will be squashed like a used-up tube (there will be five dead in this train crash). So then, the thought is running away as if Kant or Hegel were chasing it or, worse, the famous homegrown Enemy of the State author [Th.B.] with his well-chewed bubble-gum bullet by the name of Pascal (the ladies especially would love to meet him!); but turning around, the thought realizes that even the very last thing guys like his master would say or do is barely worth a quickly polished off bowl of laughter, it would be exactly what they just read in the Post or the News. And this is to make us feel at home in the Nothing. Give me something to hold on to, it will be a bumpy ride. Others got unhinged in their novels and moved too far away from their home base. They are headed directly my way, help! They are so merciless, steely, cold, and tough, they switch to different, sturdier skis at the turn they call *Heimat.* But I am already there. Ouch! And now, of course, they are looking for someone to fasten them securely, those warheads, who attack their thought costumes day after day, blowing them to shreds, and all they do is miss the gate. And this is exactly where I am desperately twisting and turning my hips, hit by my disappointments, but I cannot get around this erstwhile red but now scraped-off (those animals! They always scratched their backs on it) pole. One shouldn't talk about the dead, who, after all, are what our country is all about. Better fiddle and diddle with Mary Th., the empress, and Prince Gene, they are dead, too. How true.

Clearance merchandise cannot be exchanged, better tell Edgar right away! To get him back to his original size. Now he bounces briskly toward the edge of the forest. For the time being, Gudrun and he are still separated, his gaze, worldless, had still tossed back hers like a piece of greasy wrapping paper snuggling against a ham sandwich, except that this woman could never wrap him around her finger. And this hunk merges with nature, he carries on ridiculously on his board, but nature has patience, she keeps up with him. That's how ridiculous speed always is (says H.), an empty on and on and on, or like a slope near Kitzbühel with family homes squeezed together like freshly dyed Easter eggs in a moldy carton, quite a sight! A hen comes with it free of charge, since there is room in the carton for many more eggs. Nowadays you have to put on gloves just to touch the earth. The winds pluck the harp of trees, and low and behold, folks get tuned up, they get turned on, and the setting suggests a rural harmony called yodeling. It sounds as if one is about to crack up, but it is to be sung in unison. Edgar's gaze gets stuck on something; it tears itself away again. One figure, A, still glowing a bit in the sun (see fig. 3), amid the trees, who wants to be spelled in capital letters. The man embarks on his journey. Figuring the length of the slope and the speed of gliding down, it shouldn't take long. On his mind a few scraps of conversations with journalists trying to get smart with him; in the dining room regulars at the sports table standing up politely as a fire is thrown at them, it is, yes, it is the Olympic flame, and it flies past Edgar's cute face. A tennis star is cooking spaghetti in a TV commercial, she is the leading lady Punch, so to speak, Steffi gets away with anything, there is plenty talk about her, as opposed to Edgar, who besides his death left little for the general public to criticize. Who did it to him? Three in the morning as he returned from a boozy birthday party. That would have been punishment enough, but why did the street have to come on to him so different, so childish, so dumb, so idiotic? A street he had known for ten years! Edgar throws his hands up in front of his face. Why was that house there? And why did the speedometer show 120? I can explain that: Yes, it was US, we kicked it, so it would go higher, that punching-bag face. If we only had the patience to turn the wheel of fortune at the right time, we could make it around the curve. But what we'd get to eat then would be pretty burnt. Whatever it is, we don't like the taste of it. It tastes like gas, like meat put through the grinder. The gloves are already soaked to the bone with our blood. We might as well be dead. Yes, that's my point. Providence means keep your eye on the road. You are not an island.

Edgar has no memory of the grave, the gate through which he was dispatched. Some of the time is missing, a few figures are missing, they kept him company there while they or their friends, the animals, devoured intestines. So many hungry stomachs. The punishment of the dead is that they must let everything happen to them and watch themselves being whipped into soap by Oprah. The evening lays on earth like a dog, with endless patience, he knows someone will call him. There is also no memory of Edgar eating his way through himself in order to get out—anyway, he could not have reached all parts of his body with his mouth. Neither did other dead folk signal him, he knows nothing of the ax applied to relatives in family graves because the clay soil was not putrefactive enough. Nor did snakes dare to enter his body, he never cared much about them; you'd have to strike those graceful petting animals, who stroke you with their entire body, really hard, to get them to open their jaws and let go of you. There comes the next road warrior, ready to join us, the interred, I mean, the undeterred, who know all the bypasses when the arteries are blocked, without waiting until the mourning period had ended for the fool before him who let himself be caught. Jawbones knock brightly against each other, eyes roll out of their sockets, they want to see a different program and participate in the vote for the top car of the year. Hair grows and grows (a widespread legend, spread probably because doctors prefer to substitute technically installed gizmos, from prostheses to pacemakers, for man's natural regenerative mechanisms; none of those disappear in the ground, those vampires of steel and plastic stay unless they get ripped out of the patient before the funeral. Then only the body is left as its own prosthesis, which has copied and replaced its own nature!), like a soft scarf the hair enwraps its aircraft carrier, the body, fingernails, teeth can be found in this heavy mass, gold jewelry left on the dead woman, which now cuts into her neck. One can hear the grinding of the jaws, and the soul gets recharged. The night is clear for takeoff! In the case of Edgar, the body came along, as if in the infinity of possible relationships among the millions of dead, one or the other could be put together again with a few substitute parts from strangers, so that at least for one the beginning could fall together with the arrival; the beginning stands to stay: an edifice constructed and construed from the top floor down through the air until it finds our hidden land and our hideous roots; Germany, for example, it is right around the corner. Our house is there, and it devours its tenants so that it can alienate us forever. We enter the kitchen, but we can't find the light switch. We lie down in our bed, but there are already a few million people who love us as little as we love ourselves.

There, below the serpentine road, three wanderers, still pretty small, in knickerbockers. Even from that far away they take the piss out of our unusually clad lad. They also disapprove of his preparations to schuss in a beeline right down the mountain meadows directly toward them. Such a grand beginning is bound to amount to little, he should be kept within bounds, this rolling stone with no more home. Even if the mountains do not want to come to us, no one should want himself to be what is coming at any cost, lifting himself out of the depth of the earth, and then that high! Those mountain climbers calmly cross streets, but they won't let their homes, their rooms, be on even just one single water vein. They keep moving their beds until they die and miss the edge for climbing into them. Ghosts meddle in everything, and even worse, they endlessly delay their final disappearance. Never will we rest in peace, and never will we be able to leave others be: Knickerbockers, knee socks, hiking shoes, checkered shirts with armpit sweat stains, parka strapped to the backpack, yes, I see, this parka is from the new fall mail-order collection.

The earth is about to turn blue from the cold, but not quite yet. Fire-gilded youth, our only ace, is played out in the boutiques and sport shops, it trumps, and we, the older ones, we have long been aced out. Where did we get all that stuff? It flares up in colorful catalogs, those spheres of luminescence, and our eyes throw the echo back, all this should make young people wild and dark, in no more than three or four letters anyone can understand, who got all his senses and no mind yet for making any sense. They stroll here, they stroll there, our young, smartly closeted, I mean clothed, figures, appearing three sizes larger than they really are under their wraps, enveloped in a golden glow wherever it gets difficult and steep, yes—right there, where we had already opened the doors for them—there now their darling politician (frozen, unfortunately, but still, as if tailor-made for the pleasure of young men!) radiating out of the walls of rock, which would be made of Caucasian walnut or Ikea gold in the homes of common folks. What does this lustrous one have to say on such a clear day? "If I stand behind him, I can't see what he's got in front." That is Big as opposed to small. And the biggest thing about him are his teeth, the teeth of a rustic field marshal who already mail-ordered his field from the catalog of history, they shine between red cheeks into the light, the Bud, which is a shame, because it hides the real butt. Darkness, by contrast, reveals everything, because the dead are at our mercy. This young leader: such growth that came too late, for he truly would have belonged in a different time, maybe the Greeks, no, that would still be too close to us. Our lives are self-produced. The teeth are fletched, they are ablaze, they partially hide the somewhat lopsided facial construction, which still wants to put its stamp on us. Someday he will spread us on his bun if we don't first kick him in the ass. The poplar-lined road over there, those poplars, like all trees, are sick and dead, yet no one passing through escapes this growth. Then the sun, which talks to the wanderer with its smile. The brightness is not flattering to him; the dark might still be more merciful. No, we do not disguise ourselves. We dress like this leader; like animals, trembling witnesses who can't believe that it is we who've got the knife, we look at the mass-produced expression molded, fabricated, and distributed worldwide by that man from his own expression. We are lucky if he does not deport us along with it, toll-free and no returns accepted. The socially climbing organisms on this earth are already moving toward him, and those rushing to him from below, peddling, paddling with their roots, are trying to be even faster. The Führer. We'd all be looking for him with a needle in the haystack should someone like him disappear from the screen. Austria had constructed such a man before (and kept the blueprints just in case), and as the tremendous uproar caused by this piece of work has been quenched, they were dug up, those blueprints, and submitted for a virulent populist movement, for a third republic, brought out from the depth, but still a bit from the top down.

Something bursts forth from the gravelly riverbed, down there, out of the bushes, which will soon let off the steam of the evening fog: There, the small wooden bridge in front of the nonhouse, whence the old peasant woman, the last survivor of a family of drunkards and suicides, suddenly also passed out of there, pulled out like a cork from an empty bottle, down there on a plot that didn't sell and, in the meantime, went to seed, something unholy is stirring. It is always cold there, and even dogs don't like to pass by, they steer clear of it. What kind of fertilizer produces the intense dark green of the grass? A sort of restricted area line has been drawn around the remnants of the house. From about two hundred meters to the other side, the pounding of construction machinery. The pickax of a new settler burrows in the earth, cement mixers—if necessary, their noise will turn against anyone who says no to it, in principle and in writing. It is not only the wanderers who bring motion into the landscape. Soon, by the way, they will fall behind, as Edgar Gstranz will have started, with the number 1. The only one in the running. Finally, a reliable way to win. Clouds, in futile fury, tear into each other. A thunderstorm? At this time of day and year?, Edgar asks himself, climbing up. But there doesn't seem to be anything else to suggest a storm. Edgar does not understand the clouds, and the wanderers who are waiting for him to greet them don't see any at all. What nervous creatures, those clouds, spreading themselves over the land. Here is a fellow taking off with his sportswear as if he had cut himself out of a pattern to reinforce himself with cardboard, a dress-up doll whose lead is shrinking. The Swiss runner has the same intermediate time. But Edgar is the only one among them who was taken out and remodeled for the position of volunteer trainer in the fitness studio of the capital, Vienna, Nineteenth District, where the upscale suburb's daughters sport about in knee-deep water, as if carried by gentle waves, that's how easy everything comes to them. So there. Unexpectedly, something pushes through the rising autumn wind, it also wants to rise, and crashes into our heads. It has not yet eaten and wants to suck this pitiful place dry.

Something is brewing, up there, in the mountains. Spit it out, right now! The awakened one sets out for the village. The trees bend, but they do not break. Wind. Let him go there! And us. Let us not be split like the vampire with a stake through the heart, let us be in Styria! That is where we want to be found.

3

The deck chair lovingly carries this young woman who secluded herself in the mountains to study for her comps. Such dialogue with books and papers pushes all other phenomena into the background. Nature is present, but thinking is future bound, long arguments with oneself lie in between. Light comes and goes, but thinking gets something to just come out that doesn't much like to disappear again. Gudrun Bichler comes from Graz, where she lived with her cat in the small, old prewar apartment that belonged to her parents, who had moved to the suburbs (the cat of the dead young woman is taken care of, so reader, don't start that now! I won't get into that grind, not there, where we all got grounded and ground on principle for insufficient reason and made to sit apart forever, in grade school, for disruptive talking with each other! That applies especially to me!), yes, that Gudrun, she spends herself, her head wrapped around her thinking, which separates her once and for all from all the others who are solidly down to earth: those smilers on billboards, pasted onto an abstract design done up in bright colors to make sure we get the message ("we stand for Austria"), advertising nothing but their own constructions. Thus they con humankind, which just wants cheap flights and is generally determined to fight for discounts for everything. Until the members of the warring cartels, damaged by accidents in matters of life and love, become available at bargain prices. Gudrun, for her part, has been cast out of the only unity that exists, the unity of the living (to many she even is: invisible, doesn't need her own seat), she doesn't know herself what's going on. Should she want to book a special fare, she would not know whom to turn to.

The only way out for those left behind all alone: They escape to some place only to find out that they can't stand living there either. Beyond reproaches and recognition, a spot is left for them where they can keep their eyes glued to the floor whenever someone greets them or wants to chat with them, some of the old folks in this inn, who never keep quiet, for they know: For them, the silence is about to start. Trees, whose shadows black you out. The masses who would rather stand out travel elsewhere. Step into the sun, blink into more glaring light, where they can be more powerful witnesses of our civilization and let themselves be waited on, because a call has reached them, a calling to Greece, Anatolia, California, but wherever one looks there is uncertainty whether it would not be more splendid elsewhere. No, they would rather stay here and boss others around.

There still is the memory of the bathroom door, which hasn't been wiped clean in weeks, the package of razor blades ripped open quickly, the inadvertent cut in the thumb; the dark night that has all of us stitched together gapes open a bit, the water crashes into the tub, then the steam trying to deny Gudrun her mirror image, no need for a mirror image if you no longer cast a shadow. What can life do with this spoiled offspring who was supposed to study but could not swim in this pool of sharks, the university, all the way to the turn against herself? Mustn't think about it too long while the most demanding animals are jumping on you from behind: just one little taste! And right in front of you a splashy new waterspout luring you with the depth of foreign, singing, blessed spirits, maybe you should do it after all (think big!). Outside, a few seniors, ancient trees hardly bearing, doing aerobics. If they were trees of life they'd have to watch out lest they lose their branches as well. It was spring then and aesthetic categories were "in," which no one understood though all are listed right here, black on white. As well as the mistakes you could commit, e.g., here and now, against them. Chapters like this in all those books changed the young woman's tune, no more fifths, her range shriveled to the keynote. For a long time, this woman had unconsciously tuned herself to death, travelers should not be stopped, and all the lovely overtones that prevent us from identifying the tone of the bell also added to this depressive, tuned-out state. Thus, Gudrun B., in all that clinking and clanking to the point of harshness, is perceivable as no more than a bon ton of the Creator (according to his own practical guide!). She probably was confused, what else would cause such self-abuse, I don't know either why anyone would kill themself, some indicate it in advance, in a roundabout way that they took to avoid the crowds, others don't say anything. A matter of taste. An extra pinch of salt won't take the spice out of living, too many cooks could never stir us the way this one has just spoiled our meal. The prior blackout is a last resistance, the body switches to zero, the difference disappears, a telegram reaches the nerves and gets picked up once but not the next time; life bends over the counter and rails at the clerk because he can't find the COD package, well then, it will just have to be left there. The last heartbeat—this student did not live a second too long but not one too short either—soon the young body will be ready for viewing. The blood runs out of her wrists and into the slimy pond around her. Electric impulses of her nerves flail about desperately in their tiny boats, those abandoned travelers, they had booked until the end and now they are put on this insufficient ground, how fast that can happen sometimes! Some of the dead know their destination, others act rashly because they would rather not know exactly where they are headed now. Like a last rebuke the blade jumped between the tendons Gudrun needed before for playing the piano into the soft part as if it were mounting a horse. Like a cowboy trying to ride the skittish steed, just don't get thrown off!, the metal bites into the tender hand holders, those hinges, perfectly made for newspapers, books, journals, and now becoming the pivots of a revolving door that spits out people, though not into a warm hall, the clinking of glasses, laughter, the buzz of voices (as someone would say to capture a mood everyone experienced but would never be able to describe in just three words, even though there is a prize to win—a fountain pen, which you'll be able to fill completely!), but rather out into the night, to a place for those faded on a piece of paper, on a stone, on clay, shards, metal. Imagine yourself having started on this great trip, but what expects you is not a four-star hotel; instead, a razor-sharp existential divide ejects you (a few ounces of cheap sausage) in small slices out into the night. You could never be put together again in this nightmare. You are suddenly deprived of all your charms. The white body of an animal, which never shone anyway, sinks to the ground; the hair still tries to hold the line, it spreads out on the hot pond. There it stays until the sound of a bell, which is no longer heard. This young woman studied too much, or rather tried to author studies herself, but never found the starting point to where the road of life for those in need for knowledge begins, where this woman mostly found plain needy folks like herself. Reading and writing were never her forte, then why this maniacal sinking into thinking, into this unholy sea she practically sold her soul to: the Humanities? We, too, tend to believe that it isn't worth it. It took years of quasi-impotence for Gudrun to realize this. She won't be missed in the village of knowledge. Her essence had long flown out when her mother with a duplicate key befell the apartment and rushed to her daughter, the shore of all the flooding. This was not a roaring mountain torrent either, but a shaggy pool no longer warm underfoot. Without white swans and majestically strolling pedestrians, a last rescue team, tapping the water for its carrying capacity, who suddenly stop in resignation and throw a crinkled cigarette pack into the pool.

The wind now challenges the trees more fiercely. They bend forward, all in one direction as if they were wandering along a country road. Styria is a protected zone where the forest forces the storm onto devious paths. Those primordial woods dream of the dead like hungry bodies of food. The decomposed, the devastated, embattled in fierce fights for resurrection, throw themselves into action as if they had to contest retroactive rent increases. Gudrun, who felt but had not believed such things for a long time (she almost turned into a root herself but was pulled), lifts her head from her book and listens while technology advances: Even in summer this Edgar Gstranz doesn't have to walk on foot across the mountain pasture! Strange cloud formations have a tough time today getting ahead of each other. If the Wirtin didn't know better, she'd say it was the *Föhn,* that idiot wind, but it is too chilly for that. She had appeared already three times at the front door among her leisurely mingling guests, looking at the sky she would love to prewash at 60°C for it to be squeaky rather than just clean. She recounts her orders and writes something on a notepad. Is this the calculative approach, Gudrun asks herself in her deck chair, stretched out on tenterhooks of thinking. It is the inexperienced like herself who still want to be in control only to finally put themselves in the hands of others in white smocks, people with helmets who are connected by a rectangle of bars. The individual item gets loaded into a neutrally gray van and then buried somewhere after all monitoring of the patient had stopped. Over and done. Earth must have knocked once on this young woman's coffin as the last claim no one could finally contest. There must have been deformed feet in black stockings shuffling along, back then, years ago, pity, she could not be down there with them then. The whole family together! The trees are wagging their leaves as the uncanny starts encircling the earth; earlier it had been sniffing around ferociously in Germany and Austria, all the way into the farthest nooks and crannies. Since those countries closed down their death factories, they have focused on feeling, it is the media's drug dropped nightly into the gorges of our eyes. Now Gudrun should slowly get acquainted with her fellow dead, all of them frequently wounded objects like her, but since she never had the money to dress in halfway decent clothes, she does not particularly like those phantoms' look of decay. She wants to return because she didn't get her due share of life. They (who?) should let her live on earth again. Everyone would like that, after all. Along the bus route changes loom ahead, stops are suddenly shifted, people are waiting in vain, wondering where the bus stop sign and the small schedule protected by a small roof have vanished.

When the wild is not wild enough, it can get even wilder on a whitewater tour in Alaska. But there is no need to go that far. Did you just leave your childhood in my absence? Well, then you will understand why I suddenly miss compliments so much, surely I am more enticing than the branches of industry! So now I've completed this gift to the ladies and I am transferring it into your presence, but why does this piece of work, whose skin (which can be transported in ceramides, but only as ashes), which I purchased in a store, have to fall over again and again? Something roams around the house that does not mind being wild and dark and having been exported from the above-mentioned shop in the city: this young man in leaderhosen and leather jacket, who came out so provocatively yet doesn't come on to anyone not his age and, speaking of coming, please, have a potential partner come for us from his supplier, too! Showing on his darling not yet wasted face as it withdraws a little, then forges ahead again, is absolute closeness maintaining distance. A marking lights up inside him that, in the long run, keeps Gudrun at a distance from him: an information board at the train station, but her train took off quite a while ago, no need to crane her neck, this man doesn't go for her, he didn't come to pick her up; once again there is nothing but language for her to wantonly devour, but not the desired attendant lips, hard as the earth around a freshly dug-up grave. As open as the display is spread out before her, this ground is not solid, it does not carry. At an unbefitting pace Gudrun now walks over to the house, her books tucked under her arms, ever so cautious that nothing breaks. The spirit of the dead can be destroyed so easily, everyone thinks that nothing can hurt them. So the dead, quite offended, rather shoos his self back into the narrow chamber, which, even in his lifetime, he could not escape farther than the Canary Islands. All that barking and whining was to no avail. The lobby is dry, sunny, empty. The pensioners went to the beach or rather its variant, the mountains. Here, too, there is no lack of swimmers splashing about, swooshing and snorting, just that here they do it in hiking shoes and with hiking poles. Vacationeers are under constant exam stress: will they stand their ground if someone bites into their laughter to test if it is real? They are all beside themselves before the mountain massif. Gudrun has a dry roll hard as a rock and a shriveled apple, she doesn't know where from, in her jute tote, which in the meantime has replaced the plastic innovations of several centuries. Where did she get this, her only piece of luggage? All she remembers is waking up in a deck chair on the small patch of grass under the fruit trees, as if spat out by an animal that is now sniffing her calves from afar with a hyena's elongated neck; now it sneaks up on her, then, scared by the half-choked scream from her throat, it withdraws again with raised hackles. But it never leaves for good. It surrounds her with its self-assured expertise in cracking a thighbone with one bite. Or maybe it is waiting farther ahead, right where the stairway's twilight begins, the animal a figure of surveillance without any sense of time? Gudrun seems to consist of peculiarities, but she doesn't rest on them for she can't find any rest. As if this house were a hole devouring her over and over again. How on earth did she get here? A different, newly invented law of nature seems to have heaved her here, the ground is suddenly furrowed like a field staring at her with the suggestive glance of one who obviously hauled their fruit to this place just for us and then dumped earth on it—a gaze animals also have at times when all they want to tell us is that we humans may use their body and its products as we wish: another dimension of being without self-consciousness. As if Gudrun wanted to invade another person's dreams. Did the animal have a taste of her under the earth and snag a rest of life that he then dragged back into reality, a bloody cadaver with the intestines hanging out? Over there, where the innkeeper set up her improvised reception, spots are flitting by, as if the bars in front of a lioness had dropped. But the beast has been locked up for so long that its body was crossed out several times by the whiplashes of the Nothing, of Time. And in those spots, beyond the thousand bars no world—yes, go ahead, read the poem!—it doesn't cost us the world to vacation here, only flitting spots of light and shadows of branches aimlessly chasing about, their images playing catch on the ground, and that is when Gudrun feels a horrible pain on the level of her heart. She squirms, bends over the railing, gasps for air in horror—an athlete driving herself to the finish line with the last of her strength—she reaches for the scalpel that seems to pierce her, finds nothing, no matter how far-reaching she is. She must get up to her room, the last refuge, but where is it? She can hardly get over this unauthorized, bold invasion of her innermost self, where a mouth is pried opened and about to begin its aria for the second time. But no sound comes out, and there is no one around. She knows she must go up the stairs, directly toward a Something, so that this gash inside her can be grouted. Below, shouts of children are flying about, finally living sounds, a mother catches them lovingly and tosses them forcefully back into the baby-tooth-lined mouth that produced them. The sounds return all the sounder. Gudrun pulls, drags herself up the rails, sometimes it takes months, even years, to get beyond oneself. You never know what's waiting out there.

A dark hallway. Antlers of deer and horns of mountain goats, whose tender flesh once went through mortal fear but has been eaten in the meantime, impaling themselves on the walls from where they plunge into sleep, birds during descent, pushing through clouds: a stuffed goshawk and some buzzards. A black cock and a grouse. Who worked himself out of his element here, sports? We don't know anything more elementary than that. Somebody is here, even though the house seems to be deserted. The old folks are proving their mettle on the adventure trail, where the fir and its rapid decay in step with human life will be the topic of their discussion. This is the danger: If man dies, this tree dies, too! Of course, no one is in their room at this time of day. But up ahead something is moving, from a common place covered with red ash the muted sound of bouncing balls comes all the way to the front of the landing. Step by step Gudrun drags herself up the stairs, she has to get there, even though she does not know which room is hers. Whatever, the noise is coming from above, it seems to wash its hands and slap cream on its face. Suddenly light-footed again, the student moves through the corridor, just listening. So here you are, dead, and no suitcase packed for the hospital; it is altogether different from those not infrequent moments of happiness, when a young father-to-be escorts his wife to the car, the luggage had been joyously prepared long ago, smooth goings finally show results, isn't life wonderful, even if one has to shake people attack-style out of their sleep or others out of their bodies. It is for a good cause, after all. How come others always do the right thing as a matter of course? Bursting with life they can get it to vibrate like a tongue under a snappy mushroom hat or a light blue baby bonnet, until the larger tones can be finally spit out. Oh yes, life, children, grandchildren, sucklings! And once again I was not drawn, loser that I am.

Suddenly the sound of voices, and a young woman has risen. In Styria there seems to be a place, the carrier of the Real, why else would people exhibit such frozen stares, it can't just be the iodine-poor and calcium-rich water. So much blood wasted here, just in the forest, this young woman also splashed it all around as if she was preparing for an overdue spring-cleaning inside herself. But it wasn't that big a drama after all. Though this woman tries to catch up with her memory, something is holding her back at the tail of her T-shirt, so that she can't even think back to her death. Now she has become the indisputable center of her solitary circumstances, there is no moving forward, no going back, the compass needle rotates, it won't point north. One of those strange phenomena, which was even examined yesterday, when an old gentleman had put a compass in her hand to settle arguments about the name of a mountain. General amazement: Gudrun took the compass in her hand, and instantly the needle shifted into a permanent state of quivering agitation! Not like with the others, in whose hands the needle stayed steadily turned north, yes, the North, where all our myths and our mission come from, so we grab our raging bulls by their horns and get them to wreck other peoples' markets before their bears can invade us. At this hour the old man and the old woman are still wondering how this strange magnetic effect could have happened and why only to this nice student we met here! Maybe she stood on an especially strong water vein that pounded with its fists against the earth's surface, so that they would start digging right there—no, not to build a chapel of grace but a swimming pool. So that our blessed Mother of God can finally try out her bathing suit. Ever since that experiment which made the earth act like a hysterical patient who had been disturbed in her permanent sleep (twitching alpha waves mess up the tiny lifelines, ant trails on their backs), the two old people don't feel safe anymore. A claim challenged them, where before there was only acclaim and a smile and, for starters, it killed their appetite. They suspect an inexplicable force being right among them. Not even sleep's powerful plowing through this evil scheme could deliver them from the web, wherein some sort of spider seems to hold them captive. With limp fingers they drum on their closed eyes, as something is trying to force its way in, a power over their being, something that still must be refused, but there it knocks again, this time resolutely, on the door to their pensioners' end-of-life habitat. Something is afoot, something is up in arms underground, maybe the German army. Did they install a secret spy facility for Europe, so that they can escape the East, that constant threat of a fateful blow by the uncivilized against our geographical independence and latitude? No. That something shakes its head with a smile. They have two more guesses, but then the fully automated wheel of fortune will speed ahead, slicing off part of the next contestant's face and then his whole head. For the advance of technology can also be abused against us, as the atom has shown. It hasn't received good press in years, because we believe we must take its precious natural power to be a disease threatening our children and us. We, the parents of nature! An ax in everybody's hands will do to spare the next generations their entrances;

trees also abandon their locations and go away. We prefer beauty in our own shape and form to inhabit the earth forever.

We hear: Gudrun Bichler started to study philosophy but could not finish. It is not she who seeks, she is the object of the search. There she sits and calculates the angle in which the thinkers' thoughts pelt down on her. Suddenly a shadow on the book, the fleeting thought, I've read this again and again for a long time, but how long has it really been? An apple drops softly into the grass. As if someone put away their book to doze. What has been prompted to her has not been promised to her. There still is a minimum of resistance in her. The skin bulged, tightened, as the razor blade bit into her. In death, that gall wasp at long last slips into Gudrun's sex she rejected so vehemently up to now.

4

Sleep does not simply mean turning on the sultry red light in the darkroom, so that either the unconscious body can quietly search around inside itself or, in case it wants to go to the brain cinema, it can get fired up by the shrill ballpark screams of its dreaming consciousness that finds itself quite interesting and wants to show off. No, inside the room there is nothing but darkness, but outside the warning light is on, may sleep not abuse people when they are defenseless. And the door to the self should not simply be torn open, just because something pretty was discovered there to adorn yourself with. No light, please!, it will ruin the film, the photos with all the experiences imprinted on them as bright parts and shadows, those scanty cadres our Gudrun for instance sent into the field to start warming up there. They might be deployed later or maybe not. But the game had almost always been canceled before. Gudrun Bichler breathes audibly. Something that's calling is near, but that infernal sound seems to have passed through her beyond the auditory threshold. Something that settled here still wrapped in sleep wants to be kept; it reveals a naming from a book, though there is nothing but a spot left blank. This student waits for the name that was called out to her. Nothing. No repeat. Then, with a key she found in her natural fiber tote, she unlocks the door to the room she suddenly finds herself standing in front of, she does not know why. She is hardly inside when the door bangs against her ribs, as someone right behind her seems to push his way in, someone who is even more in a hurry to get home than she. But there isn't anyone. Who threw himself against the door? Inside, everything seems unfamiliar to her as well, even though she seems to lodge here, the imitation country-style bed with the checkered linens, the somewhat older armoire, which seems to come from the stock of another inn or the farmer's personal property: cheap mass-produced furniture. Though the peasant sometimes breaks out of people's mouths, it no longer surrounds them, or just as the ghost of the original, which in the meantime comes across as quaint to us and our children, who still have the opportunity to spend their vacations on a farm. It is a quotient farmers subtract from themselves to show how few of them are actually left, the farming milieu can't even be kept long enough until the Brussels bureaucrats take a look at it as proof that it is still present in some way, so that the arriving guest—like a god demanding overly high standards from his subjects—won't skittishly flee on the spot again. Meticulous order in this room, at least temporarily, Gudrun opens the armoire, no luggage, nothing, but she has the key, apparently she seems to dwell here, at least temporarily. She checked in here, but there is no trace of her presence, as if she had been turned off, a switch that will tip over any moment. The washstand with the jug: Just for show. The shared bathroom is in the hallway, which makes the price so reasonable. Food mostly self-produced.

The cliffs look down on the inn. The tourists look up the cliffs. Gudrun takes her tattered book from her bag and puts it on the table: there, the first trace of use. Gudrun contemplates the still-life for a while, then she shyly puts it away again, the stillness and the life, nobody noticed she had any anyway. The young woman stands in the middle of the room, a stranger, not set up to stay. Pause. A glance into the stained mirror above the table, the glance instantly puts itself around her throat, but she cannot get a grip on herself. She has no right to such getawayward behavior, she knows that, actually, she should enclose only herself, in her embarrassment, she shouldn't even be here, she escaped someone (on an unmarked trail), whom she still owes the rent, she does not belong here, since the last time she disappeared so quickly she couldn't even pay for the room. The kind of advances the furnishings dare in this place, Gudrun actually should not allow them, she should elude the objects' forwardness, the arrival of something that is neither present nor to come, it is past and yet: now. Words can be milestones. And, not unlike the weather, they are difficult to avoid. A noise outside, maybe the mason in charge of caulking the cracks? He seals them up so that the horrible moment that threatens Fräulein Bichler cannot enter. Why does Gudrun stay here in the first place? She could call her mother, but she does not lay hands on her minimal assets, parents, brother, a few women friends from the university, from childhood, something is holding her back. She has no rope to pull herself out of this strange state of absorption and no idea how close something is or how far, for this woman is not inside herself, she is here but not at home here. Nor is she anywhere. No vacancies at the moment. No answer comes to her or goes beyond her. Gudrun takes the bag, puts it down again, sits down again, wants out again, then, undecided, sitting down again, an uninvited guest of herself, who is not quite sure if she is welcome. What kind of relationship with her own presence can she get into without regrets? As if she entered some place only to find out: She is already there, but no one is around to fight her for it, to race her to the seat not taken, the dangerous one above the tires, where only legless people would sit comfortably. She must have been forgotten or nature wasted her on no one less than herself and now she must expose herself as a poor, unpublished entertainment. It is not like TV, where words lash out loudly like whips, disempowering themselves. The last thing left of Gudrun, besides memory, seems to be something with writing on it, her name and two dates on a stone, a small cross, but where? Sometimes the unlucky strike lucky, as the cigarette promised, sometimes they strike out. Mind you, had I published a novel, they would say the same about me. But let's keep going, because, under the disapproving eyes of this know-it-all woman, whose hobby was correcting others, dissing the carefree pairs of eyes and lips who—beaming in the light of cosmetics, embrace each other lovingly—had thrown around the vomit of language with much less concern than she, Gudrun, that pussyfoot woman, can now hear very clearly a sound coming from the hallway. Yes, somebody must be there, no doubt. Now, finally, she wants to go ask about herself, since she knows nothing about herself. In case of amnesia, a mountain tour should better be avoided, for after the loss of memory its attendant body might also get lost. You crash, you plummet way down, but at the same time you are still standing up there, looking for yourself, because everything happened so fast. Now there is definitely some disturbance, and a pale Gudrun opens the door, there, isn't there someone else, also sick and out of his mind, an existential hit, who took himself off the hit list, also without luck, he couldn't be found in time to fight his last stand.

Well, who'll tell you if not I: A shadowy figure, slightly bent over, stands in front of the hallway window that is embellished by a small ceramic vase, a local product, albeit with a crack from some time ago. And this figure of a young man, which must have doggedly walked itself here, also seems to be some sort of a cracked pot. It does not move. Stands like a statue whose walking papers have not yet been stamped. It cannot be easy to hold this position, left hand in an almost relaxed angle propped up on the hip. A statue that, unfortunately, seems to have fallen ill. This man is not about to move, at least not his legs, two rigid, fleshy bars anchored in the ground, a stand-in for Arnold Schwarzenegger, who made all the right moves as far away from here as he could. The man shows himself in a crass, glaring nakedness; his disguise, which isn't one, reveals what we have to expect and keep him as. His head seems to think nothing. The skin is light pink, as if dyed, painted on, like any beauty, it does not come from a cosmetics shop, indeed, it must come from inside. I would have never thought that this is possible, but doesn't fire also glow in the sky and gets thrown on us as a sun only because a celestial body keeps exploding? Something controls the young man from the center of his crotch, where his partly swollen sex has appeared through the curtain of hair to check whether there will be an entrance applause where only bottomlessness is waiting; down there, the thing that surrendered has to be taken in the hand when the wish to live wants to draw some power from the pump. That man, that timed-out being, quite obviously got in touch with great feelings through a nozzle, when gas was still toxic and in its zeal could wipe out hundreds of filthy piles of life before they melted away by themselves. It is noisy yet silent, that piece of sex bobbing on this young man, a spectacle of nature and its freedom to climb up again and again on a human scaffold, as if it had just been untied from its frame, an animal that does not yet quite know what to do with its freedom. It stinks through the dust of this never aired hallway, and its gorgeous nature is in full view on the floor, for as he was dying, the young man soiled himself, so now small piles are covering the planks, laying a track to the staircase, a shitty runner installed by this figure under the influence of (or elevated by) the weightlessness of the gas. It must have been very toxic gas, what else could have caused such vermilion skin? Something evil whizzed out of the spigot, the sex's veins are all swollen from anger, and what had accumulated inside had begun to move, blood!, it started to slide, a badly moored load, then the lifeboat tilted in the waves, the precious cargo slipped back again, a few crystal-clear drops still peeking over the sex's rim, gradually drying up, leaving behind an unnatural glow, festiveness, the gift of gab, a splashy performer who, at the last moment, could not complete his act. As if this man had put plenty of Vaseline all over himself and his popping lifeline in order to speed up his slide into the unknown from the bench where he had already been stored for so long, so this in every sense and for all senses drop-dead handsome young man tore his clothes from his body, dead as he already was, but he didn't know it. That's how much fun suicide can be, just like waiting for the downhill at the start house, if you deduct life's tragedy prior to it. Farmers do that with the milk quota, they deduct from it as much as they can to show how impoverished they are. Some feces still sticks to the dead young man, it ran down one thigh, the excretions have all dried up by now, but this humpbacked world, this *Bucklige Welt* (don't worry, this is actually the name of a beautiful part of Lower Austria), this arched manhood, a testament to his last living willy, we are all waiting for it to come, to come up with something more than a name, with life itself that grows on that stem for us to consume, this is how one might imagine it, if poets are to be believed, who sometimes sadly go to pots dumping their verbal torrents all over us, but we had just put our modest mental capital in our savings account, so we could later waste it on the hot pins and needles of daytime television, what did I actually want to say? Just no superfluous fluids! Alright, so this human shit sticks to everything everywhere and it has dried up completely, this product of death, not unlike money and the word, which also belong to the integrated school of death. Well now, an unmovable youth! No more trails leading through him, he carries his hunting ground on his body, a territory that is only half awake in the dew and fog of this hour—his cock is raised, ready to shoot anytime it wants to, but the owner shows no sign of emotion, I mean, motion. His sex suits the dead man, for a man's sex will be the sole survivor, so then women will also have to become men, someone worries in a slowly expiring letter to the editor. Trees that tall! And amid all that stench and the swarming flies the young man's still-life works like a charm. He was running around as a dead man, poisoned by gas! Imagine having the right to take this dead man in your hand and examine it thoroughly, between thumb, fore-, and middle finger, a stroll, like an early morning walk into damp grass, refreshing! For the diet-conscious, a sip from this deceased youth is also available sugar-free. Since he can no longer talk, we can feel free to talk him up!

In the meantime we have Citygas light, many would have been annoyed had it already existed in their time. They would have had to choose something else to die from or breathe in to be able to breathe again, and nothing would have happened to them. This spot right here at the window is both an educational and a memorial site, the rigid nude bending forward, beyond his penis, which wants to look out the window, too, but cannot quite make it, too bad, it can only suggest a somewhat more liberated, more liberal baroque statue forever on the verge of looking out the window into the distance. The statue of a fighter that went through decades of strokes with chisel and graver and the meager product of all those efforts: a naked young man, his scree chute, his rock massif still crusted with stinking excrement, got stuck in his own consciousness; we surely won't need a special style in which to imagine him. Frontally, he looks straight ahead out of gazeless, vacuous, shadow-ringed eyes toward the swept corner of the hallway, lured by a still dripping-wet but already clearly developed photograph—the freeness of a woman's body lifted from a tub—that alternate route in order to safeguard the distance to the ultimate goal the man really wants to take but cannot always find. Instead, the call is near, the feminine is needed for the rapture, thus the faraway one must not leave the dead man altogether. This is rape! Gudrun backs away from this organ peeled out of infinity so impetuously, offering nature pure as a sign that this is a good thing, like organic food or all-natural cosmetics or simply a stroll together, yet still alone, you got it. This is how you see the face of God, dead-on, I mean: it is to die for. But those blots on the floor and on those crimson thighs! The heat rising from this man's sex terrifies Gudrun in her unfeelingness, it is as if stones were hitting her, that clumsy rock climber of thinking who did not even hang on to any thought as a memento of herself. When the opportunity arises, we can also become quite massive, that is, when we take over another person's sleep.

Gudrun intervenes in this death by approaching the pole that pins this man's body down for good. She wants to pierce her heart with it, hoping that it will finally bring about the vampire's death and at the same time extract from herself all that half-chewed and spit-out knowledge, which is of no use to anyone but still seems to give her a kind of life. Yet in our country the great ideas are taken from the dead, never from the living. They are taken from Kant, Hegel, Schopenhauer, and Joseph M. Hauer. The injuries of the dead young man, the poison under his skin, are red-hot, his body is ice-cold, the sex is his antlers, with which he tries to decorate his wall, a timid try. The mortally wounded skin glows, it seems to contract around the stake of flesh, to offer it with appealing audacity, a plant wrapped in skin, a bouquet that is a last attempt to pull itself up on the rope ladder of blood, out of the soil's hair roots, the only trump this body can play to possibly birth himself again from this lethargic dream of death. Many have been sent into the gas, but maybe this young man of all people, who took care of his own fate, was the one nickel too many in Uncle Dagobert's silo? Amazing, how interesting and multilayered such a piece of sex really is, you can peel it like a fruit, it has a solid, hard core, and all this is supposed to be sunk in the morass of time? Some are more adept at looking than Gudrun, others have practiced eating and drinking, that haute école of the dressage of ovens, oh yes, the average person always demands the extraordinary.

The student hears light steps. The fields outside are buzzing with buzzards, animals who might soon take off with us. Clanking and clanging from the kitchen below, money seems to turn into time, which folks here want to spend eating. Empty bottles make each other chime. Then a rustling sound, something rises, Gudrun can't see it from where she is, but a bit of wind has slipped under a discarded empty plastic bag and now it tumbles around inside, a shiny little animal emerges in the play of air, it swipes with a swooshing sound across the decorative rocks, a glittering speck of sunlight gets caught in the animal's skin. Nothing, or maybe it actually is something used just now by a higher power that wishes to protect itself with this plastic skin from who knows what kinds of sensations, but here the plastic itself is the beast raging against itself! If humans were self-procured property how much better care they would take of themselves! Hesitatingly, Gudrun moves toward the man who has erected himself here, her almost halting gait knowing already it won't find its destination but rather brush past it once again. The stillness of this reddishly tinged shape encourages Gudrun a bit, maybe this man will take a raincheck on his flight and cash it in later, when Gudrun will have gotten used to him a bit. That's how it has always been, the present was over quickly, the few fellow students—civil servants retired in advance pussyfooting their way in—as soon as they laboriously begged and bedded down next to her (like children wanting a go-cart Porsche), had hardly gone through a couple of pushcart motions before they bowed out again, and poor Gudrun Bichler, for months to come, had to give herself again and again to what had passed. Who cares about her neediness. Waiting is a woman's job, except when it is a matter of a special color for a car. Now the wind outside still has even higher things in mind and pounces atop the trees. Gudrun sees the firs' tops bending while she must get through a door through which her life's lilliput-train had not taken her. Because it collided earlier with several German thinkers who for their part had been forgotten during a complicated operation inside a few Greeks and stopped without having ever arrived. Not even a fragment, not worth the effort of reading. But here, in this piece of male flesh sans garb, the long-searched-for word might fall through the crossword puzzle sieve and wake up again as prey that had long fought with itself—and in the process charged itself with meaning like the plastic bag with pure wind, coming to life as *Being* and simultaneously as *Time,* present and future, to wit in the inexperienced arms of a dead student. No *thing* has such merciful intentions, let alone a human being. In this terrible ineptitude, which had already tempted Gudrun to hook up with herself (even electricity would retreat from such a deadly box!), in this clumsiness, which is paired so often—sadly, always to no avail when ladies get set to consent in such a complicated manner—with audacity (a name- as well as care-less Imaginary punches you forcefully in the shoulder to finally get things moving, while you are still trying to fill in a missing word), Gudrun throws herself at this raspberry-colored young gasometer and almost falls out the window on the other side. This flesh in its immobile position did not stick, at least it did not stick to its promise. The flesh of a stranger is there to make others feel even lonelier in their nativeness than they've ever been. Greatness definitely goes through a lot in these small times. Light comes through the window and turns Gudrun Bichler into the shelf-warmer who warms up so poorly that it can't even raise the shutter with its own strength anymore. This naked body of the seemingly neglected Titan (all those hands once reaching out for him on-screen, but such a big screen makes an estimate difficult. You have to step back a bit to see anything at all) has been briefly visible, a tease, no more. But no causes also have their effects, so this man can keep his sex and possibly show it off in a different form in a different place, I mean, he certainly can put a tooth next to it or a few square centimeters of intimate skin. He can come on to another being that wants to be overcome by him; this is why women undress pretty freely even when they are still outside. So that finally they can erase themselves completely. As if they had never been here. Their homework lies half done in their stained exercise books. Topless bras and spaghetti straps were not invented for nothing, let them see what is being prepared, al dente, in a wrap of sumptuous hair, for you and you and you, mein Herr, as you hear and take steps.

Desperately playing the unself-conscious one, Gudrun Bichler goes to the window, nothing and no one is holding her back. Maybe she is not an obstacle after all, maybe it was she who simply walked through a human figure. She turns around. No one is there. But from her room, which she left empty before, sounds of gaiety are seeping through, or is someone crying in there? Sometimes the difference is hard to tell. Did someone go in behind her back? The young man's appearance was crudely carnal, whereas the people in the inn looked to Gudrun more like the photographs she took with a tourist's sense of obligation, the way you want to capture things as a visitor that would be of no interest whatsoever back home. That reddish man had curves everywhere, and his gaze was firm, a camera could have captured it really well, since he didn't blink once. Confidently, this flesh entrusted itself to Gudrun's waiting, indulging itself in the bliss of forgetting, all body. Sadly, he is gone now, and Gudrun is all alone. But in that room someone is breathing two parts, or singing a duet with someone, he also might whistle as he breathes through his incisors, it's hard to tell from the outside. Gudrun bends down to the keyhole to see if the naked iceman with his airborne p[r]ick, which he could well use to work a bit more on himself (uprooting it?) might have entered the room, but she would have noticed. Let's have a look, she probably thinks, trusting the possibility that finally someone might have passed himself on to her, like a shopping cart. At least that she will take in hand. She will not fail again. So now, having instinctively assumed a posture similar to the young man's earlier on, she peeks through the keyhole and on the other side of it her glance, prepared like a delicious dish, a blink of an eye that stretches endlessly, enters as the rightful main tenant and drops from her face into the room. Stumblingly, the glance gets on its feet and sees that which does not see and does not ask.

5

Karin Frenzel deposited her old mother among the trash of outdoor furniture, so that the landscape would imprint itself on the woman a bit, but the stamp presses against a pad gone dry long ago. It's been quite a while since this mother has let in new impressions that, ages ago, had been hammered by the hard hitter war into the wrong board, a nail into nobody's coffin, because all the coffins were already taken. Sometimes old familiar stuff still gets flushed up by memory, and in a steady stream the dirty water in life's sink spills over the daughter and her outfit, which, modeled after a baby's bodysuit, had actually been purchased for running, but she's no longer in the run. Though Karin, still a relatively young person in her mother's opinion, should keep running as long as she can, and that means always toward her mother, who, to the latter's endless cheers that reveal inner amazement about the child daring to express herself freely, keeps catching it in the two hand nets of her arms and shakes the last expression of an own will out of it, like a dog the life out of a prey it holds on to tightly by the neck. And where is this daughter running now? Into the off, composed of the jolly folks who, dragged ahead by their dogs, are pulling on the leashes of their conversations, which keep circling around and around Germania's North (their place of origin), from whose borders those very tourists on their part bravely give tongue to the strangers: That is where Frau Karin ran to in vain, because they rarely let her talk, this daughter, who doesn't know from which fount her accidental friends here draw their personal data and defenders of their deeds. In any event, they primarily stick up for themselves, those vacationers, a front beyond the timber line of sixty years, and they categorically speak out against most of those the world could do without, those should be sent to the front of our cold countries: Countries whose owners never owned up to their history, why should they, just because the craftier ones apparently won? This is how new wars break out between nations. Fit to be tied together, our guests roam through the world with their hound dogs. This is how strong the bonds of love can be. Karin has no pet tearing at her, the animal is already inside her, but it obeys only the mother's every word. So far Karin hasn't actually met it, that animal, she can feel it twisting and looking for a treat, a reward in all the customary places her mommy put them. Where others have their built-in free will, which they occasionally have doctors check to see whether it is still flexible in all directions, someone had tied an animal inside Karin, which keeps eating its way to the exit without ever getting out into the open. After all, it has always been nicely pampered with Purina puppy chow for just that purpose.

As a closed hiking group, the vacationers now walk over to the open rock shop where you can get those big stones for throwing. Playfully, the woolly walking aids, the vacationers' attendants, throw their legs against the tree trunks and splash some urine on them. The air is already veiled a bit in autumnness. Soon the fog's protective covers will be thrown, with autumnal storms shaking up nature underneath until winter sacks it altogether. What the other female tourists see as a dog leash, with which they attach themselves to their most beloved one who keep pulling toward adventures and must be yanked back, seems juicy life itself to Karin. Doesn't she sit right in the middle of the midday meal, actually this is already a fall menu!, life is something shaking her axis with which she wangled it until now, maybe a new ice age is coming, which will probably cover fifty square centimeters, if that axis gets pulled at long enough. Inside it scratches and snarls, a draft comes in from outside, so we put on cool warm clothes. Karin is too heavy a burden on herself for someone to drag out for free use, only to leave her again after a brief visit. A Herr Doctor in the hospital makes himself available just for that, but no more. Let's come closer to hear more, as we enjoy our own calling as a dramatist: Karin Frenzel, pretty average, colored hair, glasses, business major, secretary in the sales department of an international office equipment firm, five years ago computer training together with sixteen-to-twenty-year-olds. Well, that should be enough! Any robber of life would take a look at Karin's orderliness and, assuming that she is a stone without inscription (the chisel slipped at the first letter and left nothing but a hole), throw her back into the pond, where she could not even attract a single circle for a pleasant chat.

Karin Frenzel, a fairly tall, middle-aged woman—out of whom her mother had fished her favorite candies and sucked them dry long ago; like a crocheted toilet-paper wrap the old woman slips herself over that old bag of a daughter in case someone wanted to carry her away. For good. Hold it, wasn't there a marriage? Herr Frenzel died of cancer years ago, a quiet man, he seemed in a permanent slumber even when he was alive. Her conjugal enframing exacted quite a bit from Karin, we just don't know what, there are always those quiet folks who won't tell. Most of the time she felt like a bird that gets squashed with bare hands, so that the blood can also be consumed as gravy to a main dish. But even pussyfooters like her enjoy the rustic life, though she'd rather not set foot in a stable. Just don't lose your footing, you never know what's afoot. That Herr Frenzel. A middle manager who meddled in everything and, like a citadel, occupied his wife's harbor to make sure she could not take off. Any mention of him hurts. Someone who did not disown her mother yet did not insist on keeping her own name either can expect a gorgeous view of Snow Alp from here and have it throw sparks on her specs, they'll be fine, they won't get scratched. And exactly that person did not get up on her hind legs soon enough so that her sex could finally be seen.

Here you can always enjoy all kinds of comforting lights in the distance, while on the horrible sea, or with any other force of nature at whose mercy you are, there are no spotlights like here, on this apple tree. And not even a baby's head appears at the exit of such a person: Karin F., no wonder she never delivered herself to a stranger, since her own family, after several bloody arguments, remained such strangers to her. Foreignness can mean attractive closeness when you are young, but where is Karin now? Because she is her mother's property, she does nothing that's not proper. Her mailbox at the reception is always empty. Food still is the greatest admirer of Frau Frenzel, it reciprocates her affection, still, her female colleagues don't like coming over. Nobody wants to ingest anything at her home, for her mother's pampering made the leaves fall too soon from the sapling Karin, so that people always feel they are being watched as if through dry brush. For that bland gravy for the lamb ragout Karin recently stood in the kitchen for hours on end. It took her four days to prepare the hors d'oeuvres and then just a few minutes to throw them to the guests, who growlingly lunged at them from their doghouses and, after a polite period of time, quickly excused themselves for more unrestrained amusements, chewing ferociously on their harnesses. So here we are again. Shadows pass by, light glistens on the slopes. A house stands up. It let itself get photographed in front of a lovely green hill and is now handed around on the cold platter of our perception. Inside most people there is a knotty, gnarly self, big enough for a dozen other people, but still, they take flight from Frau Frenzel, who does not have such a self to show for herself, not even in a picture in which she makes a characteristic gesture or in another one that actually captures her character. Nevertheless, most of the guests are self-made. Karin on the other hand is a mass product, albeit not to her mother. Maybe Karin's guests sensed their hostess not paying much attention to their vivid accounts, well, she had to constantly run into the kitchen, where something sizzling in the guise of its own fat was in the process of being retrained for unbeingness. The way they gobble and snap, those guests! Leaving deep impressions in the hostess's heels. But they heal quickly!

This is how life works far from here, actually: from here on in. Those women save themselves until coffee time, then they break down the barrier, cheering themselves, who are their own team and even have their own mates, and jump at the Cointreau and the cognac to thoroughly diss those not present. They hardly ever let Karin join in. Then they leave again. Words get driven through people, as if they presented no obstacle. As if the arms of those victims were spread wide and they would soon be as scabby as all those busy mid-level employees from the nails drilled through the center of their palms by daily life with its nail gun. This is how lambs à la Karin Frenzel get milk-fed and then milked dry. Actually, they have no say, not even the craftier ones, whose homes look as if they had founded a city there. No one could smash the pane of glass that protects them from their neighbors' emergency call. Yes, Karin, the employee and her lady colleagues. The most anyone would pay for their presence in flesh and blood are a crispy roast and an Alpen cabin lay-ee-odle-lay with a shot. The shots schuss right through their casings and so the guests return home again, where they will once again blow their shawms, saucily, shamelessly, a mating call they made up in advance for their partners, who are to come with their delivery forceps and force a bit of stale life out of the shell. In front of those partners, they can then put their whole weight in the balance, huffing and howling, whatever their choice, they always get screwed. So now they fall asleep. They've got no game, but they always want to shoot at others.

Snippets of conversation twirl like smoke through the mountainscape, the high valley goes on and on, and the people march on. The wind carries a touch of autumn, even a trace of winter. But the landscape is not yet ready to be broken by winter. It gets compared to the guidebook and must render an account as to whether it stands in the right spot and has not yet been damaged by illegal landfills (which after all is also human trash). So now I come in with my stamper—an example of technical reproducibility—and void nature completely, and then I stomp a few times all over the paper on which I had stamped her two thousand times as punishment and leave my footprints there. Now she is done and gone, nature. Now they can't credit her with an order that would dwarf anything I made, and this is something I can't tolerate. Because I have no human contacts and not many things I'd enjoy! Karin Frenzel has removed herself a few steps and picks up a few ounces of panoramic view at the hot dog stand behind the fence, both view and dog are presented to her in still hot, bite-size pieces. The animals have nothing against their being mentioned here, after all, this is why they were recycled. Karin is wearing this new jogging suit with appliqués, which actually are the most important thing about it, appeals (how do I get to the appeals court? Help!) to our attention. They came in the next higher price category, the rest of the suit comes along rather listlessly. One can see those adornments from afar. A walk to the mountain creek is under consideration, so that the suit wouldn't have to be seen by just one person but in the company of softly bubbling conversations and bared moods. Here we are, the creek is right down there. Applause. It roars, this is a fact we also agreed upon. The little jerry-rigged wooden bridge had been joylessly cropped by the servants of the forest to give it an antique look. The trail descends sharply, pinecones, needles, candy wraps, everything just lying around, people line up in single file, here one can only proceed one after the other. But they stop repeatedly to catch their breath and throw foggy bits of conversation to each other. The downward climb is pretty steep, below, the spray spins around as if in the drum of a primeval washing machine, shreds of fog fly upward from the slavering flews of apocalyptic hounds leaping at the tamer members of their species who, unimpressed by nature, sniff for the wildness that seems to have left itself here. The first old ladies stay behind at a spot where walking isn't quite as strenuous, they sit down, a harmonious congregation, their feet are sitting already in health and comfort shoes. Only the strongest and most courageous are still hanging in on the last leg. Soon the talking will have to stop, because the creek roars so loudly through the twisted brush that you can hardly understand your own words. Steps are caught lovingly by carpets of needles. Slowly nature dares to unfold, she takes the helm, only to lose it instantly to a few hobby photographers. There comes the threshold where wildness is no longer us, not the people but, attention, nature, will you please pull yourself together, now that all of us are looking: forest, water, wilderness. On the way back we'll experience it all over again, that, as soon as the experience has been tamed, memory, wagging its tail, leaps at us, filled with joy that a future something did not happen, which could have easily been a horror. Yes, now it goes downward again toward the creek; the jungle of firs is thinning, and thrifty ground-cover plants are leisurely scribbling away to settle accounts later with trees in the balance sheets of Alpine Landscape.

The narrow trail makes another small serpentine curve, a rivulet gurgles, it gets almost drowned out by its big brother below (were it not for the built-in noise protection, thanks to the whim of the hilly terrain shielding the mountain creek somewhat and curbing its roar, we wouldn't hear the little brook at all or that which impedes it), with which it will soon merge. Somewhere up there must be one of the countless springs. The stronger ones among them were hemmed in by Vienna's water-supply system. Under pretexts the last three of the older participants stop here, it is too steep for them after all. They take a relaxing cigarette break. Caution, fire hazard!, then they'll get back to the short climb. Karin Frenzel, beckoned by the depth, continues alone. The fact of being younger than the others is especially noticeable between 2:00 and 4:00 p.m., a time our seniors and senioras like to take a siesta. The trickle that bleeds here over the forest floor flows into a cracked concrete basin, from where it throws itself out again through a sort of drain. There the rivulet is not far from completing its daily goal, the roaring creek, into which it seems to project itself already, as it moves pretty quickly. Water had been dammed up in this basin, what for? Maybe a small power plant? A swimming pool is unlikely, who would swim here? Or water their garden? The stone rubble of a ruin flickers brightly between the trees, which is easily said and yet so hard to grasp: Is that a there there or is that elsewhere? There is dark water in the basin, curdled, black, even though the rivulet meanders through it quite briskly. But the new blood doesn't seem to have a chance against this long-established brew. Can't see the bottom, Karin thinks, as she moves closer curiously. Bending over it, a dull, blackened shard of a mirror seems to look at her, but inside or, rather, underneath it, streaks of algae or other plants are floating this way and that before they gather above their roots ready to attack. The basin is about two meters deep, no, deeper, but the water in it—and it doesn't get even close to the rim—appears to be climbing light-footedly, sometimes breathing heavily, straight down into earth's jaws. The surface of the water moves gently, as if dead animals were still learning how to swim. A few leaves float lazily on top: Oak. Karin Frenzel stares at them, then she realizes what bothers her. Nowhere is there a foliage tree around here! Only the dark firs on the edges of a monoculture forest. This isn't possible, where do these leaves come from, nobody would have put them there. Who or what would have thrown itself into the basin, out of which an indescribably foul smell is rising, who beat up nature to a pulp here? The trees are not reflected in the dark metal of the water, neither does Karin's face leave any usable imprint, it gets lost instantly in the shimmering impenetrability that dissolves anything approaching it, as if the basin were filled with acid or another destructive substance. The leaves lie completely immobile on the water screen, at the very least they would have to circle or paddle around a bit; after all, there is some flow-through and feed-into the basin. Leadenly this executioner's block of water had been fit into the basin, nothing sparkles, nothing shines, which usually is water's favorite hobby.

In that liquid and the forest's thin pubic hair that closes off the forest's body as it splits toward the creek and rises again on the opposite bank to become impenetrably thick and fleshy again, something is growing there that we had sacrificed to our usage long ago. Fathom-deep humus of fir and pine needles, that noiseless layer under the feet, and then that black rock of water, it would smash you to pieces if you jumped into it, Karin was convinced of that. There is absolute silence, one would have to at least hear the rapids under the arched rock below, or is it actually an ark loaded with desperate guests pulling at the end of their rope to get it going again, an angry customer base? At least one would make out the foamy water beating against the drum of the machine, that quiet sawing, when the washer computer jumps to the next cycle. But every move gets immediately caught in the trap of silence. The water lives its own life, it takes an endless breath, it is connected to our heart-lung machine, as we enjoy life in the open air, we would tear our ribcage open to be able to absorb this mighty lump of nature. Frau Frenzel shudders before so much silent coldness. She stares at the three masterless leaves, and, almost as a reflex, holds her tiny transistor radio to her ear, which she always takes with her, so that music pulses some of the life force through her, shaking her, maybe she, too, would then be able sometime to drop a few of those leaflets filled with great scores. A Herr Kurt Ostbahn responds nearly instantly on the small home appliance, and this popular local singer admonishes Karin in his nice way to buy some of his hot discs so that he and his sound can keep her backbone straight. He throws his sopping chunks into the wild, that singer of wage- and salary workers, so that they can retrieve those meaty shreds as ready-to-eat bytes between their teeth out of the void of their desires; his live audience (taped in the dining hall) claps and bangs along rhythmically, pumping blood; pumping the Austrian Blues. Anytime. It doesn't help. Karin at that point can be neither cheered up nor shocked; she turns off the radio after a few minutes. The silence that follows seems to be even denser, more impenetrable than before.

The water waits in complete stillness. Isn't there another, louder sound, Karin must have imagined it, because it is not really any louder. Maybe an echo in her ears from the brief racket on the radio, that cloth she threw over the landscape, but it is already revealed again. It sounds like children's shouts, a brief, fierce yelling, a whim of the air trying to surf sound waves? Those must be preschool children, school started quite a while ago. Or are those village kids? Is it a field trip? Isn't this the season for retirees only, who always are in season. It costs less now to stay here, and the time for seniors is rather limited anyway. That howling. It hangs in the air for a moment contemplating whether it should lower itself. It couldn't have been children. So much worldly noise would have dispersed everything foreboding about this landscape whereas, on the contrary, the woods, the water, here, in front of Karin, seem to have moved together, closing ranks even more tightly, forming an impenetrable phalanx that has advanced a few meters, camouflaged with branches, like an army. And right into the center of this nature combat squad, someone must have cut a window. Into another dimension? Did the landscape itself become the TV, rather than shining through it on the local news? Nature, this incalculable cargo, which makes Karin wheeze and gasp for breath, this having arrived at a railhead, this presence of some entity wishing to inhabit us, it pushes with all its might to get inside Karin, it tries every single orifice, as if this living yet invisible entity wanted to get through the entry gates of a rock concert and is forced back by some guards or agents who must shield the stars that are up there in the sky for folks like us to look at and long for, but not to get a hold of.

The air often plays tricks on us in the mountains. Sometimes it is impossible to define the source of a sound. A short, bright bark, it wants to go for the kill, kill Karin or maybe just time, the hour Karin thought she spent there, which, in fact, was only a few minutes. The howl presented itself briefly and immediately left the highly valued stage of the water across which it resounded. The woman's hair stands on end. That howl could have brought gigantic herds to a standstill, and it could have done it without the sight of the animal that goes with it. Frau Frenzel turns away, her peregrination takes a turn, too; both flee in a headless panic. Sometimes it is ourselves who create the dangers, please do not step too close to the chasm or it will be the last thing you greet, and you'll have no more time for postcards. Right behind the last curve it goes down meters deep next to the bridge. There you have the highly active, heavy water of the mountain creek, which keeps tossing it up in the air with great effort and catching it right away, over and over again, a game we know from certain nightmare scenarios in which we have to play the water. The air stands still instantly, the radio also has had to stop its program. It gets turned on again instantly, nervously and shakily (Karin almost doesn't find the button), the battery yawns ill-omenedly, the woman should decide herself if on or off, always those consumer rush hours, and then, one moment later, another singer takes care of continued carefreeness with a new song. But let's not drag him through the filth of this fiction here. Nonetheless, now that small pile lies right here in front of us, the radio fires us up and pukes a few more times into our palms.

Isn't that a woman up there on the bridge? Could it even be that, in conflict with aesthetics, she wears a very similar suit as our Karin F.? Let's get closer, could it be the same? Karin Frenzel accelerates her pace, thinking, the road goes straight ahead, she presses the pedal and, in slow motion, comes to a standstill in midair, because here it goes down steep and deep. Karin throws her head back, opens her jaws to scream, everything stays where it is, except her, but she sees, she sees that down there—which, by a whim of gravity, is now an Up—a woman who emanates the bewitching shimmer of good taste's eternity in matters of fashion is leaning against the railing, a bright glow, because this woman also seems to be Karin! A prize-winning stranger. Awarded with a price tag that says this suit was reduced not only for Karin, others could have also bought it at the summer sale. Alright, so Karin's mouth is wide open, a thin, screaming bird appears between her lips, yes, here we can see it already: Language is hazmat stuff we've loaded onto our hazmat vehicle, but it won't be deployed today anymore.

Wind, the accomplice. It carries all the weight of those—our inarticulate—screams. Here the sharp-edged rocks are rhinestones worked into the necklace that collars nature, whom we try to jerk away from us if she gets too close to us. Quite a job! The mountain torrent rolls in its bed, it feels good because it just ate. Where does the foam on its swells come from? What delicate something that tolerates soft water only rinsed here once more extra softly? The mountains enclosing the creek flare like an uncontrollable fire. The mini-radio flies along right next to Karin. The gadget and its owner are in the dead spot where sound cannot fulfill its purpose—that is, caringly waking the listener with a song. The falling woman can jump as much as she wants against the potlid on top of her, it won't lift, the valve won't either, she is locked inside the stew. The landscape suddenly turned soundproof, as if all this time it had been a house that suddenly disappeared. Something more powerful protects the woman's freefall. The wind comes up again like a wall with this body hanging on it, holding on by the fingertips only. It seems as if the wind has suddenly stopped as well, a photograph just made, of an ocean with a surfer on top of it frozen in motion. Did the wind get collected in a gigantic faucet, where it is waiting to be set free? Does nature rest in one grip of the hand, which could quickly turn its grip on us? Karin, thrown ungently but safely landed now, indeed considerably loosened up, rises in her new jogger look, appetizing like chocolate icing. She is just a bit breathless. It seems to her that she looks a little blurred in her own photograph. Gasping for breath, she sits up and there, yes, right there, that woman from before still stands there. Because of that woman she ventured so far out to the edge of the cliff. Without further thought, or at least catching her breath, Karin pitches a "Grüß Gott" to the woman near the water. The greeting falls on the wet, foam-covered ground. Can't hear a word in the roar of that creek, Karin! The two words drip into nature's house, this long-lived house, which would love nothing more than to turn us all into leaves so that we would stick to our stems and not trample all over places marked "Private." We are, after all, the model for nature, as such we were created, therefore we should treat her in an exemplary fashion, as environmentalists prompt us, paraphrasing the proprietors of nature. Property is something solid, while nature embodies *Panta rei.*

She must have sensed that Karin would come down here, this stranger, because now she turns around casually, unfazed, playing leisurely with the tassels of her suit, which stand out loudly against the creek's white foam, and Karin invites her into her gaze. Too late to slam another door. A sharp jet of air zooms through Karin's incisors because that woman is HERSELF! No similarity one could respond to politely or kiddingly: It is—words won't help, they would only harm here—it is Karin in person, who encountered herself, who had to step in front of herself, to look at herself, to see herself in the suit. If only she had looked better after herself up on the rock! No one jumping to her assistance. The silent ones shall be passed over in silence on Judgment Day or whenever, but here, on the bank of a midsized wild creek, where the air had gotten noticeably cooler, no, colder, Karin Frenzel encountered Karin Frenzel. Nature hasn't been playful for a long time, we made sure of that, so how come that a woman who first was off-balance and then careened straight toward the center of the earth, how come that an average woman throws her flesh to another woman only to realize: the other one has already eaten it? Here you offer yourself to another person, and she actually accepts! Has this stranger, no, this strange me, been sent by the tourist office so that we will take better care of our property? So that we are careful in these encounters with the highest, encounters with the six- to ten-thousand-footers and ravines of our *Heimat?* Karin stands there frozen in her paltriness and doesn't ask herself, as she is busy taking in and throwing out her breath, if this strange double could now also randomly imprint her face like a stamp on any other woman. She asks herself nothing. We all feel we are unique, don't we? And we don't want to be separated from life, we have known it for so long. What will Karin's mother think of these strange transmigrations of a face, is the first thing Karin asks herself as she once again manages the artistic creation of a word. This stranger can't possibly be a biological sister. What does that smiling face want? The wind, maybe also in shock, has settled down as well. Not one needle stirs, only the creek rages relentlessly. Now comfortably seated, the wind seems to have unwrapped its afternoon snack, because the stench of spoiled, foul flesh rises from the stranger's seat, unpleasantly sweet, like candy. This is how moods are created, that wind sure knows its business! Carrion, caught in leaking boxes, wafts across from the second Karin, a vague swaying of figures behind her, or is it just a play of shadows drawn to a watering place or manger where, in this country, baby Jesus can occasionally be found, so that people, instead of tearing each other to pieces, can slaughter this only begotten unisex Gott. Hyperreal the tossed-out plastic bag on the wet pebbles, a glittering ghost of consumption. It looks as if some sort of figures had gone astray here, like Karin, they ate something, and now they are waiting in the woods for someone to lead them back out again. A presence somewhere over there, to your left, came along with the strange Karin, who now presses herself under the snacking wind, a quietly dozing intermission-filling creature who wants to collect the last gasps of Karin's breath in the empty yogurt cup in its hand and take it away. What sort of caravan has arrived here at the exact same time—down to the last hundredth of a skiing second—as Karin's fall; who wants to settle here as judge, as savior of our home-spawned Gretchens, to make use of us inhabitants and the habits inhabiting us? Waiting behind this strange woman might be others who need companions in order to become dangerous. As if lifeboatsmen had pushed off from shore. As if now stronger hooks were digging into human flesh, to save it, of course. But the can opener jammed and people can only get halfway out, they are stuck in their container, no one else wants to retain them. The essential entities cannot completely join us, they are caught in the present and cannot become what has been, but neither can they become presence. Instead, they want to make our homeland unhomely. Out of sheer obstinacy they want to obtain a final score in overtime in this still tied game in which we leisurely tossed around their skulls and bones and stopped only to grab their rugs and necklaces, their gold teeth, paintings, and stamp collections. Far from forests we wreaked havoc, but now this split has opened up, exercise doesn't help, our last substitutes are already running into the field (and they all look like us!), the blood squeaks in their shoes like a newborn colony of mice, kick-off whistle, the game that rested until now gets going instantly, the young ingenue enters and exits, and the opposing players, not yet in full swing but already with our visages on their faces, lift their dark wings, the last rays of sun still glistening around their edges before they parashoot down and OPEN UP. No, a parasol is no protection against a ghostly downpour.

Like a handful of leaves a swarm of shadows gets thrown over Karin Frenzel and settles in the valley. It is getting colder, nature gets more forbidding, seems to sharply lock herself in. The slopes take on a sterner face, more deeply furrowed than usual; the mountains want to squeeze everything they've got out of themselves, and why not, they'll show those wanderers! The wrinkles turn bluish across the alpine skin, the mountains have aged, gotten more rugged toward its visitors within a few minutes. Blackberries work on their bushes, splashing dark colors around. Whatever knew itself at least no longer knows another. Frau Frenzel isn't pretty enough to come out in two copies, her fellow vacationers would say. The other player in this singular double, Karin Two, who seems to have been taken from another dimension for comparison and dispension lightly bends her knees, as if she wanted to warm up first, as if she had to get used to that intricate outfit they threw her in at the last moment, as she, holding her nose and squeezing her eyelids together, pushed through the space-time continuum to leave the old one behind and to possibly become, if she conducts herself and controls her prey well, an unpleasant but constant habit. This sportswear's mission is to simulate the thrill of speed to its owner while she sits in her deck chair, knitting or reading, but the more we read in this fashion-conscious buyer of those all-the-more perishable goods (taste spoils sooner than flesh), the more her copy commands respect. There still must be more to a person, clothes already deducted, than meets the eye; and in this case, even though the model is quite plain, not counting the clothes, it must have taken quite a while to duplicate her. The powers seem to be pretty powerful. They brand their choices and put them under the strictest control; they are intended for later shoots. This is why they mustn't move. Most are already copies of photographs, but some are originals. This copy of Karin (or is Karin the copy?) is an excursion into still water that also sucks in Karin at a toe-dipping pace; the water in the basin rises slowly, which has been noticeable for some time. Not as in cooking, when it rises to the brim, bubbling and burbling and throwing out the noodles to make more room for itself, no, rising, it seems to get colder and darker in its cracked concrete confinement, which it soon will lose, if it keeps rising at that speed. Karin feels already as if she were entering the boat of her flesh, ready to take off; she gets pulled away, the glassy surface—with the three unbending leaves on top of it presenting themselves to her in relief—approaches her like a sheet of ice, beckoning her to get on it, though knowing full well she might also break through it. Land is left behind, though Karin still stands there as if nailed to the ground. The three oak signets exert an irresistible pull on her, attention, the program about Canada has already started, but that's another leaf, and only losers are in it. Hands are twitching like dogs on a leash ready to lunge at the leaves and their ribs, as if there were bones with some flesh still hanging on them. A wolf looks greedily out of the dogface, back at the person. Nature is a knockout. No reflexes on the surface, even when she gets clobbered. Those leaves are not paper that can patiently soak it all up and then softly let itself go down again. They seem to be made of featherweight plastic, not a single drop washes over them. Dry. No void of an interruption saves the woman who stepped up to the basin. Memory comes to a halt, the mind is out in the open, it stops while its house breaks away, toward the water: Memory, in this primal stream, is an entire continent, in view of what amassed on our debit account; but it became incontinent, our dear memory, out there at sea, because it hadn't been collected in time. The last of all innocent victims is dead, so in a twister out of the void the tongue of nothingness slurps up all those carefree folks gathered at the office party and spits them into familiar reality, where they have already longingly waited for themselves. The bowlers and the castle tourists, the minigolf players and the museum visitors, registering surprisedly a tiny wound on them, are quickly taken off the playing field again to rest, but that really wouldn't have been necessary for a bagatelle like a few million dead! And something invades them, it does not change their own exterior nature but rather takes from them every other nature wherein they wanted to settle. Karin Frenzel was the first to pick up her mail here, in the form of a package she was to be burdened with, even though she doesn't know her address anymore. In doing so, the strange woman who is herself split apart, transforming into a rockfall of mismatched I's, each of them still featuring Karin's face, each figure wearing her sweet but nonetheless hot jogging suit. None of those colorful accessories are particularly unique or special in any way. Now this strange yet so familiar figure seems to smile at her (a little weirdly, oh, right, the mirror shows you in reverse, while Karin, for the first time, sees herself as she really is, which takes two, because only a lover can lie to you so blatantly, supposedly to spare your feelings), and Karin catches herself smiling as well, or was she the first to smile and that mirage was only her personified image? There is no wind to play with the hair of the two women. They do not yet get to know each other by their affections. The water still rises, but it has slowed down some as if it knew: I'll get to the top any moment and then I can finally climb out. As if a water treader (but upward from down below, a water mounter!) had wanted to rise up and come for a long time, as if the water had wanted one thing only, to give itself. As if it could no longer contain itself. Dark herds race shadowlike across the pastures, darker shadows, some even in the shape of bears, close on their heels. Karin Frenzel comes in two, there wasn't enough for a trinity, it is by sheer coincidence that we now use the name of our God, who, on his tireless search for temporary help in his restoration and rest-stop enterprises, has already sent millions of people for personal use to his God's acre, so that they can work for him there, breaking up the loam with their flimsy little shovels, until HE, a new Golem, swaying, spinning, stomping, starts once again to dance our Austrian *Ländler.* Yet people always only create themselves, no wonder the consumption of materials is so high. At least they want to become something better in their children, but they can't pull it off.

A deep gorge, a waterspout, the tongue of an invisible ant bear, opens in the concrete basin, as if a lickadileaking drain deep down were sucking a lane, a tunnel, into the water and taking everything with it that enters it in a precariously wobbly vehicle. It creates a quiet vortex, perfectly round, an indentation on the surface, the leaves still don't move, but there is a suction, which seems unable to hold on to itself, as if it were addicted to her, the suction starts to pull at Karin, an interruption in the empty- and timeless-ness, a leaden surface blocking a malevolent force must now yield to it, bending at the edges, softly, sluggishly, ashen, it's only a question of time when the material, this metallic water, will give and pull Karin out of herself and down. Maybe a person will stay out there as a shell or in the shell of a car filled with travel companions (isn't that a larger vehicle, a gigantic bus, approaching her?), but whatever Karin had agreed upon with her Creator, her mother, at their journey's start will have disappeared—devoured, digested, a clearing that receives no more light because the latter didn't receive clearance for the shorter runway. This woman knows one thing and one thing only, that not for anything must she take the water's hand held out to her that, for some inexplicable reason, had become the hand of her strange double. She senses that it would make her flare up and disappear completely as if in a pale fire that wouldn't come from a tame hearth and incinerate a tamed herd, innocence incarnate, lightning striking one's only possession. Those soft, woolly backs! Just as we had gotten used to the real, which is as rare as the simple, it is taken from us again. This strange memory, this bundle of fat and bones made up with Karin's features, this winning Something wants to take on Karin as her child, as a live-in companion of her Self. A mommy and a certain quickness would be needed right away to watch over this child! It always wants to make some mischief. How the teeth of that strange Karin woman are shining now, she is shaken by a noiseless laughing fit, for no apparent reason, since her partner's hair stood up in horror, don't they both see the same thing? Karin One's head gets bent at the neck, one can't see by whom or from what, it is turned toward her colleague's glistening incisors; but a closer look at those only insufficiently pearly killer tools reveals that every other beast has better ones, here we see only the dull, gray fillings, ancient amalgamations of crusts of earth, a row of letters on a piece of paper, thunderheadlines that say little about that terrible car crash on the Niederalpl but still offer every reader a small piece of bared throat. Surely everyone, even if they couldn't kill anyone, has experienced or done exciting things to others, which should have been published instead in today's paper! Karin, the daughter, thus herself a typical copy, a reiteration (Language, you, the good about humans! You, the goods!), can see it clearly: Down to the fillings in her teeth that second woman is herself! That stranger seems to want to take her place whatever it takes, but not to merge with her, just the opposite, to continue as a second one in her—Karen's—interior and completely independent of her: In Karin One, Karin Two had captured a historic space (almost with a shower and toilet!) where every five minutes, as in a 24/7 cinema, a car crash is served up that does its crashing thing and disappears again, all inside!, the second Karin seems to want to find in the Nothing she came from a second chance to dwell. Is Karin F. the stranger's hotel room she is entitled to, which she booked? And which she will not leave, because that stranger, too, is entitled to room service. Everything that could have possibly been taken from her at one time or another should now be retrieved to her between Karin's teeth, and since she seems to be addicted to ecstasy, the kind only life and its drinks can induce, that life will now finally be tasted, drunk, at least bitten into. Oh, if only one had the right to throw something out, but we are melded into superfluity! Wait, more bodies have lined up there. Worry and fear fill the dark water, nature's parade ground, where people parade, half- or completely naked—water, one singular pretext to show off and multiply that follows baring oneself: this need for the needlessness of being more than one but not having to be. Here is your chance to cut a good figure, Frau Karin, and you already have shown us a second figure! So then Frau Frenzel must be handed over to the water and that water creature, because she and the water belong to each other, Karin knows that instinctively. That middle-aged woman known to be closed tight as a clam shall become the opening for the in-between world of insanity?, of common sense?, of second residences? She must be sucked up by this water vacuum, this vacuum cleaner of remembrance, right into her second being, sowing discord, harvesting water, declaring desires, even getting herself a second car, but one outside any middle-class categories that could lead directly to a categorical war of dark insinuations and accusations. A foreign essence insists on Karin's presence. No doubt an account will be kept, whether that woman presented here in the coldwater bath (an equation and one unknown, one plain, one purl, one Christ and his own son, whom he produced by passing through Mary like water through a pipe!) may stay there long enough for her to be measured and afterward be missed. Greedily the water takes what belongs to it, it becomes a garment that tightly encloses Karin. No wonder, this woman is an open space in the water intended to be the same size as her body, issued forth from seeds. From seeds thrown by one mother right between two cars just before they crashed. This is why nothing can become of her, not even in the water, that cheap elixir of life. The water sucks Karin, who knows her competitive price, into the site of the mother, and the water also spits her out again, she unfolds in a freezing cold that rolls over her as a cold wave, snow!, the first snow!, the woman spreads her wings, they sparkle like a plastic raincoat, she gasps for breath, snatches at edibles in the air, a sharp draft cuts into her mouth, flutters around there, treading water. Kicking wildly, Karin tries to hold on to the balloon of her first I, but it gets torn from her hand. Distinctions fade in this sinking Titanica, electricity blows out, one bulb after the other, before they all explode. Deuce, tie, blackout. Following this: Excursion Return to One's Own Essence, but as much as one keeps shaking at one's own being, it will always be two halves, the so-called unequals, the wave throws Karin several times around herself, that takes some time, T/O for me, and as she became part of nothingness, of death, she reappears again, as two, but still alone. Not in herself but still at home.

Nature begins to howl and toss frozen water around (even without considerable wind impact snow weighs between 30 and 150 kg/m^3, with wind: up to 250 kg!). They want to take her toy away! She is inconsolable, even though she was promised new ones in the shape of avalanches and Alpen-louches—the notorious rockfalls and other duds. The creases in the jogging suit, which would attract negative attention in a slimmer woman, stand still. The food rests peacefully in the body. Eating is like Getting Executed At The Table, the only delight Karin allows herself, which doesn't mean she wants to experience herself twice. The stranger: a lady, who doesn't have to promise Karin any sacred spring, since she is already submerged in it up to her waist. Her torso, stuck on the surface, rests on it like a garden gnome mistakenly placed atop the water. Her hair wet, hanging down, lacquered plaster, the water snuggling up against her hips, she is not reflected in it. That water doesn't do any good, it doesn't quench, it doesn't serve any sport. It rises again and again before it calms down again, an unruly strain of hair not wanting to get back into the hairdo, a book that cannot hold its pages. The women are facing each other, blood dripping from them occasionally, then no more. Not everything gets better with age. No crowd to admire it, nothing to brag about humanness that would dare to come out to bite its master, its mistress; something that would, in turning around, turn against its owner with bared teeth, no longer tolerating its dependence on them in matters nutritional. The innermost nature of humans: The catch—it has the same face as you and I. This is why no one recognizes it.

Even though Karin stands more or less secure at the edge of the basin, she knows that she actually lies on the bottom of it, with crushed bones and torn vessels, that she will never hold a son—that superior being, that master key to femininity—in her shredded lap. None was promised to her either. No breath of anything in her cold, old hands. The son doesn't breathe because he never came. The wind is getting stronger and stronger, a fierce breath, a white whisp across the mountains' flanks; shadows fluttering in the ravines, those skin folds oiled with human wax, lest they get sore from all the dreck. On swaying mats, the undocumented uncannies are trying to sail away on this small spot of water, which is an entire ocean to the bodiless, who first have to painstakingly calculate every possible route. Karin does not want to come along, no matter what, that much she is sure of. Something is pulling on her, something overripe, overeager, wants to finally drop from the branch to be eaten in the lap of this dear worldling. But no one will ever be sitting there, and Karin finds this swaying fare horrific, since it already has a few bruises. The water nixie Karin Two, that Sleeping Beasty Castle on a shard of water mirror, is now sinking slowly. Earlier she could still be seen from her hips up, now the water is already rising to her waist. She earnestly beckons Karin to follow her, for it seems that only voluntarily can you deliver yourself from, nay, to your essence, be in unity with yourself and die. If you are not finished living, the repast can be returned to the kitchen, it can always be reheated again and again, so that what has passed can become a singularity and return each time worse than before. So why travel far, if one can be met at the very same time right there on that Niederalpl. Nevertheless, in this Other Woman, who she also is, Karin wants to overcome the Other and finally become herself. History, after all has proven that one wants to destroy the *Heimat* in the Other, rather than gaining a second homeland! The railing high up on the bridge—its birch skin peeling off like a human sunburn—now shows human fingers on its mistreated skin. Hands. Two wanderers have entered the bridge, and Karin also enters again what she takes to be herself. Her counterimage has walled herself up to her shoulders in the basin and now sinks faster and faster. This duplicate woman's chin is stretched forward, as if she wanted to load a few more breaths onto the dump truck of her body, but the cargo has already started to slip. Most probably that woman doesn't need any air, since she doesn't exist at all, Karin thinks with relief (a dream she is not, she wouldn't look like me then!). Yet Karin can't move. To the degree that her opponent, that goalkeeper for the proof of Karin's singularity, keeps sinking, the air presses against Karin's body and condemns her to immobility. She can't even lift her arms. It is as if an entire tour bus laid on top of her and spit her out, half-eaten, onto the glaring meadow. A last gurgle in the water, the surface closes, the three leaves are pulled down without resistance, a short rattle, a drum flourish of fluid that converges in the center of the instrument, then everything has disappeared. The water smoothens again after it briefly cleaned its feathers. Now it is still, so let us greet the rising wind.

This water took some beating. But it doesn't show it. As much as Karin feared her sinking into and with the other, at the last moment, as the light turned away from the water's surface, she knows with absolute certainty that in the sinking of the other she has ultimately lost herself. She tries to jump into the sunk woman's final breath to make it her own, a last memento of herself, since no one but her mother would probably still be thinking of her. Such an exchange of wordless and also unappreciated goods does not take place. The strange woman went underground, out of sight, and at the same time Karin, the little boat, pushes herself off a bank she no longer knows, she throws herself toward another bank she knows even less than herself, it could be anywhere. Karen's futures are already underwater, the air boils up for a moment, as folks with golden blond dyed perms (how graceful the water is by comparison!) won't stay in their hideouts any longer, as glittering bluish eye-shadows no longer want to remain on the eyelids of a woman in a photo, are glad to join us, strapped, as we are, to the roof of an ambulance. The torrent surges. Women are walking there. So are two men. Those are creatures who arrived with boxes of misery. We don't know them, and their room reservations did not seem to have made it to the reception. A crashed woman can be seen lying under the bridge, hollodrio, who composed our song, destroyed it, and just dumped it in the woods?

From the height of the bridge all eyes are looking down on the fallen Karin, as if she had already been taken off the playing field, yet she was only a substitute player, always just waiting for her call. Underwater an apparition whimpers one last time, like an animal whose food had been taken away, then silence. Yet this original, this Karin One under the lump of water, can hear how down below, way down below, a mass of people, a human massif, bigger than the Snow Alp over there, wants to come up out of its earthly dimension, out of this Disneyland below the dawn of day, a mass that could never be fully counted, let alone grasped. Karin begs desperately to be forgotten or, at the very least, please, not to be seized by this emergence of masses beyond scale, this allied alien-nation. She, Karin, will not let herself be pulled by the leg! Two eyes however are already fixed on her, the headlights of a giant machine that, filled with other travelers, wants to hit the road. Now it does, with a bang, the hikers on the bridge scream, they wave and gesticulate, articulate, as an invisible wingbeat crashes over them, almost tearing their hair from their heads. A storm rises. We wade away, straining to hold the few things we saved in a package up above our heads, through a vast pile of glasses and dentures torn from the jaws of humankind, which can never keep its trap shut. As if an entire mountain were setting off from the shore, Karin reaches down into the depth; groping for her vanished self, she grabs nothing but slippery algae, feels nothing but ice-cold water in the spaces between, and freezes like a horse that gets a piece of steel driven up its anus to make it pose nicely for the slaughterer. Motionless, she awaits her disappearance, which had announced itself for years in trifles, negligences, all directed at her, every single one registered, of course. Now is the time to find the emergency exit out of herself so that she can step into the water, who knows how long time as such will last. Has she, Karin, already chosen the way out and now she lies down there, burst open, her bowels next to her? Why does her existence request forgetting again and again, it might just as well request a good red wine or a schnapps?

The double is gone, but she touched Karin and has been entered in Karin's service record; strapped in mother's bridles it leads abruptly downward, and this is also where Karin is detained. Something might want to get out of there in the future that, however, will not be loved either. Our loved ones are definitely taking too many liberties, aren't they? Karin, inside herself, wades back to the embankment. Her sight can be pulled out again. The vacationing woman's cocker spaniel, golden like leaves before they fall, begging for attention gracelessly like a sleeping infant, barks brightly downward, demandingly. Frau Frenzel lies there, we hurry after her. The heavyweight pet hops around, weightily showing the way everyone would have taken anyway. Self-important voices drone like helicopters. They represent the negative to this positively dispositioned animal. Did Frau Frenzel fall off there? Let's hurry there! A sensation! From afar more and more sounds of life, we hear information offered about the spoiled dog's love and living habits, a dog whistle is blown, the full passion of a well-trained animal lover flares up and lights the scene. Karin has plunged down there, but now she's already trying to get back on her feet, thank God. A few excited women, their skirts and slacks rolled up like murderesses taking a Kneipp footbath in blood, gushing about the blond animal and its most subtle stirrings, wade across the narrow marked trail toward the crashed woman. Animality gets crushed under caresses and born again in countless plush variations. The women slide, scramble down hurriedly, they wave, they call, entwined in the rigging of their speeches like Laocoön with his sons. Our Karin returned home again, she just doesn't know from where and as how many she comes. Eagerly the blond beast cozies up to her, to no avail as usual. Distractedly Frau Frenzel strokes the head of this companion of strangers, she is, after all, a stranger to her own self. Limbs hurting, she gets up supported by others, questioned, written down and off in longhand. Only now, time-delayed, does she hear the dog's infernal barking and pats the head that yells at her. She is given many a hand, but she shakes off those supporting buttresses as in a dream. She can walk by herself, if somewhat painfully, noticing only after a few seconds that she is already walking up the mountain, the fellow vacationers behind her to catch her in case she'd want to go where she doesn't belong. Karin Frenzel climbs up the slope, leaving behind the rushing of the torrent, and soon she again comes across the group of people who'd been so concerned about her. A hawk couldn't manage any faster and would get a bit of meat for it, shadowed by an entire forest.

6

Stumbling, the gaze gets back on its legs and sees how people fall out of their time-will-tell-continuum—a gathering of screaming tenants who no longer recognize their mothers and must carry their seed still in their arms—a fall of angels that finally pulls itself together propels itself with a jellied pike dive roll through the bell jar. A swarm of splinters sinking in slow motion, a small mound on the floor: The room breathes! The entire room breathes with the young woman bent down to the keyhole out in the hallway. It is a bit risky to peek just like that into a strange room, but every risk is well invested when the bank of one's own life is at low ebb—that is, when there hasn't been anything coming in for quite a while. So then Gudrun Bichler risks only a glance into the room that she knows is hers, and she sees herself, a little accountant of a Catholic youth group, and what she just sees is someone taking some liberties with her, storming her mound, her bunny hill, wedeling to and fro excitedly. Someone is cutting sharp edges into her. Soft snow flurries about, accumulates to a Mound of Venus that cannot be cleared. Gudrun's hair flies upward, seized by a sudden breeze. A timid sensation sneaks away from her and through the keyhole into the room, where a something without her doing anything—as if the arms of a robot, inserted into it at the behest of several trendy, fundamentally honest magazines, were steering it, letting Gudrun's nature burrow and rage to the point of insatiability. As if reaching into a tempest with bare hands. As if Gudrun's mere presence outside could unleash an overflow of *being* that would have to drain off somewhere and she, a totally normal young woman, was to shoot, beset with the cumbersome parcels of her sensations, which are still costly for her even though they are second- or third-hand goods, smack into the room. Those natural horrors. How do they arrive breathlessly inside the women, and then always too late? A soft-landing crashing against hard flesh that aged and carefully saved itself at fixed interest rates. What's with that wet thicket lashing against her legs? To show them off all the better? Self-indulgent creatures in mighty miniskirts. Bouncing about inside themselves like the dashing, newly bought elementary part. Any moment now it could light up red and implode. Wonderful, highly developed intelligences that get a raffia skirt put over them, so to speak, as a lampshade that highlights the blaze of bulbs even better so that afterward the gentlemen can read in their savings accounts how much of themselves they had already withdrawn. And what does the new young Party-Führer have to say against the so-called urban elite, small-town cock-tail-in-handler that he is himself. Thus the sensitive female being grows right in front of Gudrun, gentle, snow-white, simply great, a mount, all know or have read about it, no one wants to get inside, only high up on top of it, and like a sunny morning, yes, on a wonderful day like today it is clad in a chic wraparound something or a latex hot-dog skin around the thighs. Take cover!

Yes, it is Gudrun, but she would never wear such a super-short miniskirt. Hold it!, already in the old Sargasso-Sarajevo did the girls in swimsuited lineups parade past their strict Argonaut judges in slow but unrelenting motion. Rounds of artillery fire, suspended for a while, now tearing—not into the hall, not into the bathing flesh wrapped in molecular synthetics (which makes me think: Why did man always have to breed so many races of himself and variations of everything he got his hands on? They barely fit into the framework that the Lord of the Worlds and the Word kindly placed at our disposal. Molecules are also our buddies, in flux, by now we have to accept them as natural, even though we put them together anew a thousand times), the shots hit farther away, in front of the doors to the casino, striking the old, mourning women whose headscarves could offer them little protection, who still wanted to walk around one last time and look at everything, the old goat in tow at this very moment, don't worry, meet them, they happen only as an image, boots are already stomping into their cadavers, from which the steel springs of youth had been meticulously removed before, no one wants to accidentally swallow the fish bones; and the terminator with the imitation Ray-Bans and the imitation golfing haircut (or could it have been a Gulf War cut?) puts his cowboy boot right into the body pasture, pushing it down, it squooshes gently under his sole and, yessirree, the sales go up! Without those many illustrious magazines, that young man, that universal soldier who, in his milder depth even speaks a little English, would not know how sinister one has to look in such a moment. Gaze into the second camera we posted in the hall: like phantoms, brightly bouncing human projections, this is how those fun bodies in their feast-for-the-eye latexes fire themselves at us, and we are allowed, men and women, everyone, fiercely embattled down to the flattered foundation, but not really endangered, to be part of it, as we get to the Misselection in the fiercely embattled Sarajevo, superwomen, classy babes! Even in the West, where the sun still keeps setting, they still seem ready to be taken for a ride, even when they walk, those lovelies, a still completely unopened jar of pickled plums!: gliding along, spellbound by their own one hundred percent fully elastic gorgeousness. How grandiose, how self-aggrandizing; at that moment thunder, lightning, boom!, all those young bathing beauties are breaking through the clouds, the flesh throws itself into the battle of hot bikinis, the battle sounds increase, we don't want to die in this besieged city, we knockouts, who could still become models before that, if we can make it here, we, such splendid, splendid makes, polished in a mirror-finishing school, who can stir up quite a furor in a photo. Every one of us worth a true fighter or, if not, a poop singer or downhill killer (who doesn't know where his body ends and his ego begins). Discreetly snow-covered piles to step and piss into. Blood is running through the streets, but here on the runway it's all tits and ass, because: Attention!, this here is a special offer of fresh, not even once slaughtered bodies, who, daring, daring, stand up for their pictures until our reactions catch up with them and we want to act out our stirrings: Today you get a dozen for the price of one, take me and let that one go! Titillating beyond words those leg oars punting along, above them the wavy, bushy hair curling up to the leader self-consciously, one likes this make better than that one, another prefers the black one over there, with lightning flashing between her lips. *Geschmack und Ohrfeigen* . . . Taste and slaps in the face ain't the same, as we say here. Threatening as helm bushes the beauty queens point the way, yes, winners all of them, just for showing up here at all!, a human vessel's bow every single blown-up hair creation on every one of those wave-brushed, foam-sculpted Helanca Helenas. All those Bermuda triangles plow their splashy furrows, with so much hair growing on them you can't see the fathomless depths underneath, through the Sargasso Sea of spectators. Let us leave those volumized wastelands and take a look at what's going on outside, where I'll embed myself, get my head bashed in, and report.

At this time not much. A few old women looking sullenly and silently into the wooded area that they sadly had to leave, but we don't look at them, we mimic our heroes, and their photo flashes hurl us into the pool, not glistening, not sparking, we again come up to the surface that seems to be made of wood. Apollo has left long ago, he doesn't want to be witness to our most recent ineptitude. He has a new task: Pop music speaks through him now! Such superhuman brightness keeps pushing us back into darkness, but not him. Not him. He is recognized. Photos are held up to him with much shrieking and howling. Carefully, the old women once again clean up the outside of their essence the way they always do, before they have to take it off, their flayed Marsyas hide. Then, overcome, they sink to the ground like leaves laboriously gathered, cattle feed under the sickle, we'll wait for the repeat in slow motion, it's just smoke and mirrors for the eyes: Not to worry, nothing more real crashes here than an animal on the highway in the glare of high-beam lights, mesmerized, tensed up, a moment in which all molecular chains get comfortably settled all at once, to hold us back with their bodies. But then they still collapse under the tires of history, which those young fighters roll in front of themselves in order to nail them into the widespread hands of their sporty Jeeps (in the hall applause bursts forth, yessirree, the white long-legged stalks proceed faster now, they are almost running, bouncing along ostrich-style, way ahead of all other living beings and ways of living, throwing their excitedly jumping protrusions against the famous life-support Elastane. Oiled sex pliers dig in, they reach deep into the breadbasket. Oh yes, it is what you see: These young female bodies want to finally cast off their deadly clinch so that they can sign a modeling contract in Paris,

Rome, or Milan! Hurry up with the shooting! Or they'll be too late getting to the bouncer of the eternal!) So now, here we are again, a somewhat too bulky student in a Styrian vacation spot bends down to the keyhole of her room. In such a position, any buckvault would land far beyond her, outside the playing field. Life can vanish any time, color in a lovely face, well, it's gone now anyway, the runway with the Misses to be, who at this point do not have to overcome any more serious inner inhibitions, retreats with one, two, or three gulps into the television set, the image implodes in a circle of fire, where the one, the only one, has been sleeping and here we go, fanfare, flourish: Little Butter Fingers empty their horns of plenty over this candidate, then over that one who, under the miscellaneous glances that fluttered cheerfully as butterflies out of all those judges' flies, seems to have won. Hold it, until I can get a better look at them! I can't get off that quickly, poor dented tankertop me, I guard the hoard of language! Now I'll count out my voice one more time, it's already lying on the ground and I can see very clearly: Here grows a woman's essence! And it does so out of a bathing suit, like smoke, whirling around, cradling flowers, providing air from the pumped-up hair wound around the unbloody head, and yes, let's have some air also from those juiced-up plump lips below the palisades of mascaraed lashes with their wooden, doll-like clatter, oh dear, is this what Gudrun gets to see? Or does she see something completely different? I can't really tell, because whatever it was, it withdrew a tenth of a second ago into this small box right here and continues closed to the public somewhere, wherever History, grinning stupidly, but sure of victory as always, has just arrived with its luggage and is already chasing the staff around, because they made the mistake of letting it in at all. And since we don't want to come along in swim gear and double-quick time, she'll just go it alone: The washing machine spins bloody laundry now, and owing to good weather the event takes place outdoors. We home viewers have had already enough news from that country, which just returned to the main dish, death, we've had it as our guest, now we want to be served something else, because we crave variety and grab each other in the resounding FOX hole of the senses, but this is an instrument not everyone can play, be it as it may, an uncertain Gudrun Bichler for one cannot. Now we are getting to the essentiality and we'll try to screw in the second version.

Gudrun ("The Student") bends down to the insect-shaped hole in the door to rest a bit, to snuggle against the sight that will present itself to her, and whoops!, almost falls, eyes first, into the room. As if we were condemned forever to become what we see. Yet the moderator only introduces us: The viewer gets mutated into a TV image of himself, and what does Gudrun see in this strange room that is apparently her own? Herself in the mirror of Creation as she lays herself down for the Highest, and He still has the nerve to insist that it is He who lays all, nay, lays it all down for humans. And she spoons a good helping of it all onto her eye baskets, which press against the firn so that their owner won't sink into this ice-cold whiteness, this infinite uniformity of sugar snow on the surface (the large, cup-shaped crystals were formed from the outside by the accumulation of water vapor and have very little cohesion), that stretches out glitzily all the way to the horizon where it seems to grow even farther. So here are those who simply belong in the picture of the dangerous, they execute their make-up and become Miss Croatia (by being able to explode their own image for one moment, because it used to reach much farther, across all of Yugoslavia), look at their bouncing boobs waving like crazy from the tops of their boob traps, that's a new pennant I didn't even know. Did you see that? Anyway, those sharp high heels drilling themselves into the floor, which gets nailed together by them, an endless earworm, into a coffin, this hollow-sounding wood, a gnarled witness of belonging to this brand-new country—international recognition guaranteed any time—with the first name *Jungsammafeschsamma,* better known as Hellzapoppin, and the family name Levis, Lee, Super, or Diesel. The miss gives a mean finger and throws her imperturbable fun-body—surrounded by countless pairs of whistling lips jumping around, sitting pretty, giving paw (they probably have "one eye too many" [H.], so that in case they get blinded like Oedipus, which, however, would give them too much honor, they still have an extra one to cast on us women—into the supermarket display case, jeez, is that cold!, where, faster than the observer slowly freezing to death could bat an eye, this rump with the little forest gets the bathing suit twined around the haunches like a bright red special-sale banderole, and—since we're getting straight down to the nitty-gritty now—torn off and thrown into the fleshpot with all the others. Super! *Listeria monocytogenes!* Soup!). All the others are molten down to a dirty white spot, eternal flocks of spectators, as we could call ourselves without rhyme but with good reason, but did not do for this contest, and standing in front of a closed door, peeking, like Gudrun, into the room behind it. It finally arrived, the running meter gaze, still two sizes too big for this Topless Bra. If not even you fit in, who else would in your place?

Where might those two people be headed, struggling as they are with themselves and each other, Gudrun asks herself at her lookout. They lift their legs as if walking through underbrush, that is, on pin(e)s and needles. A ballet of bugs that makes you laugh. The man seems vaguely familiar, what will happen to his words when he won't need them anymore, he mumbles something, but it can't be understood through the door. Now the woman also whispers. Isn't that the athlete who chases across the rivers and into the trees, who has music as fuel infused through earphones and who, consistently on the move, a stretch-wrapped muscle package without return address, wrapped in polyvinyl, has been taking himself every day since we've been here, with surfboard or mountain bike to the pastures of sports? Well? Is it him or not? Gudrun knows him from sight, but her approaches, even before they could get to the poles of his glances on which it surely would be easy to get hooked, were always slipping off his rolling buns or got tangled up in the three-sizes-too-large sweatshorts. Not a good start. As always, the student gives up before her little cadaver of language could be carried out only to be slit open without mercy. She wouldn't know what she could talk about with the guy. This knight stomps off every morning at the crack of dawn, with all his equipment tightly assembled and pressed against his body, without a word and shadowed by a helmet. Over it the soft ice of sweatshirt and T-shirt, as if he were revealed as one single assemblage, the One and the Same, in short: a God, who has time for one believer, himself, who ingests himself, an aluminum wrapped holy communion: a multienergy bar!, it's the only way for him to know what a loving sight and a balanced diet can effect. There, in the tabernacle shrine, his own presence, and how it shines in all its belonging to the Now. Well now, this young guest—and it is only by accident that no maiden has yet transformed him into a stag, maybe because for Diana it's already too cold for a swim—has been brought to a standstill, and maybe it is Gudrun who is supposed to be transformed? The man expands right here of all places, in this guest room that isn't his. This ever-ready self-transformer, i.e., just now he transformed himself again, Gudrun notices, he has unpacked his pocket rocket, this glaring male incarnation, which no priest could change back into a wafer. Just now it is taken out of the Tupperware box by a sweet lady's hand and—the colorful picture shines all the way to us in the hallway—lifted to the lady's face, perhaps so she could read the label and date of expiration? Now the man raises his gaze and lets it cross a blink of Gudrun's eyes in the keyhole. The woman can be seen only from behind, almost like a shadow that starts to blur in the twilight. Then, like a doll's broken eyes, the man's gaze topples backward into the head and the female figure that comes with it, his leading lady, pushes herself somewhat more advantageously into the picture. Without a sound she moves into the field of vision; as if on tracks, her presentness gets carried around and stops: time to kneel for the holy transubstantiation, ring, little bell, ringalingaling!, Gudrun's eyes adjust the focus, carbonated acid fizzes from the eyes' glasses, and time and space extend like an animal that just got up and stretches its limbs. Then they stumble, space and time, as each wants to yield to the other and get all tangled up in one another, they wouldn't want to run away, time and space, each in the other, opposite direction, against the law? Well, the main thing is they are coming back again and we can finally get on. In this mundane guest room, table, chair, washstand, closet, nothing else, Gudrun Bichler appears a second time and this time inside, on the bed. At the moment, she is observed by herself as her body gets peeled out of the top of the gray sweatcloth—some homespun veil like the saint's?—she is wearing, it could be a proof of God's presence if there weren't millions of them, made in Nowhere. And the word became like flesh, quickly perishable, a widely traveled vacuum pack, whose only pact with reality seems to be death. From the outside Gudrun now sees a cross section of herself, aslant, from behind the door, what got into her? A rubber knife just got into her (or could it have been the sausage itself?) exposing a pink slice of herself, laced with gentle veins of fat. And jumping out of the whiteness of the flesh like something improper, I mean like some property not owned by anyone, the pointed nipple that leaps into the man's hand and bites it with a growl. In return it is made to appear all the more distinctly by this young man who seems to be a creator of bodies all around, for this is now the second time he made this one. The flesh makes no effort to escape the fort wherein it is imprisoned. The assured deployment of the flesh by this dick (he's got the licks!) can be counted on shortly. The bosom bags chockful with undeliverable mail are swinging on the second Gudrun inside the room, so now let's play it once again. A whistling sound, almost ultrasound. Where wood is chopped splinters must fall and, laughing out loud, the white teeth jump over the lips' hurdles like lambs and the young man's head has also surfaced again, now look at that, the sun-tanned hand, just for the fun of it, gets the female flesh to swing, clubbing it a bit, thick and fast the flesh has it coming now, and that, pale girlfriend, is nice and boyish, well meant actually. With playful ease the clouds, those billows of dough, are swung about, tossed up, and caught again. It's so easy that the whole Easy Jet is now at risk. The woman tries to hold back the laboring hands, but love's labor mustn't be lost. She wasn't really serious, because—as seen through the keyhole—she is already kneading her own dough, cuts out a little figure that quickly grows under her fingers, takes shape, that is, quite simply, the measure beyond all measure, no, there has to be an end somewhere, the meaty creature can't grow any further. This is how it gets served to the woman in the room who is totally identical with the woman outside, and already—hair falling over her face like earth over a coffin—the woman in the room bends forward, puts her mouth over the meat pocket, and gets to the essential, it's hard to tell who, overcoming tremendous internal difficulties, devours what, and there is the most wonderful reciprocity of sensation and consumption, which unfortunately isn't always the same. Then each takes another shot and—higgledy-piggledy to the pop, both spend their ammo with a vengeance. We dead awaken, a sizable glob of being gets poured into our houses, into the dunce caps of their roofs, and into this small, pointed little hat right here, no longer quite as hard, standing at the borders of the village, where it powered down and finally showered off, puffing, foaming, directly into the mouth of this young woman. That young top gun racer finally fired himself off. The logs plop into place, a helpless lathing, a stacking site ready for the forklift, no, this woman won't need a knife. The knife is for all of us.

Laughing and neck-biting with remarkable recklessness, the young man bends over the woman from whom he has temporarily withdrawn his member, apparently he still wants to do a lot with it, for now his mouth nibbles its way down her spine and, laughing into the wasteland that's been torn apart by the impact, his face reappears between her sturdy legs, their bark pulled down at some point, who knows when, a torn stocking here, a shoe with the foot yanked off there; now the woman also laughs, her mouth wide open, but no sound can be heard; neither of the two wants to retreat as long as he might resurrect again. Everything is okay, I assure you, both of them, man and woman, have equal parts in the affair, don't you huff and puff at me or I'll blow the roof off your joint! Fanfare! Blow! Incuntescent the inky black wire-hair wherein the man burrows his lips, then his face, a recusant toy car, it seems to have started up just now, into Gudrun's doppelgänger, and this Gudrun Two pounds and pants and palpitates with all she's got. This hit is not a miss, no stray steel ball hurled itself out of the flipper and into the temple, the throat, the neck. *Es geht eine Träne auf Reisen,* . . . tralala . . . . "A Tear Goes on a Journey," croons the singer. Better take a partner along. The two human orifices whence voice-less words are dropping lightly, not meant seriously, as, say, wafts of hay reapers like to throw at each other for fun, offer inaudible, indis-pensable answers to questions their bodies seemed to have asked, but I didn't quite understand the body language. In Gudrun everything that belongs here seems to be in its right place, it's warming up, it's getting warmer, white thighs bounce across the tennis court, over them a little white skirt, behind it a horseshow takes place at this time, too, we also built a golf course with funds from public research and development for our Newest *Länder* in our Bundesrepublik, because people are so healthy, they need an outlet for their discontinued model, a sell-out for sure. And they'll definitely need an ice-skating rink, I think, the water is already up to our hot soles, which cut up many a mean floor, quick, back into the body again, before it dares to continue by itself—the life in the making inside it is closer to it than the one on the make because of it. Gudrun bends her back like a toy bow, screaming and laughing, as the young man kindly keeps on task, he burrows and bites and licks all the water Gudrun produced. White cups, sponsored by the dairy in-dustry, are given to ur-healthy pubertianas, who couldn't possibly get any healthier, even if they would get sick before; health is our ideal, simple as that! On the rink fence revelations everyone can read, where to get all that fab fenceable stuff—so now everything is in full view of the spectators, and Gudrun Two has also been spread open by a cheerful record-keeping observer who, knowing that his economy keeps a firm hand on his asset for the moment in order to—as his earned interest has risen—deliver a second time, so now Gudrun has been opened wide, and a light-hardened raging god—her partner in an exhibition fight he copied in the guerrilla woods of the high-rising praecipes of the consumer protection bureau of *Being,* where, for starters all those tight-fitted thighs and calves and hips were wriggling and writhing on the test bench of eyes—scouts into this innermost, most interesting part of that woman whom he wants to spackle one more time real good until every crack in her is filled. He'll still do her alright. Slaps her all over her body using well-directed little flesh patties with his flat hand, slosh dripping from it. An animal gets its reward, already it rolls over playfully over onto its back, we like that, it could take quite some time before the two of them will have acknowledged to themselves that the traffic has slowed down already and, Burnout!, will be over soon. It is possible to cross the street now before a new wave comes rolling in forgetting to get off the gas that was given to it so generously. Bright light hits the fighter, his face remains a bit mean, dark, his skin seems doused in red, sinews pop out beefily—fresh kneadable plasticine and, why this loud, this last act?, the guests are already leaving!, he chucks his stalk (celery, c'est la vie, as they say here, where long ago Egypt lived with an entire chosen people and applauded in the theaters), full force into the woman, he grew in a woman, after all, but one certainly must not get ingrown there! That seems to be a joke, because right away this fellow pulls his wiener back out again, seasons it a bit with his hand, checks somewhat roughly whether the pocket is moist enough, that is, if it's got enough juice, and then he disappears once more with his part, which isn't lost and can't get lost, it has grown, it is homegrown, in the charred-black ringlets of desirability that met him just as much of the way as was necessary but not far enough to make it all too comfortable for him. Gudrun's eyes at the keyhole pop out voluptuously: Firm parallel bodies have taken up their posts! Their personal advantages have been highlighted and have drawn excessive benefits that, nonetheless, will somehow, somewhere fit the bill. But never mind how it started, get ready now: This young hotshot goes on shooting again and again, a bestowment of his ownness, destined as he was for such stints, with which he wishes to have his say, right or wrong, on a festively glossy paper that, however, has already been accomplished by someone else, today, Thursday, when the new mags come out; so there he is, a moment ago still coated skintight in old and horribly beat-up blue cotton, now crashing into this soft aberrance, whose breasts had already dropped down her ribcage, which does not appeal to us though by now is no longer an impression to take along but rather one to cut short. We have all seen that movie before.

At long last Gudrun can shake off this piece of hers that she is playing but did not stage herself, she can rip it out of her eyes like a contact lens, a contact ad that once again led to nothing, even though for the past three weeks it has appeared, curiously enough, on her pupils. The young woman wants to tear open the door, which was stuck earlier, rush into the room, into the desolation that had been settled without her knowledge or intention. She doesn't knock. It is her room after all. A dog barks outside. They don't know each other, it would be nice if they did. Gudrun feels something nudging her gently—like a small animal that jumped at her playfully from the ceiling—to "fall with the door into the house" as they say here, or "cut to the chase" as you might put it (maybe also to me), into the uninhabited room. But to her own surprise, she resists it vigorously. She does not want to go in there. That is, she does not want to visit herself, seeing that she already has a visitor. A light hand moves her forward, go on in! Big, freshly painted windows are your eyes, but that's no reason to stare with such wide-open eyes! Gudrun knows she must not enter this room under any circumstances, but she does not know why. One moment of silence please, then: Hurried steps are running down the stairs and fade away on the ground floor. Bright light comes through the hallway window. Someone kept the TV tabernacle running, but the light couldn't escape fast enough. Light to light, beginning of the beginning, what is born of God is God. Spellbound, Gudrun stops in her tracks. It would be better to turn around and go home, but whereto? She bends down again hesitatingly to take another peek, the room is shadowless, noonish, waits, ready to enclose anyone hanging out there for decoration, but he, she, left and took with them whatever there was. The bed is freshly made and waits for a new guest, is it her, Gudrun Bichler? The blanket is unruffled. A tiny piece of chocolate, if you closed one eye tightly you could see it, lies on the pillow, a small gift, which the eye knows how to find now, for the chocolate is a silvery little kiss, I have frequently mentioned it, but the TV has done it so many more times!, so then, a hole in time, anybody could have torn who recognized Franzi, our swimming champ who's always on top, in every picture. But there is no one around. The closet shelves and drawers have been freshly lined with brown wrapping paper, which can also be seen, as its door is open a crack. Gudrun thinks she can hear something, but she must be wrong. And yet: Somewhere a body has been uncorked so that it can breathe!

7

Young and exuberant about himself, Edgar lights the lights, the spotlights on where he will burst onto the scene on his alpine skateboard, chasing his lost dreams, which he won't find, since he left them in the changing room at the fitness center, and then he will find himself, framed by the alps, on a fast track down. The ditches are sprinkled with firs clawing the remaining spots of earth, and here, too: sudden dense fog, something tramping up the hill, something that is still faceless and elsewhere with its thoughts. The earth shakes from the melee in her chest, so many people, that it almost blasts the stony ground under her feet. Yes. It feels tight around her chest. We squeezed all the air out of her, even though we have already taken so many people out of her. She still didn't get any lighter for it. But this Edgar Gstranz clearly is a showpiece you can exhibit on a pillow of moss; riding on the storm, the curators, the accurators, are swirling above him, those who chose him to be a perpetual traveler, who carries himself in his luggage to serve someone as a meal on his journey, ready, set, and down we go. Streaks of sunlight, sifted through trees, make one feel as if in a jail punished for something that does not want to stop (and so the punishment does not end either), stripe the landscape like egg liqueur in fruit ice cream, so that it becomes a local specialty. To make us have an even better time, feel our innocence even more sweetly. Nice and clean the beams that hit us, and we are beaming that we are on vacation. Edgar Gstranz wore himself smooth on the edges of rocks, he mounted everything there is to mount and can't run away from him, now he's got his model board on wheels, which already proved successful in winter with just minor modifications in masses of snow, now he also wants to mow down the cropped grass with his own mojo. That board will be a su-per business! Folks will be able to vanquish their own molds as soon as they step on it! They will smash their forms and they will rise and shine, it won't be the first time that something comes crawling out of them that brings a storm and turns into a tempest. Cutting through countries with knives and chasing clouds, thus came, thundering like bells, the New Humans, the innocent, dragging their dust-raising manes behind them, which reeked of human flesh: Those are regions man can penetrate, if he tries. He lets flesh die and instantly resurrect it again on himself. And those clouds that do not carry flying bells, were they not blown to us after a long journey from way back when? Did they not suddenly arrive on their vehicles to make the immortals stored as ashes in their depots mortal again? While Edgar is still climbing up vigorously in powerful strides in order to hurtle down again, bent bodies descend out of the clouds in order to meet him, let's see whether they can catch up with him. Sport is clear, it is the given we often give up, for it is clear to us: We don't belong to the winners. But it is among those sharp peaks that an ace wants to operate. Just think of all the things he already took on! At this point of the trek the entire horizon is there to take in, panting bodies pulling themselves up the mountain on an invisible rip line, for a long time they were lying in smoke turning black, their conditions are not the best. The young men are singing in the muffle kiln of the firm J. A. Topf and Sons. Maybe they are not even worthy of being Edgar's opponents!

Brighter than the whole world is this day, mightily we storm, side dishes to this natural phenomenon, carried by the hands of strangers, to the snack bar. Without us, there won't be a meal ready for us. Without us making the area passable, it won't be transportable, that is, it can't be carried along for us to the television set so that it can also be shown to those not able to walk, to arouse their ambition, which will probably not make a lot of sense to them. Okay, the animals' four-legged mobility might be useful for sexual intercourse, get a grip on yourself, so now you groped and gripe that you are useless. We are meticulously lit by the sun, that spotlight on the hidden, but it seems to me it's already getting a bit overcast. The mountain will be silent now, just wait, it still flashes and glistens for the sun, even though the press beleaguered it repeatedly. Frantic rescue teams will set out to press their heads, their ears, against the moss to check whether someone is around, a mountain surfer, a city slicker, who slipped into something from where he can't get out again. Something bright spills out into Edgar's eyes, just a moment please! He keeps climbing, remembering something that did not happen at all. Could nature have carried him away so far that a stranger's memory was knocking at the door, which earlier had been his and he had just moved to Unknown? Instinctively Edgar turns around, could it be that he was still there, his eyes once again having been bigger than the plate with his favorite sights, the wish an Oedipus of the thought, but they will tear all three eyes out of him, just don't risk another peek! For a moment a titanic tour bus floats by without a sound, a ship in the alps, but it quickly disappears again, and the gaze goes home disappointedly.

A group consisting of three older men encounters Edgar, whose torso emerged at the white ribbon of the serpentine shoulder, in order to cross the Alpenstraße; in short—unexpectedly shooting upward in their midst (they are already descending), he flutters among them, a fallen eagle, still holding in his beak the liver of one always coming up short at the finish line. The tails of the parkas tied around their waists rise sluggishly in the breeze only to fall right back asleep. This apparition is not a superstition, it is as clear as day, soon it will be dark. One of them wears a baseball cap backward, he evidently set out for the mountains to stay forever young. It is a melody not heard often by the workmen between heaven and earth, who keep knocking at the rock to pull themselves up on it (and no, it ain't heaven's gate) or, gratinated with snowfields, melt into a giant surprise dish. Yesterday we got ice cream, today we want something less perishable. Just for that we are still hanging around the counter with melting eye-pits, loose as snow drifts that have not set yet. The cold bites. Nature despises anything new because she is so old herself. Every year when she turns green again, she envies folks that visit her, for they can drive away again. How do peaks hide their shoddiness, those blobs of human shit, aluminum foil, cans sinking wasted into the gravel, their labels faded, they don't know themselves anymore. This can, for example, wants to talk to us but can't do it anymore. No Indian here to shed a tear.

So far we are clear about the wanderers: They hid their lights under the bushel, and now, with their heads under this bucket of daily worries and cares, they have advanced to the *Kaiserbankerl,* the emperor's little bench at the *Höllengraben,* the hell hole, where you can see but not yet pick the edelweiss. From here the kaiser always shot his chamois. Fog patches are creeping in, lifting their fists menacingly, because Edgar did not yet visit his grandparents and denied the name of their cheap village. He really should look up their forgotten faces some time, I think, just to try, besides sleeping, a new form of absence (even though one is right there!). Such coming and going, that's nature for you!

Never silence. Nature wakes, but awake it is not. Maybe it is already later than we will have thought. The ozone hole a memento of the grief we can't feel about anything lost, thus we mourn something that is not and has never been known. In the distance the rumbling of a heavy vehicle, it probably has loaded wood. The loggers take this road up to the mountain pasture, where they are to shave the landscape. It's been shorn already by the vacationers. The droning in the lower regions continues for quite some time, until the vehicle has fought its way up the serpentine road, but its stench has already entered into a solid relationship with the mountain air. The eyes of the houses in the valley blink cheerfully, because the sun has thrown some confetti at them. So what's this now, those crackles in the air? It doesn't sound like a truck, it is clear yet puzzling, I mean, it sounds so concrete, but the source, where it would have to come from, is nowhere to be seen even though it seems to bubble. As if hair, complete with baseball cap, damp, sweaty at the temples, the forehead, were suddenly standing on end, as if a nameless fear filtered through the slopes of the mountains and could never be put together correctly again no matter how often we might get together leisurely at their feet or on their heads. Our gaze no longer reaches as far as before, because that which tacked it to the rock back then, when we were young, so that others could step into it in order to climb up, got rusty, broken, even the postcards showing it have yellowed, and now the light leans idly against the clouds, looking at us expectantly. But our dull pupils can no longer invite it to sit down in us for a moment.

Well, it will get here very soon, the vehicle, the wanderers have heard it for quite a while and turned around several times to see if it was close, a few times it could fool them with sound and smoke, but not anymore. The driver dead-tired not wanting anything, the fellow passenger dying for beer and schnapps, both their hides boarded up only makeshiftly against several tons of gigantic roped-together logs, which were once alive and, as a last sign that this indeed has been the case, now have a shred of red fabric tied to their asses! How pitifully these native giants carry their earthly sign that says they simply are too big! Too big to can for human consumption? And man: Never too big for his canned tunes, which now have gone to his head for good. Yes, technology must be man's balls, such a saw has more power than any native hunk of a trunk from the Styrian jungle that serves our environment as a table or credenza. Let's have those two pieces of furniture swim with the stream of nature, even if they were made of plastic! Let's wrap them in paper, and there it is again, the harmlessness of products we just wrapped in nature; it is as if a tiger would put on a nylon plush coat and stick a Steiff tag in his ear. Or to put it another way: Give flowers again, but first take off their plastic feed sack. We have already destroyed so much nature in everything dead, even if we could decorate our homes with living animals, everything would still be dead, including us. Athletes squeeze into the forest's niches and refuse a bit of breath, which, however, came suffocatively from the truck's anus; it is a friendly mouth just wanting to put a little heat on us. The air will be good again in no time, as soon as the transport has disappeared in the distance and rolled onto the highway. Schnapps, once fruit jingling in branches, circulates amid those folks and holds them together. What was healthy once is not so anymore. Instead, it went up in flames, smashed by the forge, yes, everyone can change, it's never too late. Edgar is already outside, a fellow who might soon have a new relationship or not, the wheels of his car are already working on it.

For a moment, the loggers' faces wearily rose toward the recreational hikers, before they go for another swig. The liquid hops about in the bottle and waves of nonrecognition go through the few bodies, soon they won't recognize themselves either. Mysterious, the many ways of getting to rest on a journey and such rest, too, can be in peace. At the same time a few million dead tug angrily at their lid, and that lid is smoke. They, too, want to become, salted and seasoned, a pleasure to people again, wouldn't that be wunderbar! You just wait, that kind of growth will have to get approved sometime! Dead mountain climbers, buried in the unknown land of crevasses, ruins of life take an extra peek at life itself at its peak, which to them Edgar Gstranz embodies to perfection. Would that you could at least *have* been someone like him once! Bet you could open up the earth like a cloud split by lightning. Glide just once across the grassy surface into the budding Light! None of the hikers has any idea that Edgar has been heading for the longest time into the growing darkness, where something will appear in its preservedness, something he'd never seen in his lifetime. But for now, nature still blossoms delightedly, and those all-natural guys who busily fertilized themselves with alcohol, an absolutely natural product, rattle by on heavy dual tires, axes left weighty consequences on their skin, in their flesh, which is finite, which finally is healthy again after two fingers have been hacked off already. One of them, the front seat passenger, turns around briefly, letting his gaze graze on this artful alliance of nature and synthetics, i.e., Edgar, then the turn and this short version of an athlete is gone, as if flushed away even though the athlete is still there, his oomph not yet gone. That's how it goes with our beloved dead. A moment ago there still was the coziest place in the world, a human in the flesh, who had never been hewn, one might say: an original, and now all there is are trunks, there is the light gray gravel of the logging road, there are the red veins of iron at the blast areas, there are teeth falling, bridges are built, but what purpose is it supposed to serve? And whom do we serve? Why do women in deck chairs wait for their cute hikers or join them right away? There is equipment that pays you right back for such leisure, there is home equipment, which will ultimately have to be paid, to lock in our bodies and throw away the key, and Edgar, too, tucked his equipment under his arm to stand on top of it later. He and his framework, *Gestell* the philosopher calls it, belong together, for on top of it his being-there is to be brought to dazzling light. Edgar will be so fast that to anyone seeing him he will seem a fleeting trick of light. The wheels keep running hard. Beauty on tracks, meals on wheels for a distant entity that already takes Edgar's measurements. He has been laid out on a serving cart and prepared for the crumbling teeth of the dead, if they hadn't already been knocked out of them. And now the dead themselves break out of their empire, where they also speak foreign languages, but without tags pinned, glued to their naked, scrawny ribs that say so. Thus we believe the dead don't understand us, just because we don't understand them. The creatures fade in and then they crawl out of themselves, they are coming out because they have a sense for the plastical, which we consist of when we, squeezed into Hula-Hoop benzene rings, show off boldly, and this is exactly when we disappear the fastest in our bodily vessels that the dead have poured us into. They found the right size alright, only we think that we would need the next smaller size, because we want to get thinner soon like the moon: If we could choose, what would we be offered? Our own figure that fights with us as to what we will get to eat and with whom we want to share ourselves, but what's best is not to share at all. Even though we might be drawn toward love occasionally, love is not drawn to us. We are just the drafts of the dead, and only when we are dead ourselves are we completed and others can get the picture of us. They can milk it for all its worth, but they won't squeeze much out of it, we already creamed off most of it. Having a life and a car, a tune that enchantingly ensnares the heart until the heart sac, the airbag, is in shreds. It's a fact: So many dead are left with no pictures of them. And their families have also been wasted. Who thinks of them now in a pure tone that crawls around the edges of the clouds until someone puts it back into the Walkman, the Eternal Wanderer on the battery strip? Thus, they stand up and at the last moment they throw that airbag cover over them as a sign by which they should be recognized later when they will rise and hover above others. And sometimes it so happens that one of us gets underneath, right into the danger zone (even though the Dangerous Place was held for someone worthier than him!), no matter how fast he races down, into the fir, the one and only tree waiting for him there. We put our arms around it or let ourselves be chained to it.

Right away the hunchbacked mountain pasture will slide down, the earth is already stretching herself mischievously. The wandering threesome suddenly find themselves face to face with Edgar. The older men instinctively stiffen, a jolt tears through them, they pull themselves together. Their watches do not only measure time, they also measure their heartbeat, as if anyone cared about their lives, everything has already been counted off in advance anyway. The valley below them suddenly lies in deep shadows. As if an evil thought had overcome it. For a moment the village, whose one and only brochure, its muscles trembling from the effort of holding its stately, flower-framed balconies under our nose, drops out of its conception as a vacation spot. Eyes are looking through the windows, how did it suddenly get so dark? A late thunderstorm? The evening would not sneak in at such an early hour! Only the meadows still lie there in their richest green, dotted here and there by a creature bubbling up like a spring, in athletic but somewhat scorched leisure wear, working itself out of its bind, bound as it is in elastic branding, and crawling, scratching, and looking for support, trying hard to climb up the grassy gradient.

Hurry home, granddads, where your women are waiting for you in deck chairs to tie themselves to you, their companions, again! To pull on you like animals on their posts. Don't they ever give up? Lovely, how the water foams under the bridge. The alps press like madness against these wanderers who, unfortunately, must now part for good with Edgar and his loose sweatpants flapping in the wind labeled with names that leave us completely cold—those names cry for their place of origin, the USA, out of whose chest they were torn away too soon. The names of our dead? Don't know them. Don't have to. *"Wir sind ein Amerikaner."* So we just keep going, to the inn, down to the right, to the peaks it's up. So there, the building ground's already staked, while Edgar still hears the steps of his mountain colleagues crunching in the slippery gravel of the forest road and their hiking shoes' leather whistling and the breeches creaking overloudly on the inside of the thighs; the ground has already been staked, the empty door without a building erected, and something will come through it even though it could also go around it, since there is no house there yet. A fear that stiffens the limbs. The crack of a whip. Already something is coming closer, and suddenly, for only a very brief moment, Edgar longs to be back with those men he just met, who evidently are so solidly anchored in their lives, a thread has quickly been moored, but that knight of the Alps, Edgar, that highlander is far too high-handed to grasp it. Thus he sent off the three men without paying attention to the addresses on their caps' labels. He has much better addresses on his pants. The road, that light snake, it looked short before, the stretch that still had to be climbed, now, below the hairpin turn still more serpentine bends, many more than Edgar thought. Now and then they seem to push backward like whirls in water, as if something flowed from those bends, something they had to fight against. A maelstrom, a maximalstrom carrying broken, distorted beings. How come the parts of this snake look so rigid, as if it were to shed its skin in a moment and throw its dress at Edgar's feet because it bought it in the wrong color? The overlook with the heavy logs collected for their transport should long have been coming up, there, where the forester's sons must have got the idea to shoot each other with pistols filled with water bullets and where they indeed implemented this idea, because no one, not even the forest service, wanted to keep them and, maybe later, translate them into the standard language that was a foreign one to them. Now the forester has no more children, but he still has: his gun. If we wait a bit, he might be coming, too. How come there is another curve leading higher, doesn't Edgar know the way in his sleep? As if an invisible hand had quickly put one more peak on this medium foothill up there to the right, next to Hohe Veitsch mountain facing the blinding Tormäuer mountain panorama. Someone who no longer liked the alpine shop with its limited selection and simply sat down next to it. Someone uninvited. It simply wants to offer us more, that deardevil entity.

Who has the ripest trout in the creek, that is one of the fundamental questions now that the shady gardens are competing with each other as to what they have to offer us. And we tolerate this and other questions, also the questions about people we don't like to remember while we celebrate festivals of plights, sorry, lights, during which we beasts with our dandelions, those lions' teeth, link up in chains. What kind of people are they anyway? Edgar Gstranz is utterly dumbfounded, he's abusing his brain to think, and he gives some thought to the three wanderers from before, who have long since disappeared behind the curve, aha, there they are again! As if a film had been rewound, a bend of the road duplicated, the road a spiral, a spectral staircase, and there, those three from before are entering the mountain a second time. Again, one can hear the creaking of their hiking boots, the squeaking of their knickers as if something squished around in there, a life-juice pump! Or could Edgar have lost his way? For how did he end up on this *Hausberg,* these home slopes, where he is no longer at home, which seem twice as high than the ones he already knows? Suddenly not a step, no cap's peak, no swinging arm of the doubled mountain climbers, as if a cataract had pulled the hikers down, awash in spray. Not a sound. Whose home, or even second home, will this new mountain be? Who could acquire property here, in this made New *Heimat,* it is not even parceled out. Edgar stands still amid his steps, which seem to be frozen to his body, but the steps climb higher and higher up his body, a veritable flood. So there he was, mounting the landscape as usual, but then also trampling all over it. Why has something been doubled here? Because even the oldest among us happily exploited it for themselves and the young need new fires, new dangers to roast their tenderloins in? Nothing around here to fire you up to stay, yet stay he must. Something grabbed Edgar's arm, even though there is no one here except him, and all of a sudden he is down. The earth underneath him is beyond herself with joy that in the end she managed a joke this young man did not yet know, to wit: that she, the earth, may lie here! Now suddenly the information on the trail map that you would be the only one here should no longer be valid?

The whitish gray of the gravel road seems to be getting close to its return into the mother rock, which holds out its gaping, bleeding gash, iron red, rust red, brutally detonated out of its habitat of several millennia. Around 5 after 3:00 p.m. Edgar G. briefly lies down in the landscape's bed, as if lost in the Nothing, around 7 after 3 fear rips him out of the daydream he seemed to have dwelled in all this time. Something wants to get him! Aimlessly he runs uphill a stretch, everything is unknown to him even though he has known this area for many years. It is as if a left hand grabbed him at the throat while the right one held the weapon. While Edgar's eyes get used to the onset of dusk, he jumps into the snackhappy knife. Alright, everything has been well tossed together. Incessantly barfing all over him, the two satellites of his Walkman suddenly drop out of his ears, from where it just rattled like the snake. All the stops have been pulled out. Suddenly a wanderer comes out from behind a bush, he seems familiar to Edgar, it is as if he looked into a mirror. The wanderer must have left his water behind the bush, or did he think he would find India and discovered America, which only Edgar is permitted to embody exclusively in his athletic shoes and pants?

Edgar squints his eyes, a bright beam emerges from the last curve, bright earth, it blinds him, it pulls on him, as if he were participating in an invisible tug of war. Nature had better not get too close to him! Where does the light, the noise come from? Big city sound in this deserted place? No way could a city have been built behind the bending of the truth, behind the bend of the mountains lined up as in military formation, not even if a giant child had scattered the pieces. There wouldn't be any room for it. A serving of violence but made of sugar and coconut flakes has been dumped on Edgar, who stands there totally still, with trembling flanks. He has torn the music device from his body, the tape with which he threaded such beautiful music through his head had ripped, but now the beat comes twice as fast out of the box, twice as many sounds than usual, that heavy device, the brush that stirs up the sounds in the drums, is shaken furiously at the belly of the beast as if someone shook his fist in front of Edgar's eyes. Then the tape stops. Cookie boxes, eggshells, sausage skins flutter down, settle again on the shoulder of the road, their rest area after the picnic that was included in the package deal. And here we are back to the familiar platform, in wide format, whereas Edgar is rather in top form. The mountains move up, this is the training ground where they belong. And there go the men again, the journeying men. One bends down to tie his shoelace, the other wipes off his sweat and takes a deep breath, and the third one calmly does his business, which actually was taken from him almost sixty years ago. And there the first one bends down to roll up his rug, which a neighbor had pulled out from under him, lest our feet get entangled in it. Was that what held on to Edgar's leg before? For a moment he gets stuck in nature like old chewing gum, our Edgar Gstranz, because beings are playing with him, their absolute existence minimum, as we once played with them and for them at that. They will soon get back at us. But we are no longer here, we are out of town. We can always claim we were on vacation.

8

The empty room stands at attention in front of Gudrun, no land more beautiful. Nothing in it that marks Gudrun as one of God's Children, so why the many pictures of saints in Catholic elementary school? She still wouldn't have found her way back home later to see the light, to separate the pure from the heavy. Gudrun can see the nature of both; both are too much for her, and she is looking for the light switch. As if it was not the window that was open, as if it was she, Gudrun, the open, you could simply walk through. How can one be brought to shine, at least made translucent? As a child she still experienced one of those X-ray machines in the shoe store, it surely must have been the last one in use in her provincial, sprawlingly around several parks constructed city. The mother and the saleslady, with Gudrun in the middle, checked through the circular window whether the shoes fit and did not pinch anywhere. Whether the flesh's wanderlust would not burst the shoes. What a shock seeing your own skeleton, at least a small part of it! The little bones rested quietly and at no charge in their place, they found their room in the soft flesh. But this hotel room, here, today—the moment has come that the pieces of furniture seem to hang limp like wilted flowers. No light refracts in Gudrun's eyes. Something is crawling into her skull, a memory, but the mind is not open today. For one moment the forgetting can almost be felt physically, it wants to jump out of Gudrun's head and flee, as far as possible: from the memory of another, much narrower room with tons of earth pressing against it, so that one had to finally, malleably, abandon oneself to it. A timid exchange between the clay, enclosing the bodies as if it had been burned in an oven to become their pots, and of animals gently knocking at the coffin boards. And a soft pull in the limbs to finally get expelled into the earth and merge with it. The earth is of this world, a good housewife's soft repast you sink into before you could even digest what would have become of you. It happened just like that to the many millions of happily, recklessly wasted human beings. It almost makes you a relative of leaves and grasses, as you sense that they, too, want to work their way through the ground. Try as she might, in her lifetime Gudrun could not manage to become a solidly defined person. Some people are funny that way, there are no bars enclosing them, but where most want to shine so that those small specks of light, those soft drops of love, will be thrown at them, there are others who want nothing more than to get out of those precise squares on that floor plan that enclose the kitchen and the nursery and the bathroom (all living cells are pretty wet!). All they want is to leave, even when they want to fix them up with a knight in iron panties or Anna-Lisa Psycho, who want to make us laugh during a short stay in the infirmary that's always too short anyway. But the masks are made of cardboard and soon turn into pulp from all the spittle. Even adventure pools can do that, that's how easy it is, and before you know it you are sliding, squeaking and splashing, down a stalk of flesh and in leaves of skin into the chasm of lust, which is about as lusty as a bulging tin can: You want to forbid it to open the lid, the consumption of its content will make you sick if you don't heat it up sufficiently and eat it right away, still standing. In front of the garbage can. How do they say? An overfull head is usually empty when it is to give something of itself. That symbolizes the female orgasm pretty well, I think, which is constantly threatened with consumption and fainting, a hurricane in whose eye you get lost if you did not provide in time for sufficient levity and colorful straws with which to keep your beverage on the ground or discipline it in some other way, as lady snake charmers do. The head must not be too heavy when it is to be hurled away, otherwise it just drops. And for a woman there is no gain in losing. So and so much is her value, which has our quiet approval since her actions are cheap. There are no charity bazaars where she can be presented for petting. This hotel room, however, where we find ourselves with Gudrun, is not a cage, it is there to take us by the hand, to protect and peruse us.

Gudrun can't console herself on herself, for again and again, as soon as she lies down, those dark wastelands being torn out of the earth keep crossing her mind without any one moment she could hold on to. She tries calling her buddies for help none of whom can get off their butts, as they are locked into their books. The thoughts come rushing in like stag beetles, but their pincers don't grasp anything in this cloudiness, this petrification, where even fossils resist being forced to give themselves to the earth. Everyone sleeps alone there. Memorial stones are piled up behind the forehead, but nothing is written on them anymore. All inscriptions have been expunged, at the latest during the summer, when the last human transports were dispatched. They were driven out of childhood land, life's picnic area, in front of our Opa and Oma and into a wooden sea of barracks without windows, parceled goods jammed underneath forgetful electric light, those magic waves, water waves of thoughts, they flow like clouds but they don't illuminate anything that is not already an illusion. Let's not think about it anymore, then it will escape us, which might be better than if it came along to make us prevent its escape over and over again, already ventilating while doing it, as to how we could, after enough fresh air supply and the subsequent clearing, create new fires out in the open we have reached at long last, thus blazing away even more blissfully than ever before. The repossessor has nothing to say to this. Like us he is bound by his signature on the lease, this time however it is he who was rented. Now tell me why Gudrun chose such a compact apartment while her grandparents, that grandiose duo, were raging firmly in all those vastest of vastnesses. The grandfather threw several people to the ground and didn't pick them up again. Then he once spent five days in the same place because at first there was not yet the kind of human transport by which around three hundred people could have arrived. The light shoots, by putting pressure on the eyeballs, out of them, so that one can see how they were shaped before this happened to them. Now only the empty boxes are left. Red-rimmed clouds like eyes tired from reading, the shadow of horrendous fires in the sky we won't have to regret because we made sure that during our flight we kept our hot clothes and our skin, all hot with lust, away from our bodies like a wet raincoat lest something forgets us and we suddenly become the forgotten ones. Which means nothing else than anyone, whoever it maybe, is allowed to slip into our skin and feel like us. Poor Gudrun, this is exactly what happened to her, I am afraid, and now it swirls her around in the flow of events, throws her summersaulting in her own blood that is seasoned with a tubful of water; she has forgotten her knowledge, she does not love her origin and therefore she gets drained and dressed, a local game presented on a sample plate of alpine specialties, our very own creation. This land dresses itself up with a passion and exhibits itself in brochures! Just take a look at what it did with its many creative natives! In their loving dealings with them it devoured them completely. Everybody has to watch out for himself lest he gets left over.

Someone perpetually arriving, like Gudrun here in the Hotel Alpenrose, where she, at her young age, is an exception, whose curse is still the bloody monthly rule, which does not please those elderly, who eye her, close enough as they are, distrustfully. Will she even take from them what's left of their lives and throw it to the birds as feed? Envy. Jealousy. Mistrust. Why don't old folks know anymore how humans can be put together, prettily arranged, and then placed again within reach of others? People generally lack the respect for the simplest bodily processes. Yapping mongrel thoughts snap from the deck chairs in the garden toward the window Gudrun pushed wide open and leans out of now breathing deeply, they are panting after the bitches in heat, still wriggling their rumps inside the old women, who are trying in vain to hide from the world the bulged inertia of their wombs. Here no one escaped from anywhere, they all came voluntarily. The guestroom has settled down with a placid sigh and stretches its legs out. Outside nothing but utter everydayness, including the noises. The *Heimat* shows its peculiarities that are its property, and the guests are presently so relaxed, they even allow a peek into their family lives as they tear open the doors of their cars, which are their favorite relatives. In turn the cars sometimes tear them wide open. And what do we do with all the aliens waiting with their permanent alienational cards in their fists at the edge of the clearing for someone to unlock the door to our landscape? Just looking at it comes at a cost, but it doesn't pay off, elaborates the duchess in her Land Rover, a formidable woman in contrast to her timidly tight-lipped serfs, no wonder, she owns everything here, as far as the eye can reach, and she refuses the sale of a few lots for the planned chairlift. It doesn't add up, no matter how often one does the math for her, she sees the truth behind it and does not free her property to be exploited and used by others. They would drive directly into the fire, and even their ghosts would still appear to us even though, many of them as there are, they had never done it before. This fine know-it-all woman wants to have her quiet before the storm.

A thick hedge separates the property, especially the manicured garden of the Wirtin, from the rugged landscape outside. People enter the woods through a stile. The old access road is barely used, grass grows in the middle, between the vehicle tracks, which people love to use even without cars. The hedge consists of evergreen substances, thujas, yews, privets, a never-rusting cemetery fence of shrubbery, as it is very popular and tried and tested in these parts. An impenetrable safety net only the dead can slip through, that's how dense it is, the living would get their clothes torn. Anyone who has to protect his property, and even if it was just fifty square meters, checks the gardeners' catalogs for those sorts of woods, which immediately start crawling toward and entwining in each other as soon as you put them in, it gets them sharp and going, that's when you release them on your neighbors. They ravish each other nonstop, yet they never vanish, they get fatter and fatter and merge into the typical local shadow growth. Those evergreen revenants (never went away!) shield the True, or rather, they screen it. The gigantic black dog got through nonetheless, an animal can always slip in, because the branches thin out, turning brown and shriveling toward the lower end, where less sun can get through; the plants bathe their legs in their own droppings, a centimeter-thick layer of feathered needle-leaves. The dog sniffs here and there, busily, seemingly at random, as dogs are wont to do. He seems unduly excited and then, as if he wanted to wave his hat and say hello, he lets out a howling scream. As if something ripped his origin out of his canine jaws. He raises his eyes, which take off only unwillingly (maybe a friend will still come here at the last moment who wants to be taken along into death, wouldn't it be nice to be petted under the earth and maybe even still stroked as a soap, or get petted oneself!), up to Gudrun's window, a veil blows over the animal's dark pupils and, rising quickly, up and away, like a storm: This veil won't settle anywhere but will always stay in motion, spun around and pulled away by an invisible suction. The animal's gaze hits Gudrun right in the face, and suddenly, still rising, the howl cuts off abruptly, the beast could not finish the tone cleanly. Aghast, the gaze returns to the dog who emitted it! the eyes turn inward, and the canine body collapses on the ground as if a bullet had struck him in the center of the forehead. The body is still in a shooting mode, legs ready to barrel ahead are still pawing the ground, but the path it wanted to traverse broke away between the paws, the return is blocked, the beast, caught as if between two worlds, collapses like a house of cards. The dark body bleeds into the hedge and disappears from Gudrun's field of vision; she feels as if a return was blocked for her, too. An invisible fault line surrounds this house, this garden, this landscape, but even farther ahead no path opens up either. The latter had been hidden well by the local population's friendly behavior toward foreign guests, because horrific crimes lie behind them and only the well-known local amiability could ensure that not every foreigner stumbled over them right away. All eyes are directed toward the vendors' trays with their colorful postcards, no one checks what lies behind those people selling their *Heimat,* whether everything really is as wonderful, they are all lying through their teeth after all, as it is pictured here.

In any case, Gudrun will not reheat her oven, even though she let herself fall into the hot bathwater. Then she would have to be able to run the jet flame of life instead of water, which practically is nothing. You can hardly see it, but if you inhale it, wow, you can surely feel what's to it! Air, water, gas unfold like a greeting, bringing the addressee's body and life to a glow. Humans become their own memorials, so that we, in turn, don't have to remember them. It is not us who get shoved into and vanish in these memorial ovens, rather a herd of patient humans, who all had to die of suffocation, are shoved out of the ovens; the ventilation has now been actuated, the train of events runs right on schedule, but now the train is running right into us, a messenger of the greeting, that was sent so that I can write something about it fifty years later. (A movie would have been better, I think, the dead could have been removed much faster on its caterpillar tracks.) Gudrun, the student, starts up abruptly, as if she had lifted herself out of the water a second time, but this time all by herself, Undine comes and complains once again, but quite likably in her implacability. She finds herself back on the bed again. Did she sink into a brief sleep? She does not remember. How long could she have slept? The sun did not cover any noteworthy distance. Gudrun misses a piece of memory from her colorful treasures that flutter on the clothesline and gently brush her face that is just on the verge of awakening. The room has changed. It still is meticulously neat, the blanket is still stretched smooth, hardly showing a trace of Gudrun, but there are touches of colors that were not there before, or were they? Here lies a child's torn little dress, a few splashes of blood can be seen at the hem, and there: a wide-open purse. Here a single shoe with something white sticking out of it and making itself noticed, even though Gudrun does not want to see it all too closely. A baggy sweater juts out from underneath the bed, it seems it got stuck halfway because, as Gudrun bends over to check if there is more, she notices that the sweater ends in the middle, as if it were in a photograph, no, not cut off, but rather the picture, how shall I put it, well, just a part of the sweater is in the picture. The rest of it that hasn't been moved into the picture also dropped out of our eyes' endlessly friendly shouts of welcome to reality. A greeting that cannot be reciprocated, for there is no one there with whom this being could click his invisible glass. Well, cheers! Automatically, Gudrun feels for the cut-off edge, but the hand feels nothing. No cut. No unstitched threads of wool. The sweater, somewhat soiled at the neckline, simply ceases to be, that is, it ends in a straight line. Maybe it continues in a different place? How can one help it to return to this faraway place? Or get the return that remained behind to be welcomed again by our reality? And now that Gudrun also takes a closer look at the other reminiscences, she notices that one puffy sleeve of the blood-spattered little dress is missing a whole wedge, it just stops at the intersection of a coordinate system, where the enervated cartographer might have flung down the pencil, whereby different objects just in the process of emerging simply got stuck. Some entity, rustling in the distance, kept a piece of it instead of leaving it all here, the symptoms of the earthly by which we generally orientate ourselves. The wind rose has just been drawn, we suddenly notice, and it is pure coincidence that we are here and the others are not. Gudrun takes a deep breath and shakes herself. This wide-open purse, a shabby woman's bag, it has the suggestion of a handle alright, but in between the handle is missing, it is not, like a brook or water running from the faucet, something that IS in flux only and is always the same in motion. Perhaps things attain their complete existence only through the movement of the person to whom they belong or once belonged. And since the persons disappeared, the objects that keep their traces also exist only in part or not at all anymore, even if they are laid out right in front of us. Their owners deliberately imprinted themselves on their possessions, one gigantic heap of products that escaped from the workshop of life, so much so that those things could not completely find their way back into reality. The things were strangers before they belonged to anybody, now they are friends, they are at home here, without having a home. Their relations who granted them such a homey relationship have been torn from our midst, thus their greetings, their unconcealed belongings, no matter how often we beatify them, all those innocent dead and their legacies do not want to stay any longer. A wanderer comes into view, becomes a sight, but it changes depending how fast the wanderer walks. He walks out of the picture, but his backpack and the right heel of his hiking shoe stayed. Vice versa, a hand could have torn the wanderer out of the picture and his shoe hasn't got it yet, now it wanders around among us, looking for his master, the one without a car, the one without a roof over his head. At best he was a cyclist, like my papa.

Gudrun strokes her forehead, she pulls her knees to her body and twines her arms around them. Maybe the owners of those hand-tamed accessories are already on their way to gather up these objects again? The owners might not yet know where they forgot their stuff, but maybe they are looking for them? And isn't Gudrun lost if not forgotten? Could it be her belongings are looking for HER? Books that suddenly rise, stretching their necks and, like gray geese always on the wrong track, running toward her to greet her with their cackling? Is this greeting just a remembrance, or could it even be what actually creates Gudrun? She has no luggage, but perhaps her luggage is already looking for her? Is it downstairs right now, settling the bill with the Wirtin? Will the two pairs of jeans she once owned come toward her whom they had missed for so long, whose bulges and folds they still remember so clearly, hugging her any moment now? Are they waiting somewhere, floating in a river, but the pole of the enervated fisher of men, who ultimately wants to have a bigger fish to fight, already fumbles for them hesitatingly, so that they might, with a flic-flac jump that had once crashed into the Nothing, swing themselves back into the present where they could, at long last, burgeon again. They rested for so long, neatly folded in mother's closet like hands still greedily clasped around the dead daughter, but now they can get up again and slip through an invisible hole in an invisible fence. Many people stop dead in the middle of a word and give up, when they have to recite a poem, as soon as they realize what they just said. But it is harder still to put a complete stop to oneself.

Inside the room Gudrun wanders about, completely at a loss. She stares at her shadow, which has been placed neatly on the scrubbed floorboards, she still has another one to throw into the basket, it dances on the rim of it, will it make it through the relatively small hole? For a moment that seems an eternity, it wiggles about on the metal rim, caught in the Nothing, balancing unsteadily on the iron ring, suspended between the here and now, it flares up like a dark flame, the shadow, then it suddenly breaks off in a perfectly straight line without anything else having moved into the picture. Something originally belonging together had folded at the cutting line, the ball remained lying on top of the basket, the already greeted can't find the greeter anymore, the present has only been presentification, and now, determinedly, swings up forward onto the ground, but only the upper body arrives, the lower one has been lost, has vanished, and the high bar is that straight line that again separates arriving from staying, once and for all. Something, however, has been erased by us trying to destroy every last trace of it, it suddenly returns, still on its high horse. You just can't finish it off.

The clatter of dishes from the kitchen below restores some of Gudrun's composure. She stares at her unfinished shadow and the objects cut off by an invisible blade. Maybe there is a natural explanation for this phenomenon, maybe it was an awning set in motion and lowered by an electric motor that cut off a segment of the sun. But that does not explain the heartbreaking smile of those cut-off things nor that those things had been segmented randomly, at various places, without any system whatsoever. Gudrun does not dare to go to the window to check whether something striped, beach-chair-like, shoved itself in front of the sun, something nice to rest in, but not for us, who want to be fit and constantly in motion. For deep down Gudrun feels that she won't find anything that the essence of a thing or a thinglike being, a soul hidden in the flesh mistakenly pierced with a fork, would want to get here to bring the missing parts. And more than worrying about something missing, Gudrun fears it might return. For when reality gets overloaded, when we are complete, we'll all fall, together with the elevator floor, down into the endless dark shaft, and that does not have a floor. We are still falling.

A novel phenomenon, a spectacle nature presents to herself, since many times her more modest dramas have not been acknowledged? Gudrun throws herself at the door, opens it abruptly, and calls out into the hallway. She presses herself against the wall, as if she wanted to make a splash. Her call sounds thin, like a barely turned on faucet, but it seems she was heard, for emerging in the wooden rusticity of the staircase is the head of a girl dressed in a dirndl, which, like the waving of a hat, promises resuscitation, now it all goes very quickly, the dirndlette gains ground, the comfortable orthopedic shoes and open heels and toes set foot on the narrow corridor, and this combination chambermaid/waitress-model swiftly plows ahead, toward the source of the greeting, Gudrun presses herself against the wall, so the girl can get by her, greets shyly and points to her room, but the dirndlette simply bastes herself past her with vigorous running stitches, already her gait gets more hesitating, her determination slowed down as if by a strong headwind, she almost stumbles, looks around, and, quite close to Gudrun now, pushes open the door to Gudrun's room, who can feel the draft on her cheek, swings her body resolutely halfway inside, shrugs her shoulders, quickly swings around again, the short skirt, boisterously, busily always around her, the maiden rattles at the door across, which, however, is locked, she also tries the next one. Gudrun stands there, but she does not seem to be at home. The girl rushes closely by her, almost right through Gudrun, who desperately reaches for the coverlet to pull it off so that something, anything, would move in the room, but like a patient plushy done up for grabs, it cannot keep off by itself, she cannot get her cuddle blanket, the dark changing bag, over her head. The chambermaid gets into a bit of a spin, her run, so determined a moment ago, flows into several small brooks and trickles away. The handy maid stops, then hurries to the hallway window and peers down, but no one seems to be there either. That scream doesn't seem to have a place for which it was meant, nor can it find someone who might have emitted it. At a loss, interrupting the greeting, noticeably less resolute, the girl, an empty-handed maid, turns around and goes back again, passing Gudrun very closely, who, throwing herself forward with desperate shyness, tries to catch her by the sleeve, which is running through her fingers like a foreign breath in a foreign throat. The dirndled Fräulein did feel the grasp on her sleeve, for even though it was just a helpless tug, its effect was rather fierce, after all, land and flesh were hidden under the sleeve. The flesh works against Gudrun, the rustic waitress is thrown into a spin, a whirligig that had been set in motion. For a moment bones knock against bones, careful now! they spoil rather quickly, something blows directly into the girl, possibly a guardian angel, and, invisibly, someone, a noncorporeal unit of being, sowing, by winged sleights of hand, his seeds into the country woman. The latter falls into an increasingly intense sway, subjected to a nothingness that can't bear comparison to the guests' ridiculous tips, staggers backward toward the stairs again, set on fire by a flame, and visibly consumed, and almost falling down the stairs, the irregular drumming of her heels down the stairs can be heard for a long time, a sputtering clip-clop, on the stone-chip floor of the lobby, the plastic heels sound hollow—like reality's greasy dandruff, the steps pile up at the reception; which giant was rubbing his hands here, fuzzy specks of earth cover the floor, shavings of what we are made of, an intermediate value in the addition, but it mounts up.

Gudrun stands there. A bird briefly knocks its wings against the bay window in the breakfast room, it probably didn't pay attention to the paper silhouette of a bird there. The guest doesn't want to see anything dead besides what's lying on their plate. The animal must have confused air corridors and taken a wrong turn, into the wrong path of infinity. It might also have reached an altitude where its eye was blinded by some sort of glare so that it almost crashed in a nosedive. The wind tapped the bird lightly on the shoulder and bounced it around in the air, its body being so light! Landing on both legs, not elegant but nailing it. *Gekacherlt,* parallel style, in ski jumpers' lingo. As if drunk the feathered aviator staggers in another direction, flutters for a moment as if unconscious. Then, still reeling a little, it spirals itself up and away. It won't be soon before anyone will be able to look down on it again.

Gudrun's generator, the Creator Spirit who does not know the cause of his effect; industrious by nature, he sometimes lacks persistence. Oh well, a proof of subjection he is not, but neither is he driven solely by a force all his own. He welcomes rest before work much more than the rest afterward. Gudrun, running down the stairway, accelerates her speed of flow. The light looks away distractedly. Cold cuts of woods pile up on the railing, looking down on Gudrun are the heads of dead animals with impressive burdens they never complain about, because death demanded it of them. Black cocks and mountain cocks, cockamaniacs and cock-whatchamacallthems, other alpine inhabitants, two, three hazel grouse with paper scraps hanging on them, indicating when and where they found their death, poor things. A snow grouse. And another one there. They must have been pouring like crazy from nature's dispenser. The animals in this hallway minded their own business long ago, and now the shop is closed. Chamois with vacant eyes. Some joker put a cigarette into one of the chamois's snout. A shadow of smoke lies on the rustic wallpaper, something pulls upward and remains completely rigid at the same time, as if rooted to the spot. In place of blood, something else moved into leftover body parts of these animals and bolted its furniture into the ground, the way it is done on ships, something immovable, a terrible form of being, staler than artificially colored lemonade left standing for a day, leaving it to the bare air. The heads on the wall raise, something moved into them, which makes even death seem bearable, the lesser evil. Set off against them we appear pretty plump and juicy, like cyclists, whose heads can be seen gliding by behind a low poster wall, soundless, bodiless. The heads, cut off, still have to work, we leave them unbridled, but they neither stir nor regenerate. It is an inhuman way of dwelling, but then again it was dust taken from the earth to produce it, that archenemy of every housewife, which will always be what has been, since it had already been removed before it came to be again. A horrible opponent who only becomes visible after it has accumulated several layers, a certain thickness. But even though it always comes to new life whenever it touches the earth, it still ends up, as what has been and what will come, in the garbage bag of a female who subdued it.

9

Past the vacant stare of those animals Gudrun glides down the stairwell. Her breath hardly meets anyone, it is a pneumatic elevator without the pneuma. This young woman is whole, yet everything is missing, or is it the missing that is whole? Not part inside a part but as a whole in the whole, this bird angel fluttering down the stairway! A waft of life, just barely, but sufficient for Gudrun's being to seem complete again, and she carries herself with a certain ceremoniousness, her own relic, uhm, speaking of dust: the housewife stuffs it into her irrational soul, albeit in this case she is a housemaid. Work that flushes itself down the black toilet hole of fast forgetting and losing oneself? And with that Nothing she created, the housewife ultimately covers only herself, a whole woman, who nonetheless stands with modest pride behind herself. And finally, she will work herself to nothing, even though she is still visible, serving her wild supper at the table and the host breaks, ouch, that went right through a God, scared the living hell out of him! And thus Gudrun also became dust of the earth and earth herself, dry matter, and irrational as she is to find out from the thinkers what the heck they thought was jumping out of their heads, there she comes again, made in someone's image that turned out wrong to boot; because before the years she died, the mini was up and coming again (with women being so small already, now their clothes are also shrinking!), in the meantime it went away again only to come back halfway down the thigh. Always ready: to push the elevator button so that it moves up again. Where has the dust, Gudrun, been kept in the meantime? She wouldn't want something like herself put into her, because she wants tighter thighs and to pay herself the rest in cash. But maybe in this case less would even be more. Gudrun is bone from bone, and she won't let herself be chased back behind the gate through which the flesh was hurriedly lugged from the basement, sent through the examination, and stacked on the bargain table. Hands are already pulling and pushing, reaching for Gudrun through the walls, opening her up, leafing through her, tugging at her for where the soul is hidden, one could use one for oneself, but the deal ain't no steal. Okay. Gudrun runs. Hands are groping for her, and all she knows is: run! Something's reaching for her from the wall, she feels a waft of air on her cheek, touches brushing by her, smudges on her right calf, hasty greetings that could not be completed because the address on the postcard was missing. Words get loaded, where is her shield, her sword?, ribbons are thrown like nooses, like lassos, with restless fervor, creatures grope their way out of the stream, why not, anglers are constantly groping around in the river in order to pull something out. Like some creature that has not yet properly unfolded, a Japanese paper coquetry dropped in the middle of making it, and now a joint sticks out helplessly here, a hinge there, ready to swing themselves out of lifelessness and into an animal or other creature, Gudrun darts off in a panic. The settling of accounts at her death was overhasty, for there still was a stretch of present to travel, a coupon that will be redeemed now. The invisible hands reach for her, but they miss, Gudrun has arrived in the lobby. Everyone, after all, is to themselves their most read book, even though they get ideas from another book. There we already have the glass cabinet with all the skiing cups won by the children of the innkeeper, who resolutely goes for profit even with her own children. No one has to sacrifice their leisure time for that, because for those young carpenters and plumbers, leisure time activities have long become their real work. This house and this lobby were not simply imagined by me, one has to consider that they are actually very hard on their inhabitants, especially the floor. A tree is just about to grow out of Gudrun's hair, its roots have already wound themselves, like threads, cosmic thongs, into this rich growth and hold the student, who now stumbles and falls, down to the floor, too hurried was her run down the staircase, or was it even her hair that suddenly dragged her back into the invisible, into utter uncertainty. Gudrun Bichler falls backward into a time warp, where she rushes after herself with almost (not quite) the speed of light, so that she can't stop but rather runs back into the past, the unchangeable. Gudrun, however, can't put the brakes on and falls, slips, a figure skater who kept spinning in the same spot too long and now the sewer cover to the Nothing breaks in underneath her—from the kitchen the breathless voice of the chambermaid who shrilly reports something that's briefly interrupted by interjections, outside one can't understand a word of it, maybe the words are also running backward—okay, now she lands sprawling on the floor, our Gudrun Bichler, sliding halfway across the brick floor. Something twitches inside her, it wants to come out, we do have the sole claim to our essence, it's similar to homoeopathy. No one has ever seen it, but many claim they felt something after they swallowed the little pill.

With her last bit of strength Gudrun hangs on to the front door and leans against it. She thinks she will need more strength than usual, but the door flies open like clouds forcefully shoved by the wind, and Gudrun, turned off earlier, gets turned on again, and now it is her turn to tune in to what's shown at this time. But she, the autotimer, ticks differently now, and she is different, on a different scale. I, unfortunately, am only half an hour older than before, but Gudrun instantly turned fifty years younger, the same and yet she is another and in another place. She runs and she is running out. A sort of container seems to have been moved behind the door to receive the human cargo together with the high-piled time this cargo has used already, but time here is nothing but bulk trash. This woman's presence will suddenly be plunged into a completely different light, should she be the so-and-so-many-millionth visitor, who will get honored with a bouquet of flowers and ten centimeters extra time, a round sum in any case, which will be presented to her, the earth gets so much from us, why shouldn't she spring for something for a change? Let bodies spring, which she usually encases in motionlessness? Our jubilaress for one, who sees the light for the fraction of a moment, the clearing in the dark! The uptightness of this student, who did not know how to live—or die, for that matter, being our dear jubilee guest (at the speed we get the goods in, a jubilee is due every second, the flowers and gift baskets are thrown to us from the assembly line!), makes her lighten up for half the bat of an eye, ooohhhhh, how beautiful! Gudrun surprises and scares herself, after all, it has been only a bit over twenty years since she got habituated to the everydayness, and now those twenty years of habits can't manage to keep the openness of this space open for even one second. But since Gudrun has completed a round sum of dead folks with herself, she gets ushered out into the open, compliments of the invisible, though this openness is nothing but said container, inside of which we conduct our celebration, and there, behind the door that leads again into the open, the world outside is filled with ordinariness that we would happily pick up if only we weren't dead! If only we were able one more time to come, to touch something solid, hard, that we did not buy but stole from our own body, with our own hands (a vain unveiling)! Not to be dead, just once!

Built into the container is an abandoned street, which is easy to miss, if one takes the wrong turn at the intersection. A few small shops, all closed. Dusty street signs. Beyond the last two houses, which seem to be in somewhat better condition, the street widens a bit and runs in a straight line all the way to a brick wall at its end. It is a hidden street. It is not possible to access it by car, and by foot only by going through a garbage-filled backyard known only to residents. This alley seems to have been built in as if by magic. The familiar residential area is suddenly changed, and strange faces look at us through soiled curtain veils. Shutters over the shop windows rolled down for years, the way they look. A last resistance from the signs, Jewelry, Furs, Delicatessen, which can still hold their ground, the shutters of the watch and jewelry store have a hole that has been crudely barred, but one can still look inside. Shielding the eyes from the dusty sun, one can see a couple of wristwatches and some pieces of jewelry, business seems to have dried up in this store, but the watches are still running! Only the time is totally different. The chimneys are set off darkly against the leaden sky. It suddenly got cold. Winter. An icy wind blows through a discarded newspaper and throws it rustling against the wall of a house, at which it presses itself as if it were afraid someone might pick it up to wrap the lost time in it and bring it into service again. On the ground the snow has melted into gray islands of slush. In the center of the street are the traces of countless feet, tracks left to rest here (that way one could forego graves), they have already evaporated around the edges.

And even though one can still see the traces running down the street, a rivulet of humans in the middle of the road, lined by facades in various shades of gray (no, here is one yellowish beige, on it a sign relatively luxurious for this area, gold on black: a plumbing company plus junkyard business), a trickle from the time of a flood that is already seeping away, so people must have been coming through not all that long ago. Are these droves the carriers of those tracks, the ones who rattle the track rods, the originators, who, with their shattered lives, supply us with festive occasions to this day? They vanished so thoroughly, as if their legacies were fossils in stone, primal beings whose movements had been obliterated millennia ago, and only the bones, those reasonable celestial souls, are still supplying the pneumatic market with nothing but air. Coming from one mouth, moving only thin strips of paper at best. Even the negatives of those beings have been destroyed, and the negatives of their names in the Register of Millions of Deeds to boot (the reason why we are thinking of them constantly and therefore never).

As soon as the self-closing mechanism of the door went into effect, the present is once again bathed in a completely different light. A place appears through the window, because Gudrun, who is no longer Gudrun, who indeed is no more, suddenly finds herself in a room looking down the desolate street stretched out once again in ghostly abandonment. Gudrun still can't get over the fact that she has overcome her state of fleshlessness. Like the demiurge, our chancellor, who, secretly moved merely by watching one daytime soap, believes he is moving on his own. Same with humans. Here we have an urban room, cozy, but old-fashioned and furnished pretty simply. Dust on the furniture. Everything dusky and threadbare, no light coming in, but it is not dark either, everything seems to be what it is. Suddenly, outside, a tempest is coming down out of nowhere, it did not give advance notice by a thunderstroke. Gudrun suspects that someone will show up after the storm, perhaps the previous occupant. The touch of a stranger hovers over everything, the hand of a middleman, who will charge his fees because the disappeared tenants did not earn, thus did not deserve, what they got. It seems to be one of those typical Viennese tenement flats of the period between the two world wars, where Gudrun has been assigned to live on a trial basis; the model apartment has been built into this Minimundus Museum in place of all the other dwellings, and it is dull as if made of lead that choked anything radiating. Your voucher's half-life has expired, *mein Herr, gnädige Frau!* You can try to hang on as much as you want, those walls feel several kilometers thick, they swallow any sound and they have to, for Gudrun feels as if those millions of beings, whom she, a prize-winning arrival, had beaten out, pressed her against the walls angrily in order to beat her now in return into a fluffy batter: a plutonium cookie to be thrown to the Mickey Mouse hellhound named after that cookie brand. Those millions, within, behind the walls of this room, they want the student who was retrieved into the middle of the room, desperately clinging round the back of a chair, they want to take her out again, but maybe this time in such a way that no one ever will remember her, thus she would finally be the same as they, the shadowy! Whoever annihilated these hecatombs of people did not consider, could not have known perhaps, that with this passage through fire they would receive perpetual power which would coalesce with us who are still here and hurl us, who are turning to you with this letter, out into a howling tornado, where no memorials will find us, where presidents and chancellors will speak, sing, drink, and laugh. We, the underexposed, now it is us ourselves who are the light, but we don't shine on us, for how does the singer sing, the party is over. Done. Gone. Finished. Cut. Our memorial mugs are empty. The Bock is in the beer, the whining in the wine, the open is open once again, getting lighter by the hour, now it has even acquired the right to an eternal light, the cultivated citizen cultivates nothing less than his self-proclaimed innocence and Gudrun—that is, her representative on earth—stands here in her slip in front of a chair cleaning a pair of pantyhose in the washbowl. It has the side effect of also getting the hands clean in the process.

Outside the room a young man walks by in the direction of the hallway toilet, he is in his undershirt, suspenders dangling in front. Whistling a little tune about fate, he looks through the window, which is covered on the inside with thin tissue paper, *direttissima* at Gudrun. She knows the young man out there, that's obvious. She knows him, she just remembers, from summer vacation in some sunny place. A mountain inn? A bed and breakfast? A group of young people standing in front of the house. All wearing the outfits of mountain climbers and hikers, solid alpine boots, Alpenstocks studded with small insignias, woolen caps or felt hats, parkas tied around the waste, all laughing cockily behind round sunglasses that swallow their eyes, and that young man is a special show-off. He had climbed a few steps down the ditch and picked a twiglet of edelweiss. So folks are around here at times, but their existence gets ignored. The young man flips his hat down his neck and laughs, his teeth are flashing, they blur a bit in his face, almost shifting for a moment, as if they'd been broken out by a blow or kick, as if they were falling through the frame of the lips, no!, at his age he couldn't really have dentures already! Then everything is okay again. And now he is here, in front of her door, since Gudrun knew him during a past long summer, it evidently drove him madly to this place. And Gudrun thinks: could I be THE PLACE? From outside she can hear the key put into the toilet door, then the grinding stops and the dark silhouette approaches anew, it advances, oh God, the head bends as if it wanted to return to the I, and there the young man stands again, pressing his face to the window, shading his field of vision, shielding it jealously and staring at Gudrun washing her nylons. They stare at each other, the young man outside, the young woman, bent slightly, inside. Due to circumstances it so happened that her breasts inside the capsule of her shiny pink satin bra folded forward. Her hair falling into her slightly flushed face, now she straightens up impatiently and pushes it behind her ears. Instantly the man outside flashes a smile, and even through the tissue paper on the window one can see the instantly thrilled glow of his teeth. As if he had a small lamp in his mouth, which he, with his bodily powers, could work up to a certain reflective strength that refracts in the enticing figure of the girl inside. What does the dream tell in which two people are sitting? In the compartment that runs into the undiscovered country: The young man has his bicycle tools with him because later he might repair his bike in the courtyard. The tools include a leather strap with loops that hold the screwdrivers and screw-wenches, neatly arranged by size: All these tools consist of bones! Cleaned ulnar, radius, and metatarsal bones, others I can't see at the moment. And, as I said, arranged according to size in the loops, handy to use. Otherwise, I can't see anything unusual about the young man. Except that a few other bones, white and bleached, are scattered about on the floor as if thrown away, torn open with strange abruptness like the door of a train compartment, where we have to let a new passenger in even though it is ours. But I would not see that if I were Gudrun Bichler, for all she can see, strictly speaking, through the tissue paper pasted around the sharp edges of the window, is a floating face. It just proves that people are able to adopt an alien nature if they could not keep their own. And already the room with the two people gets carried away. Utterly senseless how the railroad tracks are laid out, as if to put the reins on the landscape out from under the frozen morass, they don't fit anyway, and will be plowed up with all the people they hacked out of the Nothing, blond God, you've got quite a way to accept an alien nature! Out of this world! You have to stand up on your tiptoes to be able to look over your hobodies with blood running out of their ears, the bludgeons get quite a workout, and it's always by the ears you start to cut, torture, skin them alive, because they can't sing and play such cool pop songs as you do with your ancient lyra, still the same old song. The Most High is closest to the one that's already high up, thus your song climbs up the charts, holding on there with an ice pick, pimple-picked faces are glued to the window, looking forward to the children's camp they were allowed to be sent to, where even more German youngsters are waiting to bravely forge ahead, with folks on the march in their ears. This is about *Endkampf,* the final battle in mounting, screaming, and stomping! Okay. The young folks are busy for the moment, but here, in this room, see for yourself: A young man finds himself and his form and leaves it there.

A knuckle knocks briefly against the glass. Gudrun straightens herself, a strap of her slip slipped over her upper arm, she raises the whole arm to readjust the thin ribbon. She's got a live man at the frontline of her eyes! Or not? Her pursed lips lure him in so that one word may lead to the next. There stands the young barbarian with his warmth looking for an oven to put it in. Let others have their mind and eat it, too; those pushing and shoving behind him at the checkout, they shot the blood juice of the masses that's been treaded under booted kicks up their veins, and now he, they are looking for a place where they can empty that juice in peace and quiet. They will be hot for ten years, and then they will get cold again. Woe, when this breed's hot fermenting sex rockets upward, it will kick in the glass pane cover of our brooder's fire alarm and pop out so that everything will come into being, while we'll be the only ones to escape this fate and thus able to continue our slumber. This athletic young man behind the window, e.g., has risen already, which means his turn is first. He took his sex into his lap, so it won't get lost amid an entirely annihilated lineage or panic. Those many dead are a huge heap of *Volk,* who even has to supply its own police to make sure it stays within the borders, the togetherness of the vacation camp. The old BS about Eurydice won't do anymore, for the living are repasts chewed up by the teeth of time, angels of history running backward from the start, no one snaps at them, but you can't break them out either. Birth to some is already the high point of their existence. Never again will they be attended to as much, the dead. So then, the man knocks at the glass pane, it sounds as if many behind him were knocking with him. Now all that's left to do is tying off the threads of fate! The window is not an obstacle, the door is open, and Edgar, that's his name I decided once and for all, flows milkily into the room where little-girlish pussycat pictures hang on the walls getting lapped up instantly by the milky way so many followed. The relief is here, the fork punches the time clock, a spark of grease jumps off the exposed plate, where the last souvenir photos get burned, we are looking for contact, yessir, there it is, people just have to do much work on their bodies, so that they acquire a certain shape. The door is open now, the being enters, opens up right away, no holds barred. It is a welcome guest, for it arrived according to specification, tall, slim, and naturally blond. Feet are networked into a steady trickle of commemorations, the connection works, the source finds the current, the head is a big box truck of thinking, but it doesn't do it any good: Half a tennis ball has been put over the connector of the prime mover, and the fans are cheering cheering cheering. The nets are raised to pull the millions into our hungry traps. Lots of pictures are taken, even though those millions could not even cast their own pictures in the mirror. No reason to kick over the traces, for the tracks can be redrawn by dead hands over and over again, a spectacle around which an entire German forest darkens, that godpiece of the Germans as they keep raging like two converging rivers. And we must get into the act as well. We entangle ourselves to a web of wimpy wieners whining that it was not us Ösies, the Österreicher, we Austrians to begin with, we: the Ur-Volk. This isn't our fault. We are just the neighbors. We don't know if anyone's at home over there, we haven't seen one in quite a while.

10

If the root is sacred, why not also the branches? Or the raised arms of a people raving that it grew, like a tree, over the other peoples? This tree at any rate has gotten too big for us, and now, at 5:45 p.m. it would have to break through the ceiling. The young man for whom Gudrun Bichler opens the door, had half his head slide off him, despite the surface roughness of his dreamy inclination. The skull like a sheet of paper that had been cut off with precision along a sharp line drawn with a ruler, and Gudrun sees: It was not because of the privacy shield of tissue paper pasted over the pane or the steam on it, no, the young man's head is split open along an imagined breaking line with almost an entire half missing. On the side where something is missing, there is absolutely nothing. As if someone reached for a glass placed usually to the right side of the plate and it still stands there, but the thirsty person can no longer see it, or, even stranger, he can no longer GRASP it! So here the appearance puts us on hold forever and then it is incomplete to boot. Wow, now that head, thoughts must have been working in there like worms! A street corner got in its way and broke it open, a milestone, and what does Gudrun do, she takes a left turn to go home empty-handed once again. This student, if she turns her head to the mirror, is not an appearance to turn heads, she is awkward, an investor who can't offer anything but a taut, healthy body, that runs noiselessly in the wheels of the joints and on the leashes of those entitled to claim the right to gracefulness and pushed-out breasts and held-in bellies and, long hair, hehe!; but the lines often get caught in that machinery, what do you call those that give humans quite a bit of leeway for running or, as is the case right now, teeter into the coercions of embraces? Living corpses. Women like Gudrun are not desired, for they are too tightly entangled in their pupae threads. A strong wind is howling outside. It tears the last sounds out of the mouths and beats them around the heads of the folks that passed by and disappeared behind the fork in the road. A squall bursts into the clanking street lanterns and dries the last footprint in the snow slush. The cheap displays in the shop windows darken, a sharply outlined cloud has moved in front of the sun, a foehn cloud, it glows up bright red around the edges.

The man with nothing on his right side, no pet, not even himself, for he is quasi-folded: a man whose life is finished, in whom the spine of memory has been folded back a bit, as if he still tried to turn the page but didn't get to finish reading the book. So here is this young man, his body discarded almost unused, but when it was thrown out, it still was good. Quite a pity, isn't it? His hair still thick, a wild mess, whole clumps falling out as if tousled, as lovers like to do, though in other parts still solidly in place. This apple core still has plenty of apple to it! And the joint capsules firmly hold back their flesh if, imagining itself unbound, it wants to disappear for a bit. What's more, the flesh is even growing! Surprising the happy fella with his very self! On the branches of the hips, it already bursts the skin, lures with passions that, like joint fluid, drip out with gelatinous clarity since someone, doctors, nurses, helpers, broke open those firm thighs, burrowing inside them with claws of steel. This son was doomed and dumped into the garbage, blood-water running from his side, but in return he now leads us closer to Gudrun, lighting the scene like rotted wood. Pulls her slip over her head. And the straps also pull back her shoulders, so that her breasts come out like folding wheels. A body can also be used as a luggage cart or like the famous Knirps folding umbrella. Once is enough, and the woman exits the compartment. Then you dry yourself off and leave again, but only after you jumpstarted the woman. And a second hand that more or less comes out of Nothing, since one half of the young man is almost completely gone, pulls Gudrun's somewhat worn cotton panties down her knees, while life shines in the woman's eyes and senses, and she learns that sometimes one has to line up in front if there is no room in the back. The wheels rattle, one hand, which unfortunately is not there, goes on a journey and kneads the roast and lifeless vegetables under the anthill of the sex, where the pine needles of pubic hair had been woven and arched into a small heap, into a bite to eat that's grabbed between the lips and chewed; and even in the place where the man's face had been cut off, Gudrun can still feel the strong teeth. Her body is in the making, but it is not the body of the Lord.

Still, it emerges, barely tasting of anything, in the mouth of a young man who skillfully opened Gudrun and now works his way further into her with his tongue rolled into a cone. Her primordial playgrounds are laid out before him, and now the screws of the nipples are turned so that the little vehicle can start moving; springs are squeaking that protect us from an all-too-hard landing in the other. The counter Gudrun is open now, the counter guard went down. No need to forego fake freedom! The dead shall also live! In its daily workplace now, the man's member stands up, a pole of rotting wood, in which animals played for a pale lager and lost. Rising through the dark of this trinity, long since turned to humus, of the male sex, which once may have been a temerity, is the head, still well supplied with blood, of the crucified, an arrogant Christ, who hasn't got time to head to Galilee for three more days so that he can be there on the third day. His soul, locked into a plump piece of flesh at the end of a hose, wants to finally get out and look around whether it would like to stay here. Thus the body is prepared and shaped in a way that during its stay it can strike as well, since it has been awakened anyway.

A little glob of liquid, bright as a plastic bag of Mildessa wine sauerkraut, has been added, and the sausage rages, a sledgehammer, a battering ram against the teeth of the girl who, tipped over from the chair, dragged down by the hair, had been slammed to the floor, so that she, uncanny upper of a cannery (also does bodywork!), gets this spicy sausage bite tossed at her once and then keeps going for it over and over again. With the young woman's jaws open wide, the flesh gets pushed in, not that it existed at all for her!, but a part of the man's prick is also missing, and still, Gudrun's gums are almost torn by whatever comes rowing through the flow of her saliva. Now we have to leave this gentleman for a moment, for he retreats for strategic reasons, so that death can have its effect on this most stubborn spot of life. How would this body have died, if, as with Jesus, life had still been inside it? That is the question. Because then death would have gained control over that redeemer with his bobbing balls and his busily backward-tilting and somewhat indecisively forward-pushing (nothing found again!) pecker, which would be counterproductive, and thus the death list was conned with cunning. This young man's body might have died (it must have, cut randomly in half, how could it be so agile?), but the beam of his power has once again come over him, that's how it looks, and he dispatches his meaty, somewhat stringy shaft into Gudrun's mouth, so that he, the man, who no longer exists to the left, may at least sit to the right of whomever until the end; but this is in the crossfire of a stinking television channel, thus he does not sit for long but fires away. Only then does he look at what he jabbed into.

It is the soft flesh, yuk, deep-frozen!, ready-to-eat!, of a woman, that will perish from its own sluggishness, but here we also have a slugger's balls throwing a jab directly in Gudrun's chin! Hello! But there are different strokes for different folks, and here Gudrun has this fellow's balls banging whoosh!, whoosh!, into one of the cups 36C or some other assessable size, from where teats and udders must first be lifted. To that end the attendant male had to make a half-turn propeller-style on top of the woman, that's pretty obvious, one has to just imagine it visually and converted to narrow gauge. Look here, the lower back rotated like a grinder blade, and promptly the dead youth was stung by the visible, perhaps the flesh of the psychical, the bite swells up red, only one single bone of the young man will not be broken. And just this one wants to get into the woman's sex, which gets kneaded by fingers and teeth, and this only works when this Crucifixated rotates halfway around his axis so that his earthy cloaca orifice, dug up by busy bugger-bugs, is right in front of Gudrun Bichler's eyes and nose, an antsy hill leading right into this lord, and yes, now those shy, ravenous animals are crawling one by one out of their burial mound to leisurely check out Gudrun; so then, we are looking at a small mound, piled up by industrious little buggers, and, as mentioned before, smack in the middle a darkly outlined little hole for this winged little war vet Isidor Cupido Jelinek, a dashing dead he, sure thing, and then at the hairy bread bag beating against Gudrun's chin and then, with the soul his only clothing, the last member in a long chain of dead members, which couldn't possibly have vanished all at once. So where did they all end up, since we don't know anything at all about them today? This one member settled inside Gudrun. Well then, poking around now in this Austrian mix of treats, a national specialty, is this elegant young human's elementary particle, which we absolutely still have to get for our natty wardrobe, then it rudely pulls back and, after its owner rolled over in his grave once again almost full circle, closes this mouth with a long kiss, until Gudrun had sucked the ultimate pleasure out of this dead man's mouth. A few teeth don't mind coming along, since they were already sitting quite loosely in the earth. Cheek is pressed against cheek, the young man's tongue licks across the woman's skin in rough, sketchy strokes, as if to do her one more time, and with an abrupt move he hands her his love bone and the pneuma it contains, which, for its part now, also has the urge to suck in and blow out some in Gudrun's suction hose, depending on what's been turned on. For Gudrun, this stick of flesh is quite amusing, albeit incomprehensible, like a ghostly apparition, if only she knew what a stream could burst out of there! There now is some burrowing, if a bit clumsily, in the young man's stiffened crotch, fingers rush to their workplaces as ordered and indicated, entrails fall into a certain design, Ms. Jane Doe signs for us all the still totally blank documents, she picks up the pen, it's already spilling and spitting, her hand is completely overrun with it!

We don't have any more room!, the next future gets divined from the pattern of fallen flesh debris; and around the swollen cock Gudrun is falling apart like a blown-up city, whose rusty pipes and reinforcements, tubes and cables had been broken, torn open, exploding into a pyre of Mikado sticks, a gigantic hay cart of bones pointing every which way, and instantly the hand of the scattered young man gets into action to arrange the woman in proper order, while she must not move anything, not one skinfold, not one delicate patch of cellulite rice. The dead youth, as we can see much better now, is horribly mangled. He'd been intubated and mechanically ventilated once, I can tell by the hole in his neck, pupils narrowed on both sides, round, IV catheters placed on both arms, thorax resistant, on abdomen ca. 25-cm-long OR wound after laparotomy, upper midline, with three basal drainage tubes (moderately filled), 2-by-2-cm contusion above the upper right iliac spine, dermabrasion above the iliac crest, pelvis resistant, basal urinary catheters, urine macroscopically tinged with blood, wound above the knee, length ca. 3 cm, closed with interrupted button sutures, however: Skull wrecked anyway, lung thorax ditto, and so on.

And now this young man pulls the woman's bones that are in better shape out of the heap and places them, like fish bones, next to each other on the edge of his plate, and doing so his mien blows UP. Teeth pull out of the lips, well, the woman's soul can buzz off now, too, as her body suffers, getting ripped apart, and from there straight into the arms of papa Franz, the chancellor, who is now making his famously nimble speech about millions of other dead. That puffed-up big wheel no longer entrusts the pneuma of life inside their bones to his Father and to his Holy Spirit, instead he prefers saving us all with a brand-new monument. The blackish, not very clean body of the dead young man is extremely swollen between the thighs, since his flesh no longer holds properly together, having been patched together hastily and then undone again. The killed youth took off his soul, had to take it off, in return this woman now receives her bridegroom. The soul (clothes!) drops softly on the pile, bra going splinters, a smashed yogurt cup, the healthy flesh, smelling lightly of sweat, garnished with dots and bluish-blackish spots, slides itself between the fingers of the Governor of the Feast and gets twirled, what a triumph of eternal rest in peace! Deutschland (sans Goethe). *Das Volk.* Now available in a brand-new collection of *Plattenbau* apartment buildings! No borders between yes to death and no to death. This smutty, double-barreled formation! Rocking like toddlers, toys and animals, knowing full well they are made of plastic and plush. What?!, those marmeladish nipples getting suddenly hard as stones? Bouncing around together but not catching each other? What can be done about that? One happy to hear the voice of the other, and the two balls of white pizza dough are getting slapped against, wound around each other, and feasted on. What all of those rescued only after death have in common: They recognize each other like a pair of boobs, though they actually know each other far too little, not to speak of the ribs, those are serial fractures with pleural effusions on both sides and multiple contusions as well as an atelectasis of the right inferior lobe! Oh, by the way, is this a liver rupture in the area of the seventh segment? I don't know, but I see displaced fractures of the R superior and inferior pubic bone as well as multiple contusions. What do they still want here, those looney boobs? Whatever, now they get bitten, pinched, and tossed around, it makes the decorative cherries almost hop off. Until the spoon finally digs in and they get inserted in the mouth, to suck them dry and spit them out again later. What a blast when they leave the light and wander into the throat (and out of it again) of a person whose light has long gone out as well.

There is a suspicion that different systems are intermingling here, but they are natural, I think, maybe even nutritional, considering that the principal actors are no longer alive and therefore reluctant or unable to receive letters. In the meantime, the young man has also disrobed, and sitting down in the sludge of his clothes, he smears it on himself. Gudrun's flesh falls over him like water, he splashes it around a bit, his toy animal bounces atop the waves but still drives in bravely each time and then out again. But first the respiratory symptomatology must be improved! A wind is coming up, but the young man's stalk doesn't drop into the leaves. A hand, emerging like a deer out of the clearing of his sex, scenting and probing the lay of the land, plays with Gudrun's hair that's standing up on her sex, plucking it, we see all this from his, the man's, standpoint, even though he no longer stands a chance either, he has reached the end of his road. Brotherly rough, with a few sunny summers in stock, which haven't been bought and had to be put back on the shelf, Gudrun's sex-mount gets lifted and torn open at the fold, she must let go of some more hair in the process. A big breath blows into it, a small, round red head shyly dares to come out, wheedling its way into the fleshy but apparently still uninhabited alley that leads into Gudrun; her lodging structure gets seized up and down, then the white traveler, whose head is red all over, stands at the entrance and says hello from the bottom of his satisfied heart. A special burgomaster for one single construction site, where nothing but flesh gets pounded like *Schnitzel* meat. This young man wants to see how and where the flesh got creased so that he can fold it again the same way when he is done pressing it.

This flesh is not an honest dead, it cannot decide what state it wants to be in, a state of excitement or a state of quiet. Anything, and we mean absolutely anything, is welcome that would raise and reveal and then revive this ruined flesh, ripped as it is by wounds. Now the young man wants to see this student Gudrun spread wide open one more time, but this time lying on her back. So he turns her around, unfolds the white body's arms like sleeves, and inspects it up close. Like a bristling animal that has eaten and now wants to lift its leg, he is quickly pulled away from the entrance again. Nevertheless, he can still yank up the bundle of flesh by the hair and devour it, and what once was flesh has already fallen through the grill. The unhooked member tore the flesh off its body, it is hot, air!, the body no longer does anything, it rests like nature, but its locomotive, this device clouded over with hot steam, it pulls and pulls the flesh down the road that had already been traveled earlier by that human herd, toilsomely, though not tolerated. We almost drowned like salad, in vitamins, had we not burned them during sex and our fingers to boot. Why on earth did we have to chase around the flesh in us so much? Good heavens, that small piece of flesh! And so much fuss about it. It has had it, and that's all she wrote. Now the dead youth tosses it, almost sloppily, into the woman. He tenses up in his hinges, a door into the Nothing that out- and overdid itself and now looks back to its house, removing itself from it with lightning speed, it already doesn't recognize its entrance that had loyally served the house through all those years as a hole, a recess, a Nothing in the earth. With a last effort the body, a door-leaf in the wind, swings forward, rises, as if in animalistic fear, on its tiptoes, as if it wanted to become a gust about to howl, and slams itself shut. The Germans, after all, also look incessantly for a new master, because they don't know their own metes and bounds into which they always want to rush together. Not even with the help of Botho's, Martin's, Kurt's, Hänschen's, and Herbert's accomplished rinsing and flushing can they get rid of them again, the dead. Even though we have been held up against the light a hundred times and we even looked through ourselves to see if something still sticks to us, love with its singular look or God knows who or what. Even when we lay ourselves aside after an undisturbed anesthesia devoid of history: nothing left to show our origin, we come straight out of the washing machine, but we don't put the lime hydrate in there, quite the contrary, we want to get it all out with Calgonite! Even our water is too hard for the fuzzy lining of our slippers.

Gudrun Bichler awakens twisting and excreting. She lies there, crumpled like a used tissue on the corridor in a dark, dusty corner next to the toilet door. Downstairs the approaching voices of returning hotel guests. Expectantly turned up barking of dogs. Soon food will be served, a hearty *Speck* and *Wurst* afternoon snack, way to go!, flesh is not always our adversary who wants to be demolished—sometimes, when it shakes us to the core, we quite welcome it. A thread of saliva trickles from the corner of Gudrun's mouth. Her jeans lie next to her. Her mound of Venus is bloated, having grown to at least triple its size, a fleecy, sleepy giant mountain, where something seems to have gone to battle for its meal, the meat course, no, rather the fish course. There is no one around. But it does not hurt, it is a strange, nettle-stung feeling, a swollen little meatball planted on the ground, which, instead of sizzling as it should, because of taming? shaming?, has gotten rather puffy, numb instead. Diagnosis: too well done. A penetrating fishy odor elbows its way into the air, it is the marrow that ran out of the bone, the pneumatic seed. The bone, which is extremely hard in that place, has a fracture, the inserted guide pin has to be moved forward with a hammer, only then can the fracture be threaded. Unfortunately, nothing could be revived by this procedure, even though the two sacral rods were inserted and fixed with nut and counternut. And yet a wound has opened up again in Gudrun's sex with a bit of earth and juice rippling out of it. And a child's whimper comes out of her mouth. A lance or something like that must have rammed into her, moaning, the young woman presses her hand against the gash between her legs.

The trophy heads on the other hand are bursting with recklessness, there, hanging on their walls, one gets quite daring, once dumped by death's shovels into the establishments of the citizens. Overloud jarring noises are coming up from the kitchen. Steps are dragging something heavy, perhaps half of a pig from the cold room, for dinner. A few drinks are served in the garden at tables, which are still in the sun, as Gudrun can see, she has pulled herself up to the windowsill with great effort. From the hips down she is naked, as if paralyzed, and smeared all over with soft earth. Her labia are wide open, and she is dripping onto the dusty floor. No pearl coming out of that oyster. With difficulty, as if to hold on to the rebate she received for her life, the woman turns around, okay, that worked. She looks for her room, can't remember which door belongs to it. She presses herself against the wall, picks up her jeans, and holds them in front of her sex. The body is incomplete compared to the one that resides inside. Gudrun tears open the door to her room, which she seems to have found after all, after almost an eternity, but is it really hers? Hasn't the furniture she already didn't recognize earlier been rearranged? Something might want her, as a sign that she is giving up now, to briefly knock at the floor, as if to invite someone to get set in her for a bit. The way competitive athletes do, though they request to let them be at the very last moment. The next time the door will open, and the apparition will be solidified. What will it want. Tea or coffee? Yes, the one with the dark grounds, like blood coagulated long ago.

11

The soft rustling high up in the treetops shoos tourists from all around into their lodgings. The forest shivers, as can be heard from the sounds of firs, spruces, and larches; grasses tremble lightly as in a fever. The weather is in good hands with nature, where else would it get that kind of attention? People are running this way and that. General gathering at the inn, while way up high hawks and buzzards are tracing their figures clawed into the sky. The demanding mountain ridge has been folded and unfolded for the guests, who will want to look at it later while having their coffee. With powerful kicks alpine boots are removing the stones, it rumbles behind the scenery, because a new setting is about to move in, thunder and storm, gusts of over a hundred kilometers per hour on Blahstoan mountain. The guests want to switch to other amusements and thus become less and less reserved than they had been during the day. The windows on the ground level are open outward, the sun, now lower, throws its glaring projection beam onto the glistening dragonfly wings of the panes, the geraniums sunbathe in their pots. The hikers for their part have folded their wings, merry, hungry, and thirsty they pour from the forest trail into the shady garden.

We, however, advance much deeper into the mountains, but we swim against the stream that sucks in all those creatures on their descent, and now, fletching their predator's teeth, they rush toward us, upward, up the mountain road, illuminated like saints by the afternoon light that also reveals our essence, and so we quickly catch up with Edgar Gstranz. He woke up, curled up like a wounded ant. He remembered climbing up the mountain with his alpine skateboard and meeting a group of hikers approaching him. He knows nothing about himself since then. He appears as if he'd been wiped off his path: as if he'd been called upon to sweep the forest floor so that he can stand on it again. As Edgar, rubbing his eyes, gets up on his feet, he feels as if, in doing so, he was also leaving his shape. The skateboard is the only thing he holds on to now, this alpine washboard that gives the ground a sound thrashing; wherever it sweeps across, the rotted surface gets sanded down, even erased, and only the underneath, well stocked with mere shadows of names, shows up. Our dead were revealed as their blanket corroded because of the excessively acidic new detergent! Edgar hugs his board, his not-calibrated device that only seems ready to accept him once he has left his shape. In the immediately following downhill this racer might be returned to life again, he can outrun himself if he hurries up, but even the light stands still, as if frozen in permafrost, it can't get out of its source, so that time itself freezes up for Edgar. And before he knows it, his essence is already farther down quite a ways (while Edgar must stay after all)—a selection of maleness that is to compete against the farm league club Logos—and walking with bent head and rosy-tinted head down the road.

Only hesitatingly the confused man dares to look up after a while: In the distance, more powerful beings than he desecrate the blueness of the starry sky by letting themselves be thrown, their arms stretched out wide and nailed to a sort of surfboard, from an airplane, how else could I put it. But they, too, come to a standstill in midair! Time passes for Edgar but not for those air divers. Has Edgar disappeared and only now the aeroknights are really thawing out? Or is it the other way around? Horrified, the trees swing their plumage, which we already took off almost completely anyway, as those Kung Fuzzies are strewn from the airplane into the House of Gods (and our knees are trembling like Jell-O, godfeed as it's called here). So Godspeed to all. But before that, the birds of heaven will pick up those sperm donors of eternity (they do have something to give us!). Flying fortresses make such a thing possible, they junk the jocks or simply drop them. Helmets are flashing, plastic rattles like the wings of gigantic birds of prey hit from below by a rush of wind, on which they let themselves be carried for a while. Humans on their boards offer themselves as appetizers! All those plastic overalls, the kind also worn by Edgar: They seem indestructible in their powerful Day-Glo tones, a polyphonic scream of artificial giant molecules, and above them, in the mighty cool pond of light, the parachute whereunder the athlete who is lined up for baptism skydives down the angel's hem and free-falls together with his cutting board on which he is served. Within three minutes his glow will fade and he will be blown away by the storm, thus cooling down, a star among stars. And now comes the Dove and picks him up. Or why not experience our Anke Huber full strength. Yes, those athletes with their young faces strained as if they were ready to cry, not to speak of the older ones who have long been without love for others. It is those others out of whose arms they now wrestle themselves resolutely, they have their own children, even grandchildren, but they still kick around like babies in their Sundays' dusk, yoked to this time, when even THE FOREIGNER learns to take a hike.

Thus the Undefeated hurl down into the Untouched, even Jesus, after all, is in need of salvation. Experience guides them, the zipper, the rip cord screeches, Ayrton, the racing Son of God, yes, yes, he, Senna!, is the first to hit the wall, he tears the heavens open and walks through the air corridor to his tap, turns it on, too, a human stream shoots out, the jumpers' clothes crackle. All those Austrian throwing stars, who want to become real stars so that they can keep up internationally. Now! Their weenies crowned with little pennants showing which way the wind blows are moving upward, not constricted by any thought in its birthday suit. Just like the sky and the earth can merge during a thunderstorm, the jock, nailed to his board, sails jerkily into our field of vision, in a few seconds he has aged many years, he somersaults one last time and now lands rather roughly, crashing into the ground, his darling face that meets all criteria, appears every day, only much younger, in commercials, and now that we have heard his name mentioned several times in the news, we have finally really, really heard him. Any woman would want to marry him or, at least once, flash her blondness right in front of him. Only for him would she sow discord into her sex, pricked into a light blue hue for a change today, which, in casual agitation and ready to break lose, shrieks angrily from behind the latex front back into the body that asked a bit too much from it. Why doesn't this woman get any attention? Doesn't she sit every Monday at 8:15 p.m. in front of the television set! She isn't worthy of this God coming down from his greatness to put on her flesh like a sandal. Though she wouldn't mind loosening his flesh, this sudden blowhard lets it be known.

Edgar Gstranz has completely forgotten how he got here. He can't even remember having sat down. The men, who'd already passed him once, are still up there at the same distance from him as before. They haven't come even one meter closer, that's at least what it looks like. Edgar feels as if he has experienced something that has already happened for a second time, a repetition compulsion, like a melody you can't get out of your head. Maybe the wanderers turned back while he slept because they wanted to climb up a second time. The three men stand completely still and stare down to him, no, now they move jerkily, they even seem to dissolve to nothing for some tenths of a second and then come back again from nothingness: Are they even the same? Of course, their clothing is exactly the same, Edgar remembers almost hyperclearly every little twig of edelweiss under the hatband, the small pins nailed in quiet simplicity to their hiking poles. A small late harvest of men just staring at Edgar. Now two of them take off their backpacks, they open them, and at that moment Edgar, without prior warning, is horrorstruck. Did they return to get him? In this solitude no one would see or notice anything. Did those men come specifically for him? A beginning, the corner of a wall, bends into Edgar's mouth, he gags, spits, his sex suddenly takes shape, like a sign of the athletic God Becker or God Schumacher or rather God Wendlinger, like a pole with a trail sign, on top on his latex skin. The laboriously arranged pile of snakes paddles with its stumpy wings, the bomb is primed and tilts in the direction of the target, its hairy scribblings get mowed into straight strips, an inscription, a cloudsy-pudgy sky- or lawn writing for whom this explosive cargo is intended, and Edgar gets yanked in the direction of his rocket, how ridiculous the surfboard has suddenly become, which can apply its full power downhill only! So now Edgar's cock, which hadn't slept in a soft bed, as it was tied to Edgar's belly in tear-proof nylon stretch, jumps out of its privacy, it dwelled everywhere and nowhere and now it sticks its bulging head all keyed up out the window. After all, this young man has lived for so long without love, but only for Austria's alpine team when he was driven up the wall of a building in a fast automobile, up to, yes indeed, up to the first-floor window, which he had scaled resoundingly in his hard, shiny auto body to peek in window after window, waving, snotting, shaking off buckets of slime until the small respiratory track, which had led so invitingly into the landscape, was definitely too slippery for walking. Until even Edgar's sex (for whom life seemed to be too minor, too narrow) could produce only tired, limp movements, not dead, but neither alive, not old and not young. Just at this moment a dreggy puddle wants to dribble out of Edgar, spreading a strong odor, and Edgar, a pretty ridiculous sight, throws away his Alpine Milky Way board—the Milka brand, yes, ours is lilac colored, we Alpenfolk are not as old-fashioned as you might think, ladies and gentlemen, we produce Europe's cutting-edge snacks and chocolates!, e.g., our star swimmer Franzi, for one, knows that, just listen to her lilac commercial break!, and he, too, the young shepherd, fiddles like crazy with his tricot, which, I believe, also belongs to Nestlé, which serves us its candy-bar jingles today, like every day, at our TV pavilion. Edgar G. reaches into his leotard from the top and then tries immediately, through the pants' legs that reach midthigh with no distance to the flesh, like attached rowhouses, to grab and relieve himself, even though barehandedly. His brush, dipped in all the way to the handle, will not keep still, it blobs from the inside into the sheath, balking and spitting, in no time will it—so hard, the whitewash can follow in tenths of a second—rip the case apart like a plastic baggie in which you impatiently dig for food. There! It's the one and only way that works, now Edgar tears the steely tricot (dyed in a bright red rust-preventing color) from his body, suspenders down, the attached pantie part right behind, it can't be fast enough for the man, he throws his sheath as if it were a burning Loch *Nessus* robe as far away from him as possible. His hands—a praying man who has managed to establish a relation to himself, for he once again feels like a god—are clenched, one around the shaft of the penis, the other around the testicles; a dead insect, already prepared for transport by the faunal forest rangers, he ejects himself, jerking and jolting, a hesitatingly departing train into the pointed, pesky alpine grass he imbues with himself.

A sticky rug, smelling intensely from rotting innards, spreads under his hands, he reaches into it, burrows in his juice, smears it around in his palms, grabs whole fistfuls of his product, as if for quality inspection, and wipes it in still-untouched slubs of grass, which, however, cannot increase his sentience anymore. A rug of hum(an)mus! How quiet it is here, as in a happy soul that threw off its super-hot swimming trunks! How beautifully secluded it was in that boy's skin of athletic fabric, but what happened to the oversized sweatpants? and how vulnerable is the champ now, this dreamy, taciturn participant, who's been asleep for years in his grave, whose member will not be lost so long as there are Milky Ways and the God Mars who mass-produces them and him. Look how this young man, completely naked down to his clumpy sneakers, this white Savior, spent himself for nature. But nobody wanted to receive it on its tongue, the holy host, which in the meantime solidified into a translucent egg-doughy, teeny thin piecelet of skin. You deal it out, you've got to be able to take it as well. Edgar Gstranz: I call him on my cellphone. If only he had a child's shovel, he would dig himself a hollow—a young hero lying there as if flung from a great height, spread helplessly around his molehilly sex, he kneads his trembling little sac again a bit, pulling out some hair, and as it screams, rocking it gently, offering it to the emptiness all around (hoping someone would cover it with something more protective than hair and thin Lycra). So now let arms and legs get some rest and spare us the rest. Quite matter-of-factly Edgar wipes off the rest of the goo with the palm of his hand and smears it onto the green putrescence of the grass panicles he had squashed with his weight. Breathing heavily after emitting a piercing whistle, he lies there for some time, a human cross of flesh, which will remain quite sensitive to anything touching it. He hasn't been splashed there as a memorial. Is he a landmark for the other dead, who might appear any moment for their topping-out ceremonies? One can hear the rattling of their motors from afar and see the funny little maypoles (from one moment to the next they could transform into enormous jungle giants!), which they, those agile homebuilders of a seemingly infinite time, are dragging in to top off the rustling crests of flesh, the only settlements the dead could ever construct and tear down again. Edgar is spread out there, defenseless, laid out there for anyone to take. And his stubby-tailed flesh worm has also lain down, a little bit curled, calm now on its eiderdown cushion to present itself to the groping hand that wants to get down to it from above, like a jewel on a pillow that's been beaten into foam.

Then the miraculous is suddenly gone, as if driven off by an air current; but they are waiting, barking and pulling on their rip cords, the souls or whatever they are, they revel in hundreds of years. So of course, they have the time to come tomorrow. At the moment nobody pays attention to their doings. Edgar notices only after a few minutes, which he spent spread out on the ground breathing heavily like a runner who had his prototype pulled from under his feet, that the air is clear again, right now no strange figures can be seen. The wind has come up a bit again and, drying off his sweat, puts a soft, hair-caressing film of coldness over Edgar's totally bare skin. Completely without his synthetic costume, just in his original skin, Edgar doesn't feel sufficiently armed. He is thinking about those young men he was always good friends with, mounted on their mountain bikes, show-jumping over improvised boards they placed over mounds of stones and earth, spinning around high up in the air, letting their super-wide knee-length pants flutter in the wind and then breaking one of their legs: Silence in the magic castle of the family, who would actually brand numbers into their sons' left hands so that they would be recognized even in the air. Attention, life is on a roll here and plays a bit of Jerk in the Box! In and out! Off and on! Hip and hop! Those dudes jumping into the light, flashing about on their boards, trying out their spins and twists and rotations a hundred times with laughing, failed landings when the board shoots off from under the soles, with the sun-giddy oblivion of jumping fish (but spawning, birthing is always up to the others, right?), of sliding and gliding and caprioling, why should they ever become conscious of their own or anyone else's condition?

Edgar's skins don't crackle, they are still too freshly shed. He wiggles himself back into them, rolling his hips and sack-hopping; the elastic sticks to the sweaty body, it doesn't want to slip. Try putting on a wet bathing suit! His cock gets a rather loveless treatment, Edgar stuffs it in as into a plastic bag, then pulls the suspenders up his torso, wiggles his hips slalom-stylishly, pulls the unitard still higher, and slips his arms in. His face is red all over, but he doesn't dare to look if someone saw him and where his outer trousers are. Then he shakes out his legs, and his boyish face below the hair clicks back into its framed cool. Finally, he picks up his sporting board. Pro forma a few gymnastic movements, for potential passers-by, so it looks as if he were just warming up a bit. Yes, Edgar is back again, he has his comeback, in front of an elegant backdrop of rock, stone, and ice on the stems of our glances, which we nailed to the water ourselves and froze, so we won't notice the time passed in the meantime. Now someone (a hand?) rips those stems out of the rock again so that those coming after us can regain a foothold without tearing their hands on us. All those faces that will follow us, all their thoughts, fired back in flight like balls that jump at us spitting with rage and bursting close to our face. They have been fried in sizzling human fat, those hand grenades of future faces, who will want to wander here, innocents, consenting rescuables. Their killing hasn't been cleared yet because our quota has already been met. But we will appeal.

A slight pain in Edgar's ankle moves up through his spine, the man has no idea where he could have hurt himself. He still doesn't quite know where he is, remembering vaguely having been in a totally different place not so long ago, which he doesn't recall having seen before either, even though he has known these mountains since childhood. Once, back then (?), they were even here with the entire alpine team, the snow conditions are always good up there. Edgar had just let his penis run through his fingers like a rope, which never held a wanderer, since on the other end there is never anybody who would at least wait until it is properly fastened. Alright, now Edgar descends into the world. We, however, would rather ascend, we are quickly approaching the rim of the full bushel that extinguished our glow before it could show us the way through the night. And that light was our very essence, which we miss now that we need it most.

Edgar doesn't even have to climb any higher, he can climb in with us right here. He doesn't go to the highest mountain station, it's pretty late already. He steps on his board that is to bring broken records back to him even before he actually broke them. Before that he blew his nose vigorously into a colorful kerchief out of the fanny pack (which he had also torn off his body earlier) and took a sip out of the hip flask, an isometric, isotropic beverage, Isostar Nirostra, it flushes a person without dissolving their insides, I think this is exactly the desired effect. But Edgar takes only one sip. Away with this charitable means of forgetting, let's hit the slope! In colorful pictures fate is acted out, sometimes fate wears a peaked red cap to cover up the burnt ears: This young man escaped the oven at the last moment, as we can see, and now he elevates himself to Highest Judge as to which air duct shall propel us along with lightning speed, us, the young, we are the fastest, because first of all we are a thought, but it is this first thought that counts! In sinking, the fabulous fabric presses itself onto our body again, the tongue is sucked into the throat, something, probably the speed itself, deforms our face, we tumble, we fall, hey, that silver bikini with the matching little jacket is totally stunning and that airy workout dress with the striped top even more so, all we need now are the right moves for it! So let's put on our arms and ears and then carefully together behind us! Jump! Dive into the deep, which has been conveniently prepared for us, everything water, guaranteed, meters deep; and what will happen to the Unsavable, the Unchangeable, the Eternal ones we are going to find there? We could wait till we are blue all over for their mercy to save us because we did not give it the opportunity of a prior ministerial examination. Oh, we forgot our state-approved lifeguard badge back home. Well, then we just have to let the herd go without us; for a long time their patient backs shine beyond the ramp. At night one can see for miles the red-rimmed sky whereunder the inhabitants of our village observe those of another.

Edgar hobbles into his track, but on his board, he will finally stand still. No reporter picks up the mike, a pity, really, no? The situation gets much easier for Edgar as soon as he steps on his board. He still has to push a bit at the start, quasi-running beside himself spurring himself on, topping it off with a few chunks of energy from the dextrose box, stop, here are still one or two clumps of grass to slow you down, but they are quickly cleared, he already picks up speed, quite a guy!, the mountain still keeps nudging him. Stay a little longer, yes, you too, bad swimmer, please, stay! I would like to introduce the following persons to you, who after fifty years are luckily back on their feet again: because they only swim where they can also stand. They only kill the seriously ill or those who are almost dead already anyway. And afterward they kill everything else. I am not making a statement about them, the prophets of the Third Reich, but about that which is ON THEM: their clothes, their jeans and jackets. And if you ask them about those, they erroneously assume you asked them about themselves and their answer is a yes. (How says the Eternal Judge? The executed action had to have been the outflow of pure compassion with the patient! Because the salvation by needle must happen absolutely painlessly, tell that to Herr Gott, he'll get the hiccups from laughing, he used a funnel to speed up the breezing of life into man, but we haven't yet come up with THAT funnel.) So then Edgar races toward his origin, there is a hole, down there in the cavern in the rock above the river, where the bats live, that is where it drives him. Because he wants to get to the bottom of himself at all costs, even at the risk of hitting rock bottom, and then get to the bottom of everything else.

Oh, dwelling, yes, dwelling! The body doesn't waste a thought on it because it always has it with him. Still, some distance has to be covered now and then, down into the air bath, where the swollen costume of nerves that's been tickled and splashed on is to be blow-dried. But that's it. Done. Finished. More and more people are forming in the air, Edgar almost brushes against them as he races by. From the windows in the ground shy beings who made their exit years ago (hardly noticed by the public) are looking up to Edgar, who hits and runs over the bumps in the ground even before he takes a good look at them, flattening them as best as possible so that they won't throw him off course, but soon he is moving too fast to be able to deliberately effect his slide. Such pleasure, the cooling of the head wind. Edgar is no longer in some farm league, he is a league of his own, no longer some farm jock, he is a shock jock all on his own. He got placed in the air all by himself, so now he belongs to the assets again; his face is open, turned toward the bluish distance, but he will not lose the ground under his feet. However, there are faces who wake up under Edgar's foot-breadth, more and more faces growing out of the grass like self-inflating moldy mushrooms, and already Edgar moves over their angels' seeds. Just now he ripped up a woman's right cheek and it changes under the pressure into a man's. A branch of the past, which could have also taken a different course, pops out, terrified, the face retreats into the ground. Edgar probably could not quite see what it was, maybe it was just a leaf. But already another face emerges right there, its forehead wrinkled with pain, as if someone had pulled it out of the ground by the hair to reunite it with the limbs. So grow together if you think you belong together, but let me sleep! The eyelids of the face emerging on the ground are lifted a bit by the traction, and a glance appears on the threshold; that look is a crushing blow, all of us had relatives once whom we simply lost again. Edgar knows: Once he looks this face—which still seems to consist of half of foliage and grass—in the eye, he will have been brought back to where he came from. Like angels, all sorts of creatures under the ground get resurrected from the condition they were led to, which they apparently could not get used to. Limbs come to limbs to unite. None of the faces wants to remain in the ground, but they did not imagine this lift-off being so painful, those faces are distorted beyond all recognition! Wouldn't recognize your own brother and he is also here! He, too, a piece of the red-colored sky that stretches for miles and miles. Endless the mass of people wanting to leave the ground. And all of them apparently in extreme pain.

A sort of tension spreads like wildfire under Edgar's feet, time just fizzes through its riverbed that flows toward the future, but it does not extinguish the human fire; and now, spurred on by a vague horror, Edgar's feet are getting faster and faster. They glide along like a water-skier wanting to escape the boat that pulls and keeps him above the water; if he let go of the rope, he'd sink without fail, departed and separated from his own sporting device. Thus Edgar holds himself up straight and even tries to increase his speed by twisting and turning his body. Down there already is the brook, you could catch its white rush beyond the hill if there weren't so much wind music in the ear that it cannot bring itself to be still. A white hand glides out of the ground as if by chance, trying to grab the board, it could be turned into a small sound box, they are probably thinking down there, wherefrom—how comforting!—their resurrection could be announced to them, and interminably at that, every hour until the dead fall to their knees pleading for quiet. But the angels have already been dispatched to Ikea to look for a new loudspeaker they also have learned to fear in advance as The Place. After all, they must do whatever HE says, and what HE says, is the Invisible, the Name, the Son: He walks, as he was told to, with the dead, through this door. And Edgar is the door, he is outside time, he just doesn't know it. Desperately, the Disobedient reach for the board, but God raps them on the knuckles. If they succeeded in veering the board just a bit, Edgar would be thrown off his course and the universe would stand still. But for today he manages to get away, the route was not long enough. Luckily, he did not get any higher before. Those below were not able to adjust and communicate to each other that he got started, Timekeeping did not plant a sensor in the ground. The very last face just before the last curve of the forest road, which has to be crossed by foot, does not even manage to show up, to emerge from the freshly sealed surface. Only the mouth can be seen, a greenish bubble, it could also be just a plantain leaf, foliage, offered with a tired gesture. Yes, the white gravelly road is a danger, because Edgar has to jump off its bank where the clump of grass hangs over, shoulder his board, and walk across in order to finish the last leg of his course to the brook more leisurely. No one could jump on a board over this embankment, about two meters high, which was formed when the street was blasted out of the mother rock, they would break their neck. But where does this grassy trap really come from, those pony bangs, might they hide a couple of thoughts? Could it be a forehead, may we use this image? The beings that suffered want to be put in order again, and therefore one is descending now, an Edgar Gstranz, a pleasure, whose hair is blowing in the wind, some hairbrain, he.

There comes Edgar, nothing but a faint noise for those furthest departed, but nonetheless a jolly voice in the chorus of darkness, through which they snake their way more cheerfully now. But what's that sitting there up ahead, frightening Edgar and all of us? Might even get caught by his zipping soles? Would the wanderers from before be taking a break in their wandering so close to the sheltering inn? What are they eating there that they don't want to take home? Three middle-aged men, whose voices don't yet seem to have risen, for there is absolute silence among them. The men, as Edgar, racing closer, can see, have formed a group, stretched out as a kind of foothills to the homeyness of the inn; and they are sharing something. Ham and bread? Sausage or cheese? The young athlete, so tightly stuffed into his, let's say, somewhat overstretched latex, might he also become nourishment? Is this what he has been destined for? That he should now kindly retrieve himself? A stick whereon his human flesh roasts? Human plastic, a tough paste, poured as filling into the emptiness of the created, which it could never fill up, no matter how busily the fire raged through the corridors of the high-capacity furnaces (the one with three and the one with the eight muffles), sniffing around in all corners for anyone it left out; the fire flows, it almost turns into water again, its old archenemy. If we managed to freeze it, time would also stand still; but what would those poor specters do then, don't they always want to step quietly inside us? Twisting fingers are already reaching for Edgar, windblown facial features are already looking for him in the blaze, one can hardly see the street, because at the last moment the dead themselves had blown into the fire.

Here the forest is already thinning a bit. Broadleaf trees with their lighter greens mingle with the spruce. Edgar approaches almost in flight, overcoming his fear, perhaps also to dispel it, he throws a cursory greeting to those serious men, like a handful of seeds that will quickly ask for more light so that they could finally turn into something. Somewhat clumsily he jumps off his coaster, our young man, but then he bends quite elegantly down to his board, and catching it in the nick of time, just before the step down to the street, he lifts it up, jumps up high in a powerful motion that lets him stand for a moment as if drenched in light, something invisible brought into view, and lands with a loud scrunch, almost still on the gravel bank, actually right next to it, where he will be served to the guests right away. He hugs his serving tray to himself, in a moment he will slip it under him again for the last stretch. It almost isn't worth it, but since he feels so good just now. . . . For a moment the sun plays on that particular bulge with which his penis warms up for him once more under the latex, like on a sharp ridge of rock. His arms thrown high up in the air like one and a half wings (one is wrapped around the board), Edgar is in pure bliss. So, ever the athlete, he is to cross the street in one bouncing leap when the men rise with an apologizing gesture, as if they wanted to invite Edgar into a messy room and would actually prefer, for his sake rather than for theirs, to hold him in check at the door, with his back to the room. Edgar's leg muscles work like pistons, jamming into the gravel and instantly pushing off again. The young man muscles across the street, which, after all, is only two and a half meters wide, maybe three, standardized for just one large lumber-carrying vehicle, he runs and runs to cross it but does not get ahead. He tries to pick up momentum over and over again, sweat splashes like rain from his face, he pants, his semen stops in progress, and looks, why the organs in this boiling pot are spinning around like crazy, high time to turn down the gas.

The group of wanderers stands still. Cardboard comrades just leaning against nature and quite conspicuously not a part of it. They can't be made out clearly, even though Edgar is very close to them now. And it's not even that dark yet! As if someone had tried to erase their features but could not wipe them all off. Much can be seen only in outlines, but these are the men from before, no doubt, Edgar identifies them by their clothes. They have disposable faces, easy to pass. But how is it that Edgar can't keep rolling past the water one of the men sprays on him, no shame whatsoever? As if he blasted the sidewalk in front of a restaurant with a hose, with a smile on his face! Something cold, which should be steaming hot, inscribes the gravel road with a dark meander pattern, cold liquid spraying out of one of the wanderers, who even swings his sprinkler around cockily to create a prettier pattern. To his left, his fellow wanderers remain in what seems to be darkness. The rivulet flows out of only one of them, how could that much ever get into him? It seems to Edgar that the man would have to be completely emptied by now, and still his water, passed, keeps settling the dust. That fellow is pouring himself out completely. And his features are fading more and more, the more he fluidifies himself; it seems he wants to separate himself from his life, this wanderer, by separating from his urinary fluid and, at the same time, also from his seeds; we, in the meantime, are getting older by several years while only seconds pass for this man. The other two hikers seem to follow this spectacle of nature with great interest. At the same time, however, they are also separating themselves from their traveling companion, with whom they were associated. Didn't I once see that face pictured in the newspaper, in the gossip column, isn't he one of the sons of God? And his colleagues, their feet pawing in that spring, are mixing the juice with the dust into a mush wherefrom new humans could spring, if only our cameras had flashlights to ignite the dust with a spark. The flow finally stops, forming lumps like spoiled milk, and its originator has lost all his features. Far be it from me to malign birthing just because it is reserved for women, but here, right here, a man accomplished something extraordinary, something wonderful! He shoved a messy mass that could displace us all into the alpine oven! What happened? An alpine accident, even though the mountains had been specifically removed from here, where they were before, and set up again over there? The paying guest and plastic consumer has rights! What kind of people are these? Darkly they stand together. Their eyes wander around, and now they grab Edgar by the neck.

His muscles go limp, as if he, too, had abruptly emptied himself. As if someone had opened him midair, midjump, at ether's summit, to figure out whether something could also be sown into him. But unfortunately, it had already gotten much too tight under the athletic clothing. The young man came down to us, and earlier, in the meadow, he even brought forth himself! Edgar's gleaming birthing shaft had been subject to other, invisible powers as he poured himself out onto the earth. Those men, by the way, seemed to have enjoyed it, even though they wouldn't really want a repeat. They want Edgar himself! There they have one who died but rose again, one whose passing was thoroughly upset by his second coming, and they won't let go of him again so quickly. And Edgar suddenly knows: He is an intermediate depository for something still to come in order to import death into the world once and for all. A dangerous product, for which any hazardous waste storage facility would be too small. No special sports arena has been provided for it in the municipal budget. Edgar can't even take in any more air for breathing, he is running out of it, desperately, with both hands he tears open the aerosphere around, opens his mouth in tortured gasps for breath. The human tableau before him is coming apart at the seams—there an arm is stuck, hardly noticeable, too low to the torso, and there, that botched body's legs don't match, and doesn't the third one have two left legs? Even with two different shoes! From what pile did he pick those? Where would articles of daily use be thrown out together with their owners? Nonetheless, this human threesome, triad, trinity (albeit not in unity, I think) still seems to want to remain one entity, one moldy, gigantic mushroom formation that flies up when stepped on, I said it already: a giant puffball, a puffball colony! A rancid bio-being, so let's take a look at it, let's engage our ocular express service! What did Edgar get into? Like a torrent from a much bigger hose, Edgar pelts smack into those half-finished folks and finishes them off. They splatter in all directions. Edgar's killer board is nailed to the soles of his feet, and maybe he was called upon specifically to perform this act of salvation, who knows. We, his biggest fans, cheer him on from the wayside, a heck of a guy, the way he schussed down earlier! The men who once were fathers marvel at someone who became the way they once were, unfortunately he is not their son. As for us, there is nothing left to be desired. We can actually swim a few rounds on it later this evening in the indoor pool of the neighboring village.

But each of the elderly hikers brought his board as well, a matter of honor! They, however, misused the boards for their own purposes, those ungestalts. It often requires a brutal wedge to subdue nature, and pick and rope are not always at hand—but anyone can carry a picnic board. What are those faded faces eating, one doesn't even have a mouth anymore? Yes, and anyway: How easily they sit in their carcasses with their limbs not even fitting together. Old farts! They eat with their own fingers and—oh no, this can't be, they are eating their own fingers! Yes, exactly, now that they can finally open themselves up to us, it's clearly visible: They are cutting into themselves with their jackknives, severing their own fingers and ingesting them. They take their own flesh back again and, for protection, all the way inside by devouring it. We did not deviate from the truth here. It isn't mere speculation: Those wanderers consume themselves! They gorge as if they had to drive themselves away from themselves, getting themselves into safety. After all, they know what they are capable of. Drinking goes along with it, the goblet is placed a bit to the side, and it has a monogram carved into it, the name of its former owner, who bequeathed it, well, not personally and specifically, but still, to the University of Graz, so that the students can learn from him to swallow the bitter medicine. The names of the deceased lineage had once been engraved in Gothic letters, worn smooth now, by countless hands, so that the member that starts with J, alpha and omega in one, can find his head in case he needs one again. Jesus was also the fruit of a human, don't we forget it, he looked like and had the name of a native-born, although he was an only, not naturally begotten child. His father is credited with having some mercy, but personally I don't believe it.

Thus, this skull is meant to serve as a pedagogical tool at a university, where the putting on of people and the putting in of seeds into souls is being practiced as well as how to get the most out of free health insurance. At the medical school of the University of Graz this engraved skull is an absolute must as a teaching tool. Whenever this institution is offered less meaningful objects, it refuses them right off. Youth must be allowed to research. Some people will also, if no ventral dislocation has occurred, get screwed or blocked from behind, where the man transforms into the woman. Afterward, after problem-free general anesthesia, disposed of. Thus, the young medical apprentices strut through the arena, the amphitheater, necks charmingly turned and twisted. Their focus in winter is skiing, and popular aquatic sports in summer, for everything that lives can be recognized as long as it (still) moves. Team spirit clings to them, but—hold it!—I see now it's not team spirit that clings to them. What clung here were jackets with three white stripes on each side and sleeve, they also come with cool hoods, why are you giving me that look, what can I do about it? The curious eyes of those young people, who are supposed to gather from this skull what's not written on it in black and white, have now, somewhat furtively, overestimated, at least overstretched themselves on the deceased who once owned this skull, that's okay, they are still learning, after all. Where did the tender, elongated hind legs, the longing hindsights of history, keep themselves hidden all this time? Nowhere. Everything's gone. For no one can aspire not to have done what has happened already. Nevertheless, the good, the better, and the bestial ones put more teeth into it, one today, another tomorrow. So that they can bite better and faster and drive the course of time exactly in our direction and right in front of our muzzle flashes. We don't care.

One of the wayfarers has already come a big step closer to Edgar, he once was a furrier and now he wants to hold out to the young man his bloody skin, once warm and cuddly, now a pack of wraps (it is the family-size package, for he once had a family, too). Okay, now we've got one at least! One of those types on a revenge expedition, which the victims of the pesticide are still undertaking, what's the use? Stay with us, for evening wants to fall, momentarily the players, all refreshed, will run onto the field. Edgar lifts his free arm to protect his face (clicking behind him are sports magazines, and those are now inserted into the human weapon!), the other arm still clings to his racing board. A gust of wind comes up as well and presses what's left of the three strangers' faces to the respective skull, which looks like scaffolding underneath and brings out the strangeness of those strangers even more. An oar reaches for Edgar to push him out into the river, in the distance a dog barks from deep down in his throat, the ferry pushes hard to get off in time, for soul and flesh are produced separately and put together only in the final assembly process, and that process leads to nothing but ice-cold, bottomless water. The ferry whizzes toward the young man, one can already hear the prow cutting razor-sharp into the waves, and there, at the very last moment, Edgar, rowing and reeling, gets himself out of this, let's hope, final invisible embrace, as well. From the boat, the greedy white hands of a few young fellows, it's only what's left of them anyway, were fishing for Edgar with their finger-boathooks; their once bushy heads are shaved now, and the shoulders sticking steeply out of their bed of muscles have been denuded. Those guys come from 174 Untere Donaustrasse in Vienna's second district; we welcome them with a flourish. For they don't lie on a stretcher in a hospital, nor do they (but you may still guess a third time) hang on the wall in a church. They are completely unknown to us but, nevertheless, with a twitch around their empty eye sockets, as if something were still in there, a mien that wants to cry, those are still almost kids, after all, they point something against Edgar, some sort of hunting knife. Well, so what, this young skateboarder is a winner, the audience loves him! Gorging the space in voracious strides he quickly gains ground, meter by meter, the meteorologists are flabbergasted how fast that happens with him. He quasi-wheels himself, a tracing wheel with which the patterns are drawn on the inscrutable human design (how flat we have actually been made . . . !) of skin, bones, and hair, and he whizzes closely past us on his rolling board, off and away into the distance. Those good people scared Edgar, but now their diligent eyes have already let go of him and he quickly picks up speed, even though he will be back in his hotel room in no time anyway. However, his tacking seam has been torn open by an experienced tailor's hand, and soon, I fear, the tacking will be continued some other place by someone else and no loving eye will remote control the rolling wheel. Oh Edgar, you won't get much farther today! Here's already the good path along which the hotel guests are heading for dinner. You better get off or the older folks among us might complain that they collided not so gently with One who Came and Ran them over. The sun is setting in the west. My God, how long that's taking again today. In the restless beam of its last glow Edgar can't be seen clearly anymore. Slowly, but sorely, famished, that is, we arrive at the dining room. Edgar, yes and no, has also arrived, but then again he hasn't. His sex stands again, in pain. He looks around for where he could hide—the young fellow is currently staying near Mürzzuschlag, where he is extremely busy with sports, while his body knows how to keep busy just with itself. Right now, for example, it knocks from inside against the latex, whereunder its flag of joy over a sold-out event has adorned itself with raw flesh.

12

The mortal remains of thorn birds are thrown on the tables to the scraping of metal skewers that spread their legs apart and the giggling of cucumber and tomato slices and salad leaves with droplets of water coyly mirroring human eyes. Today's menu features home-raised fried chicken. How happily they used to shuffle about outside. Karin Frenzel is no chapel where people of lower or weaker standing would like to convene. The fun-loving make extra sure to stay clear of that woman, who always comes by herself or with her mother. She sits down quietly, always in the same place, the variety of the meal in front of her. Karin Frenzel is a female éminence grise, a woman widowed for a while who accepts orders from the pope, the archbishop, and her mother, but also from others if they act determinedly. Actually, she shimmers quite calmly and lovingly, not what one would assume reading this. A hot-air balloon standing in the sky, life's simply not blowing under her dirndl skirt anymore, nothing to be done about that. Or, to put it another way: Not everyone makes noise when driving. Today a dress for a change, Karin? Something her mother urged her to put on, you are always wearing pants! Don't you have anything else to wear? Now I don't want to say that it was the walls that swallowed every single sound coming from Karin's shawm, most of the time only dead animals or glasses are put to one's lips, but today something has changed. Karin notices it as soon as she enters the restaurant. It sounds as if the walls were throwing back Karin's voice with a tiny delay, whatever she says to her mother, to whose right she sitteth (left from where I am). The sounds separate from Karin like everything else that comes into contact with her, but they don't run away right away as usual, they sit down in the dining room with a life of their own. Doesn't anyone notice but her? The sound as when a lighter or match is held to the outpouring gas, whoosh! The bunches of fir twigs, figureheads of the *Heuriger* taverns aflush with the young wines this time of year, are afire this time, this one time only. A thin trickle of gasoline has found its way to a fuse, the walls inside are still pure white and decorated with skulls; men and women are singing their old song, every song deals with the sorrow of the respective other, the priest raises his arm, the lace-trimmed robe slips back and reveals the blanched flesh; the stiff brocade chasuble bobs along with the movement a bit, but whom or what does the man raise now? Not what we know, and we still break out into a hymn of praise about how stretch- and kneadable the new plasticine turned out to be, the stuff humans are made of. For decades we have been decimated by traffic, and still so many are left, what for do we need the new nuclear power plant next door? (Dixit Heidi, pixit Elfi.) Such slithy and snuggly stuff can get to God much more cheaply by car. And it also acquired a new, blonde faith, the faith in itself: God is also quite curious about it, since he does not yet know it. Today you are hearing a short version of Christinanity on the radio, but Karin Frenzel hears something else, she suddenly hears—Boom!, under the billowing brocade crème puff that is her skirt, the rustling of kindling wood that catches fire and goes up in flames. This woman doesn't think twice jumping up in the middle of dinner. Astonished looks meet her fleetingly but then run embarrassed out of the room. Her mother instantly pulls her back with a particular and often applied look, really now! What's going on?, impatience, a flame blast, sit down, what's wrong with you? Karin Frenzel's darling nature gains the lower hand, soft, small, awkward, it beats out the tiny flames underneath the dirndl skirt and screams because it burned itself a little; but the wind thus fanned up is already blowing out of its fold and the skirt's hem bobs imperceptibly. Karin sits down again. The cake cover lowers itself politely over her delicacies turned rancid. No bloody threads of gunk crying anywhere anymore. That Frau Frenzel is beyond the storied monthly menses and therefore beyond history. The world is even and empty. Motherhood sadly is no longer possible. What a change once history, instead of pulling us on its raft, which can be rented, into its stream, suddenly breaks through the riverbank, the wall of time, a chisel that pries us open in a different spot than the designated one, and no child's head appears with little wings pasted on it. Why doesn't this woman finally call on Christ, so that all those tiny tykes can peek more confidently out of their bunting?, no, our nature enters, sounding hollow and tearing the flesh off the bones of us mothers of history and daughters of natural history, like of all those chickens that are to be eaten right here right now. As usual Karin sits at the first table to the right (as seen from the door), almost under the crucifix, her mother has spread her out next to herself together with the motherly needles. Asbestos fiber. Very thin. Very mean. And in the event of Karin spitting fire, the mother will steam it out on the spot. And now the daughter burns all over! The ladies recommend quite a few things to each other, but it is not recommendable to befriend them, as the hotel guests already know. Those two women always reveal themselves to the fellow guests on the spot and in toto, even if it's just a matter of selecting a good bottle of sweet wine for some fun on a Saturday. Other preferences? Green or mixed salad as devotional object, served sufficiently devoutly? Everything fresh, a lot from the Wirtin's garden or as good as. The mother exudes brutal breeding warmth whatever she does, and now she has set her daughter on fire by mistake, who else could it have been?

All that has been denied the poor young hen on the plate. Even before she was ready to breed, she was already ready to be breaded and fried, too bad for her, lucky for us. And for Karin, the word of the mother is the Law, no matter how often she produces a few soft, soothing sounds to calm her mother, hoping to be rocked like a doll. The mother always flies off the handle right away, she knows full well that her daughter is stiff as a stick; the world would split if anyone were to sniff at the style of her clothes. The décor isn't much better either. As if on command the guests look through their empty glasses at the Authentic, their shiny, shimmering snowy slope, which slowly but surely inclines toward the More, they are embarrassed by Karin's mother, who doesn't hear so well anymore and speaks much too loudly, full plates, empty glasses. Both women are waging a never-tiring battle against each other. Patterns are drawn or burned into Karin Frenzel's base, the torches are lit along the landing strip, Karin's language moves restlessly inside her portable cage where her mother has locked her up. And on this ordinary quad of all places, where the commands of the mother are engraved like words no one wants to know, in a plate, a knife and fork, a cup, an entire colony of bees is preparing for its landing. There is humming all around. Something is different than usual today. Something wants to come; suddenly, the atomaticized drone of the people's conversations seems to have become a separate living entity. Is she the only one feeling so hot? Karin Frenzel pulls the pretty brocade neckerchief out of her blouse and throws it beside her onto the bench. A hot flash? The mother briefly talks about it as if everyone except her daughter is going to die from it. The mother suggests opening the window and closing the body or opening the body and closing the window, I don't know which. This daughter is a planned child, therefore I will try to approach her most soft-footedly or not at all. Karin sheepishly studies, or rather pretends to look at, the menu, which lies there so that conversation topics can be sown among people. So that they can be spared the cruelties of nature since they do incessantly ingest natural products. Nature would not want to assault her own! The small, swiftly revolving doors of the mouth (today the Mother is the goal—I mean the doorkeeper) let those swift chunks of meat incessantly inside, one or the other gets pulled out again by the mother and put at the edge of the plate, well, that chicken croaked from old age, the mother berates the poor animal and everyone who worked so hard raising it. There is a religion that presents your own life to you as being against you and drops its horribly mutilated God on top of it to boot, a twig of parsley or a candied fruit for decoration on the quivering pudding of our joints once we finally acquire the proper appearance, which, glistening and seething, an unnatural substance, performs its chopped sit spin on a piece of food. It looks good but wouldn't have been necessary.

Nothing but food marks the time of aging. Outside, through the window, dusk has set in, glass clinks. With a daring step followed by a jump something gets into the room, noticed only by Karin, the one most out of it. She is the only one who knows: Only looking can generate a sight, and thus, her hair disheveled, she stares at the wall, from where a herd storms out, leaving their heads behind on the go. Hanging around are the tourists who, this early in the evening, are already showing all possible stages of imbibition; if they get wrung out, they surrender without a fight, those negatives of soles, which have been shaken out or washed down a million times already, it's something that seeps in over and over again while walking, some kind of water, which, poured into the tub, transforms into acid, wherein the bodies keep fantasizing for a while and then dissolve into pure words, no more riddles. Because television has solved them a thousand times already. Laughter springs up to the chamois horns and the daily blessings of the sacred buck. There, the surge of something new, the flames rage faster and faster—they, too, want nothing but consume—up to the crowned heads, those formations of former life, which we can perceive only as objects now. But isn't life still locked up in them? Something scuttles like ants under the skulls' bony bowls. And why can only Frau Frenzel, Karin, hear it? But this evening a light draft keeps blowing through the dining hall, sweeping scraps into laps, the compote into the compost, even the dietary meal especially prepared for those with gastric troubles and bilious complaints, a specialty of the house, clinks in the bowls as if frozen inside a strictly forbidden icing of fat. As powerful as nature is, something is still not quite right with her, forgeries are also quite likely, and I don't mean the infamous blood chocolate, Europe's *Mutterkuchen,* the mother-cake, known to you as the afterbirth, or the mealy bug yogurt, no, nature always covers up everything with herself anyway. But we can see now what she's got buried under herself: an umbrella of sorts, a cap of cold lamellae shielding her from below, because she, too, wears a cool skirt, just like our Karin. Did someone leave a window open, which causes such a strong draft? Well, it's not really a draft that's blowing here, inciting the flames to ever new exercises as part of its fitness training. The Crucified fidgets restlessly on his strength-training device, but not because he wants to get down, he rather requests to be admired and worshipped. After all, this home trainer sucked all of us, just the way we are here, out of women's naked, shaved wombs and threw us into the Great Austrian Church, where He set them on fire, but afterward He closed the curtain so that our spirits won't be consumed completely, just a small part of us. Then the God sits down with us for a little talk and takes the rest away from us, too. He makes us hand ourselves over voluntarily. He is robbing us, hello! But we don't notice, because he performs the miracle of nature every day right before our eyes, for the starting time please refer to the enclosed folded hands.

There is the sound of salt pretzel sticks crackling out of their packages and the image on the TV screen. Karin flinches, does she have hearing problems? The crackling of the cellophane, the slipping of the pretzel sticks, the impetuousness of the reporter, who brought along a colleague because the news was too horrible for one alone: It sounds as if tree trunks were driven through a drainpipe, rubbing against each other, pushing, shoving each other, just to get more quickly into the flow of traffic and catch the green light. Then they will crush anything in their waterway. For Karin, all of this sneaks much too loudly into her ears, which she now covers with the Lenten veil of her hands. The mother throws questions at the neighboring table that will be answered by the newscaster right away. Can't talk to her magnificence, the daughter today. She's afraid even of her own plate, and there are actually black spots on it, yes, yes, those are seared mushrooms and scorched veggies, folks eat and eat, they grab such comfort offerings the same way they reach for their partner and hug them. They don't feel that they are ice-cold underneath, as all the flattering could not light their fire. So now, this plate must be degreased, the mother works hard on it, all that's missing is her putting on her work clothes. Resolutely she presses the bread with her fork against the plate, so that it can also graze in the grease before she polishes it off herself. With a conspiratory twinkle the TV opens its Cyclops eye to a live presentation. Dead Africans take a running jump, dead Austrians make off over the guardrails. A flush of light jumps out, a breath sets in. All heads raise themselves to this mountain of information, which is thrown into the well of every spectator and arrives (they are late) with a splash. Where are the toothpicks? Calm, quiet well, steep fortress, sleep, sleep in the snow, the mob with the dogs has already arrived, it's been tried many times to wean them from human flesh but they just love eating it too much. And frequent consumption has got them on the right track with fresh nourishment flowing through over and over again, always fresh supplies. The cheap-eaters undertake a long trek to show their participation certificates that confirm with a sigh the demise of an entire fauna and flora, so now it is they who can move in instead. Open your mouth and close your eyes.

Karin Frenzel rises as if she were about to give a witty speech, but all she wants is to show her silence, which would not be noticed otherwise; the woman even puts a finger to her lips. Right then a call from the outside. He or she or whatever ejected it caused a rip, as if some huge fabric had been torn apart, but how should one make those diners understand that they would have to listen to a non-noise. For this call amid the noise was actually the opposite of a sound, it was something very quiet. Something wants to get in here! And Karin has the feeling she must smooth the way for it (our blessed Bavarian mystic Resi from Konnersreuth already believed this kind of thing, she ate only holy hosts. But it was the daily communion with the pork roast that finished her off), maybe bring this entity to the regulars' table, where the family register is kept safe. Incidentally, I am also one of those whom people would rather not hear from. The hunters are shooting in, thus signing in before the bullets come floating along on their wings. But who'd want to follow someone who is beside herself? Walking, apart from the others, by her own side? What does this woman want who now gets dragged by her mother back onto the cushy tushy? Karin F. doesn't seem to like it on this much rapped mare's bum that had been kicked in the flanks, whipped and shodded with reverse backward-pointing horseshoes by an amateur handyman, for she jumps up again right away, pointing to something only she can see; sheepishly the guests return to their food and libation, could it be that the old goat is already drunk? But she hardly drinks! The old hag next to her is getting excited, giggling louder and louder, her laughter drowning out the wondrously dead silence, which for one moment walked into the hall looking around. No problem. The (bad) weather confession is next. Frau Karin just stands there, still like a well, letting little loud stones drop into her, she is allowed to do that. The conversations start burbling again, and every wave, moved by a bit of language, gets to roll, slowly at first, hardly a ripple in the black pond of silence, toward the talkers, but then the wave emerges a little out of the smoothness, spits out some foam, ok, the teeth are clean, now the beast rises, its tough tendons we put back on the shore, and then the betting on the weather forecast is already on, today was unusually warm and sunny for this time of year and might well have to quit due to a technical KO in the massive chunks of water. Now a tremor in the sky, a window flies open, nature wants to talk to us. Can't do it on the phone. For a moment a hand can be seen on the windowsill, but no friend who gave it to someone, no pane of glass nature didn't shatter already, no target she hadn't shot at already. The beast comes in, strangely twisted. This giant black shaggy dog, who had been acquired for the guests' entertainment, a friendly beast, his size alone generates comfort. According to the following specifications of various guests, condiment caddies of pickled plastic get passed around. A lady had just produced an exalted nature theater with her spaniel, who now gets a piece of meat from the plate held out to him. Enthusiastic cheers, one to nothing from the small old-ladies-clique in close vicinity, as the beast smells the roast and comes out from under the table. Now one animal's eye stares into the other's, the watchdog has a bad limp, one side seems to be paralyzed and his eyes have a dull veil, as if his lower back were broken, he hobbles toward his seasonal friend, who holes up under the table again with a howl. The dog of the house's hind legs fold, and he falls on his side in the middle of the dining room. Agitated calls for the proprietress, running, concern, in beautiful frailness the old ladies sink into each other, comfort their own two-legged and four-legged loved ones, talk to the patient's despondency, let carbonate pearls roll toward its lips, but it bears its teeth and gnarls from deep down in its throat, and all this under the table to boot. Its fright seems to want to change into whining any moment, as the growl twists itself into a bright, high howl. In the meantime, a crowd of animal lovers has formed around the dark pond of the black dog in the middle, there are still calls for the mistress of the house, who seems to be busy somewhere else. The gorgeous beast lies panting on its side, his dully veiled eyes directed into the Nowhere. Isn't there a hairless spot in his side? Did anyone beat this dog? But he doesn't seem to be hurt. Karin Frenzel gropes for the back of her chair, a woman ready to leave making sure she didn't leave her purse hanging there. But what she can feel is oddly soft, Karin's fingers have to get used to it that her fumbling with a chair hit something not made of wood. She turns around: There is hair growing on her chair! One spot, a tuft of short, soft black hair growing on the mass-produced, peasant-style clobbered-together country inn chair. Karin's hand retreats immediately into the seclusion of the sleeve only to come back out right away again to check once more. Hair like curtain decorations, maybe everything here was made of hair once and got long since abraded and bald everywhere except for this one spot on the back of the chair. You can't really see (Karin bent down to this black spot) whether an animal or a person had left behind this private part—after all it's just a small, shapeless spot—definitely a tuft of hair. As to its nature, this soft spot that once grew on something living is essentially ambivalent, it doesn't point to a specific life, it could have belonged to any kind of life. And Karin applies herself to this mini-wig as something that had nothing to do with life. She is absolutely certain that this is only a hairy piece of wood, and there is no danger coming from that. And right she is, it turns out that the reason for this unexpected cuddliness is that apparently human or animal hair got stuck to the gooey dirt on the back of the chair, which formed a sort of pelt on this piece of furniture. Or isn't it? Could it be something else? Could it be a part of the soft belly of a beast that rose right among the diners, offering his sex that indicates whether the animal is alive and well? Or at least a signpost, this way to nature, that way to humans who are completely denaturized, thus to the inanimate, you decide! But consider: You will have to get used to its silence.

The inn's dog is surrounded by a dense cluster of people. And now they disperse, laughing, as if the dog had performed a stunt, which ends herewith, for the gigantic beast jumps up again, shakes himself inside his fur, you'd almost expect to see drops of water scattering away, but it's dry on the outside. The eyes are also coming back again, they sprout like clover out of the head, life reenters, two windows light up, and the beast hops cheerfully, awkwardly out of the room. Relieved laughter, so, everybody, return to your seats! They might get cold. Absent-mindedly, Karin also sits back down on her dangerous chair and submerges in the mother's amniotic fluid lapping round her to the hum of the thermostat, the fluid is kept warm in a thermos bottle. Something however is left over, a crossover, a thin bridge, which got stuffed into Karen's mouth like a dessert, while all the others have long finished eating. Lots of words all around picturize their owners' imagination; the curtain in front of the event that took place has been torn somewhat in front of the temple where folks are now consuming God, who has received three stars in the dining temples guide, to allow passage to the next restaurant. Sitting there are the diners, who have already degusted everything that's been served to them, and now they must get down to devouring each other. Their fat-ass Michelin guide must have gone apeshit with them. How dare they. . . . First, they order a miracle to happen, God should be handed to them as the main course, neatly sealed in a piece of wafer, and then they turn away from him and eat their own human comrades! I must say, when I addressed Christ by his true Name, I did not mean that, out of fear of him, you should simply save all of nature, it is enough to get the one into safety who was put in your hands, heated almost to the boiling point. But that one you'll drop instantly, of course. Just as you are not automatically saved, except if you are still a child or, as in our case, a dog. There God's great soft arms reach out for us, and it is right and just to say: I, Karin. But this dress most definitely does not look good on me.

Becalmed, in bliss, the guests have returned to their food, and Frau Frenzel also lowers her head into the holy sober water font anyone can have installed in the previously cleared community table, if they want to. A badass sacrament absolutely everyone can partake in. But from the pier of this inn a hot wave flushes out of that woman, that monster, whose bloodstream is about to break off. A blaze bursts from this bowl of substance, by which even ninety-year-old men can irrefutably distinguish the real women from the fake ones, and the flame smacks Karin in the face. What a flop, how freakish femininity is when it inhabits a monster, whose blood has turned ice cold or even coagulated into a pleroma, just so that women can become brides again. The seed can still slip in there, too. And the eaters' heat joins in as well, within which they find communion. Blazing over Karin's head are the trembling bunches of ostrich feathers from a chimney that won't ever die down; short and frizzly, the bunches of fire are coming together to play like the bushes on human sex, reeking as repulsively, as if stinking hair were burning, there, on the molding of the paneling that for once was cut directly out of wood, not that precast stuff, that's already for shit even before it gets shaped and shipped. The guests gather under this dark heaven, this canopy, under which, amid chiming, clinking, and clouding, the food is carried in. They hit each other over the head with the leftovers of the day. Their insides take a bath, telling each other that their experiences feel like the saving grace of baptism. Besides Windex, the streak-free glass cleaner, more shameless pairs of lips snuggle against the windows from outside, caressing them, tongues dancing out, pressing against the window facade, they want to get into the warmer bodysack in there, but there still is a thin membrane in between. That brings the blood, for which we now want to use DEUTSCHLAND as a symbol, to a boil. This country brought forth so many dominant figures and then did away with them that it makes other countries with all their famous folks rather dormant worlds by comparison! There was so much coming and going, a constant, rippling unrest in the stream, an exchange of students in the school of life, yessirree! It's solid stock they come from!, that's why Germans work so hard, because there is constant movement in their reactor fluid and they melt down all the time. They accuse! That's how it is with blood, it won't stop, and water is even faster, because it is thinner and slimmer than even we would like to be. The swamps stand still, but you, dear one, you flow, and you, dear German-Austria, Deutsch-Österreich, taramtamtam, exude booziness to boot, because your gourmet guzzlers suck up so much blood sludge in those sausages or they smear it all over them, they get more gorgeous by the day. Come on now, no one could seriously request that Frau Karin Frenzel fix the malfunction in the oven with her bare hands. Sure, she's employed here, she doesn't know who hired her, but they can't really expect her to burrow in the blood sludge like a shithouse scrubber. Something's jammed in the TV set's incinerator. Gotta rake through the embers. Karin jumps up. The mother pulls her back to her seat. So what is it now? The mother decided Karin's first hour, she will do the same with her last. The daughter, whose voice is her only document, all others were taken away from her, does not have to worry about a thing. Mama will take care of it. There still isn't anyone but Karin who has noticed any strange elements here in this heavenly beautiful landscape. Yet the bleeding heart of Jesus is also pretty swollen and can hardly wait to spill its embarrassment of riches all over the diners, who, unfortunately are already half gone. By contrast, the dead are really livening up the night now. The mother calmly continues to eat, a snail that destroys the ground she feeds off. One would have to use force to tear her from where she has dug into. How shall one put it: The spirits of the dead contain the big All within themselves and are themselves not contained anywhere? Karin, to avoid having to peek outside all the time through windows studded with human fingernails, keeps her eyes fixed on the floor. This way she doesn't have to see how knife and fork get pushed into the meat, vanquishing death over and over again. There, the rustic rug, isn't it a human hide that has rolled itself up like a little pet? The contours of its former owner are still clearly recognizable as shadows, and just now this owner flexes his muscles, a runner—thrown there by an angry salesman in front of an undecided customer—in preparation of jumping up again to sound the fire alarm for himself. Only one thin, small glass has to be smashed beforehand, then the sand starts running through the timer. Caution! Like whips those rolled-up cadaver garment-bags could hurl themselves over the diners and smash them. They might want to gain their final historic importance, which is still pending. By chance we were caught grazing gently at the scene of the incident, feeding exactly at the place where grass must have grown over it long ago. In this intimate closeness to our sustenance, we stay put. The voices of the church resound across the pasture, hollow as usual. Life at its fullest, no more, no less, is what these things (or whatever they are) want to get back to again; crudely reassembled as figures, they want at long last to wade ashore. They were riding long enough in the same boat with all those proudly unborn ones, whom the church would much rather take care of. And for all those sweet babies the dead always have to play the older siblings and keep an eye on them! All those counterimages of what could have become of them, had they been permitted to take over the parents' businesses, don't make good fellow travelers. Like us, history must reach for the sky but hits the ceiling when it realizes that it also consists of corpses. And now they get pulled down like carnival streamers. Dust avalanches rise, they darken the rustic lamps and also the many little table lights, which were purchased primarily as ornaments. Yes, if we have one culture, we have many, and it is either a table- or fruit-growing culture.

Women settle in Karin F., there is no way she can prevent it, and they all are also Karin. It's not that the face of this already somewhat oldish woman is so pretty that all of them would want to look like her. Like the toss of an omelet interrupted too soon, Frau Frenzel seems slapped onto the wall, and she pushes against it as if she wanted to disappear in it. She is completely beside herself, not even the mother can bring her back. The daughter has already departed into herself!

One could also say, she went out of her mind. Clinking sounds, a changeover of power between an older couple at the next table, unscathed both, he not a widower, she not a widow, what's more, they just exchanged their car a week ago in Rüsselsheim, they now experience a new four-stroke sensation and would rather look out into the parking area than into other humans. Karin's mother is embarrassed. She pretends to look under the table for a bright far faraway, which, however, is outside. The daughter gets a mother's multivalent tug at the hem of her skirt to let go of it immediately. Because Karin has lifted the frayed hem as if she needed to wade through endless depths of water. One can see the relatively long-legged, tenacious cotton underpants under which an exhausted being is trying to wade on land, which at the moment can be delayed as far as we are concerned: We can only listen and enjoy. The clinking of flatware. A hard object falls into a bowl at the same time as my metallic scream. There, Frau Karin Frenzel gets screwed into a bright light as if it were herself: Colored concentric rings pull her in like a fleshen, photographic lens, ever faster—all waltzes!, very friendly, please, before you vanish completely! At home, before running off, we commit to memory the wooden scraping of the clogs, doctors like them, too. Nurse Jutta, we need to sterilize and cover everything around the area now, this pelvis is instable.

Unreality can also be concluded from the figures now standing in the light of autumn falling through the leaves, who have crawled to the shore of the table; those cannot be distinguished from Karin Frenzel. Thus, many people make the mistake of thinking it is she. Frau Frenzel will be seen frequently, but it never will really be in a way that invites interpretation; believe you me, once she lost her bloody curse, she got herself a new one. So. Why does this song end now?, the *Vaterland* tends to be seen here as a *Mutti,* albeit only the mommy parent of banks, let's be honest: Thinking of your homeland gives you such a snuggly feeling. But this *Heimat* is a fake mother, a woman whose skin has turned already cold and whose blood is immovable, solidified (even today this land is so die-hardened it defies admitting its mistakes). This nice, homey-cozy, woodsy-cutesy land with the round pompoms on many of its churches, a playful animal, it rolled onto its back just to be able to feel the steel drive into it, the terror in the raw. Being so close to it, a woman like Karin Frenzel cannot be expected to take it all lying down. Does she want to become a terror, too?, a child of this land, who is now greeted by the father of this land with a wave from the TV?, a secret signal only she understands at this time?, it's only meant for her, what an honor! The cadaveric juice that curdled inside the places we saw suddenly bursts out of this woman, pulsing beneath kicks, arching like a ceiling, a calcified coverlet Karin has wrapped around herself for protection, then she stands up, all of us have to stand up sooner or later. No matter how soft we have bedded ourselves, now we must be operated on. So Karin jumps up and onto the chair as well, lifts her skirt, and utters a wood-clacking sound similar to a *Baumkraxler,* a tree climber (that's a toy children once used to enjoy, a small wood-carved figure that climbed along a wooden stick, up and down, depending how one held the stick. My papa once bought me one, at the Kalvarienberg Market, Vienna, Seventeenth District). Yessir, they are running into the field, all the bodies who are Karin morphed into hollow bodies, spinning themselves into ice cream cones, diving, with the urgency of the last word, which must mean something, into the dead flesh, slipping into the *Muttermund,* the "mother mouth," i.e., the uterine orifice, which isn't bloody at all but, quite the contrary, bloodless, empty, a stone. They suck us dry, the dead! Already on arrival they are no longer responsive. Thereupon rebirthing on the operating table. Why did we plus Karin have to be born in this country, which constantly pretends to unite us (plus hundreds of thousands of tourists) with nature or, if there is none, with a hospital; well, in any case with a place, where one finally finds some rest and "lets one's soul dangle" as they say here for "relax," as if the soul were the only dick that still dares to come to us here. Here's my answer: The dead will simply have to eat and digest themselves. No one will throw a side dish into their coffin or wherever they might lie anymore. Tons of ashes are piled up in small heaps—those were people, all of them, swaying shadows of sisters and brothers, oh dear, no Christians among them!, who are now looking for their unborn grandchildren, clumsy as surfers under whose legs the waves froze in all the rosy colors of dawn and fruit gardens, per Captain Igloo's permafrost. Can't faze a seaman, tells us a popular German *Lied,* for he stands strong with both legs atop the automated yogurt cliffs and looks down into the valley, where folks together with their golf- and tennis balls (they absolutely refuse to stop, those guys!) are fluttering down—some chocolate sprinkles on top of it all.

All gray, all fey they appear, that Frenzelite Sisterhood, an order of ghoulish, mulish nuns who are simply useless, because any emergency service to life, for healing, helping, and real living, has been denied to this sister. She takes more than she gives, and now she even pulls down her underpants in front of everybody. The mother shrieks and in rhythm with it pulls the undies back up again, in perfect harmony with the four-lipped foreign language the daughter suddenly speaks in tongues, no one, not even she understands any of it. This Mother Inferior, now on the table, complaining, and it is not the food she's upset about. Like an illuminated, if not at all pretty face, the daughter's sex appears mischievously above the panties' waistband that is grasped so frantically. One would have hardly dared to ask for this locality, and yet the cute tousled treetops are popping up now, rustling softly, the little hairs directly at the slit sticking together a bit in moist, thinning (is all this really blood?) curlies, and the point is to pay careful attention to this place and its traffic signals, something that should have been done much earlier; in any event, no one could avoid asking about the farthest gone, that bloodless mouth through which a new fire suddenly rages in the wake of new road users. When you are taken to a hospital, you have to check your sense of shame at the door, the doctors want to get into your innermost part! There the threading of a fracture is a painstaking process, because the interfragmentary piece is partly positioned laterally to the direction of the impact, thus closing the medullary space of the distal portion. After the guide wire has been properly placed, the distal portion is drilled out with the flexible drill shaft, let this be said once and for all!

Anyway, Karin lifted a gate for anyone to drive through, no doubt she rather likes showing herself to her audience, discovers a special taste to it that is not on the list, even though these days you can get ice cream of almost any shape and flavor. What a wicked menoposter child exposing herself here well-nigh in her birthday suit. This woman really is too old for that. You'd expect her any moment now to lift up the Styrofoam cup and bestow the lethal host according to Austrian tradition (this land bestows guaranteed eternal peace to this day, as it has always done, sometimes more, sometimes less, we don't need a "Wall" to separate the doers from the donors). The nurse practitioner grabs the full bottle of life and exchanges it for an empty one, receives the deposit, and immediately loses it again: that oral medicator (sister terminator), already the water gurgles in the laid-up's lung, knocking off the breath that made itself all too comfortable there, that is, for seventy-something years. Brutal, how you, as an old-timer, inborn and -bred, simply get thrown out of yourself! When you're so accustomed to yourself! The lung, unfortunately, does not have a built-in drain. The geezer's life already flaps pretty loosely in its hinges, but it still wants to go dancing, hey, the chief physician has announced a staff party for this evening. Thus, they obediently swing their haunches, the doctors and the nurses, with whom the former are dancing cheek to cheek, as their reward. Let the old Pepper's lonely hearts press their fingers raw on their tubes and bells, the nurses would rather press themselves against the good doctor, all they need now is their girdles slipping out from under their skirts. Our Karin, by contrast, already travels in brighter far-aways, she took out her lush furry grasspatch for a taste, nibbling on her own blades, so that she would finally find herself digestible. Women know no pity, not even with death, with whom they are best friends, the most hopeless are all they need. Their compassion has already gone to sleep or become so numb that anyone who gets hit over the head with it must immediately be taken to a hospital. There are more nurses there! No mercy! The medical plumbers have already packed up their wrenches. The nurse has already thoroughly emptied the oral cavity siphon, squirting it deep down to the bottom of a wet lung to the point of total breathlessness of the thusly overirrigated individual. Or, as a better understandable image, also for the boys: No spark of life whatsoever itching in the exhaust anymore. Now they undulate along in white uniforms, those waves of death that, after a few minutes of rigidity, have already thawed again; a sparkling instrument scoops them out of their sorting bucket (one raspberry with scratchadildo, with whipped cream on top, please), all power into our hands, we are all brothers and, above all: sisters, forward, march!, colleagues, ladies and gentlemen, altogether now, we will hurl the Rohypnol out of our peasant women's hands, which once bandaged granddad's chapped feet (a disgusting job, no one else wants to do it), except that at some point these hands turned, unnoticed (right, Sister Gabi?, Sister Helga) into eagle claws that now are throwing eggs at death and, as a small reward, get Sacher torte in return. They rip their prey out of their long-legged beds, where the childish whining had just come from, a continuous howling sound proceeds from our Karin F., a sound that welts a hundred brushstrokes through the costume of our nerves. Those farmerdaughters! Building themselves up to firm- and fatness, Dianas caught while bathing, with sadly just one single naughty gaze dropping by in the last quarter of an hour. Yet how many stag heads grace the walls around here! And all that was caused by one plump female bather! No pity in this sturdy, buxom piece of work, one who expels men into unreachable distances only to latch onto them yet again with the cranked-up harness of her hips, those lusted-after know-it-alls, those droll dudes, masters over life and death, pulling them to herself by the slings of their rubber pants for a little smooch, over and over again. Who wouldn't like such an employer all in white who is so very wise. Yes, and his cart dogs with the handcarts, those are our practical, fully accredited dianeticaresses (that's what became of the goddess, read more about it tomorrow!), surrounded by their assistants, who are far, very far below them, standing up to their ankles in bloody, pussy muck. Nevertheless, those nurses' aides also deserve our full respect. If, however, you make the effort to look at them, you can see: This and that Herr Doctor stole away from them like an animal, I don't necessarily want to say like a stag. Well, well, look at that!, with a proficient kick that tips the chair of life to get a better look inside the dead-to-be's jaws if something valuable might be found there, one of our helpless wards gets unloaded from himself down the dark adventure slide, okay, done. Wash hands. Nice. An infinite void emerges, I think, when a goddess wants to bathe. The drill drives into the toothless mouth. Tonight there will be yet another party where everyone, including the least of my sister aspirants, can participate, even those not yet fully trained as well as the untrained. Royal bodies in white and the smartly scrubbed nurses join us, crackling with energy. Those shed-bred furies, those bloody pussies, who now are on top of the table in the shape of their stand-in Karin F., shedding their fur and spitting out slurs. All those well-greased douchebags rise and rage without rhyme or reason. They got electricity for their birthday, and now they can try it out: a concentrated charge of death. Karin Frenzel gets bigger by the minute since she just stepped on the table and also on her toes in doing so, and never a mother of pearls, she sinks her *Mutterkorn,* her ergot, her "mother-corn" in her native language, into the gorge of her cunt, which, still at rest at the time but unwittingly dancing along just a bit, simply wants to rub in just about anything. But in a moment she will see herself surrounded again by all those nice faces, no worries, she'll get a grip on herself again! So many old women among them, a wide field to practice. Dead before they lived. Creatures that fill me with horror. Fear of the order that I will have to step up to again to compete without ever having been picked for a team. I am a dandelion stalk in a child's hand. Doesn't work, dear folks!, I still want to be inserted somewhere, or rather the other way around.

On her table, Karin pumps and puffs herself up with her bare cunt to such a degree that it feels as if, in counterpoint to her horrific dance, she keeps stomping on a bellows to boot. Under the armpits sweat runs into her T-shirt. Flesh is a unique commodity and cannot be replaced by anything. This is why Karin Frenzel is so consumed by herself. Her feet paw the tabletop, tip-tap-toe as if they had eyes to avoid the plates, yet at some point the glasses and utensils start flying around. But what are those utensils actually doing? Gradual drilling to 14 mm, after measuring length, insertion of a Howmedica nail, length 40 mm, thickness 12 mm. That's what they are doing right now. This body, shy and half-heartedly ruffled to appear somewhat adorned as well, tramples down all of eternity, that starry fabric I created (or should I rather create another thirty eons, a huge number of lights I can populate with my heroines?), okay, so now the small glass jug meant for the ladylike pouring of wine has broken as well. A big body of calm, even rapid water could easily cover all these shards and food leftovers. And thus a jet emerges out of Karin to feed the stream. And thus slow boats—which, nonetheless, make Frau Frenzel's swollen cunt, eager for recognition, look small and poor by comparison—the dead, end up with us again, whence they had once set off. People slip below the edge of the screen, even though they had jumped up to examine the genitals of an older woman up close and unhurried. Now they have disappeared again, the spectators, and the dead are teetering nearer. All of them wear Karin's body and face, it's easy-wear for them. Those swollen lips, *Schamlippen,* lips of shame, we call them, revealing themselves in front of everyone, can surely wake the dead, and sure enough those dead are blowing in. As if a thumb had squashed this sex and ladled something out of this female fullness, some sort of rubber dolphin bobbing, riding on a lake of blood. Yes, that feminine fullness, it comes up to the rim of the father, who's already been full to the brim for the longest time. And to the extent that these pumped-up shapes rise out of Karin, she collapses. There might be unconscious stuff in her, too, maybe she will always be young and fem/male, so that she can go on producing treasures of that size, but she will not be able to burst mother's eternal chains (which are just spiderwebs for the rest of us); and to the extent of such magnitude letting itself be moved and melted so as to release dead figures, the desire for rest is growing as well. So it's fairly easy for the mother amid the tremendous ruckus roused in the dining hall to take in the sail of the skirt's hem and the daughter herself and pull her down from the table again. That's it. Enough. Can't do anything else for the patient right now. The fracture seems to be axially aligned, the length, as far as can be assessed from the fracture fragments, appears to be the same on both sides. But the patient probably won't make it. Frau Karin Frenzel suffered a setback, she got flambéed in front of everybody, and now the flames must be beaten down again. But even when this female blaze will have been extinguished, it might turn out that there still won't be any quiet. Or just the opposite: nothing but quiet. Then perhaps the desire of this eternal daughter will have grown all the way to the ceiling, continued to sprawl outside the window as a trellis, captured nature in one sweeping rhetorical gesture, and what has been will have become insubstantial. Or the true will have acquired substance. Karin was able to eternalize one moment inside herself, it might have been her last, that's why I hope so much that it was worth it.

13

This poor toppled body behind the door, it receives light only from a hallway lamp in a dirty blond plastic socket, the kitchenette is to the right over there. A Baby-Supernova washing machine is fitted underneath the sink and just vomited. But there was no one around to free the laundry from its oppressive situation. This little bit of light stayed with the body, still lighting some fire under the human leftover. The light does not jump up or rise slowly, rather it spreads downward like a veil, giving the body the very last feel of heaven, albeit far below the level of the few gentlemen who had briefly swept it into heaven; now the body suggests something watery because the proteins have coagulated. The young nurse lying here has taken off her body and is now free, if not of her own free will. She issued no son who might breathe everlastingness but a sort of son, still a boy, who popped her off. Look: in tight, feetless latex pants, wildly patterned, which has not retained the shape of the body (according to regulations, one would have had to press a button to call for the body of the nurse), bare feet in orthopedic slippers, legs spread as only the absence of will can manage it, upper body in a colorful T-shirt bent backward in an angle nature could not accomplish, this is how the woman sucks the last light into her wounded throat someone penetrated (for cash) all the way down to the ground, whence life leaps, splashing and giggling among glittering air bubbles, right out of the temple, driving herself in front of her, a Goose Girl, who is her own animal, which she shoos away. Now the rest of the light also gets there in a hurry for a better view. A fly sits on the pupil looking back, it wants to get to the bottom of looking, is it safe to jump?, but the water remains dark and motionless in its chamber. For out of this water a body is to be delivered. The water police drive their barge through the moist eye, which is still attached to matter, since it recorded so much during its lifetime, also with a camera. Unfortunately, the popular camcorder was too expensive.

The apprentice from Building 3 took off with 470 Schillings and change, a sprinkling of squashed cells and some hairy fluff brushed to the right, through the flight of courtyards that flow through the housing complex of Vienna's Meidling district. The young woman knew the fellow, for she once put a band-aid on his infected forehead under the blow-dried locks (cool in the disco!) where life had dug itself into the pits of picked zits. So he felt justified in bypassing the Creator, who breathes the spirit of life into the balloon of being until it bursts (because the Creator is so boozed up with life), and hammering himself into his girlfriend, who, as a side dish, had tried to feed him a nobler way of life. That doesn't cost him his young, virile strength, the flesh is not something that should be saved. Why was it made not to last? Can be defeated by the weirdest creatures so quickly? It is such a tiny light that everyone can carry it inside himself without it weighing down the hiking gear. A breath of sweetness flows from this little lamp onto the lips of the dead woman, which retreated, startled, from the teeth. In this general deluge it so happened that her colleague, Ms. Brunner, who was supposed to pick up the victim for the night shift, traveled today from another part of the city directly to Lainz, the hospital and nursing home, where her mother had fallen ill. So no rescuer descended from heaven and the apprentice came up the stairs to the seventh heaven, where he assumed he would get the rest of what he still needed to afford the eighth heaven, a moped of his very own. Is there no money in the house? That causes the expulsion from life's paradise, even though the crime series is running tonight, ahead of which those flamingos are running, while the drums are creaking and crashing behind them, until life's hot rhythm sizzles on the stove top and the excess drops are bouncing about. That's not how it goes with us, that's why we have to watch it. We might even be able to go there. But the young nurse Gudrun Bichler can no longer do that. She takes her immortal soul, packs it into the travel kit right next to that moisture cream that's so hotly wooed in public (more hotly wooed than Gudrun, in any case) and the nail clippers, the tweezers, and the eau de parfum sample from the global firm Revlon, introduced by Byron the bulb (pace Pynchon). Life got atomized in Gudrun by means of a switchblade knife, which an apprentice let dart out of Apollonian locks, an act of power like all acts through which future states manifest themselves. There it goes, female flesh, which was the same as that of any human, splashing onto the coconut runner, creating a fibrous red track across the small hallway. The apprentice, however, leaves the human rocket he pulverized right there; he wouldn't know what to do with such perfection, anyway, the body would also be too heavy for him. No God is helping him to pull himself up by his own blood tracks. The little bit of money had been in an old cookie jar, but what is the condition of that person now?

Like cliffs the public housing buildings rise up to the sky, as if the streets were folded into mountains, fine dust covers the canyons where humans get lost and found again as mummies. Only their devices still have juice, because the electric bill was paid by standing order. Heating pipes animate the foxes' dens, warmth rushes in, the burnt wastes of those with a zest for life are dashed through these pipes. Once human lives are completed, they are chased upstairs and bundled, like their waste. They rush upstairs, the old, where they rot most brutally, but their chunks are suddenly awakened, unwittingly they rise and run into the half-dark staircase where earlier, as a final dress rehearsal, the chicken bones of young girls and boys had been tossed. Someone had picked their bones and thrown them, after having impaled them on his sex—this exterior essence of the State (that hot dog thing twitching underneath a load of spicy mustard, which still wants to go on spritzing and begetting,—bang!, the Vienna sausage right into the delicate little crescent roll. Severed and freed from the body, it flew off immediately. Children's ghosts! Little girls have been torn apart. They won't be filled anymore with sons who might later take away from their mothers some of the breath of life everlasting. A small child has been murdered!), the licked-out, scratched-out husk into the shaft, next to the elevator door, from which the paint is peeling. Calmly and tied into bundles the dead stream upward, for they crave light, which in this building they find only at the very top. Inside their torn chicken skin still the aftertaste of matter, whence it sings as from some hill still alive with the sound of

Muzak or within which it bangs as in a great crime episode or whence it laughs as in Villach or Mainz, where folks, in order to get away from themselves, are climbing like humangous animal herds out of the waters to the shore but get pulled back down again and again by their body weight. Come on, let's make a human being in our image!

Downstairs, Gudrun leans next to the small co-op store, where folks got coupons before the workers movement, out of forgetfulness, broke up this system in order to make a few bogus corporations out of it in Liechtenstein, yes, the labor syndictraitors also think they are in paradise when they can separate from what they created and, confused by demonstrations, grasp what's there for their taking and save it, on their bare arms, in thick briefcases of immense length and width, offshore to Switzerland or the Cayman Islands or South Africa. Mind you, they all were real angels once, and now, admiring their own beauty, they have crossed the line. People are still eating today! Here, on the paper-covered display windows, our special offers, discounts! Luckily, someone cuts people some slack for once, the rope simply pulls too hard around their necks and the interest rates also constrict them pretty badly. So what, the fall sun warms us up as we go broke and Gudrun shuffles her feet idly in the sand. Housewives hurry past her, their feet swollen and footloose their husbands, who always leave at night and return in the morning. They barely finish their meals and gone they are. Go, go! What's Gudrun waiting for, who was once actually a student of philosophy and on vacation? She is waiting for a blessed spirit, who had the body strapped around it only for a while and now it is undone, the body, I mean. Our Gudrun has become a gatherer of the dead, albeit not out of passion but rather because it has been inseminated in her, as only a father can inseminate, that she should fill matter still wrapped in the trappings of memory into those people on earth who were taken from it. There are no words to describe how wretchedly folks were robbed of their features, their looks; they simply must come back so that at least some of their light can be saved! Raise the bushel, but higher the glasses. Cheers to Jesus and bottoms up! How lackluster they are, those thieves who, starting in July 1938, come to the furrier's, e.g., as commissarial custodian (name: Herr Karl Kolarik), and that means they come daily for just a quarter of an hour to check the cash register (even though the owner of the store was shot through the neck and shoulders on 5/7/1915 in the Carpathian Mountains) and, latest news!, pay the dispossessed owner his weekly check for life; but the disloyal custodian who deceives Jesus and wants the vineyards for himself (let others cry that they haven't found an animal to gut! He's got himself his own sacrificial bird to feather his nest and suck the blood out of its throat!), soon enough he will take his own, Herr Koralik, his life, and serve it to his SS superior on a platter, where the sweet remnants are still twitching and where wife and child must also become food. Certain angels are chosen and fill the world with forgetfulness, for they want to keep the secret of resurrection to themselves.

Gudrun looks upward, the legs promised to her for inside the tasteless elastic pants will soon show up, one can already hear health clattering in the clogs, at least the service to the aged tender flesh in the geriatric ward of Lainz hospital—a matter close to the heart of the city government and the whole homeland's holy covenant has been canceled today once and for all—such special nursing care calls for a whole woman, most of all her motherly hands. The rest of her, a very small light, we don't really need. A trolley, our Bim in local lingo, hurtles around the curve, it sends up sparks from the tracks like Karlitschek the stallion racing with his cart through a long-forgotten town, in front of which, like lingerie in a cheap strip show, the iron curtains came down with a clash, today a town aglow with small, faint light, it still carries the same name as before but completely cored, deboned, thoroughly purged of dead thinking, cleaned out and made sizzling hot again for the tourists, ice-cold goons who first have to shovel a big helping of Kafka into themselves, as if they were his gravydiggers; or they already come in twos, since one could never eat so much food all by himself, frat packs from the Golden West, binge-banging for a couple of coins a few steins of sturdy blond chicks all through the night. But let's not skimp on the mayo now!

So then it thunders along, the red public transport vehicle of the city of Vienna, where the bodies, changed toward the fatter, idler, hitch themselves up to the grab handles to pull their own cart out of the mud, and there the ghost ship of a nurse pops out of the surrounding darkness, which has been whipped up especially for the sex offenders. So that they won't lose their balls before they can still abuse them. In the meantime the victim, made of angelic material, an art teacher, in front of whom surge the graceful waves in the display windows of needlework shops, inviting endless looking—how she loved knitting during her lifetime!, how she enjoys the sight of the yarns and wool, she can try out everything without the saleswomen noticing the slight stabs: death one huge hobby mart, where the consumers and the devourers, who consume themselves with their yearning for more pleasant activities than those they executed in their lives, are floating around, fluttering against the lamps; life- and love-unions made in anger no longer fit and have to be reknitted; but we, nature's colorful snacks, have already altered time in our lifetime for an eternal fit! The sexy pants, trained on no one whom it might concern, sashays down to the impatient colleague Gudrun, who is none other than the murdered woman, now the second time around, but this time in toto, unharmed, I know that's hard to understand, but anyway, those pants draw attention to the wearer. So the dead nurse pit-a-pats down the stairs: First of all, a scarf must be crocheted, so one won't have to see the waste of what has only recently been poured down the gullet and is now trickling out of the neck's organic waste bin. Her sister is waiting at the main entrance for the rushing nurse. The latter stops abruptly, hand pressed bashfully against the laryngeal cartilage, which unfortunately was damaged, so there, that's her a second time? Could this be the meaning of dying? That in the end the body is as dark and inert as everything else? That the blessed spirits have to look for sustenance under the buzzing powerlines of mothers, getting hit by electric shocks and other blows, new body garb for the last lawyers' last supper in celebration of Judgment Day? But all that the *Defuncti* get to ingest are snakes slithering about in the cesspools of their graves that, as soon as one wraps oneself in them, start drilling into their new masters and mistresses for the inner linings, because the body husks during their lifetime also always wanted to have more allocated to them than they could stuff down their throat. Envy and murder!

The second Gudrun has been created and unites with the first, who knows how many more of them there are, of course there is a difference in clothing and: the first Gudrun is more goal- oriented! Because she has a mission—since her thoroughly healthy appearance immediately catches the attention of the felled and sadly not quite as slender fir, Gudrun Two; besides, there is some air pollution all around the roots of this treelet in the form of all kinds of colorful lichen and vines printed on the cheap, skintight leggings. It's difficult to pay attention to pretty wrapping when the purchased object was cheaper than the paper that wrapped it. Having to decompose under these pants presents big challenges to the chemical industry, but someday it will manage to burst even our hot dog skins, not to worry. In the warm dust of the streets, amid the blots of spit in the archway to the public housing project of the municipality of Vienna, whose coat of arms (a cross that no one will take from it, it is dedicated to all the betrayed dead in these Red fox dens) is proudly displayed high above, pointing to eons of everlasting courtyards, looking backward also an angel who does not want to see his grave but rather incites the mourners to get under the earth quickly as well, so that he, too, can spit on someone, this then is where the two women unite, the still half-alive (?) ghost Gudrun with the freshly killed Gudrun, a rare case, admonishing people to better stay away from court cases. While the student—a carcass, a clothes bag who would much rather move up in an airplane with other bright and bushy busybodies—lies on the floor in a rural hotel, a woman risen from the dead, a young murder victim, pours into this body form that was handed to her, and they become one, a third something, a vampirized being of the third order with an Annunciation. About two thousand years ago something must also have gotten angry with Christ and caused his death, so that he would dwell among us ever since, undead like his entire religion, which does not want to become really dead; with their leading employees and managers, he and his club are punished enough. It probably happened to him because he was so undecided. Because he was so undecoded, he did not want to admit having been human like you and me. Everyone always wants to be and receive something better than they are and have. We speak of bride and bridegroom, when something, even though it constantly argues, seems to belong together, nonetheless. Thus Gudrun becomes the bride (the bridegroom) of Gudrun, one steps down the stairs and into the other like a puddle of dust and bones, on which the forgotten wishes float and flicker like streaks of oil. At that moment a force is sent to this in-between-being that reawakens its body.

A hoarse kind of barking resounds from this Church of Unification. Gudrun, a student of philosophy, can throw around kilos of revitalizers in the handy variety pack. Juices welling out of the screen, food products deliciously processed in that final repository, the television set that annunciates to us what we should consist of so that we may continue to exist in front of the blue flickering tabernacle of our Lord, Herr State Network President: Brothers and sisters descended to us, and how did we treat them? They had to leave all their belongings in their uptown homes, their business reserves, their family resources, and then they were put onto trains, whereon they had already lost all human traits even before they passed through the fire and arrived in the chimney (yes, they were simply erased before they could sign up for the playground, where people and German shepherds played with them on the drilling/killing field, rather than the other way around), and taken eastward to the empire of the rising sun (luckily not to our middle kingdom, we would not have wanted them in our midst right next to our middle-class rentals), so that someone could reinvigorate himself with their souls, glasses, fur coats, and dentures. You vivify yourself and get vilified for it for fifty years and counting. No one hears how the two human railcars get coupled together, even though a world premiere is being prepared here. The bodies twitch and squeak in the coupling joints. It was not *Arbeit* that set this young nurse free but an apprentice who, in turn, has not yet been set free by the apprenticeship certification exam that would have qualified him to be released into the public. Where the father rides roughshod over the son. And then a young woman student gifted her nurse with what it takes to be part of the world: life!, substituting for the Creator, and not only that! This life has been kept in the original packaging of the body, in the tight pants that are specialized in the processes of outlining and shaping, and in the comparatively oversized T-shirt. So this simple woman has it better than the Lord Jesus, who, his followers believe, has risen in his own body. They have not considered that heaven is not a refrigerator, therefore flesh cannot be let in, no matter how well-hung it is, accompanied by thunder, lightning, earthquakes, and darting snakes, piercing lances cracking bones. One has to come up with another form for it so that people who are dead won't also have to stay dead just because they cannot be recognized on account of simple formal mistakes. Most of them were hardly known to the public during their lifetime. As for our young nurse: Her body has not been discovered at this time, and the apprentice is still on the loose, a cub having just practiced karate in her coochie, and then the finishing razor cut!, he roams through the atrocities of the heavy traffic, which, sadly, he can't join, since the heisted cash is not sufficient. Thus disadvantaged, he can barely get a pair of jeans for the loot, and only at the discount store at that. So then his friends will just have to treat him to the disco. He can't be a big spender anymore, up and running as his body is now, for he has practiced in the meantime: No doubt this dick played around some in the nurse's slit with the tricky clit and slippy bits 'n bobs he hadn't known before, just out of curiosity. For those few urine-bedewed hairs and the raised harelip, for this split bulb of slimy flesh, most brutally kneaded by the apprentice's fingers until the last drop had been squeezed out, it was hardly worth it that the fingers slipped in all by themselves; nonetheless—this flesh-plant can be spread apart a bit and the apprentice looks inside, into the void, into the nothingness of that woman, where the rocket propulsion ought to be or the firewood for the volcano, the common abridged image of woman, this one, however, isn't one. Here he can only puke, the apprenticing punk. Here nothing flickers anymore. This sex education was a bore like all education, this darkness does not clear up. Just something yellow running out, quickly shut it before life might shoot out of there. The guy slides a thin, goldish ring from the five-and-dime on his finger, the kind that brands animals as property. But those sausage-skin pants were pretty hard to pull down and back up again, that plastic stuff sticks like glue, after all, they are designed to create the impression that women were born in such jogging pants, that's how well they fit into them. Everyone has the right to a view that hides nothing but, on the contrary, highlights the unearthly delights of this body's demise. Though in fact there is nothing behind it, the flesh cannot rise, that's for sure, according to someone who knows it now. This apprentice, however, cannot bear the secret of the flesh and hurries to the jeans store to cover his own body with them. He is no longer young enough to believe whatever gets sent into the world by means of antennas from the roof. An alien power is what he is himself.

As with freshly lubed joints, Gudrun Bichler, out of whom someone just treated himself to a good swig, is gliding along the walls into the Empire of the Night. Folks have mounted huge dishes on their buildings to thoroughly milk this night like all previous ones, letting voices and pictures run into their homes as if out of udders, and already the first marks of Cain are flaring up, it will be a late night once again. The first commercial voices, which rested so securely inside themselves, are zapped off in the middle of a shriek (the commercial is always longer than the serial offender film framing it, millions want to take a look-see what is happening in another wastewater channel. The darts of dusk slip into the nurse's licked-out husk. The discarded remnant of a snake lies on the floor, and a soft foot steps consolingly on its head, Lord Almighty, Gudrun must go back to a tenement unit, but which one? She darts like an amphibian. The uniform biotope of city birds storms around her all confused: live feed but dead nonetheless! Open to eternity (an endless stairwell covered with a roof of clouds). On her way Gudrun might take a quick look into the Amalienbad, the city's historic indoor swimming pool. The damp tiles have been painted over with streaks of light through which her feet stride. A child learning how to swim on a kind of gallows screams and reaches for something outside itself. The pool is not busy, at this time it's mostly a retiree swim, folks already thrust far out on the tides of time, but they still get their fashion presented in high-end magazines, sweet fruit hanging too high for arms that are no longer easy to lift. But swimming in a group improves performance, it includes you once more in the light that is thrown on all of us. Not everyone is yet ready to pass through this gate between domains where the lifeguard is posted, Master of life and death. Already a child's body sinks to the ground like a helpless crab, where it still wobbles sideward a little before it lies down, waiting in spider position, arms and legs pulled around itself; no one notices. That's how fast one can loosen the mesh of the life net! By luring people into the chasm with images of themselves. The spider bite of the undead nurse, who, after all, has to practice sometime or other, paralyzed the little boy; the child actually dried up in the water, and then, already transformed into a different element that had picked itself out of the easy-to-crack crab shell, it moved to a slanted ramp, where it was selected as a double, at this famous ramp that segregates the nonswimmers' from the swimmers' pool, and quickly climbed by auto-forklift back up to the rim of the tiled wall again. Watch out, this boy is no longer what he used to be, what will his mother say this evening when she feels his teeth dig into her softer side for his pocket money? What creature winged his steps?

Gudrun, the goddess through whom the storm raged, threw an old, discarded life she got her fingers on, into the boy. She batted only one eyelash; cleansed by her death, she sees the essence of the world wearing a hot bikini and standing on the three-meter diving board. It bobs and tips. It hops up a bit and twists around itself like hair wanting to be curled around a small, heated rod, absolutely the finest fiber that can be twined with natural material. From now on and with immediate effect, Gudrun can threaten with death, and this trick works because she is so much like God. Because her foundation is blood, which she freely wastes. That she looks like a goddess not even the lifeguard, sword of the community, Gudrun's natural and first enemy—that is, if he could identify her as a notorious murderess—is ready to buy. Thus all he sees is a young woman of average shape, watching, shoes in her hands, she probably wants to leave at any moment, watching the aquatic activities, those spindly swarms of humans crisscrossing the pool, now and then a presence jumps among them to grab them, rises between their legs, if they are at all worth it, and releases screams from the pelvic scissors. Then everything gets gnawed off. A child that stepped into this pool has already been transformed, and still more bodies are beckoning, albeit most of them old and already rotted, tickets that don't make an entry desirable; let me through, the water tells Gudrun, I carry anything anywhere, just tell me what. There are no obstacles for me. Nothing can stop me. Dams, those advocates of human matter, are embossed by me and carry my image on them. I can carry tons of flesh, weightless, wriggling packages, I can't feel them at all, it's quite similar for my colleague, the chimney. It transports incredible masses of people without really feeling any of it, most still carry their parents' stamp, the mark of the mother, the testiclament of the father, no matter, all together they can easily tear down the fence of fire and rush on, leaving behind all those feeble little houses that once were their bodies. Practically no resistance is to be expected from them, it's not even worth duct-taping their fly right under their nose.

It is getting light in this vivarium, where lumps of flesh paddle, calling out to each other the stories of their diseases even as they can hardly save enough breath in their lungs to remain on the surface and invent lies. Most of the women swimming here haven't been subjected to the lunar rhythm for a long time, no discretion softens the gazes aimed at them like pebbles. The geezers would rather cast their eyes on the plumper little bloodsausagettes, wherein the ovaries sweat and toil, small organs compared to the whole body, but they are capable of a lot! They tempt and tease with bent finger hooks. What passionate arousals they manage to scratch out of those slack bellies, roots in search of moist, dark earth, soil to plant and enlarge oneself!, feeling their way out of the leg holes blindly but still determinedly: thin little legs and then the popular third standing leg, the slack white little weenie skin keen to gift itself all the more generously. Today it could soften at least a paper plate, that's how strong it feels. Yes, life goes on further than we would have thought, or it collapses right at the start due to wobbly scaffolding! Those young room attendant fräuleins (they simply attend to every room they appear in with their juicy brushes of the best, frizzy bio-hair!) can make history go on further than themselves, that is, in their embryos and the end products they become, even though history is threatened to go out at any moment in every single being who must die. A deplorable permanent condition. There isn't always enough human flesh to feed them. All this is accomplished by those ovarianates harnessed in their swim gear, their crest, still fresh or freshly dyed, shimmering like the light refracted in the helmetlike rim of the tiled pool. No tiny humans jumping out of there who might be gods or goddesses.

The waterspout of a scream cuts through the deep water like a suction tub immersed there briefly. The curled-up body of a child has been sighted at the bottom, formed by a father's, a mother's blow so horrible that this body slipped out of the swimming trunks dismembered, in pieces. An arm, frayed, drifts along half a meter away from the body. This blow was no trumpet blast announcing the popular program *Know Thyself in a Melody,* it was already the shoulder punch in the relay race to eternity, we are all Firsts, we hit something earlier, the lifeguard dives down like a screwdriver, he hadn't noticed any of it. He can't understand it, he's been looking there all the time. The retirees' feet trample, in a final drumroll, downward into the deep, panicking they whirl to the edge of the pool, tired ship's-spooked-screws wanting to escape something they just suspect but don't know. Actually, they would have been next in line! The lifeguard pukes into the water but has no room for it, tightly enclosed in water as he is, as if he were cast in plaster. The child's body is completely torn apart, a piece of the wing drifts by, which a giant had taken out of the fridge but didn't like, so he simply spread the pieces around. As soon as the lifeguard gets a hold of the child, it practically melts in his hands. The parts drift between streaks of blood, smears of red paint lazily working their way through the chlorine-calmed waves, the dimensions of this child's body can't even be guessed anymore, was it killed so that it could live? For the sin of the world to die in its stead? Water: Doors opening all by themselves, descents, stairs, shafts. A gigantic reservoir one cannot drink, an executioner's block of water. Who can tell the Celsius degrees the godless talk about when they have to say something at the Gate, a password? The retirees get cold easily. On their big swim day, they get heated up better than other swimmers here, in an element where the world ends. There will still be a lot of talk about this one dead child, black letters will be thrown at him like small clots of soil. And strangely, his jeans and his sweater and his shoes, a product of the Swabian Adidasses who are flooding the world with their crowns of Creation (if I interpret the logo correctly), those are not where the boy left them, in the locker room, where the satchel with its now orphaned books and notebooks is also found, instead they are found at the edge of the pool, and those, too, are slashed, torn, and soiled. As if some sort of being had opened and then shut those low gates into the open to boot. But practically anyone gets in here with us.

But the infinite millions who are also dead no eye has ever seen. How did they get through this narrow door, which is equipped with a self-locking mechanism, into the Great Hall, where their reincarnation is under discussion? How come only three of us have passed this test until now? One dead soul might not be enough to speak for so many.

Where are they all? It must be no less than all.

14

No, actually, the faces of those older women, who sit there so self-assured in the dining hall of the Alpenrose were not presented to them to pick and choose, they must have washed up, flotsam that crept ashore, discarded: saved go-fetch-it sticks, but no one running after them, pawns never picked up, drawing behind them a trail of cheap cosmetics. But now these women are really left high and dry at both ends, wrapped around themselves, cellulose samples for nothing and no one. Mummies soon after they've been mommies, whose children had been smashed like eggshells in war and peace, through crimes and punishments. Frau Karin Frenzel is also somewhat dried out: the slimy gunk of this erstwhile slyish fruit de mer still shimmers for a while in the sun (above an operating table?), then it hardens, we are not to get the slightest flashback of it anymore. Those big mammals once raved softly in the wheel of their pleasures, rolled about, spread themselves, and sprayed their fluids; now hardly a trace is left of them in the sand, while in the distance the daughters are already opening their arms boldly for the *Erlkönige,* the Alder Kings (that's a horse named after a car because it is so fast. Brush up on your Goethe and think Mercedes). The *Muttis* treat themselves to their vacation here in the country, but increasingly they get skipped over. They basically are gymnastic equipment, as the one and only daughter already practices diligently with the flesh wherefrom she came in order to dangle sometime later as a gift on the Christmas tree (just her new hairdo created by a fuel rod) for the final hit into the nursing home. Just take a look inside the new *Brigitte* or *Petra* magazines, how young flesh strikes its final repository, the old woman! Oh well, that's youth for you, at least on paper, it consists of clothing, which is eyed passionately, but this frame doesn‘t keep what was promised to it. Endless restlessness inside the sportswear, then a movement emerges to feed its *being there,* a trusting animal that presents itself from its best Lycra sides when it swooshes through the air. Afterward the boys and girls pack themselves up again. Every time their firm flesh touches paper, it grows, charming monuments à la Boris and Steffi, now there are more, many more of them. We notice an oversupply of juice and alcoholic beverages. The bodies' windows fly open again, the journals' wings swoosh, too, we called them for 80 Schillings, and they came with People! Creatures whose build glides over them in gentle waves, spawns of health, nonaging procreative prospects who claim the following for themselves: sanitized soil, hosed gravel, a guaranteed homegrown, ingrown region (meaning: self-engendered, native, immovable). And please—no wigs, no snapping with your dentures made of iron, you gaping crevAsses! Makes no difference if the unity of the former two Germanies may be trinified by a Father or must come up with the next round of shutting up, beating up, or burning down—those pukes spit out by vampires, forever young to boot, they can befall us now. Oh, golden age of youth, we spread our legs for you! Where is the stake to which we can tie their hands like boats or drive right through their heart? I am afraid that even then they won't pay attention to us in the darkness of our graves. Up to now we could always blame other folks for everything, but now—the blood that spurts from the glossy pages is the fuel that enfeebled us older Karin-cretins, who did not give birth to those children or anything else for that matter, from the start. That Mineral Oil Light no longer lubes us semi-senioras. We don't push through the cocoon, the new beauty treatment that encases us in a thin layer of plaster and mortar, the circumstances in our bowels, dislocated and contorted, break the cold bowl in which our limbs rest. No brewskies here and we are skrewed. The hospital waits for us poor beasts, our health insurance moans over us, increases the premium, a Mother Mary wringing her hands facing so many sons and daughters nailed to the blue cross, blowing down their dying like gusts of winds that make the insurance authorizations rattle in the draft. As for us who no longer have to be amicably attended to, we've got to take the bones left over from the surgery. For the beast in us that also wants to feed there's nothing left. Let it lie down in peace, head between its front paws, at home, where scenting from whence the wind blows is cut off. Let's hope it is benign and won't have to be cut out of us.

In the meantime, Karin Frenzel, denaturalized all of a sudden (and without the lubricant of guilt), has thoroughly unlearned bleeding. She finished in a draw. The umpire lowers the flag but: as she crawls out into the night, into a long summer, in which the bathing suits are coming out of the closet so that the bodies gain worldwide attention (tall and slim), her time runs backward—something is wrong here, and blood shoots out of her again, as in the good old time. At first, she hardly notices that she had once again been pushed into the period of fibrous fem-care products wherein rests, chock-full like milk in the unmilked udder (the cow after all howls with pain!), the silage feed of fluid-retaining plastic, always ultra, but whereto? Thus it has to be replaced, the blood. But how, if not by stealing it? From a plastic bag! The law of youth is a hot rhythm, to which it moves, unmoved. For the man the time for it must be anytime, for the woman it is only once a month. It runs down Karin's legs, takes a good rest in the elastic bands of the white knee socks and the still somewhat pulled-down panties, both of which she wears with her dirndl in defiance of age. Her head floats brightly above it, a gruesome revelation, what with the white threads of the first aid bandage flying off of it, late summer's old goatssammer, borne away like the lines of a paraglider.

The wrinkles that had been worked up honestly by the face seem overcome, for now, as the woman storms out into the night, her expression, which earlier reflected and enacted only weakness, smoothens out. Any trace of that woman is currently erased. Does her hand grow out of the grave like the child's, so that at least one would know where she is buried? Sorry, I don't know. In the weakness of her blood Karin quickly throws off her lid that kept her inside herself for all those years. She melts around the rim, that murky cup that's suddenly all fluid with nothing holding her together anymore. What's that? A melody and stomping, still? The machine's been started again? I hear: There is this creature sounding in all its daze, producing its thin, helpless insect tone, heard only by its own kind so that they know which part to attack, for they've already tasted blood in this broken bowl and want to see much more blood flowing. So that there'll be enough for dessert, too. War! War! This time it starts right in the hospital. But now Karin first wants to drink her lemonade. The sexes open up recklessly. Stand up now so that eternity can see your face, which you took so much trouble to conserve, it might be you who's been selected to form a long female row, a hunting route, skirts above the head at the express wish of the father physician-in-chief, whether child or old woman, for the Father gave them this conformation, so that you, Madam, remind him always of the union of man and woman, though actually He formed each as individual beings. In short, one should replace you with a younger model, the highest God may reach inside you to steer your organs with His Spirit over the cliff. Yes, because men always want something new, but history can also be made for many other reasons! Which is also based on the change of instruments with which the people in those countries that simply can't be helped are laying into each other, as if they didn't have any economic subsidies and export quotas to lose.

The light gets thrown through the door onto the parking lot, which once was a vegetated garden. It had been cut off from nature, that virtuoso who constantly practices the fiddle to play to our feelings. One look back: Sitting there is Karin's mother who chose *Gemütlichkeit,* throwing lightning flashes at her daughter, who cowers next to her in a sort of bushel; hidden under it there's even some tasty gravy as a burial gift. Fog rises outside. No one has noticed a creature sintering out of that windowless tent Time, through this actually nonpermeable wall, which at best can be walked through only backward, straight into memories, where people throw indiscretions at each other and dig themselves greedily into someone else's flesh, where they want to be digested. And rightly so, given the magnitude of the treasures they proffer! Yes, women love with their guts, here, where they dropped you can read them. You, our loyal trees, you still stand strong, the sight of so much blood can't frighten you off.

Not the slightest bit astonished, Karin Frenzel looks back at herself crouching conspicuously next to her mother, a small light that at most could serve the buried as a means of orientation and at the same time gliding through the door into the open, guided and framed by a chain of lights of all kinds of skeletons ghosted out of the closet, meant to beautify the entrance to the restaurant. The two creatures, mother and daughter, hammer and anvil (better to be the anvil, you don't have to rise above life so grimly), are lavished with food by the waitress and watered with a bit of juice. Still, those two lives are not very fruitful. The bloody series ends in this pulp mag, in which the humiliated woman, amid shouts of pity from the male audience, this wander woman in miniskirt or—depending on the season and the matching men for each, I mean, the match that lights the fire—in hiking pants tried to keep the hatches of her easily damageable armor shut, out of which she'd been shooting all those years with a woman's special charms, weapons—which basically are nothing but rubber tubes, suction pumps, rubber pants, diapers—know how to find their way through all the leaking and shrieking. No wonder our male colleagues triumph when they can finally tear down our iron belt lock, which sometimes lets us women come out quite loverly, so they can jerk off the curtain rod on the spot. All I am saying: Something tore here, and right away the whole curtain comes down in a cloud of dust, burying man and woman who briefly lit it up with their flashlights. Sand whirls up. The woman puts on her show, and blood drips from the swaddle wrap. We're surely making fools of ourselves.

It is as if Karin were a radio that has increased its signal range. The music of the blood rages in her head, and straight back to the veins shall it go right now, is what the newscaster has to say about what follows the report of the accident: the lamb of the music program after the killer of the evening news. The woman yanks her face to the side and wheezes, she can hear it super clear in her soundbox, that dark space, between two earplugs, where people let themselves be bubble bathed and sugarcoated. The house that she just left even though she still seems to be present there—one look into the rearview mirror is enough, she doesn't even have to turn around—united all its highlights: Sitting in chairs, at tables, are the evening guests, ready for action. They are painted with bright fresh color. Killed roasts toss about as if they were still alive and turn between jaws. Young, strong wine pours after them. Karin, the peak-a-pee, a watercraft with her eyes pushing forward like oars at the boat, steering her female nature here and there between the dust-covered thujas and yews of the hedge, dives through a life driven through the organic waste of thousands of meals, a bird caught in its song. A moment later all of that is behind her. With the pole of her new completely transparent being, whereunder her blood vessels are calling for help, because they can't let loose even once a month, and now they suddenly have to unexpectedly give all they've got, Karin Frenzel pushes off the shore. Out into the faraway! The dead live longer! But as for us, we'd rather not die. That's how we want our women: letting us look inside them, check out all the nooks and crannies, but on the outside there should still be something to nibble or lick, a boundary that highlights all those daring barings. Pink cotton candy, secrets that only the Self-Originated Father, the Great Immovable in *Newsweek* and *Time* and *People* (please fill in any missing items) can expose. An innate wild propensity underlies all this. Karin's thighs have been replaced almost completely by fat, a bitter by-product of life's excitements long ago. So far, no candidate has scored any points, but the contenders, the worldly ones, who nonetheless play otherworldly tennis or golf, have all been touched by a ghastly being that spread its trail of blood all across the parking lot in search of totally new intimacies, under no circumstances should one intimate any interest in it. In a robbed image, the man finds a substitute for what he is entitled to and gets constantly taken away from him, for the allure of front-page beauties, to whom he has a justified claim—how they shine through the night, how they get pulled up by an arm and held in front of the face ready to be consumed right out of the paper, warmed up by admiration!

An automobile zips by on the state highway outside, it represents the audacious attempt to completely undress oneself behind a radar screen, a flasher! His father: silence, an important member of the Eightfold, which the driver has to examine in spirit if the motor starts to stammer. Plumes leap up high, with their helpless, threatening gestures trees temper the fire of their hurried visitor. A hand of nothing, of fog, pulls the animal chased by dogs through the finish line. A being in a dirndl races over the deep tracks of soil, over the graves of tires torn open and not filled again, yes, here nature set herself up as the mistress erasing with the rubber everything that's ever been scribbled on the ground.

However, the car's driver stops suddenly, a horse that spooked and didn't know why. Smashing, how all the devices that usually look into the inner life of the car have stopped on their slim horsepower-ankles and even refrained from giving warning signals. No oil? No fuel? Nix *Ennoia?* Should the night traveler let something enter that wants to drink, only this time out of him? Should he recharge himself? Who'd come to save this pneumatic sex with a jack from down below? So many questions and no shop open. Night is made especially for the motorist. It has been produced for him, the racy driver, so that he, in the heat of his cool, can load a bit of flesh onto his horns. The crises that grow to superhuman dimensions in it make for the allure of the night, otherwise it might as well always be day. When it's over, you don't know if you'll separate again or understand each other even better. No one has yet decided whether he wants to drop all inhibitions just because he dropped his pants, I beg your pardon, this really was below the belt! The darkness collapses like a badly pitched tent. The driver hesitates in his Fourfold, he looks at the clock on the dashboard. Must he really remain without wine or women for the rest of the day, today of all days, because his new car simply stopped? He would certainly get his usual place at the Stag later, but first he should be able to have it work out in another being, who should, I beg you, be slim, youthful, and, like him, also delicate.

Suddenly, with one stroke, the fog gets pulled upward, the night decided to be clear. Calmly waiting: a silent motor that's been pulled out of circulation and doesn't really have any problems. The adventurer at the wheel discharges his duties, which consist of approaching a woman's most private spaces: He played tennis all afternoon in a multipurpose hall that was erected by the municipality to siphon the bloody foam off the streets and put people like him into cold storage, so that at some point they can be fed back as fertilizer to the soil they had abused. And so that new descendants, who would be anything but prudish, their clothes lifted up into the uncertain, could sow themselves into the insufficient ground, a ritual sacrifice to rip the means for the altars of road construction out of the flesh. This cheeky driver won't let himself be kept in check. In the clubhouse at the feet of the mountains he had been served well until recently. Traffic scrimped and saved him. Truth be told, he was just passing through to his more elegant hotel. He wanted to avoid this tiny village via the bypass, but his vehicle must have taken something so that the track rod can satisfy itself for once. Here, heroes are promised lonely women, who keep bashfully to the side for the moment. None of them will be able to resist this automobile. Perhaps a dance's swings are waiting, rustic pleasures, a piece of property belonging to the *Sonderklasse,* or one that is owned by the bank. In such places there always are a few bored young grass widows with child, with those you can crash and crush wide-open feelings. The driver looks into the mirror above the passenger seat and opens his shirt collar. Meanwhile the car, big and hulky, buries itself to serve as a bunker. The trees throw off some foliage. There is a noise. Listen, it sounds like a dog panting, as it follows a treacherous track, which it has to look for again and again. The driver scents, then responds with a dark howl, which he has drawn for years from his cassette recorder, which now surfaces from a slight slit next to the hole for the cigarette lighter. Something has been initiated, a sort of birth. It doesn't know itself, but it comes to the fore. The antenna has been pulled out and would, if one let it, smash the Austrian Radio traffic info with its music, which can make mincemeat out of this (any) traveler to boot. His thin brainpan bursts under a terrible blow into a hail of splitters, while his desire, knowing nothing about it, just waits a little. From somewhere the sensors of a foreign presence get dipped into this expectant night watch, wherefrom, unexpectedly, sprays the colorful juice of life as fresh as it had been drawn from colorful magazines and videos. This juice settled in the white knee socks of the being, the woman, who'd done away with right and wrong in equal measure. Now all that this power, whose name had once been Karin Frenzel, has to do is skewer herself on the good shepherd staff of a stranger, who was actually looking for quite a different herd or at least for the one dainty, stray lamb. In order to make herself happy, let this oldish woman betake herself outside of humanity, if you please, with her life's expectations and excretions, to a place where the man—an equipment manager in the changing room of modernity that's been crushed by athletic training shoes—gets the newest models out of illuminated niches, this gym expert of intimacies, whose passions were mistakenly cut off while secretly peeking through the keyhole. At least he was left with pretty images. Now a creature is crawling in, the forest suddenly breathes loudly, it puffs, it pants, no gump that one, where does it still get all that gumption? One can already see through its leaves.

A stinking trace approaches the vehicle, a trace splattering deadly aqua vitae, an ostracized female, Karin's twin sister in a way, whose lively, albeit monstrous original lovingly bends just now over her elderly mother in the dining hall of the inn, to check behind her back dentures that something didn't get stuck there after all, a fish bone, whatever, that betrays the terrific bite of that woman. One final overview behind the lifelines, and there creeps the unnaturality of a woman over the straight right, which is what the car and its track stability mean for every one of us. Only when the track subsides do you notice that you've lost the way. Watch out for the watchman of the road, and yet he lets this creature enter the space of history, which in fact is a hyster[i]a.

It stinks of old chalk and dirty sponge water that absorbed all the blood, this sponge, after all, has never been washed. Women and children are targeted with bold, bright colors, and already their bodies splash onto the concrete that deals with their various wounds more openly than their fellow citizens. Every Tom, Dick, and Harry has access to the crises of women, if he summons them to pass muster between rear peep and aperture front: No, this model doesn't appeal to him, and neither does that one. Off with it, the bullet gets loaded to place itself in this meat so that a few people can win once again. Hectoliters of blood, intraocular fluid, pus, tissue fluid are leaking out, how could all this ever be stopped? (Male war dead never give the impression of "leaking out," they seem to hold together to the very end like sleeves, their bodies are simply better toned!). How sweetly and yet clumsily women throw themselves at the last moment over their little children, who are even softer than they are, not even the TV can completely gloss over it, though it is flat as a plate that wants to be filled. You can pile as much food on it as you like. No doubt, history is sometimes a little bit feminine, well, we ladies do have our own herstory once a month, which we relish as long as we can. Though we do have to dam ourselves up a bit, I think. Anyone who wants to, can (re)press it down, all it takes is entering a flower shop to pin his love interest with something much heavier or a jewelry shop to saddle her with an even heavier choker.

Like an angel the precious vehicle now opens its wings but turns away at the same time and wraps its hood-head in veils of fumes rising from the warm motor. Something, less than nothing, drags itself over dirt and gravel, a thing, a creature different from the rest. A woman's face smoothened as if by several sequential miracles, a small lamp that would love to blow out every other light of life. A fellow countrywoman without a country has come across the mountains, spreading her terrible snugness (she has all the time in the world united in her) like crumbs out of bags into her own track. Well, the alpine grasslands are definitely cuckoo! Mats for apparatus gymnastics or summersaulting. Freshly slaughtered meat, far away from us, does not have to endure many glances anymore, such as those of the butcher in charge for example, and this flesh has had to endure quite a lot up to this moment as well. Now it bloats, trichinous, the eyes of parasites look into the blue, something bulges out of its house of torture, swells up, it won't put on the shoe of life anymore, that's gotten too small for it.

With a soft sleeve the radio sweeps incessantly through the warm, lightly preheated interior, the cassette will be inserted in a moment, because we don't let anything be forced on us. Filled with our favorite rhythms, our bleak legacy, the little that will be left of us, will look even more pitiful when we'll finally be quiet. The hand of a seasoned tennis player reaches for the door, almost automatically. The teasing creature that wants to get in hasn't yet shown its appreciation of this attention in the rearview mirror: The car's pinion timidly flaps open, and a human chunk in a dirndl, a stone with an illegible slip of paper hanging on it (it weathered and withered long enough in the storms raging through it, the mystery of the flesh in general—and in particular: if and why it appeals to anyone) gets thrown in without further ado and lands on the passenger seat. So that's what held sway earlier over the great legs, the sight of those! A gigantic smoothened, steam-pressed being, whose real age drained off into the ungainly elasticized pants and knee socks. Underneath, the smooth cerebral/uterine bloodbag from where all the trains, at the whistle blow of the GYN stationmaster, to which the women's bodies react like recruits, have been taken out of service completely. More blood puddles and gobs of slime on the floor, they spread quickly, oh God, someone's dying here, quick, the flesh off the skin! Right then the woman who has just been abducted from the Nothing shoots, at a signal of the invisible umpire, who always looks the other way when a line has been crossed, right into this intimate hole where the rackets of tennis sluggers hold on to each other in fear. A brownishly smeared piece of paper that's been flipped between a small thumb and its index flies upward. Music swings back and forth like windshield wipers, to quickly measure time, which will probably be missed afterward. No one could resist this unbodily body. All those severed passions that were blown in here by the wind, they turn the man, the Creator, the Redeemer into unbodily matter, so that in principle he will have created ALL. The two creatures rise on each other and instantly start fighting like insects. Antennas are buzzing, legs kicking, female forms are becoming dangerous. Main thing, come out of your shell, even though you'll get erased in the process because you had to use the rubber.

A silky mass of hair immediately weaves across all doors, jams every outlet. That woman almost seems to have her natural hair color again. I'll be darned. It's Honey Blonde No. 3 by L'Oréal, something a company has chlorified to ultimate lightness once and for all. Go ahead, take some sample locks to pick your look and he'll pick all your locks! The perfect nest for every budding tryst. Besides, with this silken curtain the head can be pinned at any time to the backrest or smashed with the force of a pop song against the windshield. The open flesh of the former Karin Frenzel, which does not have the coroner's stamp because everything slipped through the controls all killed flesh must otherwise endure, sinks soundlessly onto the motorist. In the fucking rush of the hour, the man behind the wheel (and the guest devouring her meal or his life's sustenance falls out) must not speak to the passenger so that his warhead doesn't get distracted! With the gravedigger shovels of female thighs this driver gets locked in his grave, whence he can't get himself out anymore. It is as if an avalanche of carrion were thrown into his face. This isn't quite how he imagined a custard pie battle. On his face, where the body's stony and then again soft deposit has been thrown so abruptly, it now draws its constantly widening circles that promptly solidify into flesh. The man's sex gets whacked with a sort of swatter. Shreds of pants, ripped apart as if by a claw, drop onto the feet in the athletic sneakers. Something impales itself on the proud friendship device. The flesh around it is already burning but still keeps looking ever more desperately for the ungraspable, the rag ball, the birdie that landed in an alien being. Deft punch, well done! The man's torso rears back, he simply can't grasp this woman. She did him in. Something tender drops close to the tennis faker (he won't become Boris but pretends to. When the model is that famous, it also rubs off a little on the imitation), a curtain that shrouds him at the same time as it exposes him to the scent of female fungus odors. A whirlwind of fiber-flattering foam, as has been demonstrated to us several times when wooing us with the example of an angora sweater (Is it new? No, washed with Woolite). The transparency of feelings has been utterly removed, otherwise the TV would look at us and not we at the TV, yes, we would be mirrored on the screen, if only our intentions were not so easy to see through that we present no obstacle to the gaze, not even as specters.

With shirtsleeves, without the help of a governmental show of strength, the appearance of a woman (in her mid-fifties!) subdues the driver. The shirt quickly ties his arms, so that the cheery (bleach) Blond Beast in him, which seems to be determined to act according to its designation (the manual in four-color printing lies next to him), can come out safely. After all, today's evening news was, as usual, completely devoted to it and its deeds, as much as Karin Frenzel was in a position to hear and see. So let us kneel before Pooch, the animal, the blow-dryer's howling waves straighten out before it and its stick, so shut up! Sit! This magic wand has been in a deep freeze long enough to have hardened like a folded newspaper that's used to fix wobbling furniture and punish unruly tamer animals just for peeing. It's a horrible thing to say, but it does not mean contempt for man and his indisputable capabilities (even though he always has only despised me, I don't give tit[s] for tat, I shouldn't even give a shit, it makes no difference when you must try all your life to keep such horrors at arm's length.) After all, the horror's reach is 20 cm and in some cases even farther. So we still have some air between us and that scrubby tree, which has its foliage at the wrong end. In our case this means approximately midfield, no insult to the system the pneumatics will throw their souls into, which up to now have served them as clothing, on the occasion of the world's end. Ours are already right in here, ladies, in the Salvation Army's collection bags of compassion, which we customarily tour, southbound, from where the upper crust let themselves be picked up by air ambulance, leaving others to at best pick through their color-print rags. Then they'll also have to bundle them themselves. The clothes we summoned made us women into fully functioning human beings fit for service because we, too, get mustered: In our case here, a tennis outfit from a registered company, in this case on a man, gets completely bent out of shape.

Carrion, which is generated by female illnesses and still carries the smell of its womb with which it was buried while still quietly dripping into the coffin lining (did you know that the uterus can resist decomposition the longest—up to one and a half years?) proudly like a quality seal pelt, pelts like crushed bones through the windows into the car. Bait on a fox track. The animals like to intermingle and enjoy it tremendously every time. Out of such biofuel, corpse wax of the Wild Type is no longer possible, not even with unspeakable artistry, to prepare any body for passion; and no camping stove could produce a tasty meal from the powdered soups of several people trained by television to dissolve in each other in a rapid boil.

The man's rudderless club, with which he practiced reaching deliverance at least as often as the Austrian bishops' conference did with live human beings looking questioningly for salvation, gets the door slammed under its nose. It rises angrily, the club, stomps into the arena, throws its fiery head, looking for the ring that frames the tautly stretched paper through which he intends to jump on the spot. But today all worries are removed from him as easily as a panty liner is taken out of the StayFresh box. An ordinary motion if getting moved is what you want. It screeches between the teeth of an *Über*-voice, it bursts out of a hard, fashionable mouth whose lipstick color doesn't want to fit the woman of that age. Why should only the young become mates? After all, the freedom of choice has been taken from all of us. Instead, there are catalogs, in which people, vividly made up, have been designated for immediate consumption by the body-building police, a pointer in the direction of Adam (the feminine brings forth beings, but the masculine forms, I mean formulizes, them) will do, no need to undress. The comparison is meant to make you insecure! And you, too! Truth be told, stinking fat (the *Campylobacter coli* distribution is something like that: Tonsils 24.66 percent, bile fluid 2.66 percent, feces 61.33 percent, and we ate all that!) enfolds the person like a second skin, inside and out, and on these premises, he can't look around anymore for what he wants to eat and what nags at him because he hasn't yet been able to buy it. Let's give him the chance to get over it.

The auto-pilot screams. His visible world seems to be covered by fire, really, he's never felt that much foreign flesh around him! Less would have been more here. Moreover, the figural defects could have been described much more precisely from a greater distance. It is imperative to promptly knock off this tender, spoiled, zoonosis-infected flesh—like the mountain the climber, because the mountain also wants to go to sleep sometime. And this person never advances again. This mounting takes too long. As if this man had become the woman's robe, no, no, the other way around, the shoe is on the other foot: it is her oozing, rotted mass besetting him as his own personal climate disaster. Something land-based lands on him, a meat meteorite, a Pershing, a pesticillin missile that, cleaning and disinfecting every TV-featured building, crashes into the airshaft, extinguishing a few percent of Iraqi and shrieking Iraquois women on horseback, it's all one and the same, news and featured film, gone they are, as if they, as if we had never been there. Dangerously poisonous, suffocankerous mash runs down the man's muscles. He once was a mother's psychic potpourri, but like all material beings he could neither grasp an insight nor absorb it, though he didn't make an effort either. Instead he nicked plenty of notches into his nature, he'll always stay wet behind his weenie. He barks out loud in horror and delivers a stool sample. His small world with the reclining seats as extras gets consumed by fire, ultimately it is his ignorance, his ignorance of the Father who sets the world as well as its destruction in motion. That's a discrepancy, a discreet *Panzer* that would not let him see the feminine even if it stood before him, telling him the lotto numbers, the lookout is too small, actually not much more than a small hole. The unknown's breath is taken away, whereof his mother could not be the cause, she is in the nursing home, on the contrary, she first gave it to him (oh, Mercedes! Well, at least the first atomic bombs bore the names of men, albeit very small ones), the enlivening breath of pneuma, in our case *Pneus,* tires that is, how they once delighted the child at his first ride on the tricycle. A body dissolves like ice that could no longer make it to the freezer. Others, aliens, are entrusted with taking care of our car, and we pay them well. They step up to check how much oil or air is contained in it. What flows in our vehicles is antiblood, a juice in their muscles that pulls them forward without letting them bulge, gasoline, a juice without tension—a rousing spark is generated without impregnating anything, and yet, all those fruit are lying by the wayside, where we passed, in their blood.

Is it possible? This Father still gets into the panties of this woman, even though toys will do as well. His cock crows three times into the apparition, tears open the flesh that hasn't even assumed concrete contours yet, not even to do him a favor, it simply hasn't had enough time. This woman will soon be completely dried up. Luckily there are germs that are sensitive to it. Personally, I wouldn't depend on it, this one's still got enough juice. Yes, the umpire can hardly believe it: Even though a motorist who's got his faith pasted to the windows (don't turn around, it is I! I swear that's what stands out here) fell victim to a horrible apparition, he keeps jabbing his little stick until the very last moment, the way he learned it in a skid-control course, into the loose flesh. Not only his own flesh and blood shall rise, he also wants to create the woman for it; he'll teach her that he alone is God and except him no other one exists. Enlightened by this Sophia, he shall, in turn, recognize the Higher One: the God of Abraham, Isaac, and Jacob, but I haven't even told you and him the name of God. There are more pressing things to do: to butter up this woman and spread her in small portions or to start from scratch again. But when the likes of him prick us, we don't bleed. We always bleed at the wrong time anyway, and if we get something in our pants, it won't, unfortunately, always be panty liners.

Since the music, after a brief struggle, surrendered to the rock-solid motorist, he is busily co-conducting it with his boner (please get things back in order again!). The female matter that fills the car's interior has developed into a pretty hairy element that, in the meantime, wove the whole vehicle shut. A twine of misdirected cells and a few more ungainly vessels to be noticed on the woman that, loaded with this man's fire, swiftly leave for Lilliput, are not the stuff that dreams are made of. A drum roll, because the act is difficult, but this piece of goods, Woman (it can also be mail-ordered from the most distant regions, even with return and exchange options!), gets ground up wham-bam between the loins of this thumping machine. Wandering from the height of an Austrian tennis court that, on account of the darkness, has been relocated to the car comes a hunky-gory racket man, and with a firm grip on his handle he wanders straight through the product he chose as a partner to win this one set. His body, Jesus!, is brought down from above, the stand-in knight hops and drips only a little anymore, and like water through a pipe, he moves through this quintessence of a woman who simply is everywhere, above and below, left and right. He and his semen! He splashed about everywhere, without getting even the slightest impression of this woman, he got his body from above, and now he is taken off the cross. Yes, now I can see it clearly, something lifts itself up, a product, logically, of the Logos, the primal ground, which this Love-game player fertilized fruitlessly long enough with his favorite balls. He hardly ever scored with any of them, and his patient, inborn, burnt-in essence now turns against father and mother evenhandedly. This thing on man's end still shakes itself out rigorously, one hand gives him a hand at it, squeezing it until only dark water, a tiny back-alley playground for fish, flows out. You, dear reader, receive here a strange piece of writing. You are still puzzling, and in the meantime, from the boner-sling, the sweet particles are squirting out already. Unfortunately, they are fattening, fatiguing, or get you fucked into the family way. The unformed fleshen plug that hasn't even earned the name Woman yet, yes, THAT ONE, with the multivitamin!, the bloated one in the white lace blouse and those ridiculous white knee socks (she even tied a small apron somewhere around the midriff or where the middle is assumed to be in this carnal apparition, a fig leaf?, which hides nothing but nothing and wild curls), this bait that laid itself out now swallows the endurance-stiffened beast, that plucky bundle of joy, which actually should have eaten it up, the bait, the fun fare, and then spit it out again contemptuously. Now this zealous amateur athlete has actually shed his whole sheath and merged into that woman. Women had always been his element where he swimmingly wagged his wiener. Music has been squeezed into the car's warm interior, filled with the steam of blood and stinking from intestines, superfluous?, yes, but thank you, we take sweetener squeezed from the tubes of Radio Music as the (one and) only atmosphere. It enlivens the "place" (a possible euphemism for God just watching it all, doing nothing). Heaven and earth must have a good relationship with each other, or one would not voluntarily make room for the other and we would start to slip if we wanted to follow this road to the end.

The man is the woman's death squad, but the woman is man's death sentence. At the moment of death, the woman withdraws her body from the man, the man can't do much with his anymore either. Oh Mama! Finally, she can make her last and best supper with him out of it! She also made life, for God's sake, while the man simply kept cruising. Now she takes revenge and bends over the baby carriage, where the hoarific decedent coughs and swallows water, but even the water would rather march through the air and cut off the breath unwittingly. This traffic light is out again, and the motorist doesn't know what to do: So, one really dies only once, I would have never thought it of us. HIS sex must be removed. But if it accommodates me, it is quite welcome to stay.

My domestic circumstances prompt me to tell the truth at least once: This vacationer seems to have been ravaged as if by an ax, a mower, or electric clippers; lying in front of his car, his eyes are wide open, one completely torn out (an anticosmic, anticosmetic fundamental stance, which speaks for ascesis rather than emphatic libertinage!), his pants, his underpants, which he tried to take off voluntarily, are hanging in shreds around his ankles. His torso including the arms is bound with remnants of the shirt, the entire front section bare, as if readied to be rescued immediately or scaffolded for reanimation. Maybe his sex, which had been ripped out with the roots, still tried to confer with the father confessor of Reason. It wouldn't have done it any good. A human mass keeps pushing forward until it has blasted its scale; it puts itself out of operation over and over again, when it collides with another continent, which has the necessary strength. Who or what does still exist when we let ourselves be consumed by our desire for it? It disappears right in front of our nose. We, too, will disappear. But a new catalog is quickly bought, and already we are consumed by wanting something altogether different. A place where at least the stars could save themselves, I hope, so that empty eye sockets can follow their movements even in the face of death. It will be captured by cameras. Vanished from the bloody compost of pubic hair is the grub that grinded away for so long, ladies, ladies!, under our ferocious supervision. Perhaps it turned into what it wanted to be, the bud, the base of everything that wants to continue to grow in nature and gets wrecked. The sex is a plant that gets devoured by its own roots again and again. Now everything waits for the new building that should feature an erotic moment, if you please, before we move in ourselves to let it whirl us into an infinite rotating motion. Until all emotional fog will have been blasted away from us, subdued by the centrifugal force, yes, exactly: let's flee from the other, as long as there's still time! The motor is dying down now, its battery empties, because the high beams were on. Hearts of humans get hurt until they have no heart themselves.

Panting, its nose close to the ground, scenting and sensing, a being runs off in a beeline, in a rag of a dirndl dress, that is to say, enveloped in a sort of lampshade made of human skin, as worn, even bigger and more beautifully, by Frau Carolin Reiber, under whose bushel, in the evening, at 8:20 sharp, a grave light, weak and easily perishable, will glow once again. The figure hurries down a stony road rolling into the cooling night. Leaves a pile of trace, an excretion that she, diligent housewife that she is, also left, of course, around sink and stove. A steaming pyre of bones. Dogs bark, the being barks back. She has stuffed a few scraps of flesh into her apron pocket, a souvenir of times when even she still followed the monthly rules, when her body window was still entered and exited at least once a week. We would be more cautious entering a car: there we brush off our shoes and step on the rubber protection before we rev ourselves up and race toward the alps. Ah, grand alpine world: the inn is far, yes, back there, that's where it's parked for now. Jesus Christ, the Highest Native incarnate, hangs on the wall. With Jesus, that semibared body, nakedness, in contrast to God, the essence is beingness, in short: The being has been bared, bloody shreds of loin cloths have also been elegantly folded backward, so that the alien knows itself and can take on the Father by his drapery of human flesh (angels, plunging dead folks, raging devils tie the women to trees and strangle them with their own pantyhose, because they, the demons, were not let into the newest club with the brightest, sharpest axes of light—that's how, as an angry God, you must become active on this side of Eden. Personally, I think their old-fashioned carrot-pants are to blame for the guys failing to get in and being humiliated to such an extent), which is its all and our fall. Why did he have to wear such a short skirt, that God? Quickly down with it, too! They go into Mary's wash, right with her sheets, her dirty laundry, into her slurping and blurping front loader, which the church also loves, that's why it always comes out so clean. Approaching a woman in such a measly clothing substitute to just grasp and touch her won't do. We ought to wear a solid logo, clearly visible on our jackets and jeans, otherwise it's all a no-go.

The bloody, ripped out genital lump has been placed neatly next to the dead body. Animals inspect and first take what they don't have to bite off. The rest is also up for grabs. Flies graze in the blood-clotted pubic hair. They should actually be sleeping by now. A light must have attracted them. Round, rigid eyes rest without blinking on the throat that's been bitten into and abandoned. The thyroid cartilage can be crammed down to the core. The jackdaws and rooks that recently, in a public spectacle of nature's reign, relieved entire flocks of lambs of their eyes, leaving just the bare stumps, are still waiting a bit, in case someone is approaching. Then they will also start moving, picking up the human seed and doing nothing with it in the end, that's still more than we ever did. A hot dog in gravy, this white martyr lies there, the loin-wrapped, zapped body whose midwife went missing so that he could never really rid himself of himself and the desires that pestered him. Who stands by him now, the eternal player on the red court, the cinder track (also: called the Tart[ari]an track)? He had to lower his standards with regard to cheese, wine, and humans while, as mentioned earlier, he had already lost all sense of scale sometime before. You simply must look whom you invite into the car that has already had its fill anyway. Who'll still believe this man now, how big his member was during his life? Soon his license plate number will be reported, and the search will be on for a monster. There, just go over there and check the license plate, lately black on white, there are, after all, smaller unions than that with the Lord and/or man and woman, there is the European Union: a group of people who labored really hard and reached beyond themselves: twenty thousand completely different marmalade jars! Still, many of them got nothing and nothing of God's body either. Interpol searches for brides for the demiurge, our chancellor, whose name today is Franz Vranitzky and tomorrow Mr. Minister Soandso, they are to be handed over, the brides, but this gentleman doesn't even want them. Europa! That man and his poodle, the foreign minister, borderbuster, Iron Curtain raiser, or ferryman who only must be stabilized now so that he won't wobble, the two of them got us to say "Yes" to them and all the bridegrooms that were provided for us in the fleet of vehicles, where our souls get serviced in due time. No one's going to wait for them. But whoever comes too soon will be penalized as a net payer. The material will be delivered to matter, the carnal we've always returned to the earth. So now we are incorporated and doubly innocent. So that we belong to the inhabited world again and are even able to inhabit others for as low a rent as possible.

And to prove that I am right, here is the menu of the universe so you can pick your favorite decedent from the past: TODAY'S WINNER IS THE FURRIER STERN. Hurrah! As soon as tomorrow he will bring you a confirmation for the PARTY that he wants to sell to you, no one should say, you not pay enough attention. But you must find out from responsible PARTY official if you must have professional license, but I think not, because new ordinance say it can be brought later, I not know if this is also for furriers. There is someone with who you can talk, he licensed plumber, very nice man. And you also very important to bring a copy of certificate of apprenticeship and of apprentice health insurance document! Just make sure you have it all together! Still: Not good season for furriers, because fur sellers so busy, like in high season and stupid Christians buy like crazy of poor, who must emigrate. Watch out you not have to stay behind all alone and not find business to incorpsorate. Yes, how was it with those bodies, they won't be much trouble once all of them will have gone up in smoke without anyone even catching their names. Now, now Ms. Author, stop indulging yourself in such triumphant warmth! No one has to see so much infertility as you contain. Better you restrain yourself a bit.

15

Dripping from sweat Edgar Gstranz flings himself into the kick turn, the last inhibition threshold, where an embankment that's been completely chewed up by a Caterpillar, edges forward once more before the back of a slowly rising beast comes unexpectedly into view: the roof of the inn. Edgar's room is worked in there about shoulder level. Any power could lift him now and piggyback him around, in that regard he resembles a rising flood of fellow citizens—their votes always produce huge majorities and then they wonder how they suddenly left history behind them, which they—supportive pillars—had just stretched out above them forcefully and felt it punch its powerful straight rights into them. Well, they really didn't want that much of the same as they stood in front of the movie house in the evening, being bored to death because the same film was shown every day. Edgar has learned to trust timekeeping. His sports equipment has been thoroughly tested. His feet shaking, this remote-controlled son of the Alps slid across the terrain to the finish line; now his limbs are practically slipping through the wind so fast it's as if they were skidding through a thin curtain into another continuum, where the TV watcher lifts the gauze in front of the window only to sink powerlessly back into their comfortable chair. So then, here, too: the same film he didn't want to see at the movie house to begin with! A harbinger of the snow wind jumps light-footedly from the mountain peaks. Below, where one can hardly see anything anymore, the slope merges with the dark; the flatware clicks, a bad dream takes hold of the people forcefully and nibbles on them a little. This athlete, a horse not yet broke, whose Party will certainly show him the ropes that will still break his neck, has surely been prepared more appetizingly on his surf plate. He can almost hear the laughter of our dear in- and outlandish guests. A lectern must still be climbed with great effort, the crowd, a body of water, a wide stream that the Prince of the Party, with a quick reach for the holster, wound around his hip: his code of [ch]arms: his blue fake freedom scarf. Loamy, sluggish water murmurs in front of him and threatens to overflow him. That's just what he was waiting for, that big boy blue! Impishly he dips a custom-made foot into this metallic human plain, the water is like liquid loam, as if it wanted to pelt him with people in turn, it is viscous, brackish. When our speaker steps into the mud with pieces of flotsam sticking out of it, turning with great difficulty in the rapids caused by them, then it parts, the sludge, it comes up to the speaker's hip, and pounding against his sex that lies somewhat below the slimy surface of the stream are human hearts with thousands of tentacles grabbing in this liquid metallic mush at HIM? Where are the helpers? Here are helpers, midwives fumbling with HIS zipper, who is the first to get it open? Yessirree! Party officials at their reserved TV table, hopping around with each other to relentless polka and *Ländler* music, their woody loins rubbing each other the wrong way. Or this woman right here, with her usually quite normal modes of behavior, there's suddenly something quite sassy about her, the way she stretches herself high above the water, a steely bridge, from where you can let yourself be thrown, tied only to a rubber band. Where have I seen that face recently? Doesn't matter. The young Führer feels well under the pall of people, but it's no longer okay with him when those countless fish mouths under the water's horny surface that no sunlight can get to glisten are snatching at his flesh, cannibal fish sliding their jaws under his pants and shaking his flesh if something's in it for them. A smarmy, swarming *Gesinnungsgemeinschaft,* a community of conviction, still kids, but members already; in colorful swimming trunks, that's how they play between their riverbanks, now they have even got a punt, and as soon as they start poling they hook right into their neighbor on this vast body of water with a wooden crackle that echoes from the steep shore. The shore is kept open for those blond youth (some have no hair at all, apparently for no reason, maybe so that nothing sticks to their heads) from 8:00 a.m. to 5:00 p.m., then the boat rental closes: all young chubby cheeks, licking ice cream, sucking at words, boys and girls, but also many old folks, hanging on the words that bubble from the lips of our big little rascal and then get spit out. The utmost is granted to them: once a day a KitKat break! The bigger ones among them, each a bloody debt head sitting in the stripped skeletons of their single-family homes plus garages, are put out to pasture by their (ring)leader, at the tennis club, for that matter, where they can chase their own tails, it's the only way it pays! Their Party issues a stay-fresh guarantee, the young candidates are quickly replaced as soon as they start to smell. Every one of them's got a garishly furbished package of cookies, wafers, or some other shit wrapped around them like a coat, the flood they all have become is rising, and they fear for what's been promised to them, that they may stay a bit longer inside their package and have father's milk chocolate melt into them: The masses stand up to their knees in excrements! The folks that elected HIM as their Ringführer get repackaged and laid out as fresh bait again. This sleek man wants only fresh flesh, the old one gets paid off in cash faster than newspapers could wake us up with their rustling. He jumps full length out of the murky masses of water, holding onto the bait, his jerking heart, what will it catch next? Whatever escapes his flight is pounced on by the youths jumping like dolphins from their dugout, whose longing lengthens their bodies. A furrow that's not been (for)given and forgotten by a woman is left as their wake. The water was like wood, just as hard to split, but now it gapes wide open, a leadenly resting mass coffin. These fellows will have their bellies split open as soon as they fall back into the flume. Bits and pieces of paper are floating on top like the back fins of countless smaller fish that followed the big ones, snitching pieces of cadaver out of their mouths. They pick up the scent. Anything far and near not wanting to hop along gets stuffed into the pipe and smoked, the ashes will be emptied again discreetly in a place where we are not. Watch out, full speed ahead! Steel-blue scarfs are blowing like swords off the muscular fabric made by the Mothers. Sometimes the fellows also rope-harness themselves to the dirty equipment of their Freedom Party head to scrub it clean with their rough tongues. Raging storms drive all those ready to storm troopers onward. Moving melodies are hummed into the storm that will take the twisted bodies out of and along with it up from the muddy stream.

Edgar Gstranz pants in pursuit of his grinning models who either breathe through gills or not at all, but whose teeth—unfortunately, I must be frank here, sometimes grow a bit crookedly out of their mouths. But now they have to take care lest their hands or whatever other limbs will grow out of the graves to boot. Not to worry: Mommy will be there again, hitting them with her crop. To be sure, fresh soil gets thrown over it all, but hands and extremities come out over and over again. So the guys turn the old story around and beat up their mothers (those are women who try to prevent their children's road to death with their own bodies, but the children want death, oh yes, delicious, cool, firn! Like a eucalyptus candy, they want to suck their mommy's twat whence they were thrown out once before!). But hold it, there still is mother's best friend, that nice Frau *Heimat,* whom those hunks can beat with their unbeatable nature, actually, they all have about the same: all under forty and with as much as possible neighing HP (with whatever type of drivable saucer in which you can catch your own spume, when the hand, restless as it is, slips on the wheel. And then the wall of that house racing toward you like a folded-down ironing board!). Up, up, onward! And the ass saved into the tightness of the jeans, where one can guess the furrow along which folks poke around in this climbing rock. Where is the hitch? A deep rift separates the head climber from the others, who all want to get to him anyway. They are dangling out there in the open, these cronies, they are hanging in the wall, that's why they are called hangers-on, but there, in the back, where the seat of blue pants or the white tennis butt is wiggling, that's where one's very essence ripens, and many a fella feels up his Führer quite brazenly. And he can't do anything about it, he is stuck in the wall hanging next to his photo. The healthy beasts kick their legs and sparkle from saliva. The loins shake like sieves, and again some super- or normal boys throw themselves onto the red clay, where they smack their balls and brag that they've been around, but their rackets hit only themselves, and on top of it all, they were caught in their own net. Nothing slower than a BMW could get in the way of these hicks, and nothing smaller than an electrified stream spreads in front of them, outflow from the lake, a packet of cables they flow into, until they are a universally criticized mass. That really gets them going! The more fiercely they get grilled, the deeper they bite into the bridle that was put on them so that the Herr Party-Führer can ride them all the better. They wag and wedel under him, suck up to him, hard stuff drips from the armed pits of newspaper clippings that they paste into scrapbooks. Sport handed them their leader prepackaged as a jogging morning gift, he is constantly written about, photographed. And if anyone dangles, I mean droops, he must immediately be stiffened with blood, so that their heavy fraternal oath holds up real good. The chancellor himself used to be a swift pitcher. The functionaries are substituted until even their softer parts are torn by clapping spurs and hacking boots. High screams ripple out of deep sleep, loins tighten, and the little cocks click in the light wheat or dark wires of hair.

Now listen to the truth: The Party chief who keeps bashing but is never abashed can enter our public tennis court any time, he just has to say the password. But where we, his *Volk*-fortification, are on our knees looking for the ball is not where he wants to go. He always wants to be where we are, just higher. He wants to enter a few levels above us, with his horse-powered bratmobile, so that logos and life can be coupled, and all things generated thereof made into a clay court, where the bones can bleach in peace. This is where he wants to take the whip with triumphant audacity. But regrettably, no chance!, this exceptional being was not accepted. Two whole votes short. I am telling you why: This club has long been blocked up by the kind of tribe who always keep their mouth open until our cute little rascal pisses in there for real; and in case of rain, the game will again take place inside, that is: inside them. They'll find out through what kind of waves (which they themselves made), into which Red Sea, their Father led them once again! But then it will be too late. They can never take root on a tennis court. Such people, just because the Red Sea released them in the nick of time, always have to show off their cargo of history! For all to look and see: Nothing has been cut off from them anyway. Only the thread of life could no longer be sutured, it could open up again any time. Besides: Ultimately, the ball was played too high! Thus opinionates a high functionary of this beautiful white sport who wishes to remain anonymous. He says something like that: It's best to keep your distance from all the victims of the Raging Reich as far as you can piss when they sing with their souls, for they want to hold, always and everywhere, even in the barbecue smoke inside the special event tent, their International History hour, which has been common knowledge for the longest time, it's been written, after all, with beer, puked and pissed into the sand.

Those misbegotten, not to be forgotten, constantly want to pick our scabs for all to see that our flesh underneath has stayed HEIL, and that means WHOLE! But in the future it won't be so easy to keep or tell the good from the bad, confessions alone won't help, no matter how somber we look when we make them, pouring them from one pan of the scale into the other. Something always goes sideways. Though we have been entrusted with the maintenance of penance, others will follow us who will no longer let themselves be crossed. But now the most painful of all: We no longer have the Mercedes subsidiary either. That star, unfortunately, has been taken away from us. Others have been sitting for the longest time now on the fool's throne of History who by all accounts actually make themselves heard: Hey, guys, do your felling somewhere else! Otherwise, a Germanic (family) tree might drop on your head! Don't worry, the show will go on in a moment: Thighs are pressed together, trunks come well to the fore, as the young athletes, grabbing each other by the neck, bend down to the member of the lineage, the only one that lives here, the only one allowed to stay. It's not unusual to spread it apart and see whether it's really one's own, still and calm, the one from before and not suddenly something foreign snapping at it.

Edgar Gstranz is one of those. And he was called upon one day, when he still was on skis—and a modest man came gliding in. Then he temporarily reached the lowest rung of local greatness. In their quiet alpine hole everyone picks the one they know from film, radio, and TV, where blond women (Claudia Schiffer, a bunny from another star!) rather than clouds are all over us or threaten us with the snow-capped mountain crests of their white teeth, which, somewhat bloody from lipstick, are exposed by the candidates' broadest smiles, in the glacial crevasses of society columns, whose stalagtits we stuff in our mouth and suck dry, as if they were from Häagen-Dazs or Dairy Queen and thus for every penis a bonus. So, okay. What's next? We push the button, and instantly the Austrian state TV anchors get to the bottom of everything, and what does this land, dipped into over and over again by cold but forever whining Wienies have to say to it all? Thirsty! A Fresca, Coke, or Sprite, please! Crammed into a circle of ambiguities, folks roll the dice, begging for cable or satellite dishes for their self-images, which are then presented to them by Levi's, Lee, Diesel, or Super, packaged in fresh fotos. After all, the Roman crucifiers also covered their parts with their loincloths, brand-name facing front, when they began to cross a god with themselves. Then the donated clothes were distributed by the Salvation Army and the protective visors of their cool caps were turned backward once and for all.

As if drunk, Edgar spills punch all over the place. A former high-performance athlete in the shadow of tall trees pouring himself into the electorate. Folk music surround-sounds his slogan, but so is pop music, in the rustic disco, where this champ hooked up to the Wild Hunter's Führerbuggy, fired up night after night by a wild bunch reeking from the same stable, wreaking havoc in and out of their hip jogging suits, out of sheer enthusiasm. Between his dear listeners a small lake of wine, sweat, and tears and lots, lots of laughs for the multicolor medium that once produced some spirit, which, however, immediately disappeared. Dudes and dolls, you need so many outlets for the flood of all your favorite music. How do you relieve yourself when they're all blocked at the same time? One time our Edgar has also been clocked in his sport vehicle—the brand-new candidate for councilman was just saying a few words (in that party they say: Charge for change, there's plenty to charge the old parties with, but not us!, we'd rather kick and lick your ass)—that means no more falling asleep in the dark, you mountain sons, but rather: Wake up! Get up! Wash up! Clean up with Mr. Clean, the Magic Eraser of History, make the bed and grab your ankles in front of it, because a sinewy hand gestured toward the treasured disciple Edgar, an index finger beckoned, lightning struck, and in a second Edgar Gstranz is as good as new! Looking at a theodolite (that's a device that, however one turns it, always points to God), you can clearly see, where the deus ex machina, the god of this new Party, pointed from his fast chariot, the chosen one must slit his skin and take it off to the sirens' rousing roar. Apollo told him to do it. There is more and more talk these days about folks taking off their clothes lest they are recognized only by their clothes. Nature is truly intoxicating. Lord of hosts! That god did his business exactly in the place where young people pulled his pants down, see: the picture of a Man. The tongues of the faithful dart out to [ap]praise the death of a lamb, of all lambs, the amount is written on the sticker, and there comes our TV Inspector Rex, more German shepherds are coming out of their front yards and the single-family-home garages that are slowly outgrown by their cars, just take a look at how the chariots gleam under the slobber of the rust-protection shampoos! Thus, human flesh rises and shows its innards, look here, they're up for grabs! Doors open, the sexes are open for business, fanfare!, they get pulled out of their pants and stuck into the darkness, and a hunky host who is the perfect product of skiing, climbing, and tennis hurls his twitching laser beams after them, those faceless sexes who want nothing but to multiply so that the hall rental was worth the money. This dance floor has a super lay-out, and we can get brighter and brasher so that they'll find us in the field guide when the time has come for a hand to grab us once again.

From high above Edgar now looks down on his valley, which has something biological about it, the way it twists and turns from the hips. This is exactly what *HEIMAT* is all about: it has grown below us until it lay down again in the bullet hail of our guns. So then we pull ourselves up the mountain on our safety ropes, a T-bar between our thighs, a board under the ass, sunglasses over this strong sucking and blowing from which our values seek shelter in vain inside their snazzy little thinking caps, and so we go, full speed ahead!

But all this gets thwarted for the shyest of shy, the ghosts of the dead, who are not buried in legalities, real or invented, and are already coming after this young athlete. They have shrunk from a huge mass to a narrow, indignantly puckered mouth-slit and chase Edgar into an airflow smelling of cheesy dead body fat, which, according to an unwritten natural law, should blow nicely behind him. The new time, which measures even one-hundredth of a second, is not pulling him along, rather it is the old one pulling at him. That one stinks a little, but it's still okay. The night gets high on this young living body, whose skin it'll quickly get off his back to stuff new flesh into the sausage casing. Or it will put him into the chest of the earth so that future generations can still benefit from him, digging for his skull. Because down there is where they push and shove, the high and the hammered, who didn't know nothing about nothing and, furthermore, faked their expiration by at least fifty years. In the meantime, almost all of them are on their way into the Nothing, into humus, animals gnaw on them and multiply in their flesh, splash about in their juice. Our innocence is that pure, it paddled for decades in Grüner Veltliner until the notorious glycol incident. Somehow some car juice got into that. For every memorial we have to roll the dice so that we can start anew (e.g., that British parachuter in the Frein, Styria, near Mürzsteg in the crotch between the Mur and Mürz River furrow, right around the corner from here, that's where they killed him with their hunting knives and teentsy cutlery, which usually sleep peacefully in the drawer's steely smell—they sharpened them on their lederhosens, and well, how shall I put it, there he was, rolled up in his ripped ropes, all ready to eat, this captured whale of a rollmops, and they just kept stabbing him with their switchblades. And this is how those folks took care of their paratrooper, their dearly departed, as they call him today as cheerful little wrinkles appear in the corner of their eyes, the pointed seven-dwarf cap of the skier who still brazenly executes the prewar stem turn, along with the rustic diehard's Styrian hat decorated with the traditional *Gamsbart,* the chamois's tuft of hair, put daringly aslant on the dwarves' heads: this is how back then they first went to get bombed and then let their SASsy chuter slip through the heavy drapes—with which those guys guard what's theirs, so that no one would go through the roof and create a hole—into the Nothing. Then they deep-froze him in small packages, lest it smell there fifty years later from this heavy feed for the media to get wind of. Delicate hot flushes rise in the tourists when we lift the pot lids. All signs indicate oven-fresh food. I'll be darned! Waiter, the lottery numbers, please! It costs something, after all, to keep this landscape broom clean until the skeletons sparkle radiantly white, the screams slip at night on the smoothened, thoroughly cleansed road and land on an innocent house wall. And those Safe-Travels daggers in the traffic news carry the speedy driver today as every day over all cloud-covered heights, surpassing eaglelike even the sun, over the southeast beltway and finally put him down again gently, so that we can calmly cut ourselves a slice off of him. He's been steaming in the jam long enough.

Edgar Gstranz was a CANDIDATE, emphasis mine, but he sadly lost to the local wholesale butcher of the Christel Party, who had the votes of his church's lovely voices, a wonderful Mayday choir devoted to our Holy Virgin, because he fed the poor folks in the nursing home with dogfood at no charge, stacking his dough to the melodic tune of the miraculous multiplication of bread in accounts full of black money. And the bishop has a good laugh about it. Nowadays our Edgar comes here only for vacation, but many people still know him from way back when he ran his campaign, high on cocaine, guzzling beer and champagne, his thundering voice resounding through smoke, a face to remember in those days. But sadly, it has passed. Only occasionally the voice rings out of someone else's mug, even though this is not welcome, for a new candidate has long since been found. And Edgar at that time clearly was in overdrive. Before that, the party's top guns always liked to have their picture taken with him and the spirit of the sport, which is always recognizable by its clothes (nothing underneath). Out of sight, out of mind. Maybe it will work out better next time, Edgar! We wish you all the luck. You got the young people's votes handed to you like a punishing rod, yes, our youths, they are getting louder and louder, they drift, kicking in their diaper pants and railing against their playpenitentiaries (vocational school, apprenticeship, upward-climbing school toward the waterfall, named "the Dead Wench," *das tote Weib*), their clothes get ripped by rocks, a thunderstorm rages and calms down again, and we women must not stand back, we need to buy something new every year because the skirt length is different now, but we'll probably stick forever to our super-minis; for out in the country no one buys a pig in a poke. And also the short pants, skin-tight, dedicated to biking, urine-marbled memorial stones, which are still in fashion today and will continue to be for the next ten years. They are so practical: for our roots to remain visible forever, those make us cling to what is ours, mean signposts pointing downward, where we bring anyone who cannot muster the necessary elasticity. Now it is us again, and we will continue that way! Dragging the dead out of their beds! Laughingly, we embrace the world, which is not crumbling soap made from human corpses, this ain't no long-running soap, it's the awesome staircase in our very own international blockbuster TV series "*Wetten, daß . . .*" and that means "Betcha!" and similar diversions and deflections. Yes, the world, and the way everything is attached to it, it's there to be mounted only by us, the carefully groomed, with wiggling asses and whipped hair-creme dressings foaming from head-Tortes with *Schlag*.

Just now the essence of the young mountain lovers was struck by the lightning flash of a camera. Sorry about that! So there they stand, lifting their rough loden jackets slightly at the hem as if they had to paddle across their very own whitewater that had at some point been poured to them as vinum veritatis; there they stand, these two sons of the Alps, who, one week apart, smashed their skull bowls with their work tools and exposed their brains (which resulted in a small heap of darkness that gets pulled out of the shadow with a scrubber, that's at least one domestic tool every unemployed female of this region must employ once we will have had an employment policy as before, *Arbeit* that really makes us *frei*). Anyway, the hunter kids stand next to each other arm in arm and support with their respective free hand the blood-caked rests that were left of their heads. They are not ungamely, those young masters, who (at least one of them) had been so afraid of failing the exam, and now they are falling with a howl out of the clear blue sky. Bone splinters gleam brightly in the sludgy stuff, an eye jiggles like vanilla ice cream on a stick. But tired they are not, going home they are not. Now they turn the alpine hunk mass of their bodies toward each other, the air hugs them kindly, and they resolutely make themselves noticed to the others who also populate this dance floor, for as their coffin clothes have been gnawed off by underground fauna and the tooth of time, they are, unfortunately, not wearing pants.

Doesn't matter. Now the Loden Yodels (a local big band?) have already fallen all over them, cheering, nibbling at their breast flaps, which stretch like latex across their ribs, but down there: Down there their white disco-sticks stand out, bouncing lithely up and down, testicles jumping at each other like growling wirehaired pointers, slapping each other playfully, things held in hand a thousand times, on top the small, half-stiff decorative flagpoles, each sticking in its own fruit cup, they understand each other's language and mien, the way they peek, their heads all red, out of the bullet case. How many times did these brothers, to the loud stomping of the animals all around them in the stable, where no one saw it, where the parents' cold curses, the father's oxwhip, the mother's punch (while she, that angel of the family, twirled her sons' little flame-throwers between her right thumb and forefinger) could not reach them, because sometimes the parents wanted to try out their weapons against each other as well, how many times did those brothers rub themselves raw on each other and devoured each other cooingly like loving pigeon throats. Now the two of them rise, lifting their moist, soaked wicks up to the navel, they start to glow, and already they, those eager finger pointers who always point to their own disgrace, have advanced to the other's wall. But that stands already in no-man's land. The first drops are falling! In the drizzle of the putrefying rain, they press the right buttons, and they defiantly rub against each other, the eager messengers, because they have something to tell us. That you should have a good time as long as there still is life in the cockerel. It's also what the transistor radio tells us in the kitchen. Makes you want to bite right into it until the blood comes out! Then the big older brother, whose prick woke up expectantly, turns the younger one around (he always teased the younger one that he'd never pass the hard woodsman's exam even though the little one should be used to the darkness in the woods, after all, he had to squeeze himself, supervised by the older one, into every dog's muzzle in the village, while the big brother dealt him a few good slaps on the bouncing white tassels tied around his woolly sack). Okay, and now, with his harmlessly shiny meat and potato mien, the older brother tries to squeeze himself into the younger one, even though it's already pretty full in there. Then a triple salto mortale from a squat into the infinite, his own brother's boundaries have finally been broken, and that calls for celebration, here we go!

So then the little brother gets punched in the back with the fist to open himself up to the older one, who with his vehicle clears the endless way into the snow and the Nothing. But the little one will be the first to kill himself. Meanwhile, the little idiot, who is absolutely unable to memorize anything about hunting or the management of trees, who remembers nothing and therefore must feel it, may scuttle about with his subjugated, pinched birdie out in the open and drop some poop. After the exploration of his behind, which gets fucktified by big brother in ways that defy translation, the little one, when it's his turn, may also let go and scatter himself onto the barn floor as fodder for eternity. Even in death will he be the one in front. There, you've gotta see this, here's the older one, looking once again for a starter for his abuses, bending his little brother, turn and drink!, he knocks him with his Titan (such a huge vehicle is driven only by one who absolutely can't get out of his shell any other way) to his knees, pushes his blood-soaked head that no one wants to spoon up anymore downward, and mixes for the last time—but the first time that a local celebrity like Edgar Gstranz watches this special performance—his syrup with the brother's water into a quite acceptable drink. Those pitiable boys crouch in front of a hedge and drink from each another, yeah, no one escapes hardship; those two young fellows are the pre-unthinkable, well, you can also simply call it "human," and there is also "son of man" who fits the description, here we even have two pieces of him. Oh my, it's that long that the forester boys have been six feet under! How time passes! Buried in the double-stacked grave. If you've still got a brother, be happy and get inside him as much as possible. He is, after all, the only one to be left of his series. A pain as if from an instrument in the back, the loins, where some muscles are already somewhat decayed, are getting weak. You've gotta see this!, the strained grin of the bared, soiled ass is still a bit repulsive to the older one, but then his hunting tool disappears—which he knows how to use, especially on himself, beyond death, when somewhere a target pops up—all the way down the partly upturned shaft in the brother's well. Their mother, after all, forged them together by the padlocks dangling from their white bellies, which she personally sharpened and oiled again and again. Screams escape the mouths unwillingly, throats tighten with a click, crowing gun cocks; surging waves hit the tender loins, sweeping everything along, and here he comes, the brother, foam pelting from the groins, atta boy!, such sensitivity! Like a comet-tailed stud, whom his father could never break in and chase through the streets with anything ridable that had several gears. There are threats, poundings, mountings, over and over again. The umbilical cords get entangled, waves wander through the black smoked chunks, there's pouring out and pushing in, the bar with the good Styrian beer is open, yes, those two brothers were given to each other as promotional gifts and by coincidence they are also the only ones ever given to them by their parents. They weren't exactly advertisements for their profession. Here—where their moldy belly flesh glows pallidly among the animals under the hayloft from where it's raining straws, while the backbenchers bob their butts and the blind urges up front grope stiffly for the ground to sow themselves. Right here, where nothing grows but the grazing sex, whose muzzle snaps, shoots, and sprays, sprays over and over again, until the floor whereon the animals stand, totally floored, almost disappears under the layers of slime—the chain of this family ends. One of them pulls on it, and all at once they are all gone.

Edgar gets hailed, they want him to hook up with them. After all, he's also got his padlock! Anything sharp that can always be sharpened again if needed will get in. Spruces twenty meters tall are shaking as if they had grown up on the dance floor, while their colleagues, God willing, for God's sake, have been felled long ago. That's permitted. There, a bit farther from the inn, that's where it is, the now-orphaned dance floor, where an occasional country fair spectacle of war takes place, an exercise for the long-extinct Yugoslavia, which once bordered this state, yes, and exactly over there, you can listen to the orchestra, where folks enjoy sticking knives into each other. Bells can be heard ringing from the chapel farther in the back, beyond the curve, at the bridge, where the rocks push so close together that they seem to crush you between them when you drive through them on the logging road that is closed to civilians and amateurs. The soil is loamy in these canyons. Some call on God in person and push little bouquets behind the wooden bars, where the Lord sits in the slammer, God as possessor, like the thief as the possessed, are both nearly out of control with excitement over what the offering box might hold. In his soothing way God instructs the candidate to come back the next Sunday, it opens at 10:00 a.m., when the priest from the neighboring village arrives as visiting host and to show the host. Maybe there will be some revenue, too. In the meantime, there is darkness, which, nevertheless, gets busily stepped and driven into. Edgar Gstranz hurries along with swinging muscles and sacs (that's a muscle God blew at to make it a bit fuller) that could shut down any moment now. Behind him he hears, also in the fifth—the so-called animal gear in the GTI that runs on pure alcohol, a panting and gasping and a nervousness that doesn't cause insecurity—takes hold of his lively loins, which are so plump and slaphappy under the latex, it makes you want to slap them, too. The two young hunters sink back into their pleasures, abandoning themselves all the way to their slam-bang death, that is, one showed the way, dying before the other, with the other following him as the singing part of the duo. Oh yes, and passing on, a friend, a famous athlete, also spends the night there, close to them, the strangers who were next to him in the soil, in self-assured soliditarity. Soon we will celebrate the deads' topping out. From the moment the traditional May tree gets hoisted to the roof, there is no more remembering the dead, now that the fiddlers are off the roof one can see what's coming sooner than others, since it's always oneself who has it coming. The night gets cruised through, the auto body shines, the young man, almost city slick now, observes what life has to offer him, white rings around the tree trunks to keep away from them while driving. Okay, soon the cruisade will be done with, one more reflecting aluminum ring, a spin at the wheel, the swing flies forward one more time and then backward, too, and why is there a house, there was never a house here, oh no, there it is again, the loamy stream of the road, the water reaches almost to the knee, sluggish sand lines the banks, and here, a bridge, it ends after a thousand-plus meters, somewhere in the distance, the water is littered with garbage, how many people have already thrown themselves in there!, as if an ancient film projector had spit it all out in fits of spasms. And then that muddy river simply tilts up, into the driver's face, the water rages and resounds, the protective wraps of the ice cream cones, even the small caps covering them for hygienic reasons, are flying, framed in thousands of tons of water, around Edgar's ears, still more water gets pulled over the self-closing eyelids, a coin gets placed on top of them so that he can pay the entrance fee later, there is the delphinarium, take a look at that fish, uhm, mammal, now he jumps, just like that, over a whole man (discover nature in action right here!), the man is the spitting image of the one last week, it might even be him. He's got to wear that shoe now. And he beats, bangs himself into a single-family home to boot. Better not try to beat that.

Thrown as lightning by two dead brothers' hands, Edgar falls against the low stilts of the dance floor, his roller board careens away from him, turns upward, and lands amid discarded paper cups and plates and Coke cans. The beloved board, one from the Sixpack, which shall be our last dwelling six feet under, is immediately surrounded by two pieces of human refuse, which absolutely wants to get away from here but doesn't yet know exactly how. Recently, even a sky-surfer dropped on the head of a woman who was dead before she could get to the feminine ending of this unexpected sea of desires (falling from the sky like a star just once!). Refuse and death, however, are ours, they show up reliably wherever we float in the filthy, stinking water, where we and our trash are swimming and drifting toward that tunnel ahead (the broken hull of our house) through which the subway roars today.

The two hunters' sons have already covered the distance from the cozy to the uncanny, now they can also show it to Edgar. Without hesitation the stumps of their hands grope his athletic suit, what a drag, it's got no opening. Where's Edgar's origin to put the jimmy in? Where is the spring, the whitish cloud of water, where one can dock the mouth? Come back, everything's forgiven! The brotherly, the mountain lovers throw the panting athlete on their backs and squat on his swirling legs, they keep his trunk hanging from the cutting-board floor, also the head with the hair standing on end, which is just about to brush against the floor's memory. Edgar's mouth is wide open and screams, while far away at the inn the food pelts onto the plates, a daughter expressly bred seedless, named Karin Frenzel, softly slumped in the seat next to her mother, wipes her plate with bread as if she wanted to disappear in the sparkling surface, she is just pissed, that's all, that she can no longer see her mirror image there, nor in the knife's polished edge. Maybe she is no longer herself? How come the hall is suddenly packed with people? Where does the awful stench filling the room come from? Do they have a stockpile somewhere here where a hand can reach in any time and whip the guests forward as if blown away by rainsqualls? Edgar is finally brought out as well, to breathe into the palm of his hand and, since he belonged all his life to the ungrounded, learn to come out of himself at least now that he is in danger of drowning.

The two forest spirits, the aborted shooting stars, snap their centimeters-long horn nails against the latex cast of the sculpted legs, a hill, though, to be mastered only with climbing irons or nitric acid. Sharp, horny claws damage the fabric, which is durable but not indestructible. Ready for action, the two corpses test their last teeth on the force between them, the interface between two body-blocks wherein reactions explode one after the other but still remain with Edgar. The teeth fall out, but they undo the seam like a razor blade, there is living flesh marching toward them in the opposite direction, oho!, that's flesh forthcoming.

We haven't had that down in the ground for a long time, there our flesh was always just lying there, ready-to-eat meat for all those tiny subterranean creatures, mostly maggots and worms. The seam is slit open in a jiffy, and Edgar jumps out. Small bites are taken out of him. A few measures of folk music, wind players from the Ötztal Valley sink their lips and teeth into folks who always think they are at that moment missing out on something better, maybe the Zillertal Valley Skirt-Chaser Band (as for myself, that's the biggest disappointment since I became a Rapid Vienna soccer team fan—what am I doing in the Austrian TV's sports studio, moi, a loser, isn't this supposed to be a gay show?), and Edgar's constant companion, who holds on to him and often enough was also held by him, that dick gets thoroughly gnawed off now. The brothers tear the best bites out of each other's mouth. The gateway opens, the dead walk through patiently, even at times when the cashier's office might be closed; Edgar's arms try to swing upward to cover himself and the secluded little path into him, but the arms have no strength, overly burdened by souvenirs and old ambitions, covered by futile desires for status, which once almost got him to be councilman. An evil friendship guides the hunter boys' hands and balls. What's been played into their hands, which they can't pass to the teammate? A heavy, sluggish piece of meat, an empty belly, intestines everywhere, two hands dripping with blood, this passive, very specific weight that's been put politely into the small plates of their palms. Above it, bluish, reckless, wrapped in a subtle, smelly vapor, the tunnel, watched over by the thighs like slackers who have nothing to do. Like a broken branch Edgar's genital bone tilted forward, it has a tap built into the cask that dangles directly into the forester candidates' wide-open mouths, which are snapping at it from both sides. Those louts have obligations! And what are they doing instead? Gone fishing at the edge of the woods. They suck the heavenly fire out of a pair of peel-off plastic pants. From above, high up on the cliffs of the rotting tunnel entrance, juice is dripping into them, they carelessly wipe it off with their sleeves. A tarp rises in the wind, an angrily fluttering bird. Three names are called up. Edgar cannot carry his body to term, even though he did not have it all that long. He is totally stripped now, the top of the bodysuit, along the median strip, is unstitched all the way up to the notch, where the little turtleneck peeks out. His rod, his roots, his lineage are one, something that returns home religiously, to where it is alone in the homey darkness of itself, a dead thing sprinkling the lawn with itself. Meanly, it snapped at anything trying to come close to him. Unless a pretty woman, her hair flowing from the parting long after we already turned away from her again, was connected to that term. And now the Edgar meat is revealed top to bottom and torn open for taking, stretched out as it is on the soft floor. Immediately, the greedy teeth of two fellow dead rush into Edgar's ant- and worm-filled pouch, the teeth of two wanderers who lost the way and panicked, graze off everything to pave a new path for themselves, where they will once again lack politeness toward their wandering comrade. What's wrong with our fellow traveler? Didn't he watch out? Well, why did he have to let himself be served so deliciously on his board? Naked and prostrate he hangs from the high-heeled wooden floor. Edgar's soft flesh is used like some kind of God's acre where the shovels sing their way in up to the elbow, groundbreakingly, down to the fundamental tone of the floor. God prepared this garden, but since then the dead have stirred it up pretty good. A narrow descent leads inside Edgar Gstranz, into the dark words that must be said at the gate. The partition had been bashed in with a hatchet, the halves gape open, and a completely changed being rises naked out of the plastic peels of the pants. Its name was Edgar. But it is Edgar no more. It is the name of many folks taking a walk to the bridge from where the bodies get thrown into the river.

With ease, while walking, a wanderer strips himself, who at long last dropped his requisite, those few boards that were to protect him under the earth. He uses his member freely for the purpose of being presented on billboards as sport and image, as man in the flesh or in tube amplifiers, who likes to play all his instruments or at least listen to the music. It was unavoidable that the earth finally took him. Everyone back to his producer, Philips, Grundig, Sony, those Walkmen for the walking dead, because everything material gets transferred to the bank, where it toils and still gets cut down until its account comes to nothing, or even less than nothing, because it did not grow along with its master, for not even the Lord hands it to his own in their sleep. The carnal and the material, however, belong to the earth, Edgar will be seen quite frequently, but it is not him.

16

Hail to you in your nobility, Mother. Your concessional mammarchy has always given us the strength to think foreign lands through to the end by slipping into their bellies and—everyone a cuckoo throwing another woman's children out of their nest—effortlessly covering thousands of kilometers in order to take possession of this gigantic stretch that is paved with the dead. Just so that we can stay children forever and nest wherever we want. We are running out of names for our prey.

First responders swarm around the overturned vehicle, which does not move because it had this terrible accident. Ants, beetles with ropes and heavy equipment surrounding the wreck. Confident of victory, proud women are standing on the terrace, stirring in their *Torte* base, they have the best view. The victims of this badly ending excursion have already been removed. Giggling, they crept out of their larvae and spread around the area. At long last, they can see the sights that close to the living at 5:00 p.m. That's how they are, the dead, sure of success and victory, just like us: instead of trampling their earthly cocoon and taking the ghost ride, they even pump themselves up in their plastic bags of skin wherein they were stored: maybe because they are annoyed that they did not put themselves into a sturdy aluminum lunchbox. They pop themselves stepping on them. But they duck down quickly—everywhere there's some authority and an autobody with a door that should have been pushed open in time to jump out—under a *Gestell,* a framework, the highest in a wreckage of racks rattling in the wind, from whose highest part the figures flap loosely like laundry, were there more supposed to perish?, a *Gestell,* with their names hung up on it, which could cause problems for them. Directly after death it's still possible to feel like a gem in hand for all to see, but the Name ("the Word") is not forthcoming, no one seems to know it anymore, even though the accident happened recently, well, in fact, just now. That old woman—toll the bells, you'll hear that at least—like a miracle, hardly anything happened to her. She sits dazed in the meadow, her purse in her lap, which she holds on to as if it were a small animal, well, you never know who might sit down next to you, and still not chastened, she pulls on her vocal cords yelling for her daughter, who seems to have slipped away from her forever, even though so much love had been sowed into her never-changing features. Helpers in their colorful leisure wear make great efforts, I have to say, that the daughter, one Frau Frenzel, won't go to sleep for good on this foreign ground. The daughter does not breathe. She already looks waxen. Her body a wobbly, rubbery chick in an invisible chicken slaughterhouse where it's already been hooked up and moved along in a waiting line. And those wide-open eyes, look at those eyes! Like two dark raisins pressed into the facial dough, but where are the impressions those eyes are actually supposed to take in? People act as if this well that is a human being must hold something; they have encountered it in medical TV series, the concerned look of the powerful one, the diagnostician brought in from the prairie, who provides the name for that which *Is.* At her age the mother cannot build any more nests, so her child should return to the single-family home, which consists of two women, as the mother emphatically demands from the amateur players of the rescue squad, it doesn't work that fast, the ambulance will be here shortly, however, the lady is dead or as good as! Under the rustling of some protective plastic stuff with the crusaders' notorious cross painted on it in red, the saviory knights finally rush in. Their horses were stuck in the traffic jam, and now, with their front legs, they dig into the ground, not for nothing did the crashed vehicle get stuck in the middle of a meadow. Tightly packed, the crowd of gawkers follows, they certainly won't forget this quickly; although they are allowed to look, they were looked at by the cameras with utter contempt. Seeing themselves on the air will wreck their evening. The TV rushes to the site, giving all of them a license plate, a transferable number plate with "horrible" and "accident" written on it, usable for multiple events. A tight ring around the daughter who seems to be dead, no breath, no movement, but hold it, a barely perceptible movement, the wind whose hand she escapes? The mother shrieks and howls, two supporting pillars step up to her and throw their arms like shawls around her shoulders. Brace yourself! Your daughter is dead or very seriously injured. Amazing, how smartly the soul works itself out of the body, but hold it, you simply can't make even one step without being watched, here, in this forest of curious bystanders. A black beetle crawls out of the prostrate woman's right nostril. If every revival were always this easy, every dead would happily go for it. Sure thing, this is the very reason why many of our fellow citizens are so vivicious, because even death backs off from them at the last moment, as soon as he sees their homes. The crowds stop dead in the middle of their conversations and buck full force. That black critter, a spider?, comes out leisurely, like a name that's been thrown in the well, the fount of a foreign faith, and suddenly it was still just a stone. In this case a trickle of blood working its way out of the nose, a moment ago it seemed to be a bug with tiny, swirly legs. Some blood runs out of the nose and congeals into a strangely formed spot, as if the will quietly wanted to pull the life out of the body. But blood does not transform that quickly into something mineral. It does not become motionless that quickly. In theory, this woman should be dead considering the condition of the young man who sat next to her in the minivan. The doctor looks, lights, taps, wiggles, budges the joints, peeks, injects, and listens. The body in front of him does not at all fall apart at the joints, even though earlier it sure looked that way. Go figure. The mother flexes her muscles, she will not let her baby gem get away from her, after all, she sat on its *being* early enough! Slowly her conviction gets chipperer again, as her child, presumed dead, now already pretty perky again, hurries back to the oasis, Punica, Prunica, where it will soon be drinking fruit juice, one is never too old for that. Frau Frenzel Jr. sits up to set herself up anew. Tears shoot out of the mother's eyes and mind as Karin, the eternal daughter, straightens herself, unbelievable. Like water suddenly shooting from a hose, life pulsates back into the tight rubber pouch, and the tube proudly rises, spurting toward the rescuers. The doctor, the assistants, are pretty amazed. Where a second ago was still no breath at all, an almost unnatural rosy sheen lies on the cheeks now, as if death absolutely wanted to leave behind a lesson. The frequently crucified, doctor and helper, speaks with beautiful, serene conviction about the limits of his knowledge, that eternal joy and everlasting combination of commodity and money that must be presented in a sealed envelope. But how did that black animal get into the victim's nose? We already know it was a clotty bit of blood. It just squats there, darkly, right under the rim of the nostril, the hole seems unnaturally enlarged by this blood spot. The woman's only sickness was life, still, that spot! She seems to have gotten away with one thrust of nosebleed. The blood clot lies there on the slope to the lips, on the edge of the forest where the nostril, a tunnel, leads into the skull. The mother has already gotten a handkerchief with which she polishes around the upper lip, but the spot does not want to disappear. The mother is dead sure that the daughter got away with this trifle, while all around the dead are brought in, to whom the daughter actually belongs as well. But it is strange how the hard, faithful rock of a nose won't let go of its black pet, many helpfully offered tissues notwithstanding. The spruces stretch, it was midmorning. Now that's already an hour ago. Now almost a whole day. The vehicles do their best to follow their colleagues' suit and experience something similarly dramatic. The grass slowly comes up again at the scene of the accident, the wreckage has been towed off. Funerals are pending, all the wounded people who'd been lined up by Globus and have now been taken off the field will be sunk into the ground soon enough, and new players are already running out of their quarters; in these moments they look at us and our sleeping world, that is to say, it will soon go to sleep and be woken up again, and most guests got up today as well and put on their sports clothes to push themselves to wellness once again.

But hold it, an obstacle, where usually there was none, has put itself in the way on the fitness trail, and they who know the area by heart—after all, their index fingers have been trained on the map since they retired—look at the strangest face of a quite sporty car they have never before seen here and that has set up camp there. It stands next to the inn's parking lot and blocks half of the access road, even though there would have been spaces available in the lot. Only for guests of the Hotel Alpenrose, who are strolling under the apple trees. As if someone discarded his car there. A fivesome of procreation-resistant nonfemales, a party of older men not looking for a match, because every one of them would be a matchless catch, chased after, no doubt, by many birds at any time. Not that they dislike delicacies, but what's offered them here they disdain because it comes for free. Those oldish men had planned a hike, they are already dressed for it, even the parkas are tied around their waist, only the gentlemen's feet are still in their soft slippers, two of them are still fussing around with their hiking boots, which got all muddy during a short downpour yesterday (two of them decided to stay home after all, since the weather doesn't seem all that promising, those two want to go mushroom picking closer by and not climb up any higher for once, besides, there is an afternoon sports program on TV starting at 3:00, which these geezers also get a kick out of. So, the three more courageous wanderers want to get started right away, specifically, those men are the Thankful (Obliging?), the Liberated, and the Ferryman, as is written somewhere. It is they who will meet Edgar Gstranz later on his descent. Today there is an auction of the narrator, you can thank me, the author of the day for it! When we encounter those three gentlemen, they will no longer be those who went on their way in the morning. At first their efforts and good behavior shall get them high up the mountains, yes, they, who can also be called the Sons of the Middle, their middle years being quite a while behind them. What follows are their incomprehensible civil names and honorary titles, wherein they are still allowed to move about freely. What does the wanderer want? Although the world is beautifully done, it is still dominated by the contradiction between desire and knowledge. And the wanderer, upward and downward, is the in-between.

This vehicle won't open by itself. A couple of angels' arms would come in handy now, since no one has a key or knows the owner. The windows are totally opaque, one can't tell from what. There are no curtains drawn, still, one can't look in, the gathered folks get a shot of indefinable fear poured into them by the chrome- and paint-sparkling spirit shoppe. As if the car belonged to some previously existing person who simply went away and left something unlocked behind that nobody can open. A few guests who only came in for breakfast want to leave now without having eaten, they don't know what drives them away but they feel as if ropes were tied to their lower backs, rubber slings, and they are not getting far. They keep crisscrossing the garden, where something seems to rot: There is an unrelenting smell that sticks to its regulations and respects the fence. As if thrown by flame-throwers the roses spew out of the branches, they are especially succulent this year—or is it only today, the way they are subjected to the sun, which like a fist presses their heads slowly to their chest. It takes so little to be dead, and yet death is so difficult to grasp. Those roses with their tantalizing secret! They bow toward the ground from all their weight, they want to enter this parked car, they climb, this is no fairy tale!, over the door as if to take home a soul who, however, read on a sign that, sad to say, it must stay outside. As if the vehicle has been standing there for weeks. But it's been here only since last night, no one saw it before. A group of travelers breaks out, and as if chained to their walking sticks, they plod along with great effort via a gigantic detour through the garden beds, a small expedition that attempts to get out through the garden gate through a hole in the hedge that the leader professes to know. But they can't find the way through and keep roaming aimlessly through the lettuce and the cabbage, constantly stepping into something that leaves dark marks on their shoes. The inn seems somewhat sunken in the topsoil. How come the vegetables plumped out so rampantly almost reaching up to people's knees? Isn't that building lower than yesterday? A gentleman who is concerned about the mist that seems to have set on the windowpanes, shades his eyes, and looks for a clue inside the car but cannot find one. All windows are fogged up as if an entire herd were alive in there. One onlooker points out to the other that with great difficulty one can make out the handle of a tennis racket through the back window. But no door opens, no net is stretched, no balls are flying onto the court like bad angels, well, can you believe it, the hood is still warm! As if this best of man's friends has revived itself a little, and isn't that a hand right in there? The hand does not correspond to the female kind. This shiny, steely work of man, now the object of fear for those who manufactured it, even though it is their work, a sculpture of themselves, who were always so crazy about traveling, all in all an image, like everything, of what our hands, answering to the name of God, produce. And next month a payment is due again, which no one would spend for a human being.

Already the curious are stepping back again, stomping with sports-shod heels the people behind them, as if their looks were stones that, tossed, leave a concentric circling in the air. Those air rings are now rolling toward them, bringing something along that the gapers do not want to touch at any price. Overloud, all of a sudden the din of voices in the garden, which is a mosquitoes' dance floor, but the buzzing does not come from the insects, it has multiplied with raw glee, hanging around the vacationers' heads and swarming merrily here and there. Already the first bites zap their targets, and people slap their devastated flesh, where only less demanding creatures could still find any blood. Where does this film on the windows in which we are not allowed to perform come from? It looks grimier than cast-off bodily vapors, which would be easy to wash off. But it is inside! Yes, as if it were not supposed to come off! And as if one could hold on to it, a smell so dense and strong and proud, the last to waft out of the *Wurst* of Time, which seems locked inside this container; it smells of blood, so it can't be ghosts doing their thing in the steel-made, steelily conceived, well—thing. The blood: a reddish-brown streak on the rear window points to it, some claim to have seen it, others not. As if a desperate finger wanted to nibble at the glass, to get the smell of life and licentiousness on the lips and lick it, but the car's heart remains silent. This is no inn, after all, maybe we can drill through the sheet metal (two men are already on their way to the tool shed), maybe it can be dug out, for what? So that people fill it up with even more dirt, and the floor covers must be washed because someone got their muck all over this beautiful car. But the dirt comes from the inside. Who would, on entering a car, make sure not to mess it up just because it belongs to somebody else? Oh, I see, this doom buggy is supposed to have made the mess all on its own! That's how it is with the inside of people, the heart its motor and habitat of many demons, all of whom advanced when all good spirits were expelled. The red streak could have been the fleeting but stubborn reflection of a rear light. Perhaps someone is trying to back up from outside the magic circle around the inn's garden into the parking lot, but the motor keeps stalling for some inexplicable reason. They couldn't get in anyway, because this idiot here is blocking the entrance. Such luculent, bright creatures, those cruisers, so shiny, so smooth! Let's talk about them instead, bless those hearts that can be switched on and off!

Finally, the newcomer drives away again to lie down in the grass somewhere else, but surely, something will crawl over his face there, too; so then, impatiently, he gets back on the highway again, the bypass of this place, which is his own homeplace, while driving he pushes some buttons so that he won't have to hear anything and will see only what's absolutely necessary. Something wild lurks in this landscape, the road runs along the clear river, which throws itself sobbingly over its gravel bed, mowed meadows stretch up the slopes, interrupted by dark blots of trees, woolly clouds pull across the sky as if everybody were reading the paper at the same time, murmuring and meandering at the feet, a small brook skips down along the path, jumps waggishly into a hollow tree trunk, and gets caught, as if by an assistant coach giving a hand to the water sports enthusiast, in a moss-covered trough. Isn't the grass wild today, tangled, as if a giant hand had wiped itself off on it? For once nature is not her usual fragrant self for her strict lords and masters, the Green Party, which nevertheless is the only one willing to pay for admission. The guests don't know what to do. Should somebody call the police? The anointed kings of the road, those gentlemen of the Automobile Touring Club, who also like to get their palms greased before they try to squeeze you in? There is something intimate about this car, which one does not dare to get into. As if something inside there were looking for its sex untiringly in order to gravel its driveway, the way you quickly go to get some milk, which you then spill unintentionally as you casually swing the jug. That fleshy, capless sex had already started to get a good night's uninterrupted sleep, and it had locked the door behind it. The rest of us wear caps with the visor in the back and jostle each other, splashing handfuls of fluids, like children in the paddle pool. We stick our white canes into the drinking trough and suck each other dry, gargling, bubbling, regurgitating. No one spares the other.

Let's not have a dog rip up our pillows now! There, an overbearing tower, Mother Frenzel, is one of the last ones to get out of her warm seat to make sure that everything's OK and she's the one to deal out the KOs. All her acquaintances are already in the garden, powwowing their heads off. What d'ya mean, they follow their nature, who's still got something in reserve, a tire?, which took us by surprise, because we took ourselves to be the only ones in her talon. Rooms in the hotel are still available, but no one asks about that. Karin clings limply to her mother, maybe still a consequence of the accident? It wouldn't be surprising. But the old woman: not at all an invisible lady, even though she is quite spooky, today she actually seems fresh. Something helped her system along, everyone recognizes Jesus their own way, only the mother recognizes him all the way—he is her daughter! He is a woman, others are saying it, too. To the degree that her child is wilted, the mother seems pumped up. Or did the daughter take the wrong path and make it back to the hotel only early in the morning? Well, that's the way the cookie crumbles. The night is for sleeping, the day for all kinds of things. It isn't far off, this night, weighing on many a memory. A howling as if from severe chastisements still churns in everyone's bones, but there is no mention of it. A howling as if death himself had died. Probably cats. Or another force of abstention, which broke its own one-way path. Jesus!, that vehicle!, as if it never stopped guzzling, and gobbling, an organic creature but, like Jesus, giving off nothing; at long last, our culture, totally devoted to the automobile, managed to produce its own divinity; it had to come, after the kilometers-long list of debts and deaths. A very special god had to hurry here who taketh away this devouring of its precious children, of which Austria's inhabitants have made themselves guilty, let's not talk about it anymore. Can't accuse Austria's fabled Formula 1 racetrack of laziness. Proudly the mother pounds her chest, which causes her daughter to almost slump down from under Frau Frenzel's arms, so she must be brought back again to her mother's favorite battleground and tickled awake underneath the plumage, a hen who doesn't really want to fight anymore, well, we really didn't count on it either. I think there is a catch to this gender. The daughter—her mother's torn, battered peacock tail—gets dragged over the gravel, leaving no trace to blur. With great effort, Karin F. lifts her head, she ran along here not long ago, her head must have been hanging very low, her tongue shoots forward against her will, a panting sound whizzes through the teeth, startled, a hand is held over it like a cover of bread over a partly rotten sausage in which pathogenic germs unleashed a storm of protest: They want to eat it themselves, it is theirs! The grass seems to have shot up high, become a thicket, matted, here and there it looks washed out, bled into the gravel of the driveway, a spectrum of colors swirling from every blade, contours dissolve as if the lawn was painted on, oh, how much lesser the image than the living thing, but we enjoy pictures so much longer. Those figures, for their part lesser than the created world we destroyed with them, are dearer to us and our badly constructed legs (not bent enough on the low end!), which want to finally rest, dearer than whatever is alive. We learned about them in school so we can once again feel stronger than they: We can look at those pictures even while lying down as the grass whooshes whistling past our ears. They, the murdered, who don't seem to have a clear picture of their state, are sinking, locked by our living eyes in a transparent Snow White elevator down and then six feet under the ground. What little value there is to innocence! Soon enough people will get a TV built into their coffins, I think, and show off as creators of the world among their fellow dead, because they know who won the last World Cup. Let us rather follow our nature outside! Let us come out of our shell for once! Karin resists her own steps, but the mother wants her close by, even though there is hardly any blood left in Karin, that tempest in a teapot that usually boils over right away. Mother wants to set the tone, a tuning fork must have been stuck into her neck. So, here we go right into the fellow guests' noisy yet muted conjectures! So, what's with this car, an outrage, that's what it is, putting it here, putting us on and out like that; truth be told, we don't warm up to anyone as intensely as to our licenses, they can occasionally be taken from us, but our drives stay with us all the way, there's no one we talk to with such intimacy, and a beautiful name on our license plate usually completes the works. The mother wants to break it—no, not the car, break up the gathering, we had planned a little hike for this afternoon, she tells a random acquaintance, but that one turns her periscope to a different eye level. How lucky that God is invisible! No, we do not glorify the invisible, but we want to look at it at least once.

The visible is trouble enough. Like an entire cheerful clubhouse the police arrives, but it can't get through. Screeching and crackling, the device reports of threatening things on the highway. The broken part could not yet be repaired. They walk around the illegally parked vehicle and back again. Other than that it is quite fogged up, there is nothing to discover. In this case we first need to reorient ourselves. Piece by piece the guests lose control over themselves. What used to be happy satisfaction, with the food, the area, the beautiful countryside, all offered and obvious, has now been somewhat poisoned for them. It wasn't part of the deal that we wouldn't get to drive our car out and around and back in again. The selling point was precisely the assurance that we were free to do anything, we are on vacation, for God's sake. What sleeps there, deep in the ground, and is there any ground under us at all? Suddenly people are popping up (as if the hedge had shot them out) who have never been seen here before. They are just walking around. Now and then two get intimate with each other, but they couldn't have come here from our simple, shimmering white country road.

Who selected them, on whose request? Who brought them here, like those two young fellows, for example, they wear lederhosen and white shirts, nobody young wears something like this today. What kind of skins are their pants cut from? They come across stiff as a board, as if they had been glued with congealed juices, and yet the two men move gracefully inside them, as if they were cast in their pants, a spring wobbling out of dark soil, escaping a hand that seeks to gather, to harvest the grapes of water. Idly the men switch from standing leg to free leg and back again. Whatever confinements they might come from, now they have all the time in the world to use for nothing. They both have dark hair that now merges in one dark spot, they are putting their heads together, whispering, muttering about something. That, too, isn't something the young superboys who are flying today—living em-dashers—through the air, they always talk loudly and instantly bang every one of their experiences smack on the table (a hardened newspaper), faster, faster, it only upsets them when something fails to materialize, not when it finally comes back again, like, say, the fashion of the seventies. These guys are different, and now that taciturn student joins them as well, the one who always sits in her deck chair staring into her books; these three youngsters walk as if they just came to life and are still all soft, in and through each other. The light is deceiving. An illusion! A trick of the senses! That's not the way to learn to feel! A robust septuagenarian approaches the young folks, asking them something, and gets the answer, "We are looking for the third goal." There is always some tension when youth doesn't want to provide information. And the question was put so politely! Mistrust and fear accompany, why?, the retiree's next steps, who joins his waiting, watching wife again: Us oldies still take an active interest in the young, whom we expect to hurl us as far as possible away from the looming grave. Then how come that only now do these two elderlies—just as they believe themselves to be especially far away from sleep in the bright light of the day or sleep in the dark of the earth or sleep deep down in the ground today—suddenly feel so close to the grave? Warm and happily fulfilled, they snuck up on those youngsters, whose somewhat antiquated clothes might have inspired their friendliness, an intimacy not befitting their age, yes, indeed, a cockiness even—now, let's not make the world an enemy at the last moment, so far everything has gone so well!—and the open road that could have led to a little chat has been buried in a rockfall. Mud flows toward the old couple, mud with lumps of grass and branches sticking out like hair. The country road, sun-soaked, friendly a moment ago, rises, yawns, and suddenly comes toward them. The old couple reconsiders their modest question and does not dare to communicate a second time, the mail was already undeliverable the first time. The young men were not unfriendly at all, but the two old folks, after their brief one or two plain, meaningless words, virtually long for such a broad-ranging organization of the impudent, who usually race along, making a lot of noise, thrusting their flanks and heads, trusting calves hemmed in by artificial colors, the girls always in the fantasy shapes of their casual dresses, freshly cleaned shop windows, they've got nothing to sell to the oldies, but nevertheless, such transactions should not be missing in our streets: There the old folks get pelted into the bin, where they still can try to dance one last time on its rim, but afterward they can also get up again, so that someone can thumb through them until the binder that once channeled them into the Raging Empire is all tattered and one can see, how their, our mold-stained, unbleached linen underwear tears, out of which, originally, a new curtain for the temple was to be sown. Now even an old married couple must have had an experience at their age. I don't know which one, for it is kept inside them, deep inside. Tonight, tomorrow morning, the day after tomorrow, or never, someone could press forward into those two oldies and ask them about the absence of The Word, a simple question as before, but they would rather go on owing us The Word, our war generation, it pumps itself up on credit, with a heart pacemaker, since their heart has always taken too small steps: Well, then, some kind of shrilly squeaking laughter will literally split the two elderly's sides—a higher ministry, an even higher administration, and the reach for their presence will soon result in their absence. Only then will they be allowed to appear, but this time for real, a rare pleasure! But already it is today as if they had never lived. Only by their right-angled crosses could we have seen them win.

17

Europe's offspring has already been bred. However, it is still hovering two thousand meters above us, wherefrom it glideth down to us on its kite frames—the angels angrily throw stones after them. Then it can see what it got inside itself as it falls through a waterfall, pops and scatters its innards as if by the hand of coincidence, it does not even need that much education. Indeed, it is astonishing that there still are youngsters who do not hop on their snowboarding dishes this way and that way across the multipeaked roof of Berlin's famed Tempodrome, juggling gravity on the go. Laughter from a perceived power that is recognizable only by its impact. Entrails for the hellhound, who pants clumsily after them, licking up their remnants: This alpine valley is an ultrasounding echo chamber, wherefrom human popcorn gets hurled up in the air and tossed back down again until the mountain eventually stuffs it all down its maw. A final look up: The All is the beginning of everything, and the human being is the beginning of everything that still must become when it has practiced enough. Can you hear me, boys and girls, this is Father August P., doesn't matter if you keep falling! You'll make it. Still, it won't change the fact that you athletes, men or women, are not imperishable and eternal. But there is comfort in that even the son of an unnamed human, in the following simply called Son of Man, had become and was capable of suffering, forever, had come into being, sans time, sans will, sans plan. Consider the following, if you will: The last cable car leaves at 4:30 p.m. That still leaves you two hours to roll around in the snow bowl with the steep walls and show off your clothes that were polished by your lives, that's also why your pants are so shiny.

Karin Frenzel—her mother calls her a little wild and out of it today, still rather quiet—has come, almost tiptoeing under her dirndl bell, too close to the car. She extends a hesitating hand, unnoticed, for the mother threw herself with deadly bravado into the maelstrom of a pretty one-sided conversation with a totally unknown woman and now gets tossed from dung peak to dung peak into finity, without being aware of it; the mother does not even notice whether her brain is coming or going, her stream of thoughts is that rapid and her canoe so small—it must have been for her to have power over at least one person, for the others don't bow to her singing, instead they bow out as fast as they can. No one noticed that Frau Frenzel Jun. touched the car door with her fingertips, an advance only men are entitled to, women had better polish and relish the outer body. The invasion, that burden of responsibility between the shoulders, is only permitted to the masters of passenger cars' transmissions, those gentlemen who would bend every vehicle into shape between the thighs, if they could just open it. The shiny door has hardly been touched, and already it starts slipping through the fingers, namely an oozy, dark trickle—a woman screams shrilly, prematurely, blood! All of it soon dissolves in laughter, because: what we have here is a swarm of insects, no, hey, those are winged ants! How did they get through the screws and polish on the surface? The sealing looks so smooth, yet it appears to be just a net, over which, with an elegant backhand, such and similar creatures creep in to catch their breath and each other and at this time of year, they are usually swarming in July, so what do I care? A lively dark patch of seething insects. Pushing against each other with wings that shimmer in the sunlight, hanging on the door in a dense, bubbly bunch. And new ones keep welling up, it is a bit like wetness, somewhat disgusting to be sure, their delicate flying membranes deployed as if against a rain they are themselves and at the same time is still to come, they put themselves up like flying umbrellas, these bugs, the sun doesn't seem to mind, for she gives them a last glow, the next ones scurry onto the runways while the vanguard already took off; they take the air as it comes, and folks laugh, relieved (could it be these creatures had blocked the door—a living duct tape?), they follow them with their eyes, still turning pale like cumulus clouds, because it's beyond them what these bugaboos are up to now. The swarm breathes itself here and there, a delicate cirrostratus in the air, it stops, searches; the young lederhosenites, those newcomers who nonetheless (huge human success) were an instant hit, lift their eyes, the insect ball seems to have passed itself to them, and now they pass on the beastly cloud with the bats of their rigid, lash-lined looks, without stirring, they look directly into it, and the whole cloud of inflight ants gets into a spin, they turn on each other, lumping together in a wingskin ball as if they, all those cute creepy-crawlies, who usually just scuddle on the ground, came to one single, firm decision, that is, all those tiny bodies in concert—one breathing, thinking decision, and there they are, balled up into a rock, already falling from the sky, with no more will, no existence. The lump of animals went down to the ground, one unique singularity, which consisted of tiny individuals now falling apart into a pile of ash particles; can't recognize one single one if you stir around in the pile with the toecap, as some particularly curious are doing now, yessirree, I see: Natural history hobbyists appearing on the scene and busily exploring this phenomenon, indeed: Not a single ant recognizable as such. That peaceful holiday-giddy clan, a very rare sight when it swirls like fog around the buildings, has been torn apart to nothing but dust, ash flakes, globs of soot.

While people are still staring into space and then again back down at the ground and their jobs have already been rationalized away by the Green Project because they contributed nothing to any of it, those natural observers, who don't draw any conclusions from nature other than that there will soon be an end to it—avoid plastic waste, or all of us could burn up in our meltdowns under all those colorful processed cheese pictures—one of Karin's hands, this time unnoticed by the bystanders, sneaks back to the car door. A gentle grip, flowers and fruit lift their heads, the garden presses flesh out of the ground, it wrings itself out, a butcher shop that suddenly has merchandise arriving again; and ever so carefully, as if this sporty BMW—which, under the swift freestyle strokes its erstwhile master had slammed into its transmission, just climbed ashore dripping and panting—could turn around the last moment and pull her back into the chasm or at least—before its own drowning into another dimension—would bite her in the hand; Karin F. steps back, letting this form under her hand jump up and trustingly nestle its head in her, Karin's palm. This Bavarian *Ur*form, also one of the forms like the cube, octahedron, pyramid, not to forget the cyanides for the skin, a formation (for self-protection) which humans will probably appear in, once they will have turned into ashes, etc.; all those formings that are contained in the simple line of the Iota. That car is simply a dream, a pure One- and All-ness, is what I want to say. Take a break! A higher mind must inhabit the metal that gets blown at here and lets out a dull, half-hearted tone (it's not quite alive yet, the metal of our cars, so keep stroking!), a trumpet that water got into; it is as incomprehensible as those mistakes that are always born of women, as incomprehensible as the kinds of humans that exist, okay, so the car door does swing open, someone must have counted backward into the basso continuo, time gets written in reverse numbers that look back on what has been but never could have been, those many dead who are on its conscience, and for those there exists only one organization, and a very weak one to boot. Who is to represent the interests of the dead? I will have to reorient myself in that formation once again, it doesn't matter, those present step back, as if it hadn't been curiosity that made them step forward before, come on now, open the door, voyeuriders, and on to the cold buffet! What's been laid to waste here can now be cannibalized by you, Herr Chief of the Chamber of Commerce, yes, you, chef among cooks of the books.

Icy breath exhalations—lecherously, language gets spit out by the bystanders, like the ribs of the man, who became woman, who in turn produced a line of men again: vomited by the gawkers who pushed up very close, spitting, drooling, venomizing. Something self-generated must have lodged itself here to hibernate and brought and started its own generator, its Creator Spirit. A human comes out of another one and gets separated, split in one stroke, and right then the animal also begins to decay. You can do without wine, it is offered and dies in our throats. But the flesh is sure to rot, even as in the supermarket the expiration date has been falsified so often that somebody finally had the idea to move it back to a time at the beginning of the world, when that poor animal wasn't even born yet: In the BMW now the penetrating smell of flesh, not as carrion, rather it is the warm, dull smell of swollen flesh coming from the fleshly rod of Moses by which bodies get transformed, they are to get bigger, so that no one notices that the two young men with their lederhosen hooked up together have stuck their hands from above into those pants and are now strolling ever so tenderly, carefully over themselves, sometimes they run back a stretch, knead themselves hard, and take a delicate walk on their balls, solid shoes not needed for that. They enter the squash court, where, alas, they will be crushed, so what, they stroke their penis shafts from back to front, it's not a forced march after all what they start here with their hoodless sex that really would need more protection. A car door bursts open: Tightly wrapped in themselves, thick streaks, like dry ice wafting, whole mountains of carnal pleasures wooshing out. We get the opportunity to talk to each other about it, but we don't seize it. A woman's cutting voice stitches her own monument and sticks in a few needles for special effect. The others are silent as if in reference to their ownmost shock, which they can't remember, way back when they, too, were created with a magic wand, carried and then cruelly expelled from mother's tent, the maternity dress. Their secret can't even be suggested in words, even though they are totally normal human beings, as millions, no, billions can be found everywhere. Every one of those is such a humangous secret. There isn't much to see yet, for Karin's body blocks the view into the car's interior, she bends forward over the passenger seat, only her dirndl-covered butt and her sturdy legs can be seen from the outside. May she have free rein, folks didn't pay admission that would entitle them to see her, that abandoned Shell shell, no, not abandoned, the tank is still half full. Anybody there? What brother, what sister has been packed in, parked there, and released again? An appearance usually has a certain form, namely the appearance of invisibility. As if anyone could throw their own television image against the wall like a plate full of food and then see something there, whose name he'd even be less likely able to tell. Maybe we can be woman for a moment because we labored in pain! And a being arrived, which could be called gentle in only very few places, I don't mean places like . . . .

Body branches frozen stiff, no, they are not frozen, still, they are totally stiff, catching the bystanders' eyes immediately, aiming right at their eyeballs, and the people resent such contrivances, they can't bear the sight. Is this a human being? And if so, how is it equipped? Not definable, that horrid object of skewered flesh poking in all directions—

as if some fowl monstrosity had been produced for more convenient consumption: wings, thighs, drumsticks stuck together, a multiarmed fleshness, just human-seized, it was the product of the ten strokes for the one and only mark, which Frau Karin Frenzel received on the eternal Ten Best list of hobby dressmakers, but for this misbegotten human flesh with a sort of goose-bumpy skin, she might as well get herself a few slaps in the face. The curious young sports-freaks foam over the Tempodrome's rims with such energy, as if they could change water into blood, locusts, gushing, swarming over this venue set up for them in what seems to be snow, as they breeze in on unwieldy roller skates, winged contraptions, boards on wheels, sometimes playfully exhibiting their bellies, zipping through the grass, speaking of grass, those young show-offs should get the gas, uhm, grass under their equipment changed into flesh once, then you'll see how they deal with human competition. Now we take this letter of the alphabet out of the magic microwave and look at it: No, oh yes! All flesh turns into grass. So then all grass can also become flesh, as so much has already been put into it. Anyway, you can always make a soup out of it. In the bowls of their hands the two young lederhosen buggers lift up their sexes and bless themselves, those How-To procurers of flesh and How Big, weigh them in their palms and ponder what for. A colleague in the car, whom creation could well have omitted, a tennis player and skier, well, okay, creation left him there half-finished anyway, he is coming, he is coming. What did creation order him before?: Seek yourself, and if you get far enough on slippery slopes, try the same on the racing bike or perhaps standing on your head. Equipment, however, was quite obviously of no use to the carneculturist in the BMW. An oldish woman, gimme a break!, clotted, curdled blood, a lump of perpetually soured milk, a heavy embodiment of No Thought whatsoever, in short: Frau Karin Frenzel deboned it, she birthed this don't-touch-me flesh-made plant (without anyone rolling in her loins), now she also begat this substance, which was both origin and goal of her lust, that she didn't even know existed. But yes, indeed, it does, and if it doesn't want to give in if stepped on, it was discovered that you can even skate on it, the elementary. Who else but Karin could it have been, other than her no one approached the vehicle so brazenly. That old maid, how could she even have wandered, from one to the next, up and down the pyramid of living beings, quite a siren that Karin, now she has turned out to be a test alarm! Lately, she also sings, the man stands like a stud being pulled by his sex, and then this supermasculine sex gets covered by the body of this aging girl, the drain gets plugged, the woman swells rhythmically and puts inside herself the seed, which, however, can no longer be watered with a *Stein* of liquid blood. Yes, it congests without ever having flown. Karin, the uterine gravel turned to stone, desiccated on her own. Here now, without the loving liquid coating of feminine diapers, each of them bearing the likeness of one of their wearers like Veronica's veil, here you have it: the product in its cotton-padded nest. A night music of flesh, everyone recognizes the melody, even though this being can't even (not yet?) be recognized as human. But neither is it an animal. It sleeps without wanting to, and it was awake, also without having wanted it, and it can no longer find an exit.

That which no one can handle, the corporeal, has finally come home. It is imperishable, for, as much as there has been killed of it, there still is enough in the goulash canon to ladle it out. We don't want to and cannot list all its names, the name Jelinek might stand for millions, but it doesn't want to. There is enough light to roll this hybrid human cone on its back, if that's what it is, but no one dares to help Karin, please step back and let our police do their work, what, you're not going to? Have they perhaps done it once too often? So then the oldish dirndl-wearer grabs the bull by the horn, throws herself on it, pulls at it, rolls the meatball—it is, as mentioned, pretty unwieldy—for better insertion. There is no head on this fresh carcass, no one could know where it would be. Screams resound in the people's carryings-on, they jump back, their voices cutting holes into this experience, which corresponds to the long past and finally surfacing maneuvers aimed at getting to the field of honor; they jump back from that scruffy automobile, which was a tremendous surprise for them, not something that's usually said about this make. The Bayerische Motoren Werke engine plant cannot be held responsible for the content of its vessels of clay, but this time they really baffled us. In Munich, they somehow succeeded in manufacturing artificial life or, rather unfortunately, in destroying it again right away during engine ignition. Or it must have been a completely uncivilized fellow who wrecked this person, if indeed it was one, beyond all recognition and, together with other human weasels, stuck it back together as a completely new creature. For the time being it is still covered by the upended bushel of the sports car, the press has not yet arrived to photograph this totally new deconstructedness, this wagonload of humans, with several people sitting inside, and there is also room for the dog and lots of luggage!, in order to throw them in the face of the folks in the famous southern German BMW Four-Cylinder Highrise all the way up to the executives' floor. But for the light of this son of man, one so elegantly garbed in his own words, his crisply fried rabbit's tail, to shine out at last, Frau Frenzel must first push her tootle-butt into reverse gear and make room for the gaze and the fetters of explainability, and then we will finally have lost it, the shell game for life, which everyone, except the One, who always knows where all the life is, or at least has got to, simply has to lose, it is the immeasurable that is proven by all our measurements: Herr Gauleiter, if possible at all, in person! Assuming that you are not aware of the following circumstance, I take the liberty. You might not know at all how excruciating it is for old folks and children to be NOT PERMITTED TO ENTER the nearby or even more distant city park. Just because one IS.

Yes, thinking is nothing without thoughts, seeing is nothing without what has happened. The dirndl colossus, the dirndl clod retreats from this brazen car Klo into which someone threw himself, apparently in toto without first chopping himself in the shredder, and we have not provided any softening or whitening rinses here either. But here it has magically popped up again, the colossus—the flower-patterned dirndl dame, so meatily wrapped for consumption, emerges, and she looks almost young again, the cheeks are red, the eyes spark, yes, at her age the girl-woman is almost ready to proudly turn her back to someone looking at her, oh yes, she is as often the cause of gazes as raw milk is the cause of poisonings. And throws some herself, well aimed, like snowballs: the gaze creates the woman, a man's a man. Karin's hair has lost its gray threads, all fresh again it rolls itself into a cannoli, however, there is a certain rancid taste to it just by looking at it. Oh well, the true age can't ever be totally denied. As if it were puffed up with tallow, a yellowish, fatty substance, cheeks plumped up, backs of hands bloated, a paradise story made of dough is what this body hidden under the flowered dirndl seems to be, the dress seems a bit tight, as if the wearer had stuffed herself for three days, well no, three years. A carnivalkyrie, our Karin, with gaudily colored sugary sprinkles scattered all over her apron and face, her breasts loaded as if with milk, canons ready to shoot at sparrows; the lederhosen boys, allowed to see this, open their lips longingly, tongues flicking, a reflex request for a white jet squirted into their mouths as Karin has risen from under her body-pod-sail with new suppleness. No thin joint branch cracking anymore, a cloudy, chilly squall blowing into the damp postpartum confinement wherefrom Karin seems to have alighted. A bunch of blood grapes, a plump mother without ever having been a mother, a being of feeling, that's Karin Frenzel, her body is pumped up like a tick's husk, head just a tiny pendant, no more, and what is that? Son of a gun! Her hair has turned suddenly pitch-black, it was a sort of brownish gray before, sloppily colored over. Her lips open smackingly, a thread of mucus weather-flagging from her chin, skin stretched so taut it almost seems transparent, as if the sun never doodled around on it, and Karen blushes intensely. Roses rise on her cheeks as if embroidered, such glowing purity emanates from her, what marvelous unripeness suddenly hangs on her flesh-happy white arms, from which, like shining splints of a split branch, the lace of the puffy dirndl blouse is sparkling away, the last white wisps of fume from a cold exhaust that is visibly warming up now. Her hand this giant dirndled doll (hasn't it even grown a bit?) wipes off on a clump of grass, a hand with blood seeping from it, the crowd edges gingerly toward the car but ultimately does not dare to get all the way to it, that's okay, we still can see enough. Proud like an earthworm, the shapeless lump of flesh that's coming forward there, the parts growing out of it like branches, three, three! disproportionally huge genital monstrosities, misshapen, at first just their contours carved out of the meat lump, hardly identifiable in their various stages of wakefulness, and yet now that creature is completely lifeless again. Maybe it's got three masculinities since it can also execute three athletic disciplines at near champion level? And all that on this dead human-(animal-?)tree, this log boat: All we have to do is sit down in it, grab our oars to plunge the blades into the dark stream, and mix it all up in there. Some force must have first pulled up this human stump and then smashed it to the ground, and then this new force, with the help of a plastic explosive in an envelope, piled up a few other creatures and wedged them together, loose but still stable like Lego bricks, so you can feel like God and develop new forms out of the old ones, can you tell me please, might the Herr Gott be saying, you have ruined my train station plus the bus shelter, the carport, and the church? Why don't you try something beautiful yourselves! You have received plenty of material from me, after all, fathers, mothers, sisters, daughters, sons, and the roots of all of them, too, all those offshoots of the All, you can make everything, anything, *Alles* out of it all, and then I'll simply drive through it with the four-cylinder, just like that, at the drop of a hat, livedon'tletlive, so that for once you could see how that feels! Through man and woman. Let's leave some space! An additional aide is coming, it might be the one it all comes down to.

Maybe Karin F. has already discovered it and, egotistically, has applied it all to herself, not to her only relative, the mother, who, nearly one with the stucco, leans against the wall of the house, almost choking to death wedged into the ploys of the two lederhosen boys, but for the time being they keep their wieners in the quiver, though still keep rubbing them perhaps to give shape to this force and with their fingers bring their fruit into being. Their skin so smooth, young! Wowee!, you could press them, just as they are, onto a helluva gravure print, next to them none of us, man or woman, would pass thru as just a human being. And yet, everyone is entitled to compare his construction to theirs. Each of their rods is limber without showing how they function, like a snake, that is, beginning and end at once, both were located near a small Polish town, today a History-Disneyland, that has already been featured in several movies and, as a true-to-scale model, we could even take it home with our eyes.

Karin, I mean, her double, has appeared, a femme dompteuse who suggests the sort of flesh that goes around in the amusement park of this summer vacation spot. A rejuvenated figure. Fluid running from her footprints into the ground, indiscernible whether coming out of Karin's flesh or rising directly from the ground, in any case it is some sort of blood fluid, intraocular fluid, secretion congealed and liquefied again. The ground squelches juicily under the steps of the cool colossolita, trotting along, throwing back her head, yes, the world can turn a human into a beast alright, but a woman must sing to it, an Austro-Circe, Steffi? Gitti?, oh dear: A high, bellish voice thus peels out of the cracks of her throat and confectionizes a folksong, a German one, *ohwiewohl, werhatdich*—ohhowwell, whostruckyou. You could practice for hours on end and still not sing as beautifully as she. The sweet figure of this song stands like the cross of the white magic elk above Karin's head (see the image on the Jägermeister bottle of what once was also known as Hermann Göring Schnapps), the way she stomps natively through the grass, elevated in the backhoe shovel of her existence above the heads of the crowd that now looks up to her, even though she was reasonable enough to stay on the ground and simply stomp ahead.

And when folks lowered their heads again—wasn't there that winged swarm of ants from before, it can't just have turned to ashes—they see this ruined young male body in the car, nothing else. It so happens that this naked corpse has actually been torn to shreds, its limbs scattered quite shapelessly, but otherwise there is nothing special about this decedent. A crime has been committed, unfortunately, the perpetrator(s) have not yet been identified, right now the site is all that is sensational, but everything will probably come to light soon. Where are the clothes of this naked decedent? He is well nourished, groomed, no purplish red marks yet of livor mortis, but rigor mortis is distinct, that's strange. Screeches, accusations, and questions ramp up like a storm, unsettling and unsettledness, a horrible murder seems to have been committed, with sickly finesse, only a madman could have raged here, we must leave right away, do you see how this figure is wrapped in nothing but flesh! We show our shock in multiple ways. It bends us forward like the storm the trees, then, as soon as it gets us in the crown it abates again, but humans can't easily be straightened again. Instead, complete strangers let their voices do the work on the farm. Everyone saw it. This barge on wheels bereft of all good spirits shamelessly exposed its fleshy fruit and its pigpen stench so that all the many words we produced could at long last become flesh.

Pressing a dripping package she retrieved to her breasts, Karin Frenzel retreats. The crowd presses after her. That woman removed something from the car, Herr Inspector, Sir. This dripping thing has no name, and if it does, it is so ghastly, it cannot be granted the word until proven worthy. The car will soon want to race against others, its impatient driver obviously didn't have the time to wait here endlessly, so the wait was shortened. Folks waft like dried hay out of their shorts and comfortable carnevaults, a wind is coming up, like eyes, words glaze in death, trees get torn out of the ground, only the fingertips of their roots still hang on to the soil, so let's call this super set of wheels our house! Oh no, it hurls fire from under its stud-hood, our house would never do that! The elements are said to be simple, but fire all by itself is very complicated. It swallows up everything and still keeps going. Fire is very open somehow, I think, everyone can see it, but whatever vanishes in it becomes the hidden once and for all. Well, no, fire does not think for a moment! Now its tide, playfully picking on everything and everyone, licks its way through the open door, what once had been flesh disappears, and letters are crawling toward me. Sadly, my house of language has collapsed. Language is both energetic and productive as well as veiling all at once, not unlike the fire disgorged by the skull that Frau Frenzel now carries around: Engraved in it in big old German script is the letter J, its generic name, it does not need anything else for the young conformants to stew in their own juices, for the anatomy exam is hard. But they can do it three times, deny this skull three times and crow three times to boot. The young doctors-to-be believe everything they see. I am the Eternal One, says the skull, but that is not what they believe. They can see clearly that this is not the case, the writing is blurred, weathered. Every one of the students is their own person, and that person is honestly tired from all those studies and hobbies. Nevertheless, Karin has an inkling of what it takes to be on the move, sometimes yes, sometimes no, it is similarly complicated as the interplay of four, six, yes, even eight or twelve cylinders to get some life into something. Everyone check their appearance, here the hem's uneven, there the blouse is poorly ironed, and a dark greasy ring of matter has settled around the collar. One could be a perfect piece of creation, but already the clothing mars the glow of our image. Yes, the sex of man stinks and wiggles, and disheveled like that it takes on its reign, I mean, in that state it assumes its place above the human's reign. In the meantime, let's put its fruit into this barn on wheels, where the fire devoured its chaff, while the full-bodied wheat, an athletic young man, the ne plus ultra of being, is now restored in plain view.

His murky flood gushes through the opened door, the frozen matter dissolved in the heat of the flames, extremities gracefully annexed themselves to the body again, a few bloody strains of hair are still wafting about, that car was like a uterus for alien flesh born just now. The icy breath has vanished. Rising from its embryonic contortion, a being arises slowly behind the wheel, behind which the sheer Nothing, a boxing glove of air, the airbag, aims for his forehead. Nothing comes of it. Relieved laughter from the crowd, did they all fall victim to a collective madness? Did that crazy woman, who's got more inside her than she can carry and gets carried around in toto by her mother to boot, drive all of them out of their mind? A BMW driver, and no one else, surfaces behind the wheel, rubbing his eyes. What did so many of them want in this situation? Well, duh, that he removes his car of course. First he had to dump his cargo here so that it would arrive in time for the wake-up call at the incinerator. There the flames unite the bodies into one single one, before they, with the help of a traditional practice that tames the flames in a few combustion chambers like a crack the whip, make flesh-pollen dust out of it. What breath will pull us, revived, out of the ground and into the jungle?

A breath of eau de toilette. It is the prerequisite for quite a few to turn around, and then the "O" adds the finishing touches. We see the cause of such good things, a young, athletic man, and watch a bit longer, with a second look. This man will have to learn sacrifice, melancholy, grief, because we can't grasp him. We are half letters only, yielding no content, our frugal way of life is like the mole's, who has moved under the earth for good. Nevertheless, we still reserved the place above, the dangerous tennis court, for 10:30 a.m., where we are all that's needed. A woman, of her six powers she's got only one left, and that's the one to blow herself up to extreme fullness, so now that oldish dirndled gal floats away, as if she were a soul ready to receive at least thirty charges and thus transform into a battery; this antediluvian babe does not turn around for her prey, whom she saved with her secret breath and then quickly threw in the freezer. It's all going down much deeper, also from our den, where we can dry out miserably before anyone sees us. This man had just slumbered in his coffin, whose windows have been cleaned streak-free to make them clear and invisible, a feeling well known to Frau Frenzel, as she is always and to anyone except to her mother so invisible, it makes you think you look into the Nothing. An icy frost just broke off from her, so now Karin can grow and go for a stroll. No one will be able to see God and stay alive, so instead people break with Him, before He can even show himself. This car has always been taken care of so lovingly. Its windows were reluctant to dissolve, to let go again of the image they already had in their clutches just for us to understand it. There is the angel again, in White Dressing, he wants to get in now, hard as a frozen chicken leg, his apparition brushes against the car door. His words stay sealed in this car with the extras, which, however, are not words, except for the words: Victory for Gerhard Berger! Okay, so after the treatment with Windex and Mr. Clean, the whole perfect nature of a young man appears, more beautiful than in the most beautiful commercial. He reveals, opens himself (first touch the paper with your nose, then slide the paper away until you are completely exhausted by all the riches you can see there, congratulations, you just discovered *the* Natural and your head will roll in a moment). Not long ago, the young man in the white tennis shorts had been served amid the frozen vegetables of golf and tennis balls, and now he gets up again, cool as a cucumber—nothing but a rigid food packet in nutrient solution, together with a special hot sauce from the vacuum-cleaner baggie. As if sucked into it, this alert driver, whose hair is receding a bit from this road god's forehead (Caution! Or someone might pop out of there, too!), jumps buoyantly out onto the lawn, while the onlookers come closer, curious, after all, that little imperfection at the hairline reconciles the older ladies, who had roamed the damaged woods for weeks, with him again. Hesitating at first, they want to flick him from their gaze like a poster that offers the unattainable to their target group, for no one would waste as much as a directional arrow on them that would show them, under God's rigid eye, the way to the john. At the very least, those ladies demand from a man the charm of a talk show host. This car could easily have metal a few millimeters thicker, just like the really big nocturnal beasts have it, thinks the driver, who in disembarking, instantly becomes a pedestrian again. And you? What are you still doing standing here, so no one can get through?

The eaudor of the aftershave sprinkles the mountain meadows and springs into the reasonable noses of the new guests, who draw close to the misfit, who obviously wants to duck out, he cleared the crossing, after all. Well now, they won't let him get off that easily. They are still horrified. Since when does all this wild stuff have access to everything? We do have fences that'll put the brakes on his run and get his ankles to bleed and snap, that is, if they work, those fences. The roaring, raging sounds of a poor fat *Volk* can be heard coming from somewhere, but this noise, too, can come only from the man who just alighted from the car. He actually increases his noises, though strangely, they can't be properly ascribed to him. This man himself is noise that booms out everywhere, even as he bounces through the grass absolutely soundlessly on his brand-name sneakers. This is how it works with light: You hold your face over a hidden lightbulb, and every impartial viewer would think it is you shining all on your own! That's Christianity for you: half substance, half warmth, and you can't see where all this is coming from. But you know you must go to church. This athlete won't permit any of the ladies here to touch so much as the hem of his shorts to make them believe what they can't see. As if lubed by their longing, the retirettes reach out their arms to the man, he must be wearing winged shoes the way he treads, almost in slow motion. His movements seem strangely delayed, as opposed to the black gazelle Wilma Rudolph, who could pick up unbelievable speed within the shortest time. She is dead now, she outraced herself. Just about ready to vanish, this man pulled off a finissage of his riches, so that at least he'd leave behind an impression. He takes a little time for stretching, straddling, busting his nuts. Everyone looks on, fascinated at how he gets himself to glow by friction. The radioactive shines on its own, this man gives off more than he is under the sun of his only slightly forged logo. What does his hidden essence say, which is of special interest to us since we are not allowed to touch his body? Unfortunately, for most of us, the most important persons can be admired only behind a matted, wadded sheet of glass. This woman, for example, I pick her out and let her drip off: Her summery native linen suit is all askew, she was in such a hurry to stumble here. From the depth of the skirt hem her legs are marking time, they tread the water in their own veins, that is, from the ankles always slightly downward. Bluish venation on calves and thighs. She wants to accuse this man of spoiling the ride of today's excursion for her, her heart is heavy, how many trips will she still be able to make in this life? The minibus, a Chrysler Voyager, has had to wait outside and wag its tail, what else could it do? Though now surely we can get started. But no sooner than the complainant faces this master player—not to be confused with the player Muster, Thomas, our King of Clay—with a gooseneck stretch, she shies away from him again as if she had disturbed a new god in the middle of creating a human and noticed too late a whole host of thirty about to race toward her, a master-race, whose first official act will be to dominate her, since, pitiful as she is, she could not be her own master and dare to step forward. She doesn't dare say a single word. Oh no, a whole bus is coming this way! Help! I am dying! And before that I'll have to expose myself in a hospital! Certain bad memories come over the old woman, since she has always kept silent even when she shouldn't have. Self-reproaches, an all-encompassing fatigue due to a vague old guilt that has never been settled. Perhaps out of pettiness and weakness she can or will not speak to the charges. The greatness of this man alighting from the car is immeasurable, even though he also looks quite average somehow. Two other young men, their naked bodies clad in nothing but lederhosen, have peeled themselves off the building's wall, shadows turned flesh, they simply had to become bodies today, you can tell just looking at them, and coincidentally, the history of our country will also be grilled today in the flesh. And what that meat contained can be read off the feces we excrete. So then, what can and cannot be expected from the dead? They'd already been such a body, so they can be it again. Maybe it is their radiant eyes the man from the BMW has been seeking so intensely that he got out voluntarily—he can reach the two youths' sun-warmed skin with his chewed-off fingertips and stamp it blue like cattle for slaughter. Step closer: Now you can already see that these fingertips have no texture, they are smooth like fins. Human fingerprints often carry their only secrets, but that man is a riddle to us altogether, even though he seems quite (re)-solved; he came to us from far, far away, we saw him and won him, now he is playing for our club and even does promos for our hand-raised Styrian slaughter cattle, oh, that white wonder! A calf sacrificing itself for itself! And now the man looks, with a look that should get pulled out of his skull because it hurts him so much, at this old woman, whose partner, as happens so often with older married couples, stays noticeably back behind his spouse. He is put to shame by so much youth and snatches, way back in the pecking order behind other curious folks, at chunks of meat left for him. The births of misshapen animals in this area are said to have increased considerably, though yesterday there was talk about only one petrified calf. The old man just heard that for weeks only stillbirths were brought into this world, cattle are dying out! If animals die, we unpalatables will also die, he says, and in doing so already earned his keep for the day. Is there an illegal dump for rotten meat somewhere close by? The man from the car still doesn't seem to know who he is up against here with himself, in the flesh, he does not yet really know himself, this Frankenstein product that could tempt other physicians to follow suit, and still teetering a little, he tests his manhood this way and that only to pack it in again and take with him.

Our Frau Karin Frenzel fixates the alightened one as if with a jackknife, and it seems as if a power was driven into him. It is a power different from the tiger's in his tank, for which he had been looking incessantly at every gas station.

His prior life opens up to him like a stage, balls fly high up, unstoppably high, there is also a basket standing in a schoolyard, and young people, screaming with joy like our chancellor, who just got out of his austerity package, are jumping up to the basket, put something in there and get it again, and then, immediately afterward, a warm summer rain, a crossroad, a disappearance. So, what's going on with your car, will it stand here until tomorrow?, ask the people strolling by, who have their own appearances, which got too big for them, haunting them.

Herewith that moment is over for good. The new guest will no longer deny himself to his audience. Many are waiting for a match with him, there are even lists of all sports fasillyties in the region, they are available at the reception. Still, he can't leave, he first has to get some substance, gasoline, he explains with a laugh. Someone gets a canister and smarmily also a hose from one of the guests, who has been a hustler all his life, so he knows what to do; there, he already purses his lips, now this cone needs to be fitted into the face, and those lips are sucking, lest the young man be dissatisfied with him, the substance of life from the hose, just don't swallow it!, the picture would be erased before it's been completely painted. How nice for this fairly oldish man being accepted as such a nimble servant! His wife, the lady who got so upset earlier, has resigned herself to stepping back into her group of seniors, her husband obeys higher orders now to fake every possible similarity to a younger man. Conversations murmur along again softly, but also increasingly relaxed, they jump over the stones, that dick who kept us here so long will drive off any moment now, and then we, too, can storm away. The most impatient ones break away from the crowd to get ready for their ride, we'll be on our way shortly, well, finally.

The old man keeps sucking and reroutes, puffing and blowing, fluids from one blood vessel to the other. In the meantime, Karin Frenzel has reached the edge of the forest, with the cliff towering above it, relentlessly demanding self-sacrifice from the hikers, throwing rocks at them to get even more attention from them. And now this rock stretches itself, a sleeper, clumsily and yet persistently wanting to get up to visit its dear guests once for a change. Didn't it just thunder? No, that can't be. Now Karin F. turns around one more time, her gaze meets the younger driver, it is like this TV encounter with the new laundry detergent, which, however, ruins the fabric at the same time. Frau Frenzel looks as if she'd already dissolved under her clothes without waiting for the fabric to fall apart. A hair band covers what would have been gray roots before, it wouldn't have been necessary now, because, oddly enough, Karin has eerily darkened. On the one hand, Frau Frenzel is fading away, on the other she stands out more distinctly than ever. Those constantly reappearing dark spots on a human are the result of not having studied carefully enough the instructions that are handed out in the hospital when you are delivered into the hands of your mother. Neither a thousand years of *Reich* 'n' riches nor a thousand years of wretchedness would have happened to us had we read what was expected from us. Like leaves we flurried, just like that. Well, snow can do it, too.

Otherwise, we did nothing, content with miniscules. The crowd runs a fairly straight line, like deer, just not as shyly, to its wildlife feeding. Their feed is checkered, no, that's the fabric of Karin's dirndl. In sudden panic, as if the animals were behind rather than inside her, her cooling water runs out of Karin in front of all those people, that kind of thing happens to her from time to time now. Straight into the white knee socks. What happened to Karin? You'll find out in the next episode, it was the horror of being mixed in, dangled up in everything, pure impure nature she can no longer set herself apart from: THE STANDING ONE, in short: THE UNCREATED or, rather, The Unbecoming One. Karin F. is an unfinished one and has been all her life. I say, as a cue to her entrance: She is the second human being who perished as if she had never been, and therefore she has never been. Jesus, by the way, was the first trick played on us. The mother shadows her daughter to prevent the worst: that the daughter could crawl ashore, dragging the afterbirth behind her like a parachute. Then the mother would have to heave up her child with great effort back to the saints' sphere of light, but doing so, Mommy will have to make and break a lot of wind for the canopy that came out of the mother to open up again. All the deep-freeze treats robbed from the mother have thawed before anyone's eyes and are running out of Karin Frenzel. The latter has slipped, as you can see in the picture (fig. 3b) out of the hands of her motherly seller—who would not, however, want to marry her, Karin, off a second time—and thawed on the spot. Reality is certainly cold but not that cold. Hoofs are stomping. A vehicle cranks up its joints and drives off with a loud howl, one can hear the gravel crackle as it gets blown up in the air. Then the song of the powerful engine fades away in the distance and quickly intermingles with the howl of a heavy motor bike meticulously smearing its thread as it leans into the curve of a detour, the two merge, dancing tenderly around each other with their heavy and yet easy-to-spread bodies, now they are racing together, God save the alpine lands of the Bavarians, Italians, and Austrians, maybe from there someone will come once again soon to judge us, but at least save us for tourism. We will sit to his left, for there won't be any room left on his right. That's where careers are made. *Sakradi!* Christ Almighty! I spoke too soon, that's not some friendly barking of two basically harmless, good-natured animals circling around each other, one of them, by its sound the motorbike, revs up in a rage, its even-keel sounds escalating for a moment to a holler, which indicates not a weakness of the vehicle but rather of one of the drivers, then a crash, clash, clanking, folks in the inn's garden saying to each other: That was some crash, clashing, and clanking! They jump up, look at the sky up close, to the earth from afar, watching, which makes no sense, because, unfortunately, the site of the occurrence is not visible from here. Some are already racing to their vehicles to be the first at the scene, something like, back when, at the twenty-four-evermore race of Le Mans: Over there, it must have happened in the hairpin curve right after the engine house of the volunteer firefighters, the steep road threw two or three people, poor prisoners of their own flesh, possibly right through an ex[sh]it hole into the ground, at least that's how it sounded. The guests can't get there fast enough and rev up their own motors, which might drive them into the ditch as well, but why on earth do people have to listen to such unstable advisers. Silence reigns at the moment. The aggregates' eyes are cast down, asking their owners for a little patience until they start up again, and all those vehicle holders—delighted by so much softness of their comrades in sports, who are in such good form today that for once they can generously let their opponents win—are happy to grant them the grace of late patience, but can't wait after all and quickly disappear.

In the meantime, all sorts of accusations are delivered by the mother to the daughter. It seems to me that a quick rain shower is on the way. The sky has clouded over. Karin, that fourth tiny light on the advent wreath, is spotted from the eyes' prayer corners. How to turn off the daughter's starter again, after she let all her water in and then let it out again? The mother is unendable, the daughter unamendable. Come, Creator Spirit, Manfred Porsche, Busento Ferrari, or whatever your name is! You originated as pure light, so do something with it! Oh, I see, you made such a beautiful vehicle out of it, not bad! You figured the natural is the controllable, it just needs to be produced, so that we get a background (one can also eternalize deterioration, and that is why all your products are now coming with me, nice and easy, to the car cemetery, pardon the question, but has the new PORSCHE Targa, with which I would have loved to cover my bareness, arrived?). You instinctively understood: All that people want and what a mother also wants for her child and a child from its mother is plain and simple: Godspeed!

18

At night they sleep restlessly amid the whisper of leaves and needles. With needles they fought against the truthfulness of nature: The area was inoculated with a monoculture, and now the fir repels any other tree that wants to join as a newcomer. Karin F. is finished for now with bloody or otherwise somehow wet appearances. For many reasons dear to them, quiet is important to the guests. Karin, too, is to lie, leaden as the area, in the dust of her clothing. The activities of insects has intensified, it is an invasion. One steps on earwigs, ants, variations of beetles on lettuce leaves, wasps, flies. Something's crackling, fluttering all the time, and once again some room must be combed for animals at the guests' request. Someone's got to be able to find that wasp's nest, yes, there it is, in the corner of the curtain rod, this address is located on our approach slope. All that mumbo jumbo about countries where hetacombs of dead are buried, what's that all about? Can you please tell me where those countries are, you betcha, I won't find them! Karin wears her jogging suit again and shyly enters the kitchen to get a bottle of mineral water, with the help of such ordinariness, she tries to make herself unhappened. The water's murky flood falls immediately from above through the wasteland of her body, foamy bubbles are floating around inside the woman who sloughed and spilled herself today in view of everyone. But her desiccated body does not absorb anything, and the flood gets passed on in the hollow Bakelite capsules of the kidneys that float in her renal pelvis, to be removed sometime. The nicely wood-paneled corridor opens up darkly, it crackles under the step of our fellow sister K., who lets herself enter into an entirely novel appearance. Being all there has never been her way, anyway. She presses herself, flat as a photo, against the wall, as footsteps come up the stairs, hesitate, turn back again, and rattle down, the maid probably forgot something. Karin bends out the window, the landscape lies motionless before her, the woman scans every centimeter for life. It seems to her that lately she can see better in the dark than in the light. She startles as she sees, motionless, quiet like herself, that young student standing at the wall across, so close that Karin would only have to reach out her hand to touch her, like a bouquet of flowers you put on your own grave. The two women lend each other, casually as if lending each other a handkerchief, a long look, their pupils glue themselves to each other, transfer pictures that had the paper layer of reality pulled off their skin. The lovely, gentle road of a video device is unrolled, they have it good! Every motorist stuck in traffic dreams of having his own rolled-up road with him that he could race along all by himself. Karin sees, yes, she actually sees herself on the wall remaining at the scene of an accident she can't remember. Quietly she walks out of herself. She hears a noise racing toward her and then through her, there, where she just was and where now only her "aura" sticks. The noise glides lightly, like a knife—appropriate light is thrown at her like an aurora borealis—and: There, standing tall right in front of her, a girl, not young, not old, and breaking out of her eyes a beam with appearances that throw Karin back to the site of the accident. She suddenly has the third eye and the second sight! And the car is turned over, the metal still reverberating like a giant drum, booming all around her, the screaming of people has not even started yet, and there she already sees herself, sitting and following the goings-on with sparkling eyes and bared teeth, and she also sees the mother, how she, completely powerless all of a sudden, gets catapulted out of the car like a freshly caught fish, then loses her control temporarily, but bobbing up again with eerie speed for her age, she immediately picks up the thread, pulls it out swiftly, this Ariadne thread made of tear-proof plastic, starts up the flywheel, and shoots the daughter back into life, wherein the latter, however, never had a place the first time around. Where does this beam come from, it's already late and everything is dark? It comes out of the eyes of that young woman here, zipping, possessed by a burning zeal into the wall, practically drilling itself in, it smells burnt, the picture doesn't settle for calmly taking its place, it burns up the screen, and retracting the billowing flames, it burns the projector, too. That girl, isn't she the student who always stares into her books?, it burns the pupils of her white glowing eyes, which throw around images like others toss peanut shells, and those images are not too shy to let a blooming body wither under their attack. Now the young woman pushes herself off the wall and moves toward Karin, walking through Karin to a door, and Karin follows on her heels, caught in cataleptic horror, hypnotized, oh yes, dealing with glances has to be learned! The student is already reaching for the doorknob, and Karin follows right behind. The two women force themselves into a room where an old married couple are planning the further progression of their illness. The two somnambulistic women, intoxicated by their own brightness, step over the threshold into the dark hotel room, their affairs are as important to me as my own. How will those women be received there? A hand, an old hand drops softly like a fruit, almost inaudibly like a piece of clothing, it had just reached for a glass on the night table, however, instead of the teeth deposited there, a piranha seemed to be swimming in it. The old man in the bed, whose opinions the newspapers did not want to print today either, startles abruptly. He crosses his heart, what's with his bedmate, that loving person whom he nonetheless would like to be a little less lively? His wife slumped all of a sudden. The two white nervous women in the door cackle inaudibly, one learning from the other to handle the power of their glances. Circumstances will demand shortly that they depart from here again, but not so soon. From a deep squat they hurl velocity, which they froze a bit in the flurry of an image frenzy, they are, I swear, a rain of angels! Their pictures are running! That's an entirely new sport, and the two younger ones found a quiet little spot to watch themselves at it. The old man jumps up in his class of seniors and raises his hand as in school. He is stiff, wants to get up to go home, he is a man of the old school, mind you, different strokes for different folks, but only now does he get his, belatedly, as his last chance to act has taken shape. From the lamp on the nightstand he turned on, a glimmer of light falls on the white face of a woman and a fogged bottle of Römerquellen mineral water whose green, round body glistens as if a spark of light seeped through the holy grail bushel of this woman, who seems familiar to him: Lo and behold, Frau Karin F.! Her wound, in the meantime, has continued to fester conspicuously, and already a young woman assistant appears next to her with the cotton swab, whom do we see facing us here? A grail's wound with a band-aid lid: Not the faintest glimmer coming through, no, wrong. One single glimmer does break through under peculiar circumstances. World is lost, skin gets renewed. The way one can idly splash and spray with water in a big river, a woman with almost a liter of mineral water in her hand hurls life out of the old couple Philemon and Baucis, who had already finished tilling their bloody acres more than half a century ago. The radio, which someone forgot to turn off, caresses with both hands, one full of sound, the other of smoke, the bodies of the Un-father and the Un-mother, and in an instant both are asleep again. With blazing glares, pupils enlarged like burned-out circles of fire in whose center a white-robed woman struggles to her feet and knows nothing about anything, those eyes are resting places for the departed!, the two women in the door throw lumps of sleep that were weightless like dreams before. Now these two elderlies have been sleeping peacefully for the past half a century (before that they sent others to sleep), so a few centuries more won't make any difference anymore either. Like a thin branch by lightning this retiree was torn open, a wound has been torn into his side, laying bare the ribs, the heart underneath takes a leap and stands there like a one, the only grade given by the gym teachers of the dead, even though these two dead won't be forgiven. Skulls get crushed so that thoughts can become inactive in this old pair of comrades, these party comrades. The Styrian hats roll, those, too, an ancient pair that knows each other by sight, from the hook on the door. This is the appropriate clothing around here under which the tourists make their appearance, and the two old people's appearances immediately caught the two white women's eyes. Their loden coats swing, idle ventilators, above the bodies, as they get thrown on top of them, ugly to a tee, so that the corpses are all set; the coats have been worn so long that they have conserved the form of these folks, unfortunately they did not succeed in giving their owners a different look as well. Thus the two must go with their old one into the lower Leitha (a river near Pielach!).

Now it is about time to say: In Upper Austria there is a particularly large number of criminals who put heavy charges on our history account. Well, life has been lost for two of them, their clothes stay here. The dead are covered, underneath, shreds of flesh surrender to the angels who cast their scrubbers like fishing rods in order to load the darkness of those folks (created by these angels) into vats and move it by the bucket to someplace where still many more dead are dwelling underground, smearing dirt all over themselves. There, first of all, they must learn to love their neighbors. The old man weasels here and there, his gestures are remote-controlled, he is nothing but a toy car, and the two women throw a new light on the problem of automation and control. As purple spots appear on his cheeks and hiking shoes, the old man sets an example for the huge unloved masses of patriots who, for decades, have been waiting persistently for answers, yes, with a few expert movements he charges the iron bed frame with electricity and electrocutes himself and his partner, until the two fatty pieces are grilled in fetid smoke to an inedible crisp. So now two pieces of roast arch on the bed frame, and already the two delicacies are running through the sieve, Hermas, angel, conceived out of ignorance, eye of the fire, you for example, go ahead, throw one or two of your eggs in anger over it, today the meat is on the house! The audience, who can't wait for part 2 of the TV series to start, no longer gains strength from the mothers, it pays attention only to what the food has to tell them and doesn't talk about anything else either. The solstice fires pounce down from the hills, and the young men are singing now, too, they rotate their skewers. They beat their meat to the sound of mucus. Others burst into a German song as if they, too, were already caught in the forge of their Big Boy Blue's Austrian Freedom Party's campaign: They want to collect all the innocent and drag them to the feast of the lambs, from whose bloody fur they want to have white vests knit for themselves. The feet of those inhumanoids kick their way through the cold dew, but for this erstwhile stately old couple, any electoral assistance comes too late. (Yes, we are already too spoiled for choice: To be, but only when others are NOT to be!). I am so happy: Today we'll have our bonfire, poems will be read, and thoughts will be brutally crushed between boot heels. A cloud of black flour rises, piles up around the ankles, and darkens the fires that, following a tradition, are guarded so that no one steals them and carries them off to the neighboring village, where they get forcibly washed, which, however, takes several cycles. Cleaningpower has always been our problem. Oddly enough, no matter how white we get, a brown spot always remains, because we are tough shits and shut out shitloads of those who ain't like us. The old woman is dead now, she just doesn't know yet, and fights tooth and nail to get back to her husband's side, what lust for life, even among the elderly, the two women in the door double up with laughter. I have the feeling it is a serious matter when the soul looks at the water: Oh dear, nonswimmers! Each of the two women can revive the dead in their bodies, that wouldn't be bad, for all our dreams deal with the dead, but the women can also kill those dead again, anytime, many times, to reawaken them anew.

Your wife screamed, didn't you hear it? A glance of perfect strength is lowered onto the collapsed appearance in the next bed, a glass of water fell down almost soundlessly, the hand of the old woman lies next to it, cut loose, covered with the touching, reddish glow of one who showed up unexpectedly at the wrong place. Our body parts instantly assume an excess of intimacy for us if someone else can use them even just a little bit. A hand lies on the floor all by itself, it has the deepest impact on the observer. The retiree still has one at this time that he, for the fraction of a moment, yanks up to his mouth, but the scream that goes with it does not want to come. Karin Frenzel smiles down from her runway. She steps into her pedals, the wheel has been started, in which she keeps going. There is a soft rattle as she puts a single finger into the old man's neck, but his head tips forward, he has been touched by a sort of universal discontent, which constitutes the negative side of important media personalities, when haircut, tie, clothes are not right, and people rush to the phone. How much had this retiree always wished to be somebody who leaves an impression on others! Instead, it is he who gets pressed now. His neck vertebrae break. It was immediately clear to the spine that the apparitions would not want to tread their path alone. The old man has calmed down quite some time ago, but it is no longer the calm before the storm. The storm was delivered earlier, I only opened the package because it was just lying around in the checkroom. Now I'll apply the term "time" to something else. Our *Reich* is gigantic because it denies its shortcomings and passes a lot of wind instead, so that we can ex- and deport our essence as required to foreign countries as fast as possible.

A power has been conceived, and one of its new angels, Karin Frenzel, unleashed. The darkness glides around the house incessantly, a watchdog who cannot sniff evil or give mouth. At the last moment, as Karin bent over the retiree, he boldly grabbed the cloud of her breasts and pulled on it as on a window blind cord (still, not even half of heaven is coming down with it!), he took the liberty of turning the screws under Karin's jogging shirt, which a desire of nature rejuvenated into pointy, prickly rose hips. Sharply, the two nipple lancets force their way into the old man and suck the last blood out of him. It is getting light, it's the same light as every day, which we may, by act of grace, let get used to our bodies. The retiree's hands can't leave well enough alone, they just want for one last time this ultimate unfamiliarity with which sex confronts us on its unnecessary paths, better it stays where it is. Why the effort of going shopping one more time, why still a quantum of space, time, quality, or quantity, God Almighty! The old man stumbles into his next life without having cast a last glance at his longtime companion. Well, in the last years, just the headlines got him beside himself more vehemently than his partner. And she even yelled at the elements when they cast a shadow on her sleep. The two women standing over their prey, backs arched and baring their teeth like dogs, are charged with a certain tension between them, which might still be the effect of the many volts and amperes of current in the bed frame. They throw each other brief, veiled looks but avoid direct eye contact. Then they start stuffing and devouring. Whenever they choke, they heave up the flesh in brief, coughing, yowling thrusts only to instantly swallow it again. Their pelts they wrapped tightly, like the shade the lamp, around themselves, so that no one can tear open the curtain to throw a glance at their exclusive prey, which they now ingest voraciously.

The next morning nature once again pushes her supplies on us. Nature is here because we came to her, and she unpacks her horn of plenty. As usual she forgot the shampoo, the forest still looks pretty good, only the hair has gotten somewhat straggly. A bunch of people gather in front of a room whose doors are wide open, as are several mouths. I take the gift of irony, of course, it never fits: A retiree couple calculated their expenses for this spot of all places to commit their double suicide. They complied with what Creation had allotted them, but impatiently, they then forestalled nature because the estimate was running over budget by a thousand years. Maybe they made this plan because of illness and executed it in the most horrific way. The man cut off his wife's hand as if it had been a mere side table to the body. There must have been a fight, maybe panic despite the agreement, but both are lying here calmly. A confusion? With the municipality's power vibrating in their uniforms, the police shoot back and forth. A gray car waits in a discreet corner. Perhaps at the last moment the female partner did not want to follow the male's challenge to step whereto he was ordered. Maybe the old woman did not see her transport into the beyond confirmed. In the tour bus she always made sure, like several others, to get the window seat behind the driver. Or did the old woman in a fit of confusion cut off the hand herself, so that it could not grow out of the grave? Whatever. Handbags with their [be]longings pressed tightly to themselves, no thief could ever snatch them, the two dead oldies poke ahead in their holey barge to a place where *Kameraden* (and they mean com-patriots, not those commi-comrades) have opinions they won't be able to change at their age. Alright, now they race together again, they find themselves in their will to power, but they'll only get beyond themselves in 1997, no, 1998, as they announce, and then we will personally open time and space for them so that they can get a top seat in history again. After all, the old man blocked his gun barrel fifty years ago, because it did it all, devotedly, dearly beloved hand, by itself, and now this! Later, it never got to be so much fun again. Become harmless again in a few words, no, better shine above others again, better to be the shining sham itself, so that one never has been true!

The doors of the taverns open up wide, and once a year the hard berth gets prepared where the wolves' broods tangle up in balls and animals leave their droppings, it does not weigh on us. *Arbeit macht frei* is the catchphrase, yes, who built us up, us dark doggies, busily wagging our tails, foragers, groomed in forested heights, where once they let us be eagles, the empire's crest, and lie down in worship of our masters from the Wild Reich? Only many years later forks were poking around for us, who at that time were still crispy or not even born yet, brought us out of our snail shells, oh dear, how the herbal cream was dripping out of our ears then! Unfortunately, their undertaking got those two oldies to the undertaker: The current! The dentures, products of national health, glow in these pensioners' faces, who once had advanced far beyond their appearances. No need to explain here what it means, primarily for the spinal discs, to lay out all that *being*, sold by the meter on our grounds. On what ground did we now roll out this Freedom Party blue carpet? That old forgotten law of one day a year—the day of the crime—in solitary confinement in a pitch-black cell should make an interesting adventure trip for us, eh? You can also travel to Poland by panorama bus and get yourself reconstructed all new again. Or we could play hide and seek with ourselves and polish off a snack board, where the carrion is first put on the rack before it gets locked up again in our dark, lightless fat cells. What fun then, when we, the dead ringers, held together with wide leather belts, who always left our acts behind us neatly under lock and key, start rattling our neo-patriotistic rings because we want to break into something again—this statement suits me perfectly. And now I am going to arrest the truth, too.

Herr Gauleiter, you need to keep only a spark of humanity at least for the old folks and children in your heart, even though it's about us (*die Juden*), in order to provide a remedy here, and by the same token you can protect Deutschland from *Kulturschande* or, to put it bluntly, cultural shame. In the old empire there were special benches for us, but to cut off urbanites from fresh air, even if it's about us, will also make a definitely peculiar impression on those, potentially up in arms, who come to us with tourism. Are you aware that there are signs in front of public parks that deny us entrance, *ach?*

The strength she received from her mother Karin Frenzel did not relinquish just because today she tried, with a bad outcome, a handful of an outing, to Mariazell, which the dead retired couple had also booked originally, but that's a no-go. This couple now strays (the woman holding on forlornly to her hacked-off hand like a wallet or a flask with residual heat) along our wilder side and, against their usual habit, don't even dare to get into the bus. The weather is magnificent, it waits for the vacationers like cathedrals, where it always gets light, because millions of hands fiddled with it. And angels' feet step on our fingers when we want to climb up to our Savior. Only the synagogue just stands there, meanly, and pierces the Lord's side with a lance, there the chapter finally gets dark again. The synagogue does not want at all to look friendly for the foto. Let's go to Lower Austria, where the Roman

Church is the victor and walks toward Jerusalem, because from there a figure walks out of the destroyed temple, she has a fish knife, no, a sacrificial knife in her hand. I bet she wants to stab that Bed-of-Nails, our Mother Church, with it. Amazing. We are some cross to bear, alright! God is already waiting for our worship, which rises up to Him from our fore- and middle fingers like the scent of Angel Soft. And so many fans in the vans! Yes, off we go on our pilgrimage to Mariazell, which has been dedicated to His Mother, although, of course, He remains the one and only boss. The women wail below, under the cross, no one talks rationally to HIM, who escaped his fans all the way into the kitchen, where he hides in bread and water, we've had enough already ("We are fed up!"). Now we have put our hands into the sides of the lamb, and still we are incredulous, like Thomas, what prices they demand from us here. We, the Lamb's intimacies, its intestines, on this group tour, where we could contemplate in small pictures the repeatedly perforated flesh of the pope, who recently underwent yet another surgery, if we wanted to; our faces look expectantly: What does Christianity tell us today? A rose sprung up from Jesse's root. And that one ain't no rose to boot. We pigheaded rootstocks! The motherly womb of all places supposed to be paradise? Supercalifreakisticly, Karin F. steps in, right into the mother's mined mien, and we, too, step sometimes over others and explode. And all this just so we don't have to let our neighbor on the bus, whom we love like ourselves, have the window seat.

HIS mother sees the rottenness and the garbage bestowed upon her son in this place, HIS place of honor, and walks back and forth in the darkness of the rest stops to pick up banana peels, Coke cans, sausage skins, and throw them into the appropriate trashcans. God believes that his mother exists all by herself, he's already forgotten that it was HE who produced her as well! This darkness, however, is a miscarriage. This God-help-us mother has some shortcomings that need correction. Foreign voices arrive to intone their equally foreign-sounding songs to Mary. They sing at the top of their lungs, as if they were the first ones in the impractical, though washable shape of humans; but the first one there up front seems to be God Himself welcoming the people at the threshold to the Church of Grace, where His Mommy prepared a snack and hosts get thrown around like crazy. The bishop's blessings are shoved down the customers' throats so that they will continue their silence and not spill the beans about what they, in the armor of their Ecclesia, which pursues the fleeing Synagoga forever and ever, had twisted, nailed, cut, pasted, and thrown out again. The fresh good looks of the Son of Man (not to speak of the beautiful things he made with us in the advanced course!) slides as a picture into the picture, it emerges on the surface of the water of Lake Erlauf, retirees are reflected in it, so that new vacationers can be produced in their image, only reversed, this time they come from the other side, from the East. They just keep switching sides as if they had never existed as negatives. Least of all on the right, where it will remain dark a little longer, because winter is approaching. The new tourists don't want to be an imitation of an imitation of a mere picture, they want to start over from the beginning, as if nothing had ever happened. With all those fans, your bus could use an extra van for all their baggage. Though everything has been well planned, especially the meals, at this place of Our Lady, which, nestled between mountain sides and loafs of hills, so beautifully poured into the form of a basin, you could just eat it up. As soon as he boards, the guest is king and signals to the other angels around him that his place is right behind the creator with his blue driver's cap.

There it rests, the cultured pearl in the shell of the valleys, the cloudy Church of Mary, a gem that takes our breath away. Its real core is Mary with sweet baby Jesus, made of worm-eaten linden wood, blackish, but more beautifully dressed than hundreds of thousands more beautiful ones. A wooden statuette and, surging around it like a waterfall, a windfall from a horn of plenty (careful, everything is falling out, please make sure to hold it with the opening pointing upward!), a flood of clouds made of silver, rustling lace paper around a bridal bouquet of flowers. The spume splashes high up, spray-protected against the saliva of the faithful, who burst blubberingly out of themselves and all over the fleshy soul of the Mother of God. The name Maria suffices for it to become light. She is innocence incarnate, this is why we adore her so much. Angels step out of the silver lattice behind which the priest gets locked up and intones his insights in his respective native language, they could reach as deep as a shoebox if only we had a flashlight to shine into it. Holy Innocence! The Slovaks, for one, who perhaps adore

Maria the most, they just had a totally new nation body created for them, so that they can remember the old one they used to have, which already had plenty of holy dust piling up on it as *streusel*-topping. Excellent, Herr Pope, Herr Bishop! Look, there's yet another toxic swarm incessantly dropping the honey of their pious songs, which they've dutifully collected for everyone to swallow. What a diligent *Volk.* According to a holy resolution, the Self-Created One has been personally dispatched, and all this power came from none other than his own Mother. Here, among the many thousand booths, you can buy a souvenir of her, who made two hundred eighty thousand popsicles out of her very own son! We don't have any left, why don't you take this pretty glass ball instead! Now turn the miniglobe upside down, and it will snow cardboard on your heads! But there, I want to leave this as written: The light still comes crashing down, everyone who gets hit on the head by a silver club will be like new again without blemish or blame in their profile, which comes from the Father, who drags the souls into the realm below the material world. Our soul is attached with a *Knopf im Ohr,* a button in the ears of the sons of Man that rebrands us as adorable plushies.

This church has its daily bleedings. Sloshing over the rims of the wastewater buckets, high atop the crests of the waves, jubilant that the ugliness of her old, edgy regimes has been removed and splashing onto the floor are the newly created Right-minded Religionnaires, especially the women. They have a lot more time for things like this. Now please look from the tabernacle back to the portal: These women, all in freshly beaten frothy wool, chickenish downy in their self-made knits as they ride into the church on holy waterfalls, as if the saints had requested them for spring cleaning—after all, these busy little cleansing devils even managed to pull out and take out their old, horny warlords from under their sickle-y, prickly emblem (the hammer, however, of the grand executioner still hangs over them!). Stop here! Here you can take a good look at everything! Their drab clothing makes you shudder; it could be easily improved on the spot, but the women don't have time, they must step before the Mother of God so that she will be benevolent and then, after five seconds, tear her creepy-crawling brood, rotted through and through from too many monotonous years, off her teets so that the others in the litter can also get a turn. The pilgrims snap at the light that pours from the garments of the Highest Couple in the electrically charged niche, precious metal mixes with fire; remaining eternally in the shadow, however, are the rest stops for the busses, where the real matter of this trip, sheer waste—here the merrily rustling paper flags and there the sausage skins animated by the magic of softness—bend kindly over the crumpled packets underneath them, which, all depressed, are trying to peek out of the garbage cans. Cold cut wrapping, cheese paper, butter aluminum foil, thoughts suffer from it, people are also feeling down, but nevertheless they get around! And there is always some person courageous enough to express his honest, sincere opinion, which was unfortunately not possible before.

Another lofty pair, Karin, with Mother, squeeze through the marble vena porta, out of which bubbles human flesh thickened into ready-made soup. A bit of flesh rubs in the area of Karin's thighs, all in all, the two women have a lot of frictions, this ne plus ultra of intimacy. The human carpet has been unrolled before the First One, who already came here as a child and sitteth on the arm of his Mother, who let him be attached to her. Here one has to muffle (but instantly!) one's sense of hearing with a blanket in order to endure the screaming in many languages in its thick sauce of vociferociousness. Something comes into being here that keeps crawling incessantly out of the throats and makes people create a stink about each other. Help! Humanity has forgotten its bodies! No, no, a whole lot of them are lying around out there. The advantage of death is having time: after a short second of terror in the vacuum pack, wherein different *Völker,* yes, entire peoples tore off each other's skin, each taking advantage of the other's weakness, clawing into each other ever more deeply, their skin had to come off in order to separate them. And there the aluminum membrane on top pops off, the doctor gives the green light, foam sprays out of the microwave (turned on too long), and the dead, enchanting in their excess and simpleness, I mean sameness—for if a form is proven to be successful, nature produces it again and again—glide out into the darkness, one moment, please, the dead are already screaming at each other again, until finally fruit has to get stuffed in their mouth to get them to shut up: e.g., Apples (libera nos a malo—MALUM: evil, or rather the Apple!), this special offer of the serpent, who supposedly tempted the naturally perky creature, woman (the sly pot of sins that man, strong as a bear, must repeatedly reach into) with crunchy fresh fruit. Apples. Sweet Juicy Styrian. The woman looks down and recognizes her body. The man does basically the same, but he recognizes his mind: a true ghost story! And then they instantly start attacking each other with their crown corks and their *Schwedenbomben,* their Swedish bombs, those dark chocolate-glazed, white marshmallowy buns, to tear out and inspect the entrails of their closest neighbors, warm digestive repositories in a body's loving bowl, wondering how it can stay so slim with all that food. They can instantly twist us women, perpetual "wind's brides," as whirlwinds are called here, twisting us, the perpetual winds' brides of war, around their finger, like a yelping band(age) of maenads.

But why are humans so insecure when God looks out for them anyway? Maybe just because of it? Why do they rush to the rest stops, which they foul up with their food waste and excretions, spreading them all the more visibly under the shroud of light? And their constant slathering themselves with suntan lotion, I absolutely do not like that either.

A howling wind roars through the nave that swings and quivers in the onslaught. All the way to the side we find our lead characters Frenzel, who distanced themselves a bit from the rest of their tour group (earlier they had already parted with the jointly rented minibus in the parking lot kilometers away) because Karin and her Mommy want to enjoy God and His Mother, to whom they've been invited today, all by themselves in their light-filled attic. How those two surrender to each other, mother and child, you've got to have seen it! Out of this world! Karin F. handed herself over to her mother, to her this is the natural condition, which both women accept unequivocally. God and the Virgin take a deep breath, which will smell of incense when they exhale. Look, Karin, the beautiful silk fabrics above those two high Spirits! Holy perfection from a bit of semen, and Eons raised as sails, just wait, the Spirit would raise you out of your deficiencies anytime, if you just could find him! What intimate bliss under the pearl jewelry donated by the Habsburgs (the most famous of the small-minded spirits)! Plus, the crowns on the heads, likewise Small! How noble of this dynasty, whose descendant recently married a life-size human model in crème-colored brocade right here! Now this holy Ur-family romps around happily at the shopping mall of Europeanness where types like them would be desirable—and whoop-de-doo, there they are again! So that the tribes of their former lands must no longer stick their bajonettes further und further, as the Imperial Eagle once flew, now always up the creek into each other's shabbily self-wall-papered bodies. Those who sing here to God and His Mother and cross themselves and double-cross others, they will go home again soon, and there they will play an outstanding role when a Gypsy is to be burned: one of those types who never really get completely clean no matter how often they get cleansed. Folks surge with such love, they sweep away everything that's standing in their way, for they want to fulfill their fate: every one of them all on his own in his own state, where he can push the buttons for all kinds of light and on remote controls as he pleases. From the families Jesus and Habsburg, they learn what clothing, or rather nudity, makes of a person. Like religion it serves destabilization and differentiation. All our wannabe foreign ministers respond with thunderous applause, in the meantime, the space between the palms of their clapping hands has become the only one wherein they are free to maneuver, unfortunately! One has to (go to) press, then people can read, black on white, who is also unwanted here with us and must be marked for their instant return. Eyes keep moving around uneasily, always on the look-out for those and others looking just like them.

This place of pilgrimage, this battleground of opinions and cultures who all agree on one thing, to wit, that the Cathoradiating Church repels anyone who simply doesn't want to look up to her eternal light; she is the place, not to rest, but rather to puff oneself up like a cloud and start to rain gently because one can no longer take it, holding on to the only God that exists unless He comes in ethanolic form. The hymns are weighed by the air and found too light, and the air is getting dirty because it has been emitted from too many throats. The pilgrims stress and strain, then something dollsy gets disgorged and barfed onto the carpet: cone-shaped female bodies hooked up in their wired native costumes, held up by nothing but the stiff rigor of the petticoats. Now sassy little Hungarian boots sweep across cold marble steps, that woman's got paprika, our Marika, operetta star from Hungaria, Wowie! Woman! Don't be a doll, dechrysalize, Europeanize! Yes you, too! Shine your flashlight up to the Mother of God, you won't notice any difference, you teeny little light, because it's so light already, it can't get any lighter.

Who would want to taste just the seed if he can have the whole apple? The following fetters have been put on the singers: They can do anything in this church, except take bites off each other. The light laps contently round our sinner-heads. We do not want to look at it because we would recognize the evil that we are—a conflict of interest, for God actually wants to recognize the evil in us, let's give him some time! This is why he issued this or also that other commandment. On her finger Karin Frenzel wears this tiny ruby ring that once had been her engagement ring. Filled with wonder she stands where she had pushed her way to and sees that God's exposedness has disappeared completely behind a cloth of white brocade laced with a touch of gold. The mother hisses that afterward they'll stroll to the *Milchbar* and suck on a straw. After that there will be a visit to the chapel where the holy water flows and may be drawn into bottles you need to bring yourself. It will be taken home after having witnessed the perfection of a jet of water escaping from the ground that can be caught in jelly jars by members of all humankind. I prefer that the holy bankrollers of this church to whom she promised eternal life (but not the everlasting bank account) are bent over and busy, at least they won't invent dramatized fairy tales about the ritual slaughter of children (my dear little Anderl from Rinn, at the *Judenstein,* the Jew Stone, so called in memory of you in Tyrol: Unfortunately, you were pulled by the bishop in the shape of an eagle out of your ancestral manure gutter and rinsed off the dissection table together with all the blood, which, however, came from his own hands! What golden-hammered rays should we reach for now after the big communal cowering and covering up, since we are all just little lights?), whose blood came over us but came out in the wash without getting us wet. Instead, we get bombed with our Bloody hail Marys, homemade with our alpine Freedom Blue Enzian schnapps! And tomorrow we'll become the *edel*whites again, hard to reach, sprouting in rough terrain, and no one may grab at us, we would much rather grab him. Just crazy for that red, white, and blue.

Oh my, look! People are passing incessantly, like the shadows of grazing cattle, by the surge of silver that encapsulates the mother-child tableau as if it were a toxic ulcer. All that metal contracts—a tiger before the jump. Karin's little ruby ring casts a dot-shaped reflection onto one of the silver clouds, it is truly mesmerizing to watch. Blessed are those who do not see yet still believe. We, however, see by the swinging of Karin's hand, how she enjoys that salient point, as if a pointer from infinity wanted to follow her melody and her very own rhythm, as people did only with Elvis, Mick Jagger, or some other meanwhile antiquated band, blowing their own horniness over and over again. That ring is the sanctioned authority of the image. The mother falls to her knees, that's the way it is, period. It would take someone stronger than Karin—ideally, he should show up as a pair to have an impact on the mother, that pilgrimness, whose daughter in turn must grin and bear it. The light is inaccessible to Karin, but she does offer a small contribution with her dot jumping so prettily, as if drunk from itself, around the silver mountains, on this luminous common. It is hard to guard that tiny dot. That Love-Flower. The Holy Pair's veils have been thrown, they flutter down, off the lace, to uplift the ghastly singers, who, as one, flesh alone, lift each other up like waves with hooked combs gleaming on top of them. Standing there patiently is also the shape of an eagle, who put on a second head, oh yes!, that's our dear double-headed eagle! atop the tabernacle shrine, the priest singing something, Karin's shadow scurrying one last time across the silver cliffs, Yahweh the bear face and Elohim the cat face appear, the one just, the other unjust. Fire and wind burst from the mouths and sexes of the women, almost all of whom are wont to lie in wedlocked deadlock, always the catcher, never the batter in bed. And now all of a sudden the tiny red spot of light stops dead in its leaps of desire. It was aroused, and then it fell back asleep.

Karin Frenzel, who was determined to hold her daytime cotton dirndl blindly into God's flames so that it would catch fire like sanitary napkins, melt its absorbent soft core at the center, and release tremendous energies, stares at the abruptly vanished reflection in the alpine Silver Lake. Her humble treasure ended up there and simply got swallowed, her little ring! Where did it go, into which glacial crevice, which darkness? Karin bends forward, actually, the blue-and-white check of her urban faux-dirndl dress-up should have also appeared briefly as a small preprint on that arrogant Habsburg precious metal! All these women all around continue to put their warm cheeks and hands on the ground in front of it, furtively nudging each other out of view of the priest, who is celebrating Mass at the moment. Those bundles of energy, their notebooks in hand, they keep the scores, and they are already crossing out all others with powerful strokes as soon as the ink has dried with which they corrected their own after the fact. The mountain, however, remains silent to Karin's insistent knocks, who basically insists on herself for the very first time. At the same moment, the mother turns toward her, jerks her head searchingly, and turns up one of the iron corner bracings of her mouth, because she can't see her daughter, who should be standing right in front her. The mother gets into a tailspin, picture it like having a dog on a leash and suddenly all that's there is the leash and maybe the collar. The light talks right through Karin as if no one was there. Female organs flicker before this light, and they are roll called by the Spirit, who else should do it?, some are too old, and the other, the priest, is too busy swinging hosts, banging out bogus, singing, and yes, on point!, stepping on the hem of his robe. Mother searchingly rotates around her axis, where is the bone from her bone, which she always picked so thoroughly? So, there one summons all one's strength as a woman to form a female figure, proudly one lets her come into being before one's eyes, and now she disappears just like that! It isn't easy to recognize its nature, but once one makes it clear, once and for all, that one is God oneself, a very fruitful experience for a mother, then there is no more holding back, then this homemade creature is discovered before the coast of its observant mother, and one can construct, right in the muck and morass of life, a forged model colony. No matter how many human mudslides roll in here through the center aisle of the petrified, petrifying basilica, wallowing in themselves, the dirt will always stay as smooth there as if it had never been stepped on.

The spirit of life has been yanked up and out of Karin, but without strength, she is subject to the Nothing and stayed here, though then again, she is not here. The mother doesn't know how far she is allowed to go in her search message to the Red Cross, therefore she starts out softly wailing herself into the gales of songs—a second voice that has to duck under the first one, for the first is the mighty, chronic surge of the New World in the now former East, which now has passports and finally has to—late, but better than never—face itself in many tiny pictures. Sluggish, muddy, sweeping everything away, flooding every *Reich* as well as the rich. Now it's THEIR turn to rule for at least one thousand years at the Holy Sepulcher, that void, out of which the displaced, as well as the dead who once had been stuffed into it, keep leaping in a high arc of light. One shape has been raised from the grave before it was really in it, in the meantime it is already outside the portal, squinting into the sunlight: a self-carpentered fort in the stream, against which the masses separate for a while, like water against hard breasts, but then quickly clash over it. In the long run it is too strenuous to go around the Nothing that we created, so let's go right into it! It is also this light we poets can thank for our unpleasant nature, it is an imagined one, for it would be terrible if we had to be personages at some point.

19

Isn't it tedious to appear over and over again? Always taking on the character of something well known to oneself but frighteningly unknown to others, bringing oneself into view, always in the same old wishy-washy, wavy shape, always anew? Behind the student Gudrun Bichler her hair broom swishes about as if it wanted to blur something. It is actually greeting the forest, the hair, as it rises and bows on her head, flowing horizontally like a wind cone. The gases get the body to explode now and then, but inside the body of this young woman they behave more mannerly, they have transformed into fuel, at the gas station I look into her bunghole: That woman drives with biogas, for the sake of the environment, ninety-six hours max after death the musculature slackens in the same order as it stiffened before. Well, and how do you like the woolly garden? Well enough, thanks. Gudrun falls down the stairway, her feet hardly touch the ground, at the most they push against a stair a children used to do on their old-fashioned scooters. Nowadays they can serve themselves on their roller plates without the handlebar to hold on to on the good old deck. By contrast we older ones make sleep our lord and master, whom Gudrun, that loner, was able to overcome for her humble self: Sleep, why is there no truth in you, why are you deception? So Gudrun still lies occasionally in this room where she lodges, which, however, shows no trace of her logos, no idea why the Wirtin can't rent out this room: she has tried a few times, I was just told, but for some inexplicable reason no guest wanted to take it this year, they'd rather drive on to the next village, to Neuberg, the Preyn, or Mürzsteg. In Gudrun, it is sleep that observes the body, not the body sleep (the one asleep gets pulled into some kind of show while she lies helplessly before us), and when Gudrun returns home into herself, then she herself becomes the sleep. Then she is gone. Though to her it is as if she kept waking up all the time, every moment, yet also sleeping deeply, as if her sleep were a missing object?, and she could recycle and extract herself from her sleep anytime, like iron ore, which also sleeps in the ground after all. Now, during a break in her sleep (or is her waking state a break?), Gudrun steps to the window with a yawn, our Gudrun, and lowers her head out of it, as if someone had hung a string bag with groceries outside to cool. Truth be told, I wanted to keep this observation to myself, but since I have seen it, the birds don't fly all the way up anymore. One has got used to their presence as one would much rather get used to a presence that is really an absence, they always flutter up when someone approaches, you hardly notice it, their delicate air-pullups are too weak. That way they are here and yet they are not, but you hear them almost constantly. Now it's gotten so quiet, you can't ever hear the feathered creatures anymore, no, no warbling sounds can be made out! Instead, all kinds of bugs buzz around everywhere on earth. Thus, the forest sends so many greetings, it makes folks conclude that maybe they should visit it. And when you jump in the car to follow the invitation, the bystanders who casually covered their manners with their own coats or jackets without lowering their voices are hearing something like the soft plop of a cork, that small, dull noise, as if someone opened a bottle, and there, once again, a feathered friend and other fauna popped under the tires. With sparrows and other small piccolo-birds it is hardly noticeable, but yesterday, with the turkey of the Wirtin, it sounded as if someone had smashed a huge, blown-up paper bag. So now here lies the avian hash in the mush of giblets mixed in with the corn it had eaten shortly before. The animal unfolded into a kind of pillowcase that can be used, flat as it is and the way I often used it, to pull over the next bird's body, the carcass lies one meter away from it. The way it is today, a person's pain can be shown the appropriate vessels for it right away, so he knows where, if he just follows his tears, he will be rescued or not. Now I throw out a human with the bathwater and then I rapidly let out his lifeline, a flying line that I tied to him for that purpose, so that he can get a grip on his options at a glance from above, which he would then call the Truth. Hang in there.

Something's up in the air. Being human, please take over, the role of being is still open. I haven't yet unspooled it. What about those who cannot talk to us anymore? No worries, I am here.

After a while the guests notice that the animals no longer take to the air, when they, the guests, flying high with their plans du jour, are whizzing by, snapshooting the little creatures at full speed. The air has turned leaden and depresses the vacationers. In the meantime, Gudrun has acquired the character of an old acquaintance, but everyone sees someone else in her. She is the Jolly Joker around here, so to speak, people greet her, but immediately after the greeting they turn their heads embarrassedly, they mistook Gudrun for someone else, which was revealed in speech: They called her by the wrong name. Each of them has seen this student for days, but if they had to describe her, every one of those descriptions would be different from the right one: that there was no one, but still, everyone saw her, at various occasions. Right now, for example, she has joined the two lederhosened in front of the warm, harmless wall of the house, but she hasn't yet managed the right connection. Both have their right eye closed, the left one wide open, and at this moment their hands are fiddling with their sex, a daily, dear habit, carefully weighing their plums every day before they wash each other's. Will they be able to stick to it much longer? Oh yes. After all, they are sitting on it all day, on that bird that won't fly up from under them either. Their hands play in the manner of well-bred children, without fighting, they like showing off the wakened worm peeking out of the hard hosenlegs whenever they have an audience, which, however, turns away right away (not quite believing their own eyes); the two one-eyeds smile when Gudrun smiles. They let their handle, by which they want to be raised, peek out some, I have the impression that the student finds this quite normal. Like these two she has been let out from under the earth, where she has been raw food for generations of animals without losing her body, the foundation, in the process. No God has talked to her scoldingly, admonishing her that she should not keep repeating her mistakes over and over again. She was already six feet under, and now she has been brought forth again and starts all over again, freshly lifted. Just like that, and greedy for air and life, she pays the most careful attention to her observations since, as of now, no one seems to take notice of her. Only those two fellows, who are like twins (although they don't resemble each other at all), have developed their rather undesirable qualities, that is, both the same ones, goofing around incessantly with their genital parts, whose heads don't have that small pouf of skin, they are just fruits and their firm good cores. Really now, aren't they a bit too old for that! Spooky poofs! Acting just like little kids. Isn't one of them, the one on the right, the young man whose body, when Gudrun last saw him in the corridor, was vermilion and speckled with spots of excrement, probably from gas?

At least he looks exactly the same, and sure enough, as Gudrun lets her gaze wander down his legs, she notices dried splashes of muck as if the fellow had sprayed himself with light clay, but that's not clay, clay doesn't smell like that, and the little household pet she already encountered earlier, lying there on its leather pad, still a bit rolled up, curled up, has a bluish dark head, but no hat, so now the animal is being presented, there, it's already peeking from below, out of the short pants leg and gets lifted up to Gudrun (as a lap-pet?) invitingly, but right away this lovelorn beauty who would be safer in a trouser leg than in the indeterminacy of this country's history gets lowered again like a little flag that turned with the wind of a woman only to peer, shyly, but still self-confidently back at his owner again, nudging him: It also wants to play its part with the other folks here and as often as possible at that! With the other hand, which is also to get down to it, a piece gets pulled out of the knitting bag (no, those aren't needles, those are worms, and you can also find bacteria if you are looking for them), pretty roughly, I must say, as if with a needle, to this end the stiff *Hosen*-leg must also be lifted, which seems caked with ancient, disgusting sediments and an assortment of other oddities (entire generations of the dead must have worn this model of diaper pants with that German flap, the so-called *Zunge*, the "tongue," that's the absorbent core, which now has those handy folds that protect the pants by hugging them lovingly from both sides, yes, that's the kind of tongue locals love to be licked with. In fact, those pants are the model for all alpine *Hosen* ever since the popular lederhosen-browning of this land), which seem to be decorated with mushroom conks, a tree trunk pipe with the water snake of a brooklet, happily gurgling with foam, bouncing through it, incessantly splashing into the basin, okay, now a bit of a rise, getting some air, and there it is again, the snake's head, its one eye (one eye, wakest thou, one eye, sleepest thou) virtually devouring some folks, who in turn can't think of anything else anymore, Gudrun sees the small hole at the copper vitriol tip from where the flesh, piling up a puffy crater scar, has withdrawn further than usual; it is a black ash volcano leading, no, not up to, but into this flesh-hopper, that rises ever more strongly between the intensely and roughly kneading fingers. But this fleshen [gr]ass popper that has risen, it is so wondrously white and clean, only the hole is not, it looks like an old, long-forgotten ant hole in the earth where the animals raced with their load in order to consume it leisurely under the ground. And while Gudrun, somewhat embarrassed about such an overabundance of riches, turns to the other boy to her left, she sees that he does the same as his companion, just in mirror image, using the other hand. He heats up on his own flame, so that his flesh starts to boil over and floats to the surface, white, plump, hairless, but the flame has not yet gone out, the gas cannot escape. It is still blood or its equivalent flowing into the roast cut, no, the stewing meat, idly rising, clotting. And so much time passes in the interval between the onset of the heat, the tongues of fire, and the powerless, spineless, submissive rise of the pupated flesh that the carrier of this sex, just because something wants to get out of there, forgets about his own death! Though the command went out to his member (at the moment of death), when he had to let death in through all pores and openings, to blow out the flame once and for all, but since it has already been blown out and gas, the greedy oxygen inhaler that tolerates nothing, no form of life, next to it, comes hissing out of the nozzle, this young fellow resorted to the second-best solution at the last moment of near-death euphoria, that is, to jump altogether into his sex, into the last representative of his line, undo the leash and get going, all of him becoming his own sex! So his body is just an appendage of his dick and not the other way round, and hence it may for once applaud itself. This fellow took refuge in the whole lot of his line, his sex, which fucks him constantly and thus itself! This sex fucks itself because it is the last of its line, its subjectification does not change anything essential, this sex on the line is man's soul for which he is only the base; however, I would not go so far as to say, man is also his own mind. "In Styria" is inscribed on the sign, which shows the Name and the Place of the Deceased. The same goes for his comrade on the other side. And thus Gudrun doesn't know to which side she should look first. From both the left and the right, she is greeted by upright bishop's miters, those have no use for a second hat on top of them.

While the bones and feathers of dead birds speckle the lawn, clots of ancient feces disfigure the legs of the two youths, who have Gudrun wedged between them. Though the two young men, those braves, have not yet uttered a single word, they grin encouragingly at Gudrun, their colleague in death at the necro-college—where did she leave her bag with all the books and notebooks today?—and hand her from both sides the contents of their blood-and-soil authentic native *Hosen* to cast on, knit, cast off, and sew up what-do-I-know which main connecting thread. They are the fathers of their ill-bred little whipping boys who are taken to heart and scabby-queened, *Schwarzer Peter* they call the card game here, and someone always ends up with the *Peter* in his hand, and those two even have one each. As if guided by hand, Gudrun, who can't imagine anything if she is not doing it that very moment, stretches several timid fingers and reaches into the *Hosen*-leg of the man standing to her right (is he one of the forester's sons or someone else? Another student perhaps?), and he immediately puts something warmly recommended into the hand. But he is ice-cold, this heap of cock garné, as if out of the freezer, no, even somewhat colder. It's been in the ground for more than fifty years, and that's how it also feels, if it would just do something. In my opinion, boiling water, as well as machines and personal hygiene, pose a potential danger, therefore: Leave everything as is! The little bit of appetite in Gudrun is quickly overcome. It has been subdued by a *Wurst*. It is solid and good, but icy, too hard to bite into, and taking a closer look, Gudrun squatted a little for this purpose, bringing the young man's thing up close to her eyes, there are countless worm burrows, animal holes, tiny nesting places leading into this seemingly intact, plump, pig intestine sausage-skin, it's literally teeming in there with two to three centimeter-long creatures, since surface aeration does not deactivate pathogenic microorganisms. This creature here, for example, which creates such a buzz in and around itself, lives on completely different organisms. Gudrun wonders why she doesn't feel any revulsion, she is the way she is, and her intense contemplation of this white genital with its tiny narrow hole of life, its juice hole, through which life has already gone in and out, I don't know how many times (but has never been observed going out and coming back again, what a gourmet, life itself, we don't know what eateries it has checked out in the meantime), does not trigger any horror, any revulsion in her. This robust meatproduct that ran to Gudrun's market to peddle itself, this compact buffalo meatball out of its leather skin, is still well behaved, but that could change quickly now that Gudrun is taking it by the hand. The faunae want to get out, they are burning to do so, even though the fire is out and the deep freeze of a soil that's not its native habitat seems to have taken over the task. And while the poor birds and critters pop under the car tires that bop under great strain over the uneven garden terrain, thousands of those wee mites come crawling out from under the young man's skin, like blood under squeezed fingernails and run into Gudrun, joyfully greeting all those that had already scrambled there from under the ground. This pliable sex must admit it's feeling good now that it has landed in our squatting Gudrun's mouth, which—so that this white pile of flesh can really decorate its little narrow life—contracts like a rubber band around the little piece of man. Gudrun sucks and smacks, something drips from her chin, she never did that sort of thing, her performance here proves nothing whatsoever, and yet she sucks something out of this thin blade—her desire causes her considerable embarrassment—that bestows on her a sort of somnambulistic state. She blinks upward, blood runs down her chin as if her mouth had been staked by something pointy: like a burning pile of brushwood, she grows, immaterial, up the wall. Something whitish, like egg white, drips out of a pair of shorts, a mouth laughs out loudly, no, not yet, first it's the other one's turn, the second of the Diobscuri, who turns Gudrun toward him like a bunch of lettuce-coiffure or a shock of radishes, and now he drags her down into his lap, where the same takes place, just slightly varied. This festive dish gets prepared, pulled out, and stuffed into Gudrun's wide-open mouth, real big!, little man, what now?, what are you looking at me with your shiny, pretty, honest eye, from where the *There* flows. The two young leatherhoses have become quite restless, since they've finally brought their ID forth, or rather still have some forthcoming, especially the one of them, he still has one unreadable letter in the egg-dough letters of life to let swim in a mouthful of soup, this one and at the same time last letter, which nevertheless is to turn into a writing, a writing of the inarticulated, no images, no, images would always mean only themselves and always announce only themselves (the inarticulated: the sound of a scream lasting till today?). It first must be learned, such writing: The brushwood crackles and wrings its hands in the fire, which has now actually turned into a real one, it turns side to side, in all directions, people appear in it who reject having been no more than a letter in a dead newspaper article, I wish I could lure their shimmering swarm out of this little pile of fire that is fed by one root, which is incomprehensible and silent. The two young fellows form a pair, a gate, one shows up above, he is the *Thinking,* the other has Gudrun's head put over his ding-a-ling, and Gudrun disappears below the horizon, a big female thought, which, even though it once gave birth to the All, went down, nonetheless. Gudrun's head turns this way, then that—similar to the boy-girl swing in one of those cute little weather-house hygrometers, that alternate hurling out the male and female sex, thereby keeping them forever separate, depending on what people scent is brewing in the air, whom to kill, whom to spare—from one young man to the other, yes, she, Gudrun is suddenly the mightiest of all, as she can test, spit out, swallow them, bring each one out of himself right where he is. Her desire means that both of these young men have to exert themselves in an automatism of constant repetition. So two applicants have appeared who playfully passed their fruit to Gudrun, which of the two will she pick? She will get herself all the folks around here, I think. It is her right, the brothers, the colleagues, or whatever they are, they have pressed their brand into her hand and mouth, and now Gudrun guards their one-and-onlies, their boy skins, which she keeps rolling to and fro in her mouth, tasting, sucking them, one moment please, now life is coming about but isn't needed, it melts, goes up in smoke, in this case, however, in sound. Each of the two plump white branches collapses with a scream, there they lie now, in their milk and their seed, still more words are coming to me, under my fingers. Help! Yes, okay. Now you better write down yours.

Or they won't be said. Starting out with a very small spark, the penises of the two deceased youngsters are growing, gaining strength, and waxing in the waxcloth of Gudrun's throat, which, after all, has been dead for quite a while and is all smooth and washed down; an unchangeable scale mark is each of these pricks, it will never ever get enlarged again, because it has been pushed out from a small Viennese room, a Final Place, and still gets pushed out, amid dust-raising sounds, while a barrel of noise and merriment is being opened on the street in front of the house. And Gudrun savors the tiny veins showing on the outside of those genital growths with even more pleasure; though she intuits rather than tastes the Sickness to Death as a deadly poison in the fluid welling from the fleshy hole in the branch. Irrationally enjoying the other, even if it were two, would be like birds, about to get run over not even considering flying off. Who can unriddle this? Like the ropes in the Indian fakir's trick, the two white death-light wicks point straight upward, and Gudrun busies herself with the play-it-again-and-somemore rise, the little sticks slump, a friendly dog's jaws open wide, and Gudrun gets thrown into the grass. She immediately gets up again, rubs her eyes, where am I, her breasts are still hanging out of her bra, she hasn't yet put them back in, and she is still washing her underwear in the basin in the kitchen of her one-room apartment, and the young man, as if unable to bear the weight of his grown-up state, wants to come in to share it with her. With the one half of his face, he stares inside over the window covering (the mist), because her boobs, blowing him an inaudible march, have fallen out of their fatty harness.

There, standing behind that fellow seems to be another one, whom she knows from somewhere. Did she see him on a vacation that's already over, or will she be seeing him during one that's still to come? In the disco, in the reading room? Gudrun Bichler holds her hands over her fruits, which unknown eyes are biting into and for that very purpose had come out of her *Brustkorb,* her "breast basket," the ribcage, that is, maybe also to get some split. The young man in front of the window sniffs at the woman, albeit with his eyes. Foam emerges from the corners of his mouth, as if he had already wolfed down those fruits, which she offers him on a silver platter so to speak, but why is the foam so dark, did the guy just eat blueberries? Why does this murky juice trickle out of his mouth like a thread he lost while speaking? And what's with the dark rope now passing his lips? What's that all about? Now one can hear the surge of waves, oh no, it's just a rivulet of talk thrown out of its bed, the little brook's murmur is coming closer, I can hear it already, it's moving up the staircase, a laugh gets caught in the railing, then flutters ahead a little again. Gudrun stands up on her tiptoes, who is coming now, the youth in front of the window also grudgingly unglues his eyes (which must have been held by corrective contact lenses so they wouldn't fall out in the process) from Gudrun's white tits with the blotchy raspberry buttons, distractedly licking the clotting in the corner of his mouth, which, however, seems to be colorfast. Gudrun stretches, lifts up lackadaisically the shiny weave of her satin brassiere, and stuffs the two mystery-mongers that played such tricks on the young man's glances carelessly back into their husks, wipes distractedly some splashes of water from her arm: Apparently there is a laughing, screaming, joking group coming up the stairs, they make a racket as if they filled up the entire staircase wall to wall, and it keeps increasing by the second, that noise. There are a few more lurking behind the compliance of the bend, right there, where the railing is broken and patched up with cord as a makeshift, higher up the handrail is missing altogether, and a piece of rope tries to substitute for it. Who's that roaring bunch of party animals climbing up there, what do they want, who else could be living up there getting so many visitors, the first ones pop up already, what on earth . . . !

In principle it's only three people, that's how God wanted it when he created himself, one of them a child, a little boy, quite obviously, in the customary latest fashion of athletic wear, teeming with crowns, stripes, jewels dropping off the crown, and those amoebic shapes that came off the Adidashing mountain stripes. Those delicious, pernicious particles, lumpy and chunky, to elephantisize his feet and thighs as much as possible, are flipping and flopping around his small body, and with every step upward, they get poured in full swing down the emptiness of the stairwell. The drops twinkle on the worn-down stairs, the child's face is completely blank and without any expression, but that noise! The hubbub of this animated little group shakes the entire house, as if behind them other footprints are pushing forward to every centimeter they left open; as if hecatombs of restaurant revenants and cheap-eaters were pressing against the exterior walls, as if every space in the staircase were occupied by stevedores on ghost rides pulling out some shocking stuff on poles, thoughts, strengths, Superiors, Inferiors, Middlings, arms, legs, extremities. This game is now coming our way, already we can see the white in the eyes, the tension of tendons set to flee, the hunger of a fleetingly wide-opened mouth, a waving arm, no, two, three, ten, one hundred: And yet, it's only Three People, actually two and a half! Now would you tell me what you want! What sewer did you just float back from, what movement moves you, what spring pulled you back with a mien of regret, what dam released you, just so you could cross the borders swimmingly!

20

The ideal aimed for is the artificial production of one single piece of organic life, which can be a match for a product grown on humans. In art, technology, science they are wrestling, bent over bowls and glasses for something creationlike, but wherever the beautiful material arises, it gets trampled, crushed, slashed, ground down, burned, poisoned, taken for a ride and dumped. Our stupid concoctions can't even come up with a single human hair, such a product is already a basket hung too high, which scientists jump up to so that their small hands, which can stay on the ball only with great effort, can put their hard-boiled egg in it. They make artificial ears, but these don't even look like the real ones. And those wigs of artificial hair are so electric, they can be used as flashlights, but not as a substitute product for those wonderful human waterfalls. However, far away from us, beyond the glacier that's slowly melting away, there are huge storehouses, filled with roaring dust clouds of frustrated dandruff, whose *Urgrund,* the primal ground, the mother scalp, was taken from them forever. There the hair-pieces are stored, torn from the ground of the skull, not raised to life from their grave, but plucked prematurely from the living bone mass, cut, shaved, that won't disturb anyone's sleep, or will it? Hair always reminds one of youth that is over! Herr Eichmann, that banal bureaucrat, who had the guts to rip people's guts out, probably lost his hair, too, without being able to figure out what to do with that gigantic warehouse he and his bureaucrat buddies planned and organized. Thus, we live amid a concentration of bodies, eyeglasses, teeth, suitcases, dolls, stuffed teddies of strangers, without it possibly being use- or harmful to us. The mangler like the horrific Mengele can't implant those things in himself, he can't let them grow on him, not even with the mint-fresh revitalizing breath of life from Tic Tac, which one might eat to test the growth. I make an exception for organ transplants. In those cases, the physician in charge has to keep the product alive, and with more care than was ever bestowed on its original owner and donor. So there are the lunchbucketeers with kidneys breathing inside them, steaming demonically (Jürg, I hope you are getting your predestined one), so helicopters ascend, easily reaching the heavens, then quickly land again; and many feet in white shoes, tenderly caressed by equally white trouser legs like especially dear relatives who just have been wronged a little, are hurriedly rattling along without toppling over the white clogs. No explanations have to be submitted, when heart-lungs are splashing, breathing, banging, brooding in tubs, brought into the world again as all-natural plantings and learning to count in millions, our doctors-nurses teams are superbly tuned in to each other. *Jawohl,* Herr Chief Physician!

Now only the warehouses, filled with biomass, an ungodly amount, which has nothing to do with biology anymore, because its dimensions alone are *über*-human (it's just that too much came together all at once, too many of the millions, who were assembled in one layer, one stratum, as the middle stratum of the earth), only those warehouses are standing there now, our clayey army; they don't clamor, they are made of dust, and our well-heeleds' never-stagnant figures shuffle in mounts of broken glasses: An entire eyeglass factory in its boundless greed to produce could not have crunched this much glass and made a floor meters deep for those trespassing in athletic shoes and standing in it. While the human dust on which those specs once hung so that shining eyes could see themselves mirrored in countless pages, or open up in amazement in the icy aqua vitae, which they dove into unauthorized, somehow foreign and ashamed that, despite such a feat, they were not accepted; so then, while this dust of humans rises toward their salvation, which, however, had to be canceled due to a European summit, where the Father was finally to reveal himself to the Son, while this giant cloud of dust then turns its attention to us, I cannot resist the impression that it now starts to tend to US as if IT were the good housewife! It wanders, eternally, unfadingly, out of the ground into the flickering light of day; a kind of magnetic force begins to reach randomly for anything metallic, and iron filings rise from flesh, a projection beam of flimmering particles, streaming through the doors, so that they will be saved, these microtomes, and then, a little later, into the horse farm filled with cheering vacationers, where they can jump apocalyptically on those who are not to blame and therefore want to have it all, at least always that which is too much for their own wallets. The dust returns to flesh again so that the dead can be themselves again and at the same time become their own successors (and heirs). Many have gone and never returned, and I don't do anyone injustice when I say that this really happened. Isn't the not-yet-real worth finally making a decision now? Nowadays you can't even show the flag for Open Fire and, oops, someone's instantly burned again, and TV, radio, newspapers lament him?, recently there were even five pieces of women, because the German youth after all these years seem finally to have been grilled through and through, after all the vacations and burgers they have enjoyed, and now they put others on the grill to devour them. Before, they called humans: *Würstchen!* Wienies! Please take a seat here and relax! Even if all that were left of the dead were molecules, you would still have to climb up a ladder to sit, the last one to arrive, on top of that heap, at the right hand of God, that's how HE makes sure his helpers will stay, after all, every craftsman has one or more hands who must do charitable work for him under the table, because they got burned and sadly exhausted their credit. Now you become a witness, how down below, at the quay, on the Danube Canal, the van that transports Ilse's grandmother and a few other grandmothers and children and grandchildren turns around the curve and disappears. Out of sight but not of mind. Ilse already has a hole in her brain from all that drilling into her head today! And it still takes a few crying children coming from the smiling dentist demonstrating toothbrushes before the effect of pure radiance has been achieved. All those distant shapes will not be seen again, even though their souls are desperately burning their eternal light to attract attention by way of smoke. What qualities that wick must have to still smolder quietly after more than fifty years, apparently still determined to reveal something, so now a door has opened this very moment, a touch of draft can be felt, cash-on-delivery packages appear at the post office, which are suddenly picked up, even though they expired long ago and should have been returned into the Nothing. A wrinkle in time that suddenly seems smoothed.

The stairwell lies still like a shaft, where the miners go down, somewhat sooty, it is an old house, for which it serves as the gullet from where people get gobbled up as a delicate filling by their own flats, where they then leisurely eat their own hearts out craving bigger wrappings, perhaps even a small house in the country. A child bounces up the stairs, swinging a bag with swim gear above its head, kicking something invisible in front of it with the new super-platform sneakers, which, like horrendous clumps, bigger than its head, leaden, have the child's feet diverlike positioned inside them. The spirit of death has thrown itself onto the child's thus solidly anchored legs, the shoes are not tied at the ankles, that's the fashion now, whatever. Nothing is reflected in the boy's pupils, no light goes in or out. Stores are filled with labels, but the child will no longer believe them even though he knows them better than the hobbies of his parents, who seem to have been cut out of the screen with a jigsaw. With his feet, the boy accurately measures the way up to the second floor. A young woman with her hair flowing down tearily stands behind the curtain watching him. As if by command all parties on the floors raise their heads from the television sets, then: "please wait until the sound of a whistle has crossed the sky, then start talking," something must have happened to the community antenna, it doesn't often happen that anything is welcomed with such unanimity as this wire contraption, including its hottest supporter, the dish high up on the roof, which has been filled with plenty of food for all of us, right above the dripping-wet linen that we'll have messed up again by tomorrow. Let's hope there are no stains after we sheep have put our heads on the block of German TV's mega-hit *Wetten daß das Wetter* . . . or: "Wanna Bet . . . (how bad it can get?)."

Hardly more than the plastic product of his physical shape is still recognizable of the boy, who had been abused in the water less than two hours ago. Even though it is pretty dark in the stairwell, a glow emanates from him as from a rotten piece of wood. Well, so then he's pretty bright already, in case he has to write an essay sometime. Merciful teachers apparently labored successfully. Inside, in the parental apartment his parents weep for the fate of a child who apparently drowned in a public pool, the face of the child is said to have been horribly disfigured. His heart seems also to have been torn out and pulled into the water like a boat. It floated a little apart from the nice, good boy; will we now have to quasi-police swimming pools for a long time or even avoid the sport altogether? And what about playgrounds?, where our dearest, the sometimes mean and naughty children, who are so precious, because they belong to us, in order to continue living for us, proceed with sand against one another? Parents must learn to keep their belongings under better control. At the moment they blaze anxiously in front of the television and show their open fire. This way they become dangerous to their neighbors. Wasn't their son also swimming there with his class today! Even at the same pool. The mother rushes to the phone just when the child she had put so much work into for years presses the doorbell outside. Any embarrassment for the authorities has been averted, the angel is already on the trolley and gone, the mother storms to the door and embraces her cold child, while the news anchor's voice trembles as he looks as if helpless, to his black-haired female partner, so she can squeeze a little of her diet mayo (yes, you may) on top of it. The double emceeing of two strong, independent spirits was once again right on target, and now we have no more change that would be small enough to pay the TV back in its own coin. Those compassionators never err on the side of malice, they always are all empathy while dropping small, nasty slips of the tongue about especially crass cruelties, which they want to be the beneficiaries of their vespertine caring attention. But in view of the ritual murder in a Viennese public pool that led to one being awarded with eternal life and forced another that was there already out of it, the illuminated spirit of this pair revives once again, and they pop up on the spot as a reverse glass painting, now, please, where can we buy the real side? Well, the main thing is, our own child is back again. Does he know anything about the horrible event that took place right near him? In the same pool and at the same time, when this poor boy would have had to be there, too, no? Okay, now this child has been handed over to his parents. It sets his eyes on his mother, but there is something wrong with those eyes, its mother could not say exactly what. I can help her: there is no reflection in the pupil, which might help to understand what is happening behind it in the head, which is what parents always know when they look at their child, this only one of many little angels, who, together with a friend who was saving for a vehicle, type: moped, will at some point strangle a twelve-year-old sometime with a garotte (self-made with two nails and a piece of rope), thereby cutting halfway through his throat. In our case, someone else beat him to it. Time is of no essence to us. The small corpse will be rolled into an old carpet. Then off we go, hop hop, up into grandmother's public housing unit, she just happens to be in the coffeehouse just now, bragging about her grandson, who is a pure soul floating invisibly above her coincidentally that very moment, it can happen when one keeps bragging about granny's bulging savings account book. The few cabinets are quickly ransacked by the kiddy perps. The children lifted the keys from their victim, its soul came out at the same time, it looks around now, takes a few steps to stretch its legs, but without a soul the child is not able to stand up. Some strength was once born in every human, it becomes just a matter of being able to apply it against one's neighbor. For only a very few know what their strength is good for other than putting a car together or breaking into or racing around with it. Yugo bombers headed for Graz? Oh no, they'd better forget about it! But that's only repacked meat, marked with a new expiration date (put into one hundred parts soya peptone bouillon incubated 18–24 hrs at 42°C, you'd be amazed what else comes of there, from just a few dead bodies, and there are many more among us!

Filled with joy, the parents embrace their apparently unharmed child in order to gear it up for their ambitions: doctor or lawyer. Like a maggoty piece of wood, the clueless little bubba strolls to his bed, which his parents had dug right next to the sofa. Mommy inquires whether she may also tear out her heart and put it on the child's plate (it comes with spaghetti). He doesn't want it? Well, then he could also have groundnuts cake for a dessert the whole family is nuts about. In despair, Mommy registers that her food has been rejected. Her child does not seem to feel he owes her any explanation, has he been at MacDonaldduck's and received fries from a dead hand out of a tabernacle, from people who wear funny hats and are not always exposing themselves down to their innermost nuclei as parents do in order to get to the ace in the hole with which they could still beat the child? Did the son weigh himself into the eternity of a burger chain's light, did he let himself, sans parents and history, let himself off the leash? A little European, formed and normed, who gets his processed food stuffed down the throat, until he speaks the language of the time and talks to the birds, because he ingested so many proteins? A little Saint Francis. Did the child mistake the ark and lined up at the wrong shelter for baptism during a flood in the Dianabad? As if saying, "Cheeseburger," the son smiles quietly in response to these questions, not for anything does he want to announce what happened, unless he'd get the car racetrack he wants.

Suddenly this place is veiled as if by Christ. The parents' movements slow down, something, whispering above us clueless folks and the gigantic web of millions of dead, many among them having been as good and beautiful as if out of the fairy tale of Sleeping Beauty, cocooned in a web of thorns, or Rapunzel (who at least lets her hair down!), gets lowered down the walls, a knit ladder, whose former owners can only limp behind beside themselves because they were broken into with boots and cudgels out of the sack. Hardly anything can be noticed from outside. The woman is worried about the look of her husband. As if darkness has broken out, she can make him out only spectrally. Outside the door someone still jumps around cheerfully, thinking he's got something to show. Then silence, little mouths pop out of it, as if they wanted to participate in this domestic entertainment. But those are just those golden throats striking out from the TV, heartthrobs who want to meet each other in a dating game show, they are showing us now how rousing they can be when they are supposed to push themselves on us on the idiot box. The entertainer makes sure to release them from any conversation, because he wants to be the only one talking. He assigns them flattering tasks for the sole purpose of giving them the opportunity to appear as members of upper-class circles, who voluntarily leave others alone. The family watches with interest, even though they hardly need to see it, those Three after all have already found themselves and don't have to let themselves be newly pumped up, they don't have to be whipped together until foamy in a dream wedding all over again, as much as they might want it, if only for the eerily beautiful dress that would then be donated to them, okay, the game is played here for money or life (others never had to confront this choice, darkness was all that was waiting for them, you stupid German television, now you have put your chips into humans like a fly its eggs, oh well, at least it's nice and warm inside you, and there you go!, the skin is already popping, there the larvae are already rising like angels, the program producer is already flying high on his success!). Television measures all of our time, we got caught in its fetters, hence our plans are so wicked and weird that, heavy with golden dreams, we don't see what lies directly in front of us:

A dark liquid is flowing down in that corner, right there, but the child's parents don't notice because they are staring into the boob tube. Something seems intent on getting down in a hurry to reach a safe place on the floor. There are two witnesses plus one piece of child. The latter is the only participant in our viewing area not looking at the screen, where visibility feels its way to the people so that they will forget their obligations and surrender, conveniently packaged, without resistance. The child has totally dark, pupil-less eyes and stares at the quickly expanding rivulet fighting its way out of the darkness of the room, while the dishwasher rotates routinely, and the beautiful porcelain chips and cracks into pieces. The father, obliged to watch over his loved ones and sniffing at the hot air produced by the Emcee (that guy must think it's all in the family wherever he passes his stink!), finally pays attention, briefly pulls himself together and asks what or where this could be, could the neighbor's bathroom have a leak? That guy already thinks he can shit all over us. The father floats from the sofa, which had just been slipcovered. He is in full flow now. But over there some new flow is brewing, someone seems to have spilled his juice of life there. The father's finger got all red when he stuck it into it. And what about that web!, which is primarily responsible for our beauty, that's why we should always use the right shampoo and conditioner: Isn't that hair? Up there, blood and hair are shooting out of the ceiling, tentacles of an entirely different existence. Quite a powerful impression. Oh dear, human mass that explodes all human measure has been channeled into this TV room and is now bursting the banks slowly but surely. Who would have thought that what is done on the screen unto the Highest of our brothers could also be done unto us and top even the entertainment value of what we just saw? At the moment, the event is still in progress, and appropriate to its scope (the appropriation of the appropriate scale. Authenticity is the measure), it rises on our trauma gauge. The father scans the wall with his fingers (in disbelief, like ten saints who supposedly personally knew Jesus and couldn't imagine he would become so famous one day), but he teeters already, the father. Now the hair is falling from the ceiling, as if hay had been loaded into a barn and diligent locals had to pick it up because it is a subsidized native product that cohabited with our thoughts, and what's more: The hair, having lived so close to the brain, must have picked up a few secrets that were subsequently wiped out by the ladies and gentlemen in Styrian suits or brightly laughing loden woolens. In addition, those people now make the ungentle, ungentile acquaintance with buttons made of human horn, oh yes, and the clothing clearly speaks *Deutsch* as well, and it also strikes when it speaks with the forked tongue of a necktie. The television speaker and his lady in black are supposed to tell us what to do and what we must see today. Their words have been scrubbed with the grooming brush. Those people have no backbone, they are to be consumed quickly, they are disposable.

The mother, a shepherdess, whose own hair stands on end, too, leaps next to the father, for her second thought is to protect her fawn, but a thick Gretchen braid, usually pinned to the neck with daggers of bone, with which a dead woman once tried in vain to disguise herself, that is, with a bone hair grip—like the bone handles of the umbrellas all Gretels also always carry with them—such a braid is now thrown like an anchor onto the mother's neck, just a moment, I see the mother already stumbling and falling! What a nuisance the history of our land becomes when we wish to put ourselves up for sale! The guests from abroad turn away and cover their heads, how should they take our measure when we constantly break our scale? They don't even want to say our holy names, well, that's how it should be, since we also are our own gods. We have no points of contact for anyone who wants to get in touch with us. Blood bubbles in blond rays turning into ever thicker tresses that blackened in the fire, okay, ready, this is it: Abraham's entire people throw down their roofs of hair, a red sea, which will not part a second time, since so many tried to drink it out of steins of skulls, an old custom around here, which entails holding the stein, finger wrestling, downing the beer, and then addressing each other like old buddies, with "*DU*." For good measure the beer also foams, only half of it is out of the bottle and so intimate already! In any event, the TV could have prevented such atrocities much sooner, because we could have watched ourselves in it, in the crosshairs of the screen. The mother, lying on the floor, feels blindly for her son, but now he suddenly seems much taller than herself. The mother stares at him for a last moment. This must be the end of the created world, who is the man who made this mess, what an asshole! But he, too, lies prostrate, as if sacrificed, on the floor. No father ("Both of us are returning from the mountain") would sacrifice his son to God, because no God would ever demand it! But WE did! The mother collapses, and the father-mother suddenly takes shape in her son. Her compassion is not very great, since in the meantime the commercials have chimed in, time for us to put our heads between the blocks of last evening's series once again and let ourselves be pissed on. Underlying those commercials is the fire of ignorance, which they want to extinguish, so that the world will finally be returned to nothingness, well, yes, the error: it isn't really the actual carrier of evil, but we shouldn't succumb to it often or we might unintentionally buy the wrong car.

Now the hair-hay, ever more tightly packed, whooshes down and smothers this model family we chose to build our house around, crushed them like the pot its flowers, filling every crack of the room. At the very end even the automobile PR must face it. One of the fabulous, shimmering vehicles puts in a word with a cheerful face about low fuel economy and high market value, in all that pneuma of human mass a small spot has been left empty, there the child stands and watches how the parents must keep themselves covered, unable to come out from under their furniture. The midsize car's spot is between Pneumatics and Somatics, a special for the middle class because hardly any commercials get made for the upscale automobiles, those Gods and Saviors, in order to avoid enraging everyone else with what they can do: produce more gas! The child parts the mass of hair with bare hands, easily, like a curtain, it steps over the parents and pushes its way through all those tresses that grew in his small world, which has been turned away from the sun far too long, a prearranged setup (already in the morning the TV often ran aimlessly through the room, but its mistress wasn't even around, she went shopping). Now we have to go to the door and take a look at other folks who are waiting there, please say hello:

In the night of November 14 to 15 of this year my parents and I were summoned out of bed and taken to a collection quarter. My seventy-five-year-old father was beaten just because he asked the agents who appeared in civilian clothes for identification. He was to report the next day to you, Herr Reichskommissar, but was not admitted. Thus, feeling completely without rights and protection, he committed suicide in this desperate situation in the garden of his small country house. In his seventy-five years, my father, who was a native Viennese, never committed any criminal act, political or unlawful, in any other way. He was completely without criminal convictions and always very much respected for his righteousness.

The room, once filled with quiet yet frequent conversations, is now a brick of human residues that upset our stomachs and block our ears, and now the antidandruff shampoo ad will also appeal to the hearts and wallets of the intruders, some of whom are just about to blast the door, at least that's what it sounds like. Maybe they, too, will think nothing of an entire family together with their belongings getting buried under an avalanche of hair. In any event, nothing will have been noticed in the staircase. Often whole mummies are lying around without ever again opening any windows or doors, it borders on zealousness to believe that anyone would be interested in anyone as soon as they have vanished. This is how all those women, for example, drop out of the world who don't really understand how to use their bodies, those flamboyant products, though they certainly get plenty of instructions for it. Everyone is a room of their own where others roam through, roughing it up at their leisure.

It is the two women leaning against the window to the courtyard, chatting, to whom the child returns. One of them is Gudrun Bichler, who stepped curiously out of her apartment in the hallway. The murdered nurse, around whose shoulder she puts her arm now, is hiding her throat behind her hand and keeps licking the excess blood from the corners of her mouth. What a big cheer will there be at her former place of work, when the murdered colleague wants to let death in and realizes that she has been in there all along, still hunting among all those white-painted caregivers and gamekeepers, and at tomorrow's staff party she'll sit in the doctors' laps, joking and laughing, until the names of all the participants will be hiding in the files like Easter eggs.

Where were we? Gudrun Bichler and the dead caregiver, the death leader and her ward, who was hauled in so that a few more jolly dollies could slip through the net's meshes and force their way through the corridors into space and time, from where they had been expelled too quickly, without consideration, without glowing lights, so then, the two women, still almost girls, peek through the filthy hallway window into the crowded yard. The next group is already waiting for their tour, men and women in inconspicuously protective street wear. The men don't hunt or fight. The women don't protect or produce. Idly they slouch around, templates who have had, now for the second time, a ground plan of humans cut out of them, shadow cuts silhouetted in the cracks of the wall from which even their classmates withdrew, nothing special about that deal, even atoms can be split. If so, many could have disappeared without the remaining people setting off their alarm systems as retrieval howls (nowadays they can be heard on every corner as soon as a car gets grabbed under its wings), then some of the disappeared could also return (without being noticed?) and lay themselves between our jaws, dripping, freshly thawed prey. But that's not possible, it would instantly start a war inside us, we would be forced to start getting acquainted with each other and become pacifists, which we always were, just differently. We announce the opening of our annual Vienna Festival so that we can do a job on the foreigners without leaving the country to do so. Such parting would be too hard on us, the family would be torn from their comfort because of a missing member. And the air traffic controllers are on strike. Why? We can't possibly miss someone we don't know. The food still tastes best at home. For that alone there must never be war again. No, we won't let ourselves go.

The two women laugh softly, combing the air with their hair. The child runs next to them, panting. Its body is covered with fine lines, where he had been torn apart in the water and then put together again, somewhat sloppily. Medical examiners and detectives bend over the earthly remains, asking themselves politely whether the perpetrator could have made any mistakes. There is absolutely no device that could dismantle a body that quickly. Only a wolf man could have committed such a horrific assault. If we wanted to dispose of a huge number of staff members who are constantly shining their lights into all corners of the room, we would surely find better, gentler means to do so. Our neighbors are brutal, right in front our eyes they spit their bloody foam onto the pavement, which is already soaked with blood through and through. Screeching females with pitchforks, men in the elegance of their combat clothes (and never do they make a killing with their stock theater of dirty little wars as a boy from the Holy Groves of LaLaLand can do every time he tears the white out of our eyes: First of all, those sneakers aren't right, and those sunglasses are a tacky designer knock-off! Herr Fighter, yes, you, with the cool sporty baseball cap modeled on a shadowy movie monster!, don't expose yourself and your nation to contempt, I am warning you! What sense does it make to step on the head of this already completely butchered peasant woman in her pitiful formlessness? Life has snuck out of her through the backdoor long ago, and you will never be a star of much light and much shadow anyway, because You Are Real! It doesn't work. One can see immediately that you were bought Made NOT originally in the USA!), children who in the future will have to hop around with half a body like sparrows, luckily their lower half was torn off, but the lower half will probably think differently about this: Why can the upper half go on living and not I?, it's awful, no feet, no legs at all: such is the ear-shattering bombshell entrance of the Possible arriving in Reality and taking a bow amid trucks kneeling in the sand. We big-spender donors were asked for goods, but we ourselves were not turned over and squeezed out. I am just synchronizing what happened today. Tomorrow it will be different again, but similar, or the other way around. For the actors to be able to enter, we will have to guide their speech to a faraway site: But it does come with a remote control! Just push a button with your index finger and every place is FORT and every other place is DA, *ja!* No one will deprive us searchers, who have already been screwtinized by another viewfinder (how does the poet put it? You don't watch TV, the TV watches you), no, no one will rob us of the pleasure of seeing ourselves, we are still HERE, SO THERE!, we are somebody again! And now it hits us, we are the ones who make three-hundred-and-seventy-five people drown yet again in a ferry disaster, among them not a single Austrian.

21

You there, unknown young woman, have you noticed that it grew dark? The night appears before the kitchen window, and as if across the windshield of a moving car, the trees' black shadows are running across the glass, stretched across it as silhouettes, nature's foil spread over everything. Though nature should actually be the reason why everything exists, the one who keeps everything going. Nothing works without nature, with her little jug, her special juju, she busily oils everything, she polishes our aging mugs, a delicate web, a clockface, each running faster than usual, projected onto the windowpane only to crumble right after along predetermined breaking points, a sun face, no, a fog face, and on it the rolling trees and bushes. Standing out at the center is the solitary figure of the dishwashing woman bending over the sink and responding only with a silent nod when a guest sticks his head into the kitchen inquiring about the off-the-menu *Wurst* that was to be grilled especially for him. So then the guest looks for the boss lady, who is in the dining room assisting the waiters. There is a buzz around the tables as people are trying to bring back to life the victims of a serious traffic accident, with everyone declaring themselves a God in white, offering their diagnosis, which, had it been followed, could have saved the victims. But in secret their veins tingle from the thrills that there were casualties and that we knew them personally and isn't it something that we were spared and can continue our own spiels. In a moment it might be possible to see the victims and their relatives, who can't yet bring their loved ones back to life inside themselves because first they have to make order in their feelings, maybe on-screen! People give no further thought to their expectations, just having them is enough. A light comes from the kitchen, a wire screen is in front of the window. Fly strips hang from the ceiling. A clock strikes. Then the same again, the same strokes. What odd time is this supposed to be? The hair of the dishwasherwoman (this time a very young one) falls over her forehead, she tosses it back with a jerk but it comes back right away, like a spring that can't be blocked, it keeps bubbling out of the forest ground over and over again. A black mark on the forehead, how disobeying water can be in its enclosedness under and above the ground, that's when the operators of the power plants get it that the world doesn't just consist of their operating. So now the girl decides to raise a foam-dripping arm to the headscarf tied under her neck, the parody of a Goddess's gesture with the power to transform, and tug the strand of hair underneath it. Here, the street, no, that's definitely impossible. Gudrun Bichler stands in the kitchen door and stares at the young dishwasher, she is the least who counts when the voters' envelopes are drawn from the urn and what comes up is only a small pile of ashes and a Bic lighter instead of her. But the dishwasher also counts as a vote, not a particularly bright one, but it burns! A smoking, sooting flame. Gudrun is only looking, she gives herself something to see, but it is an act of will, she'd rather preserve her hiding. Forlorn, she puts her book bag on a stool. When she looks up again, she can't believe that her gaze has suddenly come to life, or the whole kitchen has been imbued with life and is running or driving along. Gudrun literally gets dragged through the window by the eyes, pulled out into the night. Whoa!, now she's driving on a road, and the median strip races—a dotted line, a tentative path for small-fry and fauna (unfortunately, the animals often take the short-cut)—alongside to her left. The trees, even though just black silhouettes, thrash her face corporeally, she feels scratching branches, twigs on her cheeks, they nearly peel off her skin, her inner epidermis, which seems to renew itself differently from other people, at breakneck speed, every minute she is someone else, and afterward Gudrun feels quite weakened. Why is she already in another place, does this road get dragged along, how come the inn's cozy dining room suddenly ends in the open or, rather, is the open? The earth must have grown backward, receding earth-flesh! A street that Gudrun stumbled on only by chance still carries her out now like a ship into a stream. Only the young woman's back bent over the dishes has remained, she seems to be a cutout doll anchored in the post of her sink. Now pointed dark thujas and yews are running through the windowpanes, a black hedge with thousands of pointed hats, no lit night lamp anywhere, and Gudrun staggers into the Sudden. Only the light bulb above the sink smolders under its glass cylinder, one bulb is burned out, the second one still glows, a couple of squashed moths stuck to it. The asphalt on which the hunt is moving is clean, dry, does not reflect, the kitchen simply leads onto its spinning surface, anything could be beyond it, dirty piles of snow, mud, or dry, summerly dust.

Gudrun pins herself against the wall lest she be pulled outside, she presses her hand over her eyes, but the hand is suddenly transparent and Gudrun feels that the landscape wants to lure her, drag her outside, as if she were nothing, offering no resistance, indeed, as if she's been on that road forever, or rather as if she were the road herself or maybe merged with the hedge and disappeared, as if she didn't even exist and couldn't say anything either. And if she can't say anything, then the thing that goes with it doesn't exist either, she herself, after all, is The Thing that currently visits, besets the city. Just those monstrous calf births all week! The accidents, the dead. No one really thinks about the claims Gudrun still has on life, she doesn't either. When she moves her lips on the telephone and you think: wrong number, or when something wakes you up and you don't know what it was, what's actually going on then? Gudrun has the impression that there is a huge crowd out there in the night that wants her company. Masses of gawkers pointing fingers: Whoa, she's alive! By shouting yes!, nodding their heads, pointing with the meatless diet of their fingers. A fusion of sorts, a spot of winged ants on the wall, a zodiac, sign of nothing, a machine whose clomping one hears, it comes from its ongoingness, whose handling, however, uproots anyone in the long run—something bright, risen, but never awakened. It is quiet in the kitchen. Those beings or figures, Gudrun feels, have a completely different dimension and she belongs more to those than to the locals, for whom one constantly has to create new departments and positions. She drifted into something here, even though it's not at all easy to get her drift, no, she doesn't really get herself, let alone the books she still has to read for the exams. Opinion can be awarded the medal of speech, which confirms that one belonged to the SS Totenkopf brigade, but around here there is not the least bit of doubt anyway, because here, among the least of my brothers, no one believes that Those Out There even exist, and thus the truth about them, about us, will never be recovered, it is hiding from us, after all, and so we don't know each other. Sure, Those Out There disappeared from our midst, but of course, they never existed, therefore they could not have disappeared either. Could it be that at best the lives of Those take place below the ground? If that's correct, then why do they drag Gudrun, who did nothing to them, out onto this dark path? She listens. Does she have to really go this way all the way to the end? But already she marches or drives on, turning her back to the shadowlike woman at the sink, who is like wood, without sound and smoke. Nothing coming from that woman could lure Gudrun or even just keep her at ground level. There, the turnoff, the house numbers at the entrances, which Gudrun can't read. All the time that airflow on her legs, tugging, grabbing at her, but there is no car driving by her, yet she still feels it as if she were sitting in one, which would have to be completely transparent then. How shall I explain it, it is like an attack of rotary vertigo that turns you into a whirligig. A motioneer, a constantly shape-shifting entity looks at us fearlessly and throws us out because we are rotten to the core. But Gudrun, for some reason, was accepted, and now an insect's sucking maw lowers itself over her, it is the street's maw, which Gudrun has been staggering along for the longest time, swaying, caught in the airflow, which is caused by herself. Someone walks in front of her, some woman stands behind her, washing dishes for the time being, a constant flow of plates, glasses, silverware, but she belongs to the Here, which knows that it finally MUST say something (which I don't want to get into right now) so that future generations gain some insight and if it were only one—that all this time we have been raised by machines, to wit, by us, their glowing base, the blind followers of the up-and-coming. Good heavens, I see the result: Kitsch and superficiality, the business: Collapse!, no, then I'd rather be Ernst Jünger's seeing-eye dog than that! Well then, walking in front of Gudrun is someone who does not turn around, a man, judging by his movements, quite young and energetic. And as if the earth was awakened by his soles with every step, other shapes join him with every step, shadelike, but once the sun looks down on them, by day, a person could come out from the first shadow, then from the second, and so forth, do we want to let them continue this kind of expansion heedlessly? When we ask about them, the answer is that no one has seen them and there is no trace left behind, as the witnesses confirm in unison. None of them has clearly heard any voice saying: They are for you! Gudrun accelerates her steps, now she is already running, she feels herself smiling, finally a footing in the unhomeyness of those buildings, poles, streetlights spinning around her, the neighborhood wags around her like a storm's impatient tail, and Gudrun sets herself against the airflow that keeps her captive; her arms pull the air apart and she almost dives after that man in front of her, he's already near the end of the street, let's hope he won't enter one of those buildings, she'd never find him there! Isn't that exactly the building where she had that cheap studio apartment? Yes, exactly, that is her old lane! All the stores are closed, it is late already, there the small jewelry shop, which—that's at least how it looked—never had a single customer. But she once got her wristwatch repaired there. The young man gives the impression that he is looking for something, apparently also checking the house numbers, once he almost turns around but changes his mind, he wouldn't want to visit her, would he now? But since he hesitates, Gudrun, in a few strenuous leaps, can zap herself out of the storm and after one or two steps practically stabs herself into his back, he shrieks in fright, she wants to say something, but the word she is looking for can't be found anywhere.

A nobody-and-nowhere face turns toward her. Such a thing could easily happen if someone copied the faces of all the people who ever lived and also future ones, one on top of the other. Mr. Wittgenstone had the patience for this only with a couple of pictures of women relatives in order to prove that they stole his soul, which, however, all said and done, was written all over their face. Since that face is like any other, Gudrun knows right away that for her it is the one and only and therefore must not be lost, no matter what. She had seen this young man before, maybe even more than once. It seems to Gudrun as if this young man had always been in motion whenever she spotted him: a piece of bread to wipe the plate with, which already disappears from the scene, a smudged scribble, a fading spot, always on the go, always onward, gliding, sliding, cutting capers. A lake sometimes throws such men ashore, where they lie down for a moment only to quickly jump up again and whoosh, up on the water scooter and running down whatever makes a peep and ducking whatever ventures out from under the leaden water surface, for such men always are the first to venture into or up to or down. Remembering them is always remembering fun, splashing water, shrieking, laughing, prying, dumping all the other shit. A radiant, smiling mountain world emerges in panorama, peak after peak, which one could cover with one's thoughts, if one had any. Waves lapping against the lakeside, a flower being put in the hatband, an irritating hiking shoe pinning itself to the rock's heel. Gudrun moves her lips without a sound, this young man is every god's son, he is every son who could have every man as father, one who burns in front of her like a splinter set on fire by newspapers and at the same time—congratulations!—has stayed normal, however, as she touches him, he gets into the frenzy of the well-rested, wide-awake, Rin Tin Tin–ish, that athletic folks frequently have about them. He swirls his arms and legs as if he wanted to perform all his favorite sports at the same time, he climbs with backpack, rope, and pick into mountains splashed with sun-filled buckets and dives at the same time into the plasterlike solidified waves of the lake, no space surrounding him would remain still, no wave ejecting him would dare to lie down again. He comes to life inside himself, which at the same time burns him out, zealous as fire happens to be, which in total can burn more than 4,700 people in a total of forty-six combustion chambers in a continuous operation of twenty-four hours, simply because it was fed that much to process. And the fire returns the favor of such invigoration with increased zeal by continuing, now throwing itself into one more individual and transforming into his soles, which lick and race ahead, in circles and down the mountain, up and down and around, going on within itself, because nothing goes on anymore. The end. Not even a thought stays alive. Here we find ourselves in front of a building's gray wall, where the road seems to end, this is where Emperor Sport has lost his rights and everything has to be done standing, for which enough room has been created by knocking off everyone else around oneself. Forget about worries, it is beautiful to move people, claims the diligent fire inside the walls, first they move, rising with great effort, then they dissolve, this operation just stopped, and the Worker, having no history, makes himself something, rather than finding his home in those flames once and for all: So now he makes reinforcement wires instead of making himself. And this young man, who looks so familiar to Gudrun, thrashes his arms around and stomps the ground in always the same place in such a frenzy that it wouldn't have surprised Gudrun if that man suddenly broke through it, since he just pulled out a piece of earth like a corkscrew, and halfway he suddenly pushed it back in again as a horrible stench emanated out of the ground. Now that Gudrun has hunted him down and this is the end of the road anyway, this man does everything in one spot, running and climbing, jumping and diving, why does he go through all this trouble? As if he would miss mealtime, his last one? Oh, I see, he does it because he can't get away from his spot, as little as she, Gudrun, earlier! The young woman realizes that the man's desperate efforts are not to serve physical fitness, to keep muscles in motion, but rather that he, just like herself, is trying to get out of his own personal tornado. He simply wants to run away! Everything is dripping wet from the sweat he splashes all around him. His arms stick out like brambles, grab at Gudrun, the wall's gray shrubbery continues into a far distance, it is the distance from where the steps of a huge crowd of people that perhaps want the young man to join them are now coming closer and closer, and the man flexes his muscles in order to get away at the last moment from this dream team that's on its way to the land whence come the fingers given to us and the dreams we distribute as burial gifts to the eternal sleep. The whole city is just a toy, that's how small it is. But what seems to drive her people is gigantic, larger at any rate than the people, and they throw themselves into her, not only to take a dive but to become bigger than they are, bigger than everything she contains: her shape, in which her flash-wrapped essence gets chastised with punches of roasts, kicks of *Wursts,* and whippings of cakes. Yes, big is what we bigots would love to be, and even bigger than that! Once again, we are the up and coming. And this is how such a person comes to be, out of the Danube's moist warmth and a few of the Alps' smashed tributaries and runoffs, to wit, one whom the earth and the water brought forth as our one and only, maybe to export him, and now he lies there without breath, without motion, no, rather AS motion in this case, Adam Edgar Gstranz or whatever his name is, or rather was, unrattled, rocked by forces that, nonetheless, can be purchased any time in his sports store to fire yourself up. To quickly put some life into yourself, so that there would at least be something to be said about us: how many seconds we need for the hundred meters in order to be saved. But around here every stroll gets arranged around mealtimes, which must never be missed. Eating is our national pastime, so it can happen that inadvertently a few people get eaten as well, that also counts as sport around here. And sport, in turn, accomplishes as its most wonderful success that you don't always have to stay in one shape and suffer from your looks, because the sport market tells us about our shape and what about it should be changed and it covers our entire being, it gets recorded as gospel by a computer in a downward-sloping performance curve, we'll shit in our pants when we see that and sports medicine will have to save us. But when we put on or strap on the right stuff, we can breathe easier right away. We were brought forth by surfing, hiking, climbing, rustling in such good time that we come into being quasi BEFORE our time and now we may do it one more time, but better this time. Thanks. No problem.

This young man seems eager to jump and glide around and inside a giant toilet paper roll made of concrete and with a summersault finale perfect his balance in the bank, but please not now, the steps are getting louder and louder! And Gudrun stretches her hand out and tugs at him. She pulls him out of the storm wherein his greatness stands and stops. His suit, which wasn't the newest anyway, because the newest we only got in yesterday, his suit then hangs blowing in the wind, the only remaining question is whether he could even have prevailed in terms of color against the new patterns, which also pop up bigger and in varying shades of color variations—this time more of a peppermint green—on the newest surfboards, if the suit at least would have been kept alive: and thus Gudrun has landed again amid a sea of shiny glass splinters in the kitchen of the rural inn, the splinters wash around her ankles, they hardly twinkle in the light of one sole lightbulb; and none of them reflects even a tiny piece of Gudrun. She saved one human being, which doesn't mean the whole world. By way of thanks, she gets the hot, greasy dishwater coming up to her wrists. It protects her wrists, against whom? Who caused both her wrists to be cut open lengthwise? The water is turning deep red already, first there were only streaks, now it has become a blood soup throwing itself swaying and spinning into the drain. And a naked young man, whom Gudrun is getting to know better and better, since she has met him several times before, stands, like her, in the pile of splinters of the broken kitchen window, his thoughts running down from his forehead, hair, and hands, as if his skin were greased. He can let it rain from his member, which wants to reveal itself all the time, pump out its name that is hidden (it serves the regeneration of the Son of Man, all the sadder that I don't know him) as much as he pleases. Revealing itself in this member is the changeable becoming, as opposed to the unspeakable, which I, who am shapeless, have no intention to speak. I don't count. How can I shape, how can I speak, if I don't exist? Maybe I could raise my hand.

Maybe this young man could also push his affirmation of life far enough to become the one, for example, who bludgeons Gudrun to death and drills a sixty-four-centimeter-long stick through her anus into her abdomen? Because he had such uncontrollable aggressions? His girlfriend swam with another guy into the claypit lake, that was an hour and a half ago! Who on earth could take this. A young man should always take his position as carrier of the good, Hermes, messenger of the Gods, seriously, so now he stands there, having slipped his nudity into those superwide, baggy knee-length shorts, whereunder he presses his knees into the cushioned plantation around her sex in case he fell, and his own unique member suddenly began to stare at him and nearly choke to death on him. No, I see, it wasn't this young man I just got, it was another one who looked just like him; he now lies among the special sales items! At the moment he feels a certain relief, but it's not one of conscience. A girl's murder does have its special quality: There he scoots along now, that fellow, open to anything, on inline skates and fletches his teeth at you, poor young girl, your neighborhood, *Favoriten,* that part of Vienna is an all-too-sexualized district! Gudrun, here I can see a mushroom of foam in your mouth, that is, you involuntarily swallowed water, therefore the struggle must have started already in the claypit lake. Ooh, stop that, please! But then your soul's guide, young Herr Hermes, was not about to hold back, he punches, kicks with the winged shoes (the three decorative stripes still have to substitute for flying and even the car for now, but the next time we'll take off for sure!), and then this Hermeneut, who stands for future as well as past things, which at his mommy's he always generously ladled into his plate—he, by the way, is shaped like a man's member, pointing from the bottom up—so then this living boyscout dagger, as his Penelope Bichler woke up in the water and immediately continued weaving her thread of life, without first taking his measure, her Lord and God gets his rocks off in her womb with branches and twigs in a sort of overkill. Personally, I prefer describing car accidents, since in most cases there are several persons involved, beholding and self-withholding is my being, which I lay out in state by way of insurance forms. The branch, after all, sticks sixty-four, no, sixty-six centimeters up the young dead woman's ass, that's where he pushed his light, not under a bushel, but onto his candlestick, that's how he was taught!, this light bearer who brought light into darkness, *Licht ins Dunkel.* Austrian State TV's beloved annual Christmas telethon raises money for light. You are in the wrong place here, throw the stick into the slit provided for it, but watch out not to swallow the clit. Better spit it out! Spit at the gruesomely mutilated victims, who no longer have protective roofs on their body buildings, by getting into your vehicle right away and split, otherwise you might get an aversion to it all! The whole thing about that Gstranz fellow is difficult to explain. When Edgar Gstranz has aggressions, he can't turn back, so now all his aggressions are already gone and we can have a pleasant talk. The appreciation of life should not keep this young man, whenever he gets himself together, from doing it just for the fun of it. And all the fun and games I have to watch are there for him to enjoy his body again, it is the biggest sin if he doesn't. Unfortunately, for that purpose you have to put yourself into an unknown person, and if you don't fit in there, you will have to dig yourself a hole. This young man, maybe he will decide after all not to kill our Gudrun Bichler, not to impale her on a branch, fletch his teeth at her, or set his penis in her—which Gudrun B. may also see in all its shining glory, before a jagged hole, no star (because she will get into the *Inquirer*) is cut into her heaven—but rather keep it for himself, this diamond among the family jewels. It doesn't fit in all the way, he'll have to roll himself up in his hole. Some women hardly know this pleasure anymore. Some think that it will pass them, stop! But it wouldn't have to remain sixty-four, no, sixty-six centimeters.

All of a sudden, the foam rises above Gudrun's hands up to half of her upper arm, and as the blood is running out of her, she turns to the young man in order to establish with him a sort of interest group of two. In ceremonial stiffness Edward's cock stands before her amid an undulating cornfield of hair, which seems to be painted by a master, hair by hair. Well fortified and stolid, Edgar's legs keep him upright. Turns out, he didn't have wings on his heels after all, so he can't run away; the contours of his body are there only to look at, but the in-between suddenly blurs before Gudrun's eyes. Edgar's member is truly an experience, for it can change its position from moment to moment, it moves as if all by itself and even seems to enjoy this tiring activity. Give her one more moment, please, so that Gudrun learns to understand this mutable shape, she doesn't have much time, Edgar is already taking his staff in hand, he's found a grazer to go for the kill. The staff, however, has woken up and beats with a nervous knock-knock against Edgar's belly, it lulls the eyes of the dead to sleep, it also wakes them up again when they fall asleep, the awake the awakened, who have become suitors for Penelope B. Edgar and Gudrun embrace each other as if, thus entwined, they were crashing from the cliff, which is a place of skulls. Inside the fencing, the teeth, no, the teeth are the skull's fencing, they'd first have to be broken to get inside the inner human, into the flower-patterned, no, checkered lining of this much-described, never-reached anthropophagus: and Gudrun cuts off her hands completely, after she has already cut quite a ways into them, and she falls, like most of the dead, with Edward into the fabric of forgottenness, but whoever has seen his shirts, shorts, and jackets might not ever forget him after all. Noise from the kitchen door, laughter, there are some who want to take a nip at more glasses or get a piece of bread freshly spread, the Wirtin isn't very strict in this regard, things are pretty private here, most guests have been regulars for years, often decades. The door flies open and another hiking group of three wanderers stomp in laughing and joking good-naturedly, it seems a beautiful moment to her. What, the innkeeper is busy at the bar because a bus with package tour travelers arrived for dinner? Nowadays you've got to accept those guests, too, in order to turn a profit. On the blackboard next to the improvised reception a trip to Mariazell is advertised, no fewer than six persons, where could you get a better deal? The men help themselves to the homegrown rowanberry schnapps on the shelf, earlier the Wirtin had smilingly given them permission, and they add it properly to their tab. Already a bit buzzed, the three wanderers want to hurry to the regulars' table to play cards before others with arrogated priority rights, they seize their places, clop out again laughing, as a matter of course, and walk right through Edgar served up on his plate on wheels and Gudrun lying cut open in front of her sink, as if through, plain and simple, but now seriously: Nothing. Air. Atmosphere. Awaken, you, who are asleep and rise, for you shall appear! Be restored again! Messia oufareg namempsaiman chaldaian mosomedaea akfranai psaoua, Jesu Nazaria. And—ignoring the young dishwasherwoman and the bloody pigsty she created with her sudden suicide as well as the naked router who was so thoroughly conditioned by his Arisen that just before his death he absolutely had to do something outstandingly piggish with it (I identify *Salmonella* in 27.2 percent of the isolates from the feces and 36.4 percent from the tonsils and mesenteric lymph nodes) just to try it once—those three oldish men went to the shelf and got themselves a bottle, they did know, after all, where to find it. A cousin of the Wirtin distills the homegrown firewater himself. And a few millions are going up in smoke. By tonight the kinsman will deliver the sun that rose in those red berries, which for some will rise only tomorrow morning. Outside, the vacationers produce unhurried, grinding noises and gather information from mouth to mouth, from one human's door to the next. Then one thing becomes clear to them. Earlier they had a lead, now they lost it again. Gaily they trot back into the dining room, from where a loud hello rings out immediately as well as the slapping of cards along with lively calls, words, each of which, luckily, cannot turn into a thing. Thus nothing sleeps here groundlessly, and if they do, then only very deep under the ground and for a very long time.

22

Vacation bliss blazes from the forest where at this time, however, only few dare to go for a walk. Most people clump together at its entrance, open up their panic supplies and close them again, undecided whether they should eat the fat skin on top of their feelings or instead peel it off and throw it out. All of this just to be able to get a generous swig from their partner as long as he is still hot. Look at those trees! Signs call them by their first and last names. An educational trail that includes climbing and exercise devices keeps the feet in place and the mind connected to the elbow's supportive grip so that it will hold up—oh, stay a while, as Goethe says—when it wants to rise to the *Kronenzeitung* tabloid that's been brought along in the breast pocket of the jogging suit. Fermenting slowly in this juicy shadiness, the vacationing guest is informed on metal plates (cars, after all, also have informative number plates) about native and exotic flora that were transported here to floor us with their looks; and every self-proclaimed forest guard is lovingly protected by a timbered enframing, if in between he wants to launch himself in a giant swing onto the high bar planted there for that purpose. Then the invisible force hurls him over the bar or rather throws him out. This trail has always been visible far ahead, how come the forest body has closed over it like a giant blob of chewing gum that's been pasted over a hole? No poet penning the pinewoods' wonders could plug this hole any better. Now, does that say it all? Please, not again! Old folks pant as if the heat were put on them. All that hot air athletes create they'd want to get a whiff of just once, and then more and more of it. This forest, no one sees it unconfused once the sun's fire finally gets down all the way to the ground. Our senior citizens don't give up, they greet others of their kind who have already melted away completely in their colorful packagings. Pull-ups and vigorous arm bending and leg stretching: listening to the others puts an end to their compassion. Even the elderliest women wear their cool sport shoes to the angora sealing of their knees. There go two gray ladies walking by who do not follow the rules! They move a bit faster now because breakfast time is near. So we break off the scheduled sportive activity or save it for later.

Indifferently, the ground with its centimeter-thick layer of needles yields to the foot, because the breakfast needs a foundation. Now you would think that people who softly rock their bodies' flabby protuberances like naughty children who want to be calmed down and yet wish nothing more than to be left alone by their owners would keep far away from each other, to be by themselves in this gentle dusk. But the middle-agers still hear the hoofs of extraparliamentary opposition horses thundering in the distance and want to gallop after them. Those horrid former young folks, who rule us today and travel elsewhere with their money, farther away, where there are more dangers, or is it the distant waterfall with a beam of light falling into it?, but no, the old folks look for each other on the fitness trail and accuse the municipality of not setting up more benches along the banks, where you could deposit yourself profitably (view!) after having spent so much of yourself. Those elderlies seek mutual closeness to assure each other that they in fact come here for this kind of soilbound solitude as the transition into another dimension of homeland, namely the beer fest in the tent, the tent fest in the Here, this eternal parish fair, which is to lead seamlessly into a Christian men's and women's booze-up blast, and then indulge in it down to the ground. Homeland, your educational trails through the woods drive the vacationers like cattle into this denuded trench, which is all that's left of the wild that once was here. Now everything is neatly labeled. Nothing left for us. Nothing to be done. Like tender but insistently growing sprouts we grow beyond ourselves, and the signs grow out of the trees so that the wild and the common finally get to know each other. Heavily our profiled soles embossed by us weigh on the earth, that's all the profile we've got. The needle carpet swallows everything. Shrouds the indeterminate shapes human bodies become after many years of committing mortal caloric sins. When will these bodies finally be defined? In what dimension, which they will have reached by then? They can die any moment! Here, on our grounds, the sweat-cloth veiled ass burrowed in the cuddly pine needle blanket (Caution! Showing up now and then, if fuzzy and yellowed, even in this frequently, though vainly Downy-rinsed knit of the finely ribbed little-rascal-underwear, is also the imprint, if weak and faded, though occasionally also—O sole mio—tan face of our Savior!), yes, exactly, this is where the Messrs. Retirees retreated to. Their short break doesn't mean it's all up kaka's creek for them. On the contrary, they are still full of it. They still have lots of plans, road maps on which they are drawn, if only by hachures, and there are plenty of solitary widows, the young, orphaned singles, regrettably, have something else in mind. Not much to go kaka over. Anyway, the exhaustion of years wore down the hinges, thus the wanderers fold themselves up, and thus, grumbingly, the more mature classes of aging lords and masters save their necks from the nooses, which masterless females tried to throw over them. Better to mail order one from abroad who at least considers them stuff she can stuff herself on. People love to read each other, but unfortunately, . . . it's only the few meters they can pace out inside themselves that are actually released for publication, when the obituary must be formulated.

Tree trunks must be stepped over, plenty of effort for some senior gymnasts. Gravel flies up because the police drove up in a car extra-big for poor readers and marked with a blue light to boot: and vague speculations are expressed by people who feel useless because they didn't notice anything during the night. They grapple with ideas, but they don't grasp it. What on earth did this landscape, already somewhat bespattered by tourism, dream up for them now? Is this what folks here mean by an adventure holiday? Did the few hotels and vacation homeowners think up a new party game that involves geezers getting roasted like apples in the campfire of eternity, which they imagined was bigger somehow? The shadows of those walking are advancing only haltingly today, people are crowding the entrance, and don't touch the house, where this horror happened. Groups that paid a flat rate, everything included, now come to a halt, everyone included, they expertly touch a few leaves and deny the acid rain, since they now hold something against it, a healthy leaf that nods its head. And the good earth, so popular that we begrudge her for it: some people pulled Bach flowers out of her to make themselves feel better again. A terrible event took place here, no doubt, shadows continue to exist, since the light bulbs still work; a stone-gray van, loaded with human stuff for God's Charity, which we will have to sort out later, has already left again. But this death shrouded everything, even the words that applied to it. It is unclear even who the victims were. In the meantime, their souls have become strangers on earth without having to pay for it. The dead were apparently torn apart as if by the hand of a giant praying maniac and robbed of their best pieces, the dog can't have these long bones. Speaking of the dog: he's doubled up with his hair raised and doesn't seem to listen. A married couple electrocuted themselves on their bedframe, grilling themselves like pieces of poultry, that's the rumor. Chunks of meat, half-cooked, like half-digested lumps of a landslide, were thrown into the room, we hear. According to the date on the packaging, these two elderlies weren't even designated for consumption yet, so who changed the date of conviction that gave their life its final determination, and what confessions did they make to whom before? Chatterboxes are standing in groups, and revamped as trash bags, they spit out their guesses about this strange double suicide, which are also just barely picked bones, into them. Behind their hands discreetly shielding their mouths. This death has the effect that people can't hold back any longer and can no longer contain themselves, and suddenly startling each other, they rear up high to get a better view of what's ahead. They want to get out, but how? They stand around like colorful throw pillows after a rabbit punch: the women similar to southern hemispheres where everyone likes to be when it's the darkest and coldest here, the men desperately straining to keep their fearfulness to themselves, should death tap them next. Time's up, buddy! Not even in this utmost fear of death do they want to share anything about themselves with their wives because they always want to know the value first. Anyway, in all these years they've already picked the best out of each other's eyes where they are the darkest. Even death has to resign himself to it and make do with what's left.

There, in that gray grisly van from the county capital in front of which officials are running around in circles taking pictures, where guesses are flying about, in there the image of man as it's already been shown with painstaking precision in anatomy books has been corrected a bit upward and downward, and what's this now? The bones were put together all wrong! It looks as if . . . in the great calm and quiet of the eons who thus far have always worked together very well, there was another possible way of shaping humans, by which the brightness, the light, their essence could have been dripped into them like a paste of eggs and flour. As if a force, liberated at long last, had written the shopping list directly into the flesh, of what else was needed for this food for gods so that The God would even recognize his own creation again. Only: This time it didn't work out as well as before with the alphabet pasta bubbling out of the funnel into the soup we loved so much as children. Even though the coffins have a good foundation, both insulating and isolating, it is already dripping from inside like a thawing ground in a transitional season, when the landscape's limbs dissolve and folks' faces lead to all sorts of conclusions except the one as to what bursts out when someone nails a piece of his wife to the stick of his ax. Or did he pump her with a gun. Who gets the house and whose children are they now? The inside of the human being, the son, the father is a something that wells through the armholes, irreverent, irredeemable. Perhaps on the outside he is a little more. Puddles form on the floor of the hearse, liquid seeps, sinters out, aren't those two coffin lids rising already, because inexplicably the volume of the piles of corpses has steadily increased? Bones floating like driftwood on the surface, the private, not the public, organs (the latter better help us with car body damage) are waking up, rising up, Herr Chauffeur, hey you, Herr Civil Servant, there is a pool of goo forming around the back wheels, haven't you noticed? Something's banging around inside the coffins, kicking, forcing the lid open with its back, something kneels there, which is able to express itself, if only vaguely, in its own juice, hurling steam up to the skylight, so that it would order more light, a super-slasher spot to be thrown on it right here. As for us, we don't yet want to be put on the spot. We aren't game, can't bag us yet. Our life hasn't been eaten yet, no one even wants to just take the first bite anyway. But then! That waterfall in the casket slowly but surely turns into a spring, which could soon wash away our entire homeland. It's dripping all the way to the very last room of our nicely furnished home, where this wasn't part of the deal when we purchased the deep-freeze casket and filled it headless, headlessly, with the Sophienalpe (mother without father or husband).

The blood moves steadily. Bubbly foam rises to the surface from the fragments of those two dead, and only feelings are still expressed uncompressed by the bystanders as black milk poured over their dwellings. Restlessly the animals paw the ground, now what? Some folks no one had ever seen before remain silent, their words are still looking for accommodations, only there could they calm down and swarm out again. Conversations diverge more and more frequently and take the detour around the weather. Some turn away, dumbfounded waxen dummies. That stench is intense, like an opinion from the heart, one wants to express—if it gets rejected, its producer will have to take it back again. The twin coffins shake and sway, something shadowy coming from two creatures freed of their fetters sinter, like smoke, in a thin stream, out from under the zinc lids. The new dead no longer have the quality of the older ones, who still were showered to death by us. But then we missed them, those fellow humans, and we had to create new ones, this time, however, exactly in our image. But what's that, those old pneumatic folks, who in the meantime have turned completely into air, want to reach their homeland's fresh-air spas again. Hello! They must be hearing the radio's wake-up call, and now they don't just have to wake up but also be born anew. Their sour dough has been sitting heavily in our stomachs for decades in the form of millions of risen bits of yeast. As if a newly risen force took the shackles off the dead and they were growing in the vat, in the bucket under the bushel. But this dead couple does not yet see its truth, they lack the prerequisite for it: freedom. Though they seem to want to get it now, Emma, erstwhile Nazi maiden and her spouse, formerly SS army preserve: Death lets them loose, he lets them off the long leash and the retraction device seems to be stuck, there's simply no way to catch up with the mixed double beast. The whole day with its garish glow is just waiting for this wild pair, let loose in the open, to devour all its sun.

Come on over, you two leading characters, ring yourselves for dinner, you two half-portions, you!

The student Gudrun Bichler and the con athlete Edgar Gstranz step into the dew and grace of the day to shake off the morning cold. They warm up with an easy jog and toss up their heads, which hang on the soul's chain. Soon they will have left behind the still-stiff retiree bugs who first noticed the fire in that one room and yelled Fire!, but only after absolutely everyone had seen it, and now all of them are clumping together at the entrance to the cave. The breakfast room, usually bright and friendly like a twinkling eye: the daily breakfast routine gets disrupted from several sides: the dead, the waker-uppers and the awakened, are a bit worse for the wear, but etiquette demands that they be commemorated in a memorial service. Folks move their lips mechanically. Hardly anyone can still remember that these dead once lived among us. So then, what happened to the old, quiet couple? I think those two are going to get the other dead, who still resist going beyond themselves and, thus transforming, finally becoming themselves! They brought them a mail order catalog. The two suicides had been turned around in their own carcasses almost full circle (as if screwed the wrong way into themselves) and then left lying there like that, half done. Also charred somehow or, how shall I put it, as if they wanted to be consumed by something bigger than a fire. These days it's better not to put one's ear too close to the impulse of time, in order to listen whether time itself at least is still alive. Actually, no one should be allowed to own even a single television set.

A sound encloses the inn, which got struck like a giant bell to last until the last soft-boiled breakfast egg and the last multilayered Teflon bread arrived in the last hand. The cleaner nature gets, the more desired it is, the same goes for humans in closed spaces. The pigs roar in the sty, that's unusual, just wait, soon you, too, will be cold cuts. They scent blood. A certain odor, known to them from older brain layers, weighs heavily on this place, where does it come from? As if a knacker had dumped something from his truck, but the stench remained, it's even getting stronger, is there a candy factory around here? Folks, true to their herd mentality, laugh sheepishly, it wasn't them: Rumor has it that a car got stranded in a deserted forest parking lot, actually a green bay, where used rubbers drift in the surf and right next to them the wrappers of chocolate bars, which masqueraded as baby food and were repaid as tooth decay in the human face. Some early morning exercisers already wondered why one couldn't see into that car as the windows stubbornly remain fogged up despite the day warming up quickly. Now and then groups of two or three joggers are gathering already, circumambulating the obstacle on the educational trail that all flesh must go before it gets combed out, piled up into a haystack, and then set on fire, beautiful waves of human hair! People stand there, stunned, shading their eyes, but: nothing. Destiny's waves want to weave themselves back into life by way of an expert hair transplant, which the singer Frank Sinatra would have invented if someone else hadn't already done it and it hadn't been considerably refined since then. After a while people continue their run. On the ground men and women tie their imported manifest destiny boots. How come one can't see a thing when looking inside the car? Surely it's some con trick, which will turn out to be a new day cream for man's dearest friend, a car polish, which, however, is not to be used on windows. The dull stench makes itself felt here as well, eventually it will prove itself to be a toner for the beloved metal face. There are also barely visible streaks as if from grease on the right rear window. But we don't look too closely, it will soon become apparent that grease is not a big help either when we want to dock onto our capricious mistress with her mega-horsepower without denting her, stubborn as she often is, she doesn't always want to start up smoothly and jumps instead. The trees rustle and one can see that this goes in a certain direction. Non-natives separate at the obstacle and converge again behind it. They feel they've already gone native with us. The earth is soft, their feet rest gently, they hardly touch the ground running, as they and their Adidashing manufacturers in the Black Forest boast.

We must turn the heat on ourselves if we ran out of dough and still want to have our cake and eat it, too, on our vacation. The innkeeper had peeked out of the door several times since 6:00 a.m., scenting the air, trying to catch the drift. Making money, sure, but not at that price! Is this supernatural meat that's rotting here, even though she just fried it nice and crisp? The smell comes from the direction of the Cistercian monastery, which under its gigantic red roof hood has already attracted many visitors. Or does it come from farther away? It might well drive away the guests who darken our land like thoughts. But no, quite the opposite, a special jollity seems to break out. The stench stretches like a bedspread over house, garden, forest. Like a preseasonal blanket of snow that turns everyone into a homebody, and who would be more at home here than us. It works out well that the guests are already here before the skiers arrive, to walk ahead of us into the avalanches.

Weakly but piercingly heaven's commandments weigh on the heavy tablets, and people check whether they feel like ordering the day's specials including side dishes, everything's set to invade us poor calorie sinners. Groups are standing together talking quietly but not inaudibly about the prescriptions from their physicians and pharmacists. Soon they'll be taken off the parkour as the side effects of what they actually ingested to save themselves. They are so sick because they were focused only on the heavy stuff on their plates, which they had ordered for the purpose of stuffing themselves, even praising the Beast, which seduced them to sin. The Beast is a snake of humans formed at our *Musikantenstadl* TV show of immersive Alpine song and dance entertainment, it sang and clapped a bit, the snake, and still strikes at this hour; now, I don't consider myself an innovator, just because I always invent things to add to something that's already been expressed frequently before, nevertheless, I must tell the Austrian and German television stations, ORF and ZDF, respectively: This music is awful. Unfortunately, many of our viewers believe that they will soon get into their penultimate shape with dumbbells, jump ropes, and some clapping. But at the same time, they take meticulous care of themselves, measured by their own standards, which they still have to live up to, namely with vitamins and minerals and exactly that music. Well, that's the way they are, the older ones among us, the senior citizens, who also have a special program created just for them, which lifts its leg on them every Saturday right on time, immediately after the program for animals who want something from us. And that is for us to want them. No one leave the room! Everyone stay on their padding, the one with the wings that can be changed if needed. No one will notice.

According to the supermarkets' regulations, all meat will disappear from the shelves, night after night, as of today 3:30 p.m. And the fresh hams will show up again the next day, just to make us the butt of their jokes now, repackaged and rejuvenated like vampires. In the meantime, the expiration date has expired. Resurrection and eternal life, here they were accomplished without the hype generated by the saints, the initiates with their exclusive, blessifying innards. From man to machine—together they paste small labels onto the bags, simple as that. The circulation of blood and death, how eternally springlike they act, forever young, who'd have sterile instruments at home to do the latex agglutination test. Anyway, the first thing people do when they go shopping, they stick their fecalic fingers into the food, thus eating themselves that way. That tender, bloody substance, which has to yield to every pressure, poor us! How could we resist it? This dead, honest protein provider, no matter what's promised on the packaging, still depends on what our senses tell us, and they say YES. The flesh puffs itself up, it cuddles up to its transparent patroness, Mother of God, that looks good! That nutritious little prisoner in its protective custody, in its soft wrap, it'll never make it out of there all on its own. Thus, it abandons itself to idleness and plays catch with its maggots. The meat: Someone passing in a hurry will pick it up from its nest without looking closely where it spends its transitional period: pigs, tested positive: five in Saint Marx slaughterhouse, Vienna, three in Graz, zero in Mistelbach. To the last drop. Yes, any day could be your day of death, therefore live as if it were your last day! Everyone who still has teeth, grab it! Sit, Rinty, sit! This land is a good food recycler, it reconciles itself with itself every day anew. For it was flesh of its own flesh, which it sacrificed, this land singing of hammers futurebound, and even today it still has to keep its customers alive, those who arrive to thrive among us again or at least visit us in our butcher shop, where we've already durably processed quite a few others with our timing devices! So we're sitting directly at life's source and use Whole Foods and let ourselves be slowly cooked through by our feelings, which we would never have had before (so now, instead, we have all the more of them, we stored them in the freezer)—women, mothers, fathers, who want to find out from books about their innermost selves, their nature, because they don't know what to do with themselves—and the one to whom they mailed themselves today doesn't need them tomorrow either. Which hand throws them, those who came to us as dear guests, which hand hurls them with a big swing down into the packed yard so that we can read our past in them and the way their intestines drop to the crowded ground and then return the book to the library? Because we have already read it. "Alles Große steht im Sturm," the Black Forest philosopher exhorted his students. All that is great stands in the storm again, and Ernst also wanted to be visited by his *Jünger,* his disciples, again. Until recently, people were standing once again in hissing serpentine lines in front of his little house, knocking on the door. Those are thirty eons of error. Across the millennium, those followers and their saviors, the pope, the bishops, have not dared to pick themselves up from the baggage check, but now they are returning again as foremen in the vineyard. Because people must simply be made to fit their inventions or get clamped into the vise right away again if they don't want to fit into their trimming devices, yes, the soul is hard to pin down because it doesn't stick to one appearance. Appearances will look much better after we have pedaled enough on our bikes.

So then, this forest also became a gigantic primeval rest stop that opened up to upscale expectations. Desired folks show off their seed under their suits so that others can find bliss in their fashion. Fresh air, good *Wurst,* clean springs, fungi. Thus our war profiteers, toughened up by the newest hardening sprays, stroll straight along the borderlines and tear their sleeves on the barbed wire fence, which the leaseholder, a famous Ariel, no, aryanizer of department stores (in the meantime all dead or sold, that is, his descendants practically own the banks!), put up, so that he and his hunting party could remain undisturbed. His wife got a house on Lake Wörthersee as a present. Animals roll over, collapse like crazy, easy as falling off a log, no wonder, with those loaded hunting guests, the ones being ahead of their time, I mean those running around in front of their time. In nature people crackle with enthusiasm like flames, like fires, they flash and glare, but some of the elect can hurl the fire themselves. This trail descends steeply, keep looking! Keep running! Your mate is already far below!

Chilly, moldy smell rises from there. Rotting leaves, herbs, grasses, creatures. Rocks that seemed to have moved closely together before, barely leaving space for a logging path, split suddenly wide open. They have a moist coating, seem much darker than the light edges of the metal-veined wall of wounds, which would desperately need to be patched (it'll happen at some point), it had been blasted out of the mountains without consideration of their architectonic fault lines. Wounds in the rock, a carnage of stone. Earlier, when the two young wanderers strolled along the forest road, the sun was still beating down busily from the side of Wetterstein mountain, but it didn't hit anything. Forty meters tall, firs raise several warning fingers, they were left as a memorial for the population to remember that this had once been a jungle. Now the Union erected crosses there to crucify those who left the local state-owned industries nearby. That's for what membership fees were collected all these years. But our folks—we already took two of them (we always take at least two for the double-blind test)—they have already left the graveled road. Almost unnoticeably, they just don't yet know it, they started to slip out of hand. Perhaps it was the last time they were slipped to us. Like combed-through magazines on rainy days, wherein celebrities go off against the rails behind which the infamous gather, pelting them with their stale lives.

Edgar and Gudrun sit down on the embankment that's covered with dark, moist grass and move carefully down into the Old Moat. This steep trail is the original one, the one envisaged by the Alpinist Association for the subjugation of the surrounding mountains, and the few mountain farmers who could still nest here for a while also dragged their carts with dry goods along this path. It is as if the pair stepped inside a bell, but only to be clappered down themselves. It looks like a bomb crater, where something of considerable caliber detonated. A hole is hard to pinpoint or describe. The temperature fell a few degrees, it seems to me. The valley floor breathes loud and hard, like someone sick. Anyone climbing down there freezes over on the spot. We provide you with similes now. Tourists reach for their jackets and shawls. Something rustles softly, buried in the alder thicket. Rotates lazily around its own axis, a big animal, a small one? A common otter? Plants seem especially succulent here, chrome green proliferates around the water's murmurs. A cabin stood here once, but it burned down years ago. Wild fruit trees blossomed in the ruins now teeming with insects. Butter burr, plantain, burnets, and whatnot, giant wild fennel bushes with myriads of midges clawing into them, until the white umbels look all black and frightfully busy. Everything the valley swallowed it also keeps, and its blithely bad breath rises already. The murderers worship carrion that, like The Worker, hangs on the cross: Deliverer and Delineator, even money gets raised for Him and His buildings. The grounds are given to tolerate us on them.

An old monster that slept here sits up and opens the maternal womb, which it kept locked with a zipper. Lusciously the vines intertwine in front of its kennel, the warm air stays above, at the floodgate, the entrance to this underworld. The wanderers feel like being shaken in a dark green, steamy bottle to become effective, to make them palatable for a greedy appropriation of and transformation into someone, who intends to celebrate himself as ruthlessly as car racer Niki (the Rat King) Laudate or Thomas Muster, our King of Clay, who just got to the quarter finals, bravo! Oh, how those plants stand out, glistening, firm, strong! Magnificent! There to stay. *Dwelling* pure, which no human would want to start, for someone might come after him and get him. The stones on this old path are plastered with mosses, dotted with lichen, with several panicles of quaking grass sticking out. Yes, that's what you saw, the grass already reaching for those weather-worn stones, its gravestones, in order to bury them in turn. A barely visible Hansel and Gretel trail, strewn by an invisible hand, and below, around the blackened, jagged ruin, whence tiny stems, young but already withered, extend their gloves, oh Mama, this must really be the end! A moist shuffling, glittering of insects and their trails, dew-covered spiderwebs, sharp-edged blades the darkest green never crushed by a foot, drunk from forgetting. A runlet trickles from the rockface. The ground bubbles up under the feet, and Edgar together with Gudrun stumbles down into the ditch. Their path will be decided on this wet grass. Encouraged by its patient calm, the two stepped into the wild lawn, oh, my dear times, when the wild is more precious than the cultivated, the spoiled!, and now they are amazed by this gelatinous stringiness. It is as if they stepped on meat, fresh out of the Safeway wrapping, but already somewhat past its prime and thawing: little octopus arms, peas and carrots, put out to pasture; sloshing under their soles but still keeping its elasticity, the grass, instantly bobbing up again behind their steps. Hoisting the foot on its back, throwing it down again. A there without a there to hold it all together.

23

Edgar Gstranz looks at Gudrun Bichler at a loss, both arrived from somewhere, but they can't say from where, oh, what an imposition!, the power of memory doesn't work anymore, with whose help we could ascertain the most banal things, while we forget that books, like the open bodies of bats in the rafters, could help us preserve reality just as well. The power of the senses also has something to do with it, with whose help the two try to recognize each other in the reflection of their shadowish ideas, which, luckily, barely radiate. But they don't know who they are and who the respective other is; the dim medial light is not enough for them, they want to imitate the medium's appearance on the bluish smoke screen, at which they gape bewitched and bewildered, for they find it impossible that people can be shrunk that much, ouch, Gudrun's and Edgar's batteries have almost had it. The breathing, the almost voiceless hum from the blackened ruins gets more and more audible. Something puffs and blows rhythmically, licking itself. The burned-out ribs of the house rise and sink, the juice of life, no longer sizzling, gets pumped, black syrup to calm the bloodcake, that's about to get burned in the joints' sockets, the sizzling skillets on the body stove. For in this area, in the various vacation spots, folks want to raise their arms fiercely again. A hidden booster pump pushes the blood through the walls of plants clinging to the shattered nature. There is something else behind it. Some sorts of creatures breathing exhaustedly, gentle flesh undulating on blades of grass, and a sidelong glance from Edgar reveals the nocturnal, longing strangeness of his companion: this can't be true, she's becoming more and more transparent! Unnoticed until now, the billowing vegetation has gained entry into her flesh! And this isn't flesh anymore, is it now? Her bright sportive colors, the thin red anorak, jeans, T-shirt seem to seep away somewhere along the wayside, and the deeper she advances into the thicket of wild lettuce, buckthorn, Saint-John's-wort, wild chervil, soaking wet up to her knees, the more vehemently the last veneer of life flows out of her. Puddles, pools of color are already forming around her: a hurricane, a vegetative orgy flows into the measurability of her being, thus skimming off the last touch of attractiveness like foam: the ground drinks up Gudrun. Her protective membranes, the water wings on her thieving thoughts with which she desperately tried to steal memory, this forever bottled-up, closed book of a woman, seem to dissolve, a force that becomes immeasurability and is beyond our reach—as the gents of the OB trucks are saying here, lifting up pieces of *Torte* at the altar and throwing dark glances at the infidels, whom the sun of Christ hasn't yet reached during their *Torte* throwing—apparently starts to have an effect. The gentlemen bless their congregation as if they had winnowing shovels in their hands. Yes, this is Catholic country and yet nothing but dirt in the parish! Congrats, how God's self-shining body merges with the garment of the son who had to be crucified. Yes, their total essenceness gets dissolved, thus everything must go that is not son and has not created or at least touched the truth with his own hand, this wound that festers constantly, if it isn't quickly [ad]dressed by the Catholic Men's Association and buried with or without a stone. An ancient hit in Austrian music boxes says: What we haven't touched in person won't touch us either. The views of poor us don't get enough consideration. Maybe Gudrun will transform into a hexed woman and rise up in the air, screaming: a flying dragon on its way, well, we still have to think about that, but even such a thing would be easier for us to imagine than the truth: brain in the glass. Hundreds of children's euthanized brains in unsealed canning jars! For us this is almost as normal as the complete disappearance of people, at least something is left of the former: their preserved commemorative food for thought. And what we, what they think is far from happening. Powerless us: No one puts us on the cross, we aren't as stupid as Jesus. God is with us and our giving and taking incorporations, which we have received in place of bodies after renovation and thorough cleaning, we native children (one of us is Arnie, who is currently worshipped in a movie). So we won after all, and in the *Volk*'s music program the sighs change into roars of the common folks. They don't want to broach the subject of themselves, they don't want to brag about anything as much as Christ's cross shining over baroque altars, with which they crossed the rest of the world; okay, that's crossed out now anyway. Yes, Jessie, no one will contest any of the loot anymore!

Could Gudrun be some such piece of loot someone ventured to go for? As she walks, she seems to get heavier, more sluggish, bulging. Her cracked shell opens, if involuntarily, to her viewer, Edgar, it bleaches out, dims; up there, what's that, a BLOOD BLOUSE! A blood bag. Bulging, semitransparent like the feelings of the more literate in the letters to the editor columns, which crash and crack, secreting something that mustn't remain a secret, today we want to talk once again about this product, SlimFast!, that made our country so sensationally thin, because with its help so many citizens lost so much weight, they were just skin and bones and simply flew away, but we don't want to hear about it. Here you can actually look inside a person, checking them over, how thin they've got in no time at all, you can't even see them anymore. Looking at him—okay, but driving, taking him for a ride is no longer possible. Blood shoots upward from the ankles as if into a communicating vessel that's connected to our beautiful landscape. Look, this landscape is alive, though it has been dead for fifty years, or at least it pretended to be dead. Now it opens its eyes and receives its tribute in the death toll of the individuals who were sacrificed to traffic. That's what Gudrun envisioned in the vapors of the grass. With moist matter-of-factness she puffs herself up, a portal vein, a portal into another dimension. What does this being who must bear the cross of her own thinking have to say to us in the name of this land's inhabitants, who let us sign petitions? It says, in an ideal state it would first of all have to be more *gemütlich* than in ours. Amen! Cheers! Stop yelling like that. People might think that you and not your topmost boss were nailed to the cross. Hurry up, let's pack up and leave the picnic area or we might get stomped on by roasted chicken legs and discarded gray brain matter! That's not my idea of *Gemütlichkeit*. But the Austrian men and women had to fight so hard for it, at first no one trusted them, back then, when the nation was given to them as a present. In honor of the occasion, the double-headed eagle, who'd pulled a ligament breaking its chains, got daintily laced paper frills arranged around its drumsticks, so folks biting into or just swinging it won't notice how tough the meat is (no wonder, it's been slaughtered half a century ago!), hello!, our precious name, which generates a splendid musical echo all around the world since then, is Austria, precisely because, as mentioned earlier, her citizens are Austrians. Ta-ra-ta-ta-ta! Plato should have had light installed in the cave right from the start, yes, now that it opens, you can see it, pal!, and maybe also central heating, since we were spared the Central Committee at the last moment, after they had already requested us. Our entrance can be easily surveilled by video cameras. So that you can comfortably see on the monitors what's going on outside without having to open the door. Who casts his own shadow nowadays, when the adventurer simply proceeds to the projection room: this last straying of the past into a windowless time, where we'll capture it easily, time isn't that big after all. Reality comes, thoroughly fried, from the *Schnitzel* pan into the bonfire of TVanities, where it slowly turns into a patriotic crispy brown. With french fries and mayo. Or Catch-as-Catch-up, straight out of the tube. Have we been guilty of anything or not? It depends on the interpretation of this lovely image (shelves up to the ceiling with brains of little children!), which still must be analyzed because it is contradictory. Either we were, then our goose has been cooked at the Highest and we are taken to the barn every day to get thrashed. Or we weren't, then let's just forget everything that has never been! Then we'll feed ourselves with a few thousand kilowatt hours into the shopping net, where we can also bag our profit and take it home in no time, beware, when we are let loose, that'll be the real freedom. So in June, or whenever it was, we bought ourselves back into the European consumption zone where we—with our expiration date stinking of rot and decay, which, with immediate effect, must not be tampered with—are once again permitted to be in the front line when our pork, including its spear-swinging *Salmonella* strains, is offered and instantly offed again by other countries, who don't permit us to mess around with our old date that stinks of expiry and putrefaction, okay, so let's eat ourselves in our rage, we are clean, after all! This space is plastered with warnings of our past, and as it goes with home interiors: Sometimes you want to slap paste all over it. Only those who brought their participation certificate (don't forget the residence registration, at least ten square meters per person and residence permit) may look up at the shelves and get a taste of the things that are tugging at them, though still a bit reluctantly, and they may throw themselves on all the shadows, wherein we, the prisoners of ourselves as well as of the press from a faraway east coast where the Easter bunny lives, can still be totally ourselves. Who are the chained ones who tell it differently or just simply lost their way, who knows?

There is a little bit of life caught in the ruins of the small house, and it breathes heavily. Nothing can be seen yet, but people are rising leisurely, quietly, from their sporty bucket seats, where they crouch, pathetically thrown into their already pathetically dated clothes. They pull up their socks. They wrap their arms around their lower legs. The cords of bindweed almost rip apart soundlessly but nonetheless smack vigorously, and a door swings open. The people who fled from our memory and commemorative events by means of which we celebrated every single one of those fifty years all the way to here, where our daily news and weekly magazines aren't even available anymore, all these missing persons can no longer be kept in their confinement. At this time the talk about them is more benign than usual, but they don't know it because they were buried in a different place than their thought-organs, so then, where, pray tell, are those graves? We want to visit them. And anyway, tomorrow the talk will be about something entirely different. The ladies/gentlemen will be able to wallow in the mud of the past and tear their actual hair out from under their spa-packed coifs. Remember! We are not going to doubt ourselves now, will we? Oh yes, we will, we'll do just that for a year, at the least. Our chancellor now wants to visit the long-promised land and then return, in person, to civilization again. Men rage with anger under their memorial stones, which they threw, always the first ones, and always at others, that they weren't among the few saints back then, and today every Tom, Dick, or Harry can call them fellow travelers whereas back then they ran up to several millions. The marathon starts at the Vienna City Hall. Soon they'll all be dead, but so will we. And yet, the much-mourned ones are already forgotten amid all these lamentations and accusations; since they have been exposed for so long to the horror of our benevolence, many don't want to and can't hear it anymore, me neither, by the way. Amid our mourning glory they are long dead and gone, and we can do without the gory, though maybe here, in this shady valley that puts us on the spot, they have gathered for the very last time. The keyboard of the Never (but please, Not Again!) has now been played long enough. Now we would much rather entrust it all to the rustling tissue paper in our chancellor's throat, stretching it on the rack of a comb, blow through it and listen to it again on a fast soundtrack. Around his cabinet we can look at ourselves in the mirror while we wash our hands as if in innocence now that we have relieved ourselves. The shadiness of our forerunners' deeds, our foreshadows (they act, after all, as if they had never lived heartily because they've been loved and lauded too little), keeps us captive. It is not possible that those things could have ever been done. The picture on the screen proves that we can't be real: It replaced the light at the entrance to the cave. And the gaze in its elegant ghost garment turns around and around but never back. It is a light made by men, wow, look, that beautiful sun! Whatever it once captured can never be gotten rid of, tickets to the South are bought, and all of it, a ready-to-eat meal, shoots out of the tube, see above (please take a short break or read again), and shows us the real thing. The eye will get used to it, okay, and we do still have our brains. Once a year, during vacation, ID sees the light and misinterprets it as television. And cheers. And waves. We are being watched. The ideas have already outgrown us idiots. How can we ever get used to us, always so deep in the shadow of our grand ideas?

So. Now we are finally getting to the last stretch of the descent to the spring that gurgles and murmurs down there. Get a grip on yourself, despite all my detours, and follow me! Bring your own drinks. We don't want to reveal them too soon, our springs that feed the grapevine streaming from our telecasks. We do miss what we have lost, but it also nurtures many doubts about the exact number of six million. With this number they deceived us in a most ignoble manner. We get ourselves truth, because we simply need an element to show that we were elementarily different once. Our wanderers wander. We are frightened by their looks. As if a gigantic green bottle had suddenly been turned around, inside of which there was always a vacuum, that's how a howling, dully booming glass funnel sucks in our two young wanderers. They run faster and faster, and the deeper they get into the chasm of plants, the softer their bodies become, more transparent, greasier, even lighter, yes, that's what it looks like to me. Looking more like two thin-skinned bowling pins, quite playfully thrown by a giant hand that seems to belong to a state-run stately medium, a coo-coo guru, who's got us by the balls. That's how they are floating along, two cruise missiles, two missing links, graceful. Soap bubbles, with fogged-up, streaky outer skin. Blown-up pig bladders, that's how they rise, wearing their faces painted on natural sausage casings with the thin-threaded blood vessels still visible. That's how they are rolling down the slope, the bouncing balls of history, which apparently had a small memorial cross for the martyred erected here and that, unfortunately, at the expense of us descendants: Austrian history does not want us to look in the mirror, it simply does not want us to believe that there is something (plastic wrap and picture tubes) between us and it. It wants to reconcile itself with us! Bravo! Excellent. And of all places it is this place where at best only images could live, which the dead picked to get out again, maybe because it's cool down at the valley floor and they won't rot so fast. Or maybe they wanted to break out of their door- and bottomless time to see something else, something new for once. Who will win the fall championships? And only because of Gudrun and Edgar, that rope ladder, are they able to climb up now. Pitying ourselves because we have had to pretend so much throughout the years, we often talked to them: Our dead. And us. Like trees, we often drop our leaves, when we, hugging the sofa set, must tell each other something. And light-footed the pair Edgar/Gudrun slides, rolls down the grassy ski jump. And something walks out of the ruin and toward them.

The plants are definitely gaining too much ground. That malformation that was Gudrun takes on a comical nature: she suddenly talks incessantly, the student, as she steers through the perils. She chats on and on as if all this is nothing and what's at the bottom of it all: groundlessness. Folks anywhere don't sleep anymore, and in a last, desperate pull-up they move, in order finally to wake up, to the lowlands of German late-afternoon TV serial schmaltz, which are trying to outplay the American series in a gigantic match of aggression and repression, but they are so flat that no one can last in them except maybe an earwig. Gudrun braces herself against this diabolic virtual (?) village that pulls her down together with Edgar, whose muscles seem to have been sold at a bargain price. It doesn't work. Some kind of origin births itself there, because everything ran in reverse all the way to the beginning, which was actually meant to be the end. However, the author of this series was short of an ending, so he now takes it as a beginning and as an excuse that afterward nothing happens anymore. We prefer driving every day to A. and commemorate the dead over writing no more poems. Every fifth, well, let's say sixth, meal here with us is already a *Gedicht,* "a poem!" as the saying goes. And in the meantime, there are more poems than ever, every turn of the page an inner turmoil for the artist who wants to do it better than the others. Those liberated have long since climbed back into the cave, but we, we aren't even shackled, or we could no longer pursue our pleasures, or the pleasures will then pursue us into a kitsch-as-kitsch-canned castle at Lake Wörthersee, where we could also easily be. Yes, and the pleasures follow us all the way there! But they don't find us there because we are already looking for more, for other pleasures. After all, the point of it is that we chose them and not they us, anyone who once has been partner to a person will worriedly agree.

What did I want to say just before I cut off this section? Yes, down there is a black hole, let's take a look, mothers can cry there for their Erwin and their Isidor as long as they want to, they won't come! People have accumulated there, even children!, and the battery is fully charged; they no longer want to be in the dark and hidden. The liberators are coming; but before they get all the way down, they are already in danger of succumbing to the superior power of the truth sayers, uhm, soothsayers. Our liberators have long faced the threat of getting killed. They left us too few invented truths. Our poets should finally be allowed again to write what they want. Now that they have been on their knees before their concoctions for so long that they've been smothered by their own schmaltz, they deserve it.

The dead want to be liberated, but in order to get their lives back they have to kill the living. It'll be some disappointment when they'll notice: Their two liberators, those sidecars of life who have been activated for the increased death rate during vacation times when folks get completely restacked, aren't living anymore either! Angrily, as at water in the street that's splashed all over you, the prisoners of death lace into those two shapes, who were dumped into the cave. Whoever falls under the spell of this place will perish there, and the danger is everyone to himself. We implode into our guilt and can't be killed anymore because we've been dead for the longest time. Getting to feel at home in what we have done, with whom, and what, the chancellor proclaims to his fellow citizens, won't help either. We hesitant ones who have waited so long with our birth, just so that we schlemiels would be freed from any shadow, we knew how to get us Gudrun and Edgar, and now we dread, though not too much, in our human-leather-chair, the unknown. But the nobly crackling fire in our open fireplaces throws around its head neighing, and the apron with all the colorful motifs shrouding and shredding everything on it and written on it: Today the chef is cooking, this fire wants flesh and ever more flesh! This fire gives people a new look, but that way they can no longer get out into the open because they can no longer be seen. Are we also in danger of becoming sacrificial victims getting burned to a crisp, if not ashes, because we always present ourselves as a species endangered by cars? We lie on our backs, sunscreen with SPF 15 on our faces, turned toward the blinding void that hurls down from heaven like an ax, and the blessed victims cannot be looked at today because they are already in the hospital. That is, in the basement, in a few hundred colorful glass jars, only the best of them: the brains in their cerebral mantles! Mhmm!

And we, our sight is trained on one thing only. Lightness (from an express train waiting for the signal?, the trigger to our second stage of knowledge?), a lump of light that won't move, but we don't see where it came from or what it touches. Too bad for the sensitive person who can't take the light! He gets nothing out of it. One Herr Botho Strauß, for example, I just had his name held up to me on a piece of paper to be served with a colorful garnish, from which he, however, had already picked out the better bites and berries, he is simply too bright, and that is because he never gets out into the open. That way he simply takes himself for the real thing and hasn't even seen THE LIGHT yet, which bothers me so much when I am trying to sleep, well, maybe not him. He doesn't see the light coming from a fire! It's quite normal if someone has had enough of owning up to the guilt and would rather owe a debt to own the little house at Lake Tegernsee. To begin with, this man owes us an explanation and will have to pay up: Why always only we? Why does it still hover over us born-after sun worshippers, that hole in the stratosphere or wherever, we see it every day anyway, the invisible, springing from the lips of a concerned meteorologist to meddle in our leisure activities, oh God, animals are staring at us, skin cancers are creeping up on us! The main thing is that there is still something we fear, which we can escape all the way to the Caribbean or to the Austriasses to dive into the depths of Lake Wörthersee. Thank you, Herr Strauß, for lending me your flashlight. Now I can see I've been out in the open for the longest time, which, however, seems as big as the reach of the pencil-thin beam from your blender. For now, the ticket collector says into his little gizmo that, for starters, everyone must pay for the transportation and then not clump together like this. Move forward, please. The final stop is coming up, so it's no longer worth offering a seat to the dead and make them real by acknowledging them—that's definitely not part of the parcel, there is already tomato soup in it, good for the eyes. Just needs to be stirred.

It won't be long now and there won't be any paste left in those two *Wandervogel*-figurines to reinforce them, after Gudrun Bichler has had her say, soaked and softened herself, and swept her innermost out with energetic broom strokes. She knows nothing about herself anymore, it is as if she were already gone, she only has an inkling about exams and the university, later she will teach at a school, I have no idea how she knows this, she has even lost her name, after all, and if a piece of paper were put in front of her, she couldn't write it either. So now everything went down the drain, well, some of it ran away at the last moment. Gudrun B. remembers nothing, for days now she has been staring at the TV, and as if she had suddenly developed an extraordinary memory for all the facts, which can't forget a single crack in the cobbles but doesn't know who her own mother is, everything is real now, if only for the past three days. She opens her eyes. A Sargasso Sea took her memory away. The present delights her, for Gudrun's miraculous corpse has been raised. For the politicians to be able to stomach someone like Gudrun, like all people, they must pound their chest with their fist in all their nonstop politicking honesty, the gust of air that follows is something they might miss some day. No matter how desperately Gudrun tries to hang on to the roots and shrubs, her feet slip away from her, they stumble and slide, glide down to the valley, and that champ at her side slides even faster, after all, he has practiced for days on a rolling saucer. Nothing is left of all the words, which the philosophy student used to play with the palm of her hand instead of a racket the birdie, but this sorry sign language of a mother, whose brainless children shat into her brain. Speaking is senseless. And even if: That much truth, this delicious well-done angels' flesh, is something this country is simply not used to!

The two transparents run, roll, stumble down the mountain, weightless, as if a priest held them high above his head in a Corpus Christi procession, as the hornorary honorarians, hats pressed over their privates, sink row by row into the dust that their holy dead are made of. What does the Lord say? My father's house has many rooms. But from my father's house alone forty-nine Austrians have disappeared, now they don't need a home anymore. No God will give us hell for that. Oh yes, those Honorarities: Their wallets and mobile phones shield the pounding hearts from a stray silver bullet. But to begin with, the bullet would at least have to be gold, it wouldn't hit the right spot anyway, because our superiors' hearts are not in the right place. This thing floating high above the clergyman's head, God in the shape of a pill, who's giving an extra-extreme performance today, so high up there, what a stunt! Never is He held in higher esteem than when nothing can be done anymore, and the rest of the people rest already in their car wrecks on the side of the dusty country road. Still, you, dear flat Wafer-God, don't take away from us children of God any of our grosser than gross national product! And don't let others take anything from us either. Just for you we created a totally transparent state under whose translucent cover you can read in people's IDs whether or not we belong to your religious community and how one pours something from one hand into the other, whereby, of course, both hands must belong to oneself.

Watch out, at this moment the two creatures I created arrive at the moist valley floor. Gigantic leaves of wild lettuce shade the spring, it gurgles and bubbles amid them where they've got something to hide. Thick drops lie sloppily, like souvenirs in a junk shop, on the plant flesh. Like horses, two or three creatures, too few at any rate, raise their front legs, lashing out. Around our nature church (everyone worships her) all those small booths and kiosks have clumped together and specifically in those places where a landscape knows best how to market itself. Nature is her own souvenir, and she is also the shop where to get her. Don't be shy, don't control yourself! This blackened ruin is alive!

Men and women, transparent like Gudrun and by now also like Edgar, pour forth from the hardened larvae skin that protected them the whole time, the ruin is a breeding ground, a reservoir, for those cast off as refuse by this blessed Mother of God Nation, here they crawled through a skylight through which they had already spied on us all this time, back to the surface again, incompletely, but still almost tastefully hemmed in by the remnants of body parts, skin, and clothing, which were stripped from Gudrun and Edgar, torn off their bodies. Those teeming larvae and lemurs, teeming is an overstatement, it is a rather small group of humans, but still . . . they acquired pieces of tissue of those who back then were sent by their travel agency on their eternal wanderings, of course, it wasn't enough to sustain a body all on its own. It has been going on for years, ever since the Germans started their crime series again, the imposition that you must carry your nature inside so that you have room on the outside for your Boss jacket. Mind you, Inspector Derrick's voice is meant for show, and his thoughts separate hearsay from what he heard has been said, which, however, is not true either and has never been true. The fashion dictates of the allied factories of clothing and other donated items are applicable to only a few of us who are entitled to distribute their images so that all of us will know whom to emulate. All the pictures are a bit duller, blurrier than they were before, without an additional dimension. Come on now, set the table so that the powerful can visit us again, since we have completely renovated ourselves! However, a tennis racket can't replace a ribcage, much less mend it, not even if our hearts were beating twenty hours a day for Steffi, Boris, and Thomas. Deutschland! We love her so much that we even brought her over to us, to Lake Wolfgang, to be exact, so that it can rinse off her bloody bottom one last time. Our two traveling companions, who were let loose to let them look just once into the fire and at what it left behind, i.e., a few jelly jars with head and body parts at Steinhof sanitarium (they don't know what's happening to them!), thus they fall into the Nothing of the hidden, the veiled, the dissembled, the disguised, which is called the truth here; and the unhidden, all those quiet people at the bottom of the valley, they are throwing dice for their loot and are getting at least a few scraps of clothing each. There is much soundless, teeming wrangling over every pair of sports pants, for Gudrun's anorak, for Edgar's T-shirt. Lively larvae in an ant hill who are busily carried around. Humans in transition, yes, that is what they are, are quite peculiar about marking their stays everywhere, after all, they are fighting for visibility, those lost ones, since everything around them oozes utter unhiddenness. And by this I don't only mean women striding through the mountains in their bras until their skin is cooked to compote, forming bubbles. All the clothes, cans of music, cannonballs are shooting out from the plastic walls of TV sets, and today we are getting vapors that solidify into smoke and drive us out into the open. From catalogs, from the teleshop, buy, buy, creatures approach us, whose good sides we turn around and around to pick out something because we want to take off soon. Where we are now, in this place, you could for a long time see nothing but shadows if you tried to recognize someone. It would make no sense anyway, because you didn't know the person in question. Now they are taking their liberty, the dead, and tear the clothes off the healthy, the skin comes along voluntarily.

24

With a rattle a swarm of birds rises from the ruin, all those wings flapping like the tabs of a throwaway box. The unessential ones, all unfeatured creatures spray up. Puffballs, having been stepped on, are now spreading their seed everywhere in the forest. ASCENT FROM THE CAVE. LET'S GO, GUYS: Carrion drops from beaks into our area, for which we are still searching for an area head, so that we can find our way around, we long-awaited liberators of the dead. At least we (united, unique, now no longer stand-alone Austria) have given them a few beautiful ceremonies. Flat and without substance they look in at us, the dead, like paper cuttings pasted to a never-lit window. But stay and serenade are granted only to those who are like all the rest of us, therefore, dearly departed, do not hesitate to throw on our smart and sporty regional costumes and customs! While we locals are busy working at not having our origins recognized everywhere and that we, as far as our outfits are concerned, could absolutely be of higher descent, thus also privileged, and therefore, as of right now, entitled to always be offended by any sight. They are ready to march now, the gray sentinels of the beyond, the glass pan above the alarm button smashed this very moment. They can be like fire, consume and then skip out on the tab, after all, years ago they paid for everyone at the table of that conniving Upper Austrian World Surveyor, yes, that one, he with the long knives. Quiet men in suits, two women who, in trains long junked, had been given access to everything the Linz world court criminal [gas] chamber could hold. In death they became accustomed to the most extreme state of unhiddenness, they were driven through the town by two farting flesh peddlers who thought they were the Storm over Europe, and now they are no longer ashamed and so they show up just the way they happened to be dressed as they rose. Their glances drop shadowlike, and they take those shadows for real because it couldn't be real what happened to them back then. They couldn't imagine that those types among whom they ended up were supposed to be heroes. What happened to them could not have been true. Only their shadows are the actual *Unhidden,* and so these late returnees become our living shadows (Oh yes, go ahead, try it! Start moving! Your shadow won't follow you anymore!) and tear themselves away from the retirement they were sent into all too soon. They prevail in the clothes of two young people, and in such disguise, they can finally appear again, more real than before, when they were not tolerated here. Their gaze is already filing away on the chains, and before we can wrest from ourselves a few words of commemoration, they have already cut through the friendship ring that had chained them to us. Since Gudrun and Edgar had reached this stage of being released prematurely by death to this moist valley floor, on which the sun seems to have started to shine somewhat askew, our spirit shall not be dominated either by such bleak things, voices and moods. In the light of our Saturday evening show everybody shall be allowed to show up and we'll even provide our own images, which will make us look like C. Schiffer or C. Crawford. So then, the appearing figures are now liberating themselves and pick up exactly at the place where they had been torn away into darkness. A bridge across the Vienna Danube Canal. A square in Graz where reveille signals the deathbound to gather. Innsbruck, I now must leave thee. Linz, you were actually meant to become the Imperial City! So much truth, though this fight to death can't be expected from any of our current, hard-won prime-time locations, from which this famous operetta star, with her bouquet of flowers shrouded in the artificial ice of its plastic wrap, risks a last look for the camera at Mörbisch, that popular operetta festival town on Lake Neusiedl, to the beloved Merry Widow, a role that unfortunately she didn't get. One tenth of a second longer in the picture, prettyplease, yes, now: There! Here she is! You, Dagmar Keller, Cellar, Koller, or whatever's your name, let's call you Austria's Julie Andrews, why are you straining your crackling neck to milk one tiny moment's presence from the lens of this objectivity-bound medium, which, with its blue light, cheats me daily out of my life? Why do you work so hard, Dagmar, just to achieve this ultimate perfect presence on the TV screen, as if you, too, had wrenched yourself from the Nothing for only just as long as you could be catapulted into our living room? So now you are popping up, presenting yourself as—well, not bad—one truth among many, waving to us in our comfy cave! You, a shining emanation of the Nothing's light! And we, locked into the earth with our images whose stand-ins appear now and then in our popular country music dance show at a barn, which has hay blowing out of its brain (tickets are never available, but at least it's still sitting nicely in its place, the one piece of brain!), we gape at you, who signifies the entrance into the third dimension, as close as you are ingrained up to the neck in this milky gray stream of the screen, which is surrounded by us fans. Curtain up and lo and behold!, in broad daylight there is even a second cave! When we look at you, Frau Keller, Ms. Cellar, we are kind of looking from one cave into another, and this is exactly what you want to hide from us, I don't know why. After all, you have taken great effort with hair and armor when you entered our chamber with pointed patent-leather shoes stamping out the essence of truth: Come on in! We are waiting in our borrowed things for the appearance of your appearance, for someone like you never hides something like that!

Dear old classmate Fischböck, your time is limited, mine, too, but shorter. You sure remember the noble air we were allowed to breathe at Amerling High School and I sit next to you, busy copying from you. Today I ask favor. Am still attorney at this time. That I am not just Polish newcomer tells you our school years together. My wife is Rom. Cath. Aryan. RCA. On record. Loud and clear. Son wears cross with crooked arms. Has striven to be decent, always, so much so that today I am poor man. That is why it hurts double when get thrown in the same pot as Polish sharks. Hope for future: That prohibition of praxis can be avoided. Should my request be mistake, please consider circumstances in my favor, that bricks fell on my head (of course only figurative), so one forgets calm thinking.

Love stutters something to others who, however, don't want to hear any of its BS. The dead already saw the light; it was fire that expelled them so that they could fertilize fields, forests, and lungs with themselves. And now they voluntarily step back down into the cave the Ur-*Volk,* deutscher than Deutsch—all waltz to our tunes, Germans, too!—gave them a good roasting, before we went again, nicely, like good animals, as if we'd always been milked on time, whenever we were full of it, to the urns and threw our votes into them, to have them voided. They climb up to us, the departed, but this time they want to be more cautious and always wear skid-resistant shoes. Sport had the effect on us that our general awareness coincides with the fourth most beautiful triviality in the world, our appearance, which we know from the mirror. Our statements about our favorite club are also correct. And in the meantime, our very essence has changed as well: We want to win the match across the whole of Europe. Can't wait to see what the dead will show us today! Some patience, please! We won't let anyone play games with us: It will be the visibility of the everyday, and let's hope the sun will shine. Because no one and nothing stands behind the dead to illuminate them. Gudrun and Edgar have been completely in the grip of this storm, and from now on the dead give and take from them their memory. No one forgets the soldier either, who stands as the fifth most beautiful minor detail next to the border. As in an ant colony, the departed, in order to become visible again, converge in our two tintinnabulating necro-sextons, armed with a collection bag made of skin. An indistinct hurry-scurry, a whirling in the air, bright schools of fish are jumping, as in a Sunday afternoon series, around a nice American in a boat, heavy German actors, our trusted braves are tearing violently and with ferocious words at the doors of villas in a Munich suburb and relieve themselves in the middle of our living rooms, something pulls resolutely at Gudrun's eyeballs, at her teeth and hair. The shadows assume a more and more cheerful sweetness, who could have been robbed of his belongings here?, and where do this child's swimming trunks come from, which a young man, torn out of his human size and spat out again by a German shepherd, is now trying to put on? But he himself consists only of shreds on account of the dog's chops. Not worth taking him. He has set his mind on an impossible project, like us trying to imitate our operetta idol's hair color. His sex can't grasp the size of these trunks at all, yes, every man is ultimately inscrutable, in any case, he can't be grasped based on a pair of trunks. Who would have given him a thought back then, when he, this average man from Europe, jumped off the ramp into the next element. The elastic fiber of a former swimming pupil who once wreaked havoc in his family: His family is also lining up now for a new look, they stretch out their arms to receive the pile of clothes intended for them. A teenage star enters in front of a cyclorama, eating chocolate. Who would have thought she is a world-class swimmer! The brighter the glow from the box, the darker and more inscrutable the ideas of the TV powers that be. Franzi, the swimmer, who got somewhat sidetracked in her development. Her hair also falls on us and our children and chokes any emotion such a film should actually generate. Moved, we spoke about a dead young man intimidated by a dog: This revenant pulls up on himself the swimming trunks of the child who drowned in the Amalienbad pool and finds himself in a fix because of the depth of his sex's roots, which once dried out in the fire. But now, together with the trunks, a bit of juice, half a glass maybe, dares to venture inside again, his—the dead man's—limbs and member stretch out of the box, where our seed strain is kept germproof, it grows out into the open, and a dark liquid gets sprayed into dark plants that are showing off their growth, and holding their heads under the pipe's warm jet, they begin to really glitter under the warm KO-drops. The small swimming trunks burst like a balloon that's been blown up too much. Funny plastic speckles spritz into the air, as if blown by a gigantic breath. We are being heard! We are listened to as to what we would like to watch. We reveal everything to the pure glow of appearances without reflecting on the ultimate visionality, the ne plus ultra virtuosity of a dirndl dress, which lays out the corseted, delicate continuity of our sex in a lace-covered display window, thus our organs get back into the swaddling blanket. We are living so much and so often, we could start thinking first thing every morning about where we want to go today to carry on in public about the glowing virtuality of our ideas, so that they appear bigger and more. Gudrun Bichler's mouth opens for a scream, as she gets torn away from Edgar's side and pulled toward the impressive body requested by life once again. She has been selected. The orphaned body has aimed for something nearly impossible, and yet it has worked since being freed from its roaring, raging death trunks, and now it attaches power to itself like an extra jet on an airplane that's in a special hurry to get somewhere and we do, too—inside it. Faster! Faster!

Gudrun's head gets buried in the crotch of a stranger's venereal hose, at the bend of a stream of news that was briefly interrupted because of a disruption, but now the show goes on, ladies and gentlemen. Now we'll tell you once again what you have done, even though you don't want to hear it. Because that's how it goes: Botho, the writer, and his little friends don't want it either! Rather, let's be quiet, as he said. The news studio is packed with snazzy, witty learned folks, where we'll have the opportunity to be interrogated by this beautiful, lonesome, utter stranger. But we prefer our own beautiful home, yes, it's still most beautiful at home. Now the starter gets activated, our victims are furbished with some kind of appearance, plus a carnival medal, broad laughter resounds through the valleys when the guild cracks jokes about politicians, thus trampling itself down together with those weeds. People get drawn tightly like bow strings, they whir in front of our shining eyes, which surrender to that shinedig, because they are allowed to laugh about their superiors once a year, which is during Carnival in Villach, Carinthia. At 11:30 p.m. it's all over again. The early departed pushes Gudrun's head between his thighs, where he had his last laugh so many years ago. Shred by shred the skin gets pulled off Gudrun's ears, not out of confused love but out of madness, this newly risen throws her throat over his regenerated sex, which he stole from Edgar Gstranz, as I just noticed. Now we get to the canned goodies. You have to have seen that! Saying and hearing are two different things, I know everything only from hearsay. In any case, everything visible can always also be watched. No holds barred. And if anyone has an idea sometime, he can't realize it because all our TV titans have an awful lot of relatives who want to see their ideas realized first, before it's your turn and mine.

The dead are looking for community, but not exactly ours. Nonetheless, how uncomfortable, Gudrun's body gets blown up, tied, and the small rubber rim, her rubber mouth, with a thread of fate casually twisted around it, is handed to the young deceased to keep. And still more bodies are passed around like canapés at this premiere performance, yes,

Edgar is also offered, mouths take a bite, appetite came only with eating, and the tables deck and shit themselves with gold, good evening! The light disappears, it's getting cold, fare well only means good-bye, and the good only speed. Levers get pressed and squeeze out leverage. Values are stuffed into packs of detergent and laundered. Resolute partners inhabit and turn against us with vigorous strokes. Serves us right. Everybody knows something and tells it wherever they can. Conversations between two grow in front of an applauding audience into a biopical that holds five hundred thousand persons. Unbelievable, all that stuff-cum-ideas that get dragged in front of the camera just to become visional everywhere. Any virtuallusion must work at first take when the endless parades break out of our ground's rot in long chains of slippery stitches they are made of as they cross the screen that made them possible to begin with.

The dead got lost somewhere, no, stop, they are here now, with us, no matter who misses them. We are here and have always been gone already, shadows are interrogated by a controversial moderator and then charged to his account, they won't increase our debts. Inside our homes the sun of the film studio remains invisible, and yet even our shadows still feed on the spotlight, in which the native stars appear against payment of the symbolic. Thank you for allowing this for our low fees, Herr Intendant, but what were your intendantions for this? At least one could still recognize living beings in those shadows, but now that we turned off the TV, the shadows themselves appear without the sun's reflection that radiated from the screen before, lighting up their limbs. TV ratifies our existence. But what do the shadows seal with themselves? Are they locking the entrance to the cave? Before the light goes out, let's quickly examine our appearance in the pocket mirror of our ideas (and let's not hesitate to throw some more powder on our face until we really have lost it!), who knows if we'll find another opportunity to express them. However, since there are already as many talk shows as there are people, everyone surely will have a turn sometime to step into the sun of our attention. Yes, you bet we are something else! We first look in the rearview mirror before we swing out and cut off the superfluous threads of life of others.

25

Millions of Austrians act unconsciously. Relaxed spectators, they listen to each other reporting their actions, the essence of truth keeps changing continuously, it can hardly catch up with all that dressing and redressing. Its bloody clothes are spread all over the floors while it strolls casually along the train of thought, to whose opening the honored guests are invited by the federal president. With a good locksmith at his side, he tells the fellow federal citizens to pack all that old stuff stirring somber brooding into the bags of the used clothes collection, and the consequences? Hysterical flickering of the lights on the walls, an understanding is granted, and it shows our essence in its most beautiful dress: the idea for the thousand-year celebration. A hot costume!

The woman enters the dining room for supper. Her body is identified as belonging to Frau Karin Frenzel, who disappeared briefly in the well-known pilgrimage church and could not be found in an intensive search. Since that time, even though only a couple of hours have passed, her mother wanders around like a masterless dog, calling authorities and hospitals about her fear that her beloved child might have fallen off a horrid place. The passenger seat in the bed next to hers remained empty. Could her daughter's body have spread itself finely or divinely in the House of God? As a reflection in the silver coating of the altar figurines she was visible for one minute and gone the next. Something strange is going on here. Various areas of the mother's body are hurting: Roaming the church, something was torn away from her side, and now the spot where the band-aid used to be really burns, a coin-sized piece of skin is missing and should soon be replaced. The daughter has simply vanished. A kidnapping? Illness? None. The old mother has collapsed in the corner of the dining room, the victim of a mother layoff. Her eyes stumble across the tables, from which other eyes, yes, clearly more eyes than yesterday and the day before yesterday, which, however, seemed also to have gotten lost, glance at her fleetingly from the corner of their eyes. You don't really want to stare. Enough has happened since yesterday that need a thorough discussion. Still, no one dared to approach the locked car with the fogged-up windows, except the Automobile Association, which had run through its membership lists to check whether one member ran away. Yes, one is missing, no, false alarm! The police at their station are in a peculiar state of inactivity and would rather listen to moving songs inside their accommodations than do anything. They listen to what's beautiful, and they expel what's foreign and came from Yugoslavia, or whatever that country is called, swimming through the Mur River. On the roads, things tend to take care of themselves by way of accident. In its ghostly embarrassment of ghastly riches the vehicle still stinks, as if torn-off limbs were pressed against its kitchen window, but no one wants to look closer. The observations contradict each other, some saw someone get out, as they could swear to, the others didn't. People always want to know everything and, in good conversations, trade off opinions from the heart for opening hearts. They leave the small change on the table after they've wiped the neighbor's good drop off themselves.

The mother opens up, tart as ever, but no one is interested in adding more spice. Such conversations are better avoided, the vanished woman was so inconspicuous, one could hardly recognize her when she entered the dining room. An old woman can't be given any consideration by us when it comes to foreigner bashing. The mother talks, but nobody cares. The said and the heard are the same. Just that no one's listening, and no one offers questions. Tomorrow there'll certainly be the opportunity again for climbing another mountain or going on a bus trip. Today all you can do is laugh your head off about nothing. It is time, because it absolutely wants to be evening. Well-nigh inexhaustible supplies of food are opened. We are death. Straws are driven into the teats of milk cows who must die, so then those animals much prefer to stand up straight.

Look, a woman is coming into the dining room. What does she have in mind? Our minds are telling us it is Karin Frenzel, but today this usually clumsy woman is moving elegantly, almost flittingly, nimbly, I don't know, you almost hear flocks of birds whizzing by at her sight. It is as if she could get anywhere from here. What matters is what we think of her. The mother storms along like the wind, not even her orthopedic shoes can do their job, they run themselves down. But before the mother gets the chance to let her daughter's presence sink in, she stops short her flight into her child, it was a flight that ended up in a desert. Now the daughter is back again. The old woman had enfolded the daughter and put her hand in her, the daughter's, wound in which she, the mother, had been the sword, before she lays herself on the line, jumps off the reel, reeling, and, on a roll now, a rough, much-stepped-on footworn rug, the worry about the seemingly lost child billows out of the tough corseting products, by means of which she prevents the abundance of her gifts from sedimenting anywhere else. The daughter's absence could not have possibly been aimed at the mother, because the mother who wound and brought up the daughter every day anew is not aware of any wrongdoing on her part. This filial being, with respect to her mother, just didn't show herself for a few days, that's all. It just kept still, that being, because sometimes the mother can't take any sound that doesn't resound with herself. The whole world must be tuned in to this beautiful music, all the people who are still living are nothing but shadow boxers against the low blows of this mother, all other blows just hit randomly, because the room where these people are locked in together is small, and if anyone takes a big swing, it's always a hit. A small stuffed animal or a paper rose. But those don't scream. You can tell by a scream only when flesh gets slain in its little house of life. And where do we get hit over the head? A mistake.

The alien and yet so familiar woman enters the dining room, which is already filled by mighty antlers, gliding along silently between the tables. It's not possible to see how her legs are moving under her skirts, it's rather like the roaming of a preying animal that jerks up its head every time a little bird hits a wrong note. Dark caves the eyes, lodgings of fluids, which also permit the seeing of the hidden. And the skin in between them, which the cosmetician always fussed so much about, because it bulged and then furrowed, summer asphalt that, though hardly driven over, already had its best time behind it, time, which life had taken by its horns: This skin has stumbled and stood up right away again, good as new. The forehead is suddenly smooth. Specular! As if an alien hand had newly spackled and polished her with eternity's strap, so that this razor will get newly sharpened to drive among us and take along as many hitchhikers as possible. The shreds will then be spread in the wind. This woman won't be recognized by other people, even those who knew her well, but always by a mother's heart whose beat smashes anyone coming close to it! With an inaudible scream this new presence of a woman breaks through the molecular skin of a universal beverage, today it is good old Ovaltine that returns declining strengths it had never taken away. This daughter just appeared. A force to be reckoned with. And her mother jumps up from her seat like a dolphin and, amid loud screams of recognition, lunges at the child, who is now straightened out and back in her permanent employ again, at this absolutely wrong, in the sense of unreal, creature, so why does it bother us so much, the child could simply split!, but one meter before the lovely goal, the mother stops abruptly before so much new splendor coming from the essence of her daughter. Such glow from nothing but a housewife? Who does she think she is! A red light starts to flash in the old woman's brain, this is the theater of war between the true and the false who lock horns with each other, because no one in this country knows what distinguishes the two. To stop or to go on? Is this lustrous being standing here in front of the mother as daughter, this sudden beauty . . . does this mean that suddenly the daughter has turned out not only right but also true, something the mother would have never permitted her to become, because she herself, the mother, had never tried it out herself? The truth?? The eyes of this creature open, they actually look like bristle-covered puppet eyes with rigid pupils framed by a plastic surface you could engrave with a sharp ice-skating track, and it still wouldn't show any trace of the newly sharpened edges of the skates, the way they are fixated on its opposite underneath the rattle of the eye's hinges. Could this be the essence of truth? No wonder it isn't something you'd want to look at. This puppet creature seems to have pupated in a place where time turns back after only one or two steps and starts from the beginning again. This sexless emanciphantoma is further sharpened by her contours, which look as if traced with a pencil, but in between there is nothing but shadow and impenetrable thicket that scribbles unreadable stuff on the legs. No word gets her out of her mind, this spirit, maybe there's been a mix-up, everybody, after all, has some sort of spirit in them. With six million people lost to us, how could we think that we should still form a final definitive opinion about one single individual? With this creature it goes like this: The dirndl skirt plays catch with her shimmering knees but keeps getting kicked away by them and swings into the room while a howling siren's voice escapes her mouth. But only the mother seems to hear something, shy but grand (she seems to have grown, by the way), the daughter's presence stands tall in the room—she could get Catholics to break with their faith (an always loudly shouting majority in this country, fighting against drowning), if they were able to see her at all. But no one seems to notice her, the White Woman, a Frau Hitt or whatever's the name of that petrified queen of the Alps; meanwhile, outside, the Wild Hunt takes a short break and refuels its horses with power, the folks in the dining room would rather eat fat and carbs. They all have to move on. The hunters have perishable organs (human issues) in the car, but they won't leave the mother behind all by herself, she's been long overdue. Someone who punched (thus voided) her child all its life must finally get into the vehicle so she can see how it works. This White Woman, her *being,* her becoming, must stop for one moment until the false of her has been determined and this errant one recognized as true. Only then will she be real. For the mother, who had waited so long for a phone call from the police. So that she can steer the daughter back to her beddy. But the mother does not realize that she's about to hold a foaming, roaring river in her arms, too much to pour back into her womb. Something runs through the mother's fingers, drops from her towering rock. The figure flows out of the mother's looks, at the same time it stays here with her, she will take the essential train of her thoughts at 9:30 p.m. and then the small bus tomorrow at 8:00 a.m., or did she already do this yesterday? Come over here, her mom pulls at that lady with the spaniel, my daughter came back. The lady doesn't have to look to see nothing and, with her face turned away, hurries through Karin F. She is immediately followed by three men welded to their alpine costumes' Velcro fasteners, anyone having lived here for a while knows them by sight, but it's not them, they just look like them, I think. The men's originals lie collapsed in an ice crevasse getting sucked dry by the thirsty mountain, that is, whatever there is inside them. Life it is not. Why haven't later generations been told about it? And the earlier ones didn't find out about it either: Nothing happens without them, who were always on vacation and did nothing.

Now the White Woman F. shrieks shrilly. She shrieks into her notebook, where everything is written down, and she winds herself up like a child's toy, a flying saucer, a flywheel with one of its plastic threads getting unrolled at breakneck speed, thus catapulting a plastic wheel into the orbit of a garden plot, unfortunately not high enough so that it could circle around us eternally like the Skull and Bones killers Heinzi Hitler, Kit Kaltenbrunner, "Little Rascal" Eigruber (they've gotten soooo small in the meantime!); she flicks herself to the ceiling, this woman, where she remains, trembling, in a state of suspension. This condition is illness. The apparition of Karin Frenzel whirls around under the ceiling, like a fan with rags hanging out. She has executed herself, an unknown quantity, but now she carries on like a baby, no, baboon on the rustic ceiling, directly above the chamois horns and the good stuffed one. But why not? There are people sitting here bearded like chamois. And the shaven also slouch there, those born in stables and those who fared better in life than Jesus, and under their seats their *being,* finely sifted by them, is heaping up in ever larger piles, human sand they formed and slapped against the ceiling like herrings' souls (a medieval angler's tradition), here, you can see them still: the imprints of those souls!, there's hardly a trace of them, but they are recognizable nonetheless, shot from a child's sling, that's how easy it is. One just has to write a letter to a Herr Gauleiter, any provincial governor, that folks entered a park at their own risk, who did not pay their parking ticket and pulled it out from the machine, for which death was transferred to them as a small contribution. So, it IS true! Well, I don't want to formulate it! So there's one who should have long been removed (is this why all the others did not make a move, when he—Jesus be thanked—was picked up but not returned to us?) but owns a company, and the next moment he doesn't own it anymore. I am not so good at telling this, but anyway. What happened to the owner of this factory? None of one's business. He's got no business here. I'll try anyway: Venerable Sir! Permit me to pedal strong into this matter! Ask for support, because apply in program of aryanization the bicycle be provided, so it move faster. Application runs for weeks now and runs and runs and no second one registered. So now my turn! You, honorable Sir, know my purity, my selflessness over twenty-five years for the Austrian garment- and downsizing business. My clear-cut nationalist position has placed obstacle like evil guardian angel in front of Chamber of Commerce, so that I was stuck back into Torte because of Schuschnigg, so I must burn as candle for Anschluss. Am party member since May 1938. Since decision must be made in few days, I ask to receive me so that I can be dead in sixty years and nothing drop on my head before. *Heil!* Much more to say to this! I say nothing.

Please wait! Your gaze is quite right, look at that woman rotating under the ceiling beams of fake wood, stirring up odorous air! Serves them right, those who diligently altered the truth so that a new dress could be made of it. Stop!, now the gaze we currently direct to this guest isn't right anymore because it went in the wrong direction and is now ambling under the stars, where the plaster has come off a bit. The truth I speak is an error, but at least it is mine; maybe there is no woman hanging from the ceiling, she might just be in cold storage, while hanging-in here continues merrily, as it lands on the plate at this very moment, hot and juicy. Does this overheated mother only imagine seeing the daughter and simply casts her gaze any which way? Why would the daughter make an appearance wherever the mother's cool lizard gaze is fixated, the stain of a human being, just because it's been squashed there once? This is supposed to be a real appearance, I mean that which appears to shine? Only because the mother's everlasting power wants it that way? And what was still true years ago is no longer the case now, for we took pity on it and picked it, after years on the human back-up bench as center forward, and now we are going hog wild. Unfortunately, the team, the real thing, frequently gets tampered with, that's why they win so rarely. People run into the field! They don't understand their presence there either, but they start kicking as soon as the ball gets hurled out of the launchomat, or better yet: after the kick-off by a charming movie actress, who comes out of a German movie, yes, they do exist. Besides, I have wanted to say this for a long time: Our fleshy silence holds hidden secrets—in wine glasses, that is. Now all it takes is our water to get transformed into wine.

Something still bothers me: Something's up there on the ceiling stretching its arms out toward its mother, I can't yet see it clearly right now, in any case, it isn't Jesus, who wishes to command his mother to whom his clothes should be passed on, and the small package of immortality be sent, because he's got a bit left over. Most of them get nothing. The old woman stands up in her orthopedic shoes and tilts her head back. Now she speaks loudly and in her usual peremptory tone: Come down here, right now! The daughter's hair—meanwhile thin again—hangs down from her head covering her smoothened skull face, she should still manage a blessing with the arms: An impression of protection that's usually accomplished with armored vehicles, as a new group of people comes through the door, dressed unusually formally. Sport did not chase after them, it remained outside trying to bury its droppings, but too late. Yes! Nike, the goddess of victory, produced a limited edition! Herds of the young and younger, seriously now, Jung and Jünger, and those staying young forever have already picked up the scent, they are panting now, nose to the ground, muscles sharpened and filed to a point, at the gigantic stock of clothes that had once already belonged to someone, uh-ho! Said group, that sadly defeated group of people—where did their sneakers actually come from?—sit down at the entrance and keep silent. Until something happens and they must leave this site. The waitress raises her head above her tray with food lingering on top of it, how come, new guests?, no bus was scheduled tonight, those ain't no Hogan's Heroes. The newcomers' faces have something withered, it's hard to tell their ages, so then we estimate, as is the custom here, their budget range.

There is a soft rustle of dirndl-garb under the ceiling, the White Woman Karin changed her position a bit, but not much, sad to say, she is still connected to her mother, who now raises her voice one octave above her normal hertz and lifts it with trembling arms, she won't be able to do this for long, but is her gaze even aimed in the right direction? More and more people, but oddly not the new ones, take notice and request some brain, which the neighbor hands them politely in a glass. Who's that old hag talking to? Nothing can be noticed on the ceiling that could be published in the paper, and the guests' group photo won't be seen in any of them either. A couple of mouths open already for a big complaint and a small beef. Those present do not want anything decomposing in their midst, except on their plates. A scream emerges out of the mother, from deep layers, her essence shows itself now, that is, in nothing but the lightly grayish reference to herself. The daughter, after all, is still needed to chauffeur them back home. Karin! howls the mother, come here. The moderates, those are the ladies and gentlemen who sat down at the door like the freedom radicals, those are the ones who float freely around in the space, changing seats often, they all jump up now, craning their necks as an old woman on solid soles turns wildly around her own axis, spraying insults, orders, curses, and abuses like a lawn sprinkler out of herself. But where is the addressee? She can't possibly be where the old lady is looking. One can't hear her with hearing ears or see her with seeing eyes. So how are we to understand this thereness? A sympathetic spa-shadow colleague, who had occasionally chatted with the mother after the latter had tied the daughter's leash to the back of a bench or wherever and made her antennas receptive for a stranger's woes, if only for ten seconds, approaches her valued travel companion, takes her by one of the arms flying by, and tries to get her in a lock. Shortly after, the knife is stuck in the ground, quietly trembling, the mother aims a beaming gaze, the dictator's dagger, at the disturber of her raging calm. Her stronghold breaks up into strength, and it gets passed on without the batting of an eyelash or other galvanic jerks, and can you please pass it on as well: My daughter is up there on the ceiling, look there, the woman in the dirndl, she doesn't even own such a dress. I will instantly call somebody who is born of the flesh and not of air, as ghosts are borne of, he will understand me.

I see nothing, take it easy, answers the stranger, who is still preoccupied with this confusion. She's in the hospital, your daughter, isn't she? She'll come back, she'll get healthy again. The things our doctors have accomplished: terrific, fabulous! Taking the brain out of the skull and storing it in a totally different place! The caressing hem of a dress sinks softly over the mother, it sticks for a moment, a base hit on her forehead, slides across her face, two legs glide down the motherly bosom, like oars adrift, the rest follows weightlessly, the sinking boat, a becoming that never has been a being and not a has-been either, just a misapprehension covered in a dress since nothing is holding the dress together, not even a tailor's dummy—the hidden creeps into and over it, so that it can be seen, all prim and proper, the hiding entity, the puffy tea-cozy garment of the entire country. Is this the false in the correct dress or the correct in the false dress? All over this floating garment its frills: wilted lettuce leaves and one or two stems of ancient parsley, which cannot part the Red Sea of the soup that was cooked up here, yes, that is as much, or rather as little, impact the lost ones have on our life today! Nothing is right about this garment without people, darn! The mother pulls up the chops, she has picked up a scent, this apparition has to go. She embarrasses the mother in front of the other guests, for whom the inn is a setting to push their well-padded bodies through the mail slit of their new rustic evening outfit. But if the bodies never get licked, their secrets don't hold together either. They gape open forever, the wounds of the blessed showing their one and only beatifying content hoping for the curiosity of someone wanting to peek inside them, but more often than not, their hope is in vain. Pulling on her harness, an animal's breast propped up under the cotton-puffy dirndl blouse as worn also by natives, who tried to get themselves a new shape that way, in this shape, Karin, if it's really her, must have heard the mother, and we also heard her mighty voice. But we did not see Karin. Right now, she seems to have stood up as the hidden entity against her mother. She is back, but as usual, no one's looking. No one wants to see some kind of entity transforming into truth, which, however, is a lie—no one, that is, who sees the Austrian news river of forgetfulness flowing by him but not the unshaped falling from the ceiling right under his nose.

The apparition of an eternal daughter sinks, untouched by life, from the ceiling, the mother hisses the dear name she herself gave the daughter, which now spritzes right through the custom-cut cast-stone denture-monuments, amid the vile, the bile dammed up by them, desperately searching for a matching body: Karin! Come Here! Right Now! Flickering through the room is the thornbush flame of an aging daughter, filling it with irregularly flaming light, because no one has anything better to say than: What's she done to her looks today?, golly-gee! The mother's hair stands on end, all over her body, a wreath of rays, a halo, as if she'd been canonized and just like that, already in beatified bliss, stuck to a hot grid, breasts on a tray right next to it. Help yourself! And here the child that belongs to this godly mother: Rose lips open in a strangely familiar face and a tongue pushes itself to the front, punching the corners of the mouth so it can leisurely stretch out in the front. Eyes start glowing and shine through the foreground with such an intense light that no one would be surprised if people were suddenly sitting there as skeletons. It is a completely new kind of radiation that will surely be discovered some day. Karin Frenzel's eyebrows pull against the flow of her hairdo, which has slid off her head like smoke. An emanation that crouches jerkingly, curls, then shoots up and seems to evaporate again. In the meantime, the border has been closed. Like the light, life now also wants to leave Karin, some are already fighting for her clothes. They also want to return in local disguise, maybe then they may stay? The dress puffs out, a sail driven by the wind, flaps groaningly from one side of the mast to the other. Something light tries to glide out of the garment's openings, the shape's interior, which would like to make the idea of being spirit its own, a gift to itself, and the shape tries to gain solidness, rightness, so that this rightness as the body of Karin Frenzel—something easy for me to say but hard to describe (like THE BODY OF CHRIST)—could be recognized. As if one were to softly breathe diagonally across the slit of an organ pipe, that soft a tone: Mother, Mother, why don't you recognize me? Though not a son, I am dead but not done.

The mother staggers to the wall, presses her back against it, the waitress encircles her while childishly screaming for the boss. This woman holds up the professional rush-hour traffic of eating. The calories want to burn, fat wants to sizzle, and there, a flame out of a female figure!, a column of fire flares up, it would be more real if everyone would look there, but no one seems to notice anything. Only those few men and women at the table next to the door turn their neutral gazes toward the human fire, that's been distilled by totally harmless quartermasters into firewater, which I will run again and again as liquid dung along the innocently exposed organ parts and down their throats as long as I live, cheers! Could anyone have spilled the beans as to what we did? Well, we'll keep it all in a bottle. Oh no!, then forget it, then all you've got is vinegar for a sponge on a pole, no more drinks and no *Führerschein,* that is, no driver's license either, that permit for living and loving! Who'd walk to a date? What would there be to talk about? On the Other Side the huge pyres spread a stench that pollutes the entire area in a radius of many kilometers. This woman is burning, or at least the apparition of this woman. Her lips are already drying up, pulling back from the teeth, and the shape grins, while the lids are melting down over the eyeballs, a gape shimmering through them, a stare, that is to establish the accuracy of the ocular coordinates. Mother, please confirm, Roger and over!, just confirm, will you. And the mother drops with a scream one halftone down the hierarchy, for she might not even be a mother anymore. What's going on, is the question making the rounds, did this woman, whom we hardly ever noticed and if at all, then as insignificance personified, did she exchange her *Wesen,* her *whatness,* and notice only afterward how horrible she is and how horrible the *Wesen,* the being she always brags about having giving birth to, really was? That doesn't count now. At least this other being is nowhere to be seen right now. Thank God. The door opens, time jumps ahead, time turns back again, and Karin Frenzel enters calmly as if back from a hike that led her up to Mount Hochschwab. Folks returning from there often have this vacant gaze because there are too few charming alpine watering holes to refuel. What follows in the following is the stay of the stay of a biological daughter, I hope this time it finally is the right one. Some of us get to throw the dice twice because they got a six the first time, MAN! You rightfully inhabit the biggest flood of all, and it is already packed into showers. The daughter smiles, greets, waves into the circle, there is no noticeable difference about her, maybe she is still on the dusty bridge from one side to the other, cars speeding by her, below the subway rumbling in its casing, a dark mass of people must leave the site, they are getting removed now, soon they won't be the same anymore but rather, being the ones going under who, however, are of interest only to their relations and no one else, they will fill the ditches, because all the ovens are overloaded. Because one stay is different from another stay, there is a difference, after all, whether one is packed into a shower stall with many others or all alone in the living room, locked up cozily together with the TV, looking through its ideas and reading off a screen why one, oh God, has been forsaken and once again did not score. Whether or not one was there, it's a no-win again either way. Only at the Olympics or at our own death, being there is ALL that's asked of us.

26

If one takes the 71 trolley from Vienna's Central Cemetery, recovering one's God-knows-which millennials-old faith (where there are so many dead, there must be One who, with bats in the belfry and abandoned by all good eternal lights—they burn for up to seven days—produced them), one gets back again after a while, thoroughly shaken—and who shook Great-Grandad Isidor and Great-Grandma Betty's gravestone until it fell to the ground? And why did this new society "Shalom" not put it back up again? It's too heavy for me, I am only one bug under another stone—to the Russian monument in its Hochstrahl, that is High Jet Fountain, setting. During the summer, the fountain is lit by multicolored lights so that one finds one's way around the top-of-the-crop cave of the Red Army's dead. Back then, yes, not good back then, and still, we got off by the color of our blue eyes. Individual traffic foams around the monument like an ocean: Astra, Vectra, *WEG DA!* GET OUTTA . . . ! Opel's heavenly bodies salute the wind from the east, which must never dare to get as far west as HERE! No more war! There floats the White Woman—white, as in: blank sheet, because no one knows who she is, though she could possibly be the modeling student Gudrun Bichler, fading away like smoke out of the monument's semicircle of columns. But she is not so sure about that herself. Because she wears a long blue coat and a dainty pink umbrella. Far away the barking of spoiled dogs from the third and fourth districts, a multivoiced howling of animals, who know their ways around here and also still know their neighbors, sweeps through the canyons of the streets. As long as animals have existed, they have made noise at the worst time because they wanted to unite in the sex act or fight with each other. The impact of the screening in the movie theater across the street abates, the audience streams out of the theater, mostly young sideburned dudes in leather jackets, by means of which they like to make themselves wild, young Elvis fans, each with a little lighthouse lamp of oil stuck to the front in front of his haircliff, which now flares up from all the music as if playing Battleship (the individual young man is highly endangered but also endangering others because at any moment he could start singing and squeaking with his entire body!), after the "Gold aus heisser Kehle"— ("Gold from a Hot Throat," the German title for the King's straightforward "Loving You") had been served to them and right afterward taken away. After they had just reached for the sky of the flat, cold ceiling of the screen, those young slickers scatter quickly, shivering in the chill of the night, they raise their collar gates, the signal that they are giving up und subjecting themselves to life and the views through the bull's-eye of their God. As soon as the modeling student's illusion of herself being the movie's star has ended with the film, she pushes her way hastily through the packed rows, her little umbrella dropped in the process and retrieved and handed back to her by a nice guy. Why is she in such a hurry? No one sees her anymore or what will happen to her. The noise that she will quickly drum into the pavement with her pointed metal heels will remain unheard. Such a beautiful young piece of flesh! What a shame to throw it out. Healthy and charged with whole milk, firm and laced-in tightly with a belt so that it can show above and below all the more braggingly and signal studiously when turning, so that one wouldn't lose sight of it. Everyone else should stop. The girls in the modeling schools always wear those pointed smooth pumps, that's the dress code, and with it a weighty tome on the head that's too big to get inside the head. That's the way the girls were taught how tall they could get if they were a few centimeters too short. Let's not have them appear where they don't belong. Gudrun's hairdo is there to be seen, teased high, blond, a mountain towering above the distributer head of a rubber band that holds the hair together at the back of the head. All sorts of clips give support and hope that it will also stay there, the hair, and absolutely fabulous!, the face harries the hair from below, eyebrows raised upward with a black pencil, and what do the gentlemen have to say? That a woman's thinking goes as far as the hairline, the hiding of which is sometimes the purpose of bangs. I have often heard that expression myself. Light-handedly HE, the Herr who said this, raises the hair curtain on the forehead and strokes across it, who is ever able to grasp light? Life? The borderline between the two was still made of iron a few years ago, but also just like a curtain that, in the meantime, ended up as a bedside rug for our final rest in peace. The border between suffering and passion: We, unfortunately, must stay outside again! We get put on a leash, waiting for the gray norm, which could soon drop on our plates again as bloody chunks of meat. Only through biochemical differentiation can we recognize them as campylobacter-negative, but with absolute certainty it will be kaput some other way.

Looking back from a distance and without digressing: a bright spot of light from the entrance to the movies, with entertainment-starved folks still streaming out. But what will God do with this receding chin, this too-short upper lip that bares the oversized and somewhat crooked incisors? Did HE do all this so that maybe later some guy's mouth can better till this doll? In that case HE will still have to come up with something. Better study a few journals with beauty tips before requesting the whole assembly kit. Maybe HE hesitates to descend a second time, sending instead a cosmetics lady from the blessed country, I mean from the counter of Avon. She then pulls the veil off the soapy dead face, the blanket that was put over the cold countenance, and after having seen the dead woman in all her horrificity, she decides that the next time she'd make the face all by herself all the way from scratch. A new makeup can also turn you into a new person, only the power of mortality can destroy her again. But even if a woman might forget this, God will not forget you, you are my child, Israel, fear not! By way of massaging and blackhead squeezing a new body gets formed with nonphysical passion even if we had to dig it all out of our own bare hands. But alas, this young woman will no longer be able to be a model. Angels are rowing along, throwing the fishing line to death, asking for a package that was left there for them. Charged with banalities, the singing Elvis still in the ear, the band's hot rhythms, like a speckled band, a boa constrictor (the animal looking out of the ears with a hiss, and the music also makes the faces look so puffed because they are filled with it from within, and parasites are tingling, in step, between the legs that happily trample down anything alive), this is how the pumps clatter along on the pavement. Soon the ground will be exhausted whereunder the dead shout out warnings, unheard, rise ye, eternal gates, we are almost neighbors after all! But the gates remain shut. There are still a few stations ahead on this journey.

War originates in the body. The young white flesh gets uncorked, the cork flies out of the bottle, the revealed emerges out of the blouse, the pleated skirt, the human being is nothing but an outward form of water, you can forget the rest; but somehow one is attached to one's appearance, which has always been such a struggle, sometimes shimmering streaks of oil float on the surface, eye-shadow powder, lipstick, the stuff that gave the thing the appearance of something appealing, which, nonetheless, must be returned at death, at the box office that offered entrance into the stars and the opportunity to learn from them. Some even got a number tattooed into their upper arm so that the clothes won't get mixed up, when it gets down to the nitty-gritty, the residence permit for the profundis, all the departed, whom we had to practically dig out from under the soles of the profound natives; the whole thing is a bureaucratic desert, you'd better know your way around when the body bagger shows up with the delivery order for the top model. That girl, that student who will have cut her modeling class for the last time today, has even hung little filigree earrings of gilded tin on her ears to distract from her unperfect mouth, but the ears will get to regret it. This offspring of the Under Secretary of Commerce has got it down: Through transience to permanence, and were it only on a glossy photo, that is the profession she aspires to, God should recognize her just by her clothes when she gets there. She doesn't want people to say, we could hear her voice, but we didn't see her appearance. The second earring will be found tomorrow at Vienna's famous Naschmarkt market, a few more stations of the cross by streetcar, imagine how the earring got there all on its own. I imagine that the murderer, beloved by no one, threw it away. The young woman's cold, dead body lies in a flat grave of earth, a real grave six feet under would have been too much work. Oh, Gudrun. At least she could have been taken to one of the thousands of graves that we've already got here. What's with this *Volk* making a higher being out of just one woman? At some point order must be restored in this gigantic circus around the deceased, you, dear reader, won't get each one of them jumping through the hoops and bashing their heads in against the sun wheel (an ancient symbol!) just because you want it! This is why we chose Gudrun Bichler, so that now—with her cumbersome pink umbrella fearfully tucked under the sleeve, small purse forged into a useless weapon—she can rush out of the movie theater's last light and look into the wolf's maw. The trick doesn't work, the wolf is pretty clumsy, but he can still rough up this one-woman league. The body is a grave, many of us are whitewashed graves, floor samples of *being,* the meaning of which be anybody's guess. I only want to demonstrate in what high esteem the dead would be held here, if only we'd get them back again. Then the esteem would last until they hop back under again. In motionless motion. Good thing we removed them far away, to a distant country in the east, where no one will get to know them, since folks there, because of the cold, prefer sticking it out in their warm homes. In view of the young dead Gudrun, whose existence has been plucked, it will probably be all they would talk about for months. As if there weren't millions of dead who could tell much more interesting stories: The ultimate high lies in the realm of the senses, a bait that this young murderer jumped for every day anew. And today this Christmas ornament is suddenly close enough for him to see: The body is not an unmentionable secret, the glitter is worth nothing; today for once the body speaks with the body of Linda Evangelista (a famous model beauty of our time who wasn't born yet at the time of the deed), yes, I know what I am talking about, wet mud also often gets thrown into my face, where it instantly solidifies across my pores: So now I can finally cut an impression in the image of a beautiful female stranger. You, my dear fellow sister citizens, will have to find something else to cut. Now the gifts have been distributed, but not equally. Even today new body baits get stuffed into sausage skins and, still bleeding, hung up on the ceiling. Some are big enough to reach their bodily goals, others can't live on the high hog and must go to the movies to see other people experience such things.

The columns rise darkly as they slouch against the memorial to the Russian Unknown Soldier in order to finally fell this commemoration of the Soviet soldiers. For our population feels boxed in by this defeat, of which this monument is a constant reminder. Try to let yourself be pounced on by a monument! Guards of the dead appear, their hands tossing scorched earth. Then they open up even more hands for the tips, which, however, they have to pass on to us. Now the land of which it is supposed to remind us no longer exists. Millions of dead, simply thrown away by history, a handful over the left shoulder so that they won't return. Like accidentally spilled salt. Too much pepper is what these dead had in their asses during their lifetime, that's why they didn't stay at home. Others traveled to Poland with their cardboard luggage. And there our folks lit quite a fire under their asses. There, look, some first-class traveler is running after the departing train, he bought something at the platform. And then, even more people are coming from that direction, whom one would rather know just from hearsay or at least only in interchangeable relations and passing exchanges with us, before we'll have organized the transports of these people and sent them to the cleaners (one last time we'll do our own dirty laundry and then again, they: THE VICTORS, they'll soon get us perfectly clean, so that in a few years we can, carefreed, put on their clothes and become the victors ourselves). Only we, the imperturbable ones, perform great feats. Or rather small? We wanted a blackbird to sit on this branch and sing. Okay, little one. Here we go! Into the *Wesensgrund,* that very ground of being! Out of the *Wiesengrund!* No Adornoment will help you now. And, betcha!, no one will figure me out. Stubborn like rams who must be torn away from the sheep, hard like roots, the bodies. As they were plucked from the earth, so they also get back into it, until they start to rot and finally want to get a little active again. Someone, after all, has to carry the weight of feelings, and the Germans want to have it all, they don't relinquish it to the neighbors when it gets too heavy for them. *Weltschmerz.* That fountain has been turned off for the night, water that springs snarlingly after the deceased, like a living creature, sometimes higher, sometimes lower; the multicolored beams that light this fountain are naturally copied from nature, that is, from the beaming faces of the Viennese women and men. As if the water wanted to mimic something organic, copies of images and sounds of the living, hello again! The modeling student makes herself be heard in her pointed pumps, which have a brief chat with the pavement. Young flesh is desired. One likes to open it calmly and look at it. The hem of a dark blue coat still plays cockily with the legs. Quick steps clip-clop, end abruptly, and then the flesh gets flipped open, how naughty it looks if you only saw pictures of it heretofore! Coat and pleated skirt tipped up, so that the dumpster can hastily dump its dormant load. Where hardness confronts us, we must bear it. The murderer cannot be disabused of his belief that all this flesh was made just for him. Heedlessly he fells this figure, which could be glass, thin as it is, he kneels down and stuffs his Unflappable into the cunt. He simply doesn't give it a thought! A white flesh plant comes into bloom on its way between the columns, a young man (pushing thirty) pounces, almost unintentionally, against her shyness that holds out no longer than a tent pole punched to the ground by this man's wolfish leap, yes, he jumps sideways at this turbo-flesh that was fed and groomed by an attentive family, raised to be a beauty, but it didn't get that far, for the upper lip, as mentioned, doesn't quite get to the lower somehow; this piece of organic meat, whose breeder is a personal acquaintance, who gets the bottle held so lovingly to its milk-bubbling calf's mouth, this piece of Viennese tenderloin expires over the course of one single step, that's hardly finished before this almost brand-new life ends up as an expired item in the rummage bin for smaller animals. Poor Gudrun, she has to serve as kumbaya bag for this scumbag, all that stuff he stuffs into her! Now he can even surpass what he had promised her again and again. His stumbling cock, unloading itself in jolts, serially, is bigger than I thought. Before that, the carefully chosen outfit of blouse, pleated skirt, and even the discreet coat with nothing special to add got pulled off the girl like banana peels. A white rag of flesh is stretched out on the ground, it separates, there is fourfold thrashing by two persons, one of Gudrun B.'s breasts gets bitten, three times altogether, the perpetrator struggles to get out of this night and swipe the 12.50 Schillings from the plastic wallet. The woman must deliver the dough, let it flow, big and small, numbers two and one, because the perp used both openings. Nothing can be closed to him and after him it stays open for anyone because he smashed the door. So then anyone can come, he, however, will be leaving. Stop it! The dishes must be cleaned, you don't just throw them out after you have eaten! Then the storms peter out on their own. The peter takes cover, shakes off the drops, the thighs that will soon arrive at the table are twitching and banging under the blond bushes, now the man places them on his shoulders, one to the right, the other to the left of the head, flooded in white, but not really rinsed clean, until they sink down to the patient plate of the earth. No, the flesh is not like grass, grass becomes hay, mmm! Flesh becomes a criminal case, where flies feast, on different kinds and cuts, plus garnish, which is pulled from their own spawn. Furthermore, the flesh must pay attention to the following: slaughter hygiene, foodborne infection, storage pests, rodents, insects, birds, game, and, last but not least, pets. The back ends of the sharply pointed shoes are banging fiercely against the back of the man, who will get up in a moment. What a mess he has made with his boorish trafficator! He activates it now because he wants to turn from the right path. Angrily, a pair of hands lift the upper part with the rosy buttons, those get screwed now, something will turn on alright, but it's not music that's coming out, and a set of teeth with a noticeable dental flaw sinks one last time into skin and the lower tissue of the pale white flesh, which, as so often happens, a grandiose mother slipped on occasionally to wear as a garment. That's how softly the flesh absorbed what its mother said only to put it away again, unembossed. (Oh, dear, the daughter skipped school again today, the one she herself chose to attend, to go to a movie instead. A musical movie!) In short: Tomorrow the dental marks will be matched with rather poorly tended teeth that were never controlled by an embankment, that's why the venom could splatter so easily.

But what's even more unpardonable, malevolent fingers are simultaneously running around the neck, prying all around it before digging into the larynx, whose tender and at the same time mobile slightness can't outlast the treatment by the stranglehold. The hook settles around the neck, shudders run over the skin, ribs, and way down, where hasty, moist whispers fade into the intimate body ear, where the wham-bam-split slit gapes and gets thoroughly chewed up by the aggressor. Then the knees that kicked right in the center of the perp's pelvis come to rest, one shoe even flew off on account of the impact. So, a lady's shoe could save itself, but it will be missing when the dead are allowed to jump out of their graves. The next attempt at solving the unspeakable secret of how to open the pearly gates of one's own body without letting oneself be torn out by the suction, without being able to solve it either, will be initiated by the priest the following week, but then it will no longer be the steely, superpolyester strength of the pleated skirt and the frothy whipped cream of the nylon blouse calling for Attention!, then it'll be the wooden modesty of a refurbished wooden crate with handles; that kind of shaky stability they finally do acquire, the dead, though their path is quite strenuous in parts, they mostly have to slosh through their own slush.

So, the young dead woman gets removed from her clothes, the clothing trash even gets its own grave next to her. Her life gets routinely inspected, such customs are learned in those juvenile homes where unruly children get hit completely naked by the latest pedagogic/academic findings, like the Sterntaler girl, who in her day had to lift her pinafore whether she liked it or not. She wasn't asked. Flesh in such places is a rare dish and will, from then on, taste especially good all life long. The perp took the trouble to dig two shallow ditches, the tools are in his briefcase, even the picklock with which he broke into the house of life is a stolen one. But first the two holes of the dead woman must be viewed, albeit not long enough for the gaze to be able to calm down and get used to the many little fleshy cones, fear-driven shoots that the body tried to provide for the future of death (I think the female sexual organ is structured so intricately because, inside it, nature had thrown everything she's got into the battle, since that sex gets constantly decimated and threatened by extinction. That is also why so many cones are sprouting at its ends). A light goes around, because it also would like to go out. Pampered white flesh: thrown to the cold ground, it quickly lost its rosy character wherein Mickey Mouse still ruled, though followed closely by Elvis P. He rocks so sensuously between the hips, imitated by us frequently and futilely. But this already flight-bound life can no longer use its body as silverware to maybe pick Elvis out of his snail shell and eat him up. Yes, I mean this body here, which only yesterday learned (yes, before God's eyes, that's not even a fraction of a second, it is a negligible size) its erect gait in the modeling school.

The occupants of the Chrysler Voyager rest tired amid the greenery, they sway in their seatbelts, at least those who buckled up: toddlers, lovingly cared for at the time, are conscientiously secured and accompanied by the car through the countryside, watched by the mustering eyes of the Father, who stands in his rubber boots in the slaughterhouse: For Him we are even smaller than clostridia. Thus, we ask him: My God, what's with this bus, look at this bus! What's it doing so far on the left, it's driving much too fast! It'll never make it around this curve! Small figures behind the windows, a couple of arms getting pulled upward. Short posts, you've seen them, with perky black caps of paint, red-white-red safety flags stretched between these small arms, raised as if for a folk dance, God is already tuning his sound post to us, but there, in front, the posts are missing for a stretch of almost ten meters. There the road discontinues with a jagged edge, look, quickly!, everything's been swept away from below, yes, there is construction farther ahead, men are standing there with shovels, asphalt pavers, and heavy equipment. I think the side of the road has been frayed by the violent storms because the earth underneath has been washed out. Bending over even farther, one can see the debris of the road lying in the steep meadow to the right, though the grass has already partly risen again. A rivulet murmurs below, alder brushwood and hazelnut bushes hiding it for longer stretches again and again. Shrubs of stinging nettle and elderberry bushes standing tall. More glaring though, the plastic ribbon that's been provisionally stretched on the iron clamps of the wooden posts, well, they won't stop a minibus. Each metal hook that's been rammed into a stake has a red-white (in the meantime halfway torn down) plastic bow hanging on it, a coquettish, flashy bowtie on the prematurely grayed road shirt. And now right here of all places a tour bus came around at the narrowest part and at that speed! The license plate hails from Holland, who's got its number? No more time for the prize drawing. Up on the mountainside folks sit happily in front of glasses and plates and bacon snacks. Small figures who studiously manage to take a picture every second jump up, their sportswear, the anorak tied around their hips, flies upward like the wing stumps of a bomb and lands back on its owner again. Sunglasses get taken off. Wow! Look! Now they are driving a car directly into the water! Fingers shoot up like birds. Someone even starts to cry because the attempt to get out of the way didn't succeed down there. These vehicles make a racket like stumbling dinosaurs whose colossal skeletons get squashed together to half their size. A path is plowed into the steep, grassy slope, before that one could hear the screeching of the brakes, whoever has heard it once will never forget it. The result is a hybrid of vehicle and passengers inside, because the two merge in a crash of metal to one entity that had to fulfill its forwarding order: There they come, there the wander-creatures are already pouring out of their sheet-metal claws of their so far pretty boring accommodation including toilet in the rear part. Before, they were still completely preoccupied with themselves and the region, inattentive basically to all surrounding life, dozing, stretched in the frame of the conditions, doweled into their container, and now suddenly deep water, screeching, cracking, crunching, silence.

The Dead-Squad leaders approach unhurriedly so that the dear souls can make it to dinner on time without rushing. The first time they have to be shown the way, for where they are supposed to get to, they will hear unpronounceable words they won't be able to pronounce on the first try either. And while under this one, our most recent dead woman—to the applause of millions of Russians wasted, squandered on the *Raging Reich* (I am sure some of them had small gardens in front of their cabins, others a piano, many have also been charged by book batteries, and there, a real bike!)—the mobile folding legs get unfolded by the time runners as replacements for the ailing and the weak, who all too often are their prey, the killer still drills around doggedly in the openings of a human being who was almost brand-new, oh mama! What will the papers say, for days, months? This *being* is laid out squarely and thoroughly kneaded through, so that it is easier to chew through it, it gets examined because it has lost its naming power, its soul. And thus this leg of lamb gets thrown to the One Lamb, the lamb of all lambs, and that one says something like: It doesn't belong to my herd, but since you are here—just come along, I'll show you your feeding ground and the good water, which is also down the drain. This murderer can't take with him any part of the seventh heaven he's in right now, but he can bite off a piece of it. The flesh tears like the edge of a road where the lining sticks out. Or a pair of pants on the clothesline, whose pockets, those wrinkly sacks, were pulled out to dry faster. This paradise doesn't sell any souvenirs, but hold it!, that little earring, we'll tear that one out, we can take it with us as a memento (or did the murderer notice only later that it's worth nothing, tinsel? No, I don't think so, or he would have lifted the second one, too). And we'll take the little there is in the wallet. You could also nip off a nipple, she's still got one after all. Sadly, women are often looked at that way. They attach too much importance to their clothing, that's why special measures must be taken: You've got to go for the whole nine yards, because they've got something hidden to put out that which they're still holding back at the moment, and you can't let them get away with it. So, it's all very simple, cut to the bone and screw them, no, vice versa. Beyond their exterior, which can often be annoying, since they offer that lovely sight to everyone (but the one who may climb the mountain they want to pick themselves!, so there they stand as a great sight, and instead of letting you check them out leisurely and then chuck them out, THEY want to do the checking), they have too little to offer for their lives to be worth living. Walking around with a book on the head—gimme a break! Sometimes words are at their command, though many of them are more painful than death. So, this one woman gets moved front and center, the head rolls to the side without informing us in advance; the half-closed eyes, the half-closed mouth subject themselves without argument when a piece of living weight gets forced in that found the courage to justify this wholesome venture. The defenseless deceased gets rolled out on the floor, then the normal newspaper reader can cut himself a piece from her, maybe right now: She is not moving at the moment. And the lammergeier lifts his wings and rips open his victim, claws and beak hacking into her. Something like this isn't easy with someone alive, it's hard work, for the living imperiously demands his preservation, except his name is Jürgen Bartsch, also a unikiller, a lone traveler of those early years, whose sex was exclusively in the hands and coercive control of his mother, who kept throwing him out with the bathwater, after having merged with her son, who wasn't even really hers.

One's entire life, I think, is practically a self-service shop, and here, on the edge of the meadow, after all that crashing noise they made, the colorful fragments of humans and cars have now been arranged for viewing, still busy with themselves and screaming, or with the neighbor's suffering, or not at all anymore. And the pitiful rests of Gudrun's clothes, the chicken ribs of her umbrella, the flailing jellyfish of her skirt, the slime of her nylon blouse swimming on top, are hardly worth a bucket of warm spit. Nevertheless, she does get her own grave, that Gudrun, albeit a very shallow one, that is, in this water, where a huge chunk of the vehicle cockpit had also been thrown; the leader of this small group flew right along in his driver's seat, and all of it lies now in the bubbling water of the creek, which is still somewhat loamy and excited by the flood after all those storms. The naked dead woman, a motionless woman who'd been abused by everyone having been so moved to see the young woman lying there completely naked—at long last the long-held idea of the reformatory school has been made true, in the beginning was the word, and in many a lap one finds not mother but the Father, and I, once again, can't find my way out of this—so she gets ditched into the shallow ditch and small handfuls of earth are piled up on her. This actual realization of his thoughts jumping like bucks over all obstacles afforded the murderer a hike to the peak with many viewing points: Here the model Gudrun gets laid out in this shallow hollow (unfortunately, not a glass floor that allows for observing nature's disengaged ideas at play!), and her clothes even received a separate hole. Everything must succumb to the earth, but since the girl briefly stayed alive before she stepped out of her body, quite a bit roughed up in the delicious soft curves, she lifted her head one last time, or maybe already in her death throes, and thus a bit of earth trickled off her torso. Hence the clustering of earth clots on the lower extremities, which the murderer abused to the extreme, yes, there, where the seating is kept for this slippery, damply gleaming hall (everyone thinks that just their floor is made of marble) for the kind of session that we normally are obsessed with. But that happens in all friendliness, we immediately throw ourselves into worship, if it's the partner's wish, and mostly we enjoy the relaxed aftereffects of our sex, and that's really the least our organs can do for us when the flesh experiences its one-sided adventure even though the fire had been set on both sides. Where is the highest accumulation of soil? Over there is the highest accumulation of soil. A bit of humus aggregated there, but it won't quite do for humanity, that would have to be piled up as high as a molehill. But no one would shovel that for long if he didn't get anything out of it. This young man only did what was absolutely necessary to let his personality show a little. And then all that effort only to hide the body, whose well-made coat was completely torn apart, in this condition it could no longer be fixed by any alteration service. In their sickness and weakness people actually believe that fucking, of all things, happens between friends or, rather, under a friend. This here is the unambiguous counterexample, and in the matter of bodily screwing, it lies in the purely psychic realm of decibels beyond the Richter scale (which you can find where? In the *Buch der Richter,* the Book of Judges), whether you were able to inscribe yourself in a body before you crumpled it up and, without a trace of yourself, threw it into the garbage.

The meadow is speckled with sprinklings of colors that, though, are anything but flowers. Vehicles land in positions for which they weren't built. One European town will be waiting in vain for one of these heavy vehicles, and Austria's junk piles will have grown once again. A house will look around one day and ask itself where the bus could be that drove off from there so cheerfully. People also cry about cars, even when the insurance premiums have been paid! The guards of the dead rush to the opening of the new season, which takes place today, right now, and even the remaining pieces of clothing, which were pulled through the teeth and then spit out again in strips, get covered with earth. But the monument officer will find them quickly tomorrow morning when he goes to relieve himself, and I'll find out the moment I see him. Dressed up with her briefcase and the trench coat that goes with it, Gudrun waits at the monument for herself, uhm, so that this young dead woman can slip inside her before she cools down, before her blood sinks into the heavily damaged lower body parts. Gudrun observes the body's instantaneous revivication, the brief jerking of the upper body as it rises from the grave, spitting earth, it doesn't get much farther, the perpetrator, as mentioned earlier, didn't bother too much with the shoveling, the ground is hard, it is heavy, killing is heavy, it is hard, and anyway, the easy and the hard, the light and the heavy, are part of life, and heavily our seedy drives are hanging from us, because they, too, want to quickly till or at least hit on someone, you know us and our rock-hard and lime-rich ground well enough. Almost proudly, those lovely hidden things, Gudrun's waled, marked breasts, jump out of the makeshift grave, and they hop straight into the hands of the murderer, who nips at the budding decay, then grits his teeth and battles his way through it. At the peaks, he pulls the tips away from the upper body as far as possible and then carelessly drops them again while he looks at them with a man's entitled gaze. Unfortunately, the flesh slackens too quickly; no matter how much it gets fiddled with, it can't be cranked up again. Wasn't there a thin little twig just a moment ago, yes, there it is! Young, strong things often feel voluntarily called to good-naturedness. But then what to do with all that strength? The legs of the young dead woman, for dead she is by now, or almost, can be tucked up but not spread anymore, she already lies in the shallow earthen case, yet one can push the feet until the legs form two arches of light, and then the little twig can be rammed into a hole, wham bam, and then bingo, a little tree grows out from under the friendly cover of blond hair, though it won't bud anymore. Alright, so, this young woman can no longer show herself in the company of girls who never paid attention to the likes of us either. When will the dead stop trying to draw attention to themselves? I think that all too often they stay silent, maybe out of modesty or because people don't appreciate enough what they have or are. I now bend forward over my thoughts and try pulling on an arid branch, but it's already half the human being coming toward me, that in-between thing between here and beyond. Skinfolds flap open, wow, that's like in a fairy-tale book. A flesh panorama one has to kneel in front of and push a new slide into the slit so that one can see more, a lot more, everything. A new chapter is opened, a woman's sex smiles through the rest of the leaves, now and for all times she is preoccupied with herself.

Night clouds sweep over the semicircle of columns, blond hair twitches once more in the grip of fever, moist at the roots, this Ophelia got her withered leaves thrown after her for good measure, they are a good cover, there is no need to add more of that damn earth, but even with this thin layer of humus she won't be able to withstand the elements, our deceased, her face emerges again, pale, out of the zoo of bugs and worms. She was not allowed to keep anything that, at least covered with clothing, could still have been sent across a catwalk, surrounded by the rush of many more chic dresses and waves of applause breaking at the cliffs of piled-up coiffuriosities that sweep toward us like crests of waves gone wild. The body lies there as if it wanted to swim the backstroke. Evidently my admonitions were to no avail, so then, folks will have to drink what they brewed. Impatiently, Gudrun looks at the watch, isn't she dead yet, that young thing who inexplicably is also her, Gudrun, after all? And she's got no time to lose. What's she popping up from the ditch again, does she want to check whether all her clothes are still there? Well now, they weren't that great. The wallet is gone, ditto one earring, but that was only 17.15 Schillings, junk! Waiting with nothing but language as the midwife for a corpse, while the neon signs for the movie are slowly going out and nothing's happening in the city anymore either, is not very entertaining. Even if you just want to pick an apple you need a tool, namely a picker. Now a child in swimming trunks also approaches the dead woman, its teeth gleaming between its lips like gravestones, its hair all wet. It stumbles over a loose branch because it absolutely must read about it in the day-after-tomorrow's plus forty-years'-later evening paper (and gets reprimanded by Gudrun for it), there it says that there was an especially young dead female from a good family, and on page 3 it says that there was a bad accident in Styria involving a tour bus from Holland and a minivan from Austria. More pieces of corpses? Piece of cake! I'll gladly cut you off a few more! I cut them out of this beautiful dark monumental semicircle, against which, among others, the decomposed Russian legions and whatever other peoples who got there pressed their tired backs. From the sky heavenly chocolate icing and white dabs of creamy whipped clouds, a freeze-frame, wherefrom the berrylike thickened blood, high-proof, liquor-wobbly creme, gets infused with the piping bag into the devastated bodies, which are kept open with a spectaculum. Shuddering, the holes open, where the blessedly blissful bodies can finally meet themselves, murderers are reached for by the arms of eager women who've already got everything but them, the weather is unpredictable, because it can't be estimated how long those corpses will hold up before their stench starts rubbing the wrong way. A chaos in which my thoughts are what's still the most alive, except that I can't squeeze them out, too much blood would come out in the process, but at least they are still small, I mean the spot that must be squeezed isn't very big, and if it gets inflamed, a blaze is a long way off. At this time no papers or indications of the victim's identity have been found in her clothes.

At long last! The incandescent gas mantle rises nuclear-mushroom-bright from the hollow, the white she-wolf shoots out in long leaps and merges—still in flight, dead center of the humidifier, because a moist fog has settled over the city, it's almost drizzling, that's how dense the fog is—with the student Gudrun Bichler, who will soon be famous. Unfortunately, not under that name. No one can stand meaninglessness regarding their person; just lying still, letting the little globs of earth dance on your own breath above the grave, idling, resting, and watching the animals, until the lights are turned on above and the coffin of the next beloved person—so it stays in the family—is lowered down! Unfortunately, before that, the gravedigger often beats his shovel round our heads and hacks off our limbs if we haven't taken proper care of our own decomposition. Just vegetating, this certainly can happen to anyone. There is one who briefly felt happy because she reeled in a fat white fish and the earth wasn't even as deep as she thought. Now she is getting out. One against all the dead: For weeks captured in paper[s], jumping headlong through the hoops, the headbands that hold together the hair of the ambitious, most of the time they can't even push their fist through the delicate giftwrap of their lives, but later it will cause water damage or damage by rodents in another body. Yesterday, two pieces of Austrians perished in a hotel fire in Pittapong or wherever, plus one hundred and eighty-two pieces, mixed grill from many other nations, something like that doesn't happen every day, but when it does, it gets reported in the whole world, which threw out its free nature long ago and got it back as newsprint. The fire doesn't even shy away from Austrians, pretty courageous, considering how many of the local traffic citizens this *Volk* practically forced this fire on, threw it down their throat. Unfortunately, in the meantime this big fat story creates a bad aftertaste. The truth is not something that has passed. We want it raised again. All those dead who got burned so badly, let them surge in a new wave, walk right in, ladies and gentlemen, hold it, now it's getting really hot! We preserve so much that came down on us, that keeps coming over us, even the Lipizzaner are coming in, even the violins are crying, but we don't, not us, why shouldn't our dead be allowed to echo some of that for our tourists? In a movie? Maybe a musical? A fifty-year run guaranteed! And we, in our snazzy aerobics clothes, we who expect you? We are our very own most beloveds, and thus we even sling the suspenders lovingly over both shoulders. Our bodies go a bit haywire, they can hardly be held together by these outfits. But on the other hand, our opinion holds up pretty strong. After all, we bought an elastic wrap for it, too. At this moment, however, it must be rewired, our prized opinion. Look, Jesus, you, the tax collector, you, the mega-fundraiser, yes, you, here you can see that we really lived, so much for you pointing your finger into our cave earlier. But the flight always goes on strike just when we want to take off to paradise, and right away those fallen and those felled are back among us and want to come along as well. Yet the only thing that's going to arrive is us, right now, at an opinion, where all of this should play out, in Rimini, in Caorle, or better still Mallorca or at the brave Costa Brava.

27

Ramblers, lonely people, rangers, their shoes caked with dirt, are standing at the reception desk. The Wirtin can't understand the sudden onslaught. She is busy with account books, room maps, paper money, but as with the miracle of five loaves and two fish it seems to her that the number of rooms for the surging crowd just keeps increasing, like late spring shoots, but that's a miracle she can quickly get under control. A lot of words she simply receives and puts somewhere absent-mindedly, only to forget them again. If you asked her what she was just talking about with the young alpinist who tilts his head so weirdly you can sense: *vorwärts!,* onward, to a place we've never been before, she wouldn't know it. Therefore, permit me to address you. Outside, the trees, doll-like, are raising their arms, this is not an attack. Even the shape of the Wirtin wrests itself out of her dress. There are no high-speed feasts-on-wheels in sight that would have enabled these wandering masses to show up this time of year, the so-called bad weather threatens any moment. We certainly had enough rain this year, and the last few weeks' heavy downpours, which fell on this land like swarms of birds, chewing up its trails and roads and in fact causing an enormous expansion of the rain-drenched area, are still fresh in everyone's memory. The water slapped the people from the skin of the landscape, as if someone higher—no, not someone high, Higher!, then the blow has more force—felt bothered by them as if by vermin. Cleanliness is definitely not what has been bequeathed by us inheritance cheaters (we are cheating the Green partisans out of their Clean *Über Alles* legacy).

The marked trails and the unmarked, where folks, should they use the latter, are not much appreciated by the forestry service, least of all now during open season, are crawling through the terrain, wriggling through the forest like dark worms, but everything is underwashed, which isn't easy to notice, these mountains' reservoir spaces are full to the bursting point—not a pleasant experience for those who want to avoid us. Up there the hillside has pockets, and the one over there does, too, cracks gape in the mountain meadows, three cows plunged down from the alpine pasture. Out-of-towners harvest the forests' abundance of mushrooms, but in turn the sky trounces the land with its rain to wreck people's appetite for good, the woods have long been wasted anyway. Cold autumn, why are you so warm this year? Everyone getting here seems wildly determined to claim this terrain for themselves as if they hadn't had a vacation for years and years. Just don't squander everything you've got while you're still on the road! It has also become dangerous to take a walk. The fogs come in early, even on the sunniest day, it gets rather dark, and some who get lost do not return. That is because some trails people have known for years suddenly end. They slid down the slope. What's left of those ant runs for tourists can still be seen in the twilight, a small flashlight track, a thin, bright line that broke off, and five meters farther down, it stops altogether. The creeks' banks are sawed at, the creeks themselves slipped off their run like the seams of old-fashioned nylons on white bony legs. The Wirtin is nervous anyway, because yesterday evening three wanderers, senior sportsmen but still going strong, did not return to the inn. The innkeeper hopes they at least reached the Teachers' Shelter, erstwhile Imperial hunting lodge, of which there are many here, though it is closed now because it is late in the season; nevertheless, folks: enjoy, what there is to enjoy!, climb every mountain up to the clouds, and there, the forestry service can fortify the soil for you, e.g., grassification, reforestation, but not too much, please. For God's sake, catch those avalanches, who's at bat, who the catcher—so there you have this heavy avalanche barrier, but even storms storm in vain against the bats in your belfry, who still want to throw thoughts from an altitude of two thousand meters—and for tennis balls you've got a mesh fence that can smash your partner's felt avalanche, or do you have a deflector device, a control structure that can put the brakes on your human opponent's stroke?, and, excellent!, this portly carved balcony of the Teachers' Shelter and the wood- and provision-shed below do offer some protection. Though somewhat preoccupied and a little out of it, the Wirtin keeps going, distributing the keys, warnings, advice, small, hectographed trail maps, pointing out the bulletin board that offers bulletproof vests for the wild and excursions on the tamed trails, which are still relatively safe if you shoot through the valleys fast like the wind and could be stopped only by timber transport regulations.

Don't fall into the inland delta of the Mürz River! You'd have a grave alright, but without the coffin that goes with it, in thirty years' time vegetation will surely have changed your eternal bed quite a bit: Please enter your name on this list, and where you are going. Request mountain guides in time, those who have crashed routinely get down again by helicopter. Yes, at this time it is not advisable to climb up anywhere alone, the fogs move in rapidly as early as three in the afternoon, scarves, floods of hair that are thrown from heaven over the jungles of Styria, and we'll still have to talk about the storage of logs in dry ravines. Just a moment, here, in nature's slammer, we, the slam- and wham-bam bangers, are also at home, in a dark corner, where wives empty sacks of house dust all over us. The new guests climb up the narrow wooden stairs panting and spread out to their rooms, of which there would never be enough, as the Wirtin recalculates distraughtly, her eyebrows raised, her thoughts and premises stretched to their limit. How is it possible that, except for the retired couple who recently killed and then fried themselves in such a ghastly way, the only ones missing are the daughter of that old pain in the neck and the lady from East Germany who was in that Chrysler crash—so how are you doing, better, thank you, and you? And yet there are always new groups of people, in pairs and sometimes also alone, climbing up the trails and stairs. Cardboard luggage is piling up high behind the reception, cumbersome cargo like you haven't seen in a long time, too urban, actually, for this rural travel destination. Most guests prefer those modern light nylon backpacks they can also use for side trips. The Wirtin hasn't seen such cardboard suitcases since her childhood, when she helped her aunt in the neighboring village who already back then rented out several rooms. The

Wirtin's grandparents also had an alpine pasture, they, too, rented out rooms, to hikers in the summer and skiers in the winter. Not only are people multiplying at the moment, the suitcases, too, are building up higher and higher. Going by those, there would have to be at least two hundred new arrivals, where did they all go? The house seems empty, almost deserted, though people would have to swoop down from the air like swarms of hang gliders, they would have to stream down the stairs, the railing would have to crack and then break off. Those are overflowing human streams as in a flood, we seem to have an inexhaustible reservoir full of them, but the practice of grazing on its soft shores should actually be prohibited, as well as any sort of loosening of the soil and other land use in the endangered area; small streamlets must be cleared, and those graves certainly don't belong here, the dead would fall prematurely into the stream, no, our riverbanks must not break! We must hold them up! The ground should stay solid in the flood zone and not dug up in childish stubbornness, otherwise our soil won't be able to settle again on top of the carcasses after the next catastrophe. Animals in general have the right to reside here only provisionally.

This house would have to have shown signs of being fed up for a long time, just the way nature carried on with those three wanderers, or: let's hope not, the windows will fly away from the house because so many people are crammed in there. The innkeeper often commiserates very emotionally with the TV, but her dark premonitory feeling that rummages around dark corners with the zest of a hunting dog can't keep up with these vacationers. There are too many people here nobody ordered. They turn to this pleasant woman, turn away again, the shape of their hostess is not steep enough to schuss down on; the new guests look in all directions as if they knew what they were looking for, but in the end, they seem to be self-sufficient. They push each other away from the window spots, where they had grown into umbels to look into the darkening sky for what it had in store for them. They had pure southern weather conditions until noon. Every one of them signed up properly on the appropriate list of excursions. What is happening? Nothing indicates that storms are storming, that the weather might turn. The Wirtin putters about nervously with her doll's hands, turning her head again and again: If more violent storms were to happen this year, the bridge to the inn will be torn away, and we'll be lucky if half the riverbank won't come along in protest, maybe the entire land will break apart; there, a lady just handed the landlady a golden bracelet for safekeeping, so where to put it now? Why is this already the fifth person giving her his eyeglasses, what's she supposed to do with these glasses? Is he afraid he could lose them in the mountains? Right now, quite different things are threatening him in the mountains: The windthrow that tore into the Moasanger hillside had blown its top, it looks as if this gigantic slope has held on strenuously to its clothes, which have slipped a bit and in installments down the flanks, here the pants, there a piece of underpants, and there the hem of a tank top is showing (only very young people can dare to dress that sloppily on purpose). And where have all those unknowns gone who announced neither their arrival nor their disappearance? And even the old regulars: Since they are nowhere to be seen, they acquire an intangible dimension, where are they inside this house, which, together with a few thousand trees, clings desperately to its roots, which, worn down, tug tentatively at the washed-out earth—where on earth did they go, the woman with the spaniel and that other lady who always wears the khaki-colored long pants and the red knit vest? Where's that old one who constantly misplaces her daughter? They look like any other woman, yet curiously, they are always among the first at mealtime, *being* among *beings,* but they would certainly dare to be among those not being, these energetic ladies. And who just left the BMW standing in the driveway, and with four wide-open doors to boot? A short while ago it was locked. If someone took it . . . . People simply have no brain—let's not begrudge them this power over everything that came and that which ceased to be! Because they simply can't imagine what they are doing to others. Only when they see strangers do they know with deadly certainty: That's them, the others, now they are here!

Just a moment ago the sky was brilliantly blue, but from Höllgraben, Hell's Gorge, scattered patches of clouds and fog are approaching, intermingling, chasing each other, they can be pleased, as they bring new weather or maybe not, better not, Lord God, let this warmth, unusual for this time of year, last a bit longer! But even the smallest thing starts to grow sometime; they race here and there, the clouds and their children, as if different air currents had collided in this blue sky and met on the radio to play, there are constant disturbances on the regional station as of late, hissing, crackling, the same with the telephone. The hourly weather forecast could not be heard, so let's instead turn to the sky again! They turn their pockets inside out and let go of a few drops, our clouds, our mood setters, so let them have fun!, but over there, where the weather is coming from, something's really brewing there now, it turns darker almost imperceptibly, hark now hear—no, baby Christ is not yet on its way. It's different than usual when a thunderstorm is coming. No, you can't cut open the sky in order to read in it. You might as well buy a lottery ticket! At the moment the sun still shines, it even shines back from the reddle wall and in red at that. Beautiful weather is followed by rain, and after the rain the weather is beautiful again.

The leaves of the trees appear in the now somewhat hazy light that threatens the guests, still almost jokingly, with long fingers, as do the scattered rays of sun, which still fall through the branches, as if chiseled, flat, without depth, like a wallpaper pattern, somehow we don't like it. That's all we need, that the edges of the clouds turn the color of sulfur, some even crimson, signs of hail, the clouds seem dipped in fire, as if they could just about manage to plug up the sky's bloody discharge, but not much longer, the cloud finger is already hurting. On the stairs still the clutter and clomping of heavy shoes shuffling about the boards, the red coconut matting runner can't really muffle the noise, actually the guests are supposed to put their heavy hiking shoes downstairs, where the skis are kept in the winter, adjacent to it a sauna will be built next year. But whenever the Wirtin sticks her head around the corner to check whether anyone has acted against the regulations, not a soul can be seen. The lobby is empty, an indivisible point that is nothing and consists of nothing (whereas visitors, once they become paying guests, always insist on something, and that means right away!). This sounds again like the apprehensible inapprehensible, because there is an incessant hubbub as if from a gigantic shapeless mass of people, you can even hear a few stragglers run: Where on earth are those people? They were here just a moment ago. There can be no words or speeches without a voice to be heard. Yes, yes, we hear them, we just can't see them at present. All that can be seen are a few scattered elderly vacationers whom the Wirtin knows, but behind them, the background seems to have been set in motion, like a slope that filled its pockets with water, and since the eyes have once again been bigger than the belly, it will momentarily slide down in toto. Such restlessness, a steady arriving but no leaving! Something pushes itself up the stairs by fits and starts, the house breathes and hums to it, an almost inaudible melody between its teeth, quiet conversations emerge between the paneling, penetrating the rooms all the way to the roof, at least that's how it seems to the innkeeper, and she is a woman who is not exactly made for jokes and personalities, all of them! You can tell immediately by the tone of voice that this is not the usual blabber about always the same that usually floats up like mosquito swarms between the deck chairs in the garden, every slammed car door can cut right through them, those idle conversations about nothing and someone who is not present at the time. Something is being argued and someone defends it before even giving it a proper hearing. The steps of who knows who are seized and, still on the stairs, turned all at once as if they got caught in a turbine, which was invented near here by a Victor Kaplan. Suddenly a discarded shoe tumbles down to the ground floor, there is a hollow thump—can't those people dress and undress themselves more quietly? Since the departure of the municipality's busy gray hearse, no other vehicle could be seen arriving except for a private car that couldn't be opened for the longest time, so now it won't close anymore. Its windows are still smeared, and there one can see those dark, greasy stains all over the upholstery, but look, now the woman with the spaniel is trying to—no doubt she's back, but why does this not calm the Wirtin?—press the doors shut in passing, shaking her head indignantly, the illegally spread-apart vehicle bothers her, where does the woman suddenly come from?, no, everything is pneumatic now, and yet: the woman can't do it, neither can the dog who shuffles behind her without lifting his leg as usual on everything and everyone—those doors don't move one millimeter. The rooms of the house are increasingly penetrated by an indigence as if with half-dried, coagulating oil paint that rolls centimeters thick through the hallways. The heavy drapes in the dining room have been closed by someone, by whom?, that usually happens only on winter nights, when we, without any resistance that would dam us up, drown in the TV.

He looks like a real loafer today, our Herr Gstranz, he usually moves about so swiftly all over the terrain, always the first down, always the first up on the summit. Now he leans against the wall as if he wanted to draw himself out like these idle hours, talking to two people whom the innkeeper can't exactly recognize, but they seem to be locals. Their bulky clothing that surrounds them stiff as a board as if it would start cracking with every movement is certainly not urban, and now they each raise, as if they were twins, the right arm to the head, no, one is definitely shorter than the other, who seems to be a veritable giant, there was only one in this area who was that tall, almost two meters tall, and that one has been dead for years. Suicide, a tragedy, which folks dare to talk about only in a whisper, and both have the right eye closed and the left one open (though the skull is just mush). The father was the forester, and the forester is a rigid man, he hasn't been talking to anyone since then. Only with the head forester, who, however, is with the hunting guests from Germany up in the hunting castle, all of them glued to their binoculars, spying, vying, vulturing in the depth of the plain through the firing slits of their pale eyes: Out of sight, those cold marbles, as if they were glass! The way the weather looks, it's fair to say it looks like nothing, the hunting guests will also stay home tonight, until they can once again downgrade the natives as the carcass carriers of elks and roebucks, yes, here we pay with our very own, in-person human currency! Courtesy of the forestry, all workers are granted a vacation for part of the hunting season so that they can earn some extra money. Well, the Wirtin is too proud to check whether she knows the two men from somewhere. Still, not for the world would she step out of the house and have a word with the two, and neither would she say a word about her dear, longtime guest Mr. Gstranz, not even if she were asked to come out with what's her take on any of this.

Now the shorter of the two turns his head and upper torso a bit, he had pushed a small boutonniere of alpine flowers through the lapel hole that stands out clearly against his crude loden jacket, actually his facial features should also be traceable through the fog now, at least nebulously, but there is nothing—there are these two made up rather than made out eye-belly buttons popping against the fog. The Wirtin does not want to admit it to herself, but she cannot detect the face of this man. The skull simply breaks off beneath the hairline with the woolly shock of hair above, that last tuft of grass to hold on to, an escarpment, a rockfall, a sort of washout that permanently flushed out the signals that permanently derailed the trains. For where the spark of life jumps about excitedly in others, showing off in front of the opened windows of others, this young man has nothing; something ends, it lurks, it screams inside the house, riding on this usually so gentle air, stuck on his hobbyhorse and stick. This face has been cast off like a lizard's tail in dire emergency, when it gets grabbed at. It must be the canny reflection of a windowpane that caused the imaginary discarding of a face, the Wirtin smiles about this strange optical effect. She almost reaches for the window to close it, she would love to know which young fellow from the village has come here to chat with one of the guests, they do come now and then, especially in the fall, playing cards and bragging what power they have over chicks, animals, and machines, but their advances are often rejected, you can tell by the way they aggrandize themselves up to the bright stars. A father who lost his children—such a one can sometimes hear time rustle—still roams through the forest and lets his blood come to a boil, broken vessel that he is. I would like to assume it was him, the lonely man with his dog, who bent down before, checking the grassy scar at the side of the road between his fingers, even smelling at it. Isn't that blood? Did it finally break open, the scar? Innocent, this landscape has been tortured by rain, hail, and storm, one can tell by the ground. It can be lifted from the mother soil as if it had never been attached to it. So then, one more time: The grass can be pulled off the ground like the skin of a drowned body (incidentally, it also works with a burned one, for example with this one here, running aflame out of the subway shaft, a tornadonna, her skin flapping behind her like a raincoat! As if her body picked up a piece of paper to inscribe herself on, but the pen dropped out of her hand in the process, and the fire's whirling, wailing winds were pulling at the shreds, now with a whimper, because she forgot to decipher the scribbling on it beforehand. So, now once again the fire doesn't know whom to spare and whom to keep), the forester, who has no more children to give, puts this earth through a tough test in return, he grinds it between his fingers, then raises his eyes to the Moasanger slope: There is this wind corridor, the burned path that the storm had torn into the forest, which continues way up into the mountains, and not even half of the timber has been carted off. Now a stretch of logging road must be blasted out of the ground again, which can later be used for the cars of the vacationers, nice! Nature's still screaming. She has to turn the grinning white pine jaws unprotected toward the people, and those are slowly rotting by now. There are holes, cracks, carious spots. This ground won't stick. It will take at least thirty years before it can stick again. In an older fire corridor, the tangle of new vegetation, those treelets surely haven't yet grown very tall. Here and there a couple of firs, sometimes even larches that withstood the fire back then, are sticking out, a whim of nature, who enjoys her futility even more when she can measure herself against something greater that withstood her for a long time. Luckily, it is late in the year for more storms, but the forester stops nonetheless, in the curve where the panorama unfolds in three wind directions, only the small Schwemmkegel mountain with its open wounds protects him from the back, in front the valley spreads out, prepares itself in the pan, namely the panorama of Snow Alp from Wind Mountain all the way to the Naßkör moor, the Red Mountain face inserting itself a ways with its red ironstone, its iron beard and capricious fir coif above it, well, at least the village is farther to the east, outside the air corridor, in case the ground should loosen and lift off. The strange thing about these mountains: The same forces that built them up are also working on destroying them again.

Only the village of Tyrol below, most of its houses are deserted, abandoned, except for that old farmhouse, today a bed and breakfast, and the Saint Nepomuk chapel, below, the only ones far and wide that still reach out to us, are still holding on. Shreds of wind break loose, play together, and jump apart startled, because the peak of Hochboden pasture with its characteristic jagged peaks has bored into their flanks.

Alright. Like almost every day, the forester, just by chance, has reached the spot where his sons shot themselves just a few weeks apart, look here: the heavy log they sat on back then is no longer there, and the first son's blood was still visible when the second one settled himself rather uncomfortably (the remaining stumps of cut-off branches are quite prickly) and poured holy water from Mariazell from the thermos into the barrel of the gun. The gigantic poles of two firs—they easily measure forty meters tall, and only the upper ten meters are hairy—drill into the sky. The mountain wind howls, calling down to earth from the sky that she should come. Oh, I see, she's already on her way. There, her two harbingers, the two tree giants, lightning has split them multiple times, countersignature to the Lord, but not felled, the resinous blood ran from their primeval stem and clotted stickily. As always, the forester steps forward to the gravelly lip of the wound where the street is still snow-white, right next to the darker grooves notched by the heavy timber trucks into the logging road. If one of those vehicles were to crash, it would go down a hundred meters almost vertically, and that is exactly the same path an avalanche would take and has done so already several times, directly in the falling direction; these saplings couldn't even stop a falling chamois or an elk if they zoomed down the area with their biogas motors. The roar of one of the local autosaurs makes itself heard from much farther above, just an intimation, it still gets swallowed up in the curves, it comes from the Eisernes Törl, the Iron Gate, where there is massive logging right now, they'll take ten more minutes to get all the way down, they always drive much too fast for their tons of cargo; in this clear air every sound can be heard for kilometers, even the train can be heard in the distance, and that distance is very distant, believe me, it's at least thirty kilometers from the county seat. The forester holds his face into the wind and lets it, the old buddy, lick it. It is oddly humid for this time of year, and the forester doesn't like the wind and the clouds at all (the wind even tries to drive them apart!), the main thing is that the streams of tourists like them, who flow like lava into the land's crevices, where they pad the ruggedness of the rocks with their bodies because they looked up in the air one minute too long, those Heinis. Sometimes they are discovered only many years later. Recently the skeleton of a forty-year-old hiker was found in the offside of a hidden mountain pasture, a belated Heidi who lay down in the grass and got wolfed down by animals, skin and bone. There are such hidden, tempting places around here, but normally no one wants to be that far in the off. Oh, how tired the forester is, walking around, he hasn't spoken a word with his wife since forever, or with someone else for that matter; he will retire in the spring. Soon his successor will arrive and walk the territory with him, he'll have to talk then, like it or not, when an upright face addresses him with something easier to grasp. The new man by the way has already introduced himself and was flung into the wretchedness of his predecessor to be way past the next table at the inn, where he had difficulty in the foaming surf of beers in holding on to a kidney-shaped piece of driftwood of bacon and bread served to him by the Wirtin. The brush of raspberries and blackberries the eye falls on if you step into the chasm of the road, plus the fuzzy hair of meter-high thistles and herbage, mullein and chicory, even lady's slipper and diverse spurge plants, they could never stop anything or anyone. A fire, for example, that'll jump right across the street like nothing, like a cloud of insects, that black entity that separates at any obstacle only to close ranks again behind it even more forcefully. Nothing remains behind such a raging cloud but a tunnel of air. A hole in the wind, a black hole that sucks in anything coming near it. Even the sounds, the sons of earth.

The gigantic fellow turns his back permanently to the Wirtin, and that's good, she doesn't really want to see him face on for sure, better to remain strangers to each other before your thoughts drop to the floor with a crash at seeing something that wasn't meant for you. Except for distant sounds on the roof, it got quiet for a short time. Then this indefinable noise sets in again, this time even a bit louder.

And the thunder in the distance? Is it a rockfall, a blasting, it reverberates almost like a sustained fire by heavy artillery, but there is no military training area close by, there are still a lot of mountains in between.

28

The mountain sides have loosened up, only the sidelined in this area are still stubborn. Gudrun wakes up after a dreamless sleep in her still untouched (even by her) room. What noise is that now outside? She jumps up with a start, sweat-soaked, she has been tossing and turning—her head was bent all the way down the nape of her neck—and twitching from muscle spasms and panting like a dog, she startled out of her sleep. Her body is now exposed to a specific sequence of events. It rushes to the window, gasping through the wide-open mouth to compensate for the oxygen loss. Then, as Gudrun looks around again, no, no oxygen machine has been dropped off for her, she inadvertently lets her eyes rest for a moment on her used bed: no impression, no imprint of her body on the mattress, which isn't covered anyway. It still was covered yesterday, wasn't it? All in all, the room has not been cleaned. The beds are raw, no one has taken the bait, the closet door is open to air out, none of those checkered place mats the den mother loves to throw around to produce homeyness has been swirled across the table. A storm of fleetingness, and in fact this storm is deep red, a gentle surge seems to fly toward Gudrun, turning around at the last moment and getting away from her again, the red sea does not stay with her. Otherwise, everything is in order, isn't it? The condition of this room does not measure up to any lived-in-ness, for Gudrun's gaze avoids the (where from?) familiar objects, curving around them so that it can continue ambling on a righter path, but no such path can be found. In the speckled mirror no picture of Gudrun. I just want to ask: Aren't we happy about a small bouquet of flowers or a bedtime candy when we are away from home? Gudrun would be happy about something like that, but it's a one-sided conversation she has with her room, for there is no answer. The sky also got a bit darker, she notices, as she tries to at least get in contact with nature outside. From afar the rising and subsiding thunder of the heavy timber trucks bringing down damaged wood, and from farther above, the breadcrusty logged wood with its appetizing bark, it almost makes you want to bite right into it; when the wind is favorable even the screeching of the saws from the sawmill at the Seven Springs can be heard. A lovely hiking trail leads to it, so that bubbling joy lies ahead of us if we want it. Autumn embellished the leaves at the wayside with sparkling dew and drops of mist. The landscape seems to almost jump at Gudrun, whose gaze follows every single one of its bad manners, playfully, almost naughtily, once again deserving a good smack, but caution, it might hit back with a couple million cubic meters of rocks. As the young woman opens the window, it's quite difficult, the bolt seems to have rusted a bit, and leans out, she is struck by the heavy loads of apples weighing down the trees in the front yard; the hem of the fir forest, jealous of so much fertility, seems to have pushed forward a bit as if it wanted to look over the fence's shoulder and into Gudrun's window as well as those of the other vacationers. Such small wild ideas are also the problem of the Zillertal Skirt Chasers and other poop groups, yes, that legendary horde of stout, stolid men in bondage to their record companies, throwing musical pies wrapped in the thick skin of brutally beat-up drums, whose other clothing also exhibits peculiar colors and forms, yes, these are folks who, with their moist, nutritious musical spittle, wanted to get shrink-wrapped inside the record cover, the mantle of seventh heaven, and thus, resistant against antibiotics, popping out of their anthrax- or erysipelas-polluted flesh, call to an open-air concert to boot. So they called, and eighty thousand people, did I just put one zero too many, no, that's right, so then all of those fogeys climbed up a hill to hear the earth echo in their singing but while doing so they forgot the sky, which, insulted, brought itself to their memory with a few million specifically to surpass the humans: Five hundred million cubic meters of water!, I'll show them, the heavenly Father must have thought, who distributes the principal currents to the cables, and thus it almost happened, it wouldn't have taken much for those enrapt by the music and the mountain on which they stood without having their roots there, together with the alpine ground on which they were crammed together, hundreds of people would have slid down into the depth. That was almost too much for the mountain, it nearly threw off its entire epidermis together with the subcutaneous cell tract, just imagine: a landslide, a slipping of the soil with eighty thousand people standing on it! Aladdin's flying carpet alpine style. People are overflowing their own embankments, they slip even on more solid ground, rise up in the air, and come over us and our descendants, who'll certainly descend upon this place, too, because they don't know when and where to stop once they start singing, screaming, hand-raising, and slope-sliding. Thus, our homeland's soil gets removed and moved elsewhere just because people don't want to go without their favorite music, even in the wild.

Our embankments rupture with the screeching howl sound of amplifiers, the music surges, floods the masses, leads to a heck of a downbeat, some kind of cosmic downpour (the masses down everybody and ask only afterward who that was), no, this music is a force of nature, it gets down on you, it floors you, and then you are fucked. Watch for the masses merging with the mass of water to one singular *Projekt Lebensborn*/Fountain of Life–mash that tears foamingly into the valley, sweeping along everything that gets in its way. Pure rubble, deadbeat to the max, this is how music and listeners arrive, in the best of moods and incredibly elated, down below, fans who behaved unusually well and disciplined for more than an hour (say the police, who usually love to put strangers whom we don't personally know through the wringer), or were they also swept away by all that rip-roaring and sliding? These peculiarities of the soil, which, however, were not caused by our stuffing so many people into the ground, apparently so that they can return, fermented, into our throats, who once yelled so loudly at those people, no, it's not our fault, only the innocent weather is to blame. And because we are so refractory, we always want to return to where we came from, that is, into another person's body, where else would Edgar's audacity come from, who is now talking to his sex in a somewhat one-sided manner, yes, now I can also see him, Gudrun, of course, has spotted him already because she was finally able to open her little window and leans, still more in- than exhaling, the joints of her hands twisting ever more grotesquely, far outside. Look at me, the fellow seems to say, as amazing things go on right in front of him. His Jingling Johnny rears up, it speaks for itself, if its master is not in a position to speak for himself—and that very same now discharges itself, spraying and pattering into the rose bed in the sunniest spot in front of the house. In the garden of the Styrian friend of the house. Why is there more life in death than in life?, we ask ourselves at this point, and are looking forward to it. It will remain a nice memory for Edgar that the two young men are watching him in the process from the left and the right, even though they didn't make the extra effort of putting on their faces.

They stare nevertheless. Their bright facial massifs, those breakages grope for Edgar's little soldier, who is already starting to keep watch again, standing up, first timidly, then ever more forwardly daring to step in front of his owner, quite a cutie, who soon turns trustingly toward the two boys who want to pet it. They have to feel Edgar's prick carefully, as they cannot see him, after all. Their heads, which were their favorite habitats, sadly only half of each is still in place, well at least one half is still there, nevertheless they look at each other earnestly, they resemble each other like the seasons, that is, not at all. Something buried their facial skull deep under the back of the head with blood, brains, bone gravel, a force that penetrated them with a crash and a gigantic gush of water. Their heads, those ancient culture grounds, landed in the watershed of a catastrophe. Edgar, a deep joy pulls him this way, then that way, turns his vermin-infested water birdie, which just had flushed itself out, once again toward them. This boring drip, which nonetheless is quite a good worker, gets prayed to every evening even by us older, ravaged women, well, what do you know, it stood up here, we always looked for him somewhere else. So then, Edgar's prick comes to a halt and looks around on all sides, having a bellyful of all that rocking and rippling in his own supply pouch, what, that's supposed to be the eternal rest? But now even the earth, shaking with laughter, has started passing water, look here, on the ground, at all these muddy waters. People always want an entire ocean on the spot, I'll accept their honorable feelings, if need be as Super!, though for most of them Normal will suffice to get them where they want to be.

Gudrun sees all of this from the bird's-eye view of her window, she hears overloud the rush of the small brook that cuts its way through the meadow, there is more gravel and sand on its banks than usual. Even this smallest of the water events in this area burst its baby banks during the recent storms. Altogether, despite the beautiful weather we had for days, everything seems to be soggy, plump, overripe, almost bursting, the apples lie partly (many are still hanging) smashed in the grass, as if the Creator, Lord over Many Waters, wanted to make all these folks suffer for coming here of all places! Look at me, Edgar Gstranz laughs out loud one more time, and positions himself, his stout legs spread slightly like a torchbearer, in front of the two loden brothers, whose thinking, though preserved in bloodwater, was flushed down after all before it could be eaten; thinking is an adjustable part of the head, don't you forget it! And with this annoying fragment of a thought from a shattered head he turns against everything that's soft (he prefers hard pistes where he can cut off hundredths of seconds!), Edgar shakes his fishy-smelling, after an accident somewhat torn, balls and rod up to Gudrun, whose gaze he just found, and Gudrun musters him as if she wanted to turn him over page by page, but she does not find the Passage, maybe he doesn't have it. So there stands Edgar's penis, the Eternal Not-Asking and therefore Restless one, dimly lighting up his surrounding like the bare wood of a brittle tree trunk.

Even the ground under this Young Siegfried seems to want to contemplate now, whether something else hadn't been visiting it, farther down, bingo!, this sex of a young man, stirred up to a crumbly concrete that doesn't want to hold, which it, the ground, was allowed to hold on to for a little while, it slipped away from it temporarily, this human thing, this teddy bear plushy, in the age when only the hours walk on foot, into extinction, well at least a part of them. It's all too easy to lose track. Yet how beautiful is the search, like the cry of a blackbird! Edgar's member swings to and fro, getting more animated with every pendulum swing of the clock of life, its time, however, has long run out. Strange, and the two young men, the shorter one and the big one, have also exposed themselves quite a bit in their clothes, which used to be supervised by the parents, I must open the security lock and check: The bigger one, who also seems to be the older one, is already feeling for his, let's hope harmless, raptor in the loden leg of his Sunday suit, no, hold it, it's the short, rough leather hosen he is wearing, tough stuff, easily mistaken, since the leg has long taken on the color of the soil. And the now gray animal opens its beak that sung itself into frays and answers with still more singing and screaming, gotcha, huh, that fellow's pecker gapes all the way up to the root, ouch! There you have it. The roar of the sea might be better, but the trees aren't doing so bad either. Some locusts received their accreditation for Austria and desperately want to be heard. The giant's cock is running on empty. And the shorter one of the two leather boys faithfully copies everything the bigger one does, of course with the creeping time lag that goes with it. So the two young men reach into themselves, find a small incline that emanates an odd odor, like spilled sweets, candy, but there it is now, the long branch no one sits on anymore! Which of the two is longer? To the misfits, extinction is nothing but weakness and end. Even so, those two faceless beings pull their pale double-pronged antlers, their trophies, out of their pants and rub them vigorously against each other, well now, they are back in the game, ready to man the ship. Once racy Edgar could also do it with three Frenchmen, two Italians, and one piece of Swiss. It's all quite harmless, believe me, that's how boys play with their jackknives, and they grow bigger and bigger. But then blood flows for real! And that's a blast!, even though one could sometimes lose heart over how long it takes or how quickly it's over again. The two loden laddies get their satisfaction from each other's melancholy exhibition, earlier this went on in golden sunshine, now it happens in the Cathedral of Nature wherefrom women, who in the old days were the only ones to represent nature, have been expelled. We can hear sounds of Ow-ow from the shorter one because his brush handle was pulled at roughly. Darkness pours from the mouth of his member, you can only see it if you get very close, and it's not nice at all of the bigger one that this is what he's doing now; he and I want to see exactly how far it goes into his little buddy and how far one can rush ahead of the other without losing them. He listens at this tube (aren't they submarines, the dead?, pushing their periscopes as pallid mushrooms through the soil), lifts it a bit at its mucous mycelium, this orgy of roots, puts this suddenly black, shriveled penis handle on his palm, decomposition is like a dream figure one wants, which, however, is gone before one even had it. The flesh at the base melts away, but by contrast, the little one's erection rises, as if racing up along an umbrella pole, yet its handle below soon crumbles away from it. For a moment the little one's erect sex seems to float on the big one's palm, glowing like a lampwick, then it runs through the fingers of the bigger one and drips to the ground. The guy had more than twenty years to perfect this behavior, and at the climax, as he wants to lift the Forbidden of the little one—which he should not have ever touched—to his mouth to marvel at the hole, the darkest zone of youth, the darkest spot, where the pressure runs deep and wild, and then suck on it greedily, eyelids squeezed together, brows knit: Oh, you facial lines, why did you have to derail, just when we needed you so badly and got new locomotives, but immediately hauled them off again? So then during the earthwork the big guy has the lesser one's—the one violated all his life—whole piece of sex fall apart on him, on the bare hand! Edgar watches smilingly as the monster of a farm boy (or what- or whoever he is) clings to the little one, who seems to have such an appeal for him that the big one simply can't stop, even though the little pet sitting on his hand has become a pile of peasant cheese: this giant wants to install right now and here at all costs, pigheadedly, but then again also modestly, his power plant—it should be in a pretty area so that we can organize a sit-in against it—notices Edgar, even as he peeks upward more and more frequently to this Gudrun Bichler, unlike him such an obstacle in wintertraffic when it comes to wintercourse, since this woman always wants to close the road at the first snowfall. So now this downhill racer is really in a pickle! How is he to save himself from the loads of scree that might thunder down on him from the upper story? This woman turns herself into a volcano, which she does not want to be mounted by anyone, because before that she definitely wants to cook a little something or some bigger thing.

But this time Edgar will destroy the tollgate Bichlerville, because he's got no change, he'll just have to drive through. Because of those multiplex sights from above, his overflower has also been affected somehow. Once more Edgar lowers the head with the observer nozzle, which can also be useful for self-massage, with which the bigger one now carries out a human experiment. In the meantime, the two of them don't pay any more attention to Edgar, they act as if he weren't there at all. He, Edgar Gstranz, though he can move quickly, is—like flowing water at certain places—superfluous, a fish out of water. The giant is unstoppable. He gapes out of his noneyes at the little one's thumb-raiser, his hitchhiker, who has not developed a behavior that would protect him from his giant brother, who now rudely turns it round and round, smelling it, yes, even trying to screw the little one's member in or out, no, that really doesn't work, while all the time it is the gigantomaniac who gets explored, observed, namely by the little one, his predetermined victim, whom his mother—whose declared favorite the little one was—knotted a last traditional bow around the shirt collar; farther up, however, complete power outage, all traffic lights were out, and thus the little one didn't even have an old traffic ticket to look for to prove his existence and hang on to it, and there is nothing he could use, at least provisionally, as the brother's face, not even a carnival mask, since this master face had the beauty of his eyes broken off. Yes, and this is exactly what also happened to the servant face of the younger. But all of this doesn't seem to bother the two too much. If anything bothers the bigger one, it is that he has the smaller prick, well, that happens, while the little guy got a long, thick one, filled with a mixture of gas, where could it possibly be fed from with everything underneath just mush, pear wax, apple sauce, conjoining the soil? Where is its source, no, no need to turn around the whole (despite the relative smallness) heavy fellow for it! He won't look any better from the back either, possibly even worse. He can't hide the source back there where it leads into the bowels, he needs both hands to fend off his opponent, he can't defend himself because a dark fluid with shimmering air bubbles in it keeps running out of him incessantly, which can be teased out with a small pointed stick and by blowing through the drain: the boy's white ass has definitely more visage, for the giant in any case, than the face that was originally intended to signal, shine, and go out. For in life the big one—as it had long dawned on everyone—has been the little one's constant companion, his biggest fan and at the same time his worst adversary, which showed in all kinds of roughness that, however, ended in intimacies between the two, and nothing seems to have changed, they probably should not have been buried together, I think. It's not easy to meet someone six feet under, still, the two of them should change their clothes more frequently. But they only have one suit for their pursuits!, well, at least one each, while their bodies seem to have grown together, an old habit going back to the children's bed, and badness goes to bat in bed. They can't learn anything good from each other, and thus they also remain fellow travelers in death, they don't possess any potential to reform and not a single talent as far as I could determine. Anyway, their clothes are comfy and formfitting, who knows what it looks like underneath. Both are saturated like the leaves on a branch, yet they still want to bite more and more off each other until their white splendor has passed for good on the rotted, dried-up flowerbed that's been covered with sacks against the winter. They may own the fieriest, brightest stems, but their berries, the twosome's life, that turns rosy come summer, has long gone.

How softly enmeshed they are, a pyre of flesh, their branch-limbs pointing in all directions, their orifices (and their faces are one single orifice each, come on in, the mouth is no longer a goalkeeper, go ahead, shoot, it's just a pitiful doorman) neatly surrounded by light, because it is day, they shine like freshly cleaned windows, thus, offering their lips, they call their silent observer Edgar into their alert, soft double-formation. It is unique in its way: almost a pity that the Massif will soon let go of itself and wash away any half that's no longer a whole (pity about the heads!). Unconsoled.

Already Edgar takes a step forward to join the game of the strong, it is, as always, a boys' game, soil to soil, ashes to ashes, the young men's gestures are made and deleted again from the slip of paper where the scores are kept, that's what the boys learned from life on the surface, as evident in the space above them, where the student Gudrun Bichler still hangs around as well, now desperately spinning and pulling her eyes' fishing rod, so that this thick fish, namely the middle one, whom the two pilot fish who were supposed to show around in eternity and instead put the screws of their sex on him, okay, so that this fish would finally let himself be reeled in. His well-vascularized gift of God, which has this kind of dark yet glowing finish, does actually jerk in Gudrun's direction now and then, pointing up to her rakishly, as if his sex organ wanted to climb up on Edgar and beyond, like a vine gone wild, up the wall, while its owner would rather (as proof that he isn't drunk?) like to follow an undrawn line that doesn't want to stop anywhere, the sinker of a somber shadow line, which can't lead anywhere but directly into the ground, where nothing and no one is waiting for him, what on earth would he want there? It is women who redeem men, they do it with a device that can mix, puree, and stir, stir up men, who'd rather remain sitting in the kettle without someone fetishizing their war-diminished stock, but those two fellows down there can also carry on by themselves; both boy-bodies are stirring, they beat each other stiff like egg-white peaks, smile with the smashed little deer faces of their heads down to the loden abodes of their bodies, oh no, I just noticed, their carved deer horn buttons are the only faces they've got! And then, to top it all, those ubiquitous wildlife eyes, hammered into the lederhosen, punched into their suspenders, as constant reminders of the animal the pants are made of. There is a storm raging across the entire area; as dust devils—"wind's bridegrooms" in their case—the boys whirl toward each other not seeing the house they stand in front of; and, deceptively safe like clouds, they crash against its wall; like blown-up sails the front flaps of their pants beat against their bloated backs, smacking kisses resound once from below, then again from above, depending where they, in rapid pursuit, catch one another, from the belfry, from the wine cellar, the kisses come up against an avalanche of fermented flesh, yes, fermented, for the interaction between the two has been all too sweet from the beginning, no one may dwell in another being this way, he must always know the door to the outside and, if possible, the emergency exit, too, not just the door through which he came in. Death has also triggered another problem, I don't like to say it: incontinence in the anus area, thus the two rolling fellows, whose flesh just shone so white, get slowly covered by a brownish liquid that poured out of the anus area, creating a humiliating condition the two of them don't even notice, on the contrary, they explore each other with every newly awakening strength, spreading each other apart, holla, that causes even more amazement, oh no, not that as well: some more watery diarrhea, with which the one has already rained into the other for days, years, cannot prevent these wild grooms from being happily drenched by each other, as if their bodies were cream horns, into which one always likes to sink one's lips, and then to crawl, with the whole joystick up front, into the warmth and reemerge with a darkly frosted mouth. But where there is no door through which the blessed Jesus can walk erect, we won't need the Judge either. Or: Jesus himself is the door through which the faithful can enter the Mystery, and what do they find there? One of the most common tumors we also fall ill with, love, I take this word back and give you another one instead, except I don't know where I put it.

These two country boys through whose dropped fly grow the heavy steps they take against each other won't need another fellow player for all eternity, their soft, no rather, smudged locks play with the heavy pieces of the collapsed skulls, and even the owners of those delicacies in the process of decomposing to earth, into the earth, give the impression as if they, slaphappily, wanted to roll down the slope together at any moment, one clinging to the other as to a last saving bush, how nice!, that they are having such fun, and so the somewhat damaged blocking object (that is something meant to protect human settlements from the forces of nature and in the process can easily become a threat itself), the one true love object of Edgar Gstranz, which has a pretty clean slate except that she locked a tiny rotation of the steering wheel where he, the speed-record-breaker, should have taken the curve by dancelike leaps and bounds, hoppla, already done, turns the somewhat befogged gaze, while fiercely inhaling twenty centimeters airflow, to the facade of the house. Up there a woman's arm is waving to him, isn't it?, a woman's white arm, but with a red line through the wrist, as in no entry, no, the line instead points up the arm, all it would need is the arrow at the end if it's up or down, yes, this cultivated area of an arm has been crossed out in the book of fate, grades are no longer legible, so what, so you don't know if you flunked or not. So this modest branch of an arm beckons the young athlete, who feels provoked and, with a running start, rushes up there three stairs at once, because in the meantime, two have already found and completed each other into one entity and received a fast-drying coating of life, now one just has to be careful for a while not to touch it. Edgar G. really is superfluous down here, a fifth wheel. Looking for something requires *being THERE* to begin with. But up there something impressed itself upon Edward's memory that could be ready to sit silently next to him and not intentionally get in his way with any intentions. Ready, set, go! Yay, behind this door things are popping!, calls, screams, clouds, so graceful, so dignified, but what's that? Didn't Edgar just want to get into the house, yes, he felt as if he had already made it up the stairs in a couple of leaps, which, of course, doesn't mean that the whole house should be there to meet HIM, on the spot, helpful and at the same time discreet. Every one of us wants a little affection, after all, but if an entire house hit on us, it might easily become too much. The house is annoyed that Edgar G. did not want to come to sign autographs for such a long time. The thin, pale arm with the bit of red on it got briefly stuck in the window frame as if it wanted to throw out its stance this moment, but already the whole house hits Edgar over the head, rushing, headfirst, toward him in a split second, well look, here it comes, the full Monty, window, door, and everything, the entire horizon that delineates this house comes clapping down on Edgar like a mean-spirited double-decker top that got saddled with a substitute filling because something, a liter of beer, wine, whatever, had washed away the original one; a preview of six feet under is in progress, it whizzes and whistles, the whole house, including the student Gudrun Bichler, who is still stuck in there as a half-digested pellet, collapses over Edgar Gstranz. He splutters, rushes one, two meters up the wall like an insect, hold it!, isn't it he who crashes into the house and not the house on him? In any event, the open is now outside and Edgar is inside. Though he almost rode the bull right through the window to the gate, that's how fast he was on his way since he'd lost his way once already. The young athlete hurled himself into the house, but to him it seemed as if the house threw itself on him. Now let's watch all this again in slow motion! Edgar Gstranz is clearly out! Lightning strikes. The Arrow-Emperor. Who protects our house from us? Eternity does. We do have to leave our house for good, don't we, sometime.

Just now Gudrun Bichler had looked out the window, her gaze still floating on the wisp of sun, although the day seems to her a bit dark today. The landscape sways, spread wide like a sun-drunk butterfly, teeters toward her, Gudrun grabs her forehead, probably just one of her dizzy spells that sometimes come over her, must be her low blood pressure again. It also affects her vision. Often the human settlements she looks into seem strangely distant, with dollhouse furniture, as if they had nothing to do with her anymore, as if her childlike hand intentionally tore holes into those landscapes of tissue paper, as if all this took place in another universe, without any connection to her. Down there three young men are showing off, big as well as little, that is, one is very big, one medium, one rather small, equally childlike and ancient in their "look-at-mine" histrionics, advancing into their pants or jostling their way out into the open, then laughing soundlessly, tossing their heads, neighing voicelessly, then leisurely spread-eagling for viewing, without being able to hold still for one moment. Yet Gudrun feels nothing but a faint regret that once again she can't stand among them down there and belong, participate. Sure, she would like to run down there, but she has subjected herself to another dimension, to emptiness, and that, let me tell you, is horrible!, there you see nothing but your own breath to breathe in again: and yet Gudrun fears that someone might come who would know how to read her, that his account, however, would already be dated, but since she keeps circling around herself forever, she would at some time come across herself again. And whoever was looking for her would be gone by then. The last account, by the way, that Gudrun submitted of herself was at the age of six, when she got a pretty box of colored pencils for her birthday. So then, she does not know herself, and so that she would never be able to meet herself she killed herself, so that she won't have herself ever after, but neither will she have to miss herself. So that she, not smart, not pretty, not useful, could no longer accomplish anything either. She could run her head into a wall and wouldn't get any response from it either, at best one would give her the doctor's look and with a shrug, oh well, turn away from her again. She wouldn't turn around for herself either, even if her own mirror image came riding toward her on a Lipizzaner horse. I think that Gudrun, in truth, is her own brake shoe, so have someone else put on that shoe, if you please. It always fits, no matter whom.

I am now speaking one truth: Should you reach consciousness of yourself, that is, embrace yourself, you'd lose yourself in the same second, it is different when someone else embraces you. Then you become the shrilly ringing one and only, the greatest, the hero of a whole series that's been constructed around this one: *Man spricht Deutsch.* German is spoken here. End of truth. Gudrun touches the Sunday dress of her sex, maybe it can get somewhere, too. No one can see her anyway. Elegantly, her vulva's lips flutter up as she busily burrows around in them, looking for something, while her eyes are still fixed on the young men below, what's that, is she bleeding? It sounds as if they were talking about something important, and Gudrun is quick to collect a few scraps that she scraped out of her sexual orifice to look at them: no. First smell it: no doubt. It is earth! Old, crumbly, dark soil, even one or two white root threads can be recognized in the small clots. Or are those worms? They are not moving, or not much anyway. Is it soil erosion, but where from? How do soil and worms get into her cunt? Who tried to eradicate her and her whole family to boot, which she, for lack of time, could not yet give birth to? Eradicate her by stuffing her with soil? Was soil the only thing at hand to silence at least her female sex? Even though there is no quieter person than Gudrun! Where is the main source for this humus filling? As if through layers of plants and seeds, the student burrows deeply into her own duct, which in life had only a few flames go up in smoke, for no one wanted to stay with her long. Okay, now everything's flushed again, and the water tank can be filled anew. Gudrun's body contorts, and suddenly her whole hand is caught inside herself! How brittle this tube, this end moraine that slipped into her body or was pushed in by someone, a cavern widens and everything is so weirdly mushy, so soft, no doubt, one of the worst hazard areas of her small settlement areas is located here, the earth worked its way all the way up to here, in planning her layout, Gudrun did not take this into consideration when she started to prepare a nice grave for her body and choose the furniture she wanted to put in there; she did not consider that all of it could collapse before that time, and here we have the main portal vein for all that shoving. Gudrun is up to her elbow inside her own body, she even opens her hand in it. A cavern. A hole. A pulling pain in her wrist, as if something inside bit its way out of Gudrun's body, some blinded animal that could suddenly no longer see in the dark. The slopes of her grave hole would also have to urgently be reinforced, otherwise Gudrun's body might collapse under her hand and bury her under kilos of quicksand and motion! It happened the day before yesterday to a bus of the Munich Transport Authority, it broke through the ground atop of which the traffic always tootled and pushed itself along with the feet ever so gently, because all too often all the wheels stood still in traffic jams. I say: terrific!, if things really happen the way you imagined them. Ouch, but this bite was actually not so bad, and the following bitties aren't either, for Eternity's predatory tooth is so sharp, it almost doesn't hurt when it goes *Fass!,* Bite!, but then this pull, Life, an enraged rodent that runs down the arm and from there it jumps down with a thud, as if it didn't have the slightest obligation inside the body anymore. It is unattached, gathers last observations, thoughts, maybe it wants to write a letter to the woman who owns the pet shop, whatever happened to That Creature, that little guinea pig who just graduated from high school, so what: keenest interest in beautiful bodies and their sex parts, let's finally stand by it, ladies, it's high time! This is why Gudrun goes to the open window one last time, the arm, from all that pain, had slipped out of the vaginal sheath as if all by itself—or maybe also because it has been lubricated with so much fluid—a small pile of earth has already accumulated in front of her, and from this vole hill of earth, blood is dripping, running, flowing to the floorboards, and by looking curiously out the window one more time, Gudrun succumbs to the nullity that weighs down her chest like a clay canteen in which she had mindlessly poured herself for years, now she sweeps her books off the night table in one stroke; the thought shines back on Gudrun; if she weren't an elevation, a rock, then thinking could never do it, well then!, and she unlatches the leash on the collar so that the meaning of this stroll into death would dawn on the Nothing, today the introductory death special is half price! And while Gudrun twists her head in order to see what's peeking, still placid and a bit bloated, like small bell clappers, out of the mother-hennish lederhosen legs of the two young men down there in the cool grass, a bird, a lizard each, whatever, one literally looks at the unformed, the disordered, and if fate so ordains that she may walk her untrained eyes all the way there, several tons of earth will press against her waterless eyeballs. Where is the rest of the shooting fest, the local adage rings in Gudrun's head on her exploratory stroll, you don't have much more time, get going NOW! And Edgar, whom Gudrun knows, presents the rest of himself, and hard as one may try, five minutes before the clock strikes twelve, it is impossible to find one's way into it. It is the blue of his eyes that catches Gudrun's eye, and then her gaze descends and strikes, one last time, but even though his boner gets deboned by Gudrun's petrifying stare, having been picked out of the flesh, it climbs upward, stretching and calling up to her gaze, and while Gudrun tries hard to form a word, yes, at least one, raising her blood-soaked hand to her mouth as if she were choking on the thick white fishbone drilling into her face up an almost entire floor, this man's sex, she must have it, she must, she must, just because it eludes all rhyme and reason and is something self-activating, something proactive, how beautiful, she wants it given to her, but she won't get enough time to accept her residence permit, which has once again been refused, as Edgar holds up his high-rising knight errant with a laugh, without shame, why should he be ashamed, he is open to any favorable reception: The crowd goes wild on the edge of the ski slope, thousands of sauna visits have also been successfully completed, hey, look at me!, thus he befriends, fraternizes with his two companions, and then he honors the house wall with his jet of yellow, he has nothing important to do at the moment, for HE alone IS important. That water is nature's call. Nature meets up with it and picks that which is her essence, and everything in nature draws from her its very own essence. But this water is not water, it is blood, a sprinkler system filled with blood has been turned on. And upstairs, at the same time, in the smallest room of this inn, blood gushes from Gudrun Bichler's wrists, it pelts onto the floor with the sound of naturality, it bursts forth, human input has stopped but human outflow still functions.

Blood often runs around inside us for days and we hardly notice it. But when so much of it suddenly spurts out with such amazing force, like a rainstorm, but in such distress, even if one is to blame for it, you instinctively remember a place that is the only one where the bleeding can be stopped. Help, I am bleeding, screams Gudrun Bichler almost voicelessly—let us turn the receiver louder—but only a tiny, numb sound comes out of the thoracic apparatus, and since Lassie isn't home at the moment, she, Gudrun B., has to get help herself. She hears the clopping wooden soles of the maid's orthopedic shoes, always the same shoes at the same time (unfortunately these are not the soundless sandals of the Fisher of men!) in the hallway, still, what a saving little noise! A human being rushing to her rescue, ambulance, hospital, women's ward does not have to mean terminal! After all, Edgar in his smart Twist-and-Drink outfit did hold out his straw to her, but it didn't do, I mean, it was not meant to do HER, maybe she could have replaced her loss of fluid if she had nibbled on him, who knows, use it or lose it. Gudrun's blood pelts down to the floor, for God's sake, help me!, the pressure in Gudrun's vessels drops rapidly, her pulse speeding up simultaneously. The heart receives less blood through the coronary arteries. An ECG would indicate an ischemia of the heart muscle. And the undersupplying of the heart leads to a decreasing pulse rate. When blood pressure and heart rate drop below a critical value, the brain is undersupplied with oxygen and dextrose. Unconsciousness. Brain death. High time. So at least get her to Jesus on time. I just remembered, yesterday two people again burned alive. Think of it now, because: The slower-beating heart can simply fail, even without any preceding ventricular fibrillation. Blood circulation and breathing come to a halt if a big vessel was hit, it can happen within a couple of minutes. The maid's steps are coming closer, the clatter is very close now, directly in front of the door, poor girl, has to run around the whole day, up and down the stairs, for nothing at all, but this time the running will have made sense and Gudrun will be restored at the last moment, right? Apparently, at this very moment the girl does not hear her, Gudrun, who could also call out the window for Edgar and the two boys to do something immediately, but the maid is closer to her, right there, directly in front of the door, her cross-country gait has already brought her down the hallway to her!, Gudrun! Help! Help! There, right behind the door, there is a friendly arbor, which will surely receive Gudrun right away, and with the last of her strength she lunges to the door, tears it open so that someone could ligature her, Gudrun's, arm. As a matter of fact, she should long have been unconscious, almost dead, well, there is the door, it's gonna be okay, but there, what's that, what's crashing toward her, more horrifying than anything else so far:

A wall of earth tips over into her face! A young woman who has opened her arteries is now gallantly embraced and received by the earth. Yes, here we go now, down into the ground! The elevator will be here shortly!

A split-second earlier, as she threw the door open, indeed, the very same second Gudrun heard, or rather felt, instead of the maid's friendly pitter-patter, an unholy racket, an unbelievably hollow rumble, drowning out everything else, a cannonade that couldn't come from orthopedic shoes, that delicate tapping of wood. A *Windsbraut,* the legend's "wind's bride," whirlwind incarnate, howls out in fury, someone tore off her black veil, an unimaginable mass of water drives through the garden, through all the plants, trees, and seeds that have to bow to her, and one can see—more briefly than it takes an eye to blink—how the milk gets into the cow, the vine into the branch, and the sugar into the cane, says God. So therefore, you can't just remove people from the earth, where would that get us if we regarded humans no different than a drop in a bucket of manure! Or else, at some point, a hole underground will come to every one of us, or at least its filling. Gudrun's soul toils in the shape of the elk, aka jelinek in Czech, kept under control as a prey of death. Trailed by evil, roaming the earth is whatever comes from the blows of your breath, Father, it seeks to escape the bitter chaos and does not know in what shape it should come. It comes as fire and as a house for no one, it simply gets torched by some boys. And so it goes. I just don't know what. I devote these lines to my dead ones: The girl's wooden patter disappears again behind a wall of EARTH, it can hardly be heard anymore, it is already half digested. And the EARTH stands up with great effort, groaning, of superhuman size, a shaft of EARTH advances toward Gudrun who, in her bodybox, descends into the pit, droning, pounding, cracking, howling horrifically. The ground quakes in the upheaval. Two soundwaves crawl toward each other, rise up, hiss at each other like snakes, but cause no interferences and nothing similar either, one of the vibrations comes to rest like a whip. Wall-like and high as a house, the EARTH bursts out of its pit all over Gudrun and slams shut again on her body. Once more she presses her lifeless wrists, which she, after all, had cut herself, against this cold, cartilaginous womb, her face, her whole body, whose secret she, Gudrun, had opened herself and with nothing but a razorblade at that. Something or someone, Gudrun can't tell anymore what or who, scurries away behind the earth wall of Gudrun's grave, with little pitter-patter steps it escapes this (inadvertently?) poured-out, covered-over earth gate, behind which a woman weeps, weeps, weeps and gets prepared as a little snack for the Nothing, since prey she was already anyway. Where is the jar with the paprika strips? What I am trying to say, everything is earth, and if not, we'll turn it into it. And whatever is not earth will still return to it sometime, sometimes sooner, sometimes later. Our calls are looking out whether that point has been reached, no, we still have a little time. There are others ahead of us to screw a ski binding on death and step in. We'll show them. How else could they cross our mountainous ranges of cruelty?

29

No man is an island of the blessed, but a country is certainly free to be something like that. The country has a right to buildings through which it expresses its position. Trawls, ever since they have existed, were always used to fish for sometimes more, sometimes fewer people, and now the position of the big buildings can strive for salvation, that is their right as the foundational structure of the populace: Little slimeballs jump quickly out of their doors and into their cars. This city, this landscape are of such stand-out quality that it takes extreme effort to jump over them. The city for example magically attracts foreigners, more foreign foreigners, yes, and even the foreignest folks to this day, for whom I must make room now. At 10:00 a.m., when the guided tour begins, they get sucked into the empty space so vigorously, it tears the bats out of their hands, because we've always been the better hitters. The empty space that's been created has such a magnetic pull, let me tell you, at bottom not even buildings can really fill this space; and where so many people were missing, we filled in, we settled in the Dead City, so that the buildings stay nice and warm inside and, moreover, can't fall over so easily. Thus, in the buildings, thousands of soreheads, pole in their nutshells (hard on the outside, soft core inside!), on a leaden lake filled with stinking water and, even though the boat is their own skin, a trophy of the Nothing, which naturally was the first thing they saved, still tips over all the time. So then they get stuck in the metallic water mass like a spoon in the pudding, scramble out of it, tangled, caught up in each other's stakes. Foreign countries don't care enough about our personalities! They would rather come to us to let themselves be taken care of. That's why we soon waltz them home again. In our stew we always swim on top. And what we can't swallow there, we bury in the ground like dogs, so that we can bomb-shelter provisions for a feast at which humans will be eaten once again. Yes, sirree! Have it all! Left two three, right two three! Take the lead, twirl the girl, and then turn! Atta boy.

Vienna's Ringstrasse rolls like a mushy lava stream under the weight of a few streetcar lines and supported by a few mutually contradictory but constant objectives and obstructions of a couple of hundreds of thousands of cars, but nonetheless enjoying it, and it has its belly scratched by the parade on May 1, an old custom. One can walk on its side lanes but also drive. And I am taking the minimal trouble of talking about and walking you through it, only to call your attention to our approaching a point where we might as well have walked if we weren't living too far away. Originally, our bodies were bred for walking upright with the intention of making us into something better than a beast. Gracefulness, however, was driven out of us, instead, our feelings frolic freely in our nature, shaking their heads in disbelief, they dig their fangs into the last remnants of compassion, which they grab out of our guts, where we get our thoughts tailor-made; they race like hunting dogs, those feelings that sometimes tear us apart at night, because we secretly watched a Goddess (nickname: the Truth) bathing and saw nothing, because instead of her, we ate our heart out. Under our soles the dead are raising their tired backs and straightening their shoulders one last time so that we can better step on them. How else should we screw the hooks into the walls of our mountains for hanging people on them; until the dead, air-dried, are finally ready to eat and we can shove their guts into our mouths. The meat must rest thoroughly under our butts or else it is too tough. I am so glad we are on the RIGHT side! It's beyond belief! Why am I saying this? Meanwhile, a ghastly site reveals itself to me, the basement of the so-called Art History Museum (across the street one for good *Völkerkunde*—only good old ancient ethnicities are exhibited there), come, take a look, but not close up, we don't have much time, later we still have to see the glazed brains at Steinhof Psychiatric Hospital; well, what can I say, the museum is simply megahuge, the entrance alone! Inside, in hall after hall after hall, the cracked molds of humans are exhibited. You can see how they were intended, had they been able to escape us and our insecticide. As it became apparent that it was not good, we, the Gods, smashed these beautiful molds but never got around to making new ones. Thus, those people could have never existed before either. But before that, before they were never there, we could still photograph as well as measure them and their life spans so that they would find out before their death how they, in order to please us, should never have looked. Today no one would believe what raging frenzy had once taken hold of this city, and this because of people who from today's standpoint appeared normal, ordinary from the outside. No dogshit on it, hands not yet grilled on a charged chain-link fence, no whip marks, the postage that could have gotten them to the Kingdom to come, nothing would have done them any good. Luckily, we never had to pay a surcharge later, we got off uncharged. Those folks, after having been counted by big, soft motherly hands were sent to vacation camp, where work was for free. ARBEIT: smaller! more expensive! (like the Eurobanana). At first they lived here, then they were shown the door. That door was almost a revolving door. Nowadays, we come into being like semiconductor crystals, which help to transport thoughts faster than they were thought (in that case, not only would it never have been us back then, but we would have never thought of such a thing either) in a sterile, empty space, held together by nothing but a mutual attraction, which captures our only form, the uniform, yes, we are always becoming, beings always beginning, because we must also be the form for all the others. Everything just us! A reminder of the truth: This screaming world gets weighed on the newest baby scale, but we, Germaniacs! Glacier mummies!, only we also sing, dance, and drink to it, busting our nuts on it. Smug mugs head into the night, where they suck on the black milk of a poet and then spit it into our glasses because one sip of it is already too much for us—a milk that seems to frighten even our curly-haired child Truth, even though this milk is our purest national product when we, on our knees, wish to present something to the European Union. For the child there is too much crying in it. But now we must use our whole body to stub out this blue Truth baby with the blocked heart vessels, so that it never grows up.

The allure of the exhibits makes them bounce off the walls, staggering butterflies, each their own pure race, one male and one female example, classified and nailed to the wall here. Unfortunately, in our school of life we let so many people flunk, no daddy came and fixed it. They haven't met our class's classy objective, the blond locks, the blue glances, and all that reproduced as cookies, with raisins and arancini, and with it the dreaded limobastonade on bare soles. We stuff ourselves with all this for what we call a *Brettljause,* a snack served on a wooden board, you need six *Brettl* for one human snack, and we top it with our self-aggrandizement, the purpose thereof: only then are we granted the right to exist, the final stage of our development—so then, for now, we happily made it through the preliminary stages: but, unfortunately, our style of expression is still somewhat underdeveloped, thus we need this ancestral hall to remind us how we should never look, not even today. Alright, so now we've got an idea of this. The foreigners bolt screaming out the doors. So then, in this most heavily bolted spaciousness of the museum's basement, we are showing how we must not be in Austria, so that we can be. Imagine if we should have had to save the children of Israel from the plague of snakes on their march through the desert! We would have finally been at the right address with our gas and would not have to stand there dumbstruck, like a three-legged dog on TV no one wants to have. We look at the exhibits: Here, for example, they often show a way to be as only German shepherds might get to see in the eternal hunting grounds if they were obedient—where animals graze, lie down in green pastures, and get daily fresh water from us. We are that we are, everyone a God. And we cover our floors with ideas of whom else we could eliminate so that we can stay among ourselves, cheap afghans, that floor you, which get better and better the more we trample on them, a long-practiced method, plenty in demand and imitated. The runners hide the dead, so we conduct ourselves as misunderstood beings, no idea how all these file-boxed corpses got swept under the rug. But watch out now, you, God, that your son doesn't appear to you in human form! Yessir, this was possible in the following manner: As filing cards, people are totally flat, so over time this also happened to their bodies. Could easily be burned along with the cards, sometimes pressed like briquettes and still preserved in us like a void, like something passed on to us: Blood that got all over our native costumes. Would you like to read an article? No problem, just a minute, I'll get it right away, you'll just have to get through it, but you can also skip over it, this letter I shall traffic herewith, then the light will just have to stay red a little longer for this Nationalist compatriot: "Dear Heinz, I for one am floored by your reception everywhere. And surely, the other gentlemen, too. Or are you popular because of your big Viennese kisser? Hubba hubba lah-dee-daa! Who are these other guys, don't you ever get together with any Viennese? Humpa, humpa, humpa! I am a very good girl, haven't been at a Heurigen yet, yesterday dining with Seppl at Romer's, today Wichart's! KA BOOM. The old routine. Heinrich did the math for 2 days, then called to tell me that the place comes to about 35,000 Reichsmark, well, that hymie shmymie will have to come down in price anyway, I told him so. I took a close look at everything at Stern. Fabulous, well, that's the lifestyle of the Yabbadabbajoos! Fred! Flintstone! (What? You here, too? Well, why d'ya have to have a name like Feuerstein?) I'll do my very best! So keep your fingers crossed. Was yesterday at Giebisch, Esq., party member, very nice, will do what he can for us. WhoppeeWhoppeeYayo! Wheeler-dealers gotta go, maybe even to Dachow! TschindarassaRentatent! So then Heinemann, any more hunter's luck? How big was the buck, how-many-a-pointer? And one two three! And one two three! Kiss, kiss, smooch, your Schatz. Wanna honeybun, Heinieman, rat-a-tat-tat. Hehehe! Glass of wine? Veltliner? What a treat in that heat!" Hear ye, Israel: The Lord, our God, is the only Master and thou shalt love thy God with all thy heart and with all thy soul and with all thy mind and with all thy strength.

Deep down in the sunken space, a whole woman swims around, I mean, all in one piece, not a wholly natural woman in a human-sized mason jar filled with disinfection or conservation solutions. He who was born from a woman is born under the shelter of the law, but where can a woman find shelter from the law?, this botched-up person, who has the name Nature written on her in bleached out letters, like a negative in pyrography. A ghostly glow emanates from her as if she were the glistening light brush in an oil lamp, whose radiance had been squeezed out between two fingers as if in passing. Soapy, waxy the figure, of whose existence two generations have washed their hands off already, and more of them should nicely follow. Do you think I have sufficiently honored these human beings who once tried to live up to us through language? Good. Then we, the blind folk, are going to feel our way to the opposite side, to the open-air zone, the free air zone, we call it here, to the pool, where we want to get acquainted with this creature paddling about in formalin or whatever it is. It is the biggest exhibit, right next to this one here, and should we not love the folk next door as ourselves? But where has the yelling and squeaking of the bathers gone, whom their peeping Actaeons transform into deer and eat later: there are no colorful water balls, no lifeguard's whistles to warn us folks about swimming too far out into this propulsive analysis of water that is not water. Such hermenautics tell us that the test subject was killed for experimental purposes and subsequently preserved in this basin so that she could be opened up and one could see what creation had put in her body as provision and consumption on the road, hey, look, there's nothing special in it! God didn't come after all, to dissolve the law or the prophets, and this woman does not dissolve in her liquid, on the contrary. She finds here, among us, the fulfillment of the Old Covenant between her and us! That does not mean at all that she belongs to us long-lasting jerk[ee]s who've been resident here since the Iceman Ötzi's BCE millennia! The vacation-loving Ur-*Volk* of Germans, shapable and border-conscious (keep pushing them far away from us, those borders!), has come to a totally new beginning, and we may once again be part of it from the beginning. So then, when we Imperial Eagle-Aerie[an]s and Annies get opened up, our descendants drop out and right into the hospital. The midwife's motor hums reassuringly; she is a dedicated young woman, and what will become of this Germanic nest of eggs where no colored eggs are tolerated, unless the Easter bunny came a second time in the year and brought something? That motor, after all, also gets constant deliveries of frozen ideas to be ignited there. That way they thaw faster, and here they are in their original human shape, one woman's already swimming here. I see no difference in the strong, durable hair swimming next to the dead woman in the preservoid, southerners, northerners, maybe she once was a producer of life who was chased into bankruptcy by this original *Volk* of Germans! Deutsche!, whose digestion she upset. Only human flesh is healthy for us, but not just any, as we have stated multiple times loud and clear. People love with their guts, but they prefer to live in their small second homes, the brains, where thrills change more frequently than on TV, that's why those people always come up with new ideas as to how they can pester each other. No, those brain jars (leaky to boot) at Steinhof are not as gripping as TV. From the upper windows with the curved eyelash cornices, out of sight, out of all senses, this dead woman here looks, surrounded as she is by formaldehyde, formalin, that's what she's in; so then, from behind her host fluid—no, no alcohol served here—as a display window in which the decoration never changes, she looks at us for all eternity, because only rarely do we look at her. There you have the greatest ever work of art, a piece of life expelled from itself! Such perfection could be enviously viewed, hadn't the bosses of this museum closed the entire foundation on which it has been founded (and publicly funded) to the public. Apparently, this would be too much for us, but we aren't interested anyway. Artistic women that we are, by treating ourselves with shower gels, powder, and hair colors, we can turn ourselves into a totally new person at least once a day. It's really something absolutely everyone can create, roaring, raging as the tail end of the *Musikantenstadl*-snake—that blockbusting band's final, immersive, musical procession—rises in front of us (Dagi, diva-darling, puh-lease!, show yourself on the screen, or we'll think you are dead!) to threaten all those who dared spring from, uhm, flee from the TV like walking disindigenous creatures. The local audience, in any case, can be awakened only with great difficulty, and only by something nationalistic at best. With our mouths totally slammed shut by paint smack in the middle of our face, we girls stream every day anew into production, so that every time we look a little different from the way we were originally created. And squawking dogs, those hems, are playing with our calves, sometimes with our thighs.

In the vicinity of the dead preserved in the glasses there are still millions of bones and specimens that I can't list here due to lack of space. The earth calls the sky and tells it the following: The East Baltic person, according to his whole psychic makeup, seems to be made for Bolshevism more than any other race. Well, that's simply not true! I break into a song for thinking that is damn close to the nightingale's or the Botho goat's, I look around, I don't have a sword, but I wouldn't want to sell my brand-new coat now to buy one. The earth retunes me, I resonate, raise my hand, and insist that I can be taken as a pawn by someone who arranged a date with my most trusted confidant, the sweet German language—which, alas, no longer trusts me, I don't know why—and has been bitterly disappointed by her. That person, no matter who he is, would not get her into his desiccated bed, even today, I am afraid. In the name of my *Volk* and its petrified deeds of the mind, which were set into motion in the quarry of Mauthausen and buried the people underneath them, now I, too, am thundering a little with my words until the sky tears apart as if it were the curtain in the Temple. Those blasting operations back then in Mauthausen caused our gigantic mountain range to start sliding and rolling once and for all: strictly no injection of rainwater (better eject others!), the removal of the vegetation cover, and, of course, any kind of blasting operations. Wham Bam. Zap! Jörg. Supporting foundational pillars Ka Pow! The foundational pillars of our reconstruction, which is a new construction, are located all across Upper Carinthia, and our task is Back to the Future! Go-Go gaga Austria! We transfer ourselves into a garden patch we dug and planted in the past, and now a whole forest is approaching us. Now let's all raise our hands. The re-Germanization is completed! Going Global! Zack! Now we take the people off the playing field, roll the dice once again, buy Kaufinger Strasse, Munich and Alexanderplatz, Berlin, and since we don't know where to put it all, we plant them, as the newly acquired territories, in place of the ancestral ones, which are not allowed to use their own race now and had to let themselves be uprooted, until they got totally lost to themselves. Where on earth did we put the leash and the muzzle? Ouch, now something has bitten us. Well then, the long and the short of it: The millions of bones you'll have to imagine yourself right here, I don't have time for it, paving the way there for you, so that you, amid your bunch of racy little rascals, can easily lay out a road of bone shards; you already steamrolled everything else, waltzed right through it, always rotating to the Right, how nice, I don't want to demand too much from you. Yes, it is I. I can also do the waltz to the left. Let these go!

Why still the dull duskiness around the floor-length drapes behind which two guards whose balls no one beats to death are playing ping-pong, no, not with skulls, not with brains, but with little celluloid balls. This paper bears the words much better than you, take a lesson from it. Why on earth those long curtains? So that the guards' balls won't always slip away, gentlemen ladies! And they don't have to constantly look for them between the preserving jar of the Floating Woman and the bones, skeletons and skulls of the Dark Men and Women who placidly keep still, because all their doors, windows, balconies have been boarded up. A kind of at-restness, it seems to me, surrounds their silenced silhouettes. As I said, there is a place in Vienna where they finally found their way back home, this is how long it took since they were sent packing. Tired shapes now, they stand around here, putting stones on their own graves (some are missing ping-pong balls that they picked up secretly at night), and their flesh became a cloud and wept there in its grave, but just before, as a warm-up, it merrily jumped around in the fire, whoa!, dancing down their grand entrance stairs are our two beloved stars, Marika Röck and Paula Wessely, hey, hey, hey!, the way they throw their bones around themselves, they'd want to get the attention even of animals. Especially that Marika from Hungaria, now, that's a woman!, yummyyummyyummy! But only the scaffolding held up, a scaffold whose house was taken away: These bones here are no longer taking a walk. In questions of the so-called pure race, it's not enough to say that every tall blond person can be defined as Nordic, for folks are intermixing everywhere, and at some point, they simply can't be distinguished anymore (that's why we Austrians were so good at disappearing inside ourselves). Yes, the more foreign they seem to each other, the more enthusiastically they intermix! Why do people go on vacation? I think it's to get away from home so that, when they get there, they can do exactly what they do at home. Don't you make any stupid jokes about Ernst and Juppi now, who made a special trip here right into the TV! They sing so beautifully, and our images even come live, only smaller, of course. No, just a moment, they are also homages to themselves as role models! At any rate, that soap opera of a woman roaming around here, rocking softly without a bathing suit in her container, unfortunately was not built on the model of auntie Countess Maritza, whose operetta voice in the high alpine altitude can coleraturate everything anew, an incredibly talented woman, our Dagmar (Dagi) Koller. Sorry, but this dead woman is just a broken form for nothing, put together, show-cased, no, she doesn't suit us, she is no longer a good fit for our yodeling Nordicks unless we were to take her out and pack her, together with our lily-whitewashed vests in our overloaded suitcase. So, as we say here, let's keep this church in the village, meaning let's not go too far from our village, which we wanted to sell to the whole world as the only way to be and seem to be, that is to say, the whole world has been taken to our village and has also become a village: Ours! Take your place on the square; in your new role as a roll of dough that adapts to any form, there is a place left at the center for the foam! Here, your bowl with the *Schlag,* our locally whipped cream! Though in case you are a car I am talking to now, I enjoy doing it because you have a strong heart under the hood, I am telling you: You can pick up your registration documents immediately, which document only you! Should you no longer want to be reminded of the dead, become a remembrance yourself! Folklore as part of those nice musicians, when the spit splashes out of the brain of Hias, the singer. He sings horribly out of tune, but one can cozily tune in to even such horror, the poet got it quite right, memory granteth the sea and an LP full of wonderful German country songs. I am going shopping right away, what did I forget this time? Then again, maybe I'll spare myself the whole shopping. I am worried about myself: I enter the supermarket, I scream, I beat my chest, roll my eyes, blood comes out of me everywhere. I tried to purchase this preseasoned caraway roast here, my stomach lining screams, billions of campylo- and citrobacter bacteria or whatever they are called invade me everywhere, and on the way to the hospital I don't have to think long and hard, because I always had a good meal before, pure pleasure! If only my homeland would not be so wrapped up in itself! The hometown keeps even this museum, where this woman is floating about, constantly locked up from the inside. This is a collection of forebears, it means, our forebodings get collected here, namely that once again we are somebody who keeps dreaming in the golden sunlight until we can finally get out again. When it comes to that, nothing can hold us back. Even if someone tried to make our bed all over again and channel the flood a little. Then we'll come right away and elegantly disguised as fires this time.

Sunken humans, however, leave their peculiar containers as quite normal figures. The guards fall asleep over their instructive super-glossies in which kings and princesses are constantly woken up by jumping peas. This group of humans slipping through the door one after the other, fearfully huddled together at times and setting off in the direction of Südbahnhof Station, is getting bigger by the minute. A man who passes us very closely doesn't even say "Grüß Gott." Could it be that he was stark naked and stank of shit quite pungently? No. And there, the young man in a suit, in pursuit of what?, better send him quickly off into the world than look any longer at how old-fashioned his attire and worn the fabric is. Over there two horrified figures in skiing outfits, somewhat unfit for the season, and farther left, at the gate, like fog, a group of young people staring into a boundless void, and for that they had put on alpine climbing gear (Thermo underwear? No, I think this heat comes from something else!), those things, clinking softly, strapped to their backpacks, are climbing irons and ice picks, which stick out of the tops of those backpacks like a bizarre old-German crest. Slow and chatting, very close to the entrance, a group of three older men in baggy knickers and anoraks, those men must also want to get out to the country, but they'll have to hurry to catch the last express train, it's very late already and the local takes hours. The group, now dispersing a little in the haze of the city, seems to share a certain clue- if not helplessness, they stray here and there, separate, come together again, their searching eyes looking in all directions. There, a young woman moving very swiftly and wearing a sort of dirndl dress, races in big leaps, as if she had a goal, light-footedly, elegantly, down the flight of outdoor stairs, but then she suddenly hesitates, looks around undecidedly, she even turns back to the building, for a moment the light of the lantern in front of the Empress Maria Theresia monument is reflected in her totally lusterless eyes, I measure that gaze, it is suddenly filled with unspeakable horror, and terrified, I quickly shake it off. Filled with inconceivable bewilderment, all those people gathering, separating, and coming together again, hurry away. Even a child is among them, its arms paddling as if it were drowning. Still, as much as they might be turning and spinning about, they are all heading in the same direction and continue their dull activity: just walking away.

30

The forester takes care of quiet and order in the woods. But the growing disorder all around here doesn't bother him either. The land does not want to recover from the thunderstorms of the previous weeks; just like a stubborn patient, it throws the saving thickener, the mud, now dissolved in water, against the walls and rolls around restlessly in its bed. A fever-hot hand rises up from the valley and wipes several tons of earth and stone off to somewhere, the land did not check before whom or what it would hit with it. A group of grazing cattle gets carelessly swept off the edge, the animals tumble through the refreshing autumn wind, spinning in the air, still howling, legs down, legs up, bowels outside. Crusty earth as soon as it is sown back together cracks open again. The meadows turn brown underneath the tracks of soil transformed cockily into hardened coxcombs by the heavy clearing equipment; the topsoil, the "maternal" soil we call it here, is about to drown under tractor treads. Brooks peek curiously over their banks' crust, they already got out once, licking the mustard-yellow loam, they surely can do that a second time! They only need a trigger, a shove. Brown, muddy, the dishwater—in which the three logoi, those three humans that meant something to us (the Un-Made, the Self-Made, and He who finally made something of himself), washed their hands in all their innocence—rolls ahead between the slopes, the water sweeps away chunks, shreds, this enormous water supply must be diverted, but: where to? During the past few weeks this area alone had about a quarter of the median annual precipitation—well, there were quite beautiful days in between—but now, almost imperceptibly, it got overcast again, so for heaven's sake, where to with it all? The land is at the limit of its receptivity, of people and in general; it has enough of it all, it tells us in a sad, pleading tone of voice during the evening TV and radio programs. Everything is soaked so thoroughly, and the great weather of the past few days does not seem to have passed on much of this sogginess, this moisture, to the air: The earth has apparently lost or gambled away its evaporation bonus. Entire villages have been ravaged by floodwaters and have not fully recovered to this day. Gentle valleys filled up with floods and gravel after the water receded. Where to put all that, while the evening air is almost summerly, and walkers sit down like fieldstones under the trees to rest. People come up curiously to the cliffs and escarpments; just for the visiting strangers, the side valleys expose their flanks and present their crisp brown calves and cuts, partly sliced loaves with white skeleton bones of rocks protruding from them, all the earth having been ripped from those rocks and thrown into the valley. As if giant animals were sandwiched between those loaves for us to eat. There is too much of everything. The narrow valleys are log-jammed and up to thirty meters at that! The forester puffs his pipe and lets his dog off the leash for a bit, but the dog, who usually enjoys this rare opportunity, stays close to him, sits down on his hind legs next to his master, and looks cautiously beyond the street's break-off, beyond this ski jump: So then, a selection among people does take place indeed! But it is mean somehow that the forester was robbed of both his sons at the same time. One could have been quietly left to him by the Nothing to replicate its infinity in one person at least.

The Nothing, which the forester's two sons are playing cards with, just shrugs its shoulders indifferently. The wind at first makes itself only heard, then it shows itself. Humbly, the last foliage trees farther up the slope lower their heads, they've already been through a lot this year but don't want to be spoilsports today either, when the wave drives them on to celebrate our team. The hunting dog, that dutiful fellow, sniffs the air and lets out a loud howl that transitions into a high-pitched yelp that can ride along atop the wind down into the town of Neuberg!, let's get it out into the world, it is such an earthly sound. For a moment the forester turns away from the white undersides of the leaves, those throats of trees humbly offered to the wind, toward the animal, but the dog avoids the master's glance and looks down to the ground, almost embarrassedly, without pity for his master. Down below, driving along on a side street that turns off from the valley—across the gigantic and, since primeval times, washed-out clay cave, where thousands of bats are dwelling—and that soon merges in a big loop with the highway, is the minibus of the local trucking company, which takes tourists on various round trips, most probably they are on their way over the Wild Alps to Mariazell. The hunter asks himself if they will take the route via the village of Frein past the "Dead Woman," that icy veil of water poured down the rocks by a dead woman in endless bridal repetition; an iron cross planted in the middle of the waterfall steps forward threateningly whenever a group of people wishes to cross this water on a small bridge of rocks across which the spume sputters its rage at the young birches and maples, a water creature lives there that struggles desperately to spit out something sharp, unwielding (a fishbone?), which it swallowed. Wouldn't it be safer for the tourists to drive over the high mountain pass of the Niederalpl, no, better via the Frein, the street over the Niederalpl is especially dangerous and tricky in bad weather, the traffic alerts have been warning repeatedly since the storms. But the driver knows what he is doing, he is from here after all. Just now the last simple folks got on the bus. The forester is a man who continues on his way. And already the minibus turns noiselessly into a curve, crosses the mountain torrent, that angry child who threw out almost all its toys, so it got new ones of course, just many more that now clog its whole bed. The municipality is dawdling as usual, well, how can you recruit folks for this work when all the young men are up with the owner of the hunt, where they can get three times as much per hour, most of them take their long-announced yearly vacation at this time. While so much would have to get done here! Right now the woodsman should also check the creek, which has its source here and is the forester's biggest worry, because it's supposed to flow into the Tyrol creek but doesn't seem to feel like it: since the storms, it brazenly moved its bed. And took all the bedding with it. The new bed badly needs a cleanup. Where it is now, in the raging stillness, this both unspeakable silence and pain-filled screaming of the night of death, while the forester's sons and other sons are sleeping near and far, waiting for a noise to cut through this eternal silence, there is a new, an unfamiliar noise, was this a shriek of horror? Whose? The sons put out each other's screaming like a cigarette so that the father won't hear them. At any rate, the debris can't stay there, neither can the bed, or at least it would have to finally be put in order, new sheets and covers would have to be bought if needed. The creek with stuff foaming in it, but what is it?, can't lie down there every evening, in its stinking, grayed linens. Well then, the forester will now take a look at this, and worse, he will then call the municipality from home and raise hell, the high water's already there for the taking. Of course, he will keep silent. Below, the holiday guests who stayed home are resting in their deck chairs, soaking up the sun, those worshippers, a motley selection of humans who take God's scourge, the sun, as a stimulant, while they are trying to get away from their lives in beds not their own; yes, there they lie next to each other, while, above, the creek climbs into its new bed, getting all the soil cleared away for it.

Couldn't that wind bring snow? No, not yet. The forester presses his hat with the world champion's tuft of chamois tighter on his head and turns, face first, into the mountain wind, the dog stays at his left foot, although it got the Go! Down from the pasture slope the jungle of firs presses against the man and his animal, and suddenly this master of the hunt becomes physically conscious of this forest's gigantic primordial weight, he can feel every single tree as if it had grown out of his skin, for where once the forester's offspring kept growing, there is nothing but emptiness now after this Bethlehemitic Infanticide as only Herr H. had ordered it before. Here before him, behind him: this state-owned stately logging road the hunter is walking along with hunched shoulders, the animal panting behind him, and there the slope's gravelly spine cuts through it spikily, its entire vertebral column exposed, heavy trucks dragging along on it with creaking transmissions until the mountain side's abutments break off, well, yeah, they really won't last much longer. In the darkness someone inside the forester leafs through him as in an open ledger, there, a hand reaches inside him and turns blank pages that the forester forgot to write on, and now it is too late to leave something of himself behind, a trace. After the forester it stays blank. The hills are breaking, making waves, and the trees on the slope are doing what they usually don't do. To wit: I hear a voice, it is the voice of night's awakening, wherein his, the forester's children, are living now, which is their first vacation ever. The voice speaks to the forester in two parts, thus exposing all the forces coming out of chaos, which wanted only to be thrown into the pond as a few small stones. Thus, the mountainside darkened, a shadow fell on it, clouds piled up, and rising already is the full force of the chasm's darkness that carries the loam of the everlasting, all-consuming dampness, this now ever more active force of the water-colored roar that carries the lasting, upholds the trembling, unleashes the coming, and also makes it easier for the vacationers to stay, because it never lets them go again. The waters reign, no one else does. The airs are managed by the weather, but the water reigns all by itself.

The trees don't just rustle, they don't just stand there, they work! The forester feels as if all of a sudden something pushed this jungle, one of Europe's last and the only one in this country, no, rather lifted it out of the ground as a whole. Some might think that all those loggings were bad for us and the Brothers Tree, and this is why we should kindly leave them in the forest or wherever they live; let's instead use our forklifts to lift a multicolored vegetable gondola (all food is chemistry, the chemistry of grosseries, that is!). No, what really harries That Which Came From Above is water, which can grab our crowns that capped us, corked and screwed us up for so long, and then the entire forest to finally fell us all, yes, this hand also falls. And they'll get us by the scruff of the neck, after we had slipped so many years through the fingers of the Living One Himself, who manages the stars and arranged everything here so lovingly for a foldout. Not everything comes down to an eternal cycle of becoming and forgetting, it comes down to something coming to be but not wanting to be forgotten like this jungle here, this only one unreasonable amid nothing but reason. This forest is an infinite relationship between water and earth, and this relationship must be worked out anew.

The forester ducks his neck into the collar, an indescribable, I wanted to scribble indeterminate, not yet often used fear (even though he really has nothing to lose anymore, it won't make dying easier just because the sons went ahead of him to the viewing point and saw that there was no more point to anything) seized him by the collar. There he thought he could walk the modest road of his life all the way to the end, alone (with his wife he talked for years only about what's absolutely necessary), and now, suddenly, there, this infinite abundance of forces, and all of them are coming toward him like a fully loaded lumber vehicle! And all of them work their way downhill, that is to say, down the mountainside. This forest floor—the forester feels all of a sudden as if he had to carry it piggy-back—is incredibly heavy, the earth seems to be light only for the dead: the floor reveals all the strengths and the delicious plentitude of this landscape in its roots and even all kinds of other forces, which, however, are collectively finger-wrestling and tug-warring down the mountain, and nothing will be salvageable from this descent. The forester steps to the upper side of the road, its upper, hardly scabbed-over edge of the wound: oh no, so much of the rock underneath has been blasted away, and on this bedrock, shown here on our chart in cross-section, you can also see how and where, but not why, this wound of the road has been cut into the pulse of this landscape. In any case, a relatively shallow forest floor rests on it that is so thin that it cannot be shown to scale on our chart. As the forester is bending down, the entire forest gets packed for a moment on this alpine Hercules like a hide, hold it, wasn't that thunder just now? Yes, someone just threw the hide of a tame forest turned suddenly into a savage monster over his neck and shoulders so that he, the forester, would have to hold back this gigantic weight all by himself. Well, that's a pretty tall order. Even though the forester knows from forest- and game-checking (and game-wrecking): No one who has been thrown into *becoming* can escape this. The readiness to slip off this rocky underground is always a given. The weight of wood that presses down on it! This forest is as heavy and at the same time as light a breeze. Say what, this rain is supposed to be light, slight, insignificant, and happening outside our window for our own protection? But it was the rain that made this forest so heavy! Though they say what's coming down from above will go up again, but maybe it won't come back to his master as an alpine Golem after all, no, stop, it's coming!, the forester straightens himself, holding his sides from the effort, his face red as a lobster, struggling, wheezing for his breath, where the heck is his hipflask, his iron lung, his dog at any rate raises his hackles and lets out a dark growl: Where the forester had reached earlier into the soft forest floor like into a bag to examine the soil closely, a dark swarm of flies now rises as if from a festering wound. The man jumps back a step; and he had just wanted his dreams to play for him the LP with his sons' angelic voices. There are more and more black flies rising, buzzing and starting to dance immediately, each in one spot, like ghosts. A swarm of flies: Buzzing of dead leaves in a howling storm. Fighting against everything that's coming through the air, men, women, forest, rock, water. The forester didn't give away his sons readily, but even so, he is much less ready to give himself away. He presses his back against the escarpment, I mean the rocky shore of the street. And in turn the primeval forest's slope presses its back against him, the heaviest weight the woodsman can imagine. And this weight has become too heavy. While down below the guests are still resting in the sun, their faces turned hesitatingly—please wait a little longer!—toward autumn that turned out to be beautiful after all, while getting drinks and sandwiches served to them, the air is so clear one can look into the garden of the inn—seven hundred feet farther down nearly vertically—and almost onto the plates of those eating (even seeing whether that there is a lemonade or a cola bottle), the deputy supervisor of the forest, the forester struggles with this living dead weight of trees and others, whom he doesn't see, who are nonetheless present. And on the Other Side there are many more than here, and we, too, including this boss of the forest and all the dead animals in it, do not like giving away our relatives. Two young people who should still be here deciding to go and, therefore, settling on one of those dead white logs to shoot their brains out is something we don't like to see. But the cause of every *becoming* falling into ruin: The God of Time. And that one came too late today. Time, alas, is not after all a Styrian accordion one can stretch out and push together again. Or is it? Dark clouds can approach on the purest day, at the very best hour, if Time gets sloppy. That mass over there is stronger than ours, and if we don't want to give away our loved ones, they'll come and get us, and we'll also have to move across.

The forester has the sense of a heavy overhang as he backs off the dark swarm of flies and, waving his arms about senselessly, implores his sons not to take him along, and if they did, he'd surrender, as he did in life, only after strong resistance and not just for pocket money. But the wind has already risen, and the enormous army over there pulls the trees that they disguised themselves as (we Germans and Austrians love the forest because it is like an army and we can be its masters, thank you, Mister Canetti, I am so sorry that now you, too, are over there and not with me!) by the hair playfully, it has already loosened it a bit, and maybe all of them will fall so that there will finally be some peace. The forester, pressing himself against the threatening mountainside, has a grotesque expression of fear on his face that is not reflected anywhere, earth trickles into his collar, wet, sodden soil, the forest came over us and fell in doing so, the forest. The foliage is on top. The rain seeped away but couldn't do it all the way. Down below, the ground's decomposing skin lets nothing in anymore. In this forest no one feels safe anymore because it is hammered, it even guzzled all its "drinking money" (our telling expression for tips). The forester looks up. The forest has knitted together there. He looks down, no animals can be seen there except that swarm that just flew up. The German armed forces, the forest! It stands its ground immovably; it will not budge one foot's width of the floor. But the forester knows that's not the case anymore, can you hear it, man!, Green Party pioneer Herr Pilz (your surname isn't Mushroom for nothing), standing, as you are, on a box that's made of living wood, you, who—arduously supported from below by us delicate lamellas—rages against uncontrolled loggings. Now the weather fells you! This forest will give up its floor and strike back at the people: I am telling you now what the forest, once it comes to us, can do to us, among other things: It can lift a train's 120-ton locomotive off the tracks and throw it against the station building. And if you are in there, because you wanted to take the next train, then you are part of the fate of the world, which won't miss you at all. To this day it hasn't missed millions and millions and millions.

Already almost caught in the streams of wood and debris that stroke his hair in passing like trains roaring by, the forester fights himself out of the view of the landscape and forces his face back in the direction he is going, he has to cover quite a distance to walk the hunting grounds and look out for damages. A group of people bringing along fire for their food could have caused inestimable damages, but no worries, the soil, the wood are too soaked with water at this time. He pets his dog's head, the forester, and standing up again notices that nobody in this world looks as healthy and jolly as this young fellow who has worked his way here, where the flies slipped out of the unmoored mountainside, out of the ground up to his hips, similar to a sewage worker who leaves his work area and, sitting at the edge of the hole, takes a bit of a breather. Being extremely observant himself, the man likes to let himself be looked at in all his athletic splendor, he is the young fellow whom the loden-gray forester had always recognized from afar by the colorful picture-book clothes he always wears, an uncovered agent for the sport industry, who must be first in trying everything that will later break the customer's neck, even including a very sporty BMW, but fatality notwithstanding: Our children and grandchildren will continue to buy these and similar rolling blinders for their gray existences, to hide themselves imaginatively on the one hand and, on the other, to pull themselves up creakily and show off the splendid content of their new thermos battle wear that could inflate the store windows from the inside like sails. The outside points to the inside, that's what it's for. But why has this young man, his ears sizzling in rhythm through his cotton ear plugs (to stop cadaveric fluids running out of this body that's been buried alive), shown up here like a graceful stag? And today, unlike usually, he isn't wearing anything, at least nothing from the head to the hip, that's all there is to see of him.

The forester finds this perfectly normal. He has been so preoccupied with not having to see his sons—who tend to run around here without heads, that is, headless, as they also were in life—he still keeps changing the time for his regular patrol of the hunting grounds to avoid running into them. The dog, staying close to him, rod between his legs, which he always showcased so cheerfully for the two boys, is always a sign to the forester that the forest called the dead and nobody came, except, of course, his sons, typical. Since they were never allowed to attend the pop concerts in the district town, they always dreamed of wilder, more colorful pictures than their father, mother could offer them for real, even though they bought the sons their own TV, a devotional object for their room. This *Fernsehen,* this "far seeing," the Sacred per se, had the effect that in the meantime the Gods in heaven became as remote from the life they created as us earthlings. And so it happened as it had to happen, a simple church song and one coffin at first and another shortly after. They couldn't even do it together, the boys, it could have saved one funeral; it would have been done in one go, which at least spared their mother scrubbing the living room. At least they went outside to do it. Where the swarm of flies rose from under the ground, cleared finally for its patrol flight, who knows where to, out of the hole in the ground, in the spot where the forester's sons shot holes in their brain-pans they could never patch up again; approaching now is that Herr Schranz or whatever's his name, apparently he was lured out by a conspicuous mass of dancing black-winged beasts already on their way to Heldenplatz, Vienna's Hero Square, where they will wait for Herrn Karl Schranz to arrive in his Papa mobile to meet up with the Chancellor on the world-famous—but Herr Schranz is much more famous—(NS hi)storied balcony, then all of them will spring up at once like fountains (and just as fleeting, crowds nowadays are thinning much faster than back then because parking is expensive), throwing their arms up, cheering, chanting, shouting obscenities, booing the head of the Olympic Committee who shook off the popular athlete like a swimmer drops of water, that star on skis whom this Lord of the Rings had praised to the skies just five minutes ago. But this young man whom we see here stuck in the forest is covered with earth! It sticks to his face, his shoulders, his arms, everywhere!

His hair is filthy through and through, it looks like some dark wrought-iron work, rigid, metal twigs scratching the face, where bloody scabs, cracks, scars, dried black blood have taken over the role of the fashionable. This mute face seems to emit an incessant scream of horror, this is not the Herr Gstranz we know, this early riser, ready to go even before he wakes up, this man painted into the red of dawn, who is pure as light himself unless he'd had a late night again. This better than good truth of beauty who is who he is, something's apparently holding on to his ankles under the earth, who knows what's the cause of it, so that he can get out only to the hip, even though he desperately props himself up with his hands at the edge of the hole in the ground and despite tensing all his muscle ropes as if he had to pull an entire ship on the Danube or like a bud that wants to pop open but can't do it, he unfortunately cannot be the ambassador of the sport for his company and his party at this time. Nevertheless, he can push himself off for a moment with a pathetic little hop, his bluish bloated erection that he had so far cleverly hidden from us, now visible large as life for a moment in the dark scrub of the thistly hair: Hey, look at me, the juicy dome of a chapel wherein it bubbles (a healing spring for any fitness fanatic), with which the young man actually wanted to crown the proud cathedral of his body by sitting up on his hindlegs, begging himself with it, hey, wasn't there also a mush of soil in the opening of his penis that simply didn't want to stay in the ground?, soil ready to shoot like a geyser out of an amazingly unsightly portal to lie down on its stomach, on the death raft, then: Waiting for the next knee- to spire-high wave and bingo, off we go! Edgar evidently wanted to completely bare his somewhat inflamed, swollen orifice and spill his esprit, his Sprite on the grass, off the shiny rosy road, so that at least something would be left of him and, were it just a tiny shiny spot, where something might possibly grow sometime. The orifice quivers like the gills of a fish left high and dry, it tries in vain to spit, well (is it coming? Is it not?), so then, for a moment this young man hangs in a tie between the power of abysmal darkness and the light that's no longer what it once was either, since in that very light, lies were ascribed to Jesus, which his successors promulgated as Christ's Word: That company, however, was founded with borrowed capital that it never repaid. So there!, and now this young earthling emits a scream of horror that sends the forester, who has not uttered a single sound, back on his route, only now he is no longer walking but running, running, running. He holds his loden cape tightly around himself, but it slips through his fingers and flutters, as if pretty tired, behind him like a giant withered leaf, and mumbling to himself, a prayer perhaps, an appeal for help to his sons—the one time you need them they are, of course, not around—he is running along: resounding through his facial door left open, a crack, is an almost voiceless cry, which only unwillingly leaves the warmth of the mouth and flies into the noticeably colder autumn air, and the horrified man pauses again, breathlessly, only when he's past the bend of the road, with nothing but forest to the left and right, in front and behind him, I am now reading from the paper, the forester knows it by heart, even though long before his time it happened that this forest also flailed around stupidly and senselessly in exactly the same panic as the forester now, causing damages of around 310 million Schillings and a negative human balance of twelve persons. One never has peace and quiet, not even in death.

But for now, the fright has been overcome and the dark forest's homelandishness is looking at us, in which you can have undisturbed peace and quiet, if you are a mushroom, a rock, a leaf, not a man. Towering fir trees as far as the eye can see. They don't speak for themselves because they don't speak at all. Here the heavy power saws and the heavy vehicles, which, like the Savior, can tear open heaven and earth, have not yet started their work, but the trees are already marked. Those allowed to stay proudly carry the yellow ribbons that protect their lives around their trunks. It is the other way around with humans who came up with the idea that the Veiled Woman, the Synagogue, must be marked when she turns up and pierces the Lamb of God with the lance, so that she, the messenger of death who has killed a real, authentic lamb, can be distinguished from the church across, which catches the blood in a chalice like the sap pot the tree's blood and the heart pot ours. Then the Synagogue, licking her lance, her veil blowing like wind and smoke after her, rides off on a collapsing donkey: That's how we Christels imagine it, and that is why we must also kill this murderess again and again before she catches us. Luckily, her foreignness can be seen from afar. Isn't she standing there in front with the quite pleasant face of a middle-aged woman so that we should fear her and kill her once again? As if a beehive, no, a flyhive, if such a thing existed, would have been cracked open, presumably by the problem bear Nurmi, insects are buzzing around the forester's head, and he has to constantly try to catch the bugs, sideways, with a time-honored peasant gesture. Then, calming his own breath, he gets into the bed of the slope, it is a child's bed, a very old, almost grown-over footpath, the former mountain-climber trail to the alpine pasture, no one takes it anymore, it can hardly be seen, the markings are almost completely worn off; and this path—feet are sloshing in the waterlogged juicy grass, the leaves and herbs, with washed-out gray gravel peeking out between them—this is the path the forester climbs down, and thus he walks right toward the woman down there: a shimmering of teeth between slightly raised lips.

Standing there, as the man who is slowly regaining his strength discovers already from the distance, is a human being, so now that's something true! Horror be gone! But the closer the woodsman on his increasingly peaceful descent gets to the woman standing at the concrete basin and looking into the water musingly (the forester knows: seeing it for the first time is quite startling, he doesn't know why, maybe because it seems to be unfathomably deep, a dark, sluggish water, it might possibly be because a long time ago the basin was buried, you can't see how far down into the ground it goes, it could easily be a few meters, and the burned-down abandoned farmhouse next to it was buried up to the second-floor windows in exactly the same way. I would be delighted if this time you caught on the first time, because I didn't put much effort into the description and am not planning to repeat it), the slower the forester's steps, which get more and more hesitating the closer he gets, but surely, there is nothing uncanny about this lady. She looks like all the other women tourists, maybe her outfit is a bit too loud, too colorful for her age, and at this moment the forester recognizes her and stops dead in his tracks. Has time run out on him?

Didn't he see quite clearly the woman entering the minibus earlier? He did observe how she—and he has known her for a long time, she has vacationed here for years with her old mother—he observed clearly how she boarded the bus barely fifteen minutes ago, and the mother always kept to her very closely, practically stuck to her rear wheel, as they say. The forest ranger clearly recognized this woman as far as it was possible from way up there (but a forester is used to sizing up things over great distances), as well as her mother, she actually tried to push the daughter and squeeze herself in behind her to be the first ones to get on the bus, he couldn't help smiling about it, the forester, he sure knows the two ladies, those eternally entwined figures who also come as a two-pack in case one forgot scissors to separate them, but standing here at the basin is only the younger one, alone. How can she lean against the edge of the basin when she boarded the bus before? The forester must have made a mistake, it must be a mix-up. Or did they turn back right away, those fickle females, but then this one couldn't yet have made it all the way to here even if she ran. Whatever. One can't help wondering, though: There is this woman standing at the basin, staring into it, and now she must have scented the forester, maybe his tobacco, as his feet hardly make any noise on the soft ground, she starts up, like a jackknife that opens itself from its footbed in the air, and turns toward the hunter. She looks at him as if she wanted to sew her eyes onto him with a few basting stitches. The forester feels as if he were being visited at midnight, when it is the quietest. His hair raises, it rains from his eyes directly into the woman's eyes, the wind turns and reverts the rain, a sudden rustle in the treetops, a crash, and it drops to the ground: water, caked, frozen solid. Yet until a little while ago there were pure southern weather conditions, sunny autumn weather with rising air pressure, nothing indicating a sudden change in weather, and now out of the blue we've got these horrendous rainstorms! Caused by humid subtropical air masses from the western Mediterranean region, literally hurled by an upper air current at over two hundred kilometers' speed against the alpine comb, where they now dump all their humidity. But because we are so high up, precipitations come down in the form of snow. Loose, heavy, wet snow is falling on the tree hats and tree umbrellas and from there in thick lumps on the forester as well as the woman out there in that water enclosure where something is under guard, and we might not get back safely to our hearth anymore. In the very first moment the forester resists emitting a scream, then he immediately does. And he is already running, reluctantly but still as if he had nothing more urgent to do, to the silent woman with the ice-cold arms, into the bed she stands in, straight, quietly, peacefully, elsewhere, not only in her thoughts. Just as the world was made through an effusion from above, things down here come to be, pass, and pass away, depending on the diffusion of the weather, and are managed, among others, also by the forester and by the head forester, who have to count the trees: This one falls, this one, too, and this hand here drops tomorrow at the latest. Suddenly it is noon and evening all at once. It snows, it flows, all water of the heavens' stream, and there is no coming into being that would not capture us: For us it means death. Becoming water. Thus, we would rather send others into that bed where they must become water, or optionally, as in the case of an excursion, our offer also includes ash. Big cause, small rest. The day's blue is extinguished. My God, why did you also leave me now? Give me your hand, so I can put my little bit of mind in it before I lose it!

31

Evening falls, the inn's dining room has once again taken control of the guests' mood. The space is a veritable wrought-iron workshop for diverse characters, it even produces some totally new ones. Where else would they have come from, and in such numbers to boot? Heads jolt more restlessly than usual, as if a toy train were curving around the room, loaded with delicacies; necks turn, heavy shoes emerge under the nice waitress, they walk away again while her thoughts are still strolling among the clients, who wants schnitzel and who wants roast, who, yes, who wants the English sautéed vegetables with a fried egg on top, the dish costs 65 Austrian Schillings. Today the space is especially crowded. A batch of unusually quiet hikers occupies the unpopular table at the door where a cool gust of air forces its way in together with each new arrival: Not the right patch, the space gets added on by these new guests, so to speak, like a dress that's too short. And they also block the entrance to other newcomers. Those people don't fit among the other guests, but it's hard to say why. Though they also seem to be travelers, they have absolutely nothing touristy about them. They lack the ornaments of leisure, which the retired women proudly put around their necks for the evening. Some have equipped themselves with a daring ring construction through which they artfully stick their *Nibelung* treasure of a pure silk scarf. There are no children sitting at the reserved tables that were set especially for them, because the guests want to be amazed about themselves, how much new stuff they are still able to take in, as if for the first time. Because the first time around there was not yet as much knowing will that would have guided their hand on the trail map of their surroundings. Children look into their *Kinder* surprise eggs for a moment, until someone puts the handlebar of a moped in their hands, then their whole life becomes hollow, not much was in it anyway. Why must these nice people dress so urban here? Most of them are still pretty young, but all, men and women, are wearing suits, the women with skirts, excessively formal, some have even kept their coats on at the table, and their memory, which they keep leaving behind, must be brought to them by the Invisible Ones, because those who are visible don't want to remember anything. Not even if a transcendentist were to drill out all their teeth at once would they later want to remember such pain.

As to their behavior, it seems that the strangers did not want to wake anybody up, they are quiet, remaining among themselves, they put their heads together and whisper, clumsily, as if they bent over a TV set right at the center of their circle, watching an episode of *Ein Kessel Buntes,* A Kettle of Colors, the popular (erstwhile East German) variety show from which they had been excluded just before the show was stripped and cut to the bone, then boiled and simmered until the stock had become tasteless. Maybe this is the last episode! There, light: Somebody strips and knocks out the others in a glittery jumper. Things might go bump in the night, nay, explode at any moment in this variety show, for now voices are still calm and the bared teeth neatly crafted by human hand. Soon they will get their heads torn off for it, for the impact of these pictures gets folks all shook up. An MC shrieks shrilly, he fires off an old punch line that aged for two thousand years in deep cellars, though it can still get pointed if sharpened a bit, and the audiences' heads fly, hard and smart as one would wish, through the space, mowing down everything, they even bowl those over who haven't finished eating. Hahaha! Mm, mm, mm, mm, yay, yay, yay! Don't worry, be happy, everyone's in the midst of this sizzling entertainment, and the diners are all set, precious stones that wore off from mutual use. What can you expect from the neighbor? He can participate in the pleasure of eating and chatting, that's enough. Light spoils his plate, it's reflected in the grease, which also wants to have its share in the general contentment. The guests are blissfully cocooned in smells and fragrances and laughter, something somewhere gurgles cheerfully, which is in the best hands with us, if it doesn't come out of ourselves to begin with, tiny air bubbles, caused by the food, floating to the ceiling. Who wants to change places with us? Some headquarters might want to exchange us. We are completely entre nous, and where we are, there are no others. Now something outrageously funny is on so that the MC raises his arm to conduct himself and others, the audience thrills, roaring and screaming, it sways to the right, then left, then right again and left again, until the entire room turns into a parallelogram, shifting here, then there, at some point we'll bust the walls with the blast we'll have had today. Brewhaha! Now the musicians who played a significant part in our high jinks enter the thoroughly warmed-up tube, seventy by eighty or God knows how big (now all we need is to get shoved in there, too, and get a good roasting, just turn on the light now and then, in order to check how crisp we've gotten, our joints are the first to creak), and hard to believe that they can do that at all, and they only can because they've been scaled down to a fortieth of what's there: Now today's guests appear with their *Lieder*-singing mouths in front of us, also a feast not only for the eye, fast food, but homemade and finger-licking good, they know the recipe for success. *Erfolg,* success, spelled *Ervolk* in Austria, and now this jolly little *Er-Volk* stretches its arms out and gets its allocated History emergency kit. But if you think you can make those motley little folks disappear, think again. They don't get lost, for no one will allow them to turn off the box now that it's getting exciting. They'll box your ears for you and lead you back into the birthing channel, Austria 1, that first channel given to us to speak our mind. Today's contestants are also most reliably protected, just so they can once again invade this real, existing country, which you also embody after all, and you, too, exactly! Yes, I mean you, you embody it, and therefore it also embodies you, it made you into a body that has been glued into a TV lounger. Eventually you will be stuffed into a giant's mouth and chewed up some more, even if you will have lost your taste by then.

As a filling side dish, sickening and deafening songs are piled up on the diners, chops chew, hips grind to and fro on the brightly polished old wooden benches, maybe there'll be a dessert upstairs in our room, a contently slumbering roll of cookies. The fresh air endows our gentlemen with renewed strengths, maybe the land is so mean because it is so beautiful and loved just for its mountains. Other countries have to work harder at trotting out something, we've already got the mountains right here. One grand K-plus peak after the other, but that's also what they bring in for us, and that's why they pay off. We are happy with our modest roof, which can be up to three thousand meters high and some even more. You, wanderer, who will have been "presently out of town" here someday, proclaim it loudly that you have also seen us driving here! And then we'll have seen that we've been there already.

Knives and forks scrape screechingly across the plates. The spirit is as wily as the will, but it is not as willing. We now thank reality for its appearance and say good-bye with a mighty flourish! The tuba player plays unperturbed and convincingly, the others join in; the pack of beasts with their horselike bared dental-merry-go-rounds moves in, dangerously close to our box seat (even though the way across the screen would be much shorter!), they throw their legs way up to the upper story, aim, the projectile takes off, sways around the space, a few fellow citizens have woken up, and then a flash of lightning followed by a belter zings across the screen. Dagmar's teeth spark brightly one more time with their distress signals; a strand of hair whose white gold fights with a few Karate chops (over 18!) against the natural color, if only weakly, flies silkily, weightlessly (good God, that little bit of hair, it's nothing compared to the heavy case of the TV apparatus against which it banged earlier), as if it, the delicate strand, wanted to tear down the whole box all by itself, so that the angry spirit could finally get out. Outside, the flood is coming. It solidifies into fences and fangs, its tongue breaks like blood-red surf, which, rising, is terrified at finding its master in a Gretchen-pink lipstick and recedes babbling into the gullet, a process lasting only fractions of a second, a cinch for our Dagi, our seasoned ether waves surfer. Eyes strobe under the neon letters of a bluish eye shadow, climbing from the pupils' waves are those eyelashes we are already familiar with, blackish and stiff from fright. But what gets released here? The indecision of the German gaze, a judge's gaze that sees everything but does not want to look at anything and, in the end, will decide for something it has long decided already. Light tears into the TV diagonally, lightning struck!, a crack opens wide, the image perishes in its blood, it drowns, then darkness, radio silence, blackout, called a moment of madness. The people who had just seen the image blossom and even caught Dagmar's last bloom, she actually waved for help through the whipped cream of her dirndl blouse, and we didn't understand it but bit heartily into her, so, yes, those viewers are crumbling like burned paper. Only a few gallant gentlemen jumped up to step up to the plate, throw themselves into the fire, and even toss in more twigs to make the blood boil. But now these gentlemen throw their heads back and howl with all their nerves: Interference! The TV is dead or at least seriously wounded. Now of all times. It is always now of all times: twenty-one hrs—ready: forty-nine—go: fifty. The thick, soft snow has changed into impenetrable hard rain, and something broke in the onslaught of the flood. In the gaping ford of the conversation, which was caused by some folks streaming to the windows to look out, one can hear the murmur from the table next to the door by the urban-dressed people, well, they haven't been so quiet after all. They are discussing something, one has the impression that they have been secluded for a long time, but now they are dancing around right in front of their own eyes like a swarm of gnats. Those guests were the only ones in the room not looking up to the screen at the folkloristic strolls, and they did not shower in the spray of the medial dishwater either (and yet, no one's helping them, they drowned with all the others in this bitter aqueous humor of the TV, which is perpetually liquid, Holy Blood, people can watch how the miracle comes about, that humans are doubly present, one large, one small, well, now we must definitely get the lost ones replaced, doubly, triply at that! A continuous pleasure . . .), Dagmar's gaze hasn't caught the new guests among us either. Dagmar's pea-sized blue eyes have not grazed this group of people, they struck the wallpaper to no effect, and the pods landed on the floor. If glances could really hit!, evidently, something else is amiss here, because these people in their odd, outdated disguise, which seems to be meant for a carnival that will never happen, don't own any cars. Outside, in the parking area, there are only a few vehicles plus one, which is already familiar, everyone knows all the wheels and ways of those patrons who are prepared to do their duty. Driving certainly is a relatively simple way to get somewhere. But how did these new strangers, these stranger than strangers get here? And what will they do if there is another flood? A young woman in the center seems oddly washed out around the edges, as if she had been swimming, wrung out several times, and then soaked again forever in a water basin for so long that her colors bled into the surrounding fluid. That tank is bigger than the TV, it has to be! Oh, if only the TV could have human size! There's something audacious about this woman's innocence that can't be compared to the athletes' obstinacy—Athletes: they are those maniacs who lift the red-white-red ribbon in front of the avalanche barrier and dive through it underneath, letting out a cheer, throwing up their arms with the poles, and giving themselves another push, they race down while the barrier's plastic ribbon quickly tosses the IOU after them: Herewith I owe you a piece of life of the Advanced Class!—how this note and you can do a few million deep-powder ski runs for free! No, the lift ticket is not valid here. That is for you who race from here into eternity, amen! A small plastic hand reaches once more into the air, yes, it catches the eye: We are made of synthetics, this is how these people look, grown-up human oddities, who separated themselves as far as this, and now, after the long climb up, they want to have a bit of a breather before it's going downhill for them again. The alpine world has a big face and a massive body: the massif. Had the alpine world become flesh, it would be Jesus, who, altogether, is everything that flesh has never been but came to be: dead. It would sit here now, forming a human mountain range, where we would climb higher and higher and then be able to do divine downhill runs. Imagine, your words would become flesh like He, and just so you may duck under our whip, in case of an emergency, even apply for a residence permit! But the airy summits are not as on TV, where they explain to us that this deep, beautiful trait has dug itself deeply into us, as deep as a child's hand in its blanket or our honestly acquired laugh lines. I.e., this is a train that's left the station, namely, it's only us of all people who lived here, rented apartments, and ranted and railed against all foreign fellow citizens whom we avoided here anyway. Where our ski suits contrast with the sky, always a light trail bluer than the latter. I see, you did not anticipate so much precipitation here. Or you wouldn't have taken this trip.

A cold wind starts blowing, reality recalculates itself until it has become something unreal, and Frau Karin Frenzel enters ingenuously as if she were just coming home from a brief excursion. Since she had disappeared in front of the miraculous image of Mariazell and died afterward in a car accident (or was it the other way around?)—how long has she been missing now, her mother at any rate has tirelessly tried all this time to find that figure that is an inherent part of the unity of her being—it is high time now that she report back to the house of her hostess body. Mother will have mercy on her, she needs no miracle-working image for that. Strange, though, that all the other fellow vacationers had seen her all this time, one here, the other there, as she apparently wandered around, an unhappy creature among only happy ones. Only the mother did not catch sight of her, and if she did, she did not recognize her. Many a plate about to be served gets put down again in the old woman's pelting screams, lest it gets broken by her voice. This mother, after many years filled with rejected applications, has finally been appointed coach of her offspring, and first, she must thoroughly analyze on the monitor this new turn the daughter performed on the black ice. Mommy lunges forward, knocking over a chair. No motion in the room. Evidently, there was no negligence on the part of Frau Frenzel Jr. What does the old hag want now? Has she now lost it completely? Though one mustn't forget that also lying in this woman's hands (as in those of many others) was the decision over the fate of the *Volk,* over its living and dying in Jesu Christu natu, and she made the right decision back then, first dying then living, but why is she carrying on as if she had not seen her daughter for many days? Whereas everyone else had sighted her this morning emerging as usual from the waves of the woods, several times at that, in different spots. If that's not enough . . . . The daughter was even spotted at the dizzying scenic view to the Valley of Hell, also on the other side, at the raised blind from where one can admire the entire Snow Alp massif, length times width; of course, people don't coordinate their observations with each other (at least they won't make the effort on account of a Frau Frenzel, but they do know exactly when the show starts on TV and with whom), or they would quickly notice that every one of them caught sight of the subject at the same time at quite different places. We are not the police to investigate ourselves and our dearest guarding principles to realize too late: it was only a guardrail. Frau Frenzel made a trip to Mariazell, that's all. No one finds anything special about her appearance. She was gone for just a short time, wasn't she? Only the mother seems to have been blind to her child. People continue to play their parts, they exchange themselves because thus far they didn't quite like themselves. Blood for blood, they dock at one another, and stuff food into themselves and explosives into their letters, and when they forget to pull out the tank truck hose, then—one divine spark is enough—a column of fire whirls up that could downright burn them and thousands of others if they didn't quickly extinguish it, wine or beer, what can I get you, just in time. What do we need tables of laws for? We threw those from the Autobahn bridge! The diners would get their satisfaction if the old woman finally disappeared, she slowly spoils everyone's vacation, whose purpose it is to finally come out of oneself and not to be forced by others to look inside them. Karin Frenzel takes up a challenge: Light! Aren't these the headlights of a car shining at her? Coming toward her? Something dances boisterously on the windshield, the reflection of a very big vehicle that does not want to be left lying on the ground peacefully, even though there were attempts to bring it to a halt and down with bare hands. But no, the eco–light bulbs shine mildly and guilelessly. Utensils are put into service and spurred on to also attack the slippery, the slick, fatty body of the Ungraspable, our Federal Chancellor who after the widespread earlier interruption on the screen appears now on the Federal Bully Pulpit and speaks to our dear audiences. This Dominus Interruptus committed something unimaginable. He tried to govern this *Volk*. But it didn't do any good. Now it's raining, whipping welts on this *Volk*. The fire department has already been notified, but the streets are all gone.

Oblivious to all this, the mother stumbles toward her daughter and brakes before the poor quality of her appearance. Whoever might have produced this deficient piece of work, it certainly wasn't the mother. If only the daughter could hold still for a moment and be as she used to be as a child, her mother could take out her true treasures and pin them on herself. But the contours of this daughter, this old gal (what was her marriage all about anyway! The late Herr Frenzel had been torn out from under the wheel of a car, tasted and spit out again by the teeth of time, so that he could still get cancer, too), anyway, this gray daughter's silhouette in the stony-looking Styrofoam shell of her smacking, digesting body seems to dissolve, inexplicably, into its surrounding; its outer fencing looks so fuzzy, let's try once more then, without immediately climbing over the fence, to view her from really close up: Karin F. looks as if she had stepped out of a blurred photograph because she was afraid of getting worse on account of the degradation of firmness every human normally contains. The boat rocks briefly, attention, departure, the road spreads out before us like a dark intention, a lot of landscape lies around up for grabs, with the driver's piston arms in front of her, Karin rides, a quiet hive wherein the bees live, well, she just can't sit still, okay, whoa, it sure gets narrow up there. Why is the bus driving so fast? I hope I'll be okay! The road didn't want to be left all broken on the ground and took off all on its own. And before our eyes that unreal apparition collapses again. The mother breathes heavily. In the beginning was her word and her word was with God, but she demanded it back from Him because he did not keep an appointment: She is aware of her nourishing function, for the daughter, for the entire *Volk,* and that, mind you, for a thousand years to come, that is, an advance she takes a shot at, plus a few thousand shots of ammunition, for all the other people. The Nordic race must continue to rule here, and the birdsong of her daughter will play a major part in this choir, yes, indeed, the first voice will be hers to sing. Give me six eggs in a carton with those hollows, please, so that I can lay myself among them into the stale shell of a body, I won't be able to spread out too much there, I guess. Holy motherhood: every *Volk* must make sure to multiply, or in the end it will just be one single person, and as such he/she/they can't apply for any grants from the European Union, which none of us wanted the way it is. Blonds will be extinct in no time! We Germans and their related tribes do not subordinate ourselves, we would much rather put all others in order without having stood in the order line, we are not foreigners! We are always first. Every doctor can confirm that. We are the only thing possible. Woosh! Get this: We are the only ones sitting here, and later we still want to be somewhere else. An aging daughter was selected as the speaker for our tour group. Why her of all people? Maybe because she lost her figure? At her age there is the danger of such a gain, which, paradoxically, means a loss. This eternal daughter now rises against her mother, the seed against the carrier of its peculiarities, who else would she have got them from? We don't know the father. As part of a single-family home he simply disappeared, a two-step who simply walked away. All waltz! Squares, dance too! Circle to the left, make a turn to the right, like you always do, and all incompletes have become complete again since the Father's departure. Bliss in his eyes, he looks up into the heavenly skies, there's the beautiful figure of a serpent who was once his wife. The old crackpot's pate will crack any moment, but the pâté found its final form nonetheless—the father wasn't needed anymore: The form was overturned. Isn't this Papa sitting there? Hello, Papa! What have you been up to, taking a walk again? Did you take the bike? What are you saying? YOU ARE THE ONLY ONE WHO WANDERED FOR SUCH A LONG TIME? My father, the Eternal Jew? And those are your friends who've been walking with you for quite a while now? That's really nice! *Guten Abend gute Nacht!* (Say hello to J. B.) The mother recognizes her child, but then again, she doesn't. And this for the umpteenth time.

Having escaped eternity's workbench (a turning machine), on which something was wrongly set, so that now the appearance of Frau Karin Frenzel seems like something unfinished, whatever, that's how this woman stands here, just the way she is, in space. Her maker slams on the brakes. Something's wrong with this sentence, it isn't grounded enough, therefore it won't find an owner either. It wasn't me. But how does a human inhabit this earth? And how can they prove that where they dwell belongs to them? Caring if somewhat clumsy women jump in to separate the two women, to move between them. Because the mother starts to strike the smiling face of this woman everybody knows as "my Karin," and many men, their old ladies, and all their dogs know what they are talking about when soft fur gets ruffled by the needy breath of one's own blood and/or pet and makes everyone's hair stand on end; so the mother starts hitting this nice woman, her own daughter!, fist smack on her head, as if she first had to pound an ice track for herself to slide along that shiny path faster and faster, unbelievable that the sports channels are showing such crap without even cleaning it up afterward! This is not my child, shrieks the old woman in the highest tones but without scoring, and the tiny flames of the lesser Enlightened around her whizz down on her head, it smells from burned stuff as the holy ghost of the holy mother singed her hair, but it doesn't do any good. While some of the diners are already filling in their lottery tickets—among the minimum of six that must be right, they have never even got one in their entire life—while others feel attracted to the home game of a confused old woman punching her also oldish child as if it were a city map and, getting lost, the driver blames the map. There is the danger of the mother overshooting the mark by far. In the sky the serpent of newcomers still moves along on the access road, so that up there the gates cannot be closed yet. It's pouring. The mother tongue didn't get us much further either. She spits and kicks, the mother. As for the daughter, no sign of joy about the mother's zeal, which is devoted exclusively to her. She protects her face from the blows, but almost a little listlessly, it seems to me. Hey, doesn't she hit back now? No, but I don't see what you see.

It takes quite some time to separate the two old ladies. The mother's still kickboxing with her legs, she's got unbelievable strength, it takes three men and a couple of ruffled women to hold on to her tightly and keep her in her daughter's ties, against whom she angrily swings her stiff rod arms. There is much talk about peace and quiet, evening calm and nighttime peace. While the mother keeps repeating that this is not her daughter, she doesn't know that woman at all, said woman glides as if on ice skates along the wall, a torch race, the wind of promise rises, and the quiet people, there by the door, had asked for orientation maps to track their destined road. They must start one more time. This time for once they will win! And they have requested Karin to host them (but not toast them), to get a Führerin, who really knows the place, why shouldn't they also have their Führer, albeit a female? No people are more widely spread around the world than they, which does not mean, however, that they know their way around everywhere. A bell rings in the last round of the TV game show, alerting the guests to start with the dessert, and at a round table, eternal discussionists spread the cremation-lie to their neighbor to gorge on it, too (where do all the dead folks go? Not to us, in any case, can't pack them all into this space. Or we would have seen them when we picked up our new license plates, the ones that sound like cowbells, for our heavy metal–buddies. After all, those missing ones have moved around for decades. So, then, they would have had to come by here at some point. They did, too. But we can't possibly know everybody). Alright, so that's done, too. Hands raise, tired of this endless doing nothing! End of dream. Sleeping turns into a miss, waking into a Miss contest, and there is Hannelore, beautiful wife of megahit heartthrob Heino, or some other participant, purest innocence speaking from her face now as she looks directly into the camera while an old man is stupid enough to kiss her on both cheeks. KissClickShot. And that was a trigger moment of flashing the pictures one has of a woman and the miss-takes getting made. OMG, this old man pressed the wrong trigger and made a few hundred people sink into the ground. How on earth could this happen? Didn't he have the blueprint of a multilevel erection right in front of him: i.e., this marvelous long-haired blonde! As if she also had a bell hanging from a wheel of cheese around her neck, that's how resoundingly she can make her presence felt: just with her body, her face, and her hair. We are nothing vis-à-vis her and her melodic shades slipping unscathed through the folds of the world around her. Still, just from anger: Our strengths increase, but the outlooks fade. Because it's getting so dark outside we can't see the hand right in front of our—nonetheless still dazzled by something—eyes. Rain continues to fall and fall, forcing the earlier snow out of the way. All the brighter the screen with today's starring guest. That blondie! Oh, and her shores where the moss cushions grow almost as beautiful as on Lake Constance. We glide beyond them to the pasture, into rapture, but we must move on, toot, toot, chooga, chooga, big red car, to which our stars Claudia, Dagmar, Brigitte affixed another shiny star that is still rising: that joy to the world and this star knows only the grace of the double airbag so that even in our death, a blown-up blimp may drive into our bodies. Others die more quietly. We get in, safety plus speed on all streets, even if we don't know where we are going, because the eyes of the deceased get closed on principle, unless there is no time for it because they come in such masses, like water, and there is simply no way to find out which pharma firm to drive to with the ocular organs. Life plans get cut short because you want to take a shortcut at an intersection, but unfortunately that turnoff was not on the map. Calmly and friendly, their eyes, like children's set on a fixed point, where fun and games are on all the time, as if that were all that ever existed, the gray people are rising who have been robbed of something by a gang of puny pickpockets, those grayheads who turned out to be the big mass murderers, THE macrobiotic gassing pros per se, who, with their biogas threw the world out of its rotations and the trucks and trains off their routine routes and tracks with the scenic views and then let it all run in reverse, so to speak. In truth, they were dwarfs with high-voltage cables improperly installed in them. If their power failures had not crushed them years ago, who knows, they might have shown everything in TV's muffle oven (as a preventive screening for the healthy, how they must never look), which can effortlessly devour several hundred people per second, no need for an engineer's expert opinion on how such a thing can technically be possible. There, folks turn up and disappear again as if we had a factory that makes us new ones any time. How to tell our children. They are now in the sand, playing. And the children of the dead? They wander, a different, grueling desert sand, and get raked, weighed, counted (if not quite accounted for).

32

The dark water in the basin carries a rich load as if a whole chunk of night had dropped into its heart. And now everything, everything except the black water pane, gets covered by snow, this new, bigger load, which can be deadly for this land that is discontented even in its sleep. It could suffocate under the blanket. Helplessly, the forester kneads and wipes off his hat, squinting his eyes against the blowing snow. Yesterday a bear stole the deer's turnips from the feeding site. If he dares to do that again today the forester will pop him off, just you wait, an eye will burst soon enough. But for the moment the forester has other worries as he must confront the woman who takes place here—that's the only way to put it when someone you never longed for is not wished for today either: he could avoid her, of course, but something as mystifying as this lady, whom he apparently (thus not at all) mistook for her twin sister, must be found out, maybe that's the only reason the hunter got out of bed so early this morning. And the closer he gets to the figure at the basin, the heavier the snow is coming down, as if she attracted him with snow: the clouds just had to throw off their load right here of all places, where one would need better light. If this snow changes to rain, Lord, have mercy! The surface of the land will overexpand and tear, nature unfortunately does not limit herself to the place assigned to her, she always has to overshoot the mark we set up for her by building houses in the place they must not go beyond. Hey you, lady, is this a dark intention lying next to you, or is it just your shadow wanting to go it alone for once? Maybe, the hunter thinks, the pride written all over this female face wants the fall into this basin, and he says: You'd better not bend over so far! Or you'll fall into this ice-cold brew. Whoever might be washing himself in it hasn't changed the water in ages. Blotches dance boldly on the water, where do they come from? Pride wants nourishment and love wants clothes, that is, that all too often we want to seek shelter in someone else's skin, but more often than not, that one doesn't suit us anymore. The forester, almost losing his footing, wipes, somewhat crudely, the wet snow from his eyes, but some of it immediately gets stuck again on the thick brow pillows, the flakes burn a bit on the eyeballs, really now, who would voluntarily bathe his face in diluted vinegar, the forester's beard has already turned white as well. The snow falls so densely at the water's edge that the water, smooth as it is, as soon as it appears, will instantly fall from its shoulders. I am afraid the innocent bridal gown will then be taken off against its will.

A coincidence does not scare the forester, but any appearance, even if expected, as he expects every day his sons to appear up there on the road, can bring its own particular terror along with it. As if you stood unannounced before God's face without having washed your feet, even though they waded up to their ankles in other people's blood. You are not clean, simple as that, because on Holy Thursday you were not admitted to the building of the Pope, who was supposed to take care of the foot washing, but maybe the Church will still change her mind. Be honest now, lady, standing there, did you get off the minibus at the last moment because your mother, the epitome of an undemanding nature, tormented you to the bleeding point? Or could it be that you are back already? Your group is expected only late at night! The hunter takes one more step forward, opens his mouth to ask her, the woman raises her—what seems like veiled—head (what is this thing in front of her face?) and shows, somewhat undecidedly but more distinctly than before, her teeth in a smile, or rather a grin, her flesh shimmers almost greenish amid the whiteness of the freshly fallen snow and the wetness of the melted snow on her, no, it can't be—the eyes are closed and still she can see! She is looking at him, the forester. Her gaze is hidden under the closed lids, but the eyes are open nonetheless, this is how it seems to the hunting man: She looks out from under the closed lids as through a curtain, and the veil is a kind of skin, a second birthing caul, so to speak, which seems to enwrap her entire head (for a possible rebirth?), or does the forester just project eyes into this eyeless face because her look-seeing would not be possible otherwise. This face has no features whatsoever, and still one knows to whom it belongs, this woman is peaceful through and through, or so it seems to the forester. If he were to lose his face, he would certainly run and look for it. But as a voiceless, lusterless sun is rising, enwrapping this female shape, while snow keeps falling and falling and falling, this fog-shrouded face smiles at the forester, even though such a thing can't even be possible. Had this man mysterealized his children like this sooner, he might have found more in them than now, in this key without a hole, in this keyhole without a door, in this door without a house, at this somnambulistic roost with a liquid face (maybe because of an infestation of *Pseudomonas* it had to be pasteurized like all the other milk cartons and eggs?). Here now is the critical point of the precipitations. When the snow turns to rain—the temperature lies exactly between the solid and the liquid, the here and the there, the one and the other—we'd have higher peaks here than a few rivers, which can at most use the rain for decoration, are prepared to absorb, this would be the sixth giant wave of precipitation within a few months, and that is too much for all of us. The forester is unable to face all of this, or is it something else he does not want to confront?, whatever, he slaps his hands on his eyes so that he won't have to see this woman bending over to scoop water. Does she really want to drink it with her nonmouth, her desiccated nothingated mouth that tries to suck itself full with the powers of the waters? Meanwhile, the young crowd listens to the music they like, and indeed, their young skin consists entirely of tiny ears. And they are singing and tapping like they like it to the music they like, those young ones, because their skin's also got tiny mouths all over (B.). They power themselves with fuel, the young, they do it, as mentioned, via eyes and ears. But regular water can also be used instead, as nature is proving here, having enlarged its drainage area, whole vintages of water are collected and drained off here. The old, moss-covered retaining dams with the soft gravel banks in front, which on dry days look as if tame animals had just rolled around in them, stretching their round backs languorously out of the water, those barriers are now groaning under the weight they've never had to hold at this time of year. It's quite an atypical course the creek is running now, because it has been diverted during its free run; the creek's bed, due to the storms of the past weeks, moved elsewhere trying to find shelter, so this can't happen again. But the weather easily finds the new bed to lie in.

Thus, something gets prepared, in an ice bath, unstirred, because nature, rushing downward, can't calculate exactly where she will fall and where she will land. A warming-down wrap will be poured down, and the thick snow wrap will change into a shrieking laugh track of rain that will laugh at all of us, indeed it will have the very last laugh, because at first, a lot of people and cars in weirdly thrown together clothes and colors will meet it, but less and less frequently, folks would rather stay home in weather like this, but they will also be recovered there. The woman at the basin pulls back the ice-cold, now-wet hand and, turning to the forester, asks him why this basin was built here and why it is so deep, even though only a part of its concrete frame shows from under the earth. Do you happen to know how deep it is here? Have you ever really looked into it? You see absolutely nothing, not even under the best conditions. The water could well be five meters deep or more, you could easily lose your gaze and eyeglasses in it. But the hunter has turned around already, his white face in the direction of the falling snow, and starts—slipping, panting, his hands clawing the ground, where he still won't gain a hold—climbing up the trail, just off and away from that woman in the foam bath of the falling snow! Who is THE SECOND *BEFORE* A FIRST ONE and probably IS NOT AT ALL! "I am the door" is the most that could be said of her. Snow is pure splendor for children, no doubt, but for older folks it can become treacherous. The forester slips, slides down some, gets back on his feet again, it feels to him as if the woman were pulling him back down to her without lifting a finger. Just stands there in her upright position. So there this father knows that the only thing he ever made were his sons. And now those sons turn toward the father, their faces absorbing the last of his strength, and now they form him, the father, by funneling all that water into him like a bundle of water fingers squirting around a cattle trough, sticks of waters, their route setters at least, which are already bouncing boisterously down the wooded slope toward the forester like gentle lambs expecting their birth at any moment. The high forest pulls up its flanks, stretching upward as Thousands of Arms that are too heavy for the ground. The forester wants up, the forest wants down, it is also getting tired, after all. The whole forest wants to crash into this lonely woman down at the basin and the forester, both of whom will have become no ones, no other ones, nothing, even before the forest will have reached them. An entire forest wants to come to us as the waterborne shuttle of our dearly departed because it could never really take root atop all those dead bodies, just as an infinite number of bodies could never root here.

So Karin Frenzel takes her eyes off the dark block of water. You are practically drawn down to it! But a moment later she'd rather not have stared into the water for so long, because what appeared before her eyes was far more impressive than that flushing cistern: The forest moved forward, and in her direction to boot! The forest army advances. The hump yards farther up are rumbling, couplers crash against couplers, let's hope no one ends up between them, the braking roots, pulled at and plucked at, are squealing, there is the rumble of loose walls that were apparently torn off their structures, their foundations, and she, Karen, must now wait at this incredibly huge, incredibly lively, and, at the same time, lifeless station until her train arrives. The road between is pulpy, dirty, soily, muddy, partly mushy, and not only is her, Karen's, train coming, all trains are coming at once, and the road seems to have hit itself, and one more won't matter anymore either: that other woman, wearing the same jogging suit as her, it has turned chocolatey brown in the meantime, is also waiting at the barrier, separated from her, Karen One, only by an invisible gate; she will leave once the trains are coming, or she will come once the trains have left. It makes no sense for our Karin Frenzel to speak to that woman now, as she watches, like her, Karin, at the invisible signal, which is still on red but soon will turn blue or whatever, showing the land's true color, and people won't pay any attention at first because they don't know that the train has left the station, but when they do see it, it will be too late to jump up, then the quiet will be overwhelmed by the disquiet that's much more widespread anyway. Whoever is not on it will be against it: for this train runs by the signs, the trends, the traits of the times. All aboard! *Achtung! Abfahrt!* And it still doesn't move fast enough for this forester father, he picks up the train, the traits, like toys and carries them down in person, he takes them away from his sons, he is a murderer from the beginning because his work knits, weaves, whittles undoing. No one can be saved without the Sons, and just as he carried their paternal traits down, so he now carries the Awakened—the sons who are lying in the earth, up the slope, while sinking into the earth himself—the finites away from the infinites, the goats from the sheep, from here to the beyond.

What's with you, treating me so condescendingly, Karin F. wants to finally yell at her adversister, even though she already knows that this other woman is herself, Karin, endowed with the same bad taste and the same, very tight purse. So there they stand, these two dated baby dolls in their Barbie suits, which our Barbie, the one and only, would throw aghast from her plastic hips, like a tarantula that sat down on her cool, smooth body, and finally someone has opened our Frau Frenzel's eyes that there are many women like her, and we brought one of them, so there you are. And all the while her mother had claimed the opposite, that anaerobic trainer of sick flesh.

But at least the gruff call out of Karin's mouth effected the miracle of the other one turning away hastily and running up the slope close behind the forester, no idea why he ran off just like that earlier!, now, look at that, her legs trip over each other, just like the hunter's before, her beautiful new jogging suit is getting all muddy, slimy; now Frau Karin Frenzel's gaze glides down herself and notices that she's also gotten dirty all over, so much dirt! A whole tree could take root in her. Quite clumsily, untrained, at her age she would have to do it at least twice a week, while also paying attention to the heart, work the machines, which will constantly try to hit you. In a fitness studio you can't just stand there like a great mullein, and always just plowing and harrowing the same gentle elevations with your sneakers won't do either. Karin instinctively straightens up to assist her *Doppelgängerin,* she even yells loudly to the forester to turn around and help the lady and thus her, Karin herself, one would have to get a hold of her, the second Karin, under the armpits or push her along from behind, to get her up the hill as fast as possible.

Who is this woman so afraid of, and what does she fear so much, Karin, the First, as in the First Austrian Savings Bank, which doesn't save us or from anything either. Why is the sky so dumb dumping all that water just at the moment you recognize yourself in your own sister? How can anyone, in all that wetness and slipperiness, get up a steep, barely trodden path with lots of wet, snow-trimmed, or rather downright overloaded grass growing on it? This wet snowfall is like a dance mocking you, because the dance floor is completely empty and still you must go on dancing all by yourself. Clumsily, heavily, ludicrously, without getting any respect from all the others, who are they, those others standing around the podium, laughing at you? Sure, you can live under any condition, but not at any price, and for the price of this outfit you simply can't get another one, much less another life. Everyone's looking at you, but not because you are so beautiful, and this second Frau Karin, who evidently is as unapproachable as she, the first one, is trying in vain to keep calm, holding on to anything that's coming her way, stones, twigs, leaves, branches. That's like waking up, seemingly indifferent, just before the end of the movie while the credits are still running, the doors of the theater are already open, and the dark silhouettes of the people, a pretty huge crowd, emerge on the same screen where the stars had just alternatingly kissed and beat each other up. And as they stream out of the doors, they fall over, those paper figures someone had cut out of the air rather randomly, but they fall all over us and we into them (our contours can be seen on the screen, and those shadow cut-outs on the scene run quickly over us and out into the Nothing), and now it gets really bright. Look, this very brightness is falling now as snow, an unstable element that sticks to the soles, stopping anyone who could accompany us longer than necessary. And Frau Karin Two does not seem to want company either. Her pigeonlike butt wriggles jerkily under the bilious green sweatshirt fabric as she heaves herself up the trail, constantly pleading for mercy, like a dish that is in a hurry to come up again because its mistress does not ever want to get fat. The forest keeps throwing the ill-mannered Frau to the ground again and again, and she tries struggling to her feet again and again, scrambling upward, and now, I think, she sprained her foot, her leg's been pulled badly long ago, she doesn't know how, she only knows by whom, and still, but nonetheless, she keeps running, she is running away from herself. Karin, don't let your head hang down! And not the ass either, stand straight! The body is not a glove that, if pulled off, still preserves the human shape for a bit in case anyone wanted to make yet another human in his image. The body loses its form completely once you take it off. Splat! Now she has even plopped on her belly, this doubled person, it enhances the chances of a companion for Karin One, who is close behind her, maybe she can overtake this person where she lies. But no, that one actually heaved herself up to her feet again, and now she tries it four-handed, on all fours, like animals do. Her hands, dipping into the snow, are getting ice cold even as they are warming up the snow in the same spots, but the air is warming up a little anyway. I can see it already, the ladies will never make it up into the forest to seek their pleasure, well, then the forest will come to them. Neither of the two Frenzies are still capable of seeing how cracks are now gaping in the concrete basin and expanding into fissures, a whole spider web of fissures, how a groaning sound passes through this *Wasserhose,* these "water pants" we call it (XXXXX large), and then, then it comes, the rain. For inexplicable reasons the temperature must have risen abruptly; some kind of current in the air, a corridor whose door someone had just unlocked, someone who lives here and therefore has the key, opened up to let in the friend, the incidental visitor, the stranger, and instead something is coming that changes from friend to enemy: warmth. Because of it, the dreaded snow falls as dreaded rain. It's plopping down on those two women who are now melding into one as the snow is also melting now, the basin melts as well (it makes a lot more noise in the process than Frau Frenzel, who lunges at her twin sister and falls flat on her face because there is nothing there, no woman to whom she could still tell something, even if she were an adversary: Women are often worse than one whole man, but who beats them beats himself because they can't be made responsible, they have tried to make enough of themselves, our Father in the heavens is the only one they did not make). Everything is melting. And the forest has its floor melt away under its feet.

The water falls. And the water whereinto the snow melts with lightning speed also falls. The thawing snow combines with the heavy rain that's getting heavier by the minute. During the two hours that this rain will continue to fall, it will amount to over 250 millimeters, at the Mürz watershed almost 298 mm. Those are 300 percent above the local average. The affected region is considerably smaller than those at the time of most recent severe storms, but in some areas the rain is even heavier. Along the Mürz River record-breaking measurements will be registered. But the drainage is clogged in many small areas because the obstructed, diverted riverbeds have not yet been cleared. Debris, tree trunks, roots lie around like dirty duvets and blankets, only harder. The riverbanks have partly been rended, just as the torrent renders any rendering of Frau Frenzel impossible, she can no longer be clearly seen in the dense, ever more wildly flailing billows of rain. All one can recognize is a mud creature who, at this time, is still trying to struggle her way up the slope, even though, calm down now!, the slope is already on the way to her. All this meanwhile unrecognizable creature (that's what you get from recognizing yourself in an innocent second one, who gets nothing out of it!) would have to do is sit down and wait for the slope, this animated underman, this comic, to mount her. Of course, it is, as always, everybody else's turn in the audience, because Karin is always overlooked. Where to, but from where!: The slope is coming and it will take her along. And she can be sure that the wind, coming up in gusts now, will sweep her, water, down, whereto?

33

All previous thoughts are floating to the ground and land hard: The screaming mother Frenzel's nerves collide with the surrounding alpine world, but also with the animal world gaping in the shape of mouflons, roebucks, steinbocks, elk antlers, and chamois horns from the walls, a circle of well breds, who watched over two thousand episodes of the TV series *Universum* and are even less able than before to understand the essence of what they were. The lost daughter, an average, less-gifted saint, whirs about in exactly the same air that also roars over us now to disappear in an invisible siphon. This older woman as a homeopathic pill, an overdose of it, in the air, one *thrown,* who gets pelted with apple cores and stewed cherry pits (reproduced as incorporeal matter out of an incorporeal passion, sent by who knows whom, the box lies empty and all crumpled in the trash, the label is no longer readable, this is the box HE had taken her out of: that eternally grinning TV chef who, with his blue scarf, his soul, hovering around him, is used to sparking such Frenzies, taking them out of their lonely folds to set them on fire. That one wants to surround people with the last miracles that can still be performed in this country and then, while they are already waiting for ALL THIS, restless, rootless, flambé them in a bluish flame. Karin! This little clay pigeon amid a gigantic dilution of body parts, whose particles, finely distributed across the room, sinter down on the diners until those matters, suspended in the executionist block of air, become one substance that would also love to vanish into thin air so that it can get into the diners' bodies on one side and out of them on the other. Anyone who has experienced this country's history knows, that it, too, went in one ear and out the other. Better if one sticks to food from the start, as we've got it here, but even that gets torn out of us into the night. And there it scatters so finely, so that the nature of pork roast and roast beef is no longer understood. Who took it from them? Frau Frenzel stands there rigidly in the air: All human matter, she. A God—as evident from the effect—created all this, and now he throws it up in the air before he sucks it up again to craft new persons with his pneuma, since the old ones were used up much sooner than he would have thought. A God looks forward to paternal pleasures. You just have to connect the vacuum cleaner hose to a different place on the device and he'll blow us out—dirt—instead of sucking us. The lights have gotten weaker, they took in the sight of us, and it made them sick. And then they gave birth to something? They birthed fruit in our image that attracts fire from all sides, but they can't be our fruits, for those have been raised in the freezer. Cold and half-liquefied, nestled in vanilla ice cream, they lie on the plates. Irrevocably: Folks melt away! But new ones will surely come after them and get them.

The edges of Karin Frenzel's outskirts seem more and more alienated, but also more and more composed, all in all she is a conglomerate of body and psyche, that which we call our Right(s) we insist on and that which we call a Left, which we punch in the faces of others, when they least expect it. Then we take them for a ride. Their God, the God of the diners, who has exclusive representation of those Mercedicks in human shape here, in this province of the old double-tongued Ostmark (i.e., the Führer's Germanianized Austria and the former East German currency), it was He who ultimately created everything that came after Him in His image rather than that of its original inhabitants, spurred on in secret by His mother (please remember: This Mother of God who made Frau Karin Frenzel disappear right in front of her, so as to put her own warm breath in the former's measly spot. So that Karin's mama can see how humans can be made and made to disappear again, all in one go, but this time the right way!), this is why they call him the Creator, also the Motherfather, the Fatherless, the Demiurge and Father: Father equals Father of the Right, Demiurge, however, of the Left, that is to say, of material matters. I am convinced that the latter will survive in our markets, the Ostmark turn into the DeMark. There, a cheerful glow because this brightness is subservient to Karin, emanating from this floating apparition! The Mother of God, she-boss of all us mothers! The terrestrial mother Frenzel covers her face before this swirling blaze, this pillar of fire in the middle of the room. This does not apply to our dear guests, who are eager to see such a spectacle of alien uncanniness, and the ticket taker is already here: How a mother can fill her own daughter with panicked horror will be shown in today's evening performance. The light bulbs in the heads of the supper guests are lit and are, of course, a nuisance, too much light, the TV screen, where the rolling title appears above the caparisoned Dagmars and Co., shreds of whipped eggnog froth still sparking from the crowns of the Wild Hunt that storms off after Joki or Hias or whatever's the name of that croony, end the show, one more close-up, please, one very last time!, and now it happens that all of a sudden our spectators light up, too, well, what do you know!, the bulbs in their heads are getting quite trusting now, and at the signal from the screen they leap in, because the celebs have finally exited; like friendly dogs, all those lights jumping hither to retrieve something of their own lives, each its bloody piece of prey. Yes, here something is finally put on the table and exposed. A draft of air rises, the cheerfulness has suddenly disappeared, the commercial follows, and the uncanniness dives in and starts its free, chilling run.

Poor confused Mother F. shrieks like a thread that gets a screw drilled into it that doesn't fit in size and threatens to burst the entire formation. A sharp wind leaps through the window and times the time that, caught, stops. Trembling. Then the tape in the projector jolts, an uncanny pull forward and backward at the same time, what will it opt for? Will it go on or will it go back, or will it tear? Help! The sound is too loud. Follow our rules about quiet times! Don't flare up here, if you please, Old Mother Hubba, where so many dry substances are stored, who for their part, still want to be extinguished with countless cold beverages. The clothes have long stopped crackling like arid underbrush as the guests have pampered themselves in elastic synthetic fabrics or have let only all-natural wool or real dynamite stuff get close to them, soft fuzz, noses that nudge them in a friendly and expectantly way as to what they came up with this time. We'll quickly get a few more people ready and good enough to eat. Where, for example, will we hurl this elegant new human part that goes so well with the plaid skirt, but also the midnight skirt of hot herringbone tweed? After all those debts that humankind in our gifted twin countries, which look as much alike as one Karin and the other, has incurred, it no longer wants to press its judges' robes closely to itself to avoid brushing against anything when the candelabras with their blabbers are aimed at them. After all, the chandeliers only want to put all the guiltless humankind in the right light! Even though the bodies have not learned to chime like bells, they are still allowed to show themselves, or aren't they? Whether these ladies' Lycra slacks can now be ordered in red, green, yellow, or charcoal will be primarily determined by the figures as well as who will be defeated and taken off the board.

Steaming from all those folks in a stew that she, after all, didn't cook up herself, the young server enters, and now she almost would have thrown three portions of food like ropes in people's collars and around their hands. At the same time a spectacle of nature attracts much attention: Outside there is incessant lightning. A heavy thunderstorm. At this time of year! Maybe this, too, is art. At any rate, the waitress—the sensitive type who always senses where not to turn under any circumstances when the fried liver is all gone and doesn't dare to return so late at night—suddenly has empty hands, at which she stares aghast. Creatures have seated themselves in this room who do not belong to her station, but not to anyone else's either, they are also out in the hall, right next to the door, where normally no one wants to sit because there is such a draft. Chance customers who don't seem to find their chance, walk-in guests, not planning a walkout, but apparently set to stay. Strange bunch. Never seen before. Feet shuffle. The will must play a part in our destiny, but whoever delivered those forms must have been a lot wilier. Let's ask the girl: No, no, she doesn't mean the new guests. Back there, in the hall, something was delivered, apparently frozen, because it's steaming like a foggy brain. Over there something lies around, which at the same time is an embodied lack of presentness, but you will love it! No, she, the waitress doesn't know: But maybe the new guests brought it, then they better take it with them ASAP. It blocks the way to the exercise bikes, right next to the sauna, where the geezers work their butts off, quite a show, until their number is called again because they could not hear it the first time.

So the vacationers vacate their tables, albeit reluctantly, and stream out the door, a rapid stream trying to squeeze into a bottleneck. No one can bear it any longer in the dining room where this old woman still considers herself important, making a racket for ten, trying to pull the Other Side on a rope over to them. A strong wind has also risen, curious, sweeping along more piles of clouds it then destroys with relish. All that water gets dumped on the ground. Next the wind bears down on a car parked for two days illegally and irresponsibly, the one that for so long could not be opened, not even by the police, but now seems to stay open for all eternity. Its thickly fogged-up windows start to clear, even though the car no longer contains any secrets. Where, pray tell, did the current temperature originate, and why did it come to us of all people, to annoy us? A candylike sweetish odor rises next to the reservoir, dusts off, and stretches, somewhat tentatively. Who raised you, rousing woods, so high up there? Immense amazement is available to you for nothing before we consider and conclude this meal that will consume us. That's what it says in the brochure, something like that at any rate.

More and more frequently now, this wind lets out intermittent howls that sweep the sky in thick, billowy gusts, brushes over everything, a painter of living things who take the life out of him in turn. Beaming, more and more people are still appearing at the reception, leaving their suitcases with their cute foreign name tags; how small and colorful we are, yet our imprint might not have the slightest chance of remaining in the water that's pouring down. Yet, like these torrents, we hunt in a pack, those sharp wolf's teeth we've got from all that sweet lemonade, which took the last sheen from us. The doors to the lobby fly open with a bang, a secret, odd joy comes over the rushing crowd who, at the last moment, snatched what was left on their plates, stuffing it, already on their way, into their mouths. For your return home from the event, you can take the bus, as the agony of gluttony begins to creep from the guts to your limbs. There, next to the peasant baroque table, someone who presumably realized the necessity of *becoming* (how should one realize the presentness of a God if one doesn't even have a *Volk* that wants to search for him. The *Volk,* one bygone, who no longer owns its body and its history, has sadly disappeared, it slipped through our fingers. Unfortunately, I don't know where it is now) and also has a sense of humor, has laid something down, which seems to have grown over his head. I can't believe my eyes: Lying there are packages of human size! Cocooned shapes. Gigantic pupas, wherein insects might already be getting ready to hatch, there is already life in them that still, however, has to crawl out. For now, it is still safe and secure and here for us to procure for them once again. Who produced this life, such unfinished, unfit *being?* Where other folks have their hearts, we've got our legs, but we don't vote with them, we do that with our voice. We never did anything with our two left hands either. Nevertheless, let's get out of here! Human-sized lumps have been vomited here, pellets, hair, feathers, fur . . . stuff of an animal that had promised to be nothing but nice. And what kind of packaging material was used for those machinations? Stacked by the staircase, those larvae are cloaked in fibrous tissue. Let's hope this product is biodegradable when we wipe off the plastic tablecloths with a fast, furtive movement of the hand before we seat the awakened. The bodies of water are rising up against us already, they eat away our feet when we stick them in, and now these wild waters are even coming through our doors. In the last few hours white foam has formed atop the small village creek, bonded to the water. Chemistry. Remain seated. If it keeps raining, all of this will be delivered to your home free of charge: Fibers convoluted like brains (the cerebrum immovable like the Father, the cerebellum mobile, serpentine, like the Son), admirable like magnificent bouquets of flowers, whose genes were carefully cut to order, but we would still like to know what they consist of, so that we can look up the antidote in the environmentalists' book. In any case, we won't throw them in the river or up into the air. Let's just eat it all! Maybe it'll help us digest all that human flesh. Let's open the packages and see what's inside them. Nobody dares to. This time, the live audience—"Applause Applause," our guests read on invisible signs that are held in front of their faces—appears instead of celebrities in the holy shrine, and it is now looking at itself, well, we spectators are actually the only ones who deserve to be protected by this screen. Walking out, the eaters hesitate, where is the hidden camera that seems to shoot them just now, how else would they be on TV, since it has always been their models who appeared, in whose image they shaped themselves by the dozens and as buddies of the powerful. The pattern book will now be opened once again to see if we are slated for production.

The book gets leafed through page by page, some pages are dog-eared at the top. Here you see the most captivating article, no, just a moment, three pieces of those shrouded larvae are right here in front of us. Communality begins to spread. If this is a danger, all of us are exposed to it. These shapes are just lying around, and thus the extreme edge of horror has been reached, I at least think so. Why then is everybody laughing? Could it be that these are supposed to become our scourging rods? Now look, this can't be for real! This contexture consists of some sort of hair. No, it *is* hair! Finest hair, a natural thing. But that long, Fräulein . . . it doesn't have to be so long that it jumps like fire out of this house. A narrow path forms between the crowd, and floating through it is an aging daughter. The insect mother has collapsed, that old hornet. Now even the dumbest who still need a wide-ranging explanation by those appearing on the screen can see what it is they are seeing. And in fact, everyone sees something else. Something is wrong with Frau Frenzel Jr. Her feet do not touch the floor, yet she is walking nonetheless. Swaying back and forth between the present and eternity, right on the line that runs through the center of the small lobby area where the postcards are sold. A nurse starting her job, a schoolteacher, a busy bee, sex- and jobless, the most ridiculed being there is, a tortured female Marsyas whom Apollo drove a wind, a fart, through the strings. Until the Austrian Radio and Television station's All You Can Eat–Combo, with Woody at bass and Herbie on the alto sax, plus dum-dee-dee-dum!, some old dumb drummer, forced God to capitulate and had the goose bumps caused by the sight of Frau Frenzel stripped from His back; and while they were at it, that old cow Karin, who just wanted to hear some groovy music, had her skin taken off as well and given to another woman. She is, after all, a distant sister of death, since she does not want to use her sex voluntarily, there is nothing more boring, while the tube, in which it is boiling from passion, incessantly buckles under the brunt of all those females of our fem. sex until none of them makes it through to the end, because there is none in sight. One, two, three, now we women see our forms (which thirst for a bikini's push-up grab bags and for Ossi and Kurt with the scissor hands, who clip that piece off them) behind this pane, and we also see all the way to our organs wallowing in love, turtles in the swamp. The mothers among us, those able human beings who made their bodies available for absolutely nothing in order to selflessly produce with them the property of another, look at the White Woman Frenzel lowering her forehead in order to have the cocoons give birth against their will to what does not want to be born. Just like in the movies. Those body barrels and those dwelling in them have already been made to feel the higher power once, mothers, wifelets, vixens, men, then all of them were called Abel and killed. Please, not again! Blood is moving, it crawls out between the capillary fibers that envelop the pupas and trickles into our world of wasps, where everybody, absolutely everybody has to work, except for the mothers, they rule, and when Abel was killed, they thought about it and initiated the birth of Seth, in whom they invested their whole being once again, the *Muttis.* Those salvation mavens. All they need is their own bodies, even the smallest among us can lay hands on them, at least to move them a tad, since anything else is unable to move them, the mothers.

Wow, now even the grass is blown away! The pleasures of their stay are over for these motionless shapes, I think, because a hand with nothing to it other than that life has left it, every drop of blood and all veining slipped out of it, so now a hand extends and tugs at this clotty hair cocoon. The forms are there to be unveiled, like all forms that matter. All our readers must immediately uncover what's piling up before their perpetually preoccupied heads. Every drapery edge is reached for by the hand of an auntie who got shot by the lead weight, every dust-covered fold is grabbed by a woman who is in the mood for a man, specifically for that Herbert over there, yes him, in the tight jeans in which he tries to hide in vain. So then, after all that murdering, we carefully chose our seeds for Seth, and that is why the young ones are puffing themselves up like that in front of us, because they are the line of choice, as opposed to the other line that has been destroyed. Off with those faded sky-blue of Levis, Diesel or Petrol is where it's at, the *Föhn* blows across the sky, and then it also blow-dries the hair through the appliance named after it because it still had some strength left. This young woman, for example, who, from so much listening to lightweight LPs, has an ocean of sound waves roaring around her head, which will soon be joined by water, if it continues to rain like that, water, on which the turntable and the little surfer—her brain on top of it—will hardly hold up, so this woman was asked in an extensive survey by this magazine what women first look at on a man when, behind the glass shrine in the organic products section, the line of God, the sex of Man, this man named Seth, appears in a case of Good Humor sticks or popsuckles: Love, you Nameless One, here is your label. I just have to sew it in, the brand name, let it be protected! The abundance of waves on her appetizing, fresh-from-the oven-warm body were curled for just one purpose, that the sex organ of the man Seth can be thawed and deciphered behind its inscription in three minutes and forty-five seconds.

Now a thread of hair gets detangled by Karin Frenzel's meanwhile ageless woman's hand, and already it uncoils, the ball of hair, the *Larve,* the larva, unrolls with breakneck speed around the longitudinal axis, first one, then the next, let's see now what this *schöne Larve,* this pretty mask here, had to offer and then to hide again! Quickly the flood of hair thrusts itself upon us, pops up—a launched lifeline—to the ceiling, swirls around the room, the fly of the son of the heavenly mother flies open, the surveillance camera, the one big staring eye of God, which kept close watch as to when this being would finally rise, is turned off, the eternal light of control goes out, when do we ever control ourselves, and there, the guests are coughing because the cocoon crawls into the cockadamy fabrications inside their heads, into the nostrils, eyes, mouths, into their bleeding heart (trans)plants: Hair hair hair! Religion supersedes nature, the guests hold up their arms before their eyes, but they can't see anything because they are completely clad in hair, the eyes, too, are papered with hair; here we go, a carpet as in the Middle Age(s)—it's just that nobody wants to get to that dangerous age—covers everything, and the three larvae emerge, Father Mother Child, from their sticky casings, well, that old cardboard luggage. All one can say about them is that their Creator did not know beforehand what kind of forms would come out, or, rather: These humans were formed without them having been known before. This native son, a foster-son of the Germans, in short: the Demiurge made all this visible without knowing what it was, and they, these newly enformed, don't even know themselves! Thus, lying there on the floor before us is the Naked Horror, are hardened loaves of bread of milky-white embryonal mass, two bigger ones, one smaller, horrific all of them, and everywhere that hair, as if it had been hurled centrifugally out of a cake mixture packed with human egg white.

The labor of mothers is worth nothing, so then we'll just have to help pushing the larva hulls away. But hold it, look there, the smallest is such a cute little boy. The petrified parents get dragged to the side with ropes, the mother's blue milk ducts wiped off with a tuft of hair, there is nothing else on hand, ditto the remaining blood, the fatherbody, suffocated in the position of an embryo compressed to a roll, a marble memorial plaque to himself (you can buy a package of seeds on every corner, but getting the eggs out of the mother is quite a job, let me tell you, the artificial human looks like nothing, I mean you can't see, with what scalpels, scissors, swabs and wads, knives and hooks he was torn out of the milk and egg ducts—Spittin' image of his dad! Though he only spurted into a glass. But crawling out of that horn of plenty was the SON, the WHATSHISNAME! It's only the result that counts, if you want to make people or destroy them again), unfortunately I can't read this inscription either. The glazed pupils still show the last image that the TV, the one and only valid outfit for modern man and woman, contemptuously threw at them. But we are turning now to the shining child: THE BOY. Small blood-rushes rise before him to the pilgrims, all that fallen hair has left only a very small place for him so that he can be handed to the hotel guests qua pilgrims in something like a bunting of hair, but on their hikes, they also want to feed swans, ducks, and daws, that's included in the price. So then, they throw their bread chunks into the pond, or this beautiful chapel that was created by the drop of several hundred tons of hair. The hair of the dead, a thick curtain, pulls itself aside to make room for the performance of the raging Rom. Cath. national religion, that's all the rage again these days. Mother and Mother

Mary! All leading ladies in front of the curtain, but you in the center, Mother of God: Still sticking to your cookie face, in front of which someone is always chomping, crumbling, and goofing around, are a few torn-out, dark skeins of hair, marbling chocolate-like the biscuit cheeks, where they cover the raisin eyes a bit. You papal puppet! Now I will personally move these hair floods to the side, this MOTHER has been secretly slipped inside the Creator without Him noticing it so that she will be sown into this material body and—born and grown inside it—become the word no one wants to hear anymore: THE PLACE IN POLAND. Oh God, let's stuff a whole convent into it right away! A church! A chapel! A cathedral! Nuns!! Schools!! Hospitals! More nuns!!! Quickly replace the Murderers of God with the Mother of God! And what came afterward? Memento mori: Jean A., Sarah K., Primo L. And furthermore, the pneumatic, panting Mensch, illuminated by TV, that is his own mother whom he, from now on must beat inside himself, and likewise his playmates, the former in flesh, the latter pulp (might as well call them playing cards, which we can beat without making them bleed). This child here, still in the swimming trunks of the pneuma that's wriggling in those trunks and giggling about us, and logically, there is logos as well, the word, made of Lego blocks, with which THE CHILD already assembled thirty trucks, forty-five cars, and one gas station complete with father–fuel pump, with his soul babbling in Pre-Basic on the Nintendo screen: Hooray, it is darling Anderle of Rinn, one of God's many little representatives on earth, a student guide to him right here. You can also Google him. No kidding. He was fished out of the floods, amid the mumbling of prayers and the fumbling of elderly child abusers of the Viennese pool of Diana, while we pious shepherds (each of us a poor, curious Actaeon, who got himself from the costume shop the head of a dumb animal) have already been waiting so long to be picked up by a stronger animal, so that we can learn from it while it devours us. It simply can't be true that we are looking into the stream of events and the stream of this rain and recognize in the reflection: The wolf that tears up the Herr, the Frau Hirschel, aka Jelinek, all those little stags, is us. However, here we also call an idiot a *Hirsch* and that is us, too. And folks find it an outrage that recently the Most Reverend Herr Bishop has strictly forbidden pilgrimages to Anderle. That's why every one of the pilgrims needed to erect a little wayside memorial for the small, slaughtered child inside himself.

The Septinity of world rulers will look pretty stupid, those who monitor the press of the North American East Coast and all, all the banks in the country with one single pocketmatic camera, who drive the gnarly native ski firms into bankruptcy and then make us sign a bill of exchange that, unfortunately, never ever reached us: Anderle, they bled you dry completely, Holy Child, and still, you are back on your feet again, unbelievable! Instead of your intestines you seem to have wrapped yourself around the insides of a light bulb, bright as you shine, well, let's just call this a gutsy presentation. Innocent child, you, murdered by unknown perpetrators in the year 1462, in revenge for the Jews' alleged ritual murders of Catholic children, a martyr of the Church. May this source kindly reveal its content, and there you have it, on the spot, the Child, folks drop on their knees and stare: No, that's not on television! They produced it themselves with their own seventy-five brain cells, and it proves that we urgently need private television and private TV peep-show booths in Austria since the State simply is no longer able to give us such kinky ideas and then bring them to life, too, with the help of the well-known CRT, here meaning Catholic Ray Tube, albeit a bit flat. Television will only become private once everyone can arouse such a phantasmagoria, and I am sure that everyone envisions the same: this Holy Tyrolian Child, whose three drops of blood fell on the hand of his mother in the field—she ran back and then, instead of the food, her own child had been slaughtered, butchered, prepared, and served at the table ready to eat. Jesus, after all, this ethernal Christmess gift, has been playing it for the child for hundreds of years, the hay is already totally worn down, nonetheless, we still eat it up. And already a million times we have, hello folks!, eaten the child's flesh, drunk his blood. And so, such stories get invented, the liver, the gall, and the pancreas want them badly, because they simply cannot process that much human flesh without help anymore.

Horrendous things have always happened, and we have always admitted that they have also happened to us. Three hundred years countless pilgrims journey to Judenstein, "Jew Rock" that is, in the village of Rinn and imprint their faces on pictures of saints, I mean, they press their faces on the picture of that poor Holy Boy, Anderle of Rinn, whom they would like, if they had time, to crucify themselves some time, a point of honor, no one should be permitted to take that job away from them. We are the murderers here! Every Sunday we fight for this blood legend in church. The sheep are driven in herds into the sacred place, they roar and bleat, the knives zoom out of the cutlery drawer, each has bought a ticket for a child's fare, and the murders also take place at the reduced local rate. Holy Land Tyrol, here it says that, by the way, we also celebrate a new martyr legend, namely a certain Herrn Pepi Unterlechner, ex-Savingsbank employee of Rinn. He died of a broken heart after finding out that our bishop was awarded, right there in Rinn, a distinguished Jewish medal for his resolute action of prohibiting the Anderle Cult. This is a further abuse of the Holy Child, which, however, did not seem to harm him, for now he stands up right before our eyes, and stays that way. The rain comes down as if it had reserved seats for the Good Friday miracle, underscored by, no, magically overscored for Parzival's return, and must get there absolutely right on time. Although it is still six months to Holy Week! The Holy Child Anderle has packed his swimming trunks, also much too soon, no, he already put them on! And sure enough, here it comes, the water, that goes with them!

34

If we, quite matter-of-factly, take this open, empty car simply as a source, its doors do bulge a bit: looking sharply over the upper edge of the door one can see the indentations that must have been caused by a tremendous force. The greasy mist on the windows subdivided itself into small runlets that now form narrow ant paths through which one could peek inside the car if one were about twenty centimeters tall and stepped on the window's drainboard (one could also simply look through the open door most people oddly enough shy away from). Some don't see even the slightest trace of grease! Not that they are bad housewives, but for them it's all clear: So what. There's a car. End of story. The lines of condensation on the windows are steadily expanding. Water or a comparable element with similar adhesive force is running down, it gurgles as if the beautiful brand vehicle were one single run-off, but where does it lead to? Hold your head out, then it will drip into it, the psychic stuff, into your Christian soup that was made digestible with Mary's intimate Aroma seasoning. One can hear something ripple, whisper, and mess up the floormats. Grimy fingerprints rubber-stamped themselves onto the windows. Uh-huh, a desperate hand seems to have pressed itself against the glass. Bloody imprints are becoming more and more visible. What explanations can we offer for this? This country knows a thing or two about bloodlettings and settings for letting her children bleed. And suddenly blood (?) is supposed to be flooding this car as well? Why here of all places? Some dark liquid sloshes out of the wide-open doors. Rising higher and higher. And if the word of the saint, yes, if Freud himself wanted to return to Berggasse 19, it (the *Id?*) could even rock itself as a little boat on the waves he did not make, in fact on forty centimeters of water, to be precise, that's how high it is, and behind it you will recognize the panorama of Venice or another Mediterranean city on plywood: a boat shop! Yes, this is a boat shop (below Sigi's home). Terrific! Up to the human knee it is filled with water, this shop for sports-, family-, and designer-boats. Yessirree, this is what became of the mellow Viennese building wherein waves are now rippling because they want to become permanent waves. Look into your inside, there you will see more interesting and above all bigger ships sail away just beyond your horizon, before you even have a chance to ponder their precious cargo—hurry up or they'll be gone and must be made to reappear again with the nitro-thought-thinner of the former tenants of this building, *jaja,* keep cleaning! Like your car windows! There'd be room enough in this building to fill it up to under the roof with water because all the ex-tenants were sent off or, for the most part, abolished. Sigi and his Anny, also Lün, the dog, are gone, but also the old sisters of Herr Doctor, they were picked up, uncles and brothers, by that sinister breed, who pinned small golden eagles on themselves so one could see right off: they were as ready to survey the grandest expanses wherein to do their little business. The eagle symbolizes the measure for those to come, the length of the measuring tape is exactly one meter and ninety-three centimeters, it is short seven centimeters, but they'll come up with those, too, the black boots, in order to measure their more distant routes in the expanse of the later boat business. In case you don't own a boat, dear reader, take one of those idly bobbing up and down Berggasse, or take this car here, no problem, it just stands there anyway, take this car here and return it afterward, but clean! *Heil!* Das *Heilige,* holiness, requires a mediation of Jesus, to whom we sing a thing or two when we awake, because he stands for all of Austria, and in turn Austria steps on all the others it can't stand, who are not germs of his kind and are resistant to ampicillin, cephalothin, nitrofurantoin, streptomycin, and kanamycin to boot (In, in, into the woods they go and no Woody there to land them in his song; to read this, kindly lie down on the floor and look through a crack in the wood, that's about how low I sank): something stinking, dissolving, melting worms its way—gradually transforming the autobody into a wreck au gratin with cadaver cheese—through the doors and starts to spread outside in the grass. Everything is getting darker. Luckily time does not control our deeds. It is our secret that we squeezed eternity into ca. ten years and we've still got seconds as a special offer that we can expand into eternity if you wish. What has happened, however, is not a matter of choice. Now the water is coming. It cannot be deterred from its preference of flowing down the mountain. Unlike time, it cannot flow backward. Even though Berggasse is slightly sloping, the ground has been (spirit) leveled, so that this historic Flood could be filled in.

What makes him still think he is so healthy, Edgar that is? I don't know. He has long stopped thumbing through magazines for photos of him, where the memory of this young skier's body still lived on for a bit but soon got buried again. Many others have replaced him. They wear their colorful local costumes, those proselytes, those alpine sons—gas station attendants, gendarmes, the whole kit and caboodle converted into top-fashionists—hang out in their jeans in all shades of their splashy sportive slipperiness and attract our apologies for not getting out of their way in time. They teeter constantly on the brink of the abyss, but they never fall, because the angelic voices of the press floating above our suppressed voices hold them high up to the ceiling or drop them from there; they are what is foreign and yet so terribly familiar to us, and thus nothing can surprise them in their dark wild-life coats, yes, go ahead, take a good look at them, this is our reward: that these young men have been spirited out of their time so that they could touch down here among us, and speed is their elixir. Only God can make it happen that the *being* of these angels will not be here in the future, but He can't make it happen that He is not here whereas He is, or that He has never been after He had been here. So there. And this is why Edgar Gstranz is also present here. Because he is our God. Piercing glance, what's with the leg, it really hurts? And the right front door of the car is about to break its jaw, that's how far it has opened its mouth—yawning? Something's sleeping here. Beautiful like a thing, not a human, Edgar Gstranz, who crashed dead in his track, leaves the vehicle that does not belong to him. A bloody organic birthday-pouch complete with tennis racket turned inside out. In the car, which actually was not due to give birth, Science fully indulged itself, and reversing its natural faculties, this Alma Mater whose innate nature it is to drive—instead of taking all those dead under its wheels and then getting them a proper burial—has made them whole again. The backlight of history went out at this moment. Now they may move into the darkroom!, and the dead are back, as, for example—and more shall follow—Edgar right here, surging, surfing from an automobile back into life, and along with him thousands of tons of floodwater to keep him company. Because this bank of the Lethe River has been specially heated (and it now boils over, the thermostat was broken, I think: Our Herostrat stuffed millions of people into the combustion chambers until the Temple exploded into a shudder of sparks!) for all those pleading listeners, who look for nothing but forgetting to the beat of an insistent pounding blown into their ears by a walking man, such as each of them has also once been. The mothers in their bathing suits scream at their children, who still don't know how to swim and, shrieking with joy, splash about in the blood. They can't sink anyway, buckled up as they are in their mothers' three-viewpoint safety belts.

When the universal recyclist wants to revive the dead, that is, make use of leftover material, it turns out: Beautiful as not born of woman, the Church nevertheless needs humans, no matter where she gets them from!, the sportsman bounces out of his sporting car. An indescribable roar suddenly fills the air, and we top it off with an extra portion of two young forester fellows, who also yell: They form a group, a tableau vivant, representing a passing of passing, because they have returned like the weather, at least not unlike it. Soon after the snowfall the small snow crystals begin to change, they are losing their bite (teeth are what the dead hold on to the longest), with these abruptly changing temperatures this happens in the shortest time. Also, all the female blood flown over the years has been replaced painlessly by these streams of water and rocks that are coming down now to support the wild cravings while grazing, in case we don't want to give them anything anymore; the water must now make provisions for winter, when there will be more dead for sure, when the snow gets soggy, the snow binding dissolved, and the avalanche revanche launched. A wide stream of cartilage and albumin, viscous like magma—a urine stream, the waters of Styx—of bile and bilirubin, advances toward the clearing: the ice-cold birthwater of our young men who birthed themselves and thus started the process of gradual degradation so that their fashion photos won't show the vestiges, not even the shadow of their good luck cauls, pointed baby caps (theirs made of horn—unbreakable!), first-day-of-first-grade gift of giant candy-filled cones. Whatever disappeared in this much-discussed fluid gets fished out of it, and lo and behold, the truth it is not! The truth remains the eternally hidden, the imperishable in the crevasses. In the curve, white bodies are hurled out of the wreck, dark pouting mouths open smackingly above the faded denim-demiurge collars. Edgar—one of many young men who have been artfully wrapped into the puff-paste dough of their overseized sports jackets: with this last remembrance of life you won't rub anyone the wrong way, the stream points in the opposite direction, the truth pops like a cork out of the bubbly river of death, the body dwells beautifully in its mother with whom he is screwed, complete with nuts, on the cross, but he would prefer a better, most of all a bigger dwelling, at least one additional room beyond the ruling order of aunts, midwives, and mother, called so aptly straight from the *Volk*'s mouth (which knows women so well because it does not, under any circumstances, want to be one) Federal President, Federal Chancellor, and Federal canceller. But Edgar lost the election. Under the stream, Frau Gudrun Bichler, under the lair of the hong, no, under the hair of her thong, gets up one more time, reels round herself, a felled tree trunk: illness, her innate *being*, is history now. For Gudrun is long dead. And now she charges like the bull at the gate, riding along on a few thousand cubic meters of earth and rocks like Münchhausen on his cannonball, the ice-cold, pointed nipples now erect rubber plugs and, like suction cups, pointed at a few gents, who just got themselves their hot dish from the cold buffet, mainly scrambled eggs, a breakfast dish, lettuce-garnished, pepper-dusted, a holy grail, the wound in the egg sac can never close again because a few more eggs will be removed if the first ones can't lodge themselves there and make themselves at home. Or, if ready prematurely, they are killed. A woman is just getting anesthetized for the egg-donation, while the Rom. Cath. Holy Host(ess) lolls, content, white, disgusting on its bed of salad and red-hot Marika Rökk Hungarian Paprika stripe. But the gentlemen act as if they were taking the little bit of life for their cold coffee from the cream dispenser (even though the lives of but a few are all peaches and cream!), and here we see the first results of artificially reproduced humans who are to undo all the dead right in front of our eyes, in our case they are Edgar Gstranz and the two forester sons, we just discovered them, fit as to fiddle, in old family photographs: Their childhood up in the mountains—that surely was a happy time. In each of those we can instantly forget hundreds, thousands of dead, that is how new, how unscar[r]ed they are. Can't take my eyes off them. Oh well, we can forget about the dead anyway! My Tyrol, I miss you wherever I am. Even from the most beautiful places I am always drawn to you. Panting and puffing, a champagne bottle flies against the *Bug,* the prow, and the Bug River and against the Don, and, for all I care, against the Ob, the Yenisei, and the Irtysh. Oh, Women's Fashion! And sticking in it up to the neck: those overlooked by la mode, those light, wearable coolers for camping, among them the old cow Karin Frenzel, in whom belonging, permanence, the impertinence of the female sex ripens no more, at least she can no longer launch her eggs. Some of us are rather thought of as sisters, accessories, confidants. Our breeding, our breed stands bridled on Graben, in the heart of Vienna, my!, the way those two trot. Here they come, the apocalyptic horses in front of their original Viennese *Fiaker,* the coachman and his carriage! We ladies are completely different when we dress up and also when they cut us open: There are those who've got it and others who haven't. The knife bores, we have almost too noble notions of woman!, into the yolk, who among us wouldn't choose fertility? If only it didn't involve so much work. Why, yes, absolutely, the female, the hen, just take a look at her, is already dead beat the way she looks. This is why men prefer picking up their children at the buffet. He who has produced so many dead doesn't care much about making life either. It's the same process, after all, just reversed: Time passes in and of itself, uniformly and without relation to an object. Making children, doing away with them—all the same. The masses crowd around the white-clothed auto-psi table, they walk back and forth animatedly, wink vainly into the next dimension, into the dimension of the many Ks they'd climbed or spent already, history runs backward faster and faster, the Angel wades forward in garments soaked and washed in front of the camera with Ariel Ultra detergent, and we, the victors, scrutinize each other with freshly washed, soft-rinsed glances as if for the first time. Were we conceived by pure German-blooded people? Or, second best, were our mothers already dead when we, her children, were born? Yes, you can also choose this option here with us. Today's special! And there someone is shocked by the large amounts of bread thrown at the lobster's icy claws and the trout's shiny scales!

This young politician here, yes, this one with the career crash with death, presents himself to the needy; the blond, blue-eyed ones, who will have known nothing, absolutely nothing, they float under the ceiling, amateur pictures developed, enlarged, and crumpled up in two minutes, and yet: we must bend our heads backward because those champs are high up above us!

Anyhow: That swell Herr Chair, who, wrapped up only in the laws of his scarf, flutters about smiling into the objective that's been determined by him and is therefore vain, vile, and valid, he invited us today. We eat now and don't pay, not even later. You are welcome to bang into your boots today, Chairman Jörg, they don't fit us anyway, they are too big for us. Regulations nixed. And here they enter one more time, the Russian tap dancers, those with the beautiful blue eyes. And then comes the kick-ass German footballing club, which may also perform its routines again so that it can pull us along, even though we'd rather be campfired up and singing Viennese songs! But we'll also have plenty of time for that later, we, only we, after all, are, like God, situated outside time. We can grasp the future and the past at a glance. But we don't want to. You only have to turn around, *mein Herr,* and there they are, the deceased, here, in the bed of the river, banging their bishops, sperms sparkling all over the place. There's no denying it, the pitiful old family photos of those insignificant deport-, uhm, departed, are still in our hands, as we are now discharged and, fortunately, directly into the water. But there is nothing to see in these pictures, not even on which side we've got our spine. The rest is silence.

Today Herr Gstranz wears a hot off-the-shoulder T-shirt with extremely large armholes, so that he—shed it where shove it is due—lets you see much more of him than he's got, the top bares him for more comfortable breathing, but Edgar whips an erotic current of about a hundred volts out from his sleeve stumps, that fills exactly half a socket. Even this last bit, but absolutely the very last, he took away from the women. And now this Edgar, who exposed himself so cockily here with his tennis racket, has become the only place I want to go to, but it won't take me, so I'll just follow my tears and the brooklet will carry me away. But meanwhile it's gotten so big, it's turned into a flood with white-watered fangs! Who, like myself, belongs to life's fall collection will soon, like wilting leaves, get fanned into the air with a single movement of the hand and fall, a bad hand, with unbuttoned dress into the darkness, where the earth will collapse all over her, all of us. The clotted bloodstream of the sentenced is thinning, the terminal moraine with the last few cartilages drags itself a bit farther through the grass that straightens up again quickly behind it, the flesh miraculously gets back into some shape again, the torso, the Gestalt of the Golem, keeps growing, the mother wasp, the insect queen, the femme royal (I think it is an Audi 80000, or was it an M-series BMW?) sighs with relief that she finally got rid of her freightilization, even though her interior now needs a complete body wash with shampoo, even this tennis racket is baked into the Placentubex replenishing cream, which was made out of the gentleman driver, who had just sat in there, by way of pneumatic conversion, and what became of all this? The demiurge Gstranz, one of the ultimate, frequently injured Austrians, who almost won the prepenultimate Hahnenkamm ("Cockscomb mountain" in plain Engl.) downhill race. I mean: He simply couldn't have won the cockscomb! Because he didn't know the things above him, meanwhile he at least knows the things below him. Because he stayed in the ground for so long. With his two Trabis—remember those old East German jalopies, but anyway, these two were made from the dead bodies of the self-shot forester's sons and some pulp from newspapers—this newly released wolf runs off in a lean, sustained *Trab* (trot to you), and straight back into the earth again, or rather, this time it is the earth that's coming up to him! Note in our photograph the hair shaped to a sort of rock 'n' roll coif made of gravestone, no, not here, over there: That statue wilts! Did you notice the fatigue, the frizz, the *thrownness* of the arms through their holes like an arid, exhausted hedge? Beautiful marble figure he's got for a gravestone, our Edgar (it always looks better in a photo, doesn't it, where someone else sports it, the hairdo), while blue mold emerges from the cracked heads of the forester kids, from the craggy cracks and tears, so that the lid can barely close over their heads. And one of them even has to hold his left eye by the stalk, because eternity's constantly trying to lick it, mmhm, human face, come on, try to stay! Oh no, it's melting away. Some lines, sadly, are already gone when we rush breathlessly to the station, where the last judgment is passed on the fast food in an ad hoc court—there are simply too many speeding deaths. Rushing by, our invisible, silent companions are already going for the junk, right in the swing of their hurried steps, which must inevitably come to a halt, slower and at the same time faster than us, the living, they freeze past the midpoint of their track.

Not so the walkways here in the inn. There's still juice coming out of them, which will freeze pretty soon, that's how quickly it got cold. Whereas it has become much warmer outside, a thaw, the snow has melted, the causes of the soil breaking away are more diverse. The door is pushed open, and the folks, especially the card players at the door are looking at the newcomers, who, hands behind their backs, instantly start to run in a straight line and back and forth across the room, and only after a while it dawns on us: Some wild game has been set off and now it is all over us. It's got glass eyes and tags hanging around its necks, where and when it was shot. Thus, our heads rise and the immediate gets mediated. So now an athlete's losing it right here, and the very same board on which he came across the waters of horror slips away from under his feet. This messenger of God gets his gift of rolling emptied into a glacial groove, and there he licks it with great relish, multicolored candy sprinkles. The steep slope waits and sees it coming: Backflip, nose grab, wave jump, and hopp and hoppla! We children left home a long time ago and scattered all over the world, sometimes far away I close my eyes and cry for my Austro-Rocky Mountain high: The opinions about which brand one wants to be affiliated with are split into several camps. Try as hard as you want, it's impossible to remember the many names, the selection is nearly unlimited. And the lightning, the smashing thunder of this singular fashion by which a man in his drive for a boom sport plows through the snow on a board (in the summer over grass), strikes the reflection of the alpine fortress behind which she'd entrenched herself against disappointments: Gudrun Bichler, naked and cold as she is with her rubber udder and the vague invagination where the shit hit the fan, just regained consciousness for a moment. Now she howls and kicks with horror that she squeezed her existence out of too hot an athletic cannonball, and in fact it is so hot, this existence, that Gudrun drops it right away. Pure ray of knowledge, you walk restlessly back and forth in the den of this poor head. So far, we still know the top athletes are also here for us to learn from them, but in the end the pros will go it alone, namely to where the biggest bucks are to make a killing and get all others burned for it.

The student rises slowly behind the balustrade of the wood-paneled corridor where she took cover from the light of the big sponsor of eternity. She wipes her forehead offhandedly, had she fainted? She pulls herself up on the railing and peeks through the bull's eyes of the Austrian weathered wood that a merciful God, who granted humans the right of insight, created especially for rural inns (so that guests don't have to walk down the steps if they want to know what's cooking in the hell of the diet kitchen), skidding and gliding down there, now out, now in, but let's face it, always out of sight: Gudrun's new vacation flirt Edgar Gstranz, now rushing straight up to her. Grace and beauty in one person, what does he carry in front of him? He is an advertising medium! He looks after himself! A white woman floats toward him, lips pursed as if she held a bottle of blood-red nail polish between her teeth and sprayed it in an unsuppressed coughing fit over her wrists, from where syrupy red liquid flows down in a thin trickle. And this woman is she—or is it me: Gudrun B. Her skin is ice-cold, bluish white, and all her gashes are, like the goatsucker's beak, wide open, so that one can see she does not have a false bottom. No doubt there she is, our Gudrun Bichler. She turned up and, cool as a frozen field, shoed this horse Reality, whose foot must always be held or else it kicks, with herself.

For a short moment Gudrun is totally conscious of what is happening. She is herself, but she is stuck midway on her path because her body's wounds have not been dressed, and the ground, on which all of us stand, the mud, the loam wherein the dead are resting, had been turned inside out with great determination. This land wants to prove: There is nothing to the rumors that keep coming up again and again. Our past is simply empty, just like our wallets. Was Gudrun's life for nothing? It wasn't just taken from her but even given to another woman! Standing up is so hard. She tries, with only partial success, to get back on her feet, her head jerks, but it isn't she executing her movements voluntarily, she feels as if a fish were happily jumping back and forth inside her snapping at the Nothing on an invisible bait. She sees Edgar standing rock solid on his board making a movie about himself: "I am from Austria," the Austrorock-recycler sings to it, that singer who invented rock all over and over again so that it hangs over him like a bedside lampshade to mercifully hide him. Just pull the string and the *Lieder* singer makes his rockawieny music again. And meanwhile this retiree refuge that leads directly into the ground has been transformed into a disco whose job it is, well, to rock you. Weren't we just talking about a group of silent folks sitting at a table next to the door applauding with their upper bodies? Because in the meantime they stood up and pushed their way to the front, to the vacationers rhythmically clapping to the music, such good mood so suddenly!, folks who now put their self-assured appearance in the service of a good cause as well, because soon light will be brought into the dark by the beloved same-titled TV Xmas fundraiser, money spent, names and amounts will be called up on the screen, and when your name is called, then you, *meine Dame, mein Herr,* you must go like everyone else and spend yourself. The dead, after all, have also spent a lot of themselves. Walking can be turned into a show, as the sparkling staircase knows, over which Gudrun tries to move her bare feet. No luck. She got stuck in the wax. She is fucked. The screen is in a frenzy of fortune, as the names of the spenders are pirouetting on it. To a soundtrack that's getting even louder. Those urbanites in their old-fashioned suits, which somehow don't fit here, even though they, too, seem to be in a splendid mood: Go ahead, step, it's okay, there's nothing to dread, to the front, now you are permitted to invade the chambers of strangers, at whose doors you have knocked in vain for more than fifty years, that's the bet on our show today, ladies and gentlemen, even if you say that wasn't the deal. Wilfried and Hansi and Raini and Wolferl, the worst of the worshipped homeboys, I just now remembered his name again, it's the one who sometimes wears a colorful jogging suit on stage that looks as if a *gamsbart,* tufts of chamois hair, would grow out of it any moment. *Achtung:* Here they come! Howling! Thundering applause cue, bravos, whistling, okay, it's the last time, so let's be lenient! Austro-screeching in this Österreich-Ring (no NASCAR, but plenty of streetcars), where the pros no longer compete but even more amateurs mop the floor with each other, those fit to drive, just fit isn't enough for them unless they can throw one. *Achtung:* Hit and runners! We'll send you a first-rate Hitter again! And one much better looking than the old Führer with his beautiful hands. Our thinking can do nothing against our language that betrays our origin, *das Wilde,* the wild, it jumps out of the cage, whether the door's been left open or not, pops out like from a *Hosentürl,* the "door of trousers" to us—a "fly" or "flap" to you: so here it comes, our language, *das Wilde:* a *Fleischwolf,* "fleshwolf" (for what you call a "meat grinder"), a *Raupe* (meaning both "caterpillar" and "bulldozer"), which instantly tears up again the thing it just made. So, now the guests gather their gowns and yoke themselves into the shaft of time, none of them making the slightest dent. The light has hit them, effect before the cause, the space gets deformed by time, they storm toward each other, the guest stars, every one of them taking the view that he'd just won the room for himself. Compared to that, even the fellow who, by licking colored pencils, can tell what color they are is a poor sucker, because now the civilians, with their wandering hands and stuck-out tongues, are licking our downhillers, our senior women athletes, handicapped athletes who also got their spoonful of media medicine that made them even sicker because they had to let themselves be photographed next to a Styrian Oak, the later US Governator. Now mouths are moving to our natives' throats, and even those among us with just middling midriffs but longing, albeit lined faces are served their dessert, a veritable vanilla dream. For the last time they all bring their ear-splitting screeches, laughs, and howls all by themselves into the world, from where they pushed others who tried hanging on to the lifeboat.

The snow must go on, and today, ladies and gentlemen, it is your turn, the camera captures you, who, for your part, have not yet capeeshed the determination of this beam of light, which was born before you, still, it approaches you now courageously. Time consists of infinitely long, heavy whipping twines that are swung across us. Every loss ends at this moment and at the same time also starts again, because we've got them back again, our deceased friends, our dear candidates, in this room! Their long absences make no difference, now we look at them with expectant eyes, switch on the light of our blond hair, order the forest to be green, what the hell's going on with this scene, aha, now it turns green, the sun rises, a little more red please, yes!, perfect!, the screen is measured to see how many it can hold, and now some more have given up the ghost. The dead have the advantage of being dead already, well, so we just put together a thunderstorm and with it a mudslide of voices and barf the dead out of our bloody chops again, God and TV Gottschalk cheer loudly, someone has stolen our corpses, but the heavenly guests have already organized everything for us: Now they flow in here in a triumphal march, they carry chickens in their hands, eggs in baskets and bags, someone got a hold of five thousand farmers for the EU, where all of us are candidates, who are now streaming onto the stage singing peasant songs. This is why today almost every guest star has lost the bet, because everyone bet that not even twenty-five pieces of people would travel with their chickens to Berlin's eight-thousand-seven-hundred-sixty-four-seat Deutschland Halle. All dead, please get out now of your multifamily dwellings in Russia, Poland, and who knows in what other dumps they still rest inactively, and kindly join me here up on the stage. Totally incorrigible, the dead! Always wanting to slip in here with us so that they, too, can win for once. Well, for a start, this rising was already pretty good, let's rehearse it one more time, and then it's time to get serious, then we go on the air. Okay, you are now in the light, that means you are here and at the same time also gone, for this we must thank our sponsor, Müller Milk, several tons of this light, which, enclosed in small Styrofoam cups, we will now throw at your head. Praised be his name, I mean, praised be the name of the Lord.

35

In the mountains there are tremendous streams of materials that need only the ordering hand of an impassionate helper, who would never let himself be guided by preferences and aversions, to let go of their glacial drift, scree, soil, and their mud, all those goodies the mountains want to eat all by themselves. They did not want to give any of it to us. But now those mountains present to us—with a slight bow—not only themselves but also the entire surrounding. This is not as the vacationer envisioned it. That he, hot on the trail of a relationship to nature, does not look at her, but instead, she is throwing herself at him!

We left the forester to himself as he tried again and again—the new whitewater ditch, freshly dug up by the water itself with excruciating effort in front of his eyes—to climb up the slope and get to the street, while the dense rainfall, all that water itself, became a dam wall. As I see, the man is still crawling up the slope trying to get away from the ditch with its loosely layered scree, perhaps still trying to reach the safe street. There, he turns around a last time amid his own inner shoving and sliding: Down there, wasn't there that woman just now, her face a bit out of sorts, that is, it could not sustain the original vibes that once instilled youth in it, they slid off her, vibes and youth. The woman had to show her colors, her true face that probably sprang from a creature dammed up by the mother. Now, this very moment, as a crashing, shattering burst fills the air, the forester, who had thrown off his rucksack, who actually threw everything off so he could move ahead more easily (the dog disappeared somewhere, no one whistles for him anymore either), turns around once more, maybe he could look beyond life and what would he see?, maybe the hunter could extend his hand to her as the rain flies down like a mountain, but right there, where she just stood, no one's there anymore. This woman, beautifully outfitted in her colorful jogging suit, apparently slipped away. Instead, the water whips down all the more fiercely on the hunter, whom the deaths of his sons have already turned into a badly ravaged mass that could be swept away any moment and by any stress. Up there, those two roguish fellows—the man has almost reached the gravel road when he sees them, seemingly unconcerned, as if they were baking bread or playing cards. The sons. They'd never been this meticulous, not to say finicky, in life when they were told to do something as they are now in death. In real life they lived most of the time from the respective brother's cock to the mouth of the other. And these fleshy root bulbs, wherefrom a stringy stalk entwined in evening clouds of hair grows each of them, these rootstocks they now offer to the father in a faceless grin from the Punch and Judy stage ramp of the embankment. Here they are completely in their raging element, the boys. That's all they know how to do: killing the father with their own death, the father who, for his part, killed them already at birth! And the slope opens its maw, and the Punch and Judy crocodile, which seems to be all the world, no, all the woods, because the forest, the army is coming, reliable as the mail, toward the forester, who during his life idolized nothing but the forest, it opens its maw, the forest, and it's coming, coming, coming!

The nice round hiking hill with the masses of jungle on it lets them slide down itself now with a motion more careless than waving a fly away. The forester takes another shot at saving himself, but he ran out of schnapps. For a split-second his sons' white dickies (how small they once were! Hard to remember) offered two candles, two grave lanterns, light, or were those two bright stones on the brink of the abyss? Now the forest, forced by the elemental power of the search for a way out, marches down to the valley, it's coming, it's coming, and, coming along through the brand-new brook bed, where the old bedload, the layers of debris and old moraine residues are especially shaky since they'd already been disturbed in their sleep many times before, but this time at least once, during the severe storms of the past weeks, forcing its access to water and earth:

THE MUD. THE MONSTER.

The earth immediately gives up its resistance against the water and comes right along with it. The rain is like the guy who believes in God, he knows he won't have to worry, he'll get there one way or the other.

Like the bride of the wind, the compressed air storms ahead first. But suddenly the irrepressible force seems immobilized. The initially abrupt gradient suddenly sinks, and like an open fan, the stream of debris whisks, squirts, whirls apart at the exit gate. Oh, now the whole forester is gone, too! Towering masses of earth pushed forward through the narrowness of the new torrent bed down into the valley. The forester noticed too late, even though he should have seen it coming when he caught sight of his two favorite deceased relatives up there, where he didn't even put his seed and his essence, those forces came from up there and the forces of angels who may have once been active in this *Volk* of perpetually wannabe Germans and, rumbling in the forester's loins, at the very beginning, created these two humans who just presented their white dicks, as signs that they were the select sex, the chosen kind, as opposed to the other kind that has been abolished by us. So then all these forces worked together and annihilated everything, everything. They were sent from above, put something into the path, thus gradually loosening it, and now the forest is coming and the path is coming and the torrent is coming and altogether everything is coming.

Those crashing blasts with which the earth scattered her droppings have not been taken seriously in the dining room of the Alpenrose Inn. The rain that already extinguished the entire seed of those present with its Flood gets their attention only when it is too late, because they are waiting for the next wonderful TV program, the *Dating and Mating of Game* show. They don't hear that something else is coming to an end. But it already ended at the beginning. Just a few among the guests look in a totally different, new direction each, but only briefly, because we don't have much more time. The student Gudrun Bichler is coming down the stairway, books under her arm; with all that noise from the

TV she certainly won't be able to work, she could just as well have left the books up in her room. Walking down she unintentionally bumps into this woman who has always been on the go with her mother and stops in the middle of the stairs, apologizing somewhat monosyllabically, clumsily. The woman nods to her absentmindedly and follows Gudrun down the stairs. The older woman's gait is somewhat hesitant, as if she wanted to buckle up and still fussed with the belt, as if she didn't want to take off before she'd be safely seated. Below, the mother is waiting, and the woman on the stairs is not in a hurry to get down to her, she'll be there soon enough. She's still biding her time, dawdling. There! The trees are literally dancing on the windshield in front of her, the sun's crashing down cheerfully, Splash!, the bus that's approaching here is wide like an orchestra (aha, a driving Dutchman!), that'll soon be flying right into their faces, they won't be able to get it off the windshield. My God, it's not work one sees, when folks are dying, one can only see that the brain has lost its little helper with the hammer, the heart.

Downstairs the girl with the tray runs around, worming her way between the chairs, it's a bit tight today, there are so many guests who have never been here before. That most of the new ones have to sit at the worst tables next to the door where there is a draft does not seem to bother them, they are welcome as spectators and listeners but also as guests. So at least they accomplished that! Their hands knock playing cards onto the table, wearing it out, and in doing so, they wear themselves out—what satisfies, what strengthens them? They didn't order anything to eat, not even the famous *Brettljause* of the Alpenrose, just a few glasses are on the table, which the guests don't seem to drink from. They, the taciturn card players (something unusual for card players here), sometimes clink glasses to strike a chord. But they don't drink anything. Something bubbles out of them, but they don't manage to express it. Maybe something doesn't obey them, the vacuum cleaner or the iron broom, with which they once were removed.

Just a moment, we also have to make sure that this athlete won't stay behind by himself, who talks as little with anyone, except occasionally, rarely, with this equally taciturn student, who supposedly studies for some exams here but is rarely seen reading in her books; walking or driving by her, the young man exchanges a couple of words with her, she is, after all, the only one his age. At least before that new young group of mountain climbers arrived on the scene. (Some will ask now, what group? Who's that now? There always were just those three older mountain buffs, where are they now anyway? They are usually right on time for the meals. Don't ask me, I don't know either.) There are some who haven't even seen those serious young folks with the edelweiss under the hatband. The young hikers were probably on their way to Hohe Veitsch mountain when such clueless, unteachable, but still nosy types stopped by here. Mountain climbers like to stick with their kind, as if they'd all be bound by ingrained repetition and had known everything here forever. These young wanderers, however, were all dressed so weirdly, they had to stick out in the name of the Father and the Son, no, I think in someone else's name, by which they were defined by us as the hostile breed we savaged like thunderstorms. Four creatures of this breed at most have been let in for us to perceive, and we must make sure it isn't them who produce the perfect Human Being, but us. Right. There they sit on their bench playing with well-thumbed cards. Not even they, who are constantly on the move, dare to go out in that rain. At the fourth light they must fall. And since they don't find a finish area to slow down, they'll again swing by us who are perpetual spectators anyway. What else is there to say. Truth to tell, this Edgar Gstranz—where is his board, where is his prick—wants to split the body of Gudrun Bichler to examine her double entrance, he'd be interested in that, but not much. He could jump up those two stairs and open her, something tense might possibly wake up, unfold, whatever, he could drink the spoiled milk of life, but better to leave it. Edgar nods to Gudrun, lifts his arm casually, and is already gone. She doesn't look for him, though she could have finally given herself. In the time left to us, we say good-bye belatedly to the beautiful big dog who belonged to the house, he just dropped and died yesterday, no one knows why.

The Wirtin, who is from here, is rather worried, she knows the pitfalls and traps of this area better than her guests. All that water coming down! And all those brand-new travelers in the house. How are they supposed to get away again when the bridge will be gone, it won't take much now, the piers are already pretty cracked. The banks are still secured with sandbags, but if the rain continues like that again . . . to the innkeeper it seems even stronger than the last time. This time they'll probably have to close the highway. Let's hear what the radio has to say. The Wirtin turns the knob, but all she can hear is a distorted rustle, voices drowning, their little sound posts stretched upward as if crying for help, weird. Mixed salad of voices on the radio, nothing reasonable one could hold on to, and soon you won't hear anything from me either. Inside the TV, in the entire space, the power suddenly goes out. Darkness all around. What happened? The forest! The forest. Abruptly the Wirtin walks to the door. If the radio can't tell her more, she'll just have to look at it in person. She pushes the door handle down and steps in front of the house, the wind almost tears her out of her clothes, she must instantly lean against the squall, and that still under the canopy. What will it be like outside! The innkeeper walks down the three stairs, out of the covered area, to where the water broke loose from the sky. The pruned thick hedge, right where the dog dropped dead yesterday, bends like thin sheet tin, but strangely, no holes pop up, though the straight-standing trellis buckles—no, it rather seems like the rim of a wet clay bowl on a potter's wheel, when you put your fingers on it lightly, very gently. Alas, the falling rain is not held in any hand. It must look for the way all on its own.

The mudslide, because of its inherent motion dynamics, strives to maintain its direction of impact. Thus it can happen that it curves directly up the slope. Only under the dynamic pressure of the subsequent mud masses can a change in the direction of the massive stream be enforced. The high speeds are also incompatible with the work a mudslide must perform to overcome the friction as well as for its digging activity. Speeds of fifty to sixty kilometers per hour are nonetheless conceivable. It didn't help that this house was built slightly uphill and outside the flood zone. Maybe the memory of past catastrophes prevented the builders of this house from constructing it all the way down on the valley floor. But man configures and God controls the gearshifts. The way I know Him, He will describe the motive for all that falling completely differently to each of you. He didn't even provide for us natives a special angel who could guide us.

The Wirtin still gets whipped around as she hears the rumble as if of Foreign Armies West, then only blasting crashes, then howling, howling, howling. Her own house is coming toward her. It isn't the house, it is something that's coming toward the house, not her, its guardian. And then, at last, she is also at home.

Epilogue

To their heart's content people leaf through the books of their lives, sometimes they try to quickly conclude an unfinished chapter, but mostly they don't succeed. Then they are often tempted to instantly start a new chapter without having finished the last one. I won't make these mistakes. There's got to be an end to it, says a politician, and then, hesitatingly, measuring a grace period of two hours on his scale, someone else says the same thing, only differently. Even this gentleman can wait for two hours, then it's all over for good. But those for whom it's all over are not asked. What moves me to still add on to an end that happened years ago, so that I can still reach it, at least with my fingertips? Who'd still want to wear this dress? Many do, but then it doesn't fit. Maybe I really let the hem down too far. No one is big enough to fit into this dress. And this shoe, the one lying here, bloody, let someone else put it on if you please!

As much havoc as floods can wreak, the most unthinkable devastations are caused by mud catastrophes. Entire villages sink into mud and scree. Houses get torn off and cultures destroyed. Many mountain villages have been buried so deeply by mud streams that ground floors turned into basements, because after the mudslides it was no longer possible to clear the deposited material. So, for example, ever since the great catastrophe of the Schmittenhöhe creek in 1737, people had to walk down a few stairs to the parish church of Zell am See, whereas the square in front of the church was flat before. Or: After a thunderstorm in 1567, the Seidelwinkel creek near Rauris, flooded and blocked by debris, came down in an incredible mudslide on the village of Luggau and destroyed thirty houses, one hundred people had to choke to death in the mud.

So now we can look in the mirror, happy that this time we were not among the dead of this land either, which is evidenced by us being able to look into the mirror and not into pure Nothingness.

The Alpenrose Inn in the so-called Tyrol, Styria (it's not really a village but a place, a cluster of several scattered shacks and one larger structure renovated and used for years almost exclusively as an inn), was lifted from the ground, including all people, animals, and personnel who at that time were at the inn, then swept away and finally packaged and covered by a mudslide that broke loose from the bottleneck of a diverted mountain torrent. That really capped off a year of catastrophes. At first the floodings, the breaking off of roads (the renovation work isn't even half completed at the time of writing, small troops in yellow protective gear are standing around everywhere, raking, pouring, smoothing, adding on I don't know what, and new work is already in the planning: each and every volunteer firefighter and several pioneer units of the Austrian Federal Army are in continuous operation. Watch our special program at 6:00 p.m.), the wind damage, the cracked bridge pillars, and now all of us can drape ourselves in black cloths, because the fatalities do not stop. The mudslide dissolved, fanlike, into individual streams. The solid material remained on the ground, that is to say exactly on top of the Alpenrose Inn, which is now amid the mass of debris, though in a totally different place from where it was built originally. Raised by hell and high water. Luckily the valley gets wider in this place so that the mudslide could find a calm runoff. Because if it had got stuck in the underflow of the ditch, as happened many years ago, when the torrent still flowed through its original bed (five farmsteads with the entire dead inventory had to be given up for good then), it could have come to much heavier flooding and breakage and devastation on account of the mud pressing from behind, indeed, the entire village of K. would have been extremely endangered!

The clean-up operations dragged on for several days, the hope, however, to still come upon anything living, soon had to be given up. Just now on TV, the governor, still under the effect of the catastrophe, has promised the director of Disaster Control that he will never again build houses where nature doesn't want them. Luckily, this effect will pass quickly. Against better knowledge, in order to avoid hurting tourism, the public was informed that there could still be people alive in the rubble. The heavy clearing equipment, the excavators, the shovels, were pushed down for days into blocked areas, day and night. Stairs into the depth, where a house must be, bend over and do your work! Here, a broken beam! And here, the smashed hand of a person! We dig deeper, the steely shovels burrow ahead and come upon a sign: Hair. Human hair. It gets unearthed. All is calm. But: There is simply too much hair for the estimated number of those buried. Hair. Hair. And there, too, everything: Hair! Occasionally, one presses it, like a hand, lets it run through the fingers like a rope: is it perhaps leading us into eternity, which we've wanted to visit for a long time? There is more and more persistent, longer silence. Those working exchange strange glances and decline, almost embarrassedly, the hot dogs with mustard and bread brought to them. Nature won in a certain sense, but maybe we can wangle something of her win out of her, the hair of about two hundred persons has already been found, even though only a fracture of this figure could have stayed here, that's less than the dirt under the fingernail of someone we didn't know either, sorry! The leader of the operation walks into his makeshift office in a hastily nailed together barrack, writes something down, and comes out again. He imposes a gag order that we will neither follow nor be judged by either. We don't believe him, even though he didn't say anything. The disaster expert, who also said nothing just now, will be commended tomorrow, but his gaze will not be present.

The young conscripts are removed quickly and somewhat rashly. Now older and more experienced workers will take over. The terrain has been closed over a wide area. That's all I know.

It is allegedly written in a secret protocol, which I, therefore, haven't read either, that one of the least oddities (would this then be the gravest one?) of this strange rescue operation is supposed to be the discovery in the buried inn of a great number of dead who, according to the unanimous judgment of pathologists, must have been deceased for some, partly for a very long time when they got buried in the mudslide. Well now, one shouldn't say such imprudent things! That's simply not possible. Period. This inn, after all, was not a cemetery of the homeless! Gentlemen from the city were suddenly available and climbed around in their parkas and hiking shoes in the dirt, the rubble, and the ruins. They soon took a liking to this activity. But what they then uttered to the public was rather meager. Such folks don't like to say that they have nothing to say. And yet, none of them could forget what they had seen.

As a personal aside, where we, the tame ones, live and where still tamer ones (I hope so!) think we are dangerous: hold it, what's written here? NO DOG ALLOWED. No, here it says: NO GOD ALLOWED. Okay, now: About forty kilometers from the disaster site in the county hospital of the county capital, Mürzzuschlag, at the same time as wide areas of Styria were buried by a mudslide, fifty-three-year-old Karin F. succumbed to serious injuries caused by a serious car accident between a bus with Dutch vacationers and a minibus on the Styrian side of the Niederalpl mountain. The deceased's mother, who had not been seriously injured, was at the Alpenrose Inn at the time of the natural disaster, thus numbering among the victims of the terrible mudslides. In the meantime, the Dutch travelers could start their safe trip home in a replacement vehicle.

ELFRIEDE JELINEK was born in 1946 in Mürzzuschlag, Styria, near Vienna, where she grew up. She has received numerous awards for her literary works, which include not only novels but also plays, poetry, essays, translations, radio plays, screenplays, and opera librettos. Alongside her literary writing she has made a reputation as a dauntless polemicist with a website always poised to comment on burning issues. She was awarded the Nobel Prize in Literature in 2004 for her "musical flow of voices and counter-voices in novels and plays that, with extraordinary linguistic zeal, reveal the absurdity of society's clichés and their subjugating power."

GITTA HONEGGER's collaboration with Elfriede Jelinek began in 1992 with her translation *Death/Valley/Mountain.* Since then, her translations include Jelinek's *Jackie, Snow White, Sleeping Beauty, Rechnitz, The Merchant's Contracts, Charges (The Supplicants), Shadow (Eurydice Says), On the Royal Road: The Burgher King, Fury, rein Gold,* and numerous essays. She has also translated plays by Thomas Bernhard and Nobel Prize awardees Peter Handke and Elias Canetti, among others. She was Professor of Theater at Arizona State University and Professor of Dramaturgy and Dramatic Criticism at the Yale School of Drama. She also served as the resident dramaturg and stage director at the Yale Repertory Theater.